KU-265-257

Harold Livingston was born and brought up in Haverhill, Massachusetts. During World War II, he enlisted in the United States Army Air Force and served three years in the European theatre; in 1950–51, he again served with the USAF in the Korean War. In between, he went to Israel as one of the original American volunteers in the Israeli Air Force during the 1948 War of Independence. Following his military service, Mr Livingston attended Brandeis University. His first novel, *Coasts of the Earth*, received a Houghton Mifflin Literary Fellowship Award. Since 1960, he and his wife, Lois, and their four children have resided in Los Angeles.

Also by Harold Livingston

RIDE A TIGER

a novel by

HAROLD LIVINGSTON

Futura

To the memory of my dear friend
Stuart Alman

A *Futura* Book

Copyright © 1987 by Harold Livingston

First published in Great Britain in 1987 by
Macdonald & Co (Publishers) Ltd,
London & Sydney

This edition published in 1988 by
Futura Publications, a Division of
Macdonald & Co (Publishers) Ltd,
London & Sydney

ISBN 0 7088 3674 7

Reproduced, printed and bound in Great Britain by
Hazell Watson & Viney Limited
Member of BPCC plc
Aylesbury Bucks

Futura Publications
A Division of
Macdonald & Co (Publishers) Ltd
Greater London House
Hampstead Road
London NW1 7QX
A Pergamon Press plc company

"Dictators ride to and fro upon tigers which they dare not dismount. And the tigers are getting hungry."

—WINSTON CHURCHILL

CONTENTS

PART ONE
THE RETURN

1

CARLA thought the young man from the Foreign Ministry rather handsome. Tall, fair, a typical sabra, although these days you could hardly call any of them typical, not with all the intermarrying between Ashkenazim and Sephardim. The young man was talking with an El Al ticket agent all the way across the terminal lobby. Behind them, through the observation window, an Air France airbus taxied toward the ramp. The warm, late afternoon sun shimmered yellowly off the airplane's silver fuselage.

At a nearby table an elderly American tourist sat dozing. A copy of the *Jerusalem Post* had slid from his lap to the floor. Carla could read the headlines:

210 U.S. MARINES DEAD
IN BEIRUT BOMBING

Now, as in the morning when she first saw the story, she thought of their wives and parents. She knew what it was. It had happened to her. The futility of it all. The waste.

The tea in her half-full cup was cold. She decided not to order a fresh cup, and instead opened her compact and studied the face in the mirror. A not unattractive face, she thought, if a fifty-four-year-old woman who had allowed her gray hair to grow fully out could be called attractive.

Matronly attractive, perhaps. She was Leo Gorodetsky's daughter, all right. She had his heavy eyebrows and warm brown eyes. Well, he certainly had been an attractive enough man.

In Hebrew now, over the public-address system, a female voice announced the arrival of Air France Flight 136, nonstop service from Paris, arriving at Gate 3. The same announcement was made in French, and then English. Carla remembered Paris in the autumn. Everyone talked about Paris in the spring, but she liked it best at autumn. The air crisp and clean, not warm but not yet cold. Not like autumns in Tel Aviv, sometimes so unbearably hot.

"Mrs. Schiff . . ."

Startled, she snapped shut the compact. The young man from the Foreign Ministry gazed down at her. For the first time she noticed a scar across the top of his forehead. Several inches long, running diagonally up from his left eyebrow, quite thin, but with a red indentation Carla knew was a bullet crease. She recognized it from Avi's descriptions of gunshot wounds. Poor Avi. Such a fine surgeon, so dedicated. And so proud of their two girls. His Israeli-American daughters, he liked to say. He would have been prouder than ever now. One graduating from college next year, the other in her second year of medical school.

". . . the flight will arrive in ten minutes," the young man from the Foreign Ministry was saying.

"I'm so sorry," Carla said. "I was daydreaming."

"I said the flight is finally arriving."

Carla looked at her watch. "Only two and a half hours late. Not bad for El Al."

"Well, you know it originated in Los Angeles, and stopped in New York and London," the young man said. "And each place the security is so strict. It has to be, you know."

"Yes, of course."

"I'll be right here to help Mrs. Gorodetsky with customs and immigration," he said. "There are formalities, you know."

"That's very kind of you."

"Your father was an important man. He did much for Israel."

"His fondest wish was to settle here," Carla said.

The young man smiled uneasily and said, "I'll be at the gate if you need me."

"Thank you," she said, and he walked quickly away. She watched him, amused. He had seemed so distressed, as though unsure whether or not to make conversation. But then, she thought, what conversation can comfortably be made with a middle-aged woman awaiting an airplane bearing the remains of her American-born father. The father who had been an important man who did much for Israel. This same State of Israel in which he had so fondly wished to settle and which now, in death, welcomed him.

The Law of Return.

Not to mention three hundred million dollars. In her mind, Carla projected the figure in large, illuminated numbers on the opposite wall. The zeros spilled down over the sign GATE 5, through which the Air France passengers were now entering the terminal: $300,000,000. Was there that much money in the entire world?

Leo Gorodetsky's legacy to Israel.

Carla wondered how the money would be spent. God, I hope not in Lebanon, she thought, and smiled to herself remembering how Leo hated that word, "God." All right, Daddy, she told him in her mind, I take it back. Erase the despised word. Make it "Lord," instead. Isn't that what they called you, "Lord"? No, excuse me, it was "Czar." Czar, Lord, same thing.

So, he was dead. "Dead," she said aloud, wondering what he thought of that word. He was familiar enough with it. Dead, she thought, remembering how the word flashed before her eyes two days ago, at ten minutes past nine of a lovely, sunny, October morning. In her classroom at the university, the provost himself interrupting her in mid-lecture. A telephone call from Los Angeles. She went to his office to take the call. It was Renata, her voice as clear as though phoning from a Dizengoff Street café.

"Carla, darling . . ." Renata said, and Carla knew instantly.

"He's dead," Carla said into the phone.

"Yes," said Renata. "I knew you'd hear it on the news, or from some reporter, so I wanted to tell you first—"

"—how did it happen?"

How did it happen? What a foolish question. How would you expect it to happen to an eighty-three-year-old man? But this particular question Carla Gordon Schiff had framed in her mind since that day thirty-three years ago when she first realized how truly famous her father was—or, depending upon your point of view, infamous. When she emerged from the subway at Harvard Square and strolled blithely past the newsstand, and saw those glaring black headlines in *The Boston Globe.*

SENATE CRIME COMMITTEE TO
PROBE UNDERWORLD GAMBLING
CZAR LEO GORODETSKY

Underworld Gambling Czar? That handsome, gentle, generous man, a head shorter than his twenty-one-year-old daughter. Underworld Gambling Czar? She rushed to the nearest telephone booth. What does it mean? she asked.

She could still hear his voice. Quiet, assured, each word carefully chosen, perfectly enunciated. He loved the spoken word. Language is a tool, he once told her. A tool, when properly employed, more effective than a hundred ingenious machines.

It means, he said on the phone from New York that day in 1950, I am in the gambling business. I have no reason to be ashamed of it, nor have you. Gambling is a business, entered into for profit, just as a farmer grows corn for profit. It is a business endeavor no different from General Motors, or the telephone company, or the corner drugstore.

A business endeavor.

Yes, Carla thought now, except that you never read of the executives of those business endeavors continually meeting violent deaths at the hands of others. She recalled some of the names. Hershel Lefkowitz, Harry Wise, Thomas Stohlmeyer, Vincent Tomasino. More glaring black headlines.

A business endeavor.

Although she never articulated it to him, she had lived constantly with the fear of his name being added to the others. Not of course in recent years. The Underworld Gambling Czar had long been retired. Nearly two decades. Put out to pasture, one newsman wrote, enjoying a quiet, peaceful life in California, having outlived all his enemies, and certainly acquiring no new ones. He had slipped into comfortable obscurity, his name now only vaguely familiar, even to the people operating the glittering casinos in the prosperous cities his foresight and business acumen had made possible. When they did remember him, it was as a "pioneer." Respected, and venerated. The danger of glaring black headlines was long past.

So now when Carla asked Renata "How did it happen?" she really was not prepared for the answer she received. Although, on reflection, it did contain a certain logic. If not logic, then irony.

"Mrs. Schiff . . ." The Foreign Ministry young man again. "They're here, Mrs. Schiff."

Through the observation window Carla saw the El Al 747 parked far out on the apron, and the passengers entering the bus to be transported to the terminal. She thought she saw Renata. A glimpse of that snow-white hair, the regal bearing. How old was Renata now? Seventy, or surely close to it. Still so lovely. A lady in the truest sense, Leo used to say.

Did Renata consider the way Leo died ironic? Probably not, Carla thought. Renata probably believed it was destined to happen in precisely that manner. And now, rising, standing a moment to gaze out at the approaching bus, Carla was forced to agree. It could have happened no other way.

She walked toward the gate to meet Renata.

PART TWO
KLEYNER

—— 2 ——

IT was cold in New York this February afternoon of 1913, but warmer than all week. Warm enough to melt most of the snow, leaving only soot-encrusted patches piled haphazardly against the muddy curb of the unpaved street. The entire block of Orchard Street, from Rivington Street to Houston Street, was a mass of people, horse-drawn wagons, motor trucks, automobiles.

Pushcart peddlers plodded hopefully along their allotted block territory. Fresh-slaughtered chickens, penny paper pads, matches, candy. Genuine lead-lined cookware. Old magazines, books, yesterday's *Daily Forward,* last week's authentically koshered beef. Shoestrings and suspenders. Blouses, pants, socks, long and short underwear. Pencils, pens, ink, candles.

Shmuel The Fritzer, vendor of seltzer water for two cents plain, three cents with a squirt of strawberry, lemon, or cherry syrup. Pincus The Fish, he of the nose whose jutting tip appeared attached to his chinless jaw, creating a profile bearing an uncanny resemblance to the products he sold: mackerel, pike, herring. You can tell how fresh from the clearness of the dead eyes. The Hat Man, whose proper name not even he recalled with certainty, proceeding up one side of the street, down the other, expertly balancing atop his head a pyramid of derby hats.

From the railings of fire escapes fronting each floor of every building, laundry and bedding hung like multicolored banners. Below, the side-

walks on both sides were lined with stalls: wood planks supported by
two boxes or barrels. Fried chick-peas, hot knishes, roasted chestnuts,
cold green tomatoes. And dozens of other exotic, and not so exotic foods
producing nostril-crinkling aromas that tantalized the mouth and excited
the stomach.

The voices of the peddlers hawking their wares, a Yiddish-English-
Hebrew mélange, blended rhythmically with the shrill cries of playing
children, the nervous chatter of weary housewives, the stentorian pro-
nouncements of dour-faced Hassidim. The subjects discussed ranged
from the forthcoming inauguration of Woodrow Wilson as twenty-eighth
president of the United States to the inevitable return of the Messiah.
The price of store-purchased challah, and the arrival from the old country of unwanted relatives. To be sure, the passage just this week of the
income-tax amendment held not the slightest interest.

On the ground floor of a tenement building on the northeast corner
of Orchard Street and Rivington, sharing space with a dry-goods store,
was a one-room synagogue. One of dozens of similar Lower East Side
synagogues whose small congregations paid the rent of the room and
their rabbi's living expenses. This particular synagogue, more accurately
a *shul,* for such modest religious housing could not properly be considered a synagogue, was called Anshe Kirubz, after the Lithuanian village
of Kirubz, where most of the congregants originated.

In the *shul*'s single room, formerly an office of the Hebrew Immigration Aid Society, a coat of brush-streaked white paint now masking the
plate-glass store-front window, were six people. A young boy, a bearded
middle-aged man, and four women. The women, one a sixteen-year-old
girl, sat side by side on a narrow bench behind a plain wooden kitchen
table. Five other such benches and tables cramped the room. All faced
the rear wall, against which was placed a cupboard resembling a clothes
armoire. The cupboard doors were padlocked to safeguard the precious
contents within. The Torah.

The man and the boy stood directly in front of the cupboard. The
man's heavy black-satin yarmulke, scraggly tobacco-yellowed beard, and
black alpaca suit coat and pants marked him as a rabbi. He was not tall,
but much taller than the boy, who was very short. The tassels at each
end of the dingy white prayer shawl draped over the boy's shoulders
nearly touched the floor. The celluloid collar of his new, brown-striped
white shirt was tightly buttoned; he wore no tie. His suit coat did not
match his knickers, although both fit reasonably well despite having been
purchased secondhand.

For ten minutes now, shivering in the damp chill of the unheated
room, the boy had listened to the rabbi's singsong, age-hardened voice
intone the Hebrew bar-mitzvah liturgy. A grueling ten minutes. Eyes
aching from staring at the blue flickering flame of the single gas jet

sconced to the wall, stomach queasy from the odor of garlic and onions wafting from the rabbi's food-mottled clothes. Ribs sore where the rabbi nudged him each time it was the boy's turn to recite. Each nudge harder than the other.

The rabbi, whose name was Reb Moishe, was not actually a rabbi. He was a *melamed*, a Hebrew-school teacher, presiding over the ceremony in the same classroom he had taught this boy and dozens of other boys for the past six years. Not only for the two-dollar fee was every bar mitzvah a source of pleasure, but also because it was the very last time he would ever have to deal with the pupil. In all instances, a wholly mutual feeling.

". . . *baruch atoh Adonoi, elohaynoo melech ha olam* . . ." It seemed endless to the boy, an ordeal he endured solely to placate his mother, the older of the women. Her name was Sarah. The girl was his sister Esther. The other two women, wrinkled, bewigged, flabby ladies, were cousins, and second cousins to Sarah. All came from the same *shtetl* outside Vilna, Kirubz, and all had emigrated to America, to New York City, in the same year, 1899. Almost a year to the day before the boy, Leo, was born.

Sarah was smiling proudly at Leo, who had just then grasped the back of his head to prevent the yarmulke from sliding off. His full, thick, dark-brown hair could not comfortably accommodate the shallow skullcap. His face was thin, with sharply defined but quite symmetrical features. He was slight, almost delicate, his body so well proportioned one seldom realized how short he actually was. His eyes were a deep, warm brown that like the sudden slamming of a door could turn abruptly hard and cold. And, at this very instant, did.

Leo was thinking of his father. Chaim Gorodetsky's absence at his only son's bar mitzvah did not anger Leo, nor had Chaim's abandonment of his family. Leo understood how a man laboring fifteen hours daily, tailoring suit coats on a piece basis at the kitchen table of his own home, might, as Chaim did, one day simply vanish. And, five months later, send a penny postcard with no return address from Cincinnati, Ohio. Informing his family that all was well with him, and hoping all was well with them. That was eight months ago.

No, the abandonment did not anger the son now, but the recollection—hearing Reb Moishe's wailing chant, the Hebrew word *Adonoi*, one of the few Leo knew, and which meant God—the recollection of his father's insistence that the only way to be a Jew was to be a Good Jew. As defined by Chaim Gorodetsky, a Good Jew meant blind faith and devotion to God. That same Jewish God whose people, in return for His promise of admission to Paradise, willingly endured unimagined privation and suffering.

Which, Leo thought as Reb Moishe nudged him again, was bullshit. Bullshit all the way. Definitely, Leo was a Jew, and proud of it, and Jews were a special people. The Chosen. And he knew that once they were a great nation called Israel. But Israel was destroyed, and the people dispersed. But wherever they went, despite the persecutions and wandering, they retained their identity. Even here in America, which most Jews agreed was a thousand times better than the old country, although certainly not better than having their own land. A place of their own again, a place they belonged.

The trouble was, Leo thought, reading ineptly from the Book now, Jews would never have a country of their own. They refused to fight. If you wanted something, you had to fight for it. Not the Jews. They believed it would happen through religion. Praying, wailing, fearing the Almighty. Everybody had stories of the old country, the pogroms, the persecution. Leo never understood why the Jews had not fought back. Instead of killing their enemies they locked their doors and prayed.

The mere thought of it, the senselessness, caused Leo to momentarily lose his place. He glanced at his mother nodding with the chanting prayer. The wig on her shaved head resembled a snug red bonnet. She, Sarah, believed in God, which was stupid because look how God had treated her. Look no further than poor little Rivka, Leo's other, older sister. Dead nearly two years now since the Triangle Shirt Waist factory fire.

Rivka was the most beautiful person Leo ever knew. And the smartest. They would talk for hours about everything. History, politics, religion. Even sex. An honor student, when Rivka graduated P.S. 38 the principal begged her to continue on in high school. But the family so desperately needed money, Chaim Gorodetsky had insisted Rivka take the Triangle job.

Leo loved Rivka. And hated God for killing her. Until he realized there was no God. God did not exist. A truth revealed to Leo when their grieved mother, trying to comfort him, said, "It is God's will."

"What God?" Leo had replied. "There ain't no God."

"Blasphemer!" Sarah had cried in Yiddish. "Bite your tongue! God is your Creator!"

To which he replied, "For Christ's sake, Ma, who the hell created God?"

Earning him a stinging smash across the face, of which he was reminded now by another sharp nudge from Reb Moishe. Leo had skipped an entire passage. The Reb's little cardboard pointer indicated the proper place in the Book. Leo caught up, inspired by the knowledge that these were his last moments in this loathsome room. Five years of Hebrew lessons, four days a week, two hours a day. Seventy-five cents per week, paid whether or not the pupil regularly attended class. Few did, and certainly not Leo. His truancy record was unmatched.

Leo finished now, turning to Reb Moishe as the sour-breathed old man addressed him as Laibel. His Yiddish name, which Leo did not especially like but preferred to Kleyner, Yiddish for "little one," used only by those knowing him well enough or, occasionally, by those wishing to annoy or insult him. Only recently had he begun ignoring it, drawing finally on Rivka's too often unheeded advice about sticks and stones breaking bones, but names never hurting. Far more effective than the blind, vain rage frequently resulting in split lip or bloody nose; his tormentors were almost always bigger and stronger.

The bar mitzvah was over. Sarah Gorodetsky presented Reb Moishe a crisp new two-dollar bill. The *melamed* proclaimed her son now a man, entitled to assume such status among family and community. In Yiddish, Sarah promised the Reb that Leo would faithfully attend Friday evening and Saturday morning *Shabbes* services.

"Yeah, for sure," Leo said in English.

"He better, or I murder him!" Sarah said in Yiddish, and hustled her son from the building.

Outside on the crowded sidewalk, Leo graciously accepted the cousins' congratulations. He anticipated a gift. So did Sarah, inviting the two ladies home for some refreshment. She said to Leo, "You'll go to Rabinowitz for a nice piece of fish, Laibel. And maybe another bread."

"I can't, Ma," Leo replied in Yiddish. "I'm already late for work."

"But they know today's your bar mitzvah."

"That don't mean nothing to them," Leo said in English. He looked at his sister. "Tell her."

"Yeah, Ma," said Esther. "They don't care."

"A Gentile has no heart," Sarah said to the cousins. "For three months now my Laibel works after school making those *trayf* candles. Like a dog he works there, and they don't let him have this one special day. They should all die, the bastards!"

"They don't know no better, Ma. They need him bad," Esther said in English, this directed at Leo with a little smirk. Esther knew where Leo really worked.

"Yeah," Leo said, glaring at her. "I gotta go, Ma."

He kissed her. She proudly shouldered him around to face the cousins. "Can you imagine? He wants me not to keep my job. He says he should take care of us all by himself. I should be a lady of leisure, and his sister should stay in high school." She kissed him once more. "God should only make it happen. All right, my darling, go. When you come home you'll find chicken and *tsimmes* for you." She worked eight to eleven every evening at a Fourteenth Street cafeteria, cleaning trays, bringing leftover food home whenever possible. "You," she said harshly to Esther. "You make sure you leave enough for him."

"Sure, Ma," Esther said. "Do good today with the candles, Laibel."

"Just save me the chicken," he said to her and, mumbling good-byes to the cousins, ran off, the bar mitzvah and whatever its significance immediately and forever erased from his mind.

He cut across the vacant lots behind the construction work on Delancey, over to Allen where the El, blocking out the sunlight, made it seem like going suddenly from day to night. A train, just then rumbling overhead, showered the street with thick black dust and little pellets of dirt. He crossed Allen, then Eldridge and Forsythe, to Chrystie. He stayed on Chrystie, dodging pushcarts and vendors, hurrying past all the little stores. Glove makers, cigar manufacturers, dry goods, tailors, an optician with a giant eye hanging above the entrance. He darted in and around the crowds, off the sidewalk, on, off again, once splashing into a pothole concealed by a muddy puddle and almost stumbling straight into a mound of fresh, still steaming horse dung. "Shit!" he cried aloud, and had to smile, thinking it was exactly that.

The big clock atop the lamppost outside Lipsky's pawnshop read 2:40. In place of numbers on the white clockface, Yiddish letters spelled IRVINGLIPSKY. Leo relaxed and walked slower. The garage was not far away; he wasn't due on the job for twenty minutes. The game started at three.

On the corner of Chrystie and Broome a very pretty lady had just entered the five-story tenement building where Mendy Kaufman lived. The lady wore a gray, wide-brimmed felt hat and heavy gray cloak, and carried a little black-leather satchel like a doctor's. Leo recognized her as Miss Birnbaum, one of the visiting nurses from the Henry Street Settlement House. He was sure she was there to see Mendy. Mendy, they said, had TB. He and Leo were P.S. 38 seventh-grade classmates, good friends until last summer. When Leo was nearly caught breaking into the loft of a Second Street dress factory.

While Leo went in from an adjoining roof, Mendy waited on the street below. Leo was to toss the dresses down. He tossed them down, all right—just missing the night watchman's head. Mendy, seeing the watchman approach, had run off. Although Mendy could not possibly have warned him, Leo felt he should have done something; at the very least engaged the man in conversation loud enough to hear. Mendy simply wasn't that smart. Leo realized this, and really had no grudge—he had gotten away—but their friendship cooled.

Now, reminded by the nurse, Leo felt guilty. After all, the experience was educational. The few dollars for a handful of cheap cotton *shmattes* was not worth the risk. And if you choose a partner with neither balls *or* brains, you deserve what you get. So Mendy was not to blame, it was Leo himself. And Mendy was not a bad guy, he thought, passing the tenement stoop now, glancing in the hallway at two dirty-faced kids noisily playing stickball. Mendy agreed to the loft job only on Leo's promise to fix him up with an Allen Street whore. None would take Mendy on, not even for a dollar; they were afraid of the TB.

Leo's groin throbbed just thinking of the whores. Sitting in their chairs on the sidewalk in summer. In those thin kimonos, legs spread so you could see the insides of their thighs. In winter, tapping at you through the windows of their rooms. Fifty cents.

He had done it only twice. And with the same one, Rose, a skinny, stringy-haired brunette who spoke, when she spoke at all, only Yiddish and Russian. Always turning her head away to stare at the wall, at the same fist-sized hole in the wallpaper with the plaster crumbling and the wood lath showing through. And each of the two times it was over almost before it started, she pushing him off her. Get your pants on and get out. He went back the second time only because of Rose's next-door neighbor. A big blonde named Chana who wore black underwear so sheer you could see the blond hair between her legs. It glistened like gold. But her breasts fascinated him more. Gigantic breasts with nipples that looked an inch long. He could actually feel his head nestled against them, and the soft smoothness of her flesh, the perfumed warmth on his cheek.

"You little bum, watch where you're going!"

Shrill, Yiddish words that before Leo's very eyes transformed the beckoning face of the blonde with the inch-long nipples into the face of a wrinkled old hag standing with two others in the doorway of Klinetsky's Budapest Bakery. Leo, so engrossed, had walked right into her and knocked the mesh shopping bag from her hands. As he picked up the bag for her, she cursed him again in Yiddish.

"You stupid little dwarf!"

The bag contained vegetables and four eggs. He swung it over his head, prepared to hurl bag and contents into the nearest wall.

"Gangster!" she shrieked in Yiddish. "Cossack!"

He looked at her. An old woman in a tattered coat fastened in front with two large safety pins, afghan babushka, and ankle-high workman's shoes worn through at the soles. It was like a uniform. Even his mother wore such clothes, although hers at least were much neater.

"Now give me that!" she said in Yiddish, reaching for the bag which he had abruptly stopped swinging. She snatched it from him and pushed him roughly away.

Leo slapped the palm of his hand against his forearm in the dago "fungoola" gesture. Then he raced off, laughing at the old woman's expression of utter indignation, but glad he had not smashed the eggs. It would have been like one of Hershey's favorite sayings: swatting flies with a cannon.

Continuing toward Grand now, toward the garage, he struggled to re-create the interrupted fantasy of the time he nearly went with Chana. He had the money, the fifty cents, a bonus from Hershey for a timely warning about two Italians with ideas of heisting the game. Chana had smiled and given him the nod. But just then a man in a brand-new derby and greasy, paint-stained white overalls appeared. Chana never gave Leo even a second glance. He stood there, watching her doorway; he would wait for her to finish. The idea excited him. Then Rose tapped at him from her window, so he went with her. He looked for Chana afterward, but never saw her.

He stopped now at the corner and peered at the hand-lettered sign over the double-doored garage entrance: A-1 GARAGE & MOTOR CAR REPAIR SHOP. PROP. H.E. LEFKOWITZ. An Autocar truck, leaving, blocked an entering Model T. Leo could see the Ford driver stamping his foot on the reverse pedal. After a frustrating moment, the gear engaged. The Ford backed up enough for the truck to pass, then drove in. Business was good, Leo thought, and headed toward the garage to his after-school job.

As a lookout for a craps game.

The game, played each afternoon in an area of the garage concealed by a large sliding door, was run by the garage proprietor, Hershel Lefkowitz, otherwise known as Hershey. Leo's duties consisted of watching for trouble. From police—or anyone else—and seeing that the beat cop received his daily dollar payoff. For this, Leo earned five dollars weekly. The wages his mother believed earned in the Gentile candle factory.

Gambling had always fascinated Leo. He understood numbers. He could count before he could talk. He continually failed arithmetic in school, but could instantly compute any craps odds. The percentages never favored the player.

Only once, just once, had he played. Three years ago in a game in an Orchard Street alley. On his way to the store for bread and chicken for *Shabbes* supper, he stopped to watch, his hand jammed tight to his pocket protecting the two dimes and a quarter given him by his father for the food.

The shooter was a young man wearing a leather cap rakishly slanted just above his eyes and a handsome leather jacket. You saw that he took pride in his appearance, which Leo admired. Almost as though someone else's fingers gripped the coins, Leo brought them from his pocket and placed them on the line. The shooter rolled. A natural seven. Leo's two dimes and a quarter became four dimes and two quarters. He let it ride. He knew he would win, and was not the least excited when the shooter rolled a six, then on the very next toss matched it. Yes, of course, Leo would press one more time. The $1.80 would magically be $3.60. He would take his winnings and run. He watched the dice tumble against the brick alley wall and spin into the air. Even before they fell he was considering going just once more after this. He was that sure of a win; he had never been surer of anything in his life.

The first die settled. Six. Leo glanced smugly away. He did not have to watch the second to know it was a one. Another natural, another win.

It was another six. Two sixes. Boxcars. Crapped out. Incredulous, frozen in a half crouch, Leo watched the winners scoop up their winnings. His money. The game continued, same shooter, but Leo's pockets were empty. It was as though he had never existed. He could hear himself crying, "Hey, wait a second, it ain't right!" But the cry was only a whimper in his mind. His throat was dry, tight with fear. Tears stung his eyes. What would he tell his father? Chaim had never struck him, so Leo knew that was unlikely, but he almost wished otherwise. It would make him feel better, less the fool. He had not been unlucky, he had been a fool; only fools believe in luck. Or, if there is such a thing as luck, you make your own.

Whatever his definition of it, Leo's luck that day was good. He met Rivka coming home from work. Just paid, she gave him the forty-five cents, explaining to their parents that the Triangle Shirt Waist bosses had cut everyone's salary. So Leo got away with it. But he hated and never forgot the lonely, empty feeling of being a loser.

At 2:55 Leo entered the garage. At her desk in the little office cubicle doing the books was Hershey's wife, Edie. The tip of her tongue flicked back and forth between the account ledger and the pencil point. Leo waved to her, then stepped over to the front of the Model T. A pair of heavy work shoes attached to a pair of long, overall-clad legs extended from under the radiator. Leo kicked one of the big shoes.

"Hey . . ."

A muffled reply from beneath the car. "Yeah?"

"It's me," said Leo.

A wrench clattered metallically on the concrete floor. Hershey wiggled himself out from under the car. He looked up at Leo. "The bar-mitzvah *bocha*. So how was it?"

"Lousy, whatya think?"

Hershey grinned. "I think it was lousy." He rose, but only halfway, in a crouch leaving him nearly as tall as Leo. "So today you are a man, huh, Kleyner?" From the crouch he ruffled Leo's hair. Now he rose fully. He towered over Leo. "Come on in the office, Edie wants to see you."

When Hershel Lefkowitz called Leo "Kleyner," it was spoken with affection, not derision. Leo loved this great, strapping *Galitzianer*, he of the voice like sandpaper who had begun life in America penniless, but quickly learned the streets were indeed paved with gold for those prepared to fully adopt the language and customs of their new home. In his first four months in America, supporting himself with whatever work was available, Hershey studied English eight hours daily. A bicycle-shop handyman in the old country, he had a natural bent for the mechanical and soon became an expert combustion-engine mechanic. Finally, with some financial assistance from the lady he eventually married, Hershey purchased the A-1 Garage.

Hershey married this lady, Edith, after jilting his girlfriend of two years, Rivka Gorodetsky. Rivka took it badly. She really loved Hershey, and he loved her. But he was also a practical man. After the marriage, Hershey occasionally tried to see Rivka, but she refused. When she died in the fire, he said Kaddish for her. Additionally, he befriended Leo who regarded him if not as a father, at least a big brother.

In the office now, Hershey placed an arm fondly around Leo. He said to Edie, "Well, the kid did it."

"Yeah, today you are a man," Edie said. She winked at Hershey. "Maybe I should see if he really is?"

"Don't worry, he is," Hershey said. "I know. Huh, Kleyner?" He squeezed Leo's shoulder.

"Come on, Hersh," Leo said. He felt himself blushing; such talk in Edie's presence embarrassed him. He considered her the classiest lady he ever saw. She was thirty-three, four years older than Hershey. A big woman, with a marvelous figure, she loved clothes. She favored white, ruffled shirtwaists, worn usually with thin, men's-style bow or regular-length ties. Long, tapered skirts, generally dark in color, and never the same one two days in a row. Her brown hair was fixed in a high, tight pompadour, framing an oval face with firm features and wide-set, large brown eyes. She reminded Leo of pictures he had seen of dignified English noblewomen. Hershey as a dignified English nobleman was, of course, something else. But as a married couple Leo thought them ideal. He had already decided that if ever he married, it would be a girl like Edie.

". . . all right," she was saying. "Give us a kiss." She drew him to her.

Leo brushed his lips against her cheek, then stepped quickly away, saying to Hershey, "Time for the game, ain't it?"

"Hey, Kleyner, a little something for the bar mitzvah," Edie said. She pressed two folded one-dollar bills into his hand.

"Jesus!" said Leo. "Thanks!"

"Don't say 'Jesus,'" Edie said. "It ain't respectful."

"What's respectful?" Hershey asked. "Since when is a Jew supposed to respect Jesus?"

"Hershey," Edie said patiently, "Jesus was a Jew."

"Yeah, he was, wasn't he?" Hershey said. His voice trailed off absently. "Leo, I got to talk to you."

"Thanks again, Edie," Leo said.

"Our pleasure, darling," she said.

Leo followed Hershey across the garage floor. They were almost outside when Hershey stopped. His eyebrows, knitted reflectively, resembled an unbroken, heavy black line. "He was here again, kid. Hammer."

Leo's stomach fluttered. "Looking for me?"

"That's right," Hershey said. "Second time this week. What the hell's he want?"

"What'd he say?"

"You should go around to see him, that's what he says. Maybe he's giving you a bar-mitzvah present?"

"Fuck him," said Leo, but he knew he could not evade the issue; he had to tell Hershey something. "I promised Hammer I'd fix him up with Solly Berkowitz's sister."

Hershey's face wrinkled skeptically. He waited for Leo to explain.

Leo said, "It was all a joke. But the numb-nutted asshole believed it. One day Solly and me and Joey Farber, we was with Solly's sister, Rosalie. Down in the basement of that place on Essex that was closed up for being unsafe. 'Condemned,' that's what they call it. So Rosalie, she's showing us how her mother and father do it in bed. She's hollering and making noises and wiggling her ass and all. I look up where the window used to be, I see Hammer! He's fucking well watching us! We invite him down and say for a quarter he can try it with her. He don't have no quarter. So we say come back when he gets it. And that's what he wants, Hersh."

"He must of found the quarter, huh?"

"I guess," said Leo. "Hey, the game's already started, I think." From behind the partition, a low murmur of voices could be heard. "I better get moving." He started for the street. His lookout post, halfway to the corner, was near enough to the garage for ample warning of anything or anyone suspicious.

"Kid," Hershey called after him. "Hold it just a second." He walked over to Leo and said, "I'm thinking of opening the game earlier, Leo. Like, say, noontime."

"Keen idea," Leo said, moving away. "Give the suckers more time to lose, huh?"

"Leo, I'm trying to tell you I have to get somebody else for your job."

"What do you mean, somebody else for my job?"

"You come in after school, at three," Hershey said. "If the game starts at noon, I need somebody out there at noon, don't I?"

Leo said nothing. He did not want to believe what he was hearing.

"Well, don't I?" Hershey asked.

"I'll quit school," Leo said. "It ain't doing me no good, anyway. I'll quit."

"Your mother'd never let you."

"How much will you pay me to start at noon?"

"Seven bucks a week."

"She'll let me," Leo said. He punched Hershey playfully on the elbow and ran off to his lookout post. The idea of quitting school pleased him. And seven dollars a week. But first he knew he must deal with Hammer.

Leo felt uneasy about lying to Hershey. Perhaps it was a mistake not to confide in him. But Leo did not want to ask anyone's help. He had to handle this himself.

2.

Hammer was Bryan Murphy, a Bowery thug noted for his style of pounding his fists into the top of his victim's skull. Hence the nickname, Hammer. Leo knew precisely what Hammer wanted of him.

Money.

A few weeks before, he had hit Leo for three dollars. A week later, another two dollars. It all concerned a personal service Hammer recently rendered Leo. A service for which Leo paid Hammer the negotiated price of fifteen dollars.

To teach a man a lesson.

A man named Cohen. A greenhorn who had cleverly invested his glove-business profits in real estate, he owned the building Leo lived in. The five floors were occupied by thirty-three families, including the Sharanskys. Rachel Sharansky was a pretty young woman, a friend of Leo's sister Rivka, and Triangle Shirt Waist Company co-worker. One of the lucky. Rachel had been dismissed from work five minutes earlier than the others. She stood on the sidewalk watching them fling themselves from the upper floors like flaming moths. She was never quite right in the head afterward. One morning two years later she climbed to the tenement roof and threw herself off. Everyone said it was the Triangle tragedy.

Leo knew different.

He had seen the landlord, Cohen, accompany Rachel to the roof that morning. And saw him leave, alone. Leo then went up there himself. Rachel sat slumped against the parapet, clothes and hair disheveled, skirt above her knees, bloomers clumped around her ankles. She gazed dully at Leo. When he asked what happened, she only smiled, and continued smiling. An empty little smile that sent a tremor of fear through him. After a moment, he left. An hour later she jumped.

In Leo's mind Rachel became Rivka. It was then a question of what action to be taken. He engaged Hammer. Cohen was discovered semiconscious in the hallway of one of his tenements. Three broken ribs, a concussion, severe facial lacerations. He was unable to identify his assailant, who had attacked him from behind.

A sturdy man, the landlord rapidly recovered. Leo could never resist inquiring after his health, and what a shame the coward who beat him so badly was never caught. Oh, but he would be, Cohen promised. Such *gonifs* always were. They always made mistakes. As surely as God was in His Heaven, the son of a bitch bastard *goy* would be caught.

"How do you know he was a *goy*, Mr. Cohen?" Leo asked innocently.

"What Jew should have anything against me?" Cohen replied.

When, months later, Hammer asked Leo for a three-dollar "loan," Leo gave it to him. The following week, asked for two more dollars, Leo at first refused. Hammer threatened to telephone the precinct house: If they wanted to know about the Cohen job, just ask a certain little Jewboy. It never occurred to Hammer that Leo would have no choice but to implicate him, and Leo did not remind him. He paid, knowing it was not the last time, and knowing now what had to be done.

Three days after Hershey informed him of Hammer's most recent visit, Leo was ready. He told Hershey he would not be at work; he had errands for his mother. Late in the afternoon, carrying in his pocket a quart of whiskey wrapped in a paper bag, he went to look for Hammer. He found him just leaving a Canal Street saloon.

The very sight of the Irishman sent that familiar cold chill of anger sweeping over Leo's whole body. A feeling he knew even as a child when confronted by something or someone threatening. With the feeling, always, a certain crystal-clear awareness of precisely what to do. Each single move. As though observing himself on a stage, or on the white-sheeted wall of a nickelodeon theater.

Leo called quietly, "Hey, you was looking for me?"

Hammer was a large man, with tiny, rheumy red eyes in a bloated, habitually unshaven face. He wore a battered derby and fraying pea coat. His collarless shirt was buttoned at the top so his neck spilled over the celluloid collar ring in loose folds of skin. The tiny eyes glittered in recognition.

"Gimme five bucks."

"I ain't got but three," Leo said. He displayed the whiskey bottle. "But how about this?"

Hammer snatched the bottle. He ripped away the paper bag, uncorked it, and drank. He wiped his mouth with the back of his hand, recorked the bottle, dropped it into his own pocket. He said, "Gimme the three."

"It ain't on me," Leo said. "It's stashed."

"Where?"

"You wait here," Leo said. "I'll go get it." He started away.

Hammer slapped a vicelike grip on Leo's shoulder. "*We'll* go get it, Kikey."

"Jesus, Hammer, don't you trust me?" Leo tried to squirm loose, but Hammer held firm. "Hey, let go, huh?"

"I don't trust no Jew," Hammer said. His fingers dug deeper into Leo's flesh. "You understand, boy? You hear me good?"

Leo wanted to scream with the pain. "Hammer, please. You're killing me!"

"Where's the stash?"

Leo wanted to hold out just a little longer but could not. He felt suffocated. "Down on Division Street," he gasped. "That place they was gonna put up the shoe factory. Jesus Christ, let go!"

The iron fingers relaxed. "How much money you hid there?"

"The three bucks I told you."

"How much?"

The fingers dug into the tender flesh of Leo's collarbone. This time he did scream. "There's more! Yeah, more. I'll give it all to ya!"

Hammer removed his hand. He shoved Leo forward. "Let's go get it, then."

They started off, the huge-torsoed man and the small, slight boy. Down Canal, than over to Division. "Where'd you get the money?" Hammer asked. "Who'd you steal it off?"

Leo rubbed his aching shoulder. He was breathing normally now, and his head had cleared. "You said you wouldn't make me pay no more," he said calmly, surprised at his calmness. Surprised he was not at all afraid, thinking he should be afraid, wondering why he was not.

"Who'd you steal it off?" Hammer asked again, this time almost friendly.

"I saved it up."

"Cut the shit. Jews steal from everybody. They even stole Christ's blanket." Without breaking stride, Hammer removed the bottle from his pocket. He took a long, deep swallow. Then he placed an arm roughly over Leo's sore shoulder. "You ain't a bad kike, though. Not like some I know. They'd steal the gold right out of your teeth."

"Yeah, some of us are real bad," Leo said, wincing from the pressure of Hammer's arm. But a moment later the pressure was relieved as Hammer once more drank from the bottle. Leo wondered how much he had had before, and how much he could handle.

"At least you're honest about it," Hammer said. "More'n I say for most."

They continued toward the construction site, Hammer warming to the subject, reviling Jews and Jewishness for every crime known to humanity. During the five-block walk Leo did not have to urge him to continue drinking. By the time they arrived the bottle was empty. And it was dark, just as Leo planned.

Ignoring an oncoming horse-drawn furniture van, Hammer crossed the street. For one wishful instant Leo thought Hammer might be run down. But Hammer darted past and stood safely on the opposite sidewalk, impatiently gesturing Leo to join him. Leo glanced up and down the street, and both sidewalks. All clear, not a soul in sight. He hurried across.

The abandoned excavation was a half block long and wide, twenty feet deep, protected by a barrier of wooden sawhorses. Red-glassed kerosene lanterns hung from each sawhorse.

"Wait here," Leo said. He ducked under a sawhorse and started clambering down into the pit.

Hammer said, "You ain't getting out of my sight!" And he followed Leo down, digging his heels into the loose dirt of the steep embankment, balancing himself like a tightrope walker.

Leo marveled at how it all was working out so perfectly. Unfolding before his eyes just as he had imagined, down to the smallest detail. Even the chance he took asking Hammer to wait on top for him. Like a story in a book whose ending he had already read.

At the far end of the pit was a small corrugated-iron tool shed, part of the roof gone, the door long since torn from its hinges. "It's hid inside," Leo said. "Under the floorboards."

Hammer brushed past Leo and stumbled into the shed. He dropped to his knees and began clawing at the floorboard. Leo stepped in behind him, reached around to the wall and there, just where he had placed it two days earlier, was a spike-studded two-by-four board. Protruding three inches from the top of the board, in an uneven circle, were the razor-sharp points of twelve heavy nails. Leo gripped the handle with both hands. He raised the weapon and aimed it at the side of Hammer's head.

"Where the fuck is it?" Hammer turned just as Leo brought the board down. His drunken eyes widened in comprehension and fear. His arm moved in an upward, protective reflex. It was too late.

With all his strength, like swinging a baseball bat, Leo struck Hammer with the board. He saw it as though in a dream, every move in slow, tantalizing clarity. Turning, Hammer had exposed the entire left side of his face. The needlelike spike points drove into the soft unmuscled flesh of Hammer's neck, into his cheek, and eye. The spikes smashed the cheekbones with a sound like the crunch of brittle twigs. And then a louder sound, a squish, as a single spike plunged directly into, and through, the eye. For all its force the blow hardly seemed to jar Hammer. He remained a moment in the same kneeling position, the board imbedded in his face. Then, with a little sigh like air escaping from a toy balloon, he toppled to the floor.

In the dark Leo gazed at the body. He wondered if there was much blood, and if he should remove the board from Hammer's head. He decided not to. He knew no one would recall seeing him with Hammer. No one had paid any attention. Hammer would probably be found in the morning. One more unsolved killing. But, for Leo, a solved problem. He felt neither elation or remorse. He had simply done something that needed to be done.

He left the shack and rubbed the soles of his shoes carefully in the dirt to wipe them clean. Then, first making certain the sidewalk was empty, he climbed up out of the pit and hurried away. He did not look back, not once.

3

AT night, uptown on the Sixth Avenue El, the lighted windows of the tall midtown buildings resembled tiny yellow squares painted on a black velvet curtain. Whenever Leo went uptown, which was not often, he would concentrate on a particular set of windows and imagine it was his apartment. He was rich and famous, married to a beautiful woman. Sometimes, when not entertaining other rich and famous people, they were alone. Having cocktails on their high terrace, gazing out at the whole city. Tonight, they had just sat down to supper. Served, as Leo once saw in a moving-picture show, by a pretty maid in a frilly black uniform with a white lace apron. As in the movie, he wore a tuxedo, his beautiful wife an evening gown.

The picture disintegrated in a shrill, steel-grinding lurch as the train rolled to a stop at Fourteenth Street. Leo sat in the very last row of the car, face pressed to the window, the glass warm on his cheek from the hot day. The hottest October 5, they said, in eighteen years.

The train lurched forward again. As it picked up speed, Leo was suddenly aware of the man in the opposite seat. An elderly man with a scraggly white mustache, wearing a spotless white linen suit and straw hat, he was reading the late edition of *The World*, providing Leo a full view of the front page.

ALLIES TAKE 20,000 PRISONERS:
SMASH GERMAN FRONT. GERMANS

ADMIT LOSSES, BUT INSIST
THEIR LINES HOLDING.

This story occupied half the page. To its left, a single column with smaller headlines: ZEPPELIN RAID KILLS 300 IN LONDON. And, left of that, two more single-column stories: NURSE CAVELL SENTENCED TO DEATH, and IRISH FLEE BRITISH CONSCRIPTION. The only local news concerned a cave-in in the Herald Square area of the new crosstown subway under construction. A bulletin box on the bottom of the page announced the results of the first game of the 1915 World Series.

Leo thought the war stories always favored the Allies. The Germans weren't so bad. They fought the Czar, who was such a son of a bitch to the Jews. Leo hoped the Germans killed every goddam Russian soldier. But then, some poor bastard Jews were probably in the Russian army. The ones that hadn't gotten away to America. But Jews were in the German army, too. You didn't want them killed, either. So who the hell do you root for?

The Philadelphia Phillies, he thought, just as the man with the straw hat rustled the paper around, offering Leo a final glimpse of the World Series bulletin: RED SOX TAKE FIRST GAME.

Precisely because of that game he traveled uptown. Carrying in his buttoned shirt pocket an envelope containing $210. Money from bets on tomorrow's game Hershey was laying off with a bookie named Charley Wax. In the past year Hershey had begun accepting sports bets. The $210 represented more Boston money than Hershey cared to handle. Charley Wax had agreed to take the extra action. Boston's pitcher would not be announced until game time. Hershey had a hunch it might be their young star, George Ruth, who not only had a great arm but was the best hitting pitcher in baseball. It was like having a ten-man team.

For more than a year now, since turning fourteen, Leo had worked full time for Hershey. Persuading his mother to allow him to quit school was not easy. She wept and carried on so that he finally compromised. He would finish eighth grade. At least with that much schooling, she said, he would be almost a *mensch*. And after all, one of her children—even though a daughter—attended high school. In truth, Sarah Gorodetsky had no real basis for complaint. Leo brought home a weekly salary of twelve dollars, ten of which he faithfully gave her. This, plus her own small cafeteria salary, provided for the family quite comfortably.

By now, of course, Sarah knew Leo worked for Hershel Lefkowitz, the *Galitzianer* over on Grand Avenue with the *nafke* wife. While Sara did not boast of her son's employer to her cousins or friends, she felt a garage job certainly nothing to be ashamed of. Not like other boys his age. Stealing, or running in gangs. To be sure, Sarah was unclear on the exact nature of Leo's work. He said he was "helping" Hershel Lefkowitz, and that Lefkowitz was teaching him the business.

The man with the straw hat got off at Twenty-third Street. Leo gazed after him. Probably a store clerk, maybe a traveling salesman. Leo liked to speculate about people. Hershey claimed a man's hands and finger-nails told you everything. Clean and well cut meant pride, self-respect. Leo had discovered that eyes revealed more. A person unable to look you straight in the eye, especially while talking, was untrustworthy.

He got off at Thirty-fourth Street, and walked down the stairs, stopping at the bottom to straighten the cuffs of his knickers. He rolled each one neatly and evenly past the knees. He had not worn knickers regularly for more than a year, but Hershey wanted them worn on these uptown errands. Edie's idea. She believed knickers made Leo less conspicuous. He was carrying a lot of money, after all.

He walked two blocks west to the Hotel Marion, a small residential hotel whose lobby consisted of little more than a narrow alcove with a few pieces of tattered furniture. The only person in the lobby, a nattily attired young man not much older than Leo, sprawled in an easy chair, toothpick clenched in his teeth, reading the *Sporting News*. He regarded Leo with total disinterest.

"Yeah?"

"I come from Hershey," Leo said.

"Bar, or P.A.?"

"Huh?"

"You said you come from Hershey. So which one? Hershey Bar, or Hershey P.A." The young man pulled the toothpick from his mouth and waved it hopelessly at Leo. "What do you want?"

Leo noticed the slightest hint of a bulge under the left armpit of the young man's double-breasted pinstripe jacket. "I got something for Charley Wax."

"Watcha got for him, Shorty?"

"It's private."

"Don't tell me you owe him money?"

"I said it's private."

The young man jerked his head toward the stairway. "Room Two-oh-three." He popped the toothpick back into his mouth and resumed reading.

Leo started up the stairs. His face felt hot. His heart pounded with anger and humiliation. He stopped. He turned and peered down at the young man. "My name ain't Shorty."

The young man paid no attention. He turned the pages of the paper, at the same time sliding the toothpick from one side of his mouth to the other.

Leo said, "I said my name ain't Shorty."

"Sure thing, Shorty," said the young man, without looking up. "Whatever you say."

Leo stood uncertainly. He wanted to tell this wise guy where to get off, but knew it would accomplish nothing. A sucker play. No percentage, as Hershey would say.

He went on up the stairs and knocked at the door of 203. It was opened immediately by another young man dressed similarly to the one in the lobby—and with the same bulge under his suit coat.

"Yeah?"

"I got something for Charley Wax," Leo said.

The young man opened the door fully. The room was a blue haze of cigarette and cigar smoke. Five shirt-sleeved men sat playing poker. Charley Wax, a stout, red-faced man with stringy gray hair, accepted the envelope from Leo without looking at it, or him. Since no one seemed to pay him any further attention, Leo decided to watch a few hands. He had never seen such a big game.

Before each player was a stack of bills. Ones on top, then fives, tens, and twenties. They were playing five-card draw, dollar ante. Charley Wax opened for five dollars. The next player passed to a handsome, youngish man with thick black hair neatly cut and carefully combed. He was the only one wearing a tie. Embroidered above his shirt pocket were small black initials: AZS.

"You bet like you know what you're doing, Charley," he said. He seemed almost amused. He glanced casually at Leo standing directly behind him. "Wouldn't you say so, son?"

"Yeah," Leo said. He did not know what else to say.

Charley Wax, as though noticing Leo for the first time, said, "Beat it, kid."

"Stay for this hand," the youngish man said to Leo. "I have a hunch you'll bring me luck."

"You're gonna need it, Arnie," said Charley Wax, whose real name was Carl Waxman.

"You think so, eh?" Arnie said, winking at Leo. He flashed his cards at him: two small pair, and a picture. He called Charley Wax's opening bet, then raised it five. The other players all passed. The bet returned to Charley Wax. He raised it forty dollars.

Arnie glanced over his shoulder again at Leo. "What's your name?"

"Leo."

"You brought Charley layoff money, right?"

"Arnie, I bumped you forty," Charley said impatiently.

Arnie ignored him. He said to Leo, "Boston money?"

"Yeah," Leo said.

Arnie turned to the others. "You know what just occurred to me? Boston of the American League is playing Philadelphia of the National, right? Last year, it was Boston of the National, and Philadelphia of the American. Now what are the odds on that ever happening again?"

"Million to one," said the dealer, a thin, hollow-cheeked man.

"Will you lay it?" Arnie asked.

"You lay it," said the dealer. "I'll take it."

Arnie pulled a thick packet of folded bills from the inside pocket of his jacket draped neatly over the back of his chair. He snapped off a one-hundred-dollar note. The first Leo ever saw, crispy green, large as a book page. "I'll lay a hundred to one," he said. "And give you the next ten years to do it."

The dealer dropped two half-dollar coins into Arnie's shirt pocket. "You're on."

"Jesus, Arnie, what kind of shmuck bet is that?" someone else asked. "A hundred to win a lousy one?"

"It's the easiest dollar I'll ever make," Arnie said, facing Charley Wax now and sliding two twenties into the pot, and holding up his hand to indicate more coming. He peeled another hundred-dollar bill from the roll. "A hundred more to you, Charley."

"You really are a shmuck, Steinberger," Charley said.

"We'll soon see," Arnie said. "That is, if you ever get around to making up your mind."

Leo suddenly realized who Arnie was. Arnold Steinberger. King of the Gamblers. Everybody heard of Arnie Steinberger. A college graduate (Harvard, they said), son of a wealthy father, Arnie was Crème de la Crème. The best, the Class. Talking about him was like talking about a national hero. Like Colonel Roosevelt, or Ty Cobb. Respect, that was the word. People respected Arnie Steinberger.

Charley Wax called Arnie's hundred-dollar raise and asked for two cards. Arnie flashed his hand at Leo again, the two small pair. Then he closed the cards and placed them face down on the table.

"I'll play these."

Charley checked to the pat hand. Arnie slid five one-hundred-dollar bills into the pot. The size of the pot astounded Leo. Nearly $800—$1,300 if Charley called—and Arnold Steinberger was trying to buy it.

He did. Charley Wax had not improved his three kings. Raking in the money, Arnie turned to Leo with another wink. He handed him a five-dollar bill. "For bringing me luck."

"I didn't bring you no luck, Mr. Steinberger," Leo said. "You just played it good."

Arnie patted Leo's arm, then turned to continue the game. Leo, hoping Arnie would speak to him again, wanted to stay. But the young man tapped Leo's shoulder and jerked his head toward the door.

"See you later, Mr. Steinberger," Leo said. Arnie did not hear him, but Leo did not care. He felt good. He and Arnie Steinberger were friends. Walking down the stairs, he made up his mind to do something about the punk in the lobby. Sucker play or not, sometimes you had to do it for your own self-respect.

The lobby was empty. The *Sporting News* was folded on the armrest of the chair, the punk nowhere in sight. Leo called out for him. No answer. Probably gone for cigarettes or a drink. Leo, feeling both relief and disappointment, pondered whether or not to wait. He decided to leave. The knowledge that he had intended to confront the man was enough. He knew this was what Arnold Steinberger would have done.

All the way home, Leo thought about Arnold Steinberger. His appearance, his clothes, his speech. The ease with which he handled all that money and standing pat on two small pair to bluff out three of a kind. There was more to it than a simple poker game. It was a demonstration of the proper use of money. The power of money. Arnie Steinberger understood that power, and how to use it. It was the key to the whole world.

2.

Leo told his mother the truth when he said Hershey was teaching him the business. Hershey had taught Leo everything he knew, from driving and maintaining motor vehicles to identifying shaved dice and the unique hiss of a card dealt from the bottom. He now assisted Hershey in managing the game. They were the house.

What Hershey did not know, however, would itself fill a book. But Leo was learning it on his own. Most important, evaluating the characters of the players. He instantly recognized now and welcomed the compulsive gambler. Conversely, he discouraged the "steamers," those whose chronic loss of composure could disrupt an entire afternoon's play. He learned to be wary of the dangerous shooters, the ones who knew when to push their luck, although an occasional big winner did not displease him; it was good for business. And in that small-change game no lucky streak could break the bank. Not with a ten-dollar line-bet limit, two dollars on numbers. The percentages ground down even the luckiest player. Few ever bet the limit anyway. But it added up, and netted Hershey a modest profit.

After expenses.

Fixed payoffs for the beat cops, the precinct sergeant, the captain, the New York Democratic Club. In return, Hershey's game—like other established games throughout Manhattan in allocated territories—was both tolerated and protected. The payoffs were substantial, but no real financial sacrifice. There was enough for everyone.

More than enough, for business that summer of 1915 was so good Hershey decided to expand. He opened another, bigger game on the upper floor of a Division Street saloon. The new game soon demanded his full attention. Responsibility for the garage game therefore fell increasingly to Hershey's wife, Edie—with Leo there to assist. Ironically, the legitimate garage business continued growing. Since the Lefkowitzes had no intention of neglecting this, they began relying on Leo to manage the game.

He was a fifteen-year-old boy, a kid; and to make matters worse, a runt, a shade under five feet four. But he understood gambling, and gamblers. In turn they, the gamblers, understood he represented Hershey. They accepted his supervision. Equally important, they trusted him. They knew he ran an honest game.

He did this from no particular ethics or morality, but from the knowledge that the numbers, those vital percentages, made it mathematically impossible to beat the house. An honest game, therefore, was simply good business.

Within a year, shortly after Leo's sixteenth birthday, Hershey raised his weekly salary to twenty dollars. Enough for Sarah to quit her cafeteria job, and for Leo to move the family into a two-bedroom flat on Fourteenth Street. A bedroom for his mother, one for his sister, and an almost new, quite comfortable living-room couch for him. Best of all, their own toilet.

Esther, graduating from high school, had taken a job at a hat factory. She used most of her salary on clothes and dancing lessons. It did not help her find a man. Anyone she liked seemed automatically to earn mother Sarah's disapproval. Esther accused her mother of wanting her to become an old maid so Sarah would have someone to look after her. Privately, she confessed to Leo that the idea of marriage frightened her. Sleeping with a man frightened her. Men frightened her.

Leo was far too preoccupied with his own life that year of 1916 to dwell long on his sister's. And his own went well. He had plenty of money, a good job, good friends. Friends like Hershey and Edie whom he had come to consider his real family. He spent almost every evening in their flat on the second floor of the garage. Edie, a superb cook, would make supper for her two *bochas*, as she called Leo and Hershey.

Leo loved them both, but wished they did not argue so vehemently and often. Sometimes, after these arguments, Hershey and Edie ignored each other for days. The arguments always concerned money. Hershey banked it, or invested prudently. Saving for their future. Edie felt this was fine, but for Christ's sake couldn't they enjoy a little of it *now*?

One night she absolutely refused to cook. She wanted to dine out; she wanted to go to Rector's.

"Money thrown away," Hershey said. "I guess you don't remember the old days."

"I remember, I remember," she said. "That's why I want something now. Oy!" she said to Leo, rolling her eyes in despair. "What do you have to do to get through to him?"

"You don't piss away hard-earned money," Hershey said.

"All I'm saying is maybe once a week we can afford someplace," Edie said. "Anyplace. So it don't have to be Rector's."

Hershey said, "And after that maybe the theater? Maybe to see Jake Adler, or maybe even a moving-picture show?"

"Yeah, maybe I would," Edie said. "And what's so wrong about that?"

"And maybe some new dresses, too?" Hershey said. "A nice hat? A pair of them spiffy shoes?"

"Yeah, that, too," Edie said. "Why not?"

"Why not?" Hershey repeated to Leo. "You hear, Kleyner, 'Why not?' " He said to Edie, "Because you don't need nothing, that's why not! You got all you need. More than you need. And goddamit, stop smoking them things!"

Edie was just then lighting a fresh cigarette from the butt of the old one. She balanced the new cigarette between her lips and mashed out the old one with deliberate defiance. "Sure, by you all I need is overalls. So I can sit all day in your dirty garage and keep your lousy books."

"Hey, lady, it's your dirty garage, too," Hershey said. "And your lousy books. You're a partner, ain't you?"

"Then gimme my share once in a while!" She turned to Leo again. "You see, Kleyner, that's your friend, Mr. Hershel Lefkowitz. Your big hero. The worst *momzer* in the whole city!" She rose, gathered up all the dishes and deposited them clatteringly into the porcelain sink. Over her shoulder she said to Hershey, "The richest man in the cemetery."

"The day I'm there is the day you should look forward to," he said. "I should only be so lucky," she called back.

While Leo hated seeing Edie unhappy, he did not consider Hershey cheap, a *momzer*. He paid Leo twenty dollars a week, didn't he? Besides, in Leo's book, Hershey was always right. But Leo lived with the fear that their arguing might lead to something more serious. Breaking up, for example, although he was sure that despite the heated words they loved each other. They would never break up. They would never do that to him.

But one night Hershey did take them to Rector's. To celebrate Leo's seventeenth birthday. The finest dinner Leo ever had, with a bottle of wine that mellowed Hershey so that he put his arms around Edie and kissed her and said she was his whole life. It was the finest birthday present they could have given Leo.

Not long after that there was another argument. Leo always remembered the date, March 30, 1917, because exactly one week later the United States declared war on Germany. The argument was over shoes Edie bought. Pumps, she called them. Low-cut, black patent leather with white trimming and slender heels at least two inches high. Leo thought they looked beautiful. They cost twelve dollars. Hershey demanded she return them, which she absolutely refused. Furthermore, she said, if Hershey did not watch himself, she just might go out and find herself some fancy *shtarker* that would be happy to take care of her.

Before Hershey could reply, Leo blurted, "Jesus, Edie, don't say things like that!"

Both gazed at him, startled. He felt himself reddening and looked away, embarrassed. Then Hershey laughed. "Not to worry, kid. Before she goes finding *shtarkers*, she should find a mirror. A bathing beauty, you ain't," he said to Edie.

Leo wanted to defend her. He wanted to say Edie was the finest-looking woman in town. But he also did not want to take sides. He pushed his plate away. Roast chicken, Edie's specialty, stuffed with onions and potatoes. But he had lost his appetite. He rose from the table, walked to the window, and lit a cigarette. He had only recently started smoking. He enjoyed it, but now the cigarette tasted stale.

Suddenly he felt gentle fingers stroking the nape of his neck. Edie stood over him, bending now to kiss his forehead. Her lips were warm and soft.

"Leo, honey, it was a joke. I wouldn't go looking for no other men. Honest to God." She took his cigarette, dragged deeply on it, then put her arm around him. "Come, Kleyner, finish supper." She led him back to the table.

"We don't mean nothing, kid," Hershey said. "We just yell a lot, that's all."

"It's good exercise," Edie said.

Leo poked the chicken with his fork. Then he said, "Hersh, let her get the shoes, huh?"

Edie said quietly, "Never mind the shoes, Leo. I got plenty of shoes. I don't need no more."

"Me and you split the twelve bucks," Leo said to Hershey. "Six each."

Hershey laughed. "Kid, you are something else."

"Is it a deal?"

Hershey laughed again. "Maybe you'd like to buy her some dresses, too?"

Edie said, "Don't make fun of him. He's a *mensch*, which is more than I can say for you."

"Okay, a deal," Hershey said. "Sure, why not? It's like buying for half price. How can I refuse that kind of percentage? Now eat, you little *petzeleh*." He reached across the table and ruffled Leo's hair. "Around here, we ain't wasting no food!"

Leo ate.

A few days later, Edie left the garage early for a beauty-parlor appointment. She told Leo he was expected for supper. Boiled beef with potatoes and cabbage, one of his favorites. That evening, entering the flat, Leo could not believe his eyes.

Edie was a blonde.

The once chestnut-brown hair was a startling bright yellow. And no pompadour. The new blond hair flowed down the front of her shoulders, over the swell of her breasts. She wore a black silk kimono, and the white-trimmed black patent-leather pumps. It reminded Leo instantly of Chana, the Allen Street whore of so many years ago, only Edie was much prettier.

"You like it? She twirled completely around, then playfully pinched his cheek. She wore a new perfume, too. The scent wafted dizzyingly up from her loosely fastened kimono.

He said nothing; he could not find his voice.

She extended one foot, displaying the shoe. "Classy, huh?" She bent to kiss the top of his forehead. His nose brushed the smooth, soft V of her neck. She stepped back and laughed delightedly. "What's the matter, you can't speak?"

He gazed up at her. A thousand thoughts rushed into his mind, none translated into words.

"Well, do you or don't you like it?" she asked.

"Jesus!" he said.

"What Jesus? Just say if you like the hair?"

"I like it. Jesus Christ, yes!"

"Good. Now I'll fix supper."

"It's beautiful."

"That's better, even." She pinched his cheek again and went to the stove. Leo stood watching her. His nostrils still tingled with her perfume, blended now with talcum powder and the fragrance of her body itself.

"Hershey'll die when he sees it," she said. She stirred the beef in the pot. "He ain't coming home till later. He's over by the Democratic Club. To see some galook named Joe Sweeney that's running for councilman. I tell you, Kleyner, them Irishers are something else! It was one of them talked me into the hair. This kid in the beauty parlor, a greenhorn that's only on the job there maybe a month. She said a blonde, I'll look just like that one in the Ziegfeld show—" Edie glanced at Leo with a pleased smile.

He had half turned away so she would not notice his bulging fly. He was rock hard. He dared not move, he did not believe he could walk.

"What's her name?" Edie said. "The *nafke* that's the girlfriend of the newspaper *bocha*? Davies, that's right. Marion Davies. Hey, Kleyner, come in here and eat already, huh? It's special for you I'm making this."

"Yeah, in a second," he said. The words seemed caught in his throat. "In a second." He had turned his back fully to her now. Go down, he told himself. Jesus Christ, please go down! It would not. He hobbled out of her sight and lowered himself awkwardly onto the sofa. He sat, gasping with the pain of the erection scraping against the rough wool cloth of his trousers. He peered down at it. The buttons strained against the fly.

"You look terrible!"

He whirled, startled. She stood at the arm of the sofa, not a foot away, her body blocking the light from the pedestaled electric lamp. Under the kimono, her tall nakedness was perfectly silhouetted. He could not take his eyes from the curve of her belly, and the little hollow under the curve.

"You ain't sick, are you?" She placed her hand against his cheek. "You're hot." She sat beside him and ran her fingers over his forehead. "Leo, I think you got a fever."

He faced her. Her robe, open even further now, nearly exposed one whole breast. He looked away.

"What the hell is the matter?" she asked. "Tell me, for Christ's sake."

She cupped his chin, turned him to her. "Tell me!"

"Nothing," he said. He looked away again. "Honest to God, nothing."

"Don't lie to me, Leo."

He shook his head. He only hoped she did not notice the incredible bulge in his pants. In his mind he saw it relentlessly forcing itself through the fly, shattering the buttons, bursting into the open.

"You need a haircut," she said. She was fondling the hair at the back of his neck. His whole body throbbed. His heart pounded. He could hardly breathe. "You're a *shtarker* yourself," she said. Her breath was warm on his neck. "Anybody ever tell you?"

Unable to repress it now, he moaned and faced her, and lowered his head onto her breasts. Oh, Jesus! The soft round smoothness. The sweetness. Her fingers pressed against the back of his head, burying his face even deeper into the huge, marvelous bosom.

". . . a darling boy. Really a darling boy." Her voice was a distant echo, and muted by the hammering of his heart. And he did not care what she said, what anyone said. He wanted only to stay here, with her, like this.

It was like a dream, and he was not entirely sure it was not a dream. He closed his eyes, feeling her tongue flicking in and out of his ear, and her hand on his thigh, her fingers groping for, and then finding, his fly buttons. Unbuttoning them one by one. And then he was free, nestled in her hand. And then—in a pulsing, surging, bursting wave that made him feel as though his insides had torn loose—he exploded. The tenseness remained another throbbing instant, and then all at once vanished. He collapsed against the sofa cushion and opened his eyes long enough to see that he had splattered all over her black kimono. He was vaguely aware of her gently scolding voice.

". . . bad boy! Oh, what will I do with such a bad boy . . . ?"

And then he felt her tongue, warm and wet, licking the tip and shaft. And her voice again. ". . . oh, so tasty! So sweet! Like sugar!" He closed his eyes again and thought, I have died and gone to Heaven.

But Heaven came ten minutes later when as easily as though he never had the first orgasm he was hard again. By now she had undressed him and, naked herself, mounted him. She rode him for what seemed hours but was of course only minutes. Beautiful, impossible, ecstatic minutes. She pleaded with him to hold back. Just a little longer, another second. Please, darling! Please! He could not. But she was almost with him, breathing in abrupt, ever faster, moaning gasps, her body heaving up and down, back and forth. And then, as the moaning became a single, ever louder, endless wail of pleasure, all at once she stopped moving. Every muscle in her body, stiffening, clamped onto him like steel.

For just one instant she remained motionless, absolutely rigid. And then she screamed. A shrill, ear-piercing scream that sent Leo's stomach plummeting.

"What's the matter!" he asked. She held herself still poised over him, still imprisoning him. And then he felt her relax. She smiled down at him.

"What's the matter, he says?" She kissed him gently on the lips and rolled over so they lay side by side. "The matter, sweet Kleyner, is I came."

"But you're okay?"

"Yes, my darling, I am okay." She ran her fingers through his hair. "I am very okay." She kissed him again, then pushed herself off the couch and slipped into her kimono. She tossed his pants at him. "And so now, Mr. Leo Gorodetsky-*shtarker*, let's you and me have supper."

Leo was ravenous. He devoured the beef and potatoes, and mopped the plate dry with three slices of rich black pumpernickel. All washed down with heavy, dark Roumanian beer. Leo drank nearly a whole quart bottle himself. Edie talked endlessly. About everything. The business. The next door neighbors that had been evicted. Her childhood in Poland, and the telephone just installed in the flat. Everything except what had just happened. Leo was glad it was not mentioned, for now he wondered how he would ever again face Hershey. He had betrayed him. His best friend. He wondered if merely by looking at Leo Hershey would know. And if so, what would Hershey do? What would Leo do?

That night, exhausted and relaxed as he was, Leo tossed and turned for hours. He could still smell Edie's perfume. He was certain it had adhered itself to his own body. He was certain Hershey would somehow sense she had just been fucked. The very word itself conjured up the picture of the act. In his mind he experienced it again, each magnificent moment. And he was hard again—and unable to resist relieving himself, the orgasm every bit as intense and pleasurable as with Edie. Followed, almost immediately, by remorse.

Wondering, again, how to face Hershey. But he could do it, because he would never again betray his friend. But suppose Edie told Hershey? She might, in anger; those arguments. If she did, Leo would deny it. Hershey would believe him. Yes, everything would be fine. And he intended to make sure of it by never having anything more to do with her. It was over, finished.

The next day, and the entire following week, Edie behaved as though nothing ever happened. Although Leo's nervousness eased, he refused several supper invitations, claiming his mother insisted he eat at home. When Hershey teasingly suggested Leo must be spending his time with a girl, and Edie told Hershey to stop *yotzing* the kid, Leo knew everything was all right.

A few days later at six when the garage closed, Edie came into the back room to check the action. There were only three players, betting dimes and quarters. Edie told Leo to close the game and bring the money upstairs.

Leo dropped the bills and coins in the large tin biscuit container used as a cashbox and followed Edie into the apartment. She locked the door and put her hand on his crotch.

"Oy!" she cried. "My Kleyner's *kleyneh* is saying hello!"

The instant she touched him all his good intentions crumbled. He forgot about Hershey. About friendship, loyalty, betrayal. He forgot about everything. He cupped her breasts through her silk blouse and started lowering his head onto them.

"Later, sweetheart," she said, and pushed him gently away. "First, we take care of business. Count the money."

Bookkeeping was simple. The game opened each day with a specified amount of cash in the tin box. Today's starting sum was $50. The final count was a respectable $110.75. A profit of $60.75.

Leo prepared to enter the figure in the ledger kept for that purpose. Edie clamped her hand on his. She spoke quietly. "Put forty dollars and seventy-five cents."

"Huh?"

"Forty seventy-five is what you write."

"What do you mean?"

"I mean, darling, I am keeping twenty bucks." Edie plucked two ten-dollar bills from the stack. She flattened them neatly down on the table. "You write forty seventy-five. Hershey never knows the difference. He called me on the telephone, by the way. He ain't coming home till maybe eight." She tapped a long, manicured fingernail on the line in the ledger page. "Now do it, Kleyner, just like Edie says."

He looked at her, the blond hair piled high atop her head, the red-glistening rouged lips. The marvelous breasts straining against her blouse. He wanted to say, It ain't fair to Hershey. The words were on his tongue, but he was afraid to say them. And afraid not to.

She read his thoughts. "Now listen, Leo. You know that cheap bastard, he don't give me an extra dime. And he's making it now. *Gottenyu*, is he making it! Like it grows from a tree!" She stroked the back of Leo's hand. "Do it, darling. For me." She ran her fingers caressingly over his face. "And then we'll see if my little *boichick* is still a *shtarker*. Do it."

He did it. He wrote $40.75.

"There," said Edie. "Was that so hard?"

"No," he said.

"But this is," she said, placing her hand between his legs. She fondled him, at the same time leaning her breasts into his face. "Let's go see what you remember from the other time," she whispered.

3.

Edie was careful to skim only from sizable profits, and even then modestly. But ten dollars one day, five dollars another—sometimes less—added up. Leo knew how much he had helped her steal down to the last dollar. After three months, $532.

It was foolproof. Impossible for Hershey ever to suspect, or have reason to. Not only did he implicitly trust Leo, but the game showed a continuing profit. And, cleverly, Edie kept complaining to Hershey about no extra money for herself.

Leo serviced Edie at least once weekly, each time swearing to himself afterward that this was the last time, and that he would stop stealing from Hershey. The fact that he did not take a cent for himself made it a little easier. But each next time with Edie was as new and exciting as the last. Leo could not help himself. He was lost.

But it had to end. And, one muggy July afternoon, did.

Edie was in the garage office talking on the telephone to a doctor whose Model T was in for repairs. The doctor really wanted to discuss the news of the first Americans landing in France. His son, a National Guardsman, was among them. The doctor, himself a deserter from the Russian army, was both proud and concerned.

Edie listened patiently. Then, through the office window, she saw Hershey entering the garage. A strange hour for him, she thought vaguely; and then, noting his determined stride, his grim-set jaw and angry mouth, she knew she was in trouble.

She told the doctor to call back later. She hung up and watched Hershey approach. He opened the office door, but stood in the doorway a long, silent moment. Then he said, "Come upstairs."

He turned and walked out. Momentarily paralyzed, she sat watching him. Then she followed. Her legs felt so suddenly weak she was not sure she could climb the stairs. Hershey stood waiting at the kitchen table. He had removed Leo's account ledger from its hiding place behind the ice chest. The ledger was on the table, open. Edie shut the door and looked at him.

Hershey said, "I ran into Shnorrer Willie. He said he dropped twenty-two bucks last night. He said when he tapped out, Leo closed the game."

"So?" Edie strained to keep her voice calm.

"So last night Leo put in the ledger only a twelve-dollar take."

"That must of been all we made."

"Not if Willie taps out dropping twenty-two."

"Then we must of been losing before he played."

Hershey studied her with hard, piercing eyes. Edie felt her legs trembling. She lowered herself into a chair. "We must of been losing," she said.

"Leo said the last player was some *meshuggener* from over on Hester." Hershey spoke slowly, almost painfully. "A greenhorn tailor that lost three bucks. He said he closed the game after that. He didn't say nothing about Willie, or about Willie losing twenty-two."

"Oh, Christ!" Edie said, almost as a whisper. It was all she could think of to say.

Hershey seemed suddenly weary. He grasped the back of a chair and pulled it slowly around behind him. He sank down into it. "We treated the kid like our own," he said. "Better than our own, goddamit."

"It was maybe a mistake," Edie said. "Leo counted wrong."

"*I* don't count wrong," Hershey said. "And twelve bucks was the take, and that's what Leo put in the book. Twelve." He ran his finger across the ledger entry. "You're supposed to watch the count when I ain't here, Edie."

Now that it was clear Hershey blamed Leo, courage flowed back into Edie. "I'm supposed to watch the lousy garage, too, Hershey! So I can't be watching our sweet little Leo always. When I'm not around, almost whenever he wants, he could slip a few bucks in his pocket!"

"Edith," Hershey said, pronouncing her name in two syllables, "E-ditt," as he sometimes did when he was angry with her and straining for control. "Somebody told me they saw you by Mulberry Street. Coming out of the Bank of Italy, they said."

She felt her heart flutter. The courage drained away faster than it had returned. "Bank of Italy? *Vay iz mir!* And they saw me I suppose by Wall Street, too? Buying stocks, maybe?"

He said nothing.

"What would I be doing there?"

"That's what I'm asking you."

"Whoever said that, he's a filthy liar."

"How do you know it was a 'he'?"

"He, she, it!" Her voice rose shrilly. "It's a goddam lie! Hershey, what are you looking at me like that for?"

She never quite completed the sentence. Hershey reached across the table and backhanded her on the side of the head. The force of the blow toppled her from the chair. "Bastard!" she cried in Yiddish. "Son of a bitch! Cossack!"

Hershey rose and stepped over to her. Grasping the front of her blouse he pulled her to her feet, raising his arm to strike her again.

"Don't!" she cried. She crossed her arms protectively over her face. "Please, Hershey! No!"

"The bank? Tell me!"

She stood cowering another instant. Then, slowly, she lowered her arms. An angry red welt was rising under her right eye. Tears streamed down her cheeks forming pasty white streaks in the pancake makeup. Wisps of blond hair hung frizzily in all directions, hairpins precariously dangling like objects caught in a spider's web.

"Putting money in," she said. "I was putting money in."

"What money?"

"The money Leo stole."

"You put in the bank money *he* stole?"

She nodded.

"How much?"

"Five hundred," she said. "A little more maybe."

"How much more?"

"Ten, twenty," she said. "Honest to God, that's all."

"Whose idea? Yours, or his?"

"His," she said. "His idea."

"His," Hershey repeated dully. He stood another moment, gazing at the ledger. Then, almost delicately, he closed it. He flattened his palms on the black-and-white speckled cardboard cover.

"Don't do nothing to him, Hershey," she said. "Please."

"If it was his idea, how come you got the money?"

She stared at him. Her throat was suddenly so dry she thought she might gag. Her brain whirled; she could not think of a word to say. She wanted to turn and run, but her legs were chunks of iron pinned to the floor.

Quietly, flatly, Hershey said, "It was your idea, Edie. And I know just how you done it. You wagged that big ass in front of the kid's face. You made him so *meshugge*, if you said to, he'd jump off the bridge. You got it both ways, didn't you, you whore? You got him to steal for you, and you got some of that young *petzel* you're always so hungry for. You think I don't know, huh?"

"Hersh, there's never been nobody but you—"

"—I want the money," he said quietly. "Go to that fucking bank and get it. Right now."

"It ain't in the bank, Hersh."

"What do you mean, it ain't in the bank? Where is it?"

Her throat was dryer than ever. Her lips were so parched she could feel them cracking.

"Where is it, Edie?"

She hesitated, then turned and stepped past him into the bedroom, to the clothes closet. He watched curiously from the doorway as she brought out a wooden hangar containing her heavy winter cloth coat. It was buttoned and appeared exceptionally bulky. She unbuttoned it and removed it from the hangar. Underneath was another coat. Rich, dark lustrous fur.

"Sable, Hersh," she said. "Real sable."

"Take it back," he said.

"I can't."

"You better."

"It's hot," she said. "I bought it off a mick that did a job in a house by Central Park. It's worth at least two thousand, Hersh." Speaking, she slipped the coat off the hangar and draped it over her shoulders. "Look how pretty, Hersh." She stroked the fur, extending one sleeve toward him. "Feel it."

She ran the fur over his cheek. He said nothing, only looked at her. His eyes seemed dead. She stepped away from him now and caressed her own cheek with the fur sleeve.

"I wanted it, Hershey!" she cried. "Goddamit, I wanted it!"

Hershey hit her flush in the mouth with his closed fist. She hurtled backward, slammed into the low footboard of the bed and slid to the floor, her body jackknifed in a sitting position. Blood spurted from her nose and mouth, blotting the shiny silk lining of the coat bunched at her feet. Her head lolled forward, then up. She stared at him, dazed.

He went into the kitchen and returned with a dish towel, which he threw disdainfully into her lap. "You stay right here," he said. He started away, then stopped. "Not a single inch you move, you understand? *Die herst?*"

"Hershey, don't hurt him!" The towel, pressed to her mouth, was already bloody.

"He stole from me."

"You'll get in trouble, Hershey. It ain't worth it."

"Oh, I won't beat him up, or nothing like that," Hershey said. "I got a better idea."

She sat propped against the footboard, gazing across the bedroom into the kitchen, the door ajar as Hershey had left it. She held the towel firmly to her mouth until the bleeding stopped. Then, the sable coat cradled in her arms, she hobbled into the kitchen. She soaked another towel in cold water and began cleaning the blood-spattered coat lining.

Leo was arrested at 6:30 that same evening. Taken to the Canal Street Precinct House, he was told only that he was being brought in for questioning. When he saw Hershey seated glumly on a bench near the sergeant's desk, he knew it was a shakedown. That, or the police were putting on one of their occasional shows for the reformers.

"Hey, Hersh," Leo said, relieved. "If you ain't got enough for the bail, I can loan you some."

"That him?" the desk sergeant asked Hershey.

"That's him," said Hershey.

Before Leo could utter another word he was hustled into a small interrogation room and left alone. A plank bench, two straight-backed wooden chairs, and a knife-scarred wooden table crowded the room. On the table was a tarnished brass spittoon. He lit a cigarette and tossed the match into the spittoon. Then he sat on the bench, propping his legs up on the table. After a moment, he put the spittoon on the floor.

Only now, for the first time, did he begin feeling really nervous. Why did Hershey say "That's him"? And his voice so strange. Tight, as though the words hurt.

He was lighting his third cigarette when the door finally opened. Hershey entered, accompanied by a tall, heavy, silver-mustached man wearing a derby and rumpled blue-serge suit. Leo recognized him as Rafferty, a plainclothesman Hershey regularly paid off.

Leo suddenly realized what it was all about. Some kind of heat about the game. Maybe even shut it down a few days until things cooled.

He flipped his cigarette into the spittoon and grinned at Hershey. "So what big crime we committed, Hersh?"

Rafferty said to Hershey, "Now, you sure you want to go through with this?"

"I'm sure," Hershey said.

Rafferty motioned to someone outside the door. An instant later, accompanied by a policeman, Edie entered. Leo looked at her and drew in his breath in a loud shudder. "Edie . . . Jesus!"

The entire right side of her face was a single mass of blue-black bruises. The right eye itself was swollen shut. Her mouth was puffed grotesquely, upper lip split. She had fixed her hair, but wore the same white blouse, its pleated front now mottled with dried blood.

"He the one?" Rafferty asked her, indicating Leo.

She nodded.

"Book him," Rafferty said to the policeman.

The policeman gripped Leo's shoulder, but he squirmed away, shouting, "Book me for *what*? Hershey, what's this all about?"

Rafferty said, "You're being charged with assault and attempted robbery."

Leo heard the words, and understood them, but refused to believe they were directed at him. It was a mistake. No, a joke. A not-so-funny practical joke. "Hershey, what's he talking about?" He looked at Edie. "Edie, please!"

"Can I go?" she asked Rafferty.

"Sure, Mrs. Lefkowitz, you go on out to the waiting room," Rafferty said. "No need for you to go through any more'n you already have."

Not once had Edie looked directly at Leo, and did not now as she left. He said to Hershey, "Who did that to her?"

Hershey said to Rafferty, "Whatever charges you make, me and my wife will back up."

"Charges?" Leo screamed. "What charges?"

"Are you denying all this, boy?" Rafferty asked impatiently. "She's already signed a sworn statement."

Leo shook his head. What the hell were they talking about? Whatever it was, he knew now it was no joke. Rafferty was talking, but Leo could not hear him for the roaring in his ears. And he felt dizzy. Bile surged into his mouth. He thought he might vomit.

". . . says she caught you in the act of stealing her fine fur coat," Rafferty was saying. "You beat her up. For God's sake, son, we seen the coat. The poor thing's blood is all over the damned lining. We got you dead to rights."

Leo gripped the table to steady himself. He saw it all now, all of it: During one of their arguments, to make Hershey jealous, the stupid bitch admitted she was fucking Leo. Hershey beat her up. And then, to get even, cooked up this story and made her go along with it. Well, they wouldn't get away with it. He, Leo, was too smart for them.

His fear and confusion were gone, replaced by anger. Cool, clear-thinking anger. He said, "She's twice as big as me, and twice as strong. You think she'd just stand around and let me beat her up like that?"

"She's a female," Rafferty said. "Besides, you took her by surprise."

Leo felt clever, almost superior as he sprang the trap. "If I beat her up like you say, how come I didn't cop the coat? How come she's still got it?"

"Because Mr. Lefkowitz here walked in the door just in time to stop you," said Rafferty. "And damned lucky he did. You bloody well might have killed that poor woman!"

Leo looked at Hershey. "And I beat him up, too, I suppose?"

"You ran away like the yellow little weasel you are," Rafferty said. "Now do you still deny the charge, or do you and me go for a private talk?"

"That oughta suit you good, huh, Hersh?" Leo said. "One of them private talks. Edie and you had a nice one, I can see."

For the first time, Hershey spoke directly to Leo. He spoke quietly, almost sad. "It wasn't what went on with you and her, Leo. I know maybe that wasn't your fault, and maybe you couldn't help it. But I trusted you, and you stole from me."

Rafferty said, "Now, I don't quite get this. What is it you mean, he stole from you? You and Mrs. Lefkowitz claimed nothing's been stolen."

Hershey looked at Leo. "He knows what I mean. You don't steal off your friends. They'll forgive you everything except that. You don't steal off them, Kleyner. Never."

For the rest of his life, Leo would remember that moment. It would remain engraved in his brain like the carving on a stone monument. Containing a lesson so vivid and real it seemed written across the sky in letters of fire.

The anger that had replaced the fear was now itself replaced by a calm and comprehension Leo had never before known. He had betrayed his friend. His friend did what needed to be done, what Leo himself would have done. The only thing that could be done. He knew he had lost this friend, and regretted the loss, but knew it was deserved. Whatever his punishment, he felt was also deserved.

The judge agreed. He sentenced Leo to the maximum allowed under the law, commenting that it should be remembered that other young Americans of the defendant's age were not violating societal rules, but were instead dying in the muddy fields of Flanders.

Three years in the New York State Reformatory at Elmira.

— 4 —

HE gazed at the shaft of sunlight under the door and knew it was morning. He thought this was the third day, the last, although he could not be certain. The damp, bare stone floor was like a film of slimy wetness that had soaked through his clothes down to the skin. He pulled the blanket up over his shoulders for warmth, but it was only a half blanket and did not cover both his feet and shoulders at the same time.

Finally, he sat up. He groped for his shoes, found them, and put them on. After the first night he had learned not to sleep with shoes on. He remembered that first night all too well. Not because of the swollen feet, or the first night in the hole, but because he had nearly cried. From pain, from fear, frustration. He was glad now he had not allowed himself to cry. It proved he could take anything they gave, and more.

It began almost as soon as he walked through the Elmira gate. They took him to the deputy warden for orientation, a lecture concerning the futility of instilling American ideals into foreigners.

"I ain't no foreigner," Leo had said.

"No talking!" the guard standing beside him said.

"But I'm American," Leo said, and then gasped in eye-searing pain as the guard smashed his stick into the small of Leo's back.

"I said no talking."

"Not until you're told to," said the deputy warden, a tall, slender man of forty, totally bald but for a fringe of thick black hair. "Do you understand?"

Leo nodded.

The deputy warden, whose name was Mr. Wilmore, referring to Leo's file, compared the inmate's offense with the brutality of the Germans, those savage Huns who murdered defenseless women and babies. The calm, indulgent tone rapidly rose in anger. Finally, assigning Leo to the laundry, he ordered the guard to get him out of his sight.

The guard escorted Leo to the supply room where he was issued a flannel shirt, work shoes, and denim overalls. The overalls were far too large. He requested a smaller size.

The trusty, an Irish kid, staring smugly at a garment-filled shelf marked "S," said there were no small sizes.

At the laundry, a guard told Leo to go back and get overalls that fit. Again, the Irish kid said there were no small sizes. Leo was determined not to make trouble. Good behavior shortened your sentence.

"Okay," he said to the Irish kid. "I'll just tell the screw you run out of 'smalls.'"

"Yeah, and tell him little sheenies don't deserve nothing better," the Irish kid said. "And I see you again in my supply room, I'll punch you so hard it'll make you two inches littler than you are already!"

Leo started away. At the door, abruptly, he stopped. He walked slowly back to the counter. Perhaps it was the week of rotten, rancid food. Or the constant latrine odor in the barracks. Or being awakened each morning with screws or trusties strolling down the row of bunks slamming their sticks on the soles of your bare feet. Or simply the final realization that for the next three years he would be locked up like an animal, with other animals.

In an open box on the counter was a pair of heavy work boots. Gripping the ankle top of one shoe like an ax handle, Leo raked the metal heel cleat across the side of the Irish kid's face. Instantly, two guards seized him. He spit in one guard's face. Earning him several, almost scientifically placed blows to stomach and kidneys. Leaving him semiconscious and screaming with pain.

And three days in the hole.

In the dark, with nothing to do but wait for the screw to bring breakfast. Water, from a tin cup so rusty the corroded metal crumbled on your lips, and two slices of stale bread. No lunch. Then, when the light under the door had long since faded, supper. The same bread and water. The first day he had no appetite; the stink from the bucket turned his stomach. He kept the bucket in the farthest corner, but the room was very small.

Three days with nothing to do but think.

About what brought him here. Who, and why. He reviewed it endlessly in his mind, and was doing it again this morning of the third day. The answer was always the same. He had done it to himself. His own stupidity. His own weakness. Not Hershey's fault, not Edie's. And he no longer blamed her. She had not put a gun to his head. No, he thought, no gun to his head—and even in his misery the thought made him smile—a big, soft tit in the face.

Just then the door was flung open. Bright, blinding sunlight stabbed into his eyes. "Okay, boy," said a voice. "Up and at 'em!" In the doorway, behind the glare, an impatient guard. "Come on, let's go."

"I'm out?"

"You won't be if you don't move your ass in the next five seconds," said the guard, whose name was Scanlon. He was the same one Leo had spit at.

Scanlon took him to the empty mess hall. Breakfast was finished, but plenty of SOS remained. SOS stood for shit-on-a-shingle: scattered flakes of meat in a lumpy cream sauce, spread on hard, burnt toast. Scanlon sat with Leo, drinking coffee and smoking a cigarette. He watched Leo wolf the food.

"They give Riley a parole," Scanlon said.

"So what's that to me?" Leo said.

"Riley, the kid you went after in the supply room."

Leo swallowed down half a cup of coffee. "Because I hit him? He gets a parole?"

"You cut him so bad they had to take him to the hospital in town," Scanlon said. "The warden figured when Riley comes back, he'll go gunning for you. More trouble for everybody. He only had another two months, anyway."

"The prick should thank me," Leo said.

Scanlon said, "What I want to know is where's a little bastard like you get the balls to take on guys twice as big?"

"He insulted my religion."

"What's your religion?"

"I'm a Jew."

"Was it worth three days in the hole?"

Leo's reply was a wry look, and Scanlon grinned. Leo mopped up the remaining sauce with the last piece of toast. He was still famished.

"Yeah, I figured you for a Jew," Scanlon said. "The Jews make more trouble up here than all the rest put together."

Leo decided not to give them the satisfaction of asking for seconds. He asked for a cigarette instead. Scanlon gave him one and lit it with the tip of his own. Leo thanked him.

Scanlon shook his head sadly. "I guess it's because that's just the way Jews are." He finished his coffee and got up. "Go on back to the kitchen and report to the cook. You're on shit detail from now on."

Leo considered anything, even shit detail, better than the hole. After a week he was not so sure. The work itself was easy. Scrubbing garbage cans and cleaning drains required only a strong back and stronger stomach. But Leo was a marked man. Wherever he went, from mess hall to latrine, someone always bumped him out of line, stole his toothbrush, short-sheeted his bed, called him "Jewboy," "Peewee," "Shorty," "Sheeny." Anything to provoke him, for once you served time in the hole the slightest offense might send you back. it was a challenge to see how far the little kike could be pushed.

For months, he took it. Turned the other cheek. It would get him out of this place if not faster, at least on time. And also proving himself equal to the challenge, which was proof of self-control, common sense, and guts.

But there is a limit.

As discovered one Saturday evening by an Albany farmboy, Swenson, age sixteen. A huge hulk of a boy, serving a year for incorrigible truancy, Swenson continually rode Leo. Up to now, Leo had resisted rising to the bait. This particular evening he had just emptied a garbage bucket into the large trash bin behind the kitchen cookhouse. Swenson suddenly appeared and asked for a cigarette.

Knowing Swenson anticipated being refused, providing him an opportunity for further harassment, Leo surprised him. "Yeah, sure," he said, and extended the pack.

Momentarily disappointed, Swenson took one cigarette. But before Leo could draw away, Swenson seized his wrist, and with his free hand plucked out half the cigarettes in the pack. "Thanks, Hymie," he said, and walked off.

Leo stared at the remaining cigarettes in the pack. Then he started after Swenson. "Gimme back them butts!"

Swenson smiled smugly over his shoulder. "Fuck off, Hymie." He juggled the cigarettes in his palm and continued toward the yard.

Leo launched himself at the boy. Shoulders hunched, he slammed into him behind the knees. Swenson's knees, buckling, propelled him forward, and down. The cigarettes scattered in all directions.

"Fuck off yourself, Hunky!" Leo said. He stepped past him and scooped up the loose cigarettes, replacing them carefully into the pack. Swenson, on his back now, half sitting, watched with outraged disbelief.

Leo tucked the cigarette pack into his pocket and started away. Swenson rose. He caught up with Leo in a single stride, spun him around and, slipping one foot behind Leo's ankles, pushed him backward, hurling him to the ground. Leo rolled away from the toe of Swenson's shoe aimed at his head and scrambled to his feet. Swenson pounded a roundhouse right into Leo's chest. Leo staggered back. Swenson followed wildly with another right. Leo ducked under it, stepped inside Swenson, and arcing both fists upward like a hammer striking an anvil, smashed Swenson in the groin.

Swenson's mouth popped open. His eyes bulged. Clutching his groin, he sagged to his knees, chest heaving as he gasped for air.

"Now leave me the fuck alone," Leo said. He turned and started away again. Behind him, Swenson clambered toward the nearby trash bin. He gripped an empty garbage bucket with both hands, raised it high over his head, and hurled it at Leo's back.

The iron bucket struck Leo squarely in the small of his back. The ground rushed up at him. Then he was flat on his face, struggling for breath, and hearing a voice, hollow, distorted: "... gonna kill you now, you little midget bastard!"

Leo forced himself to roll over. He lay paralyzed, gazing up at Swenson who stood straddling him. Swenson's mouth twisted into a little grin of triumph as he slowly drew back his foot to kick Leo. Leo waited. The shoe would strike him in the mouth.

The heavy shoe toe never got started toward Leo's mouth. It froze in midair when a calm voice said, "That's enough."

"Mind your own business, Weisenfeld," said Swenson's voice.

"I said, that's enough," said the other voice.

Leo raised himself up on one elbow. Confronting Swenson was a tall, handsome boy Leo had seen around but never met. His name was Harry Weisenfeld, sometimes called The Actor because he continually combed his hair, and was so fastidious about his appearance.

"He hit me in the nuts, for Christ's sake!" Swenson said. "I'm gonna take care of him once and for all!"

"You already took care of him," Harry Weisenfeld said. "Now fuck off."

"You fuck off!" said Swenson.

Harry, nearly as tall as Swenson, said quietly, "Don't make me say it twice."

Swenson's eyes flickered with uncertainty, but he clearly intended not to back down. He said, "Tell him to apologize."

"Apologize to him," Harry said to Leo.

"Fuck him!" Leo said. "And you, too!" He started rising but fell back. He could hardly move for the stabbing pain in his spine. "I ain't apologizing to nobody!"

Harry laughed. He said to Swenson, "You heard him."

"What's so funny?" Swenson asked, indignant. "You let this little buddy of yours get away with hitting me in the balls, and you think it's funny?"

"I think you're funny," Harry said. He turned to Leo. "Can you walk?"

"Someday, somebody'll give you goddam sheenies a good lesson!" Swenson said.

Harry's left fist thudded into Swenson's belly. In the same swift fluid movement, as Swenson doubled over, Harry hit him in the face with his right. Swenson crumpled, blood gushing from his mouth.

"It sure ain't you that'll give us the lesson," Harry said disdainfully, stepping over Swenson to help Leo up. He guided Leo to the cookhouse kitchen and propped him against the wall. "For a *kleyner*, you sure got some guts," he said. He shook his head grimly.

"He's a shmuck, that Hunky," Leo said.

"You're the shmuck," Harry said. "For taking him on."

Leo pushed himself away from the wall. He stood erect now and faced Harry. "Fuck you," he said.

"I save your ass, you tell me 'Fuck you'?"

"Nobody asked you," said Leo. "I was doing good."

Harry brushed dirt from Leo's shirt, then dabbed his own handkerchief on the raw, red skin of Leo's forehead. He dangled the blood-stained handkerchief under Leo's nose. "Yeah, you had him right where he wanted you."

Leo looked at him a moment, then past him to Swenson who was up, groggily shaking his head. He glanced hatefully at Leo and Harry.

"He won't bother you no more," Harry said.

"He better fucking not," Leo said.

"That's all you have to say?"

"What the hell do you want me to say?"

"How about 'Thanks'?"

"Okay, so thanks," Leo said.

"Don't mention it," Harry said. He tucked the handkerchief into Leo's shirt pocket and walked away. Leo, gazing after him, took out the handkerchief to wipe his forehead again. It was still bleeding.

Two days later, collecting trash from Barracks C-5, Leo saw him again. Playing penny poker with four others. They sat around a blanket-covered bunk in the center of the room, one boy stationed near the door as lookout. Harry was a terrible player. Staying with weak cards, betting and raising wildly. And a poor loser, cursing his "bad luck" and insulting the winners. He was so engrossed in the game he did not notice Leo.

The big winner was Nardino, a grossly fat boy wearing his cap backward. Now, on Harry's deal, he scooped up his money and announced he was quitting.

"Bullshit!" Harry said, slamming the deck down on the blanket. "I'm out three bucks!"

"Tough," said Nardino. He rose to leave. "See you around, huh?"

"Sit down," Harry said.

"What for?" Nardino said, a little quiver of doubt in his shrill voice.

"So I can get even," said Harry.

"Come on, Harry, I'm supposed to be over at the machine shop," Nardino said. "I'm late now."

"I said, sit down," Harry said. "You're ahead, ain't you?"

Another player, annoyed at the delay, said, "He got a right to quit winners. Leave him go."

"He don't go noplace," Harry said. "Not till he gives me a chance."

"One more hand," Nardino said reluctantly. He sank down on the overturned crate serving as a chair. "But this here's the last one. Okay?"

"Ante up," said Harry, tossing in his penny ante. He shuffled, presented the deck for a cut, then dealt. Five-card stud. Harry's hand developed promisingly. King, ten, jack, all clubs, on top. Nardino's top cards, a ten and a pair of kings, had driven out everyone but Harry. Harry raised recklessly. Nardino re-raised. Several more raises were exchanged until Harry finally called. More than two dollars was in the pot. Harry grinned confidently as he prepared to deal the fifth card.

"I pull another club or a jack," he said. "You are good and fucked, *paisan*."

"Not if I pair up." Nardino was glum, almost as though hoping not to improve. Winning, he knew, would only further antagonize Harry.

Harry dealt. "Four, no help," he crowed, gleefully slapping down the card. He gripped the deck now, turned it around for luck, and dealt himself. Queen of hearts. "Busted the flush, but possible straight." He grinned at Nardino. "Kings bet."

Harry rested the deck on the blanket, then slid his hole card down onto his lap to examine it. He did this with a little shrug, shaking the sleeve of his shirt. Observing from behind, Leo almost laughed aloud. It was so clumsy. Harry now owned two hole cards, and Leo knew one was an ace. He wondered how Harry planned to dispose of the extra card.

Nardino checked. Harry reached across the blanket as though to count the pot. Brushing his sleeve against the discards, he blindly dropped the extra card. It should have fallen into the discards, but Harry's wrist bumped the bunk edge. The extra card fluttered to the floor. It lay in plain sight, momentarily unnoticed. Harry glanced down at it in horror. It was far to his right, impossible to retrieve.

"Hell of a pot," Leo said. He smiled narrowly at Harry, who looked at him and then to the floor again. At the card, which Leo's shoe now entirely concealed.

Harry smiled back at Leo. "How you doing?"

"Not bad," Leo said.

"Glad to hear it," Harry said, and then directed his attention to the game. He bet thirty cents on his possible straight. Nardino called. Harry flipped over his hole card.

The ace to the straight.

"Can I quit now?" Nardino asked.

"We can all quit," Harry said. He raked in the pot, and at the same time, in a gesture of victory, gathered up all the cards and tossed them in the air. They fell haphazardly down onto the bunk, spilled to the floor—all over Leo's shoe. Leo collected the cards and, with them, the card under his shoe. He stacked them and returned them to Harry.

"Thanks," Harry said.

"Don't mention it," Leo said.

2.

Harry agreed he was a bad poker player. He therefore had no choice but to cheat. Leo reminded him he did have a choice: don't play. Cheating was never worthwhile. You only cheated cheaters, and then only if you were smart enough to get away with it. Although Harry saw this logic he refused to commit himself to total honesty in the future. It depended on the circumstances. Leo worried about that, but from then on the two were inseparable.

It was as though each recognized in the other elements he himself lacked. For Leo, it was Harry's muscle, bravado, charm. For Harry, Leo's courage, determination, analytical thinking. Their backgrounds were similar. Children of immigrant, impoverished Jews, each now fatherless. Harry's father, after settling in Brooklyn, simply dropped dead one morning at his pushcart: God's punishment, Harry's mother insisted. The old man had just finished visiting a Brownsville *nafke*. Not only had he paid her fifty cents, he also presented her with a mother-of-pearl brooch from the cart.

Harry drifted from gang to gang, his trigger temper and impetuousness lending itself best to smaller, more controllable groups. He led a three-man gang whose specialty was "protecting" small merchants and tradesmen, and landed in Elmira when he decided to diversify this operation by burglarizing three wealthy Brooklyn Heights homes. They netted a few hundred dollars and some old jewelry. As leader, Harry demanded half the loot, emphasizing the point by beating up one uncooperative partner. Shortly afterward, Harry was arrested. Found in his possession were several items from the burglarized homes and a .32-caliber pistol previously stolen from a pawnshop. The police had received an anonymous tip.

Harry was undaunted. He intended to serve his time and move on to bigger and better things, such as someday owning a gambling casino. Like Monte Carlo. He had seen pictures of it, the opulent gaming rooms, the lush grounds. And the people, rich and sleek, for whom money existed solely for pleasure. He envisioned himself in a tuxedo, greeting his eager customers, offering them the very finest and classiest facilities. He had other, equally grandiose fantasies, but none more ambitious than Monte Carlo.

It was almost inevitable, then, they would dream up the idea of organizing a craps game within the reformatory. With Leo as "casino" manager, Harry as enforcer, they couldn't lose. Only one problem.

A bankroll.

For a fleeting, whimsical moment, Leo considered asking Hershey. A hundred dollars would be an adequate stake, even fifty. He discussed this with Harry, to whom he had confided the whole Hershey-Edie affair. But even as they talked, Leo dismissed the notion. To hell with Hershey. Edie and Hershey Lefkowitz were ancient history.

"I learned a real good lesson from that," Leo said.

"Yeah," Harry agreed. "Don't fuck Lefkowitz's wife."

Leo did briefly consider his mother a potential source. He knew she had systematically saved from what he gave her the past few years. But even with the savings, the abrupt loss of Leo's salary had forced her to move from the Fourteenth Street apartment back to Rivington, and resume the cafeteria job. No, Leo felt guilty enough for the heartache already caused his mother. He would not burden her further.

A U.S. Army major finally provided the solution. This major, a paunchy, balding man of fifty, addressed the entire student body in the mess hall. Introduced by the warden, the major stood, ran his finger around his choker collar and adjusted his pince-nez glasses, and began.

"Some months ago, Warden Collins here made a brilliant suggestion to the War Department." He paused to allow the warden a modest smile of acknowledgment, then continued. "Warden Collins believes that many of you in this institution might more effectively repay their societal debt by serving their country in its hour of need. We agree."

In the rear of the room, Harry whispered to Leo, "Jesus Christ, don't tell me they're gonna draft us?"

"Nah," said Leo. "You can't get drafted unless you're twenty-one."

Leo was correct. The major was here not to draft but to recruit. Any inmate age seventeen or over volunteering to enlist in the United States Army—and meeting the stringent physical, mental, and moral requirements—was to be granted a conditional pardon. Satisfactory performance of military duty earned a full pardon. Those interested would go into town Sunday afternoon for an interview with the sergeant at the recruiting station in the Elmira post office, open Sunday exclusively for reformatory volunteers.

Listening, Leo wondered how many would actually volunteer. One in ten, he figured. Getting out of Elmira this way was really jumping out of the frying pan. Yes, he'd make book on it. One in ten. You had to be crazy volunteering to get your head blown off.

Harry nudged him, whispering, "I got it!"

"What?" Leo asked. "Another dose of the crabs?"

"How to raise our bankroll," Harry said. He could hardly wait until they were dismissed to tell him.

Everyone clustered in the yard in little groups discussing the army proposal. Harry led Leo to a remote corner for privacy. Jabbing a finger into Leo's chest, he said, "The minute that guy said 'post office,' I knew how to get the dough."

Leo said nothing. He gazed at the others in the yard, thinking that fighting for your country maybe wasn't so crazy after all. Except, he asked himself, what the hell did my country ever do for me?

". . . so I been there, at the post office," Harry was saying. "It's in the same block with maybe a dozen stores. A hardware store, a smoke shop, a drugstore, a barbershop. And—" He paused dramatically. "And Krinsky's."

"What's Krinsky's?" Leo asked obligingly.

Harry ran his comb through his hair, then tapped Leo's cheek with the comb edge. "Krinsky's, *mein shayner bocha,* is a jewelry store."

"A jewelry store," Leo repeated.

"A jewelry store," Harry said. "Where we get the dough to bank the game."

"Just like putting your socks on in the morning?" Leo said. "We knock off the jewelry store?"

"You got it, Kleyner."

Leo looked at him. "You're serious."

"I got it all figured out," Harry said, and then added, "Well, most of it."

"What's all figured out? How about how we get into town in the first place?" Immediately, Leo answered his own question. "Oh, no! You want us to volunteer for the army?"

"Who said anything about volunteering?" Harry asked. "We get interviewed about it. Interviewed. We don't volunteer for nothing."

"You're crazy," Leo said.

"To get interviewed, we go into town, don't we?" Harry said. "To the post office."

Leo started to say he was sure now Harry was soft in the head, but instead he said, "Okay, so we're in town, and it's Sunday. How we supposed to get out of the post office and into the store?"

The comb was out of Harry's pocket once more. He slicked down his hair again. "I figured maybe you'd have some ideas," he said.

3.

The key to it was the guard, Scanlon, who Leo knew occasionally drove the school bus. From barracks gossip Leo also knew that Scanlon— married, with four young children—had a girlfriend in a small town just across the Pennsylvania state line, and was in debt to fellow guards from whom he continually borrowed. Leo was therefore reasonably sure that Scanlon, properly motivated, might be persuaded to have himself assigned to drive the prospective volunteers into Elmira.

From his two-dollar weekly pay, Leo had saved seven dollars. Harry, perennially broke, extorted three from a barracks mate. They told Scanlon they were so horny they would do anything to get laid, offering him their ten dollars if, at the post office, he turned his back long enough for them to visit an Elmira whorehouse. If Scanlon arranged for Leo and Harry to be the first two of the scheduled twenty-three boys interviewed, their brief absence afterward would never be noticed. They would be back in the post office long before the remaining interviews were concluded.

The deal was struck. Scanlon knew they were not so foolish as even to think of escape. The consequences were so severe that time in the hole was a garden party in comparison. And he, Scanlon, desperately needed the money.

The following Sunday afternoon, a warm, sunny early April day, twenty-three boys piled into the rear of an Autocar truck driven by Scanlon. He was accompanied by another guard, Fritzell. At the post office, Scanlon ordered Leo and Harry to the head of the line.

Each conversed privately for ten minutes with the recruiting sergeant. Appropriate forms were filled out, including those for parental consent, and then a local physician conducted the physical examination. He said Leo could gain a few pounds, while Harry should lose some, signed the forms and sent them to the rear of the room to wait.

Scanlon gave them permission to use the men's room. He was allowing them thirty minutes to complete their business in the whorehouse, a block away. With twenty-three boys milling about, chances of the other guard, Fritzell, seeing them were remote. If he did, Scanlon simply had to cut him in.

In the men's room, Leo yanked the recruiting papers from Harry's overall pocket and, with his own, ripped them up and flushed them down the toilet. It was almost as though he did not wish to be tempted.

They left the men's room and strolled down the marble-floored corridor to the main door, and out. They stood a moment on the post office stairs and gazed out at the deserted main thoroughfare, State Street. At a man chalking news bulletins on a large blackboard inside the plate-glass window of the *Elmira Sunday Telegraph* building. The only sound was the noisy, loose rattling of an approaching automobile. As soon as it clattered past, the music of a distant band concert was clearly heard. Probably from a park, Leo thought. A Sunday-afternoon band concert.

"That's it right there." Harry nodded at the jewelry store in the exact center of the block of storefronts across the street. In thick white scripted letters fixed to the outside of the plate-glass display window were the words KRINSKY & SON, JEWELRY AND WATCH REPAIR.

Leo was not listening to Harry; he was listening to the music. It sounded like a march. He wished he knew the name of the tune. He thought living in a small town might be pleasant. Although everything appeared so tiny—the houses, the streets—it all seemed neat and clean. Orderly, that was the word. Everything in proper order. He liked that.

The man at the *Elmira Sunday Telegraph* finished writing the bulletin and disappeared inside the building. Leo read aloud: "WILSON REJECTS POPE'S PEACE PLAN, SAYS GERMAN RULERS CANNOT BE TRUSTED." He looked at Harry and said, "Jesus, the pope is the one I wouldn't trust."

"Fuck the pope," Harry said. He nodded again at Krinsky's. "Let's do what we come for."

"After them two go," Leo said.

He referred to a young couple who had appeared, studying the jewelry-store window display. The girl, while not especially pretty, was attractive in a frilly white summer dress short enough to reveal her white-stockinged ankles and low-cut white shoes with silver buckles. The man wore a straw hat, neat brown double-breasted suit, and gray felt spats over black shoes. Out with his girl for a Sunday stroll, not a worry in the world. Leo envied him.

"Hey, you think they're casing the joint?" Harry asked. He jabbed Leo playfully in the elbow. Harry felt good now, back in action.

"Let's go," Leo said. They were halfway down the post-office steps when Leo stopped abruptly. He fingered the top of Harry's denim overalls, and then his own. "We might as well hang a sign on us, wearing these."

"We're a couple of farm boys, for Christ's sake," Harry said. "In town on the day of rest."

But they waited until the young couple moved on. They casually crossed the street, then darted into an alley leading to the rear of the buildings. The first thing Leo saw at Krinsky's back entrance was the huge circular alarm bell above the door. It looked brand-new.

He said, "I guess Krinsky don't trust nobody around here too good."

"You blame him?" Harry said. "A Jew living in this hick town?" He paced back and forth a moment, studying the door, and the two iron-grated windows on either side. Then, carefully, he tried the door. There was no give. "Bolted," he said. He looked up at the alarm bell. "And wired from inside."

Leo said, "Harry, I got us into town. Now you got to get us inside the store." But even as he spoke, he wondered why he stood here in an alley in broad daylight behind a jewelry store. It was crazy. Caught, it meant the hole. Plus, for sure, additional time. He began framing words in his mind: "Harry, forget the whole thing. Let's drag ass back to the post office. We ain't done nothing, so we can't get in no trouble." He never spoke those words, because even as he thought them he was feeling the excitement of the challenge. And, all things considered, the odds were favorable. With an edge, you were a fool not to take advantage.

Harry had clambered up on the window ledge. Balancing himself, he gripped the window bars with one hand and reached the other hand up toward the bell. Delicately, like a surgeon probing a heart valve, he tested the bell clapper arm for tension. It was very taut, but he managed to slip one finger under the arm. He pulled the arm upward, away from the bell cover, raising it several inches until it snapped off in his hand. He grinned down at Leo and lobbed the broken steel rod into the bushes on the opposite side of the alley. Then he stuffed his handkerchief under the stump of the clapper arm. Should the alarm be activated, any sound would be muffled.

Entering the store was easy. They smashed through the door with a sharp rock. In the rear office, they ignored the safe and jimmied open the rolltop desk. They found a small steel box containing some seventy dollars in bills and change. Only Leo's stern reminder of the risk of being seen from the street deterred Harry from ransacking the showroom display counters. Besides, they had what they came for. But Harry discovered a piece of jewelry on the workbench. A diamond stickpin in the form of a horseshoe.

They returned to the post office, safe and unseen. Scanlon met them in the corridor at the water fountain. He was amused. "Didn't take you long."

Leo said, "We couldn't find the place."

"It's right around the corner," Scanlon said. "The Empire Rooms."

"We must of went to the wrong street." Harry said. Nervous, he drew the comb from his pocket. The diamond stickpin, clinging to the comb teeth, fell to the marble floor. Harry bent to retrieve it. Scanlon, quicker, snatched up the object.

"Where'd you get it?" Scanlon asked quietly.

"It's mine," Harry said.

"I asked where you got it."

Leo said fast, "That's how come we didn't go to the whorehouse, Scanlon. We see this here shiny thing in the gutter. All covered up with dirt and leaves. We figure whoever lost it is sure as shit coming back to look. So we figure we better not be anyplace around. So we come back here right away."

"Yeah, that's how it happened," Harry said.

Scanlon juggled the stickpin in his palm. He looked at Harry, then at Leo, and then past them, out the post-office window, to the stores across the street. He gazed at Krinsky's a long moment. Then, with a narrow little smile at the two boys, he held the stickpin to the light.

"Real diamonds, I think." He turned the pin around and squinted at the inscription on the reverse side. " 'Edward, from Nancy.' Looks like real gold, too."

"Worth a couple hundred, I bet," Harry said. "More, maybe."

Leo said, "Listen, Scanlon, you like it, you keep it." He glanced warningly at Harry. "Ain't that right, Harry?"

"Yeah," Harry said glumly. "Sure."

"Well, now that's white of you boys," Scanlon said. He admired the pin another instant, then slipped it into his shirt pocket. "I do appreciate the thoughtfulness."

Harry had no opportunity to speak privately with Leo until they returned to the reformatory. By now he had worked himself into a rage. How could Leo have been so stupid as to actually *give* the pin away?

"You're the one that's stupid!" Leo said. "If you think Scanlon fell for that bullshit story about us finding it. In the leaves and dirt, for Christ's sake!"

Harry said, "But the goddam jeweler's sure to report it missing. And then Scanlon's got us cold!"

Leo strained for patience. "Harry, Scanlon's the only one that knows we went out. He says anything, he bags himself, don't he? We couldn't of left the post office without his permission, could we? He ain't about to admit that, is he?"

"Then why'd we give the fucking pin to him?" Harry shouted.

"You putz, we didn't give him nothing," Leo said. "He *took* it! Wouldn't you, if you was him?"

Harry thought about this a moment, then agreed. "My fault, anyway. The goddam thing falling out of my pocket like that."

"It don't matter," Leo said. He flashed the cash-box money, the seventy dollars. "We got what we wanted. We can start the game."

Harry's mind was still on Scanlon. "We should of made him kick back the ten bucks we give him to begin with," he said sadly. "The lousy *gonif!*"

Leo was wrong. The game would not be started. At least not with that seventy dollars. The jeweler, Krinsky, reported not only the stickpin theft, but the seventy dollars cash as well. Immediately, Scanlon proved himself more than simply a lousy *gonif.* He was the worst *gonif* Leo and Harry ever saw. He demanded from them the seventy dollars.

"Otherwise, gentlemen," said Scanlon, "I am forced to tell the warden how I was inspecting your bunks"—he pointed a finger at Harry, then at Leo—"and lo and behold, what do I find hiding in the mattress?" He displayed the stickpin.

"You fink on us, Scanlon, how do you explain us being out of your sight?" Harry asked.

"Aw, come on, kid," Scanlon said. "With twenty-three of you heroes going every which way in that post office, who'd blame me for not noticing that two of you disappeared for ten minutes?"

Scanlon went on to remind them that the reformatory boys were obviously under suspicion anyway. He further pointed out that although both guards insisted no one had left the premises, it would have been quite possible for two boys to slip away.

They gave him the seventy dollars. Leo believed that was the end of it. He assumed Scanlon would now dispose of the stickpin.

Leo was wrong again.

He and Harry were watching a baseball game in the yard a few days later when Scanlon approached. Harry saw him first. He nudged Leo and muttered, "If he asks for our balls, tell him we already give 'em to somebody." He smiled and said to Scanlon, "How you doing?"

Scanlon said, "Kid got a nice arm, huh?" He was talking about the pitcher, a left-hander who so far had struck out every batter he faced. "But he don't have what they call staying power. He gets tired too easy."

Leo said, "He can't hit worth a shit, neither."

Scanlon glanced around. Everyone was engrossed in the game, but he lowered his voice anyway. "I fixed it for you two to go on a work party. They're putting up a new building right in the middle of Elmira. The construction company needs six strong guys to clean up the site. Carry dirt away, and like that. A buck a day."

"Shove the job, Scanlon," Leo said. "We ain't interested." He started moving away. Scanlon pulled him back.

"I said I already fixed it." Scanlon pressed his fingers deep into Leo's arm, at the same time facing Harry. "Now listen good: I want fifty bucks. From each of you."

"Scanlon, what the Christ are you talking about?" Harry said. "You know we ain't got no fifty bucks!"

Just then, at the game, the clunk of a solid hit, followed by loud cheers from enthused spectators. The batter had lined the ball over the center-fielder's head. Scanlon said, "See, like I said, no staying power."

The batter slid safely into third. Scanlon turned to Leo and Harry again, his closed fist under their noses. He opened the fist. Nestled in his palm was the diamond stickpin. "Now when you're in town, I'm sure two smart city boys like you can figure a way of . . . well, let's say of getting more of this stuff." He closed his fist and dropped the pin into his shirt pocket.

Leo said, "And we split the profits with you, huh?"

"Fifty bucks worth," Scanlon said. "Each."

"Fuck you, Scanlon," Harry said in a level voice almost drowned out in another loud cheer from the crowd. The batter had just stolen home.

"Fuck me, huh?" Scanlon said. "No, boy, it's you that's fucked." He stepped closer, so their faces were inches apart. He bent slightly for Leo to hear. "Because you don't do like I say"—he tapped his shirt pocket—"I go and I 'find' this little bauble on you." He smiled and pointed to the pitcher now facing a fresh batter. "He ain't gonna get nobody out no more. Not after they banged him for the three-bagger, and then stole home. Watch and see."

And without another word, Scanlon walked off. Harry and Leo stood gazing after him. Harry trembled with rage. Leo, too, was angry. And frightened. But even in his anger and fear he had to admire the beautiful simplicity of the extortion. They would burglarize a place, surrender the loot to Scanlon. When they were eventually caught—which was certain—it would be useless even trying to accuse Scanlon.

"He got us, Kleyner," Harry said.

Leo hardly heard him. The crowd cheered wildly again as the new batter belted the ball past the outfielders. Leo had the feeling he had been here before, in this very place, the same circumstances.

"He got us," Harry said again. "Unless we can get that goddam jewelry back."

It was Hammer all over again, Leo thought. Hammer, the blackmailing drunk he lured into the Division Street excavation so long ago. If Hammer deserved to be killed—and not once in all those years had Leo ever doubted this—Scanlon deserved it a thousand times plus. But Scanlon was not Hammer and there was no way of safely killing him.

"He won't keep it on him no more," Harry said. "He'll stash it someplace."

Leo said nothing. He was watching the game. The batter had reached third standing up. The pitcher stood disconsolately, digging the toe of his shoe into the dirt around the mound.

"It'd have to be in his house," Harry said. "We have to find out where he lives." He laughed. "Hey, that'll be our first job for him, you know? We hit *his* house!"

Yes, Leo thought, it was Hammer all over again. Only different. "We don't need to kill him," he said. He was thinking aloud, unaware of the words.

Harry said, "Jesus, who said anything about killing him?" But Harry's eyes brightened with anticipation. "Hey, yeah, that's what to do. Knock him off!"

"He don't need to be killed," Leo said again. "And you know why? Because he's a bluffer."

"Bluffer?" Harry said. "What's he bluffing about? He showed us the jewelry, didn't he?"

"That's the bluff," Leo said. "The jewelry's worth something to him, ain't it? He can sell it. But he turns us in, he has to turn it in, too. So all he makes is the pleasure of screwing us."

It made sense; Harry relaxed. "So what are we worrying about?"

"About what he'll do to us when we tell him to fuck off," said Leo. "He'll have us in the hole every other week for picking our noses, for Christ's sake."

"Then we do have to kill him," Harry said eagerly. "We got no choice."

"You ever killed anybody, Harry?"

"No, but I know it ain't hard. Especially a cocksucker like him."

Leo wondered if Harry really could kill anybody. Yes, he decided, he could. And perhaps even enjoy it. Leo looked at him a moment, then past him to the field. The next batter had singled sharply. It seemed Scanlon was right: the pitcher would never retire the side.

"Okay?" Harry asked. "I do it?"

Leo wondered what Harry would say if he told him about Hammer. Would he believe it? Yes, Leo thought, because Harry knew Leo would not lie about something like that. And Harry would be impressed. An insect was squashed, a parasite, but Harry would be impressed.

"I'm gonna do it," Harry said, determined.

"No," said Leo. "It's a sucker play."

"Not if I get away with it."

"But you won't, Harry. It's the odds. The odds ain't no good. If we got him in a dark alley someplace, or he walked around alone." He shook his head. "No chance."

"Well, I sure ain't going on no work parties for him," Harry said. "Are you?"

"We can screw him," Leo said, and before Harry could ask how, Leo continued, "We can join the fucking army."

Harry's mouth opened in protest, then snapped shut. He studied Leo a long moment. "It gets us away from him, all right, don't it?"

"That's what I'm trying to tell you."

"Yeah," Harry said, and fell silent, thinking. Then he said, "You know something, Kleyner? You don't look so unhappy about joining the army."

"Maybe I ain't."

"How come?"

"Maybe I want to learn how to shoot a gun."

Harry pulled out his comb and smoothed down his hair. "You threw the papers away, remember?"

"They'll give us new ones."

"Yeah," Harry said slowly. "I guess maybe they will."

On the field, the left-handed pitcher suddenly regained his stuff. He blazed three strikes past one batter, and the next one popped out weakly to the catcher, ending the inning. Scanlon was wrong. The kid had staying power after all.

─── 5 ───

HARRY couldn't help laughing. Here he was at Camp Devens, in Massachusetts, shaving for a date with a hot little Jewish broad whose father owned a hardware store in Lowell while the Kleyner was on his way to France.

Leo's letter, dated July 2, 1918, was propped on the shelf against the hot-water faucet next to Harry's mirror so he could shave and read at the same time. Leo wrote from Hoboken, more than a month ago, just before the 77th Division sailed.

In the letter Leo described the six weeks of combat training, with a rifle almost as big as he was, and not an extra minute for anything, sometimes not even a piss. Up at reveille, eat, then the range for target practice. Then bayonet drill, gas-mask drill, field exercises. Over and over, until you packed in for the night too tired for anything except sleep. But Leo said he was getting good with a Springfield, so good he won a sharpshooter's badge. And looking forward to seeing France. Strange talk from the Kleyner, Harry thought. Almost as though the little bastard liked being a soldier, which Harry suspected he did.

In the mirror Harry glanced at the row of open toilet seats behind him. Only one was occupied. A Georgia cracker Harry did not especially like sat smoking a cigarette, reading *Stars & Stripes*. He seemed to be enjoying himself. Probably more than Leo right now, Harry thought, as a blob of lather splotched the YMCA stationery of Leo's letter. Harry put down the razor. He dried his fingers on a towel, folded the letter, and slipped it into his pants pocket.

He resumed shaving. Leo's letter reminded him of one recently received by the Elmira police. An anonymous letter, suggesting a certain piece of stolen jewelry might be found on the person of a certain guard named Frank Scanlon.

Leo's letter was funny, too. Not that Leo going to France was so funny, but the way it happened. Old Harry Weisenfeld getting a soft job as the Jewish chaplain's assistant, while Kleyner Leo Gorodetsky ended up a combat infantryman.

Because of God, and a rabbi.

From Elmira, they had gone directly to Camp Yaphank for processing and basic training. The first two weeks were easy. Lectures, drilling, and a lot of KP. They signed up with the Jewish chaplain for Friday night services: it excused them from KP for that day. But Leo almost immediately started arguing with the chaplain about God. Whenever anybody talked about God, or religion, it made Leo crazy. Harry couldn't care less one way or the other. You want to pray, pray. No skin off Harry's ass. Not Leo. He said he just could not understand people being that stupid.

The chaplain's name was Rosenbloom. Captain Alfred A. Rosenbloom. A tall, surprisingly good-looking thirty-two-year-old *shtarker* from Chicago. Behind his back they called him Rich Rosie; his family owned a chain of department stores. Harry could hear that last argument between Leo and Rosie as clearly as he heard the Georgia cracker talking to the rum-soaked old dogface just then settling himself on a nearby toilet seat. They were talking about Saint-Mihiel, and how the Yanks really pasted the Krauts.

Leo was such a shmuck sometimes. Rosie had said something about trusting in God. Leo had answered, "I don't believe in no God."

"You can't be a good Jew, Gorodetsky, if you don't believe in the Almighty," Rosie said.

"What do you mean, I can't be a good Jew?"

"My son, I'm not even sure you are a Jew."

Leo's face had reddened. "I'm a Jew, Rabbi. I'll always be a Jew. But I ain't buying the idea of 'God' as some kind of . . . what was it you said, a Super Something?"

"Superior Being."

"Yeah, Superior Being. A thing that controls your life. It don't make no sense."

Rosie said, "You must be a very unhappy person."

Leo had looked at Harry. "Harry, am I unhappy?"

Harry knew the rabbi needed an assistant, a nice Jewish boy, and had decided this should be none other than himself, Private Harry I. Weisenfeld. No more KP, shit details, or marching. "Leo," he said sternly, "I don't think you should talk like that to the rabbi. You got to have more respect."

Leo knew exactly what Harry was up to. He played right along. "Respect for what?"

"For the rabbi, for one thing," Harry said. "Right, sir?"

"Not for me, per se," Rosie said. "For what I represent."

"God, huh?" Leo asked.

"Yes, Gorodetsky. God."

"Well, Rabbi, don't the Kaiser say God's on his side? Don't he tell the Krauts to pray so they'll win? So they'll kill more of us, than we can kill of them?"

"It's not as simple as that—" Rosie started to say.

"—and don't we say God's on our side? Ain't that what the paper from old Black Jack Pershing said? God's on *our* side, so if we pray hard enough we can win. For Christ's sake, Rabbi, don't that tell you what a con game it all is? How can a rich, smart Jew like you get taken in by all that shit?"

Twenty-four hours later Leo was shipped to a camp in Alabama for combat training.

Harry was assigned chapel duty. He remained at Yaphank four months. Then, at Chaplain Rosenbloom's recommendation, he was promoted to corporal and transferred to Fort Devens, his boss now an old rabbi content to leave the more mundane duties of the job in Harry's capable hands. This included disbursal of chapel funds. Harry was in his element.

That evening the daughter of the hardware-store owner decided to lose her virginity. Harry encouraged the decision by lying about his imminent departure for France, and premonition of death in combat. All this happened in the living room of the girl's parents' home, a large house with a downstairs bathroom where, later, rummaging through the medicine cabinet Harry found a bicarbonate of soda tin containing $150 in tens and twenties. All in all, then, a fulfilling evening—although Harry lost every dime of the money in a poker game the very next day.

Harry was too busy avoiding the nice Jewish girl the following week to pay much attention to the big news from France. The AEF won a great victory at Saint-Mihiel. The beginning of the end for the Germans, everyone said. The war would be over no later than the spring of '19. Harry certainly hoped so. He wanted to get out of uniform, away from anything and everything military. He and Leo had made a pact. They would get into something together after the war. Their own game, perhaps; or, at the worst, working someone else's game until they saved a big enough stake for their own.

Harry wondered if Leo had visited Paris yet. Gay Paree. And Leo had promised to somehow get down to Monte Carlo to see what it really looked like. Harry had no way of knowing Leo had seen action in a small but bloody skirmish at the Aisne River, and then at Saint-Mihiel. Or that by the time Harry got around to writing him, Leo was indeed in Paris.

In a hospital.

2.

Thirty minutes after reaching the line the entire battalion advanced into the wooded area just beyond Saint-Mihiel village. At first it was very quiet. Only the dull, constant booming of artillery to the north. In between shell bursts you heard the rain spattering down on the leaves of the trees. It had rained all day, so that even in the thick woods the ground was soggy. There was so little enemy fire the unit moved forward through the trees with rifles slung.

A hundred yards in, the whole forest exploded. Mortars, machine guns, rifle fire. All around Leo, doughboys fell, some screaming in pain, others simply crumpling. He dropped to his belly and clamped his hands over his ears. It was not guns that would kill him, he thought at that instant, but the ear-shattering noise. He felt his head might split open from the noise. His whole body trembled uncontrollably. I am going to die, he thought. Jesus Christ in Heaven, they are killing me! He wanted to burrow into the wet earth; his fingers began clawing at the ground.

At the Aisne, he knew he killed Germans. At least two. He had sighted them perfectly, fired, seen them drop. He felt no elation; again, just something that needed to be done. But he also had felt no fear. For some reason, then, although being fired on, he knew he would not be hit. Now, for some reason, he was afraid. He told himself he must remain in this very spot. He would be safe.

But wait, he told himself, listening now almost curiously to the endless buzzing and shrieking overhead, thinking crazily it sounded like a thousand hives of maddened bees. Wait just a minute. I cannot stay here because if I stay here then they truly will kill me. They want to kill me. At the Aisne, when he knew he would not be killed, it was almost like a game. Now it was no longer a game. Now it was real. It even smelled different, the sharp cordite odor enveloping everything like an unseen, acrid cloud. The reality surprised him. And then, suddenly, angered him. If they want to kill me, he thought, I goddam better kill them first.

He rose, peering in disbelief at the doughboys retreating in panic. Some had even discarded their rifles. "Stop!" he yelled, not sure it was his own voice he heard. "You bastards, stop! It ain't right! We got to go the other way!"

He grasped the sleeve of one fleeing soldier. He pulled him to a stop and spun him around. "That way!" Leo screamed. "That way!"

The soldier's eyes were wide with fear. He shook his head and struggled free. He started running again, and all at once toppled forward, arms outstretched. The entire back of his head was gone, torn away in pulpy shreds of red flesh and white bone.

Leo whirled, unsure where to go, or why, knowing only that the proper direction was toward the trees, not away. He moved forward, rifle leveled. He fired, cranked back the bolt to eject the cartridge casing, cranked another shell into the chamber. And at that instant he was hit.

He felt it as a sledgehammer on his upper left elbow. It toppled him backward. He lay on his back on the ground. The entire length of his arm ached like a dull, steady toothache. His whole body seemed ponderous, heavy. He could not move. He stared up at the tree limbs and the dark gray sky. Rain fell on his face and splashed cool and wet on his dry lips.

The arm seemed encased in concrete. He tried once to lift it, but something pinned it down. He turned his head to look at it. No blood, just a small, almost rectangular hole in the upper sleeve of the shirt, as though a tailor had neatly scissored out a little cloth square. Again, he tried to move the arm. This time he screamed. The pain was like an electric shock. He lay flat again. He did not know what to do now, or what would happen to him.

But he knew he had behaved correctly. This made him feel very good about himself. A strange, new feeling he wished he could share with Harry. And with his mother, and Hershey. Hershey most of all; it would help make up for what he did. They would all be proud of him. Yes, he thought, that was the word, pride. He was proud of himself.

Now he became aware of other figures. Hurrying past, advancing, wearing oval helmets. *Poilus*. He remembered that his battalion was attached to a French regiment. He did not want the *poilus* to see Americans running away. He was ashamed of his fellow Americans, his buddies. This, not duty or bravery, was why he had not retreated, and why he tried to stop the others.

The French, however, had witnessed Leo's attempt to halt the American rout.

Private Leo Gorodetsky of the 77th Division of the American Expeditionary Force was awarded a Croix de Guerre. The citation read, ". . . for conspicuous gallantry in the act of attempting to regroup his unit."

Regroup the unit: a euphemism for soldiers fleeing in the face of the enemy. Leo knew that, but also knew he had behaved correctly. He wore the decoration with pride.

Leo's shattered arm, reset and placed in a cast, healed rapidly. He was transferred for rest and recuperation to a small American hospital in the Paris suburb of Neuilly.

By the first week of October he was completely recovered. The medic colonel revoked Leo's medical leave and cut orders assigning him to AEF HQ at Chaumont, with ten days en route, which really meant ten days in Paris. A nice gesture, but one Leo deserved: he had taught the colonel, a steady loser at the Officers' Club weekly poker game, how to spot a card cheat. Although no one in the game cheated, knowing now how to spot a cheater somehow improved the colonel's game.

Leo moved into a small Montparnasse hotel. The red and green Croix de Guerre ribbon earned him a discounted rate, in a room overlooking the boulevard. The first room of his own he ever had. He relished the privacy, the luxury of being alone. There is a difference between being alone, and being lonely. In Paris you were never lonely.

He loved Paris. The good food, the cabarets, the whores. The very smell of the city. He loved wandering about the wide, tree-lined boulevards now ankle deep in crisp autumn leaves; and at night, especially after a rain, the narrow twisting streets with the cobblestones glistening under the streetlamps, and the sound of music and laughter behind the curtained plate-glass windows of each little café a promise of a new and exciting adventure.

One brisk afternoon, the fourth day of his leave, he stopped at a small sidewalk café on Rue de Lambre. He ordered coffee and sat contentedly watching people coming and going. Across the street a startlingly attractive girl emerged from a bar, Le Flamant. Tall and willowy, with long flowing black hair, the girl clutched her skirt against the whipping wind and gripped the arm of her escort, a young American second lieutenant. A slender, handsome boy with a Rainbow Division patch.

Leo watched them walk arm in arm to a small hotel a few doors away, Hôtel des Écoles. He envied the young officer. The woman, clearly, was no whore. Everything about her spelled Class. Leo bet she was some rich man's wife enjoying a fast matinee with a Yank.

He turned to the bar again just as two women went inside. Both beautiful and chic, with that same look of Class. Leo ordered a second cup of coffee. He sat and watched the bar. Another woman, attractive as the others, arrived in a taxi. Leo drank down his coffee, placed a fifty-centime piece on the saucer, and walked across the street to Le Flamant.

A small room, noisy with chattering female voices and stuffy with the not unpleasant aroma of cigarettes and perfume. A low-hanging, tassled, red-glassed chandelier cast a soft roseate glow on the velour banquettes cramping two sides of the room. All were occupied—but for one French soldier, and two civilians—with women. As Leo entered, one civilian got up to leave. A big, burly man with a long silky mustache, he nearly collided with Leo. He smiled apologetically and hurried away.

At the far end of the room the tiny bar was vacant. Leo sat and gazed at the barmaid. A beauty, tall, blond, high-breasted. She smiled and waited patiently for him to order. It was almost like a dream, this place. Too good to be true.

"*Vin rouge,*" he said finally, pronouncing it perfectly. He liked the challenge of speaking French. What little he knew, although daily he learned more.

"*Vin rouge,*" she repeated, and poured him a glass. "*Vin rouge pour un soldat Américain. Deux francs, s'il vous plaît.*"

"*Deux?*" Leo asked, astounded; he held up two fingers.

"*Oui, m'sieur. Deux.*"

Two francs, nearly fifty cents. Leo assumed it was the Yank uniform. The French thought every American a millionaire. But he paid. He had plenty of money. Not only three months' pay, but a twenty-dollar loan repayment from the hospital night-duty sergeant. Leo had organized a craps game for the night-shift orderlies. A small game, which he did not bank, but from which he earned a few dollars loaning busted players money at ten percent weekly interest.

A deep, throaty feminine voice said in careful English, "How are you today?" She edged into the stool beside Leo, another blonde. In the dim red light her bobbed hair resembled a gold helmet.

"I'm good, thanks," Leo said, suddenly glad she spoke English. He feared making a fool of himself in French. "How are you?"

"Also good," she said. She smiled almost shyly. "You will buy me a drink?"

"Anytime," he said.

The girl ordered champagne. Leo knew then she was a whore. They were all whores. But so what? They were all beautiful. She asked him for a cigarette. He lit it for her and only then, in the match flare, noticed her throat. The prominent Adam's apple. And then she placed her fingers strokingly on his hand. Stubby, strong fingers.

She was a He.

They all were. Queers. Men in women's clothes. He had heard of this, but never seen it. He was both repelled and intrigued. She was speaking to him in French now, her voice soft and caressing. He did not understand a single word. He wondered why he simply did not get up and leave. It was almost as though he refused to believe this lovely woman not a woman. He felt her hand creeping upward now on the inside of his thigh. In his mind he saw himself getting down from the stool and walking out. Her hand inched closer. You have got to get out of here, he told himself. And answered himself, Why? If you want to find out, so find out. But I do not want to find out, he told himself. No.

"No!" he said, but so quietly that only the blonde and barmaid heard. The blonde instantly withdrew her hand. She was amused.

"What is wrong?" she asked.

"You are," he said, and slid down from the high barstool. He hurried across the room to the door. He heard the barmaid and the blonde laughing. The blonde called after him in French. And then others in the room also called to him, laughing. He knew why they laughed, and felt foolish and inferior. Outside, on the sidewalk, he immediately turned his back to the street and faced the bar, the little glass flamingo in the window. He did not want passersby to see him. He had an enormous erection.

After a moment it subsided. He faced the street again, breathing a sigh of relief. You stupid bastard, he thought, you almost did it. No, he told himself, don't be crazy. Didn't I lam out of there right away I knew it was a man? Fine, he thought, then what was the hard-on all about? Well, that was before I knew, he told himself, which was not precisely true, but true enough so that he felt he had always been in control.

And anxious now to find a woman, a real one. He knew a great place across the river near the Étoile. It had a huge parlor where the girls walked around in diaphanous gowns and brassieres with the nipples cut out. He glanced around for a taxi.

As he walked past Hôtel des Écoles, the "girl" who had been with the young Rainbow Division lieutenant burst from the door. Immediately behind her was the silky-mustached civilian from the bar. Both dashed across the street and raced off in opposite directions. An instant later a shirt-sleeved, middle-aged man appeared in the hotel doorway, shouting angrily in French at the man and the woman. But they were nearly out of sight. The middle-aged man, who was the hotel proprietor, shook his fist after them, muttered to himself, then started back into the hotel. He saw Leo.

He said in French, "One of your officers has been injured. Get him out of my hotel, or I'll call the police!"

Leo understood "officers," and "police." And, with the man gesturing him inside, the intent. His first instinct was to mind his own business. But he was curious about the young lieutenant.

The lieutenant was in a second-floor room, naked, huddled on the carpet against the bed. His uniform blouse was draped neatly over a chair, his breeches, shirt, tie, and underwear folded on the chair seat. Under the chair, placed as though for barracks inspection, his leather cavalry boots.

The lieutenant raised his head and looked at Leo. His nose and mouth were caked with blood. He was weeping. The tears mingled with the blood in red droplets that streaked down his chin and onto his chest.

"The frog bastards rolled you, huh?" Leo said quietly.

Through his tears, the lieutenant laughed self-pityingly. "The funny part is I thought I loved her," he said. "I honest to God thought I was in love with her."

"Her," Leo thought, shuddering. "You seen her before?" he asked.

"Yes, of course," said the lieutenant. "She was wonderful to me the first time." He reached a hand to Leo. "Help me, please."

Leo recoiled in disgust, but helped him. He never knew exactly why. Perhaps because the boy seemed so helpless, so pitiful. Perhaps only because it was an American in trouble. Or perhaps he merely felt sorry for another human being, even if a fairy. It might also have been the all too vivid recollection of the bar, and those "women." And his own momentary excitement in the instant before fleeing the place. The doughboy naked on the floor of a cheap Montparnasse hotel room might well be him, not the sorry young lieutenant.

Whatever the motive, Leo got him dressed and into a taxi. His name was Robert MacGowan, Jr. He asked Leo to take him to the Hotel Lancaster, to his father. MacGowan senior was a full colonel. A big, gruff, sandy-haired Irishman, a New York attorney now on Pershing's staff.

At the first glimpse of the bruised and battered boy, Colonel Mac-Gowan grinned almost proudly at Leo and said, "What's the other guy look like?"

Leo wanted to say, It wasn't no guy. He said instead, "I never seen him, sir."

But then, when MacGowan told his son to go in the other room and get cleaned up, his eyes narrowed coldly and his mouth tightened with disdain. Leo knew the old man knew what his son was.

"I appreciate your help, soldier," MacGowan said. He placed a neatly folded fifty-franc note in Leo's palm and began walking him to the door.

"You don't have to give me nothing," Leo said, returning the money.

"It's okay, son. Keep it."

MacGowan opened the door; he wanted Leo out, fast. As though Leo were some messenger boy. "I don't need your money," Leo said. He laid the bill on the coffee table. "But thanks, anyhow." He stepped into the corridor, thinking, Screw you, Colonel. You, and your fairy kid.

"Hold it!" MacGowan joined him in the corridor. "I'm sorry if I offended you."

"Nobody gets offended by money, Colonel," Leo said. "I only helped your son so he didn't get in no trouble with the MPs. I don't especially like cops."

MacGowan smiled. "Where are you from in New York?"

"Manhattan."

"East Side?"

"Where else?"

MacGowan smiled again. He pointed to the Croix de Guerre ribbon. "Where'd you get that?"

"Saint-Mihiel."

MacGowan touched the inverted-V wound stripe on Leo's sleeve. "Saint-Mihiel, too?"

"Yeah," Leo said, glad he wore the stripe; at least MacGowan knew he was no paper shuffler. He flipped the colonel a casual salute and started away.

MacGowan called after him, "How much longer do you have on your furlough?"

Leo stopped, turned. "Six days."

MacGowan walked over to him. "You know the Ritz?"

"The hotel? I seen it, sure."

"Meet me for lunch tomorrow."

Leo hesitated. He knew the invitation was out of gratitude. It made him uneasy. Besides, other than a good meal, how could it benefit him? And what the hell would they talk about?

"That's an order, soldier," MacGowan said.

On the other hand, Leo thought, knowing a staff colonel couldn't hurt. It might be like knowing a precinct captain, or a ward leader.

"Okay," Leo said, and added quietly, "Sir."

3.

The Ritz dining room was the fanciest restaurant Leo had ever seen. Crystal chandeliers, sparkling white-linen tablecloths, tuxedoed waiters. And a string orchestra playing so softly that while you heard the music, you hardly knew it was there.

Leo, unable to read the menu, asked the captain to bring him the same that MacGowan ordered. A small steak, charred on the outside, rare inside; the potatoes sliced lengthwise, puffed up, fried to a golden crisp. The best meal Leo ever had. And wine, Margaux, which he had never heard of, let alone tasted. Flowing down your throat like smooth red powder.

The wine loosened Leo up. Soon they were chatting like old friends. MacGowan seemed fascinated with Leo. Perhaps it was the difference between this rough, tough, East Side Jewish kid who had come out of Elmira to be wounded in action, decorated for valor—and MacGowan's own son, whose troubles had brought them together, and whose name was never once mentioned.

MacGowan's parents, like Leo's, were penniless immigrants. Similarly, MacGowan was born on the Lower East Side. He told Leo how he had worked his way through City College waiting table, then studied law at night while working full days as a hod carrier. Listening, Leo thought, I could do that if I wanted. Maybe I'll be a lawyer. He liked the idea. And he also liked Big Bob MacGowan, and knew MacGowan was sincere when he said, ". . . after the war, you look me up. We'll find something for you."

They had finished lunch and were walking through the hotel lobby, which was crowded with officers, mostly Yanks, all of whom seemed acquainted with Colonel MacGowan. Four young YMCA girls in their blue sailor-style dresses and blue-felt campaign hats were clustered near the revolving door. One suddenly detached herself, calling across the lobby, "Bob!"

MacGowan smiled in pleased recognition at a tall, thin girl, her heavy dark hair rolled neatly under the campaign hat. Very poised and self-assured.

"Charlotte," he said as they embraced. "When did you get over?"

"Three months ago," she said. She had large, expressive eyes in an angular, high-cheekboned face. "I tried to find you, but they said you were up in Chaumont." She spoke these last words with a quizzical glance at Leo. He was staring at her.

MacGowan introduced them. Leo, he said, was a "special friend." And

Charlotte Daniels was the daughter of an old friend and client.

"Pleased tameetcha," said Leo.

"And I am very pleased to meet you, Mr. Gorodetsky." She ran a finger over his wound stripe. "I see you've been through it."

"Yeah," he said. For an instant no one spoke. He knew they were waiting for him to continue. He was desperate to say something clever or witty, but his mind was a blank. "Yeah, I guess so," he said.

MacGowan and Charlotte chatted briefly. Leo listened, never taking his eyes from her. He loved the sound of her voice. Soft, husky, yet each single word clear and distinct. Charlotte was talking about her mother's war charity work when MacGowan suddenly realized Leo was gazing almost hypnotically at her.

"Leo, you okay?"

Leo was startled. "Who, me?"

"You were in a trance," MacGowan said.

"Yeah, I was thinking of something." Leo laughed, embarrassed.

"You were looking at this young lady like—" MacGowan groped for a phrase. "Like a cat looking at a queen," he said, and suddenly snapped his fingers. "Leo, I want to speak with Charlotte a second. You wait right here." He led Charlotte a few feet away where they talked privately.

When they returned, Charlotte announced that Colonel MacGowan had appointed her Leo's personal guide for the remaining five days of his furlough. MacGowan winked at Leo, and said, "And that's an order, soldier!"

Leo knew it was a payoff for the service he'd rendered the colonel. Especially when MacGowan said he would be grateful if Leo did not mention to Charlotte exactly how he and Leo had met. So while Leo was not quite sure what her "guide services" would consist of, and while the first three days were not exactly what he had hoped, they were a marvelous three days.

They visited the Louvre, Versailles, the Opéra, Les Halles. Notre Dame—whose grandeur Leo had to admit was awesome (even if it was a church)—and Luna Park; and, of course, the Tower. They rode a Seine barge one day, all the way to Ablon, which looked so peaceful and inviting they jumped ship and bought bread, cheese, and wine for a picnic on the river bank. Another day, they met early in the morning to stroll through the Bois de Boulogne with the fog still on the ground in fluffy little white clouds swirling around their legs.

She liked to talk. He found everything she said interesting and amusing. She told him about her Glen Cove childhood, her banker father and socialite mother. The summer house in Maine, in a place called Bar Harbor. And the school on West Seventy-eighth Street run by a stern woman named Mrs. Finch, followed by the boarding school in Northampton, Massachusetts. The formal dance, called "Prom," which was short for Promenade, at the Parker House, a hotel in Boston. A world as alien to Leo as another planet.

Alien, perhaps, but he began to believe not unattainable. It was obvious she liked him, but how much? She certainly wasn't tearing her clothes off for him. And Leo was glad of it. When it happened—and he knew it would—he wanted it to be right. An act of love, of beauty. Tenderness, and meaning.

He had never known such intense feelings, even in the beginning with Edie. With Edie, although always very exciting, the instant it was over he wanted to immediately get away from her. With Charlotte, it would be different. He would want to stay with her, care for her. He wanted to please her. He wanted to make her happy.

Now, for the first time, he fretted over his appearance. The sloppy doughboy khakis dismayed him and, he was sure, embarrassed Charlotte. He wished he were an officer, if only for the tailored uniform. But he made up for it in other ways. He opened doors for her, held her chair, stood when she approached. And, most pleasing of all to her, he struggled for improved grammar. He had become suddenly aware of his speech, the hard, rapid New Yorkese. "Dems," and "dose," and "ain'ts," and "can't nevers," "don't know nothings." It all suddenly sounded so wrong.

He asked her to help him "talk good." She laughed, and said she just loved the way he talked; it was quaint. Yeah, well he didn't like it no more, he said. She said it was a mere matter of selection, pronunciation, and vocabulary. She advised him to read more, to listen carefully, and practice.

"I'll do it," he promised. "I'll learn class."

"Leo, class isn't something you can learn. You either have it, or you don't."

"I have it," he said. "Don't worry, I have it."

She smiled.

Suddenly, it was the fourth day. Only one day left. They were sitting on the terrace of Fouquet's, watching late evening traffic on the Champs Élysées. They had planned to see a revue featuring Yvette Guilbert, but Charlotte felt a cold coming on and wanted to get to bed early. So they decided to just have a coffee, and then Charlotte would go home. A good night's sleep was the best medicine.

"We'll do Guilbert tomorrow," she said. "I'll feel more up to it."

"Tomorrow's my last day," he said.

"I know." She touched his hand lightly. "Will you miss me?"

He said nothing a moment. He was thinking that not only would he miss her, his whole life was empty without her. He wondered what she would say if he told her. Instead, he said casually, "Sure, I'll miss you."

"How much?"

"Enough."

"But how much is that?"

She sat relaxed, arms folded, the corners of her mouth crinkled in an indulgent smile. He had been planning this for four days, and was still unsure. He looked away, at two French officers flirting with a girl seated alone at the next table.

"Well, how much?" Charlotte asked. Her voice had a teasing ring that perturbed him. He lit a cigarette, drew in a long deep drag, and carefully shook out the match.

"I love you," he said. He had blurted the words, but now that they were out he felt relieved. "I do. I honest to God, do."

"Don't say things like that, Leo. Please." She glanced around as though embarrassed.

"I'll say it again," he said. "I love you."

"You're serious," she said. "My God, you are really serious."

"Jesus Christ, you think I'd say it if I wasn't?"

She stared at him an instant, then leaned back and laughed. People at nearby tables looked at them. She clamped her hands over her mouth. "Leo, I'm sorry," she said. "Pay no attention to me."

"What's so funny?"

"It was the way you said it, that's all. And the look on your face!"

"What look? I don't get it."

"It's all right." She dabbed the corner of her eye to wipe away a tear of laughter. "Don't worry about it." She stood. She pulled on her gloves and tucked her purse under her arm. "Come on, walk me home."

He looked at her, then at the French officers again. One sat with the girl now. The other remained at his table, but had just clicked glasses in a toast with his friend, and with the girl. Leo bet the three wound up together. What did they call it? Ménage? Ménage à trois?

"Leo, let's go," Charlotte said impatiently.

He mashed out his cigarette and got up. He had to arch his neck slightly to face her. She was a full three inches taller. He said, "I still don't get it."

"I know," she said. "I know you don't." She patted the back of his head and started away. After a moment, he followed.

She lived nearby in a small hotel on Rue Colisée. They walked silently until they crossed the boulevard. Then Charlotte began talking. Something about the war, and how it surely would be over soon. Leo never heard a word. All he heard was their conversation at Fouquet's, each single word ringing shamefully in his ears. He hated himself for it. He felt weak and helpless, as though walking naked in the street in a dream.

". . . tomorrow," she was saying. "You'll come over for breakfast. Nine, nine-thirty."

They were at her hotel. He ignored the gloved hand extended him in good-bye. "I want to know why you laughed."

"I wasn't laughing *at* you. Honestly."

"Don't it mean nothing to you, a guy says he loves you?"

"Doesn't it mean anything," she corrected patiently. "Of course it means something. And I'm flattered, Leo. I am terribly flattered." She moved to leave. "Tomorrow?"

"I thought you felt the same way?"

She peered down at him. In the dark her mouth was a hard thin line across the lower half of her face. "You thought I felt the same way?" she repeated slowly. "What way?"

"Like I feel about you," he said.

"I'm very much afraid, Leo, that you've mistaken kindness for something else entirely. But then, I suppose you don't know any better."

"Hey, don't get sore."

"I'm not 'sore,' " she said. "I'm disappointed."

"Okay, so maybe I shouldn't of said it. I'm sorry." He hated himself for apologizing, but thought it might help. For a moment he believed it did. She seemed to relax. She smiled, almost sadly.

"You really don't know any better, do you?" She patted his hand. "Poor little Leo," she said, and went into the hotel.

He stood watching the hotel door open, then close. He watched her walk to the desk and speak to the porter. The porter laughed, then handed her a key. Leo wondered what she said to make the porter laugh. He watched her go up the stairs, and out of sight.

All at once he understood. What he should have understood from the beginning. When she talked about being fascinated at the differences between them. "Ethnic and social differences," she had said.

Ethnic and social.

The four days so marvelous for him had been, for her, a social experiment. Like the rich Jewish ladies from uptown coming down to the Settlement House with old clothes and inspiring words for the poor ones they were so ashamed of.

Poor little Leo.

He hurried back to the boulevard. He went into the first café and drank down three fast cognacs. Then he went to the whorehouse where the girls wore the brassieres with the nipple cutouts. He chose the biggest girl in the place, a brassy blonde. He stayed with her all night, falling asleep immediately after the one and only time they made love. In the morning she said he had called her "Charlotte." He said that was the name of a girl he once knew.

PART THREE
THE TRIAD

6

ARNOLD Steinberger found it hard to believe his class at Harvard was celebrating its twentieth reunion. The invitation, propped in the lower right corner of his dresser mirror, had come in the morning mail. He studied it now, tooled-leather brush in each hand, carefully, almost rhythmically, smoothing back his full hair. The gray flecks at the temples did not displease him; he thought them rather distinguished. He wondered how his classmates looked, and imagined himself at the reunion next month. Chatting, exchanging stories, reminiscing. He tried to recall who had been voted most likely to succeed. Not him, although for sure if they took a vote today he would be a front-runner. He smiled into the mirror with the thought.

"Arnold, what is it called when one is in love with one's self?" the woman asked. She was watching him interestedly.

He looked at her in the mirror. She lay in the rumpled center of the huge circular bed. The black-silk sheets formed a backdrop for her naked body resembling portraits hung above the mirrors of old-time saloons. Black-silk sheets were her idea; he enjoyed indulging her. He set the brushes down and turned to her.

"It's called narcissism," he said.

"I think you have a touch of it."

"The fact of the matter is I was looking for what they call 'telltale wrinkles,' " he said. "I'm forty-one, you know."

"It looks well on you," she said.

Her name was Alicia. With her long black hair, and fine-boned face, and deep, dark eyes, Arnie considered her one of the most beautiful women he ever knew. She reminded him of Isis, the Egyptian goddess of fertility, or how he imagined Isis. Alicia's fertility, thankfully, was a moot point; she had never borne a child. She had certainly tried, however. Both with Arnie, and with her husband.

"When do you have to be home?" he asked.

"What time is it now?"

Arnie glanced at the wristwatch lying next to the reunion invitation. "Just after four."

"You sound like you're anxious for me to leave."

"I have an appointment at seven," he said. "In Greenport."

"You can drop me home on the way," she said.

"Of course." He strapped on the watch, a five-dollar Waltham he bought two years ago in a Chicago drugstore after leaving his Hamilton on the washbasin in a compartment on the *Twentieth Century Limited*. The Waltham not only brought him luck—he made $3,500 in a whist game on the train returning to New York—it worked better than all the expensive watches he owned. A moral to that, but he was never exactly sure what.

"Get dressed," he said, and stepped to the window. Cars and taxis on West End Avenue stretched the entire length of three blocks in either direction. From here, Arnie's penthouse, you could see all the way across the river to the Palisades. And all the way down to the piers. The big ships, guided by little tugs, easing up the channel to the piers. Smaller boats, dashing in and out, spreading behind them long streamers of frothy white wake. The view, of which he never tired, and for which he paid $400 monthly, made him feel King of all he surveyed. Well, I am King, he thought. For $400 a month, I should be.

He turned; she was smiling at him. "Something's on your mind," she said. "It can only be one of two things. Money, or sex."

"Why not both?"

She held her hand out to him. He walked over to the bed and sat down. He touched her hand, the soft smooth skin. He brought her fingers to his lips and kissed them.

"Where did you tell Phil you were?"

"Shopping."

"He must think you do a lot of shopping."

She ran her hand over his cheek. "Would you prefer I told him the truth?"

It was a little game they played, but Arnie would not bet she had not told her husband of the affair. He, the husband, was a millionaire lawyer now a municipal judge. Arnie first met Alicia at their Park Avenue home when he came to collect $10,000 the judge lost betting against Man O'

War in the 1920 Belmont. The instant he saw Alicia, who was at least twenty years younger than her fifty-year-old husband, Arnie thought any man imprudent enough to bet against Man O' War could not possibly appreciate such a beautiful lady.

As each was fond of saying, it was lust at first sight. They had agreed to simply allow the relationship to run its natural course. Just enjoy it.

Now he said, "I might be going up to Boston next month. Think you could join me?"

"Not if you're going on business, Arnold."

"My class reunion," he said. He got up and brought the invitation back to her. "They say the class of 1901 is collectively the most successful in Harvard history."

Arnie gazed at her breasts as she read the invitation. Rather small breasts, but perfectly formed. They reminded Arnie of a Cézanne still life he admired, *Fruit in a Dish*. Alicia's breasts were two delicious little pears. She returned the invitation. "Are you held up as an example of that success, Arnold?"

She spoke lightly, but he knew she disapproved his new endeavor. She preferred him as a gambler. King of the Gamblers. That to her was glamorous.

He said, "You sound like my father. Only the other day, he said I was wasting my life."

"Your father is right. I'd like to meet him someday."

"He wouldn't approve of you. Not only are you a married woman, you're a Gentile married woman."

"I'm married to a Jew," she said. "Doesn't that count?"

"I don't think so," Arnie said. "That only makes you a Jew by injection."

"I still want to meet him. I know he'd like me. We both want his son to become a solid citizen."

"Do you try to reform all your men, Alicia?"

"Only the ones I sleep with, Arnold."

"Have you any idea how much money I'll make this year?" He cupped one of her breasts, then brushed his lips against the nipple. He loved her fragrance. "Would you believe at least a half million?"

"Until the government catches up with you," she said. "What is it you're called? Bootlegger?"

"Yes, my dear. Except that *I'm* called King of the Bootleggers."

"They've promised to put every last one of you behind bars. But don't worry, darling, each and every week I'll bake you a cake with a file in it."

"You don't understand," he said seriously. "Prohibition is an unpopular law, foisted on an unwilling public. How do you think I'm making so much money?"

"I see," she said. "You're performing a public service?"

"Absolutely," he said. "And getting rich from it."

"I'll still bake you a cake." Alicia slipped out of bed and stood before him an instant, naked, then pirouetted away from his outstretched arms. She began getting dressed. She put on her garter belt, then flesh-colored silk stockings. She rolled each stocking onto her foot slowly, sensuously, up past the calf, the thigh. She knew he enjoyed watching this; it pleased her to please him.

Suddenly he pictured himself pushing her against the bed edge, pushing her gently down so she lay back on the bed with her legs touching the floor. Spreading her legs, mounting her. The idea excited him and he saw the same excitement reflected in her eyes.

"Do we have time?" she asked.

"How much time do we need?"

"Hours," she said. "Days."

"How about ten minutes?"

"Make it fifteen," she said, and held her arms out to him.

All the way back from Greenport, Arnie thought about what she said about him wasting his life. He tucked the blanket in more snugly over his stomach and knees and gazed at the silhouetted outlines of the derbys worn by the two men in the front seat. Past them, through the windshield, the Lincoln's headlights cut whitely through the night. The low, throaty, steady drone of the big motor was soothing, and reassuring.

Wasting his life? Not thirty minutes ago he sat in the living room of the home of the mayor of Greenport and handed $2,000 in cash to a United States Coast Guard chief petty officer. Payment guaranteeing safe conduct for Arnold Steinberger's merchandise.

More accurately, safe conduct for his boats, the three twenty-foot Chris Crafts with twin Packard engines that drove those boats nearly forty miles per hour.

And safety for *Westwind*.

Westwind. The ninety-foot, three-masted schooner purchased last year in the Bahamas. She picked up cargo in the Bahamas, or Bimini, Cuba—even Halifax. Then, sailing to New York, she anchored beyond the three-mile limit and off-loaded to the Chris Crafts, which raced to Greenport, to Arnie's waiting trucks.

Westwind reminded Arnie of Alicia: both so feminine, so graceful, with a style and poise all their own. Except that Alicia certainly could not deliver three thousand cases of King's Ransom Scotch plus another one thousand cases of Courvoisier. Well, Alicia delivered other, equally important items.

Wasting his life?

A man living his life precisely as he wishes certainly is not wasting it. He had tried to explain this to his father. Remembering, Arnie suddenly laughed aloud. The man seated beside the driver turned.

"What's so funny, Arnie?"

His name was Charlie Cohen, once better known as "Charlie O'Connor, the Battling Bostonian." He was a big, broken-nosed barrel-chested man whose brief ring career was notable for its 1 and 12 record.

"What's so funny, huh?" Charlie asked again.

"I was just thinking of something," Arnie said. "As a matter of fact, I was thinking of my father."

"Oh," said Charlie.

Actually, Arnie was thinking of his father *and* Alicia. The two meeting, discussing Arnie's wasted life. Of which Meyer Steinberger once said, ". . . you're living your life as you wish, Arnold? For this I sent you to college?"

Arnie loved that kind, gentle old man. If only he understood his son.

"Take it a little faster, Eddie," Arnie said, addressing the driver, a slender man of middle height named Eddie Greenberg. Arnie's bodyguard and errand runner more than a year now, sharing the duty with Charlie Cohen. Both carried licensed Smith & Wesson .32-caliber revolvers in shoulder holsters.

Charlie Cohen turned fully around to Arnie. He touched the brim of his derby, tipping the hat slightly back on his head. "I meant to tell you: some dago from the Village tried to sell merchandise to Chez When. Jannsen called me about it."

Eric Jannsen owned Chez When, an East Forty-seventh Street club, one of Arnie's first customers. A good customer, forty cases weekly of the very best. Arnie asked, "What did Jannsen tell him?"

"That you was the supplier. But the walyo said he'd be back."

"Do you know the man?"

Eddie Greenberg, glancing at Arnie in the rear view mirror, said, "I do. A punk named Bracci."

"They're coming out of the woodwork lately," Charlie said. "They're all over the place."

"Eddie, you talk to this Bracci," Arnie said. "Politely, but make him understand."

"Okay," said Eddie, edging the wheel slightly right. The headlights of a large truck loomed directly ahead on the narrow road. Another bootlegger, Arnie thought. He idly wondered who owned the truck, which rival.

Charlie said something, but Arnie did not hear over the rush of wind from the truck hurtling past. Arnie did not ask Charlie to repeat whatever he said. He did not want to talk. He wanted to just sit back and enjoy the big Lincoln's smooth ride. It was like riding on a cushion of air. And the buzz of the pneumatic tires on the new macadam road surface, a kind of music all its own. A symphony of power. Arnie loved the feeling of power provided by the car. No, he corrected himself, I love the feeling of power, period. *My* power. King of the Bootleggers was no exaggeration. He ruled supreme.

Supreme, because long before the Eighteenth Amendment became law, he had the foresight to line up every first-class club and restaurant in Manhattan. Now he was their exclusive purveyor of fine wines and spirits. Already, he had more than two-dozen distributors openly operating, even advertising. And you could not keep up with the demand.

Others of course had soon followed Arnie's example, particularly the Italians. Not the old Black Hand extortionists, but the younger ones. Better educated, brighter, most specialized in running "go-through" jobs off the Long Island and Connecticut shore: souped-up speedboats pirating small cargoes either from freighters anchored outside the limit or from contact boats unloading the cargo vessels. And these young thugs were rough, and as ruthless as the seafaring pirates of old. In the past four months six men, including two Coast Guardsmen, were killed resisting "go-throughers."

But no threat to Arnie. He was far too well organized and connected, and his people—his Jewboys—merciless. No one dared hijack an Arnold Steinberger cargo. Arnie was the acknowledged King. Untouchable. So if all that, he told himself now, is wasting your life, just give me more. All there is. Thinking about it, he suddenly felt lucky. A feeling he never failed to recognize. An almost imperceptible racing of the heart, an emptiness in the pit of the stomach, and a flush of warmth through the whole body.

Arnie knew he had to find a poker game. His next regular game was Tuesday; today was Saturday. But only last week he had received a casual invitation to a Saturday game at the stockbroker customer's home in Port Washington.

"Eddie, we're not going back to Manhattan right away," Arnie said. "Take the Port Washington cutoff."

The stockbroker was delighted to see him: a pro like Arnie Steinberger made it a game of skill and guts. Arnie played recklessly, but everything he did was right. At dawn when the game broke up he was ahead more than $7,000.

He was so exhilarated when he got home he could not sleep. For a wild moment he considered phoning Alicia. I'm sending my car over for you, he'd say. The perfect finish to a perfect night. But too early, the judge still at home. Arnie smiled to himself picturing Phil Berman's judicial aplomb when Eddie Greenberg rang the doorbell announcing he had come to take Mrs. Berman over to Mr. Steinberger's. Just for coffee, Your Honor, and a fast insertion.

Well, someday maybe, Arnie thought, standing at the window, gazing out at the river. At the docks, at a Cunard pier, passengers were boarding a liner. Arnie thought it might be the *Mauretania*. If ever I retire, he told himself, I think I would like to just ride those boats. Six days of nothing but poker. Poker, fine food and wine, beautiful women. Yes, he told himself, that is precisely how I wish to waste my life.

Absolutely.

Beyond the pier the cold morning sun glistened off the river where two stubby tugboats nudged another liner dockside. And beyond, out toward the Narrows—although you could not see them from here— were other ships. All coming to New York. All coming to drink Arnold Steinberger's liquor.

One of those unseen ships was a large passenger vessel. Originally christened *The Lone Star State*, she had been pressed into service as a troopship three years before and renamed *The President Roosevelt*. This was her fifteenth crossing, and probably most triumphant return. She was bringing home from Germany the final contingents of the AEF Army of Occupation.

2.

From bow to midship, one rail to the other, the deck of *The President Roosevelt* was packed with doughboys. All had rushed topside when some-one yelled "There she is!" "She," the Statue of Liberty, her torch poking through the tops of early-morning slate-gray clouds hovering above the Narrows.

Leo had found himself a place on the top deck near the forward stack, in Officers' Country. An artillery captain who spotted him clambering over the stairway barrier called out, "You shouldn't be up here, Ser-geant!"

Yeah, Leo said to the captain in his mind, you are one hundred and ten percent right, sir, but I am not about to get jammed down there with a thousand other guys. He turned slightly so the captain saw his wound stripe and five overseas hash marks.

He said, "Been two and a half years, sir, since I sailed out of here. When we got on at Bremen eighteen days ago, I had the flu, with a hundred and four temperature. I spent the first week at sea in sick bay. I'd sure like to get a decent look at that beautiful old lady, sir."

The captain, just as Leo knew he would, gestured him onto the deck. A big man with thinning hair and heavy jowls, he looked much older than he probably was. "Lovely sight," he said.

"Sure is," Leo said. "I never seen—saw it, this close."

"Nor I," said the captain. "When we left here last year, it was at night. Jesus, it's beautiful."

"Yeah," said Leo, who had also sailed from Hoboken at night. Twenty-eight months ago. Twenty-eight months, three weeks, and five days ago. And now he was back, and the Statue of Liberty was indeed beautiful! He thought this was how the Statue looked to his father and mother when they arrived in New York. How many years ago? Twenty-one.

". . . makes you proud to be an American, doesn't it?" the captain was saying.

"Sure does," Leo said, wondering if his father thought of it as beautiful.

And then, immediately, asked himself, Why the hell should I care what he thought? My father, he told himself, is probably dead. And if not, he should be. And, anyway, who the hell cares?

". . . a year ago, there'd have been a big sign saying 'Welcome Home,' and dozens of small boats escorting us in," the captain was saying. "Now nobody seems to give much of a damn."

"It's 1921, Captain," Leo said. "We ain't—we aren't the returning heroes no more." *Anymore*, he thought, correcting himself.

"That's for sure," said the captain. "But Army of Occupation duty was no picnic, either."

"No, sir," said Leo, wondering who the captain was trying to kid. Occupation duty was dream duty. Billeted in German houses so clean you could honest to God eat off the floor. And those Hausfraus and Fräuleins so eager to make their American occupiers comfortable. A pound of sugar made you a king. A couple of steaks, you were God himself.

Fuck you, Captain, Leo told him in his mind, and aloud said, "I got to tell you, sir, Coblenz was not a bad place."

"How long were you there?"

"Eleven months."

"You look familiar, Sergeant. Where've I seen you?"

"Could have been anyplace around there, I guess."

The captain shook his head and turned away to watch the Jersey shore. "It all looks so different. And I guess to hell it is." He turned to Leo again and said somberly, "My wife wrote me milk is fifteen cents a quart. Jesus! And how much do you think for a loaf of bread? Ten cents! And steak: forty cents a *pound*. And what about this Prohibition? They send us off to war, and when we come back, you can't buy a drink!"

"I never seen—saw, a place yet anybody that wants a drink can't find one," Leo said.

"Not if you don't care about breaking the law." The captain winked, and added, "And from what I hear, not many care."

Leo had heard the same. From Harry, who would be at the pier to meet him. Good old Handsome Harry Weisenfeld. No, Leo thought, excuse me, not Weisenfeld: *Wise*. It was now Harry Wise. The name change, Harry explained, was called Americanization. For Leo's money, Harry could change to any damn name he wanted. Wise, Unwise, Be Wise. To Leo, Harry would always be Harry, a Brownsville Jewboy. Just as Leo was a Delancey Street Jewboy.

Harry drove a truck for some guy smuggling whiskey in from Canada. Selling it at five times the price to restaurants that served it in teacups. But Harry was working the job only until Leo came home with the start-up money for their own game.

Thirteen thousand dollars, cash, the amount Leo netted from his year in Germany. Thirteen thousand dollars, a large enough sum to very comfortably finance a real game, a genuine high-stakes game. To obtain that stake, to make the Dream come true, Leo had volunteered for the Army of Occupation.

On the main deck, a sailor bellowed orders through a megaphone for everyone to form up for disembarkation. "We better get below," the captain said. He started away, then stopped. "Goddamit, Sergeant, I *know* I've seen you."

Leo knew exactly where the captain had seen him. He would have enlightened him, but did not feel like talking anymore. He wanted only to stay on this upper deck with his overcoat collar pulled up around his neck, the icy wind blowing back his hair and chilling his face as the Manhattan skyline grew larger and larger.

The Kaiserhof Hotel in Coblenz was where the captain saw him. The Kaiserhof Hotel, where Leo accumulated the $13,000. In the AEF's only officers-only casino. Managing director, Sergeant Leo Gorodetsky.

Managing director through the auspices of one Colonel John K. Strickland, C. O. of the Coblenz detachment Quartermaster Section. A good man, Colonel Strickland, even if a bit of a drunk. And a thief. And not the brightest of men. A bright man would never have accepted a brother officer's challenge to drive a staff car into Holland—*to kidnap the Kaiser.*

Both officers were drunk. And killed instantly when the colonel smashed the big Locomobile into a bridge abutment on the German side of the border.

The first order of Colonel Strickland's replacement, another colonel, was the casino's immediate closure. But by then Leo had the $13,000, and was more than ready to go home.

Now, far in the distance, Leo was sure he could see Hoboken. He imagined Harry at the pier, eagerly straining for a glimpse of the approaching troopship, impatiently awaiting Leo.

Leo, and their $13,000 stake.

He wondered how he would tell Harry. He had written him about Colonel Strickland, whom he first met in Chaumont when he was transferred to the motor pool and assigned as the colonel's chauffeur, and staying with the outfit when they moved to Coblenz. And the Kaiserhof Hotel being requisitioned for officers' quarters, and selling Colonel Strickland the idea of converting the hotel's empty wine cellar into a casino.

An instant success.

One craps table, two poker tables. Leo used German civilians as dealers and stickmen. They were hungry, smart, and far more honest than any doughboy. Each Sunday morning Leo presented Colonel Strickland a full accounting of the previous week's action. Never, of course, noting the modest percentage skimmed by Leo from the top. In return, Leo carefully ignored the sum deposited into the regimental fund by Colonel Strickland: always less than what Leo turned over to him. Leo marveled that an Indianapolis, Indiana, dry-goods-store owner became so accomplished a thief in so short a time. As Leo once wrote Harry, ". . . and I thought all the *gonifs* were in Brownsville!" However much Colonel Strickland personally profited—which Leo knew was at least twice what he, Leo, realized—the fund also profited.

Enough for everyone.

Until poor old Colonel Strickland took the crazy midnight ride that killed him. Well, at least his widow was well off. Leo was sure of that. Good luck to her.

To me, too, he had thought when he boarded *The President Roosevelt* with 130 one-hundred-dollar bills packed into a money belt.

Leo did not immediately see Harry on the pier. He heard him. "Hey, Kleyner . . . !" Instead of feeling good at the sound of Harry's voice, Leo almost wished Harry had not come to meet him. Leo just did not know how to break the news.

Harry stood behind the customs barrier, jumping up and down to attract Leo's attention. Finally, Leo saw him and yelled, "Hey!"

Harry hadn't changed a bit. The thick black hair carefully touseled to frame the handsome, square-jawed face. And still the clotheshorse: even the truck-driver's leather cap and gabardine jacket and brown wool trousers looked good on him. Custom-tailored, Leo was ready to bet.

"Lousy!" Leo shouted back. "I'm still seasick!"

"You'll get better in a hurry now!"

"Yeah," Leo said, and in his mind said, That's what *you* think, old pal. But that was the last he saw of Harry that morning because the battalion went to Camp Dix for processing and discharge. But Harry drove out to Dix and was waiting at the front gate when Sergeant Leo Gorodetsky, now *Mr.* Leo Gorodetsky, emerged.

"You ain't grown a fucking inch!" Harry said. He threw his arms around Leo and hugged him.

"Yeah, but you have!" Leo said, punching Harry's stomach. Now he was glad Harry had met him, so glad he momentarily forgot the bad news he would soon convey.

Harry picked up Leo's duffel bag, at the same time running his fingers over Leo's sergeant's chevrons. "A fucking hero, for Christ's sake! Kleyner, I'm proud of you."

"Yeah," Leo said. "Let's get the hell home."

Harry tossed the duffel bag into the bed of a brand-new REO truck, then stepped to the front and removed a crank from under the radiator. He inserted the crank and swung it hard. The motor caught, then died. Harry swung it again, harder; this time it started. Harry waved Leo into the passenger seat, replaced the crank, and got in behind the wheel.

"Nice truck," Leo said. He had to shout over the engine clatter.

"It's Epstein's!" Harry shouted back. "The guy I work for, Joey Epstein. A shmuck!" He gripped the wheel, depressed the clutch twice, pushed the gear shift into low and started off.

"He owns this truck, he ain't such a shmuck," Leo said.

"He owns *four* trucks," Harry said. "And he could use a couple more."

Harry described his job: delivering Joey Epstein's watered liquor to restaurants, nightclubs, and private customers. He made good money, twenty-five dollars a week, and had a list of *nafkes* that'd knock your socks off. Every one a sure thing. He had a room in the St. George Hotel on Twenty-third Street, six dollars a week.

"But now you're home, Kleyner, I tell Epstein to shove the job!" Harry grinned elatedly. "You and me, we're in business right?"

"Right," Leo said, saying it because he did not know how to tell Harry the truth.

"Thirteen grand," Harry said. "A real stake. First-class. I found a place I think we can run the game. A joint in Westchester, Sandy's, they call it. Sandwiches, ribs, *chozzerai* like that. And a little band for dancing. The owner, Sandy—he's a *shaygets*, but he's okay—he's hot to trot. With a little grease to the local cops, we're on our way."

Leo said, "Harry, there ain't no stake. I don't have it no more." There *isn't* any, he repeated to himself. I don't have it anymore.

They were rolling fast along the narrow road, but not fast enough to overtake a black Essex coupe spewing a steady stream of thick brown dust into the REO's windshield.

"Shit," Harry said, slowing for the Essex to get farther ahead. He looked at Leo. "What'd you say?"

"I said I don't have the stake."

Harry frowned. "Not funny, Leo."

"I lost it on the ship," Leo said.

"That still ain't funny," Harry said.

Every last dime of it, Leo was thinking, which once amounted to 130,000 dimes. One hundred and thirty thousand ten-cent pieces: $13,000.

"I lost it," Leo said again.

Blindly steering the truck, Harry stared at him. "How? How did you *lose* it?"

"Somebody took me."

"You *played*?"

"Come on, Harry, you know better," Leo said. "Only suckers play."

"Then what in the name of fuck did you do?" Harry shouted. "Give it to the French war orphans, or something!"

Harry's rage swept through the chilly truck cab like a blast of heat from an open oven. Leo said nothing for a moment. He was thinking, as he had thought at least a hundred times in the eighteen days at sea, if only he had reported sick at Bremen. He knew it was the flu; he felt it even on the train from Coblenz. He did not report sick fearing they would keep him off the ship. The fever hit him on the first night. Him, and two hundred other doughboys. He lay on his bunk, soaked with sweat, drifting in and out of hallucinated sleep, sometimes believing he was still in Coblenz, sometimes sure he was alone in a lifeboat in the open sea. And, once, he swore Edie was there, mopping his face and forehead with a cool, wet towel. He asked if Hershey still hated him, and to please tell Hershey how sorry he was. It was an army nurse. A middle-aged, deep-wrinkled woman with gold-rimmed spectacles that gleamed with the reflected light from the overhead bulb and made his eyes ache.

Leo said to Harry now, "What happened was, I got the flu." And he told him how he woke from one feverish sleep, seeing a navy medical corpsman standing over the hammock, and feeling the money belt being slid out from under him—and thinking he was hallucinating again.

But he remembered the sailor's face. Thin, acne-scarred, eyes set so close they almost seemed part of his bony nose. This sailor was not hard to find. Word spread fast about the corpsman with the bankroll that would choke a horse. His name was Garret. But by the time Leo was strong enough to leave sick bay, it was too late. Garret had just lost his last dime.

Leo's last dime.

He caught up with Garret the day before they reached New York. Down in the galley near the meat locker. Stalking him from behind, Leo smashed the sailor on the back of the head with a flashlight and dragged him into the locker. He trussed Garret's wrists with his own belt, then hung him by the shirt collar on a meat hook like a side of beef.

Even now, driving with Harry Weisenfeld through the New Jersey countryside, the very recounting of the story sent that cold chill of anger through Leo's body. Remembering how he patiently waited for Garret to wake, all the while carefully honing a meat-cutter's butcher knife. When Garret finally opened his eyes, Leo smiled pleasantly and said, "Hello, there."

Garret peered blankly at Leo. Then he felt the pressure on his wrists. He twisted around to see the knotted belt; and then, bewildered, at the expanse of the meat locker. He looked at Leo again, and all at once realized he was strung up on the hook.

"Hey, what the hell kind of joke is this?" The pitted skin of his face glistened with sweat. "Who are you?"

"You forget me so quick?"

"I never seen you—"

"Oh, sure you did." Leo's smile narrowed. With a final flourish, he ran the knife blade over the honing knife. "In sick bay. That time you pinched my money belt." He slid the knife upward and laid it flat against Garret's throat. Quietly, almost conversationally, he continued, "I saw this butcher once. In a slaughterhouse. A kosher place. They drain all the blood from the cows to make them kosher. Kosher, the meat's okay for Jews to eat."

"Hey, look, I don't—" The words choked in Garret's throat as Leo applied just the slightest pressure on the knife blade, turning it with nearly surgical precision to cut a tiny line in Garret's flesh. Garret screamed.

"Save your breath, Swabbie," Leo said quietly. "Nobody can hear you down here."

"Jesus Christ!" Garret said. "What are you doing this for? It's a mistake, for Christ's sake!"

"What's a mistake?"

"This, what you're doing!"

"Why'd you take my money?"

"I didn't take no money!" Garret shouted, then screamed again as Leo pressed the blade harder against his throat. "I swear I didn't! I swear on my mother's soul! I didn't take nothing!"

The blade cut deeper. The entire front of Garret's throat looked as though it had been painted a bright, viscous red. The blood dripped down onto the hemmed collar bib of his white B.V.D. undershirt, and then onto the blue denim shirt.

"All right, yes, all right!" he cried. "Yes, I took it! But I ain't got it no more! The truth, I swear it!"

"Yeah," Leo said. "I know."

"I'll pay it back, I swear I will," Garret said. "Every fucking cent. Honest to God!"

"You ain't got it," Leo said. "So how can you pay it back?"

"I'll do it!" Garret said. "I'll get it for you!"

"Thirteen thousand?"

"Every last cent."

Leo had gazed unseeingly at him a moment; it gave Garret hope that Leo somehow believed him, and he continued, "All of it, Sarge, so help me God!"

Leo's hesitation came from trying to understand why his anger seemed suddenly drained away, replaced by a strange, unfamiliar sadness. He said, "You swear, huh?"

"I do, I do!" Garret said, and then screamed, "Oh, no!"

Leo had swiveled the blade again so the razor-fine edge pressed once more into the bleeding, lacerated flesh. He gripped the handle so tight the tips of his fingers ached. In his mind he saw the blade slicing, angled, into Garret's jugular, the blood spurting redly. He felt quite calm, and composed. This was no different than with Hammer, or the German soldiers. Simply something that needed to be done.

But while thinking all this, he looked directly into Garret's bulging, terrorized eyes and thought also that, in truth, it was different from Hammer and the Germans. Hammer would have made endless trouble. The Germans wanted to kill him. But this stupid son of a bitch of a sailor, who most certainly deserved to be killed, posed no threat to Leo. More important, killing him would not return the money. So what do I gain? he had asked himself. Where's the percentage?

". . . so," he continued now to Harry, peering at the winter-boarded fruit and vegetable stands lining the roadside, the summer's hand-painted signs on pieces of wood or cardboard still fadingly legible: CORN, 10C DOZ. TOMATOES, 6C PD. CUKES, 12C BSKT. "So, I figured I was doing something that if I got caught for it, wasn't worth it." He glanced at Harry. Harry gazed rigidly at the road, as though he needed to concentrate on Leo's every word.

Harry said nothing, and Leo continued, "You do something without getting nothing back for it—except maybe some satisfaction—it's stupid. I mean, what's the sense of killing the guy if you don't get something out of it? You're taking a big chance yourself, and unless you're sure it's to your advantage, there just ain't no point to it. See what I mean?"

Harry looked at him. "No."

"I'm trying to tell you, Harry, that to do violence just for the hell of it is stupid. And all you get for it is more stupidness." He paused, thinking "stupidness" sounded wrong. He tried to remember the correct word, but could not, and knew that the word or words he sought were only words to make Harry feel better. He also knew nothing he said could achieve that.

Harry said, "You should have killed the prick."

"Didn't you hear what I just said?"

"It don't matter what you said, Leo. It's what you did."

"Violence for it's own sake is stupid," Leo said again, and now smiled dryly. "Gorodetsky's Law."

"Gorodetsky's Law," Harry said. The two words reverberated through the truck cab like a bitter echo. "Gorodetsky's *shit*! You let the guy go, didn't you?"

"I just left him there swinging on that hook." Leo smiled again. "Hey, for all I know, he might still be there."

Harry said nothing. He only shook his head sadly.

"But you know something?" Leo said. "I felt good about it. Like I won."

"Like you won? What'd you win, Leo, the 'good-Jew-of-the-year' prize?"

Leo pondered the question; he did not in all honesty know what he won. He only knew he had not been stupid. He hated being stupid. Charlotte Daniels, for example. Even after all this time, he felt shamed, and small. Inferior, he thought, that was the word. Inferior.

Harry was saying, ". . . the guys that won were the ones that cleaned the swabbie. The guys that won our money!"

Our money, Leo thought. Well, in a way Harry was right. He had waited nearly two years for Leo to come home with it. What Harry did not know—and what Leo never would have told him anyway—was that Leo had been considering using the money to go back to school. High school, and then maybe law school. He liked the idea of becoming a lawyer. If a man like Big Bob MacGowan could do it, so could Leo Gorodetsky.

Still thinking of that, he said, "Well, it doesn't make no difference now."

"That's for sure," Harry said sullenly.

"The world's filled with money, Harry," Leo said.

"Sure," said Harry. He jingled some change in his pocket. "We even got enough for the ferry to Manhattan."

"Don't worry about it so much," Leo said. "We'll get our share."

"We'll get our share, huh?" Harry said. "How?"

"I'll get a job. We'll start all over again."

"Listen, there's eight million guys home from the army. There ain't no work for half of them. I'm lucky I got this job."

"You disappoint me, Harry," Leo said. "I figured by now you'd have a dozen jewelry stores lined up."

Leo was kidding, but Harry took him seriously. "I made up my mind I wasn't going in for no more two-bit stuff. It ain't worth it."

"Yeah," Leo said. He was watching the filmy trails of road dust splatter into the windshield like wisps of dirty brown smoke, and thinking that Harry was right. Jewelry stores weren't worth it. But you needed money in your pocket, you had to eat. But for the fifty-dollar separation pay received at Dix, Leo was flat broke. He did not know if there was room for him with his mother and Esther; and even if there was, he had no intention of living with them.

"This guy you work for, this Epstein?" Leo asked. "You think he'd give me a job?"

7

IT took Leo exactly three days to realize Prohibition was a money tree. Less, to realize Joey Epstein was stupid and short-sighted. A big, boisterous, curly-haired *Litvak*, Joey in 1917 married the spinster daughter of the Sephardic Jewish owners of three Brooklyn furniture stores. Draft-exempt thanks to a spastic colon, Joey settled down to live happily ever after carting used furniture with his brand-new Model T truck, a wedding gift from grateful in-laws.

Now, in the early spring of 1921, Joey Epstein owned four trucks, and no longer hauled furniture. Now, in a huge metal vat on the ground floor of a rented warehouse on East Broadway, he mixed one part good Canadian whiskey with five parts low-grade American alcohol. He paid two dollars per quart for the Canadian. He charged the same two dollars for a quart of the watered product.

A five hundred percent profit.

To be sure, any man realizing a fivefold return on his investment could not reasonably be called stupid. But pasting quality labels—Gordon's, Black & White, Dewar's—on the cut bottles, Leo considered stupid. With the ever-increasing competition, customers would soon enough demand, and receive, the uncut, genuine product.

Arnold Steinberger already knew this. Arnie controlled all quality distribution and sales from Fourteenth Street to Harlem, East River to the Hudson. The Italians had the Village and Little Italy. Everything else was open.

Leo pleaded with Joey Epstein to stake out some of the unclaimed territory. Flatbush, or the Heights, both wide open. It was like finding gold in the streets. "What gold?" Epstein asked. "You think Steinberger's leaving them places alone because he don't want the *gelt*? It ain't worth it for him. If it ain't worth it for him, it sure ain't for me."

"He don't want to overextend," Leo said. "He got all he can handle right now."

"Yeah, well so do I," said Epstein. "And another thing: I happen to know a couple of wise guys that did . . . what do you call it? Overextend? Into the river they overextended themselves. Both of them. On the bottom, *die helst*? In cement. So thanks, but no thanks."

They were on the sidewalk outside the warehouse. Leo, his day's deliveries completed, was waiting for Harry to come in. They were taking some girls Harry knew to supper. Epstein was on his way home, just climbing into the secondhand Jordan sedan recently purchased from a dress manufacturer gone bankrupt. Leo had planned to present his idea more formally, and in greater detail, but decided this was as good a time as any. Now he realized it made no difference. Epstein would never understand.

"Yeah, well, it was just an idea," Leo said. "Forget it."

"It's forgot," Epstein said. He jammed his toe down on the car's self-starter rod. The engine instantly caught, rumbled, then settled smoothly. Epstein, pleased, said, "Not bad, huh? No more of them goddam hand cranks. Once I nearly busted my wrist."

Too bad it wasn't your head, Leo thought, but said, "See you tomorrow, Joey."

"Don't take no wooden nickels," Epstein said. He put the car in gear and drove off.

Leo lit a cigarette and angrily watched the car rumble up East Broadway, past the new park being built on the corner of Seward. Which was another reason Leo considered Joey stupid. The building up of the area. The warehouse was not at all concealed. Even the beat cops knew about it. They were paid off, yes, but one of these days federal agents would make a raid. Or a customer, swallowing Joey's rotgut, would cough his stomach up through his nose. Say good-bye to J. Epstein Enterprises, Inc.

When Harry arrived Leo told him of the conversation. But he had cooled off enough to admit that dumb fuck though Joey might be, he had after all given Leo a job. Three dollars a day, plus twenty percent of over-quota sales. Enough for Leo to help his mother and sister with rent and food—and for him to bunk in with Harry until he found his own place.

"You're the dumb fuck, Kleyner, not Epstein," Harry said. "For even wasting your breath on him. You oughta know better."

"Yeah, I suppose," Leo said.

"Come on, get back to the hotel and get dressed," Harry said. "We're supposed to treat these bimbos to a picture show after we eat. Hey, and wait'll you see this one you're fixed up with."

Harry went on talking, but Leo was still thinking about Joey Epstein. Even before he had spoken to him, he had the feeling of being swept up into something beyond his control. The prospect of making thousands bootlegging, tens of thousands, was so appealing it almost obscured the original purpose. To finance their Dream, their own game. This disturbed Leo. It was like looking away from the ball when it came over the plate.

". . . told her all about you," Harry was saying. "A great big redhead. You'll come up to her belly button. And she's dying to meet you." He ruffled Leo's hair. "She says she likes 'em on the small side. I told her that's you, for sure. On the small side. Get it? On the small side?"

"Fuck you, Harry."

Harry grinned. "Not me, kid, *her.*

The girl Harry fixed Leo up with was indeed a big one and did, as Harry said, have a thing for little guys. So it all worked out well, and by the end of the evening Leo's anger at Epstein had subsided.

But not his impatience. Each day more opportunities were lost. "We don't move soon," he told Harry a few days later, "there'll be nothing left."

"Listen, all you get is what Arnie Steinberger don't want," Harry said. "And if he don't want it, maybe it ain't worth having."

"Whatever it is, it's a start," Leo said. "We got to keep our eyes open for our chance."

The chance came on his second month on the job. At the Islip boat-repair yard used as a warehouse by Epstein's Canadian-whiskey distributor.

It was a crisp, clear day, and waiting for Epstein's order to be processed, Leo took a walk along the beach. He had borrowed a pair of binoculars to follow a Coast Guard cutter patrolling Rum Row.

Rum Row. Dozens of ships—large freighters, smaller fishing trawlers, private yachts—all anchored just beyond the three-mile limit, lined on the horizon like an invasion fleet. On some ships huge oilcloth placards hung from the decks advertising in sloppily painted letters the day's specials: 3,000 CASES GENUINE GORDON'S GIN. ONE-TIME OFFER OF DUBONNET, FIRST COME FIRST SERVED. 250 CASES CHIVAS REGAL.

It reminded Leo of the stalls and pushcarts on Delancey Street: the contact boats racing to the ships, negotiating their purchases, racing back, easily outrunning the slower Coast Guard cutters. And hopefully avoiding any "go-through guys."

Through the binoculars Leo watched the Coast Guard cutter speed toward a graceful three-masted schooner he knew lay well outside the three-mile limit. He also knew the schooner was Arnie Steinberger's pride and joy, *Westwind.* She was anchored, sails furled, but in his mind Leo saw her plowing majestically through the water. He saw himself on deck, sails billowing with the wind, the wind and salt spray stinging his face. He and the boat were one, all part of the same.

"Yeah," he said aloud to himself. "You'll do all that on Epstein's three bucks a day."

The Coast Guard cutter approached *Westwind,* and then all at once veered away and started back. Leo knew the Coast Guardsmen were only signaling the schooner crew they would not interfere with the contact boats unloading Arnie's cargo. What a deal, he thought. Arnold Steinberger had them all in his pocket. He owned the world.

If Leo had not strolled along the beach to watch Arnie's schooner, and not returned to the warehouse at the precise time he did, one hundred cases of King's Ransom would have been sold out from under him.

One hundred cases of King's Ransom.

The genuine article, often impossible to find and in great demand. Twenty-five dollars a case. Leo offered forty. The distributor agreed to hold the shipment one week for Leo to raise the money.

Four thousand dollars.

A small fortune, but an investment easily quadrupled.

Harry was out all that night with a blonde from the *Scandals* chorus line, so Leo had no chance to discuss the deal. Harry was also late for work the next morning. Epstein, angry about that and the spring weather turning so unexpectedly cold that two trucks would not start, ordered Leo to drive part of Harry's route. The first customer was 273 West Twenty-second Street, a small restaurant, Minotti's.

Leo headed uptown on Third Avenue, under the El, pacing a train rattling roaringly overhead. It really was cold for March, near freezing, the paper said. He wore an extra sweater under his jacket, and buttoned the truck cab's isinglass windows tight against the cold. On West Twenty-second, he swung left on Third, swerving hard to avoid a pothole, feeling the entire load shift on the canvas-enclosed truck bed, and the bottles clattering in their cases. Twenty cases, stacked behind three large divans, two lounge chairs, and an ice chest.

Avoiding the hole, he pulled wide to the left, straight toward an oncoming taxi whose driver leaned on the horn and shook his fist as Leo swung back into the right lane.

"You, too!" Leo yelled after him. He pulled closer to the curb to study the building numbers. On the ground floor window of a brownstone, printed in an arc of paint-flaked black letters, MINOTTI'S. A horse-drawn ice wagon was parked in front. The iceman had just emerged from the restaurant, ice tongs balanced on his shoulder, rivulets of water frozen to the rubber apron draped over his chest and back.

Leo waited until he left, then moved into the vacant space. He turned off the engine and checked up and down the street for cops. On one sidewalk four kids played stickball; on the other side, bundled in layers of clothing, three housewives gossiped. Leo got out and entered the restaurant.

A small place, cramped with a dozen checkerboard-clothed tables, and the pungent aroma of garlic and oregano. Empty this time of morning but for two men at a back table drinking Turkish coffee. Both young, not much older than Leo. They wore expensive suits and ties, and pearl-gray spats over gleamingly shined black shoes. Their broad-brimmed pearl-gray fedoras matched the spats.

Leo said, "Mr. Minotti?"

"Who wants him?" asked one of the men, the younger and swarthier of the two. His friend, whose complexion was much lighter, sat watching Leo as though amused.

"I got a delivery," Leo said.

"I'm Minotti," a hoarse voice called from a curtained alcove in the rear. A short, chubby, white-aproned man appeared. He was entirely bald but for a fringe of cropped gray hair. He glanced worriedly at the men, then at Leo. "What kinda delivery?"

"Ginger ale and seltzer water," said Leo. "Should I bring it in?"

"Isn't that what they pay you to do?" the older man asked. He removed his hat and carefully smoothed down thick black hair. Although only slightly older than the other, he displayed a certain calm presence immediately identifying him as the leader. The hat had shadowed deep, dark, almost cold eyes, and a handsome, strong face. His voice was quiet, but deep and self-assured, the kind of voice seldom raised, even in anger. "You figuring on bringing it through the front?"

"Wherever you want," Leo said.

Minotti glanced at the two men again. The older one nodded, and Minotti said to Leo, "Around back." He walked Leo to the front door and opened it for him. "Pull the truck in the alley." He closed the door.

Leo backed the truck into the alley and got out. Deftly avoiding a mound of frozen horse dung piled against the building wall, he climbed into the truck bed, crawled past the furniture, and slid out a case of Scotch and one of gin.

Minotti had opened the rear door that led directly into the kitchen. Leo lugged in two cases and placed them on the floor where Minotti indicated. The two men were also in the kitchen now, the swarthy one lighting a cigarette from the stove gas jet. The soft-spoken man had left his hat in the restaurant, and now in the light Leo saw on his right cheek just the slightest suggestion of a scar; it almost looked as though drawn with a pencil.

"That's forty-eight bucks," Leo said to Minotti.

"Yeah, well, send a bill," said the dark man.

"What bill?" Leo said. "I got to get cash."

Minotti said quickly, "Look, tell Epstein I'm cancelling my order. Don't make no more deliveries."

Leo said, "Okay, I'll tell him. But I need forty-eight for this here delivery."

The man with the scar stepped closer to Leo and looked down at him.

He was much taller than Leo, who backed away to face him without craning his neck.

"I'm Sal Bracci," he said.

"Pleased to meet you," Leo said, and then to Minotti, "Could I have the money, please?"

"You saying you ain't never heard of Sal Bracci?" the swarthy one asked. He flipped his cigarette through the kitchen door into the alley. "You sure are a dumb little kike, you know that?"

Bracci was watching Leo with an amused smile. He knew Leo was angry, and also knew Leo could do nothing about it. It made Leo feel even more helpless. He said to Minotti, "Mr. Minotti, I got to have the money for this."

Bracci, gesturing Minotti to be silent, removed a gin bottle from the case and held it before him as though examining the Gordon's label. Then, almost casually, he lobbed the bottle into the alley. It struck the brick alley wall in an explosion of glass fragments and splashed liquor. Bracci removed a white handkerchief from his lapel pocket and delicately wiped his hands. As though this were a signal, the swarthy one dragged the entire case out the door and one by one, with machine-like precision, hurled each bottle into the alley wall.

Leo watched, paralyzed. When it was over, with every bottle in the second case also smashed, Bracci said, "See? Nobody owes you a dime. There's no merchandise."

The swarthy one, whose name was Aldo Puglisi, laughed. "Hey, Sal, that's rich: 'no merchandise!' " He said to Leo, "Yeah, and tell your boss his stuff was no good. The bottles leaked!"

Leo strained to keep his voice calm and level. "I'll tell him." He said this to Bracci, looking directly at him, determined not to look away. It was very important for him to face Bracci in that manner.

But if Sal Bracci realized this, or even cared, he gave no indication. He said, "See you around, kid," and walked back into the kitchen.

"Jeez, Hymie, you look like you pissed your pants!" Puglisi said. He laughed again, and followed Bracci inside, slamming the door in Leo's face.

Leo stood in the alley in the broken glass and puddles of whiskey. After a moment he got in the truck and drove away. Only when he reached Third Avenue did his hands stop trembling.

2.

Joey Epstein was furious. He paid his drivers good money and expected them to protect his merchandise. He also expected them to compensate him for any losses. The forty-eight dollars would be deducted from Leo's salary in weekly installments.

Leo's first instinct was to tell Joey to shove the job up his ass in equal installments. Instead, he decided this might be the time to ask Joey to stake him the $4,000 for the one hundred cases of King's Ransom. He said, "Suppose I tell you how to make a fast ten grand?"

They were in the tiny office at the rear of the warehouse. Joey was leaning back in his chair, legs propped on the edge of the paper-cluttered rolltop desk. Reaching for a box of matches to light a cigar he nearly knocked over an ink bottle. The matchbox was empty. Leo brought a single match from his shirt, struck it on the sole of Joey's shoe, and lit the cigar for him.

"How much does it cost me?" Joey asked.

"Four," said Leo, and told him about the King's Ransom, although not the source. He offered to split the profits down the middle.

Joey listened patiently. Then he said, "You're a real *baleboss*, ain't you? If I had a nickel, kid, for every time I hear that kind of proposition, I'd be a millionaire. How do you want I should take out the forty-eight? Five a week?"

"Don't take nothing out, Joey."

"Nothing, huh?" The hard edge in Leo's voice had erased Joey's good humor.

"That's right, nothing," said Leo. "Wops muscling in on your territory is your problem, not mine."

"I guess you don't like the job, huh?"

"The job's okay," Leo said. "You ain't."

"For a little man, you got an awful big mouth."

Leo said, "Yeah, Joey, I know." He plucked the ink bottle from under the papers on the desk. He unscrewed the cap, upended the bottle, and poured the entire contents on Joey's lap.

Joey jumped from the chair, screaming, "You son of a bitch!" For an instant he stood gazing in horror at his ink-stained trousers. He looked at Leo, then back at the trousers. Gingerly, he touched the spreading black stain. Now his hand was black with dripping ink. "I'll kill you, you little bastard!"

Leo could hardly stop laughing. "Take the cleaning bill out of my pay, too, Joey," he said. He walked out and nearly collided with Harry.

Harry stared at Joey Epstein's black-glistening crotch, and said, "Jesus!" And then he also began laughing. "Hey, Joey, now you got a black dick! Now you know how the *shvartzers* feel!"

Joey looked at him with wide-eyed fury. "You bastard, you're fired, too!" Still laughing, Harry asked, "*Too?*"

Leo said, "Yeah, the shmuck fired me. He can't take a joke!"

Harry said all he regretted about losing the job was that Leo did what he, Harry, always wanted to do. Although if it were him, Harry, he would have busted a few of the *momzer's* teeth as well.

They were in the St. George hotel room they shared. Leo stood at the window, observing the Twenty-third Street traffic. Harry lay on his bed, on his stomach, cleaning Leo's .45 Colt service pistol. Leo had kept the .45—and two full ammunition clips issued him in Coblenz—simply by marking it "returned" on the quartermaster requisition form.

"Too bad this wasn't on you when you run into them *Talenas* before," Harry said. "What was his name, 'Bracci'?"

Leo turned. Harry blew into the gun muzzle and smiled at Leo. Harry was probably the only chaplain's assistant in the army with enough rifle-range time to win a sharpshooter's badge.

Leo said, "You're getting too attached to that piece."

"You don't take care of it," Harry said. "I want to be sure if we have to use it, it's ready."

Leo held his hand out for the gun. Reluctantly, Harry surrendered it. Leo slipped it into a shoe box on the closet floor.

"Leave it there, Harry. Right where it is. Okay?"

"You know your problem, Leo? You think because you killed a couple of krauts in the war, you're hot shit." Harry pushed himself off the bed and reached for a cigarette from a pack of Caporals on the night table. He rummaged around for matches.

"You and Epstein," Leo said. He brought a match from his pocket and lit it with his thumbnail. He held the flame under Harry's cigarette.

Harry dragged on the cigarette. "What me and Epstein?"

"He never has matches, either," Leo said. "Now listen, we don't find four grand in the next few days, we lose those hundred cases of King's Ransom."

"You're really something, Kleyner. We ain't got a job, or enough for supper tonight, but you're worrying about four grand."

"Yeah, well I got an idea where to get it," Leo said.

"Where? John D. Rockefeller?"

"Arnie Steinberger," Leo said.

Harry peered at him, then laughed. "You're crazy."

"Arnie's a businessman. He'll know a good business proposition."

"You're gonna go right up to him and say, 'Arnie, how's about lending me four grand? See, Arnie, I know where I can pick up these hundred cases of King's Ransom—' "

"—that's just how I'll do it," Leo said.

But two nights later, Leo admitted Harry was right. The idea was crazy. Perhaps it was a return of more springlike weather, or merely a return to reality. Leo realized that he would have been asking Arnie Steinberger to finance his own competition. Leo would have made a complete ass of himself. And now he had a better idea, anyway.

He sat at the counter of the Walgreen Drug Store on the corner of Eighty-fifth and Broadway, sipping his fourth cup of coffee, gazing through the display window at the Bretton Hall Hotel across the street. Arnie Steinberger was playing poker in one of those rooms. His regular Tuesday game.

Leo turned now to watch the counter short-order cook finish packing sandwiches and coffee. In two more minutes, Leo knew, the delivery boy would carry the food in a cardboard tray across the street to the hotel. To the poker players.

Leo glanced at the POSTAL TELEGRAPH wall clock. It was 10:58. At 10:59, the delivery boy would start away with the tray. You could keep time on him. Leo's original plan was to follow the boy into the hotel, into the elevator—straight to the poker game. He felt certain Arnie would speak with him. Arnie would appreciate Leo's *chutzpah* in approaching him.

That was the original plan. Now discarded in favor of a new, better idea, also based on *chutzpah*.

Arnold Steinberger's own *chutzpah*: playing a high-stakes game in a hotel with little or no protection. Well, not so much *chutzpah* as arrogance. Arrogance, from the belief no one dared hold up his game. Just as the Coast Guard never dared interfere with *Westwind*. The King was untouchable.

Which was the basis of Leo's new, better idea.

He had to wait until nine the next morning to present the idea to Harry. Harry had spent the night with a girl who was a magician's assistant on the vaudeville at Keith's Eighty-first Street theater. The only thing magic about her, he said, was how a guy could disappear between her legs.

Leo finally got him to stop talking about the magic girl and listen to the new idea for raising the $4,000. "You want to make big, you got to think big," he said. "My idea is big."

"I hope it ain't no jewelry store."

"A poker game."

Harry was impressed. "Whose?"

"Arnie Steinberger's."

Harry reacted exactly as Leo anticipated. "You tired of breathing, Leo?"

Leo said, "Arnie plays Tuesdays and Thursdays. At the Bretton Hall Hotel. The hotel's across the street from a Walgreen's. At eleven sharp a boy from the drugstore delivers sandwiches and coffee to the game. You can keep time on him—"

"—forget it," said Harry.

"—all one of us has to do is take the sandwich kid's place. The other one waits downstairs in a car. We walk into the room, and before anybody even blinks an eye, we stick that forty-five in Arnie's left nostril. We grab all the cash. And in that game it'll be a fortune. And we're out, and gone."

"Yeah, with twenty guys shooting at you."

"No guys shooting," Leo said. "We walk one of the players out with us to make sure that doesn't happen. Maybe even Arnie himself."

Harry said nothing, but Leo knew he was thinking hard. Leo lit a cigarette and said. "It'll work. Mostly because they just never would think anybody'd have the balls."

Harry said, "You know something, Kleyner, you sound like me? A half-assed idea like that, I mean."

Leo said nothing. The harsh truth of Harry's words shocked him. Am I that desperate? he asked himself. Yes, I am, he answered himself, hearing Harry's voice.

"Which one of us goes upstairs?"

"I'll do it," Leo said.

"Maybe it's smarter I do it."

"Not with that forty-five in your hand."

"You really think I'm that crazy, Leo? I'd go shooting up the place?"

"I'll make the hit," said Leo. "You stay in the car."

"Where do we get a car?"

"Harry, this whole town's filled with cars. We just take our pick."

"We'll need plates."

"Plates?" leo asked. "You mean license plates?"

"Yeah, Mr. Genius, I mean license plates. It don't matter the car's hot, so long as the plates ain't."

"Where do you find plates?"

"A junkyard," Harry said. "A garage. Listen, take the train up to New Rochelle and knock a set off some car parked near the station."

But Leo was not listening; he was thinking "garage," and one in particular, where they just might find the plates. And maybe even a car. A long shot, but Leo had a hunch. It would also provide him an excuse to visit an old friend. An old friend he felt obliged to visit, but thus far had not found the courage to.

3.

The sign's paint-flaked letters were faded now, but still legible: A-1 GARAGE & MOTOR CAR REPAIR SHOP. PROP. H. E. LEFKOWITZ. Through the partly open double doors Leo could see Hershey hunched over the workbench removing plugs from what looked like a large truck motor.

For nearly ten minutes, Leo had stood there on the corner of Grand and Chrystie, watching the garage across the street, composing in his mind his first words to Hershey. What could he say? What should he say? To begin with, of course, condolences about Edie.

She was dead.

More than two years ago. The big flu epidemic. Almost the first thing Leo's mother said when he came home. Had he heard about that bastard Lefkowitz? That *momzer* whose rotten lies to the police sent Leo to Elmira. And the *nafke* wife. Yes, one should not speak disrespectfully of the dead, but Sarah had to be truthful. She was glad the bitch was dead. God has his own, good way of dispensing justice.

Now, smoking his third cigarette of the past ten minutes, gazing at the garage, thinking of Edie, Leo shuddered. He felt now, again, as he had when his mother broke the news, just the slightest tightening at the base of his throat, a hollowness in his stomach. And an image of Edie flashing into his mind. The blonde hair, the black negligee. The soft, warm hand stroking his cheek. Edie dead. Hard to believe. And wrong, all wrong.

God's justice. Shit, was God's justice.

Edie dead, he thought again, the words reminding him of the terrible day they told his mother and father about the Triangle fire, about Rivka. Leo heard his mother's wail of anguish. Like a trapped, mortally wounded animal. Then, after the people left, asking in quiet disbelief, "No more Rivka? No more Rivka?"

No more Edie.

Two women walked past the garage, skirts swirling high above their ankles. The latest fashion. Edie would have worn dresses like that. God, how she loved clothes!

Thinking of clothes, he was glad he was wearing his army tunic. The sergeant's chevrons removed, of course, but the sleeve still contained their outline. He wished Hershey had seen him in uniform, with the wound stripe and Croix de Guerre ribbon.

He glanced at his reflection in a store window and slanted the visor of his new corduroy work cap rakishly over his right eye. He pulled the visor up a little higher, then flipped the cigarette into the gutter and started across the street.

The big motor on the workbench seemed to be the only item intact in the garage. Tires, wheels, engine parts were strewn everywhere, covered with a coating of thick gray dust. It looked like a junkyard. Well, Harry said go to a junkyard, although Leo thought this place more like a graveyard. Drab and dim, even on a bright sunny morning, the windows so grimy they might have been painted over. The partitioned area where the craps game was played, open now, vacant, littered with debris. Leo had heard that after Edie's death Hershey closed both games. They said he simply had no more stomach for it.

Hershey, not immediately aware of Leo, was laboriously removing the engine manifold. It was not a truck motor but a sixteen-cylinder aircraft-type engine. Before Leo could speak, Hershey sensed another presence. He turned and looked at Leo.

Leo thought Hershey hadn't changed much. Perhaps a little fleshier about the mouth, and the hair graying. And then Leo noticed his eyes. Dull, as though the light had gone out. Leo found this unsettling, for he had anticipated anger and was prepared to deal with it. For a long moment each silently studied the other.

Finally, Leo said, "What kind of engine is that?"

Hershey sighed; a long, heavy, weary sigh. He shook his head sadly, as though the question—or the questioner—was not worthy of a reply. He arranged the manifold cover carefully on the bench, then walked into the little glass-cubicled office. He sat at the desk and poured tea into a glass from a kettle on a gas hot plate.

Leo followed him into the office. He said, "Listen, I heard about Edie—"

Hershey snapped a sugar lump in two. He dropped both halves into the glass and stirred the tea with a pencil. He nodded at the engine on the workbench outside. "Twin Liberty. Goes in a boat."

Leo said, "You know, I only been back from Germany a little while. I only just heard what happened to her."

"Yeah," Hershey said quietly. He stirred the tea.

"I'm sorry about her, Hersh. Real sorry."

Hershey looked at him. "So am I, kid."

Leo brought a package of cigarettes from his tunic pocket. He offered it to Hershey. Hershey waved his hand, no. Leo said, "That's right, you don't smoke."

Hershey said nothing. Leo lit the cigarette. He took a deep drag and exhaled through his nose. "You ain't—" he started saying, then corrected himself. "You haven't changed much at all."

Hershey said, "Leo, you come here for something. What?"

"I don't want anything, Hersh," Leo said. "I'm just paying my respects."

"Bullshit."

"Honest."

"You always want something. You always got an angle."

Words of indignant denial surged to Leo's lips. But even as he framed them in his mind they sounded false. He tried to sound nonchalant. "It takes one to know one, Hersh."

Hershey was unamused. "So tell me, already: the angle?"

Hershey suddenly seemed very old and tired. Broken, Leo thought, remembering a character in a book he read at the Coblenz YMCA library, *The Count of Monte Cristo*. The hero, Edmond Dantès, was described once as a "broken man." That was Hershey, a broken man. And Leo felt somehow responsible. If what had happened between them—him, and Hershey, and Edie—had not happened, Hershey's luck, and Edie's, might somehow have turned out different.

Leo said, "There ain't—there's no angle, Hersh. I only wanted to say hello. And how sorry I am about Edie . . . and about . . . everything else."

"Yeah," Hershey said. "Everything else."

"Well, I am sorry."

"Good," said Hershey. "Maybe you learned something."

"I did."

Hershey nodded. He reached blindly for the tea and drank it down in a single swallow. Leo watched him, realizing he had come to ask for plates for a car he and Harry planned to steal, and instead was begging forgiveness.

He said, "I'm thinking of going back to school, maybe."

"That won't hurt."

"Yeah, I'm thinking about being a lawyer."

"Good profession," Hershey said.

"For a Jew, huh?" Leo smiled.

"For anybody," Hershey said.

Leo took a last drag of his cigarette. He looked around for a place to put it. Hershey reached under the stack of papers and pulled out a cracked saucer. Leo mashed out the cigarette. "I better get going," he said.

Hershey did not rise. "Take it easy, kid."

"Yeah," Leo said. He stood an awkward moment. Then, flipping Hershey a casual salute, he about-faced and started from the office. He felt Hershey's eyes on him. He was glad he had not asked for the license plates. He wanted Hershey to believe him capable of better things than stealing cars.

He stepped into the garage and all at once stopped. To leave this way, leaving things as they were, was wrong. All wrong. He turned. Hershey sat still looking at him. Leo said, "Hey, I'm glad I stopped by."

Hershey nodded.

Jesus Christ, Leo thought, do I have to get down on my hands and knees? He said, "Maybe we can have supper together sometimes."

"Sure," Hershey said.

"I'll stop by again," Leo said.

Hershey nodded once more. Leo flipped another salute, turned, and started away. He walked past the workbench, the big engine. He stopped.

"What'd you say this was for?" Leo asked.

"A boat."

"What kind of boat?"

It was as though Leo had pressed a button that suddenly aroused Hershey's interest. Hershey pushed himself out of the chair and came to the workbench. He said, "One of them little ones that goes forty, fifty miles an hour. Some *shaygets* from the Island owns it. There's two engines in it already. He wants I should put in this third one so it goes faster than the Coast Guard's. He wants it ready when he comes back from Florida next month."

"He's a bootlegger?"

"Nah, a stockbroker," Hershey said. "His wife comes in here a year ago with a brand-new Hupmobile that's got an overheated radiator. I fix it and don't charge her nothing. So last month the *bocha* comes to see me. He wants I should put a third engine in his boat." Hershey ran his gnarled fingers lovingly over the cylinders. "I'll make it so it does four hundred horses."

Fifty miles an hour, Leo thought. A contact boat that fast could carry dozens of cases of whiskey, hundreds maybe, and never get caught.

He said, "Hersh, I got an idea." He paused. What he was thinking was crazy. But not so crazy as holding up Arnie Steinberger's poker game, which was worse than crazy. Suicidal.

". . . the angle, huh?" Hershey was saying, but with amusement now, not bitterness. "Now comes the angle. I knew it."

Leo hardly heard him. An immense sense of relief had enveloped him. Relief that Hershey had indeed forgiven him, coupled with perhaps even greater relief that he had just conceived a plan to make not $4,000 but ten times that amount. More.

"So?" Hershey said. *"Nu?"*

Leo said, "Yeah, Hersh, I do have an angle." He took a deep breath. "This *shaygets* that owns the boat . . . when are you supposed to put the engine in for him?"

"I told him a couple of days," Hershey said. "By the first of the week, maybe."

"I got an idea, Hersh," Leo said. "It can make us both a lot of money."

Leo was genuinely surprised to hear Hershey reply, "So, I'm listening . . ."

8

HARRY wondered if a piece of shrapnel from Leo's arm hadn't some-how traveled up to his brain. Leo's first idea, asking Arnold Steinberger to loan them $4,000, was nothing less than silly. The second idea, heisting Arnie's poker game, while risky, Harry liked. Now Leo had a new, third, idea Harry believed the craziest of all.

They would heist *Westwind*.

Disguised as Coast Guardsmen.

But the more Harry thought about it, the more he liked it. Maybe the Kleyner was right. With Coast Guard uniforms—at least white sailor caps—and a 12-gauge shotgun, and the .45, it just might be the pushover Leo claimed. The only part of it Harry did not like was the big *Galitzianer*, Hershey.

Like him or not, Leo said, without Hershey they couldn't do the deal. Yeah, Harry had replied, and without him you wouldn't have gone to Elmira.

Bygones are bygones, Leo said. Harry certainly hoped so, because Hershey was providing the boat.

Sweet Elaine, sixty-five feet long, built for speed, originally designed as an auxiliary subchaser, with twin Libertys driving her nearly forty miles per hour. The addition now of the third Liberty gave her a draw of 1,350 horsepower. She could make fifty miles per hour.

The owner, one Carl Sanderlin, had served briefly in the navy as a reserve lieutenant commander. He was not a professional bootlegger, but a wealthy stockbroker who now envisioned himself at the helm of the fastest boat on Rum Row. A dashing and romantic figure defying the law of the land, and the United States Coast Guard.

Carl Sanderlin's plan, after adding the third Liberty, was to repaint the boat a gleaming black and temporarily rename her. Had he been in town, he would have been astounded to find *Sweet Elaine* indeed repainted.

Coast Guard gray.

With white block letters printed on either bow, CG 395, she was moored now at a slip on the far end of the Island, at Montauk. All that remained was hiring a skipper.

His name was Bill Goodwin. An old lobsterman with thick white hair and skin like pink, wrinkled parchment, he sat facing Harry and Leo in the rear booth of a Greenport diner. Harry wondered if he was as dumb as he looked.

". . . now let me get this straight," Goodwin was saying. "You got a Coast Guard vessel, but don't want a Coast Guard crew? That don't make sense."

"This is strictly a federal-government operation," Leo said. "And, to tell you the truth, Captain Goodwin, we don't exactly trust the Coast Guard. If you get what I mean?"

"Well, some of 'em might be on the take," Goodwin said. "But most are pretty honest."

"Yeah," Harry said. "But which ones?" He ran a comb through his hair, nodding sagely at Leo who had asked him to please just sit there and keep his mouth shut. Let Leo do all the talking.

With an annoyed glance at Harry, Leo said to Goodwin, "Yes, sir, that's the problem. That's why this is all so hush-hush. We got information about this French freighter unloading all its cargo, all at once, to about a dozen contact boats. We mean to confiscate the whole kit and caboodle!"

French freighter, Harry thought, impressed. You had to hand it to Leo. If Goodwin knew the boat they were after was Arnie Steinberger's, the old sailor would tell them to fuck off. He'd find out soon enough, but too late.

"An my share is ten percent?" Goodwin asked.

"Standard government payment, sir," Leo said.

Harry, unable to resist it, said, "Hey, look, you rather settle for cash, we'll give you a thousand right now." He reached in his pocket, smiling thinly at Leo who had closed his eyes in dismay. But Goodwin gestured Harry to keep his money.

"Ten percent is fine," said Goodwin. "Lot more than a thousand."

"Probably ten times more," Leo said with another annoyed glance at Harry.

"Well, we want our people to be happy," Harry said. "Ain't that right, Inspector?" he said to Leo.

"Absolutely," Leo said, and just the way he said it—like a salesman selling snake oil—Harry knew Leo was trying not to laugh; the old sailor was lapping it up. But if they pulled it off he could retire on his ten-percent cut.

After a few more details, Goodwin accepted the job. They shook hands on it, toasted the government's success with a second beer—served in a mug with no pretense—and then all three left the diner and got into the truck. A new Mack that could carry a thousand cases, also provided by Hershey. Leo driving, Goodwin in the middle, they started off for Montauk. They took a back road, a few miles longer than the main, paved route, but much less chance of being seen.

"You people sure do things strange," Goodwin said.

"It's how you have to deal with bootleggers," Leo said. "Fight them with their own weapons. You agree, Inspector?" he asked Harry.

"The only way," Harry said solemnly. He reached under the seat and pulled out the shotgun. He cracked open the breech, inserted two shells, and snapped it closed. He loved the feel of the gun, the sheen of the polished wood stock and the cold smoothness of the steel breech and barrels. It felt even better than the .45, and sobered and excited him all at the same time. Now that they were actually on their way he could hardly wait for the action to begin.

It began sooner than he expected.

A few miles outside Greenport, rounding a narrow corner, Leo jammed on the brakes and swung the wheel hard to avoid smashing broadside into another truck. A large, canvas-topped REO, hood imbedded in a tree trunk, thick white clouds of steam geysering from the radiator cap. It had skidded sideways across the width of the road, blocking it completely.

From behind the REO a man appeared. He was young, and wore a pea coat and visored naval cap. He signaled the oncoming Mack to stop.

Harry shouted to Leo, "Back it up!"

Leo shifted into reverse and floored the accelerator pedal. One hand on the wheel, the other across the rear of the front seat, he steered the truck backward toward the road bend. He swung the wheel hard and fishtailed around to head out frontward. Just as he yanked the gear-shift lever into low, a huge tree crashed down on the road. Now that side was also blocked. An instant later, another man appeared. Gray, wide-brimmed fedora pulled low over his eyes, he walked slowly toward the truck, the bottom hems of his unbuttoned double-breasted brown topcoat flapping against his legs. He cradled a Thompson, which he now leveled at the Mack windshield. Leo threw the gear into neutral and pulled up the hand brake.

"For God's sake, tell 'em who you are!" Goodwin said. His voice rose shrilly. "Show your badges!"

"This is my badge!" Harry said, raising the shotgun.

"Don't be crazy!" Leo said. His eyes fixed on the man with the machine gun, he reached blindly past Goodwin and pushed Harry's shotgun down out of sight. "Son of a bitch!" he said quietly. He recognized the man.

It was Aldo Puglisi, and he recognized Leo at the same moment. He smiled almost happily. "I'll be fucked. The little kike!" He stuck the Thompson into the Mack window; the muzzle prodded Leo's chin. Puglisi shouted to another man who now materialized from the REO. "Sal, you ain't never gonna never believe this!"

Harry whispered to Leo, "Sal . . . ? Bracci?"

Leo nodded grimly. Behind Bracci, a third man appeared. He held an ax in one hand, revolver in the other.

"Listen, Mister," Goodwin said to Puglisi, "We don't have nothing you want, we're—"

"Shut up!" Puglisi said, and smiled again at Leo. He flung Leo's door open and stepped back, gesturing everyone out.

"Well, small world, huh?" Sal Bracci said.

"Yeah," Leo said. Very carefully, arms raised, he started sliding from the seat.

"Just behave yourself, nothing'll happen," Bracci said. "All we want is the truck."

"Sure," said Leo. Hands high, he placed his feet on the running board. Directly behind him was Goodwin, and then Harry. Just as Leo's shoes touched the ground, Harry shoved Goodwin forward into Leo. Both fell sprawling to the ground at Puglisi's feet. Harry leveled the shotgun at Puglisi and fired both barrels directly into his face.

For a split instant a thin, filmy cloud of gray smoke obscured Aldo Puglisi's face. Then the smoke cleared. Puglisi remained standing, his hands still gripping the Thompson. But his head was gone, replaced now with fragmented white flesh and bone, and severed arteries. Blood spurted upward from the shredded neck like red water from a smashed fire hydrant.

But even before the headless body toppled forward, Bracci and the two other men had darted away, one firing his pistol wildly at the truck. All three rushed into the trees lining the roadside.

Leo pried the Thompson from Puglisi's fingers and crawled behind the truck's rear wheels, shouting to Goodwin, ". . . over here! Fast!"

Goodwin lay facedown on the road. A red streamer of blood trickled from his ear. The blood merged with Puglisi's, both streams forming a large viscous red puddle in the tire indentations in the dirt road.

While Leo fired a long burst from the Thompson into the roadside trees, Harry dove into the truck for more shotgun shells. "For Christ's sake, take it easy!" Harry shouted. "You'll use it all up!"

"Toss me the forty-five!" Leo said.

Harry lobbed the .45 through the open door. Leo caught it one-handed, then fired a short burst from the Thompson. Bracci and the two others, behind trees, opened fire with their pistols. The bullets peppered the truck. One shattered the windshield, spraying Harry with glass.

Harry wiggled out of the truck, rolled over on his stomach, and flopped down behind the front tire. "Hey, ain't this something, huh?" he called elatedly to Leo, and immediately rose, fired both shotgun barrels into the trees, and ducked back. Leo fired another short burst from the Thompson. Both then huddled behind the truck tires awaiting the response. There was none. The only sound was their own heavy breathing.

Leo called quietly to Harry, "Think we hit anybody?"

"Ask them," Harry said, reloading the shotgun.

Leo shouted to them, "Want to talk?"

Across the road, sitting braced against a tree trunk, Sal Bracci calmly refilled the magazine of a .32 automatic. He wished the weapon were heavier, like the big .44 he saw his father wrap in towels and bury in the vegetable garden behind their home in the old country. Sal was eight at the time, and his father was unaware Sal knew of the gun, or how his father had used it. Sal's father, a shoemaker, had killed two people with it, a man and a woman. The woman was Sal's mother. The man, a farmer, was her lover. Even the police turned their backs on the murder, but the family had to leave Sicily. They came to New York where Sal's father opened his own shoeshop. When Sal was arrested the first time, for possession of an unlicensed firearm, his father beat him and told him he was a fool. Only fools used guns. Sal never mentioned knowing about the .44. He loved and respected his father too much.

Now he looked at the two men on either side of him. The one wearing the pea coat was crouched behind a large tree. He had no weapon, and would not have known how to use it anyway. He was a sailor, an experienced helmsman, a Sicilian from Catania, Sal Bracci's birthplace. He had been in America less than a year.

The other man, whose name was Thomas Marizzi, was very young, not more than twenty, but showed no fear. To the contrary, he felt only contempt for the two Jews cowering behind the truck. Sal did not share Marizzi's contempt. Sal thought the one who killed Aldo Puglisi certainly someone to be reckoned with. If for no other reason than because he was a little crazy. Sal saw the wild light in the Jew's eyes when he blew Aldo Puglisi's face apart. Sal was not sure about the other, the small one, now calling over to them again. His voice cool and steady, as it had been when they rousted him at Minotti's. It worried Sal.

Leo was shouting, "Well, yes or no? We talk?"

In Italian, Marizzi said to Sal, "Tell them to go fuck themselves, the Jews. They can't move forward, and they can't move back. They're trapped like rats."

"Yes, but so are we," Sal replied in Italian. "How much ammo you think is left in Aldo's Thompson?"

"Maybe half a drum," Marizzi said. "Twenty, twenty-five slugs."

Sal thought about it a moment, then cupped his hands and shouted across the road. "What's there to talk about?"

"About staying alive," Leo shouted back. "All of us!"

Marizzi said to Sal, "You cover me. I'll get around behind them." He gestured with the barrel of his gun.

"Stay right where you are!" Sal said in Italian, and added in English, "They got the chopper!" He called to Leo, "I told you, all we want is the truck!"

"Yeah," Leo called back. "So do we!"

Leo ejected the Thompson drum, hefting it in his palm to gauge the weight. He said to Harry, "I don't think there's half a dozen shells left . . ."

"How much in the forty-five?" Harry asked.

"A full clip, but that's all," Leo said. "How much you have?"

Harry extended his closed fist, then opened it. Four shells. He grinned. "Do we do the Charge of the Light Brigade?"

Leo stared at him a moment, "You're not scared at all," he said, almost as an accusation.

"What's to be scared?" Harry said. "The worst they can do is kill us."

Harry's face was relaxed, and his eyes shone. *He is enjoying himself,* Leo thought. *He is enjoying himself, and I am scared. I am so scared I can hardly breathe—I was much less scared in France—and this son of a bitch Harry is enjoying himself. He is about to get his head blown off, but shows no fear whatever. He has killed one man, and is impatient to kill the others.* Thinking all this, another maxim just then flashed into Leo's mind. *Gorodetsky's Law Number Two: A man with no fear is dangerous. A menace. To himself, and everybody else.*

Now, from the trees, Sal shouted, "Okay, we'll talk!"

"Bullshit!" Harry said. "They'll blast us the second they have a chance!"

Sal called out, "Listen, I'll come out if you do the same. We'll talk."

Harry and Leo looked at each other. Leo gave Harry the Thompson. "Aim at his belly," Leo said. He tucked the .45 into his trouser waistband and peered over the top of the truck hood. From the trees, hands loosely raised, Sal had emerged. Behind Sal, the sun glinted off the muzzle of Tom Marizzi's revolver, which Leo knew was trained on him.

They met in the center of the road. For a long, silent moment each studied the other. Then Leo nodded at Puglisi's body. "I guess it's him that's leaking now, huh?"

"He was a good man," Sal said.

"They all are when they're dead," Leo said. "So talk."

"Neither of us can go anyplace. It's a standoff."

"What do you want the truck for?"

"The same thing you do."

"I doubt if it's the same thing," Leo said.

"Come on, don't shit the troops," Sal said. "You're trying to make a hit on the contact boats just like us."

"Wrong," said Leo.

Sal pointed at the body of the dead sailor, Goodwin. "He's not one of your guys; you hired him to drive a boat."

Leo glanced toward the trees. "That one in the pea coat and cap. He drives your boat?"

Sal nodded. "I imported him from the old country."

Leo turned slightly to look behind him, at Harry standing openly now, the Thompson leveled point-blank on Sal. A few feet away, in the road, the bodies of Puglisi and Goodwin.

Leo faced Sal again. "I got a proposition."

Sal said nothing.

"I don't know if you have the balls for it."

"I'm listening."

"Instead of doing a go-through, and maybe coming out with a few cases of rotgut . . . how'd you like to hit the biggest bonanza on Rum Row?"

And Leo told him of his plan to hit *Westwind* with the bogus Coast Guard cutter. They would do each other a mutual service: Leo could use a couple more guns, and of course needed a pilot for the boat.

"We combine forces, huh?" Sal said.

"Better than killing each other."

"So Steinberger kills us instead," Sal said. But he liked the idea. It was audacious. More important, it made sense. Business sense.

"You afraid of him?"

"Frankly," said Sal, "yes."

Now Leo could not help smiling. He suddenly liked the Sicilian, and admired his honesty. "Arnie won't make us. It'll happen so fast, and we'll get rid of the stuff through middle-men, he'll never know who did it."

Sal thought about it a moment. Then he extended his hand. "Okay," he said. They shook.

"What about your people?" Leo asked. "How'll they take this . . . 'combination'?"

"They do what I say," Bracci said. "What about your guy?"

"He does what I say," Leo said.

It was easier than Leo thought. Sal Bracci's sailor navigated unerringly to *Westwind*. The sky had clouded over with fog and mist, obscuring the approaching "cutter" until the last three hundred yards. The schooner's captain personally came up on deck to greet the "Coast Guardsmen."

It reminded Leo of a movie he saw in Coblenz, *The Sea Hawk*. A swashbuckling pirate boards the merchant vessel, cutting down everybody in sight. Nobody on *Westwind* was cut down exactly, although Sal

Bracci broke the captain's jaw with a pistol butt when the captain refused to open the cargo locker.

Under Harry's and Tom Marizzi's guns *Westwind*'s crew was pressed into service as stevedores. There was an anxious moment when they discovered *Sweet Elaine* could take only two hundred cases; more would swamp her. But Leo ordered both *Westwind* motor dories loaded, and *Westwind* crew members into the dories to follow *Sweet Elaine* back to shore.

Two hundred cases of Black & White Scotch, three hundred Courvoisier brandy, and two hundred Piper Heidsieck champagne were packed into the dories, which themselves were nearly awash. The dories proved the smartest move of the day. When the "convoy" hove into view of other boats and of shore, it resembled a legitimate Coast Guard sweep, CG 395 escorting confiscated cargo into port.

Ashore, on a remote sandspit, the cargo was transferred to the truck. Leo and Sal thanked the *Westwind* sailors and sent them back in the dories.

"Don't forget to give our regards to Mr. Steinberger!" Harry shouted after them.

Leo gazed fondly at the truck. It was jam-packed with whiskey. "Must be fifty grand worth here."

"More," Sal said. "The champagne itself is worth fifty."

"Arnie'll shit," Harry said.

2.

"You tell him," Eddie Greenberg said to Charlie Cohen. He pulled up the Lincoln's parking brake and switched off the ignition. He looked at Charlie and said again, "You tell him."

They were parked outside Arnold Steinberger's West End Avenue apartment building, and the doorman had just waved hello. Charlie waved back, then turned to Eddie.

"What time is it?"

"Five minutes after the last time you asked," Eddie said. "Ten past seven."

"We ain't due till eight."

"You want to wait till eight?" Eddie asked. "He ain't gonna like it, us not telling him right away."

"I read a story once," Charlie said. "This here messenger went and give the king some bad news. The king got so pissed he chopped off the guy's head."

"Yeah," Eddie said. It was certainly something to think about. They were to meet Arnie at eight to drive him to a dinner date with his father at Moscowitz & Lupowitz's, and then to the Bretton Hall for the poker game. But an hour ago the Coast Guard chief on the payroll had phoned with news of *Westwind*'s heist. It was Eddie's bad luck to answer the phone.

Eddie told the chief to call Arnie. The chief told Eddie to go and fuck himself. *He* wasn't telling Arnie nothing. Now he, Eddie—and Charlie —had to deliver the message.

They smoked a last cigarette, and then went up to tell Arnie. They could not believe how calmly he took it. He almost seemed amused. "I should have known," he said.

"You ain't mad?" Charlie asked.

"It was bound to happen," Arnie said. "What I don't like is no one knows who they are."

"Oh, we're gonna find out," Eddie said. "Don't worry about that, Arnie."

"It won't be too hard," Charlie said. "Don't forget they got to get rid of the stuff. We'll get the word."

"Fix yourselves a drink while I finish dressing."

Arnie went into the bedroom. Just before sliding open the mirrored door of the big walk-in closet he caught a glimpse of the embarrassing patch of thinning hair on the front of his head. Under the light you clearly saw scalp. He stepped back to the dresser and carefully mussed the thicker side hair over the offending area.

Yes, he thought, it certainly was bound to happen: someone making a run at *Westwind*. He had expected it before now. In truth, almost wanted it to happen. Then find and punish the perpetrators. Set an example never to be forgotten.

Now, almost as a reflex, he ran the leather-tooled brushes over his sideburns. More gray in the temples, but not unwelcome. Alicia liked it. Thinking of her, he grimaced at his image in the mirror. They had had a terrible, almost violent argument. Over a woman he smiled at in the goddam street. He wondered if Alicia was beginning to bore him. The thought saddened him. Not particularly because of Alicia but because he feared everything was beginning to bore him. This whole bootlegging *megillah*. He was King. What more can a King achieve? What higher mountains to climb? At least when he was King of The Gamblers he had never been bored.

These thoughts always made him uncomfortable, reminding him of his childhood and early youth. Bored, then, too, after achieving a goal. A sickness, he thought now, forcing himself to concentrate on the problem at hand. The *Westwind* hijackers. He touched the gray in his temples once more and wondered if the hijackers had gray hair. Probably not. Probably too young. But smart, all right. A Coast Guard cutter. Not bad. And getting away with $150,000 worth of prime liquor.

"A good haul," he said aloud to himself in the mirror. A *ganser shtick*, as his father would say. Thinking of his father, he remembered he'd promised the old man a box of Davidoff's. Meyer Steinberger smoked two cigars daily. After breakfast and dinner. And only the finest Havanas, Davidoff his preference, thirty-five cents each. Arnie himself preferred Maria Mancinis. Equal in quality, although slightly milder. Well, Arnie thought, maybe I don't have the old man's morality, but I certainly inherited his good taste. Thanks, Pa, he told him in his mind.

"Charlie!" he called. Instantly, Charlie appeared in the doorway. "Don't let me forget my old man's cigars."

"Sure thing, Arnie." Charlie stepped back, but Arnie gestured him to remain.

"You have any ideas who they were?" Arnie asked, returning to the closet and sliding open the door. Double doors on rollers, this closet was his pride and joy. Three hundred dollars to build and install, and worth every dime.

"Had to be wops," said Charlie.

Arnie said nothing a moment, concentrating on rejecting a gray flannel in favor of a blue covert he bought only last week at Brooks Brothers. Then, "Why?"

"Why?" Charlie said. "It hadda be them. Who else?"

"Why does it have to be them?" Arnie asked patiently. He placed the suit, still on its wooden hanger, carefully on the bed and returned to the closet for a tie.

"Because there ain't nobody else, Arnie," Eddie Greenberg said, just then entering the room.

"There ain't nobody else," Arnie repeated, looking at them. In their white shirts and dark suits and gray spats, they resembled a pair of penguins. Yiddish penguins, he thought, and chuckled.

"What's so funny, Arnie?" Charlie asked.

"Penguins," Arnie said.

"Penguins?" Eddie said. "What the hell you talking about, Arnie?"

"I'm fantasizing, forget it," said Arnie. He changed his mind about the blue covert, He carried it back to the closet and exchanged it for the gray flannel, and a pair of Lloyd & Haig cordovan wing-tip shoes. "Five hundred dollars to the man who brings me the names of the ones who did the job. A thousand if you do it before the end of the week." He slid a blue regimental-stripe tie from the custom-designed brass tie rack. "Eddie, what do you think of this tie?"

"Stylish, Arnie. Very stylish."

Leo liked the coffee at the Famous Hofbrau. Strong, but not bitter, and served just warm enough so the heavy aroma lingered in your mouth and throat. It was his second cup after dinner, and tasted better than the first. But then, this night, everything tasted good.

They were in a corner booth, Leo, Hershey—and Sal Bracci. Sal, arriving late, was surprised to see Hershey. He had grinned and said, "If I knew I'd be outnumbered like this, I'd have brought along one of my guys."

Hershey said, "Don't kid yourself, Bracci. A dozen Italians couldn't outnumber a single Jew."

Leo marveled at how smoothly Sal handled it. Diplomatic was the word. Like old Woodrow Wilson at the Peace Conference. Sal said, "Hey, I saw your guys in action, remember? I'm not so sure *two* dozen of us wops'd be enough." He smiled at Leo, then addressed Hershey again. "We call it respect," he said.

"We call it business," Hershey said. "And I got to tell you, I ain't happy about all that booze in my garage."

No one was more astonished than Hershey when Leo had pulled the truck into the garage, and three Italians jumped out of the back and began unloading the whiskey. At this very moment Harry and Tom Marizzi stood guard over the cases, which were stored in the partitioned area once used for the craps game. Standing guard over each other, more than the liquor.

Hershey, like Harry, did not trust the *Talenas*, but under the circumstances realized the necessity of the association. And while he did not admit it, the sudden activity—with the excitement, not to mention the potential profit—made Hershey feel better and more alive than in years. In the morning, he would drive to Islip and resurrect *Sweet Elaine*. Her owner would never be the wiser.

Leo also marveled at how quickly and almost unquestioningly Hershey joined the operation. And it pleased Leo because it said Hershey forgave him for the past—no, they forgave each other; each had been punished. Now, a fresh, new start. Friends again. Family, almost. And all this with not a single word about it ever uttered, none needed.

The dinner meeting was to discuss various options of how and where to dispose of the merchandise. And it had to be done quickly.

"I think our only real chance is to take it out of town," Sal said. "By now the whole city knows Arnie got hit. Not only won't anybody in New York buy from us, but they'll fink to Arnie the minute we're out the door."

"All right, so we'll take it to Boston," Leo said. "Or Philly."

"You know any distributors there?" Sal asked.

"We'll find some," Leo said.

Hershey said to Leo, "Your great idea all of a sudden ain't looking so great, Mr. Gorodetsky."

Leo said nothing. A picture had formed in his mind, but in fragments, each piece seeming to fly off in a different direction. But he knew it was an important picture.

Sal was saying, ". . . we might have to sell at a big discount, but it'll still be respectable money."

"Sure, just enough for our burial plots," Hershey said. He drank down an entire cup of coffee in a single swallow, then finished half a glass of water. He noticed the others looking at him. He smiled lamely. "Dry throat," he explained.

"Don't worry, we all got the same dryness," Sal said.

Leo heard the voice but not the words. The fragmented picture was coming together. A picture of how to safely dispose of the liquor, and to whom. The perfect customer, he thought, as the image of that perfect customer was all at once replaced in his mind by, of all things, an image of Charlotte Daniels. He could not understand this, although he recalled glimpsing in the *Times* an announcement of Yvette Guilbert's farewell New York appearance at the Thirty-ninth Street Theater. And, remembering, with the same cringe of shame and chagrin he always felt thinking of Charlotte, that last night in Paris, the Yvette Guilbert performance Charlotte had decided not to attend. He had torn the unused tickets in half, then again, and tossed them into the gutter. He could have given them to someone, the first doughboy he saw, but the ritual of destroying them was more gratifying. Cleansing, that was the word.

"Wake up," Hershey said, nudging Leo. "We're supposed to be talking important business, ain't we?"

"Yeah, yeah," Leo said, facing Hershey, and then Sal. He suddenly understood the connection in his mind between Charlotte and the perfect customer. When he had accepted the fact there would be no relationship between him and Charlotte, he had accepted the truth. The same truth, now, that there was only one place to go with Arnold Steinberger's stolen liquor, one customer.

"What do you want to do?" Sal asked patiently.

Leo wondered if perhaps the idea had not always been in his mind, even before they heisted *Westwind*. The idea not only was right, but so right it was worth ten times the value of the hijacked liquor. A hundred times, a thousand. He pointed a finger at Sal and said, "Check out these people you think will buy it. Get a price and we'll decide." He glanced at the wall clock. "Quarter past nine. Meet me at the garage at midnight." He pushed back his chair and rose.

"Meet you at the garage at midnight?" Sal said. "I don't get it?"

"There's something I have to do right now."

"Where you going?" Hershey asked.

"I got a date."

"A date?" Hershey said. "For Christ's sake, Leo, this ain't no time to think about your *shlong*!"

"The hell it ain't." Leo punched Hershey playfully on the shoulder. "Midnight," he said to Sal, and walked quickly away.

All the way to the door he felt their eyes on him, and a tremor of uncertainty. Suppose he was wrong? Suppose his idea did not work? In that case, Gorodetsky, he told himself, you should just take the .45 and stick it in your mouth and pull the trigger. It might, in the end, be less painful.

3.

The big POSTAL TELEGRAPH clock on the wall at Walgreen's Eighty-fifth and Broadway store read 11:00 exactly. At the far end of the counter the delivery boy packed sandwiches and coffee cartons into a cardboard carrying tray. He double-checked the order on his small yellow pad, nodded, balanced the tray in his hands, and started out.

Okay, Leo said to himself, let's go. But for a moment he did not move. He had been watching the boy from his seat at the counter near the door, and now felt frozen to the stool. His throat was dry, and his heart pounded. He realized he hesitated not so much from fear, but doubt. But no, he had thought it all out down to the smallest detail. It would work. It had to.

He got off the stool, walked out of the drugstore, and followed the delivery boy across the street to the Bretton Hall Hotel, and into the lobby, to the elevator.

"How's it going, Rufe?" the delivery boy said to the leathery-skinned old Negro elevator operator.

"Tolerable," said the operator, his voice almost lost in the metallic rattle of the folding zigzag extension gate closing. He slid the car doors shut, grasped the control lever and slammed it forward. "Can't complain," he said.

The delivery boy held the carrying tray steady with both hands as he gazed at the floral-designed domed light fixture on the elevator car ceiling and began whistling "La Paloma." He paid absolutely no attention to Leo.

"Floor?" The operator was talking to Leo.

Leo looked at him, startled.

"Floor, sir? Which floor you want?"

Leo could not find his voice. The very smallest of all the details, and he had never, not once, considered it. He had planned to simply follow the delivery boy to the room. He drew in his breath to speak, with not the slightest idea of what he would say. Just then the elevator operator spoke to the delivery boy.

"They in eight-ten tonight."

"Changed rooms, huh?"

"Regular one's being fixed over."

Leo said, "Seven, please."

He got off at the seventh floor and took the stairway to the eighth. He waited on the landing behind the fire-exit door until he heard the elevator returning for the delivery boy. Then he stepped into the corridor and walked down the hall to 810.

He stood outside the door a moment and tightened his tie. Then he tilted his corduroy work cap and straightened his suit coat. He was glad he wore the suit, which he had bought only that day at Monroe's, the first new suit he ever owned. A brown wool herringbone, eighteen dollars, with vest and extra pair of pants, alterations free. The only reason he wore it tonight was to impress Sal Bracci at the dinner meeting. A stroke of luck, all right. It was important now more than ever that he look a *mensh*.

When the door opened at his knock, and Charlie Cohen frowned down at him, Leo felt transported six years back in time. The hard looking man with the distinctive bulge under his jacket at the door, the same hazy blue tobacco smoke obscuring the shirt-sleeved poker players at the table in the center of the room.

"Yeah?" Charlie asked disinterestedly.

Leo said, "I want to talk to Arnie."

" 'Z'at so?" Charlie said. "What about?"

"About the booze that was heisted from his boat today."

At five past midnight Leo entered the garage. Hershey was at the workbench repairing a carburetor. Tom Marizzi, Thompson cradled in his lap, sat on a stool tilted back against the closed partition wall. Sal and Harry were in the office playing rummy at Hershey's desk.

Leo had simply pushed open the garage door and walked in. Marizzi glanced lazily up at him. Leo said, "Great way to guard the place."

Marizzi raised the Thompson muzzle. "If I didn't want you to, you wouldn't get far. Don't worry."

"So, how was the date?" Hershey asked.

"Not bad," said Leo. He walked past Hershey, into the office. "You play with him, Sal, you better count the cards after every shuffle." He grinned at Harry. "Who's winning?"

"Where the hell you been?" Harry asked angrily.

"I have to talk to you," Leo said. He looked at Sal. "Both of you."

Just then Tom Marizzi shouted, "Sal!"

Sal whirled around in his chair, but suddenly froze. He stared at the garage door. Harry, too, was staring at the door. On the garage floor, Hershey stood with his back to the workbench facing the door. All were looking at three men who had just entered.

Charlie Cohen, Eddie Greenberg, and Arnold Steinberger.

Arnie, camel's hair overcoat neatly belted, brown homburg set perfectly square, coolly surveyed the scene. Charlie and Eddie, hands plunged into their coat pockets, flanked Arnie.

Arnie pointed a finger at Tom Marizzi and said, "I have seven men outside."

Marizzi looked at Sal. Sal had already gauged his chances and knew they were bad. He nodded grimly. Marizzi placed the gun on the floor. Eddie Greenberg's eyes never left Marizzi's as he stepped close to him and kicked the Thompson across the floor. The gun slid over the grease-packed concrete surface with a soft scraping sound and thumped to a stop against the wall under an empty workbench.

Arnie walked toward the office. Leo stepped out to meet him. "It's in there," Leo said, indicating the partition.

"You son of a bitch!" Harry said in an almost shrill, disbelieving voice. "You sold us out!"

"What's your name?" Arnie asked Harry.

Harry's face was a mask of rage. "None of your fucking business." He moved toward Arnie, his hand dropping to his pocket. A snub-nosed .38 flashed in Charlie Cohen's hand.

"Be smart, son, and you'll live to talk about it," Arnie said quietly to Harry. Harry remained tense another moment, then all at once relaxed. His hand fell away from his pocket. He looked at Leo, who could not look him back. "He didn't sell you out," Arnie continued to Harry. "He saved your life. Open it up," he said to Leo, nodding at the partition.

Leo opened the partition. The stacked cases nearly filled the small area. Arnie entered the enclosure and walked slowly around.

Sal said to Leo, "Why'd you do it?"

"He told you," Leo said. "To save our asses."

"Everything seems to be there," Arnie said. He stepped back into the garage. "You're a bright boy," he said to Leo.

"Thanks," Leo said. "But I can't say the same for you."

"Really? Because you managed to hijack me?"

"Because if you were smart enough to do it to me, I'd be smart enough to want you in with me."

"I beg your pardon?"

"I'd want somebody that smart on my side," Leo said. He looked at Sal. "Working with me."

Sal all at once knew why Leo returned the liquor to Arnie, and why behind their backs. The kill-crazy one, Harry, would have balked almost automatically; he was too dense to see what Leo hoped to achieve. The other one, the greenhorn motor mechanic, for sure would have disapproved; he was too frightened. But Sal resented Leo's not having consulted him, although he could understand why: Leo believed the stakes too high to risk even a single dissenting vote. So Leo just went ahead and did it on his own. A brilliant move because the instant Sal heard Arnie order Tom Marizzi to put down his gun, he realized he and Leo had miscalculated. No matter where they sold the liquor, or to whom, Arnie would never rest until he hunted them down. So not only did Leo probably save their lives, he was also trying to parlay it into a huge win. Trying to convince Arnie to cut them into his organization. Yes, a brilliant move. The move of a Sicilian, not a Jew.

". . . working for me, you mean," Arnie was saying.

"With you," Leo said. "Partners."

Harry listened, astounded, as Arnie said, "Partners? What do you think of that, Charlie? He wants to be my partner."

"Yeah, you need him bad," Charlie said.

"He thinks he's being funny, but he's right. You do need me," Leo said. He looked at Sal again. Their eyes met, and held. Sal nodded almost imperceptibly. A gesture of approval, of agreement. We can read each other's minds, Leo thought, and for the first time that day felt the warm flush of confidence; it was like a sudden burst of strength. The certainty, beyond any doubt, that what he did was proper and would work.

Leo continued to Arnie, "Make all the jokes you want, but just listen to me a minute." He waved his hand at the stacked cases of whiskey. "Why the hell do you think we gave it back to you? Don't you think we could have got rid of it easy enough?" He snapped his fingers. "We didn't because we figured it's a better investment to give it back."

"You did it, lad, because you knew what would happen if you didn't," Arnie said quietly.

"No, Arnie," said Leo, liking the way "Arnie" sounded, as though they were equals. Several hours earlier at the Bretton Hall he called Arnie "Mr. Steinberger." Just as when they first met, six years before, when Leo brought the payoff money to Charlie Wax's poker game. It was different now.

Leo continued, "We gave it back to make a point. And the point is that we"—he nodded at Sal—"have combined forces. Jews and Italians. Because we know, if we don't, we end up killing each other. Which means only that other Jews and other Italians jump in to grab our action, and cut in on yours. Except they won't be as organized and controlled as us, and they'll give you nothing but a lot of headaches. And sooner or later they'll grow big enough to take you on."

It was a long speech, and Leo suddenly felt very tired. He wanted desperately to sit down, but it was important he remain on his feet. Facing Arnie as an equal. For a crazy instant he imagined that everything depended on his remaining standing. If he so much as moved, he would lose. They all would lose.

"I'll say one thing for you," Arnie said. "You have moxie."

"I got more than moxie," Leo said. "I got brains, and ideas." He pointed to Sal. "So does he. We all do," he added, sweeping his hand to include Harry and Hershey, although it was more an afterthought.

Arnie turned to Sal, "You're Bracci?"

"Yeah," Sal said.

"Does Patsy Carbo know you're dealing with Jews?"

"I don't answer to him," Sal said. "Or to anybody."

"How many men in your organization?"

"Six," said Sal, and glanced at Marizzi. "Counting him."

"How many in yours?" Arnie asked Leo.

"Just us three," Leo said, sweeping his hand toward Hershey and Harry again.

Harry said, "Goddamit, Leo, don't speak for me—"

"—Harry, shut up!" Leo said. "Just shut the fuck up!"

Harry drew in his breath angrily, but shut up. Arnie looked at Hershey. Hershey shrugged; he seemed slightly bewildered. Arnie said to Sal, "What about Tony Ruggerio?"

"Big Tony?" Sal said. "What about him?"

"He and Patsy Carbo run the Mafia, don't they?"

"The Mafia's in Sicily," Sal said. "Over here they might call themselves Mafia, but they're too disorganized. Tony and Patsy hate each other. One day they're sure to fight. They're too dumb to realize they'd be five times as strong by making peace—"

"—and combining," Arnie said, smiling. "Just as you and your young Jewish friend here are doing."

"It's bound to happen," Sal said. "And you believe it, or you wouldn't be wasting your time gabbing with us."

Arnie stood a moment, thinking. Then, abruptly, he turned and walked into the office. He sat in Hershey's chair. Charlie Cohen followed Arnie in and stood silently behind the chair. Eddie Greenberg stepped to the garage door and spoke to someone outside on the street. A car engine started, and then another. The headlights of the first car, driving past, momentarily brightened the grime-coated garage windows. The other car pulled up and parked directly outside.

Eddie resumed his position near Tom Marizzi, who had not moved one inch. Eddie grinned at Marizzi. Marizzi looked sullenly away. In the office, Charlie Cohen had just lit a cigar for Arnie. Leo, Sal, Harry, and Hershey stood before Arnie like soldiers standing inspection.

Arnie drew on the cigar and exhaled a long, thin streamer of smoke. "Maria Mancini's," he said of the cigar. "For my money, best there is. You like cigars?"

He was addressing Sal, who shook his head. "I don't even like cigarettes."

"You're smart," Arnie said, and to Leo, "So you want to form a coalition?"

"That's right," Leo replied immediately. "A coalition." An unfamiliar word, but the meaning obvious. "Yeah, a coalition."

Listening, Arnie was thinking, I don't know whether to laugh, or cry, or tell Charlie to take this little Delancey Street Jewboy outside and break his fingers. But even as he thought this, Arnie knew he admired the *chutzpah*. No, more than simple *chutzpah*; it was brains and fast thinking. Realizing the stolen liquor put them in deep, deep shit, they had given it back. Claiming to have stolen it in the first place solely to demonstrate their cleverness—and therefore their value.

So Arnold Steinberger was not in the least deceived, and suspected Leo did not himself believe he had successfully deceived anyone. But what most impressed Arnie was the realization that in similar circumstances he, Arnold Steinberger, would have done precisely the same. That being the case, these young men—the little Jewboy in particular, although the handsome Sicilian was no one's fool either—were a force to be reckoned with. Better to have them with me, Arnie told himself, than not; and going through all this again, one day when they were as strong as him. For a fleeting instant he felt, again, that disconcerting sense of being at the top with nowhere to go but down. Was he losing his grip? Was he getting too old and tired?

". . . that's what we're in business for, isn't it?" Leo was saying. "For profit. We make a coalition, we profit."

Coalition, Arnie thought. My God, how he had jumped on the word. A coalition, yet! It was like the principality of Liechtenstein offering the Allies a nonaggression pact.

"Tell me," Arnie said. "What would your contribution be to this . . . 'coalition'?"

Sal Bracci spoke first. "We already contributed." He pointed to the partitioned area; the whiskey.

"Yeah," Leo said. "And that was only the first installment."

"That's right," Sal said. "Just the beginning."

9

ONE of Eleanor Baer's earliest recollections was at age six, her father arriving home from the shoe store, pinching her cheek and saying, "Well, how is my sweet little ugly duckling today?"

All through childhood, into high school and college, she waited patiently for the ugly duckling to turn into a beautiful woman. Now, at twenty-six, while admittedly not a raving beauty, she did consider herself attractive. Tall, slender, long jet-black hair rolled tightly into a bun—she could never bring herself to trim it into a fashionable bob—with a face people termed angular. Her best features were her eyes. Large, almond-shaped, deep hazel. Someone once suggested those eyes were her saving grace.

Saving her from what? she asked herself, examining her face in the ladies' room mirror and pursing her lips to apply a hint of lip rouge. Probably from marriage, she answered herself. She smiled into the mirror. People said she had a nice smile.

A young girl entered, a college student, Ellie judged from her clothes. Bobbed, blond hair, white V-neck cotton tennis dress with knee-length pleated skirt. Flesh-colored silk stockings and black, ankle-strapped low-heeled shoes.

"Hello," the girl said. She drew a package of cigarettes from her purse. She lit a cigarette, then realized Ellie was staring at her. "Is something wrong?"

"You're not supposed to smoke in here."

"Oh, it's all right," the girl said. "Nobody cares."

I do, Ellie thought, but said nothing. Why make a federal case? They were in the ladies' room of the main, Fifth Avenue branch of the New York Public Library where Ellie was employed as an assistant librarian in the second-floor reading room. She had worked here since graduating from Barnard three years before, class of '20, and planned to remain in the public-library system her entire working life.

"The funeral is tomorrow," the girl said. She took another long drag on the cigarette, exhaling luxuriously.

"I beg your pardon?" Ellie asked.

"President Harding," the girl said. "They're burying him tomorrow. In Ohio."

"Oh, yes, of course," Ellie said. "How very sad." She had paid little attention to the tragedy, although it probably would prove a blessing for the country; not since General Grant's administration had there been such government corruption. Instantly, Ellie felt a flush of guilt. You should have respect. If not for the President of the United States, at least for the dead.

"My uncle met Coolidge once," the girl said. "He's a druggist, my uncle. In Boston."

Cerebral apoplexy, whatever that meant, killed Warren Harding. Cerebral, having to do with the cerebrum. The brain. Apoplexy of the brain. She must remember to discuss that with Leo when he picked her up tonight after work. He was always so fascinated with new words and phrases.

". . . supposed to be over a hundred out there," the girl was saying. "Awful hot for a funeral, wouldn't you say?"

"Excuse me?"

"The temperature in Ohio," the girl said. "Been over a hundred all week. A typical Midwest August, the paper said."

Ellie looked at her blankly. She had just glanced at herself in the mirror and envisioned Leo standing beside her, as on their first date two months ago when she caught a glimpse of them in the reflection of a bookstore window. She did not believe she was more than two inches taller, but the top of his head seemed hardly to reach her shoulder. She knew it was an illusion created by his standing behind her, but enough of a height difference to disturb her mother when they met tonight. She was bringing Leo home to meet her parents. She was glad she remembered to wear flat heels.

When she had first described him, her mother remarked, "You won't look good together."

Alfred Baer had said, "Don't worry how they look, Selma. He's Jewish, isn't he? And he owns his own business. Don't worry about it. He's a giant."

God, what standards! Ellie thought, watching the girl step into a stall and flush the cigarette butt down the toilet bowl. The girl left, nodding at Ellie. "Bye."

"Bye," Ellie said. She suddenly regretted allowing the girl to smoke. Rules are not made to be broken. She smiled into the mirror again and briefly practiced a series of gradually brighter smiles. That was almost the very first thing Leo Gorodetsky ever said to her. "You have a nice smile." Two months ago, when he came to the desk and asked her to suggest five books to both improve his vocabulary and "teach him something." She saw a nice-looking young man, very polite, neatly dressed, nervously sliding the brim of his straw hat around and around through his fingers.

"Teach you something about what?" she had asked. And then she smiled. "Knowledge is infinite."

That was when he said she had a nice smile. Later, she realized he complimented her smile because he did not understand knowledge being infinite and was too embarrassed to admit it. She, foolishly, had not sensed this and rambled on with five-cent philosophy. But she did recommend the books, among them *Lord Jim*, mostly because the author, Joseph Conrad, was visiting in the United States. The day Leo returned that book—which he said he stayed up all night reading—she was just leaving. He invited her for coffee. He thought if she had time perhaps they could discuss some things in the story he did not quite understand.

They went to an Automat and talked for two hours. For a boy whose schooling ended at the eighth grade, she thought him amazingly intelligent. And, obviously, ambitious. He was part owner of a garage and delivery service.

She giggled into the mirror. Four dates so far, and not once had he even tried to kiss her. Not even good night at the subway. She suspected he was too embarrassed about his height: she would have to lean down. And he had never escorted her home—all the way up to the Bronx, Kingsbridge—nor had she asked him. She was not sure how her parents would like him. They were *Deutsche Jehudim*, Leo a *Litvak*. Oil and water. But Ellie noticed her father's viewpoint slowly and slyly changing. He had an unmarried twenty-six-year-old daughter on his hands. Tonight should be interesting.

She examined her face one final time in the mirror and left the room. It was nearly lunchtime. She wondered where Leo was.

He was forty blocks south. With Harry, in a shiny new Buick sedan just pulling away from the East Broadway branch of the Bank of The Manhattan Company. Harry drove, while Leo admired a bankbook. His savings-account passbook, whose balance after this $5,500 deposit read $22,250.95.

"Not bad, huh?" he said, waving the passbook under Harry's nose.

"Terrific," Harry said, more concerned with keeping his hunched knees from tangling in the steering wheel. The car manufacturers, to attract women drivers, had pushed front seats nearly into the dashboard. He laughed suddenly, explaining, "When you were inside that bank just now I had this nutty idea of walking in and holding up the place. All they had there was that fat-assed old guard. He'd have fallen over in a dead faint!"

Leo was only half listening. He was studying the passbook page, the lovely round numerals, $22,250.95. My net worth, he thought, slipping the book into his jacket pocket and realizing that for an accurate net worth figure, you had to add another $3,300. The amount of cash in the long manila envelope locked in the bottom desk drawer in the living room of his apartment.

He had moved into a one-bedroom suite in the Hotel Hamilton on Twenty-third Street. Sixty-five dollars a month with utilities. And moved his mother and sister into a new flat also. A two-bedroom on Fourteenth Street. The forty-five-dollar monthly rent of course paid by Leo.

"Harry, for Christ's sake . . . !" he shouted. The black-and-white checkerboard design on the back of a taxi suddenly loomed up before the Buick's windshield. The taxi had stopped abruptly for some pedestrians crossing Grand Street. Harry, driving with his eyes continually flicking to the newspaper on the seat beside him, the *Daily News*, the day's entries at Bowie, saw it only at the last instant. He jammed down on the brakes. The Buick screeched to a stop, its front bumper actually touching the taxi's rear bumper.

The taxi driver opened the cab door and leaned out to glare at Harry. Harry gave him the finger, and when the taxi driver moved to leave the cab, Harry opened his door and also started to get out. The taxi driver changed his mind. He glared another instant, then closed the cab door and drove off.

"No balls," Harry laughed, shifting into low and turning right on Grand. "You hungry?"

"You know, you do that all the time."

"What?" Harry asked. "I do what all the time?"

"Like with that cab driver," Leo said. "You waste your time bothering with him. What's the point?"

"Why let the prick think he can push me around?"

"Does it cost you anything?"

"Yeah," Harry said. "My pride."

Leo started replying, then stopped. Talk about time-wasting, he thought. Why the hell am I lecturing Harry Wise? I am doing it, he answered himself, because the shmuck is my friend and I love him. The word "love" hung momentarily before Leo's eyes and startled him. The word seemed uncomfortably important. He thought he knew why.

That goddam girl. He was sure she was in love with him. He liked her and really enjoyed talking to her. But, come on, let's not be crazy. Speaking of crazy, he thought, and turned to the crazy one. He said, "You know what to do with your pride, Harry? Stick it up your ass."

"Thanks," said Harry. "So what about lunch?"

"I been invited uptown to supper," Leo said. "I don't want to spoil my appetite."

Harry grinned. "Your *mishpocheh*, huh?"

"Come on," Leo said. "All she wants is for me to meet her folks. That doesn't make us engaged."

"When it's a nice Jewish girl's folks, it does," Harry said. He nudged Leo playfully. "Hey, you had any of it yet?"

"Cut it out, huh?"

"Well, when do I get to meet her?"

"You don't."

Harry grinned again. "Sure, one look at me, and she dumps you like a hot *latke*. And speaking of *latkes*, I want to have some lunch!" He turned sharply, bumping the front wheels against the curb, and stopped. They were outside Nate's, a small restaurant Harry claimed served the best pastrami in town. "I think you really should eat. Put some lead in the pencil for the nice Jewish girl."

"Fuck you, Harry."

The grin broadened. "Not me, Kleyner. Her." Harry left the engine running as he opened the car door and got out. He closed the door and spoke to Leo through the open window. "Don't bother waiting for me, James, I'll walk back to the garage."

Leo, who had slid over behind the wheel, punched the gear into low and drove off. He shouldn't have allowed Harry's kidding to get to him. A few dates with a girl hardly meant love. He liked her, period. And the fact he hadn't made a pass at her was only a sign of respect.

He continued on Grand another block, turned into Chrystie, and stopped outside the garage. The building was newly painted, windows sparkling clean now, and a smart sign in block, black letters over the double doors read A-1 DELIVERY SERVICE.

Leo tapped the horn. One short honk, two long ones. The doors opened immediately and he drove in. The interior had been expanded, rear wall knocked down with the floor extending nearly fifty feet into the vacant lot behind the original structure. What had been a dirty, cramped shack now was a spacious, modern garage with service bays and hydraulic lifts capable of accommodating at any one time two dozen trucks and automobiles.

Three trucks, two new Fords and an older REO, were parked side by side near the entrance. Decaled on each side of the canvas, in neat scripted white letters, was A-1 DELIVERY. You had to look closely to see that the signs were on a separate canvas square buttoned onto the tarpaulin. This was always removed when the trucks were in service, revealing another sign reading U.S. CUSTOMS.

The vehicles were part of the Triad's fleet that carted liquor to and from a dozen warehouses strategically located and ingeniously disguised throughout Manhattan, Brooklyn, and Long Island. One, the largest, was in a former Cunard loading pier on Washington Street near Houston, surrounded by a chain-link fence and more heavily guarded than any bonded government warehouse.

The Triad.

Arnold Steinberger's label for the organization formed by the combination of his group, and Leo's and Sal's. The Triad controlled virtually all quality liquor dispensed in lower and mid-Manhattan, Brooklyn, and all of Long Island. It employed hundreds, including thirty-seven "soldiers," eighteen of whom were Jews supervised by Harry. The remainder, Italians, took orders directly from Sal Bracci.

Leo's prime duty was overseeing payoffs. Literally hundreds, from federal revenue agents to beat cops, all paid promptly from the personnel list kept in a small leather-bound notebook, the recipient's names in a code known only to Leo. Now, in August of 1923, monies expended on payoffs totaled nearly $300,000 annually. As Arnie Steinberger once remarked, ". . . more than five times the salary of the President of the United States."

Hershey, tinkering with the motor of one of the five new canvas-topped Ford trucks purchased just last month, was the only mechanic on the floor. The other two mechanics were out back eating their lunch. Hershey came out from behind the raised hood to greet Leo.

"So *nu*?" he said.

"*Nu* yourself," Leo said.

"You got a visitor," Hershey said to Leo. "In the office. Your sister."

"Okay," Leo said, wondering what Esther wanted. Money, probably. She had a good job with a dress manufacturer now, working in the office as a bookkeeper, but still spent everything on clothes. Still trying to find a man.

Leo started toward the office when Hershey suddenly snapped his fingers. "Oh, Leo, before I forget." He stepped toward another new Buick parked near the door, a touring car with a folding canvas roof, twin spare tires mounted in tandem on the rear. It was used only for special jobs. Hershey grasped a metal ring in the center top of the back seat and pulled open the entire backrest section.

A small compartment was built into the area behind the seat. Stacked neatly in the compartment were four cases of Dom Pérignon champagne. Hershey said, "Steinberger's *bocha*, the ape with the broken nose, what's his name—?"

"Charlie Cohen," Leo said.

"Yeah, him," Hershey said. "Well, he says Steinberger wants you for a special favor for him to take this stuff out to some people on the Island. And get paid for it from the buyer only." Hershey removed a slip of paper from his shirt pocket and extended it delicately in his grease-stained fingers to Leo. Leo unfolded the paper. On it was written "Island Country Club, Glen Cove. Phillip S. Conroy."

". . . extra special customers," Hershey was continuing. "So they should get extra special service."

"For an extra special favor to Arnie," Leo said. "Why the hell can't he do it himself?"

"He went to Saratoga with his married *shiksa*, the judge's wife," said Hershey. "He got a big mouth, this Cohen. He tells me Steinberger's having problems with the *shiksa*."

With me, too, Leo thought, but said nothing. This was not the first time Arnie asked Leo for one of these "favors." In the past few months Arnie was spending more time on his personal problems than on business. Once, when Leo objected, Arnie had smiled and said that was why he had Leo and Sal as partners. To handle things.

"All right," Leo said resignedly. He dropped the paper into his pocket and started for the office again. He was halfway there when Esther stepped out and walked to meet him.

"Hi," she said. She slipped an arm through his. "How are you?"

Leo looked at her. She was quite pretty, dressed all in white, dark hair tucked under a white cloche hat, and a white linen jacket and skirt. Virgin white, he thought, which seemed, unhappily, appropriate for her.

"Ma okay?" he asked.

"She's fine. Listen, I want you to meet somebody." Esther glanced toward the office. A tall, sandy-haired man with rimless glasses stood in the doorway. "He's a lawyer, Leo. And he has an accounting degree, too."

"He a friend of yours?"

"Kind of, yeah."

"What's 'kind of' mean?"

"I think he wants to marry me."

Leo peered into the office for a better look. The man, young, wore a dark-brown suit and stiff celluloid collar with a solid-brown, neatly knotted tie. He nervously rubbed the fingers of one hand over the fingers of the other. Leo said, "Esther, you know I never hire relatives or friends of relatives."

"You hired Bernie Kopaloff," she said.

"That was different," Leo said. Bernie Kopaloff was a nineteen-year-old Leo hired as a driver, and only at his mother's persistent nagging. He allowed this one exception because he knew it made Sarah Gorodetsky proud that her son gave her friend's son a job. Besides, the kid was tough and smart; Leo knew he would never reveal to his mother the true nature of his employer's business.

". . . an NYU graduate," Esther was saying. "You said you wanted somebody for the books."

"I said somebody good at remembering figures," Leo said. "We keep the books in our head."

"Oh, he's real good at that," Esther said. "Come on, meet him."

"Forget it," Leo said.

"At least say hello," Esther said. "His name is George. George Gerson." She pulled Leo toward the office. But at that instant, from outside, the sound of automobile engines and screeching brakes. Leo whirled. Hershey was already at the door.

"Feds!" he yelled, the message confirmed almost instantaneously from another voice outside.

"Federal agents! Open up!"

"So let them in!" Leo yelled back at Hershey. He started across the garage as Hershey opened the doors. Two men, one gripping a shotgun, burst in. Behind them two cars blocked the garage entrance. Oakland touring cars, official government vehicles. Four other men, all armed with shotguns, raced from the cars. All were dressed so similarly they almost seemed in uniform: straw hats, dark-blue double-breasted suits, black shoes.

Raids on the garage were not unusual, generally by agents on the payroll showing off for a visiting Washington boss. There was never any liquor on the premises. Leo recognized one agent, a short, stout, ruddy-faced man named Hofstetter. The other, younger than Hofstetter, Leo did not recognize. From Washington, he was sure.

"We have reason to believe these vehicles are engaged in the transporting of illegal alcohol," Hofstetter said to Leo. "Do you work here?"

"I'm the manager," Leo said, not quite completing the sentence as he noticed the other, younger agent seemed curious about the Buick touring car. In which, Leo thought angrily, there most certainly was liquor. He whispered tersely to Hofstetter, who was on the payroll at twenty-five dollars weekly. "Get him the fuck out of there!"

It was too late. The agent, whose name was Kenneth Brough and indeed from Washington, had slipped his finger into the ring and pulled down the seat back revealing the false compartment. The four champagne cases. He seemed almost surprised to have made the discovery so quickly and easily. As Leo and Hofstetter exchanged glances of dismay, Brough plucked one bottle from the case, examined the label, and nodded knowingly. He inspected several other bottles and then, with a weary sigh, he leveled the shotgun at Leo.

"All right, you're under arrest." He looked at Hofstetter. "Nice job, Gene—"

"—excuse me!" said a deep voice behind them. And George Gerson strode to the Buick. Taller than Kenneth Brough, he gazed calmly down at him. "This champagne happens to be my property—"

"—good, you're under arrest, too!" Brough said.

"—it is intended for a party," Gerson continued. "A reception in honor of the engagement of my sister to Mr. Lawrence Cranston junior. I hope that name means something to you?"

It did. Brough's eyes narrowed. "Who are you?"

"Something wrong with your hearing?" Gerson said. "I just told you: I'm Larry Cranston junior's future brother-in-law."

The name meant nothing to Leo. He was struggling to concentrate on other names—judges or magistrates for the fix. And he seethed with anger at Arnie's stupidity, sending the car here to the garage. Worse than stupidity, indifference. For an instant he wondered if it had not been deliberate.

". . . now, do you want to think about this?" Gerson was saying to Brough. "Or do I pick up the phone in that office and get Larry Cranston senior on the wire?" He smiled coolly. "Should be an interesting conversation."

Brough stood uncertainly, the shotgun still crooked in his arm. Then he said, "What's your sister's name?"

"Marion Deveraux," Gerson said. "She is twenty-three years old, and very much in love with young Cranston. They're expecting this champagne sometime today." He leaned past Brough and closed the touring car's rear seat, once again concealing the champagne. Then he slammed the car door. "Well, do I make the call or don't I?"

Brough glanced at Hofstetter, then at the other four agents standing uncertainly in the doorway. None had moved since Gerson's first mention of the magic name, Lawrence Cranston.

"What's your name?" Brough asked Gerson, now clearly unsure of himself.

Gerson placed a calling card into the agent's hand, and immediately uncapped his fountain pen which he poised over another card. "And your name, sir?"

Brough peered at Gerson an instant, then said to Hofstetter, "I thought you said you had a tip on this place!"

"We did," Hofstetter said. "But Ken, Jesus, I don't have to tell you the percentage of good tips . . ."

Brough was not listening; he had turned to Gerson again, studying the calling card. Absently, his other hand, the hand holding the shotgun, raised the barrel so the muzzle nearly touched Gerson's chin. Gerson's eyes widened but he did not flinch.

Brough said, "I'll remember you," and without another word wheeled about and walked to the door. Hofstetter looked at Leo just once. Then, breathing a sigh of relief, he hurried after Brough. The instant the men were outside, Hershey locked and barred the double doors. Before Leo could express his thanks to Gerson, Gerson's knees suddenly buckled. His whole body was trembling.

"My God!" said Esther, who had rushed from the office. "What's wrong?"

Gerson tried to speak, but now his teeth chattered. Hershey gripped his arm. "In the office," Hershey said. "Let him sit down!"

Hershey guided Gerson into the office and helped him into a chair. Esther poured water in a paper cup from the bottled dispenser near the door. She placed the cup to Gerson's lips. "Here, sweetheart, drink!"

Gerson sipped the water. He leaned back and drew in his breath in a long, heavy gasp. "When I think of that gun pointing at my neck!"

Leo said, "Who's Lawrence Cranston?"

Gerson took another long breath. "Lawrence Cranston is an assistant secretary of the treasury. In charge of the Enforcement Division." Gerson paused for yet another heaving breath. "He's their boss!"

Leo looked at him, then at Hershey and then at Esther. Then back at Gerson. "And you know this Cranston?" Leo asked, astounded.

Gerson shook his head.

"Then how—?"

"This morning's *World*," Gerson said. "On the society page. The story of Cranston's son getting engaged." He closed his eyes in sudden chagrin. "Oh, my God!" he moaned. "I gave him my card. With my real name on it!"

Leo started laughing. He hardly heard Gerson continuing, ". . . I said she was my sister!"

"I got to tell you, that was pretty damn good," Hershey said. "You are something else, *boychick!*"

" 'Pretty' good?" Leo said. "He was—" Leo groped for the word. "Magnificent! Yes, magnificent!" Now he seized Gerson's hand and shook it. "I'm Esther's brother," he said. "Leo."

"George," said Gerson. "Pleased to meet you."

2.

All the way to Glen Cove, whenever he thought of George Gerson and the federal agents, Leo laughed aloud. He had hired him on the spot. Thirty dollars a week, and never mind it was another friend of a relative. This one had the goods. Although, in truth, Leo could not see him marrying Esther. He simply did not seem her type. For one thing, too intelligent, which Leo realized might not be an exactly brotherly thought, but was nevertheless honest.

Road dust from the crowded highway swirled continually through the open car this hot sticky August afternoon. He would have to rush home for a shower and change of clothes. It made him even less eager to keep his date with Ellie. Meeting her parents was the last thing he wanted right now. For a moment he considered simply not going. When he picked her up at the library he would say he was sick. A summer cold.

"A rain check," he said aloud. "I'll take a rain check."

But he envisioned her disappointment. Him meeting her parents was important to her. She said she had told them all about him, how he was her "student." And how proud of him she was. His eagerness to learn, to improve himself. He wondered why he felt no driving sexual desire for her. She was pretty enough, and probably willing.

He thought he knew why. Because it might constitute a commitment on his part.

So what's wrong with that? he asked himself.

Plenty, he answered.

How come?

You're not ready, that's how come. There is just too much to do. For starters, setting up a game—craps and roulette—in Chez When, the East Forty-seventh Street cabaret. Leo had become friendly with the owner, Eric Janssen, who was all for it. They planned to convert the entire rear of the club. Plush carpets and furniture, and tasseled lamps over the tables like Monte Carlo.

When he wheeled the Buick into the long, curving drive of the Island Country Club, he had decided to start on the gambling room immediately. It meant a fortune in payoffs, but money well spent. He stopped under the club portico, turned off the engine, and sat a moment thinking about all this. A speakeasy within a speakeasy, and no slot machines. Slots did not belong in class establishments. But a colored doorman, he thought, glimpsing from the corner of his eye the Island Club's colored doorman coming around to open the Buick's door.

"Yes, sir?"

"Delivery for the Conroy party," Leo said. He got out of the car and opened the back door and raised the rear seat cushion.

"I'll take care of it, sir," the doorman said.

"Okay, you bring it in, but I'm supposed to see Mr. Conroy," Leo said. "Just go inside and ask the receptionist."

Leo gave the doorman a half-dollar and went inside. It resembled a hotel. A huge, marbled-floored lobby with a crystal chandelier covering half the ceiling, and bustling with people. Most of the men wore plus fours, or white duck trousers and white buck shoes. Almost all the women wore sports dresses, either plain white or gaily colored prints.

The receptionist, an attractive young woman, sat at an antique table at the far end of the lobby. To her right, folding double doors opened into a large ballroom. An orchestra's dance music blended with the party chatter of many voices.

The receptionist went into the ballroom to get Mr. Conroy for Leo. Waiting, he glanced into the room. A busy, noisy party. People dancing, or conversing in small groups, waitresses and waiters circulating with drink-filled trays. Even the servants looked tanned and sleek. Leo himself wore white flannel trousers and white shoes, and the jacket from a blue suit. He was glad now Harry talked him into buying the trousers and shoes. With the straw hat, it all made a perfectly acceptable sports outfit. While he realized his appearance meant nothing to these people, looking like a *mensh* let them know you were no goddam delivery boy. Even if you were delivering their liquor.

Mr. Conroy, Phillip S. Conroy III, twenty-four years old, whose family held substantial shares in Morgan Guaranty Trust, General Motors Corporation, and American Tobacco, was a falling-down drunk. He strode into the lobby clutching a highball glass in either hand. Short, fat, already quite bald, he resembled a red-faced infant. He placed the glasses on the receptionist's desk blotter and leaned unsteadily against the desk to write Leo a check.

"How much is it?"

"Ninety-six a case," Leo said. "Three hundred and eighty-four dollars."

"I make it out to Arnie?"

"Make it out to me," Leo said. "L. Gorodetsky." He spelled it for him.

Conroy signed the check and handed it to Leo. "There you are, Mr. Geodetsky."

"Gorodetsky," Leo said. "Thanks."

"Tell Arnie to send the same thing over Friday night," Conroy said.

"I'll ask him, I won't tell him," Leo said.

"Stout fella," said Conroy. He slapped Leo's shoulder in a friendly way, then swallowed down the contents of one glass. He placed the empty glass back on the table, picked up the other glass and left.

Leo folded the check into the bill section of his wallet and started out. A male voice behind him called out, "*Leo* Gorodetsky?"

It was Robert MacGowan, Big Bob, the AEF colonel from Paris. In golf togs, knickers, and white shirt with floral-patterned tie, he was not as imposing and looked older than his forty-six years. Leo frowned and snapped his fingers as though the name was on the tip of his tongue.

"MacGowan," MacGowan said, extending his hand. "Bob MacGowan."

"For Christ's sake!" Leo said, and shook hands. He had recognized him immediately, and while flattered to be remembered, was embarrassed MacGowan might think him a delivery boy. To correct any such misapprehension, Leo continued quickly, "Yeah, a friend of mine asked me to do him a favor and bring some champagne down here. So how you doing, Colonel?"

"I'm doing fine," said MacGowan. "Back in practice, working hard but loving it. But what about you?"

"Oh, I'm doing okay, too," Leo said. "Good job, and next year I go to night school."

"Law?" MacGowan asked. "I remember you said you were interested in the law."

"I haven't quite made up my mind," Leo said, surprised at his own words. He did not understand why he was saying this, but could not seem to stop. "Right now I just want to start with some business courses."

"Good thinking," MacGowan said. "And in the meantime, I see you're involved more in breaking the law than making it."

Leo felt himself flush. "The champagne, you mean?"

MacGowan smiled and placed a friendly hand on Leo's shoulder. "Don't worry about it, son. We're all breaking the law. The whole damn country." The smile suddenly faded. "Come over here so we can talk a minute." He guided Leo to a lobby divan, gestured him to sit, and sat next to him. "I'm still in your debt, you know."

For an instant Leo did not understand. Then he remembered. Big Bob's son. The queer. Leo felt suddenly uneasy; he actually knew what MacGowan was about to say.

"He's dead."

Leo said nothing. He did not know what to say.

"Killed in action," MacGowan said. He looked away, at three white-flanneled boys strolling across the lobby. "Five days before the Armistice."

"I'm sorry," Leo said. It was all he could think of to say.

"They gave him a Silver Star," MacGowan said. "Posthumously."

"That's very nice," Leo said.

MacGowan nodded, and for a moment seemed lost in his own thoughts. Then he nodded again, and rose. "I want you to come and see me when you have a chance." He withdrew a business card from his wallet. "We'll have another lunch. Remember the last one?"

"I sure do," said Leo. "The Ritz."

"The Ritz!" MacGowan snapped his fingers in enlightenment. "My God! Leo, you wait right here. Don't move from this spot." He hurried away, into the ballroom.

Later, remembering, Leo would swear he had foreseen it all, knew it was going to happen. Preordained was the word.

So he was not at all surprised a few moments later when MacGowan returned, accompanied by a woman. A tall, dark-haired, very attractive woman.

Charlotte Daniels.

The instant he saw her it was as though a painful and crippling injury was all at once, magically, healed. All the bitterness and anger vanished, and the fantasies of revenge. All the memories of that last terrible humiliating night five years ago in Paris. Her almost horrified expression when he told her he loved her. And the pity in her voice: *"Poor little Leo."* But now, seeing her again, none of it ever happened. He had imagined it all, or if not imagined, distorted.

He chose his words carefully, literally unable to hear his own voice for the beating of his heart. But he knew the words were correct, and grammatically proper. He was proud of that, and of his neat, fashionable appearance.

Yes, she was so delighted to see him, especially pleased at how he had changed. He had matured—and she knew he would not deny that back in Paris he was rather young and naïve—but now, just look at him. A howling success. Evidence of which, among other things, was the handsome new Buick touring car with the built-in false compartment.

She insisted he have lunch at the club. As her guest, of course, followed by a tour of the facilities. The golf course and tennis courts. They were building a swimming pool, so next year he could come out and enjoy that if he wished. As her guest, of course.

He did not recall a single thing he ate or drank, and not too much of the conversation. He thought she said she worked for her father at his Wall Street bank—or was it helping her mother with the Junior League? He did hear her mention being married and divorced, and the next man would be Mr. Right, or her name wasn't Charlotte Farnsworth Daniels. But after that he really heard or saw little. Only that marvelous, soft husky voice. Music to the ears, a symphony, from the lips of a beautiful woman whose bobbed lustrous black hair framed her perfectly tanned face like some priceless painting in a gallery.

The magic afternoon turned into a magic evening. He drove her into the city, accompanied her up to her East Fifty-seventh Street apartment and mixed drinks for them while she changed. He phoned Eric Janssen to alert him he was bringing a friend to Chez When, and would Eric please put on the dog? Which Eric did. Front-row table, everything on the house. Quite a difference now from the sad little lovesick doughboy she knew in Paris.

When he brought her home, after two A.M., and she did not invite him up for a nightcap, he was not at all disappointed. Although she excited him now far more than before, he wanted it—as before—to be right. And now the only way it could be right, and would be right, was for her to come straight out and say it. "Leo, make love to me."

He knew, when the time was right, she would.

They were in his car parked outside her building. She had asked him not to bother seeing her into the lobby. She leaned over and kissed him lightly on the lips.

"Thank you for a lovely day," she said.

"When will I see you again?"

"When do you want to?"

"Tomorrow?"

She touched his cheek. "Call me."

After she left, he got out of the car and strolled around the block. He wanted to think. Everything was falling into place. Triad business was booming, with no end in sight. In the next few months, with the opening of Chez When's gambling room, the Dream would finally start to come true. And now he found what he had believed lost.

He got back into the car and drove off. He cut up Fifty-seventh, to Fifth, and then downtown. Only when he reached Forty-second Street and passed the two stone lions on the library stairs, only then for the first time that whole afternoon and evening did he remember his date with Ellie.

3.

He was proud of the tux, the first he ever owned, and custom-tailored. But if he had known the *tsuris* of tying the goddam bow tie, he might never have bought it. He had been trying for the past ten minutes to get it right, and he was already late; twenty past seven, and he had to stop at the garage before picking up Charlotte. They were going to Harlem, to Julie Jefferson's new club, the Aladdin.

A business and pleasure evening. Jules Jefferson was a real *shtarker*. He practically ran Harlem. He wanted quality merchandise for the Aladdin. All his customers were white, well-heeled, demanding the best. The Triad had ignored Harlem, but Sal and Arnie agreed with Leo that now they should at least get a foot in the door. The numbers game, for example. Nickels and dimes, but all adding to a fortune.

All right, he told himself, carefully preparing the tie again. Calm down and you'll get it right. He folded the ends correctly, then over and through. And pulled them tight. It looked like a double-knotted shoelace.

"Harry!" he shouted.

"Yeah?" Harry called from the living room.

"I need help, goddamit!"

Harry was lying on the living-room sofa reading *Time*, a new magazine with a condensed version of all the week's news. He had a date with a girl living nearby, but was an hour early so dropped over to kill time. Now he went to the bedroom doorway to see what Leo wanted. Leo pointed grimly to the bow tie.

Harry stepped in and tied it for him. "There," he said. "You look like the cat's meow."

Leo inspected himself in the mirror. "Thanks."

"Don't mention it," Harry said. "Your high society *shiksa* will love you."

My high society *shiksa*, Leo thought. Cat's meow. It reminded him of when he first met Charlotte, when MacGowan said Leo was looking at her like a cat looking at a queen. Well, the cat was now a tiger. He had spent five of the last seven nights with her. Dinners, theater, nightclubs. Even a hansom-cab ride through the park. It was Paris all over again, only with a happy ending.

". . . lined up a manager for Chez When, I think," Harry was saying. "A guy named Gruber. Sal found him. They call him Wingy on account of his arm. Like the Kaiser's. Remember? What do they call it when it's like that?"

"Withered," Leo said, slipping on the tux jacket, which fit beautifully and decided him then and there that from now on all his clothes would be custom-tailored. "What do you know about him?"

"He ran a couple of joints down south during the war," Harry said. "He knows the ropes."

"Good," Leo said, his mind on Charlotte, who did not like him to be late.

"I want to send Gerson over there to open the books," Harry said. "I like how he works."

"Okay," said Leo, thinking they had good reason to like George Gerson's work. They kept him so busy he had little time for Esther. She had complained bitterly to Leo. One thing to give the man a job, but my God, give him also a little time to breathe. Meaning a little time to spend with Esther.

Leo was adjusting his lapel handkerchief when the doorbell rang. Harry went to the door while Leo studied himself a final time. From the living room he heard a woman's voice. He smoothed his hair down in back, twisting his neck to examine the temples.

"Leo . . ." Harry was in the doorway. "Somebody to see you." Harry seemed amused. Behind him, in the living room, her hands busy fidgeting with the clasp of her purse, was Ellie Baer.

Harry cleared his throat loudly and said, "Well, I got to go." He glanced at Leo with raised eyebrows. "Nice meeting you," he said to Ellie, and opened the living-room door to leave. Harry's face was worth a thousand words. It said that at that minute he wouldn't take all the money in the world to be in Leo's shoes. Harry closed the door quietly behind him.

For a moment Leo and Ellie stood looking at each other. Then Leo removed his watch from his vest pocket: 7:30. Ellie said, "I hope I'm not disturbing you. But I had to find out what happened. That is, if you were sick, or what."

"No, no, I'm fine," Leo said. He dropped the watch back into his pocket and came into the living room.

"You look very nice," she said.

"Thank you," he said, and started to say "Listen, I'm late," but instead said, "How've you been?"

"What happened, Leo?"

Leo could not immediately find his voice. What a bitch, he thought. What a rotten bitch! Coming here like this. Who the hell does she think she is? Talk about *chutzpah!*

He said, "What do you mean, 'What happened?' "

"You know perfectly well what I mean."

"Because I didn't show up that night?"

"Don't you think you owe me an explanation?"

He looked at his watch again: 7:31. Now he did say it. "Listen, I'm very late—"

"—couldn't we talk? Just a few minutes?"

"Tomorrow," he said. "I'll come over and see you tomorrow. You still at the library?" He stepped to the door and opened it for her. She stood looking at him. She wore heels, making her much taller.

"Please, Leo," she said. "I've missed you."

He was so angry now he needed a deep breath to compose himself. She had no right to do this. Wasn't it enough he hadn't shown up? Didn't she get the message? Worse, she was treating him like a child who had misbehaved.

R.A.1.—7

"What do you want me to say?" he asked.

"I want to know why I haven't seen you."

"I've been busy."

Her eyes glistened with rage and humiliation. "That last night, the night we were to have dinner with my parents?" she said. "I planned to come back to the city with you, to your apartment." Now a single tear rolled down her cheek, and then another. "Yes!" she cried. "To spend the night with you. To sleep with you!"

He was totally frustrated. Again he looked at his watch, but more for something to do than the time. When he looked up, she sat on the sofa, rigid, her hands tightly folded over her purse on her lap. He closed the door.

"Honest, Ellie," he said. "I'll see you tomorrow."

"Doesn't it mean anything to you?" she asked. "What it took for me to come here? To say all that?" She pushed the purse from her lap and seized his hand, pulling him to the sofa with her, covering his hand now with both of hers. "Please, Leo, must I get on my hands and knees and beg you? Is that what you want?"

For a moment he believed she actually would get on her hands and knees. He placed his free hand over hers. A mountain of hands, he thought crazily. Of fingers. He said, "What do you want me to do?"

"I want things the way they were."

"The way they were? We were friends. We went out a few times. You're acting like it was a big love affair."

"It was," she said quietly, and added, "For me."

All right, he thought, there is only one way to handle this. He pushed her away. He stood and looked down at her. "It wasn't for me," he said. He had to force each word. "So whatever it was for you, I'm sorry." He started for the door, hesitating when he realized his straw hat was in the bedroom, but quickly deciding to leave it there.

He opened the door. She had not moved from the sofa. She was weeping openly now.

"Shut the lights off when you leave," he said.

Leo felt bad for Ellie, but guiltless; he had not deceived her or been dishonest. He knew how she felt. She was in love with him, and he with Charlotte, so he knew how being in love felt. He liked to think of the past weeks with Charlotte as a courtship. For while he was crazy with desire for her, and each date ended with kisses and fondling, she always stopped it before anything happened. A sure sign, he began to believe, of her deep feeling for him. He was certain she would go to bed with him if he insisted. But he was determined that when it happened it would be at her specific request.

Or during their honeymoon.

Leo proposed one evening in late September at Charlotte's apartment.

He was waiting for her to finish dressing. They were going to Chez When for dinner and the show, and then a visit to the back room. It had been open a month now and doing very well.

He stood at the living-room window gazing out at the East River, the headlights from cars on the bridge reflecting off the surface of the water as long, shimmering yellow streaks. He heard her talking to him from the bedroom, but did not answer because he was thinking, I will just say, How'd you like to get married? No, just, Charlotte, what do you say we get married?

He had already decided they would honeymoon at Saratoga Springs. Arnie, who often went there, said it was better than the famous European spas. Old World elegance, with just enough American efficiency for first-class comfort and service. And not "restricted." Meaning Jews were welcome. Especially those with money to spend.

". . . will your friend Harry be there?" she asked, coming into the living room. She wore a gold-sequined dress with the skirt ending above the knees. A white band around her temples was startling against her black hair. Leo thought she looked like a beautiful Indian maiden.

"Harry?" he said. "I don't know. Maybe. Why?"

"I like him," she said. She twirled in a gentle pirouette to show off the dress. "How do I look?"

"Beautiful."

"Will they like me?" she asked. "The gangsters?"

He laughed. She liked to refer to Harry and Sal as his "gangster friends." He said this also made him a gangster, didn't it? Well, maybe, she said. But he was her gangster, so that made it different.

Once, when drunk, she confessed she found men like Sal and Harry exciting. She enjoyed their company. It was almost like having been kidnapped and taken to their hideout and there, shackled to a bed, gagged, ravished by them. One after the other. He remembered how her eyes shone and her lips glistened and her breath came in short, uneven gasps. And she had held her arms out to him and drawn him to her, and just as he was sure she was about to ask him to do it to her, she had pushed him away with an embarrassed laugh.

Now he said, "Charlotte, I want to talk to you." He pointed to the divan. "Sit down."

"Fix me a drink first." She sat and lit a cigarette.

He went to the cellarette and poured a martini for her from the burnished-silver shaker, then decided to have one himself. He seldom drank anything stronger than wine or beer, but now he needed a real drink. He handed her a glass and sat beside her. They clicked glasses and drank, he drinking his half down in a single swallow. He placed the glass on the end table, faced her directly, and said, "I want to marry you."

For a long, heavy moment she was silent. She stared almost blankly at him, and he thought, I should have said, I love you. But those words, if he considered them at all, lay buried deep in his throat like some long-hoarded, priceless treasure. Those words, uttered once before to this same woman, had been disastrous. He had no intention of repeating that mistake. Not until he was sure it was not a mistake.

"You're sweet," she said finally, with a soft smile. She looked at her glass, then lowered it without drinking. She smiled again. "Shouldn't we be leaving?"

"Don't I get an answer?"

"Leo, Leo, Leo," she said, as though gently chiding. "For God's sake, don't be so serious. Life is too short."

"Is that the answer?"

"The answer is, my darling sweet little bootlegger-gangster, I want to go to that club of yours and make a million dollars playing roulette." She drank down her drink and placed the empty glass on the side table. "Let's go, shall we?"

Leo could not recall a worse evening. Everything that could go wrong did. A drunken Park Avenue doctor hit Chez When's roulette table for $3,000. And then Hershey decided this was the night he would visit the club. One look at Charlotte, and Hershey called Leo aside privately to suggest that while it might be none of his business, that *shiksa* was bad news. Well, who the hell asked you? Leo shouted at him. He stalked away in a fury and for three days afterward refused to speak to Hershey.

Charlotte canceled their date the following evening. She said she had to go down to Newport to visit friends. When, two days later, she did not call, he went to her apartment. She was there, but explained she was not feeling well and had not wanted to subject him to her foul mood. They had Chinese food sent in from Ruby Foo's, and not once did she mention his marriage proposal. He brought it up.

"You know what I think, Leo?" she said. "I think you're only testing me. I think if I said yes, you'd laugh and tell me you were only testing me."

Once again, the magic, sacred words I love you rose, unspoken, to his lips. It was as if those words were the final, ultimate weapons, not to be deployed until no other option remained. For once they were used, and failed, he would be left defenseless. He said, "Why can't you take me seriously?"

"Why can't we just go on as we are?" she asked. "Why does it have to be marriage?"

Now he exploded. All the frustration of the past weeks, the sensation of walking blindfolded through a minefield. The lonely sleepless nights, wondering what she was doing, wondering if she was thinking about him. If she had a lover and if so, who, and what they did. Did she scream with pleasure when he stuck it into her, and clutch his hair, and beg him to ram it in, ram it in all the way!

It would not be that way with him. With him it would be tender, and loving, and she would grasp his face and kiss him. First gently, and then with more passion. And he would know if she was not quite ready, and hold back and wait. He would let go only when she cried, Now, darling, now! And when it was over they would lie in each other's arms, secure in the warmth and tenderness and togetherness of two people loving each other.

He said, "I'll tell you why it has to be marriage! Because I love you! I want to make love to you and wake up in the morning beside you! Goddamit, how long do you think I can keep going like this!"

He paused for breath, aware he had done it, said he loved her. All right, now she had to respond. But she remained silent, and Leo all at once heard words tumbling from his own mouth that he had never phrased in his mind.

"You know how I feel sometimes? Sometimes after I say good night to you, and I'm walking around so horny I can hardly see straight—and I don't want another woman, only you. I feel like I hate you, goddamit! And then I hate myself for feeling like that. Charlotte, you can't do this to me! I won't stand for it!"

His anger frightened her. He reminded her of a playful little puppy suddenly rabid. No, worse: a dangerous genie just released from a bottle. Dangerous. You could see it deep inside those soft brown eyes that now were blocks of fiery ice. Once, she recalled, she felt sorry for him. Not now. Now she feared him. She had gone too far. She had reached the wall. Dead end.

"I need time to think," she said. She spoke the truth, although the time she needed was to think about how best to let him down. Without hurting him. She sincerely did not want to hurt him.

For her own sake.

When Leo left that evening she promised to phone him in the morning with her answer. He started for Chez When. He needed to relax. A drink, maybe, a look over the playing action. But the instant he reached the street he felt totally drained of energy. He had all he could do to just hail a cab. He went home and fell immediately asleep.

He was awakened at nine with a telephone call. When the man identified himself, and extended an invitation to lunch at the Union League Club, Leo felt as though a thousand-pound weight was lifted from his chest.

Charlotte's father, Clark Daniels.

Obviously wishing a man-to-man talk with his future son-in-law.

4.

A tall, lean, graying man, Clark Daniels had gone directly into his uncle's bank after graduating from Princeton in 1893. Today, although relatively small by commercial standards, under Clark's leadership the First

Providence Trust Company was New York City's tenth-largest privately owned banking institution. Clark was justifiably proud of that accomplishment, and of his daughter, an only child.

She had suffered one bad marriage; he certainly did not intend her to repeat the experience. Charlotte had phoned him several hours after Leo left her apartment. She was tipsy, but after she explained her predicament Clark understood why. She thought that after Paris, Leo had matured. Well, she was mistaken. He had never given up this impossible fantasy of marrying her. And now she had allowed it to go too far, and needed help. Her father's help. Someone who could deal firmly with Leo, in the only language he understood. Clark Daniels knew how to deal with Leo's kind.

He chose the meeting site carefully. He knew the very surroundings would intimidate this brash young man. On the corner of Thirty-seventh and Park Avenue, the Union League Club dated back to the Civil War, a bastion of wealth and conservatism. You almost had to be born into a membership. Only recently had certain Catholics been accepted, and those selected most judiciously. No Jews, ever.

They met in a small, private, mahogany-paneled dining room. Clark was purposely late. He wanted Leo to sit waiting in the huge, tomb-silent lobby. And when he did arrive, he went directly to the private room and sent for Leo.

Clark was mildly surprised. He had somehow envisioned Leo a skinny, pimply, long-nosed street type. Instead he found a tastefully dressed, nice-looking young fellow who under the circumstances appeared remarkably at ease.

Clark rose from the table to shake Leo's hand and gesture him into a chair. "I presume this is your first time here at the club?"

"Yes, sir."

"I think you'll like the food," Clark said. "Can I offer you a drink?"

"No, thank you," Leo said. He unfolded the starched white-linen dinner napkin and spread it on his lap.

Clark smiled. Leo returned the smile. Then Clark said, "Would you care to order, or should we dispense with our business first?"

"Whatever you like, Mr. Daniels."

Clark wanted a drink, but felt drinking alone might put him at a disadvantage. Disadvantage? he thought. My God, this is nothing but discharging an employee or servant. He decided to cut straight to the issue.

"Charlotte says you've asked her to marry you?"

"Yes, sir."

"Well, Leo—I may call you Leo . . ."

"Please do, sir."

"I must tell you I object most strenuously. I don't know how else to put it. I consider such a marriage quite impossible."

Leo's face was impassive. He gazed ublinkingly at Clark, who was thinking, My God, what have I gotten into? I might as well have just recommended broiled Dover sole instead of sautéed sweetbreads. Clark Daniels would never know that Leo felt he had been hit by a truck, and not reacting was the greatest achievement of his life.

Clark said, "Don't you have anything to say?"

"I'd like to know why you object."

"You're not a fool," Clark said. "On the contrary, I can see you're a very intelligent man. But you're also a bootlegger. In a word, Leo, I don't want my daughter marrying a bootlegger."

"I love her," Leo said. "And she loves me. She doesn't care what I am."

"You're wrong," Clark said. "She cares very much what and who you are."

"No, sir," said Leo. "You're the one who's wrong. But if that's your main objection, then I'll quit the business this very minute."

"I see. And how would you support yourself then?"

"I have quite a bit of money. I'll get into business."

Clark shook his head impatiently. "You're not taking Charlotte's feelings into consideration. Her hopes and aspirations. No, Leo, it's a bad idea for everyone concerned."

Leo said, "Excuse me, sir, but I think that you mean it's a bad idea for you. You, personally. I know Charlotte doesn't agree."

"She asked me to tell you all this."

Leo leaned forward as though not sure he heard correctly. "She asked you?"

"Yes."

"To tell me it's a bad idea?"

"Yes."

"Why didn't she tell me herself?"

"She didn't want to hurt you."

Leo looked at the napkin in his lap. He folded it and placed it on the Wedgwood dinner plate. "Let her say it to my face," he said. "I want to hear it from her."

"Now, look, I don't want to be unkind," Clark said. "But people like you simply must learn to know your place—"

"—people like me? What does that mean?"

"Oh, I think you know very well what it means." Clark wanted to waste no more time with soft words and kid gloves. Fight fire with fire, call a spade a spade. "Your background. Your heritage."

"Before, you said it was because I was a bootlegger," Leo said. "Now it's my background."

Clark suddenly hated Leo for putting him through this. And resented Charlotte for manipulating him into it. He forced a smile. "You're determined to make this as difficult as possible for both of us, aren't you?"

Leo pushed back his chair and rose. "Let's see what she has to say. Thank you, sir, for your time." He started away. At the doorway he stopped. He waved his hand around the room. "Very nice place," he said. "Full of heritage and background. Someday I'll invite you to my synagogue. Lot of heritage there, too."

Clark sat a full five minutes after Leo left. Then he rang for a waiter. He started ordering lunch, but changed his mind and ordered a double Glenlivet instead. The fine, smoky malt liquor never tasted so good. It settled him down. Only after he emptied the glass and was considering having another did he realize it had probably been supplied by Leo Gorodetsky.

From her sixth-floor living-room window Charlotte watched the rain beat down on the roofs of cars and taxis on Fifty-seventh Street. A cold, heavy October rain drumming loudly on the windowpane. Below, at the canopied entrance, a taxi arrived. She knew it was Leo. Clark had phoned a few minutes before. Just be straightforward, he advised. In the long run it was less cruel.

In her mind she rehearsed her opening remarks. Flip and charming, she decided. She poured a drink, a short one, and drank it down. Then she loosened the belt of her fur-collared silk robe, opening it just enough to reveal the curve of her breasts. She was prepared.

She was also drunk.

"It didn't take you long," she said, ushering him in. "Can I get you a drink?"

"No, thanks," Leo said. "You were expecting me, I see?"

"Daddy phoned," she said. "Sit down, please."

He walked to the window and glanced out. "What did he say?" he asked. "Your father?"

"He likes you."

Leo said nothing. He stepped away from the window and sat on the divan. Charlotte sat down in an armchair facing him. "When did it start raining?" she asked.

"A few minutes ago."

"Yes, I see you don't have a coat. You were lucky to find a cab."

"Your father said he likes me?"

"Yes, very much."

"He has a funny way of showing it," Leo said. "He said you don't."

"I don't what?"

"Like me," Leo said. "You don't like me."

"He didn't say that, Leo." She stood. "You're sure you won't have a drink?" She walked across the room to the cellarette. "He didn't say that at all." She was speaking to the bottle, concentrating on filling precisely half the glass. "Dammit! No ice!" She glanced at him with a bright smile. "I keep filling the tray but it never seems to stay. I'll just have to get one of those electric iceboxes. What are they called? Frigidaires?"

THE TRIAD   153

Leo said, "He said you didn't want to marry me."

"That doesn't mean I don't like you."

"Love me," said Leo. "You don't love me."

She carried the glass back to the chair and sat again. "Well, that's right, Leo. I don't."

Leo drew in his breath, then released it in a long, weary sigh. "Why didn't you tell me that before?"

She said nothing a moment, watching his eyes for that coldness. But his eyes remained soft, and pained, reminding her of a stricken animal. Yes, she thought, an animal. That is exactly what he is, an animal. She felt infinitely superior, and confident.

She said quietly, "I didn't tell you before because I didn't think you'd take it too well."

"So you teased and toyed with me," he said. "That made you feel good?"

"It must have made you feel good, too," she said. "You went along with it."

"That's right," he said. "I was trying to get you into bed."

"Into bed?" She laughed harshly and drank down the rest of the gin. She set the glass firmly on the glass-topped coffee table. "Why on earth would I get into bed with you? You bore me, for God's sake. And so does this whole stupid conversation!"

"Thank you."

She pushed herself up from the chair and looked down at him. "And do you want to know something? If I did sleep with you, *if*, the only reason would be to see what it was like with a Jew."

He said nothing, only stared at her. Now she felt more superior than ever. And now she could see his eyes grow cold. There, she had done it. And she was glad. She had put him in his place. She knew it was the right way to do it, the only way. So he was a little hurt; he'd get over it.

"All right, Leo?" she said. "Now what else? What else do you want to know?"

He rose slowly. His face, absolutely expressionless, for an instant spun before her eyes. I am drunk, she thought, oh am I ever drunk. But she did not feel drunk. Except for the momentarily giddiness, she felt in complete, cool control.

He hit her. A vicious backhand across the side of the face that hurtled her backward into the coffee table. The table collapsed under her, sending her and the glass tabletop and the empty glasses and ashtrays crashing to the floor. She lay on the floor atop the broken glass gazing up at him. She felt no pain where he struck her, or in her body when she fell. No pain whatever, but rather a strange, almost pleasant warmth.

She smiled at him, and all at once felt a sharp twinge at the corner of her mouth, and a sweet-sticky moistness. She licked the corner of her lip and tasted the blood.

"Why don't you hit me again?" she said. "Wouldn't that make you feel better?" She rose up on one elbow. Her breath came in short, panting gasps. Her eyes shone with excitement. "Why don't you rape me? Yes, you rotten son of a bitch, rape me!" She screamed the last words. "You want to do it to me, do it! It's the only way you'll ever get it!"

Leo would never forget that moment. She, lying there staring wildly up at him, panting like a bitch in heat, the top of her robe open, one breast exposed, the nipple swollen and flamingly red. And the robe crunched up around her thighs all the way to the tops of her stockings attached to the white, lace-bordered garter belt.

She laughed, a shrill, almost musical laugh. "Look at you!" she cried. "You've got a hard-on as big as a house!"

Grasping her robe lapels, he pulled her to her knees. He held her with one hand and drew back the other to strike her again. Blood from the previous blow trickled down her chin. Her eyes gleamed brighter than before.

"Yes, hit me!" she cried. "Hit me!"

His hand froze in midair as he realized that he indeed intended to rape her. It unfolded as clearly and concisely in his mind as though viewing it in three dimensions through a stereopticon. He would hit her again, then tear the robe from her body and rip off her underpants. He would plant his shoe on her naked belly while he unbuttoned his fly. Then he would spread her legs apart and plunge himself into her.

My Jewish prick, he thought. She wanted to know what it was like being fucked by a Jew. She'd find out good now. But even as he thought this, his hand still poised, the flood of blind, unreasoning anger suddenly was gone, replaced by revulsion and disgust. He had never before struck a woman, and certainly never raped one. He shuddered with self-loathing and then, relieved, nearly laughed. The erection had subsided as quickly as it had risen.

He released her. She remained on her knees, staring at him. She knew. She read it in his no longer bulging fly, and in his eyes. She laughed triumphantly.

"You can't do it, can you? You don't have the guts!" Her voice dripped with disdain. " 'Gangster!' You're no gangster. You're a fraud!"

He said, "You know something? That's the first honest thing you ever said to me." He stepped past her to the door, and left.

In the hallway he heard her screaming after him, "Fraud! Fraud!" He did not wait for the elevator, but walked the six floors to the street. He could not escape fast enough.

"I'm telling you, they did something to him," Harry Wise said. He was pacing up and down the garage office, stopping only to flick his cigarette ash into the saucer on Hershey's desk. Hershey sat drinking a glass of tea, watching Harry.

"A day only he's been gone," Hershey said. "That don't mean nothing.

He found a little cooze, maybe. The kid's entitled."

"A day and a half," Harry said. "It just ain't like Leo to disappear that way." He hurled the cigarette to the floor and ground his heel into it. "Shit!"

"My clean floor!" Hershey said. "I just got it washed."

"Fuck your clean floor!" Harry grasped the handle of the candlestick telephone and jerked it off the desk with an abrupt, smooth motion that flipped the earpiece up out of the cradle and into his free hand. "Operator!" he shouted into the mouthpiece. He jiggled the cradle. "Come on, cunt, I'm in a hurry!"

Hershey got up, gesturing Harry into the chair. Harry slid into the chair and rested the telephone handle on his lap. He spoke into the mouthpiece. "Chelsea one-six-eight, and fast! Please," he added reluctantly.

Hershey said, "How come you're calling Bracci?"

Harry did not reply, but spoke into the phone. "This is Harry Wise, let me talk to Sal." He listened, his face wrinkling with impatience. Then, "Okay, but tell him I got to see him right away. I'll be down there in an hour. It's important."

Harry slammed the earpiece into the cradle. He put the telephone back on the desk and said to Hershey, "I got a hunch maybe Sal knows where Leo is."

"Sal knows where he is," Hershey repeated dubiously. "So why would Leo keep it such a secret?"

"Because maybe Sal don't want him to tell nobody where he is," Harry said. "Maybe Sal won't let him tell nobody."

"Sal won't let him?"

"Yeah, Hershey." Harry got up and stood facing Hershey. "Sal won't let him."

Hershey looked at Harry a moment. Harry was not quite as tall as Hershey, who was very tall. Hershey said, "You trying to tell me Sal wants him out of the way, or something?"

"It ain't impossible, is it? Leo's the only one of us that really trusts them dagos. They could knock him off easy."

"What would they do that for?"

"That's what I want to ask Sal," Harry said. "And he better have a good answer."

Harry brushed past Hershey, but Hershey gripped his elbow and pulled him to a stop. "You shmuck," Hershey said. "The one maybe that would knock off Leo is not Bracci. It's our 'partner,' Steinberger."

"Arnie?" Harry said. "Don't be crazy." But he frowned with sudden uncertainty. "That's crazy!"

"For Christ's sake, kid, where's your *goyisher kop*?" Hershey said. "Bracci and us got too much to lose, we start fighting each other. And, anyway, for what? Each got our own territory, and nobody bothers the other.

But Steinberger, the *macha*, he just might be thinking maybe Leo's moving too fast. Maybe he don't need Arnie so bad no more. *Die helst?*"

"Yeah," Harry said slowly. "Yeah, maybe so. Maybe so." He started out again. "Stay by the phone, I'll get back to you in a little while."

"Where you going?"

"To talk to Sal, anyway," Harry said. "We do anything, we got to do it together, don't we?"

"Do what?"

"Find out if Arnie had anything to do with Leo being gone like this."

After Harry left, Hershey picked up the butt Harry mashed out on the floor. He juggled the shredded paper and tobacco in his palm. He knew Sal would talk Harry out of doing anything foolish with Arnie, and he knew Arnie had nothing to do with Leo's disappearance. Hershey was also unconcerned about Leo's safety.

He knew where Leo was. With the rich *shiksa*, whose father Leo went to meet yesterday. Leo made Hershey promise not to say nothing about it to Harry or Sal. He wanted to surprise them. Hershey was sure that in the end the only person surprised would be Leo himself. All he hoped was that Leo got her out of his system fast. He tossed the cigarette butt in the wastebasket and went into the garage to fix a flat tire.

Hershey would have been surprised if he knew how truly fast Leo got the *shiksa* out of his system.

Overnight.

With some not inconsiderable assistance from two pretty young women, residents of a West Seventy-second Street townhouse owned by a former *Scandals* chorus dancer named Daisy White. Leo had walked all the way in the pouring rain from Charlotte's apartment. Later he claimed the rain had helped cleanse him, a kind of purge.

Daisy listened to him, the whole story, each incident punctuated with a good, stiff belt of Jack Daniel's. His own merchandise. Then she put him to bed, instructing the two girls not to leave him alone, not a single instant. Not even for the can. A man in his state needed people. To talk to if he wanted to talk, or just to be there. Daisy knew.

In the morning, over coffee with Daisy, he said he was a sadder but wiser person. "I never thought I'd make the same mistake twice," he said. "It was like seeing the same movie all over again. The same thing happened the last time with her." He waved his hand around the room and laughed dryly. "I ended up in a whorehouse."

"I'd prefer my establishment described as a place of relaxation," Daisy said.

"Excuse me," Leo said. "A place of relaxation."

"Ask any satisfied customer," she said. She poured him a second cup of coffee. "And what about this girl you like so much? The other one?"

"What other one?"

"The one you said you threw over." Daisy's voice rose teasingly. "The nice Jewish one?"

"I talked about her?"

"I'll say."

He said nothing for a moment. He had thought he dreamed it. Telling one of the girls last night that he probably deserved Charlotte Daniels's cruel treatment because of his own cruelty to Ellie Baer. And now he realized what a mistake he made in dropping Ellie. What a loss. She loved him, and for himself. In what he believed was the dream, he said he thought it would have been nice married to Ellie. She would be good for him. He needed her. They needed each other.

He had a third cup of coffee. Then he phoned Harry to come pick him up, and bring $500 in cash. Harry was there in less than thirty minutes. Leo tucked the five one-hundred-dollar bills into Daisy's brassiere, kissed her good-bye, and left with Harry.

The Buick sedan was parked at the curb. Sal stood at the open car door. "You all dried out?" he asked.

"Yeah," Leo said. He started lighting a cigarette, then put the cigarette and lighter back into his pocket. He did not feel like smoking; his throat was scratchy, and he had a slight headache. Either a cold coming on, he thought, or my little walk in the rain. Or a hangover. He got into the backseat, Harry and Sal in front, Harry driving. For a moment no one spoke. Leo thought they were awaiting an explanation and debated telling them the truth.

But neither seemed interested. Sal leaned over the rear of the front seat and faced Leo. "You know, don't you, I had to talk him"—he nodded at Harry—"out of going after Arnie?"

"Going after Arnie for what?" Leo asked.

Harry then told Leo of his suspicion that Leo's disappearance was "arranged" by Arnie. Leo closed his eyes in dismay. One of these days Harry would jump into a place from which there was no rescue. Unless they were careful he would take them all down with him.

Leo opened his eyes as Sal said, "We need Arnie."

Need, Leo thought, the word flashing before his eyes. That's what you said about Ellie, he told himself. You need her. You need each other.

". . . for right now, yeah," Harry was saying. He glanced at Leo in the rearview mirror. "But I'm telling you, I got a hunch it won't be for long." He looked at Sal now. "If Arnie ain't spending his time at the racetrack, or in a poker game, he's chasing some skirt. While we do all his dirty work, for Christ's sake!"

Sal said, "Sure, but it's us that's making the connections. The customers trust us and rather do business with us. Just be patient, okay?"

"Yeah, well, let me tell you what else I heard," Harry said. "He's losing his ass, Arnie is. They been killing him. They say he's lost the touch."

"It's called the Law of Averages," Leo said. "It catches up with all of them. Sal's right. Just be patient." He leaned forward and nudged Harry's shoulder. "Turn down Forty-second."

"What for?" Harry asked. "We're going to the garage, ain't we?"

"You are," said Leo. "I'm going to the library."

She did not immediately see him. The reading room was quite busy. A dozen people were lined at the desk. Leo stood behind a stooped, white-haired old man who clutched a yellow legal pad containing a list of numbered questions. Then it was Leo's turn. Ellie had lowered her head to write a notation on her log. Leo watched her a moment, then said, "Could you recommend a Joseph Conrad book besides *Lord Jim*?"

"Have you read *Victory*?" she replied, not looking up. For an instant her eyes remained fixed on the logbook. Now, slowly, she looked up.

"I read it," Leo said. "Recommend another."

"*The Rover*," she said. "It's his latest."

"Come and have lunch with me."

"I've already had lunch."

"Then marry me."

Ellie stared at him.

"Marry me," Leo said.

Ellie glanced around, embarrassed. "Are you serious?"

Behind Leo, a middle-aged frumpy woman with thick glasses said, "Hey, mister, this is all very romantic but I have to get home and make supper."

"In a second," Leo said, looking at Ellie. "You think I'd joke about anything like that?"

Ellie studied him. He was very tense. The frumpy woman brushed past Leo and confronted Ellie. "I'm looking for a newspaper, *The Danville Courier*."

"We don't carry it," Ellie said, and to Leo, "When?"

"Now," he said. "Today."

"For this I waited fifteen minutes?" the frumpy woman said. She stepped back and nodded at Leo. "Congratulations."

"Thank you," he said.

10

SAL cut into the veal chop. He excised a bite-sized cube and brought it to his mouth. The fat bald-headed man seated opposite him said, "Good, huh?"

"The best," Sal said.

"So eat," said Anthony Ruggerio, also known as Big Tony. He was five six and weighed 319 pounds. Twenty-seven years ago at age twenty-five he had weighed 140, but that was in Palermo where he worked as a laborer on a farm owned by a man named Giuseppe Battistini. Tony Ruggerio might today still be a farmhand had not Don Giuseppe's only daughter, a pretty girl of sixteen, unjustly identified him as the father of her unborn child.

Tony was himself the illegitimate son of a milkmaid, so to Don Giuseppe the prospect of such a son-in-law was clearly unthinkable. A practical man, he quickly chose a more desirable candidate. The true impregnator was never discovered. Understandably as it turned out, for it happened to be the Don's younger brother, the girl's uncle.

But practical as the Don was, he was equally as imprudent. Before discharging the innocent Tony, he ordered him beaten and personally administered a kick to the groin that not only crushed the right testicle, but necessitated its eventual removal. Early in the morning of the day following his hospital release, Tony stole into the Don's bedroom and looped a thin, rust-coated steel wire around the base of the sleeping man's penis. Then he woke him, nodded politely, and slowly pulled the wire tight. A washcloth previously stuffed into the Don's mouth stifled his screams. Tony had hoped to replace this washcloth with the Don's completely severed member, but the wire was not sufficiently sharp, although sharp enough so that in less than two minutes the old man lay dying in a pool of his own genital blood.

No one ever even remotely connected the ugly murder to Anthony Ruggerio, who at the time was believed hundreds of miles away in Naples. The perfect crime, made more perfect shortly thereafter by Tony's arrival in America.

Immediately, he fell in with a group of extortionists, fellow Sicilians, who discovered in him an extraordinary talent for devising cruelly ingenious methods of communicating with stubborn shopkeepers and small businessmen. His rise to leadership was almost as predictable as his accumulation of body fat. He loved food and drink, any and all kinds, and was known to consume at a single sitting as much as two pounds of pasta, as an appetizer, washed down with an entire fifth of his own strong, rich red Chianti. It was also said of him that in the old days, when not as heavy and far more agile, he sometimes enjoyed a full meal immediately prior to that day's killing or torturing. He claimed it sharpened his senses.

He sat now with Sal Bracci this pleasant Indian summer afternoon of 1924 at the back table of a small Mulberry Street family restaurant. At another table, far enough from both men not to easily overhear but close enough to clearly see, was young Thomas Marizzi. Nearby, similarly distant, were two of Big Tony's men. Both, like Marizzi, armed. Sal was not; he never carried a weapon.

The purpose of this luncheon meeting was to discuss a certain, urgent business matter, Sal's current affiliation with what Tony termed "The Jews." The gist of it was that Tony, recognizing in Sal a potential Crown Prince, believed it was time Sal returned to his own kind.

"These people are natural businessmen who are good at making money, so I understand why you've associated with them," Tony said, his gaze fixed with interest on Sal's half-eaten chop. "And I think it was smart. I think you're smart."

"Thank you," Sal said modestly. They were talking in Italian, and with a formality that was considered a sign of mutual respect.

"Do you agree?" Tony asked.

"I can't agree to anything, Don Antonio," Sal said. "Until I hear more of what you have in mind."

Tony laughed, amused. His jowls, spilling over his tight celluloid shirt collar and concealing the knot of his tie, quivered like jelly. "Yes, I heard you were a cautious one," he said. "And I've also heard you had the same conversation just last week with Pasquale Carbo."

Of the half-dozen meaningful Sicilian groups, Big Tony Ruggerio's only important rival was Patsy Carbo. And the two were blood enemies, a feud dating back some twenty years. Each, within his respective territory, had prospered—bootlegging, gambling, extortion, prostitution —but neither yet had really more than tasted the incredible riches of Manhattan north of Fourteenth Street.

The problem, of course, was Arnold Steinberger's Italian-Jewish coalition. The key to the problem was Salvatore Bracci. If Sal broke with the Triad the Jews would not have the manpower to withstand an assault. And then either Anthony Ruggerio or Pasquale Carbo, depending upon whom Sal joined, would be undisputed King.

"Yes," Sal said now. "We talked."

"He offered to take you in with him?"

"As a full partner," Sal said. He cut another piece of veal and ate it. He touched his fingers to his lips in a gesture of approval. Big Tony smiled, pleased, and deftly twirled a forkful of pasta onto his spoon. He inserted the fork into his mouth and pulled it out, empty. He rolled the pasta around his tongue and teeth. He chewed briefly and luxuriously, and then swallowed, following immediately with half a glass of wine.

"What was your answer to Patsy?"

"I said I wanted to think about it," Sal said.

Almost daintily, Tony dabbed each corner of his mouth with his napkin. He tucked the napkin back into his shirt and nodded again. "As I said, smart."

"You call it smart, I call it careful," Sal said.

"Smart, careful. In this case, the same."

"Okay," Sal said in English, and then in Italian. "So what's your proposition?"

"You bring your boys in with me," Tony said. "It makes us big enough to take on Patsy Carbo who, believe me, will waste no time stepping aside. At the same time, with you gone, the Jews are so weak they can either stay and fight, which I frankly prefer because it finishes them once and for all. Or they can step aside like Patsy." He twirled another forkful of pasta. "However it goes, you and I come out on top." He emptied the food into his mouth. Momentarily training his eyes on the ceiling, he chewed and swallowed, paused an instant for the food to reach his stomach, then drank down the remaining wine in his glass. He leaned back and belched contentedly. He smiled and said, "So you see, Salvatore, unless you come in with me, we have a problem. You and I, I mean."

Sal said nothing. Squeeze play, he was thinking. Patsy Carbo had used almost identical words.

Tony said, "So you'll think it over?"

"Yes, I will, Don Antonio," Sal said.

"But please don't take too much time."

The remainder of the lunch was spent discussing the rottenness of

American politics—next month's presidential election was in the bag for the Republicans, Calvin Coolidge's Protestant Prohibitionists—and with Tony urging Sal to find a nice Sicilian girl to marry. It was time he settled down and raised a family.

Strangely, Sal had himself been pondering that very question. And after leaving the restaurant he had Tom Marizzi drive him to Carol Beech's so he could think about it more. At least the enjoyable part. Carol was a dancer, a friend of Arnold Steinberger, whose affair with the judge's wife was over; Arnie had become simply too notorious for that lady's good name. Arnie introduced Carol to Sal some months before at Chez When. A few weeks later, at "21," Sal ran into her again. She was not a whore, and he liked her, although not enough to marry. He was not sure he respected her enough.

A woman like Leo's wife, you respected. Although he had seen her only twice in the year since Leo married her—Leo insisted on keeping business and homelife separate—Sal considered Ellie an ideal wife. And eight months pregnant. Leo wasted no time.

Sal spent the night with Carol Beech, and in the morning volunteered to start paying the apartment's monthly rent. Carol graciously declined. She preferred her independence. Before he left, Sal folded a hundred-dollar bill under her pillow.

When Sal phoned, Leo was in the bathroom shaving. A huge bathroom, white-tiled, with a separate shower stall and marbled towel racks with large, fluffy towels bearing a monogramed initial *G*, designed as a crest, surrounded by smaller initials *E* and *L*. He liked to say that when they rented this two-bedroom Riverside Drive apartment it was the bathroom that sold him. Thinking about that, he remembered the community toilet on Delancey Street, sometimes with three people lined up waiting to get in. And you could be sure whoever was inside was either reading or playing with themselves, the latter of which he had certainly done his share.

"Leo, it's for you." Ellie stood in the doorway brushing her fingers through her sleep-rumpled hair. She hated looking sloppy, even in the morning. She stepped into the bathroom and handed Leo a face towel as he groped for one near the sink.

"Thanks," he said, wiping lather from his face and studying her. She was gigantic, which he hoped meant a big baby. Tall, especially if a boy. "Who is it?"

"Your friend Sal."

She always referred to Sal or Harry as "your friend." By now, of course, she knew Leo's business was bootlegging, and had thoroughly surprised him with her apparently unqualified acceptance of it. Prohibition was after all an unpopular and unrealistic law. Breaking it was no more immoral than fixing traffic tickets. They had however agreed to keep it from her parents, who still believed Leo part-owner of a garage and delivery service. Which was not untrue.

Selma Baer had never forgiven Leo for refusing to be married by a rabbi. She had not objected to the civil ceremony at City Hall, assuming the two would shortly thereafter stand before a rabbi. After finally realizing this would never happen she sulked for months. Only when Ellie announced her pregnancy did Leo's mother-in-law warm up to him.

He patted Ellie's stomach. "Feel okay?"

"I feel fine."

"No more morning sickness?"

"Not for weeks."

"That's right," he said. "They say after the seventh month it goes away."

"I made some coffee," she said.

"Good," he said, and went into the living room to answer the phone. Sal wanted to see him as soon as possible. There was a problem he could not discuss on the phone. They arranged to meet in an hour at a Waldorf Cafeteria on Fifty-second Street. Only after he hung up and dressed and swallowed down some black coffee, did Leo remember he promised Ellie to spend the day with her, the whole day. She saw so little of him, not only during the week but weekends as well.

"I'll be back before noon," he said. "We'll take a walk along the river, or something."

"How many times have I heard that?" she asked. " 'I'll be back before noon.' "

He was at the door, slipping into his suit coat and moving to leave. "Ellie, I said I'd be back before noon." He was gone before she could reply.

He waited impatiently for a cruising taxi, wondering if it wasn't time he had a chauffeur. Arnie, after all, had a regular driver; two, although they were actually bodyguards. Harry was using Bernie Kopaloff, and Sal had Tom Marizzi. Leo, who thus far refused a bodyguard, had begun thinking that perhaps as a new father he should be more careful.

A taxi finally appeared. He got in and settled back, telling himself he was not annoyed at Ellie's injured tone, but knowing he was—but only from his own guilt. Yes, he should spend more time with her. There just did not seem to be enough hours in the day.

In the past year alone the Triad had extended its monopoly on quality liquor distribution to include all the northeastern states. And trade agreements had been made with groups in Chicago, Kansas City, Cleveland, St. Louis, and Detroit. These agreements—treaties, more literally—designated sales territories and spheres of influence, so that one organization did not interfere with or overlap the other. The Independents, comprised in New York mainly of Italian families, had up to now been successfully contained. But Leo knew they would soon feel strong enough to move.

You know, he told himself, gazing out at an empty barge moving north along the river toward the open sea, maybe I shouldn't have gotten married. Maybe it's not fair.

Not fair to who? he asked himself. Me, or her?

To both, he answered himself.

But I like being married, he thought. Almost everything about it, especially the sex. Although the very first night he was not that pleased, nor was Ellie. A virgin, the whole experience was extremely unpleasant. But after that, what a difference! She was a tiger, clawing and screaming and writhing about, and never seeming to get enough. He chuckled to himself, thinking of Ellie's sexual appetite. And how invariably, the instant he was inside her, she shouted, "Give it to me! Give it to me!" The first time she did it shocked them both. Afterward, when she apologized, Leo said, "A nice Jewish girl . . . !" They laughed for hours.

The taxi dropped Leo at the Broadway entrance of the cafeteria. Sal sat at a table near the window. Leo plucked a ticket from the machine, tucked it into his hatband, and walked through the turnstile.

"Had breakfast?" Sal asked.

"I had coffee at home," Leo said. He pointed a finger at the dark circles under Sal's eyes. "Ten gets me one you spent the night with the lady from Texas—what's her name? Caroline?"

"You only bet on sure things, don't you?"

"Arnie told me you and she hit it off."

"She's a nice kid," Sal said. "Arnie did me a favor."

"All right, five gets me one that's what you wanted to talk about," Leo said. "Arnie."

"No, not exactly."

"Then what?"

"Well, while we're on the subject of Arnie, let's talk about him," Sal said. He seemed almost eager to discuss Arnie, as though it at least temporarily postponed dealing with something more troubling. "Leo, he's getting to be a problem."

"Arnie?"

"Yeah, Arnie." Sal leaned forward. "We all have our jobs. You do the purchasing and keep everything smooth with the police and the politicians, and the judges. I handle the drivers and distribution. Harry takes care of security. Even Hershey does his job, keeping the trucks and cars moving. But, Leo, what the hell does Arnie do?" Sal answered his own question. "He collects his share, and goes his merry way. When you need him he's never around."

"He's still our partner," Leo said quietly.

"I heard he beat a Cleveland businessman out of fifty grand—with marked cards."

Leo said, "Players like Arnie don't have to cheat."

"They might if they're on a bad streak. And he is. I also heard he dumped the same fifty thousand at the track. Listen, he admitted to me he lost over two-fifty this year alone. Two-fifty, would you believe it?"

"It's his money," Leo said. "He can do whatever he likes with it. And I'll say it again, Sal. He's still our partner."

"Then let him act like it," Sal said. "Or else step aside."

They regarded each other a silent moment. It was as if an issue once considered taboo had suddenly, courageously, been addressed and no longer seemed so forbidding. Leo said, "Why don't we talk to him about it?"

"What about all our big plans for Florida?" Sal said. He referred to their decision to open a Monte Carlo–style casino outside Miami in the next two years. "Why give Arnie a free ride?"

"Let's talk to him," Leo said, and even as he spoke the image flashed into his mind of himself watching, awed, Arnie Steinberger bluff a poker pot by standing pat with two small pair. A hundred years ago. "Let's ask him that question."

"He's in Saratoga," Sal said. "He won't be back for two weeks."

"When he comes back, then."

"Yeah, we'll ask him to show us how to stack a deck," Sal said, and Leo knew immediately that Sal was concerned with something far more serious than Arnold Steinberger.

"Spill it," Leo said.

"You can read my goddam mind, can't you?" Sal said, and told Leo of his conversation yesterday with Tony Ruggerio, and Patsy Carbo before that.

When Sal finished, Leo thought about it a moment. Then he lit a cigarette. "You're in a box," he said.

"Yeah," Sal said. "Slam-bang in the middle. I go with Ruggerio, I have Carbo on my back. With Carbo, Big Tony comes after me." Sal drew in his breath to continue, then unexpectedly stopped. He seemed almost embarrassed, as though he had caught himself about to say something shocking.

Leo said it for him: "And, of course, you leave us, then we have to go after you."

Sal's face was set stonily; the little scar on his cheek, the souvenir of a back-room police interrogation, reddened. "Why do you think I'm telling you all this, Leo?"

"The same reason I'd tell you. "It's called 'self-serving.' "

"Swim together, or sink, huh?"

"You knew it would happen one day. We talked about it."

"I didn't think it'd be so soon. We're doing so good now, too, goddamit! Everything's going for us!"

The sudden anger surprised Leo. Sal seldom displayed any emotion, a characteristic Leo admired, for it almost always placed his antagonists at a disadvantage. His friends, too, on occasion; Sal's calm sometimes drove Harry wild. Leo said, "Relax. We'll figure something out."

"He wants an answer, Ruggerio," Sal said. "I can stall only so long."

"How strong do you think they really are?" Leo asked. "Big Tony, and Carbo?"

"They're organized now," Sal said. "That's the trouble."

Leo glanced out the cafeteria window. A bus had stopped for passengers, blocking all vehicles behind it. The uniformed policeman directing traffic from the glass-enclosed ten-foot-high platform in the middle of the Fifty-second Street and Broadway intersection impatiently gestured the bus driver to move on.

"How strong do they think we are?" Leo asked.

"It's the same thing, Leo. They think it's me that makes you strong. Without me, you're a pushover."

Leo wondered if Sal believed this, or merely relayed someone else's opinion. He did not want to make an issue of it. It would only make them both uncomfortable and achieve nothing.

He said, "What we have to do is get them to go after each other. Without you."

"They won't," Sal said. "They're too smart."

"Not if it's a matter of honor."

Sal smiled with genuine amusement. "You believe all that shit about Sicilian 'codes of honor'?"

"Don't you?"

"For Christ's sake, Leo, that went out with Garibaldi. It's business now. If it's not good for business, it's not good, period. They're starting to think like us."

Like us, Leo thought. Once Sal said Leo had a mind more Sicilian than any mafioso, but now it looked like he was more Jewish than old Rothschild. A *Yiddisher kop*. Business.

He said, "Would a conference with them do any good? Show how if we all work together, we all profit."

"Leo, they don't have anything we need. *We* have what *they* need, so if we come looking for peace they know right away it's out of fear. You'll see how fast they start testing our strength. I'm surprised they haven't done it already."

Leo said nothing. Three canvas-topped Ford vans rumbled past the cafeteria window, each directly behind the other. All bore on their door panels neat white-printed letters: MANHATTAN CARTAGE.

"Ten to one they're carrying booze," Sal said.

"No bet," Leo said.

Sal said, "On second thought, Tony Ruggerio and Patsy Carbo are old-timers. If one thought the other made a fool of him, maybe he would go after him."

" 'Maybe'?"

"Yeah, maybe. We get them to kill each other, Leo, they'll be too busy to worry about us. And when it's all over, too weak."

"That's what I've been saying."

"Yeah," said Sal. "It is, isn't it?"

They looked at each other a moment. Simultaneously, both smiled. Leo said, "Sink together, or swim."

Leo returned home, as promised, before noon. He and Ellie walked along the Drive. She talked about the baby, and decorating the spare bedroom as a nursery. And what they should name him. Him, because she knew it was a boy.

". . . after all," she said, patting her stomach, "only a boy could be this big. Or twins." She frowned suddenly. "My God! I never thought of that! No one I know of in my family, or yours, is a twin. No, it's only one. Steven. Steven, how does that sound?"

"What?" he asked absently.

"The name, Steven," she said. "Steven Jay."

"Fine," he said. "It sounds fine."

She chatted on, but Leo paid little attention. He was deep in thought, concentrating on Sal and that problem. The first real threat to the Triad. It had to be dealt with, and fast. And Arnie had to be consulted. But what the hell for? Leo could hear Arnie's voice: ". . . hey, kid, you handle it. That's why I made you my partner!"

". . . Leo!" Ellie had grasped his shoulder. She pointed behind them at a car, a Buick Phaeton carefully maintaining a distance of some fifty feet. "He's been there for the past ten minutes."

Leo said, "Past half hour."

"You knew it was there?"

"It's Howie Tobenkin," he said. "One of my drivers."

"But why?"

He said nothing a moment. After the talk with Sal, he had phoned Harry and asked him to recommend one of his *shtarkers* as Leo's permanent driver. A kid who was smart, tough, and trustworthy. Within an hour, Howie Tobenkin was parked outside Leo's apartment house. Now Leo answered Ellie's question.

"He's there because I want him to be."

"To follow us?"

"Yes."

"Why?"

"He'll be around from now on."

"But why?"

"Let's say it's a precaution."

She laughed. "Don't tell me you're afraid I'll have the baby right here?"

"You guessed it," he said, fast, forcing himself to laugh with her. "It wouldn't look good for the neighbors." He continued laughing, but it was a laugh of relief. He would not have to explain, at least not for the time being, the real reason for Howie's presence, with a .38 in his shoulder holster, and a sawed-off shotgun under the front seat.

Leo could never have guessed the near truth of Ellie's jesting remark about the baby being born right there. He was born twenty blocks away, two weeks later at 11:05 P.M., at the corner of Broadway and Ninety-fifth Street, and not exactly on the street, but in the backseat of a taxi en route to Lenox Hill Hospital. The taxi driver, the Irish father of five, served quite effectively—if somewhat reluctantly—as midwife.

A full-term baby, eight pounds three ounces, twenty-two and one-half inches long.

Steven Jay Gorodetsky.

Whose father was not present but was, ironically, at the moment of his son's birth, at another hospital. A small, private establishment in Brooklyn, the Lavner Clinic.

At the bedside of his critically injured friend and business associate, Salvatore Bracci, whose brutally tortured and beaten body had been discovered two hours earlier at the hospital's front entrance.

2.

Carol Beech's apartment was a large, cheery one-bedroom on the third floor of a West Eighty-seventh Street brownstone. Whenever Sal visited her, Tom Marizzi made certain the big Cadillac sedan was not followed. An excellent driver, Tom always took a different route and always double-checked the cars parked on the street.

When Sal stayed overnight, Tom went home to his own Christopher Street apartment. Returning for Sal in the morning he would press Carol's buzzer three times. A long buzz, a short one, then a longer one. The signal that he was parked outside.

This late September evening Sal and Tom Marizzi arrived at the apartment laden with groceries. A whole roast turkey, eggs, bacon, half a freshly baked ham, caviar, imported pasta, Italian bread, wine. Carol liked to cook, which pleased Sal. He enjoyed cooking himself, and tonight planned a carbonara sauce for the pasta.

Tom stayed only long enough to unpack the groceries and join Carol and Sal in a glass of Rubesco. He arranged to pick Sal up before nine the following morning. The instant Tom was gone Sal drew Carol into his arms.

"Shall we eat now, or later?" she asked.

He cupped her breast through her silk blouse. Immediately, under his fingers, the nipple hardened. And, immediately, so did he. "Later," he said. "We'll work up an appetite."

Later stretched into nearly an hour. Then, half naked, they went into the kitchen and began preparing the food. Sal switched on the radio he had bought for her, an Atwater-Kent apparently capable of receiving only one station, WEAF. So they listened to Paul Whiteman's music while they worked. Searching for a cigarette, Carol found only a crushed, empty pack. She had asked Sal to bring some, but he forgot. He had even written it down, and showed her the shopping list.

"I'll go get some," he said. "There's a store on Amsterdam I think is still open."

"Don't bother," Carol said. "I can live without them."

"Shut up," he said affectionately. "It's my fault. I never even looked at the goddam list." He slipped into his trousers and a shirt. He kissed her, and started out, only to step immediately back. He smoothed the palm of his hand into the curve of her buttock. "You know, you have the finest ass I ever squeezed. I'll be back in five minutes," he said, and hurried out again.

He was halfway down the block when he saw the car. A Cadillac, similar to his own but light brown. He saw the color under the streetlamp as it passed him. It sidled up a few feet ahead, then veered in toward the curb. Two men scrambled from the rear door on the street side. The driver's door was also open, but he remained behind the wheel, one foot planted on the curb as though to launch himself out if necessary.

"Get in, Sal." The speaker, bareheaded, was short and squat. The other was taller, and wore a straw hat. Sal immediately recognized him as Angelo Zaritto, Tony Ruggerio's number-one underboss.

They pressed him in between them on the rear seat. It was done so fast and smoothly that to an observer it would have appeared two men invited a friend on the street to join them. The driver slammed shut his door and sped off. Sal asked only once where they were taking him, and why. But all Angelo said was, "You'll see."

A useless question anyway, Sal realized, with an obvious answer. Big Tony was forcing the issue. And Sal was really not all that interested in where they were going; he would know soon enough. He was far more interested in who had fingered him, and disappointed because it could only have been Tom Marizzi.

Curiously, Sal felt no fear, but relief. Relief for Carol. A pack of cigarettes very likely had saved her life. Angelo Zaritto must have planned to hit Sal in the apartment; he never would have waited all night for Sal to leave in the morning. So if Sal had not made it so convenient for them by walking out into the street, and they had to go upstairs for him, they probably would have killed Carol, too. To make a point, convey a message. That was Tony's style.

But wait, he told himself, wait just a second. Maybe it wasn't Tom Marizzi. Maybe it was Carol. She could have tipped Big Tony easily enough. It made sense for a chagrined moment until he realized it was impossible for the Italians to even know of her existence unless informed by a third party, which could only have been Tom Marizzi.

"Yeah," he said aloud, to Angelo Zaritto. "It was Tommy, all right."

"Shut up, Sal. Just shut up," Angelo Zaritto said, which answered Sal's question, and saddened him.

They drove across the Fifty-eighth Street Bridge to Long Island City. The buzz of the car's tires on the ridged roadway reminded Sal of the sewing machine in his father's cobbler shop. The old man's fondest wish was for Sal to apprentice in the shop. The poor old bastard, Sal thought, remembering the last time the old man begged him to learn the trade, stop running with the gangs. Last time, because Sal left home then. Maybe I should have listened to the old guy, he thought, as the car drove off the bridge and along a street of darkened factories and warehouses.

The car turned in at a large, unmarked building. A door slid open. The car rolled in and stopped. Someone outside opened the car doors. Angelo Zaritto gripped Sal's arm and guided him across a long, empty floor and into a small office. The room's only furniture was a narrow benchlike table and several kitchen chairs. A single, dim light bulb hung nakedly from the ceiling; it cast a dappled shadow on a man seated at the table.

"Hello, Sal," Tony Ruggerio said quietly in Italian.

For the first time Sal felt fear, and then only because of the little smile of pleased anticipation on Tony's face. Sal knew precisely what Tony's next words would be.

"We got to teach you a lesson, kid."

"I was going to call you tomorrow." Sal spoke in English. He believed it sounded less pleading. He knew Tony wanted him to grovel.

Tony, still smiling, said, "Sure. Sure you were." He nodded to Angelo. Angelo twisted Sal's arms behind his back while another man, the short squat one, bound Sal's wrists with heavy cord. This man swung Sal around to face Angelo, who drew back his fist and plunged it like a jackhammer into Sal's stomach. It felt like a knife thrust, slicing deep into him, suffocating him. Before his eyes the whole room exploded in a burst of white, fiery sparks. Bitter, acrid bile surged up into his throat. He doubled forward, but immediately the man behind him struck him in the kidneys with a baseball bat.

Sal screamed. The sound reverberated through the room, and hollowly back into his ears. And then he was on the floor, the cement cold and hard against his face. Vaguely, he heard a voice in Italian. "Work him over good." He thought it was Tony Ruggerio, but could not be sure.

They pulled Sal to his feet. The short squat man supported him while Angelo Zaritto hit him with his fist flush in the face. Sal felt the whole side of his cheek crack.

They continued beating him. Angelo from the front, the other one behind. Sal felt a wetness inside his pants, flowing down his leg. He wondered if he had pissed himself, or if it was blood. Each time he felt himself slipping into unconsciousness, they stopped. But only long enough for him to revive.

Finally, they propped him against the wall. He realized his legs would not support his weight. He focused his eyes through the hazy gray cloud constantly obscuring his vision and saw a bulge in his left trouser leg just below the knee. He knew it was broken, and also his right arm, which he was unable to move. His mouth was so filled with blood he could not swallow without choking; and his tongue, although swollen twice its normal size, searched futilely over a vast, empty space where his front teeth should have been.

"Enough," Tony Ruggerio said in Italian. Angelo Zaritto guided Sal into a chair. Tony walked over and peered down at him. "Can you hear me, Sal?"

Tony looked so small, so very far away. Sal tried to speak but no words came. He tried to nod, but could not seem to move his head.

"He can hear you, Tony," Angelo Zaritto said. "He's a tough cookie."

"He sure is," Tony said. He spoke with genuine admiration. He said to Sal, "Now listen good, kid. Right now, you got to make me a promise. Your solemn word. You understand?"

Sal's eyes flickered with comprehension. Tony continued, "You will join my organization. No more bullshit, no more stalling. You are with me. Got it?"

Sal felt no pain, only a dull warmth through his whole body. He wanted to pass out, to sleep, but he also wanted to stay awake because he feared he might die and be unable to take his revenge. First on Tom Marizzi, and then on these animals. They were too stupid to realize that by not killing him they had guaranteed their own deaths.

"Sal . . . ?" Tony shook him impatiently.

"He hears you," Angelo Zaritto said.

"Do I have your word?" Tony asked.

Now Sal managed to nod. His neck felt loose and rubbery, but he knew he had done it. He had nodded, yes.

"Good. And to seal our bargain, you will do one other service for me." Tony said. "To prove your loyalty to me, you will kill Pasquale Carbo. As soon as you're better—and we didn't do you so bad you won't get better—you kill him. Agreed?"

Sal nodded again.

"Get him out of here," Tony said.

Angelo Zaritto and the other man dragged Sal from the room and put him in the car. Angelo sat in the backseat with Sal. Driving away, Angelo patted Sal's cheek tenderly. "You know, Sal, I didn't mean nothing personal." He was totally sincere.

A police lieutenant on the payroll had notified Harry, who rushed to Leo's apartment. It was only the second time Harry had been there; he did not like Ellie and knew the feeling was mutual. But this was an emergency. Thirty minutes after Leo and Harry left, Ellie went into labor.

Harry ordered three of his own men, and three of Sal's, to patrol the hospital round the clock. Leo remained at the hospital until Sal recovered consciousness and his injuries were assessed. A broken leg, arm, collarbone, and three ribs. Severe kidney damage. Facial lacerations requiring thirty stitches. Although too early for a realistic kidney-function prognosis, the other injuries would heal in time without complication.

Only then, a day later, knowing Sal would recover, did Leo even begin to consider their next move. He and Harry sat in Leo's car outside Lenox Hill Hospital. Parked directly behind them was Harry's Buick coupe. Harry's driver, Bernie Kopaloff, sat in the front seat with Leo's man, Howie Tobenkin. Leo had sent him into the other car so he and Harry could talk privately. Leo had just come from seeing the baby, who he thought resembled neither Ellie nor him. But then a day-old infant could hardly be expected to resemble anyone. What mattered was that he was healthy and, as the doctor said, mother and son doing just fine.

Harry was glad for Leo, and he'd give the kid a terrific present for his *bris*, but right now they had to deal with Tony Ruggerio. Allowed to get away with this, Tony would be encouraged to keep chipping away at the Triad. He would become stronger, and they weaker.

Between Sal's beating and the excitement of Steven's birth, it was not easy for Leo to concentrate. ". . . we hit the pricks now," Harry was saying. "We hit 'em good, with everything we got!"

"Harry, that's just what Ruggerio expects us to do," Leo said. "Go after him."

"That's what I'm saying," Harry said. "So let's oblige him."

"It's a trap," Leo said. "It's his chance to wipe us out. He's twice as strong as us."

"Bullshit!" Harry said. "One of our guys is worth three of them dagos. That's where he made his big mistake."

Leo gazed past Harry to the hospital stairs. Shifts were just changing, prim white-uniformed nurses coming and going. I wonder how my son is doing, Leo thought, picturing the baby in his crib in the maternity ward, the picture replaced almost instantly by Harry's stubborn-set face.

". . . think having this kid made you soft, or something. You're scared of them wops."

Leo looked at him and thought of Ellie lying pale and exhausted in her bed. Thankfully, even in all the confusion, Leo had enough presence of mind to fill Ellie's room with flowers. He had explained his absence at Steven's birth, and she understood, hoping only that what happened to his friend might bring home the reality of Leo's new responsibilities and obligations. The responsibilities of a family man.

"You're goddam right I'm scared," he said to Harry now. "But not of them, Harry—of you!"

"I'm supposed to be your partner," Harry said levelly. "I got as much to say about what we do as you."

Leo strained for patience. "First of all, you and I aren't strong enough by ourselves to move. We need Sal's people. And Arnie's, too. They won't budge unless he says so."

"Fuck Arnie!" Harry said. "He's not even here. You know where he is, Leo? In Canada, playing golf. You like that? Golf!"

"I know," said Leo. "I spoke to him this morning on the phone. He agrees with me. No hit."

"I can get Sal's guys to go with us," Harry said. "That'd give us enough."

"No hit," said Leo. "Now forget it."

"Forget it, huh? All of a sudden, you're the *baleboss*?"

Leo resented the challenging, hard edge in Harry's voice. He wanted to shout at him, make him understand, but felt very tired. Of the past forty-eight hours he had not slept more than four.

He said, "Harry, why do you always want to kill?"

"You know your trouble, Leo?" Harry said. "You always think you can solve things with your brain. Some things, you can't. Because you ain't dealing with people that use theirs."

Two nurses walked past on the sidewalk. Harry smiled at them. They did not smile back.

"I'm not the *baleboss*, Harry." Leo forced himself to keep his voice calm and quiet. "I'm your partner, just like you said. But I'm trying to make you see that instead of us killing the Italians, we have to get them to do it to each other. Ruggerio and Carbo, let them do it for us. Let them knock off each other."

"So how's that supposed to happen?" Harry asked. He brought a comb from his pocket and ran it through his hair. For the very first time Leo noticed a speck of gray at Harry's temple.

"I don't know yet how it's supposed to happen," Leo said. He glanced through the rear window at the two men in the car behind them. "I don't know yet," he said. He turned front again and faced Harry. "We have to find a way."

Harry said, "I make a deal with you, Leo. I give you until Sal's on his feet. If by then you haven't figured out how to do this idea of yours, then we do it my way. Yes?"

Leo said nothing a moment. He gazed absently at Harry's tight-buttoned celluloid collar that glistened with sweat from Harry's neck; it had even stained the knot of his red polka-dotted tie. Leo thought the tie went well with the blue shirt and white collar. A nice color combination. He smiled, thinking, I will have to get my son red polka-dotted diapers. My son, he thought, rolling the words around on his tongue. My son. He smiled again.

"What the hell's so funny?" Harry asked.

"Nothing," Leo said. "Okay, we have a deal. We wait until Sal is better.

But right now there's something else we have to do."

That something else was the traitor, Tom Marizzi.

Leo had expected Tom Marizzi to be long gone, or in hiding under Tony Ruggerio's protection. But yesterday, astonishingly, Tom Marizzi had walked into the garage—asking if anyone had seen Sal.

Now Tom Marizzi was locked up in Sal's own apartment in the Hotel Astoria, guarded by one of Harry's men and one of Sal's. Leo almost admired Tom Marizzi's coolness. He claimed he went to pick Sal up at Carol Beech's apartment that morning. Learning Sal never returned with the cigarettes, Tom drove straight to the garage to see Leo or Harry. When he heard what happened to Sal, he was "shocked." He understood immediately what he was accused of, and why Sal might believe him guilty, but swore he was innocent. Would he be standing here talking to them otherwise?

This troubled Leo. Tom Marizzi was either incredibly stupid, or ingeniously clever. Leo considered him neither. But Leo had promised Sal he would deliver the man who fingered him. At least two people knew that man's identity. One Was Tony Ruggerio. The other was Angelo Zaritto.

Two nights later Angelo Zaritto lay naked on the cold tiled floor in the bathroom of Sal Bracci's hotel apartment. His body a bloody mass of welts and bruises, his wrists bound behind him with the silk sash of Sal's dressing robe, he huddled against the side of the porcelain bathtub and watched Tom Marizzi fill the tub with steaming hot water.

"You talk, Angelo," Tom said. "Or you get a bath. In the hot water, Angelo. Real hot, like how they boil a lobster." He had really enjoyed himself this past hour. He wanted this man who had nearly killed Sal to suffer and then, slowly, die.

Sal's men had found Angelo Zaritto eating supper at his mother's Washington Street flat. They notified Harry who rushed down and took him at gunpoint. Angelo's mother thought Harry a cop. "My boy, he a gooda boy," she pleaded. "He no do nothin' that breaka da law." Harry said he couldn't help laughing, thinking how if it was his mother, she'd have given them hell for not arresting her rotten son long before this.

Harry brought Angelo Zaritto to the Astoria Hotel and turned him over to Tom Marizzi. Now, while Harry waited in the living room, Tom prepared the bath for Angelo. It would be Tom's one and only chance to prove or disprove his innocence.

"It'll get you clean at least," Tom said. He pulled Angelo by the hair to the rim of the tub and pushed his face into the scalding water. Angelo screamed.

"Do I do it again?" Tom asked, and laughed. "Like a lobster?"

Angelo had had enough. "Ask Billy Dalton!" he cried. Tom shoved Angelo's head toward the water. "I swear on my mother!"

Tom left Angelo Zaritto kneeling at the edge of the tub as he called
Harry in and ordered Angelo to repeat the name.

"Billy Dalton," Angelo said.

"What the hell does that mean?" Harry said.

"Billy Dalton, a guy from Cleveland," Angelo said. "Owns machine
shops, and like that. He's a friend of Tony's. His wife is godmother to
one of Tony's kids." Angelo paused for breath, then cowered as Tom
stepped toward him. "Honest to God! I'm telling you the truth! I told
you, on my mother's life!"

Harry said, "I still don't get it."

Angelo said, "Billy Dalton got skinned in a poker game by Arnie
Steinberger."

"Jesus!" Harry said quietly, almost a whisper. He felt his heart beat
faster. He cupped Angelo Zaritto's chin in the palm of his hand and
squeezed. Angelo gasped with pain. Harry said, "The guy that Arnie
took in that game, he's a friend of Tony's?"

Angelo nodded. Harry relaxed his grip. Angelo said, "Tony put out
a contract on Arnie. Hey, why you think Arnie ain't been in town much
lately?"

Harry stood. His hands were trembling, but from rage, not fear. He
looked at Angelo, then at Tom, then back to Angelo. He heard Angelo
Zaritto's hoarse, fear-tremored voice, and understood the words, and
hated Angelo for saying them.

". . . said if Arnie would finger Sal, the contract would get canceled."

Angelo paused for breath. Harry waited for him to continue, but
Angelo only stared at him. And then all at once Angelo Zaritto began
weeping, crying so hard his whole body shook. Harry stood there another
moment, then started away.

"I'll be right back," he said.

"What about this prick?" Tom called after him.

"Don't do nothing till I tell you," Harry said.

Harry phoned Leo who was at the hospital with Ellie. They spoke
several minutes. When Harry returned to the bathroom he seemed unhappy. He looked at Angelo, then placed the toe of his shoe against
Angelo's ear and toppled him to the floor.

"You bastards!" Angelo's words from his mouth pressed against the
tiled bathroom floor sounded like a muffled echo. "I told you what you
wanted!"

"Yeah, you told us," Harry said, and to Tom, "Let him go."

"What?" Tom was incredulous.

"I said let him go."

Harry did not like it either, but agreed with Leo. Angelo Zaritto would
never dare tell anyone he had talked. Tony Ruggerio, certain he had
convinced Sal to join him, would now wait for Sal to recover. So would

Leo and Harry. They would make their move when Sal was well enough to deal with the man who had fingered him.

Arnold Steinberger.

3

In the warm comfort of his own living room, discussing business with two of his closest associates, Arnold Steinberger's once legendary instinct failed him entirely. Never, not in the wildest stretch of his imagination, did he suspect that this early afternoon of February 10, 1925, was the next to last day of his life.

". . . if we do it," he was saying. "If, mind you. It means laying out at least a half million." He poked the log he had just added to the roaring fire in the fireplace. "The question is, is it worth it?"

Leo, standing near the window, watched Arnie adjust the fireplace screen and resume his seat in the leather wing chair. Leo said, "It is, if it gets him reelected."

The subject under discussion was an impending local election in Florida, Broward County. The incumbent sheriff, Eugene Colmar, had requested a $100,000 campaign contribution. In return, he guaranteed the Triad a free hand in establishing a nightclub-casino. The cost of this alone was an estimated $350,000.

Arnie said, "The trouble is, I don't trust him."

"We have to trust him," Sal said. He sat on the sofa across the room. "We don't have a choice, do we?"

"No," said Leo, glancing out the window at West End Avenue. It was snowing, the street white but for the crisscross black patterns of tire tracks.

Trust, Leo thought wryly. He marveled at Arnie's coolness. He turned from the window and looked at Sal. Sal was fully recovered except for some temporary trouble, as he said, with the waterworks. It was nearly four months to the day since Angelo Zaritto dumped Sal on the hospital steps. The doctors called his complete recovery a near-miracle. A phenomenal will to live. Leo knew the phenomenal will was in part the result of Sal's determination to see his enemies dead.

And the Number One Enemy sat here, smiling, relaxed, not a worry in the world.

Arnie said, "What happens if Colmar isn't reelected?"

"He's running unopposed," Leo said, and added blandly, "That's why he needs the campaign contribution."

"Look, Colmar's coming up here the day after tomorrow for the money," Sal said to Arnie. "Why not see what he has to say when he gets here? You can decide then if he's on the level."

Leo said to Arnie, "We'll take Colmar to dinner. You'll meet us at the restaurant. I'll let you know where."

"All right," Arnie said. He got up and went to the little glass-doored bar built into the wall opposite the fireplace. He splashed some seltzer into his glass. "Anybody want anything? More coffee, Sal?"

"No thanks," Sal said. He rose and carried his coffee cup to the bar. "What do you want me to do about Tony Ruggerio?"

"Nothing," Arnie said. He looked Sal directly in the eye. "Nothing at all."

"Tony knows that Sal is all better," Leo said. He joined them at the bar. "Sal can't stall much longer."

"Tony knows we've brought people in from the Midwest," Arnie said. "So he knows we're ready for him if he's foolish enough to make a move." He pointed his glass at Sal. "I think that whole sorry business with you was his one and only shot. When he realizes he failed, that it didn't panic you into going in with him, he'll crawl back under his rock." He drank down the seltzer and looked at Leo. "We don't move."

"And Patsy Carbo?" Sal said. "What do I do about him?"

"Has he been on your back?" Arnie asked.

"I expect to hear from him anytime now." Sal's mouth curled wryly. "It's his turn to take me for a little night drive."

"No," Arnie said. "Patsy might be crazy, but dumb he's not. He knows Harry is sitting over on Grand Avenue with a dozen machine guns he can't wait to try out. Our only worry now, from either Ruggerio or Patsy, is they might decide to combine."

"Big Tony and Patsy Carbo?" Sal said. "Never." He laughed unhumorously. "Not even to get rid of Jews."

"Then don't worry about it," Arnie said. "Do as I say, and sit still."

"Okay," Sal said. "If that's what you want."

"That's what I want," Arnie said. He smiled. "Tell me, how's that little girl from Texas, Carol?"

Sal's face tightened. "She went back to Texas."

"Too bad. She was a nice kid," Arnie said, and to Leo, "The wife feeling better?"

"Much," Leo said. "Thanks."

"They get that way sometimes after a baby," Arnie said. "I'm glad she's over it."

Postpartum syndrome, the doctor called it. Not all that uncommon, he said, and would pass. Which it did, but was hell on Leo while it lasted. Sometimes Ellie did nothing but stare out the window and weep for hours. Then she would all at once rage at him for not being there when she needed him.

"She's fine now," Leo said. "The kid's great."

"Sorry I couldn't make the *bris*," Arnie said. "I think that was the week I was down with the flu."

"You were in Canada playing golf," Leo said. "That was when Sal got hit, don't you remember?"

Arnie snapped his fingers. "You're right. It's a week I shouldn't easily forget."

"You're slipping, Arnie," Sal said.

"Age," Arnie said, and they stood chatting another few moments, Arnie confiding inside information about an unannounced Jack Dempsey–Gene Tunney fight. The match would inaugurate the new arena under construction on Eighth Avenue, Madison Square Garden. Arnie had already made a $25,000 bet on Tunney, a three-to-one underdog. Leo said he doubted Dempsey would agree to fight Tunney. Not until Tunney proved himself a worthier contender. Sure, Tunney chopped up Tom Gibbons last year, but Gibbons was nowhere near Dempsey's class. Dempsey wouldn't waste his time with a Tunney fight.

"How about a little side bet on it?" Arnie said to Leo.

"How much?" Leo asked.

"A grand," Arnie said.

"No bet." Leo smiled. "You're too sure of yourself."

"You're smart," Arnie said.

Leo said nothing. He only smiled again.

At four the same afternoon, in the private office of his real-estate company on the ground floor of a building on Mulberry Street, Pasquale Carbo received a telephone call.

From Arnold Steinberger.

Patsy, in the process of receiving his weekly hair trim and manicure, dismissed the barber and manicurist. Only his trusted assistant, young Albert Fiore, was allowed to remain. For practicality more than trust. Albert, American-born, could converse with Arnold Steinberger in the Jew's own language.

The Jew wanted to meet, to discuss a certain matter of mutual interest. Patsy required no translation to understand that the matter of mutual interest was the elimination of a mutual enemy, Tony Ruggerio.

Patsy Carbo was fifty years old, and no fool. He had arrived in America twenty-four years earlier, young, ambitious, strikingly handsome, and penniless. On his very first day in New York, he met and was befriended by Anthony Ruggerio.

The two were like brothers. Indeed, for a time, brothers-in-law. Tony had an older sister, a thirty-four-year-old spinster who had long abandoned all hope of marriage and children. Patsy married her. But handsome Patsy soon tired of the lady, openly consorting with other, younger women. Tony, himself a man of the world, understood these matters, but begged Patsy to consider the family's good name.

Patsy not only refused to listen, he suggested Tony not interfere in his personal life. Six months later Patsy's wife, Tony's sister, left her husband to move back in with Tony and his family. A few days afterward at four in the morning Tony smelled gas in the kitchen. He discovered his sister kneeling on the floor with her head in the oven. All the gas jets were on.

Three days after the funeral, Tony Ruggerio sent three men to kill Patsy Carbo. Tony did not know that one of those reliables was indebted to Patsy for his own life. Disassociated from Tony now, Patsy formed his own family, an organization that in less than four years rivaled Tony's as one of Little Italy's wealthiest and most powerful.

They were like brothers. Cain and Abel.

So when Patsy Carbo received Arnold Steinberger's call, he had no reason to question the Jew's motive. Tony Ruggerio's death would obviously benefit all concerned. He readily agreed to the meeting. At a restaurant in neutral ground, Lynch's, a small but excellent seafood café in Flushing. At eight sharp the following evening.

Patsy would never know that the man he and Albert Fiore talked with on the phone concerning the impending killing of Tony Ruggerio was not Arnold Steinberger. It was Leo, posing as Arnie.

George Gerson worked late at the garage that evening. He was upstairs having some supper with Hershey when Leo arrived.

"I thought you and Esther nad a date?" Leo asked.

"We did," George said glumly. He bit into a corned-beef sandwich. "Did," he said, his mouth full. "Past tense."

"He's doing the books," Hershey said. "You work him too goddam hard, Leo."

"I don't mind," George said.

"Well, then you won't mind this, either," Leo said. "I'm giving you a little vacation. In Florida."

George put the sandwich down. "What's the catch?"

"Colmar," Leo said. "Our sheriff. I want you to bring the money to him."

"I thought he was coming up here to get it?"

"He changed his mind," Leo said. He stepped across the room to the telephone on the high-pedestaled table beside the icebox. He jiggled the receiver, saying to George, "He heard it was snowing in New York."

George Gerson knew Leo well enough to understand that the flip reply was Leo's way of terminating further discussion. But Gerson knew no arrangement with the sheriff was to have been made until Arnold Steinberger met personally with the man. He listened curiously to Leo's telephone conversation.

". . . Arnie, Leo."

". . . . ."

"Eight tomorrow night," Leo said. "A place in Flushing you once recommended. Lynch's."

". . . . ."

Leo faced Gerson now as he continued into the phone, "Sal and I will pick up the sheriff at Grand Central, and bring him out to Flushing."

". . . . ."

Leo laughed and said into the phone, "Sure, we'll get him laid, too. Eight sharp, Arnie."

Leo hung up. He looked at Gerson a long moment. Gerson said, "That sheriff you were talking about? That's the same sheriff I'm bringing the money to?"

Leo looked at him another long moment. "Get the *Miami Special* in the morning, George."

"Okay," Gerson said. He was glad now he had not demanded an explanation.

At six the following evening in the Washington Hotel on West Twelfth Street, Patsy Carbo's second-in-command, Albert Fiore, left his third-floor room and walked down to the lobby. He heard his name quietly called.

Standing nervously near the vacant hotel desk was Angelo Zaritto. He gestured Albert over to a corner shadowed by a large potted rubber tree.

"What the hell do you want?" Albert asked.

"I got to talk to you," Angelo said. He glanced around the empty lobby. "It's important, Albert, no shit."

Albert looked at the clock above the desk. "Make it fast. I'm supposed to pick up the old man in ten minutes."

Angelo moistened his dry, cracked lips with his tongue. He wanted to turn and walk away.

"Come on, huh?" said Albert.

"I know where you're taking Patsy," Angelo said. "I know about it."

"You know about what?" Albert asked.

"Flushing," Angelo said. "Lynch's. Eight o'clock."

Albert tensed. He regarded Angelo narrowly. "What're you trying to tell me?"

"Jesus Christ, man, it's a setup!"

Albert said nothing.

"The minute Patsy steps into the place, he gets it," Angelo said. "Him, and anybody that's with him!"

Albert stared at him, then around the lobby, then through the dirt-streaked storefront plate-glass window to the street. Although it was too dark to clearly see outside, he knew his black Oakland sedan was parked at the curb with young Fred Conti waiting patiently at the wheel. He wondered what other cars might be parked out there.

"Angelo, I don't know what the fuck you're talking about," Albert said. "Patsy ain't going to no Flushing tonight. It's none of your goddam business, but where we're going is up to Harlem."

Angelo took in a deep, almost shuddering breath. "You guys are doing a meet with that Jew, Steinberger. He'll be there, okay, but so will Tony's guys."

Albert shook his head impatiently.

"I'm trying to help you," Angelo said. He was actually trembling. "You know fucking well what can happen to me for this!"

Albert shook his head again. "You're crazy, Angelo." But he looked away, at the window once more. He felt sick. When he turned, Angelo was at the door, pushing it open.

"You tell Patsy he owes me one," Angelo said, and left.

Albert stood a moment, thinking, then hurried to the door. He peered up and down the street. Angelo was nowhere in sight. Albert stepped out to the sidewalk and glanced carefully around again. Then he got into the Oakland.

"Mulberry Street," he said to Fred Conti. "Fast!"

Parked around the corner a block away on Eighth Avenue, facing south, was Sal Bracci's Cadillac. Sal sat in the front seat with Tom Marizzi. They watched Albert Fiore's Oakland race past. A moment later Angelo Zaritto appeared. He got into the Cadillac's backseat.

"Did he buy it?" Sal asked.

Angelo's face glistened with sweat. "I don't know," he said. He wiped his forehead with a handkerchief, and then his hands. "I think so."

"He'll buy it," Sal said. "And so will Patsy. He'll have to believe Arnie set him up for Tony. How else would Tony know about the meeting?"

"You're a prick, Sal," Angelo said hoarsely. "A real prick."

"No, the prick is Arnie," Sal said with a sour grin. "For setting Patsy up like that." He leaned over and patted Angelo's knee. "You did good, kid."

"You're a prick," Angelo said again. "Making me do this to Tony."

"Hey, what's better?" Sal asked. "This, or him finding out you sang like a canary about Steinberger fingering me?"

Angelo did not answer. He slumped back against the seat and gazed morosely out the window. Sal patted Angelo's knee again and handed him an envelope. "Five grand. Get out of town, *paisan.* Take the first train and get out."

Angelo pocketed the envelope and stepped from the car. Even in the chilly evening air he perspired. He wiped his hands again. He started away. Sal rolled down the window and called to him.

"Nothing personal," he said. "You know that, don't you, Angelo?"

Angelo Zaritto did board a train that very evening, the first one available. The *Lake Shore Limited,* to Albany and Buffalo. Leaving the 125th Street station, a woman told the conductor she thought she heard a gunshot from the lavatory. When they forced open the door they found Angelo Zaritto seated on the closed commode, his head nestled in the washbasin. The porcelain basin was filled with blood and gray brain tissue. The .32 revolver in the dead man's left hand was gripped so tightly that in prying it loose two of his fingers were broken.

Arnie never got inside the restaurant. Accompanied by Eddie Greenberg and Charlie Cohen, he casually approached the entrance. Just as Charlie reached for the door handle the headlights of an automobile flicked on. The car roared past, front and rear windows open. Arnie saw only the bright yellow muzzle flash of two Thompson submachine guns. He was dead long before the sound reached his ears. Eddie Greenberg was also killed instantly. Charlie Cohen, hit in six places, lived nearly a week, but never regained consciousness, and would have been permanently paralyzed.

One of the gunners was Albert Fiore. Safely away, he stopped at a roadhouse outside Flushing. He phoned Patsy Carbo. Patsy had remained in New York, prudently avoiding the trap he believed awaiting him in Flushing.

Albert spoke one word into the telephone. "Done."

That was the signal for the simultaneous assault by seven Carbo men on the offices of Rogers & Co., an import-export firm on Water Street owned by Anthony Ruggerio, and serving as his headquarters—and by four other Carbo men on a Turkish bathhouse on Avenue A where Tony was known to be this particular Wednesday evening.

Five of Tony's people were killed at the import-export company, and two at the Turkish bath. Patsy Carbo lost four men, two dead, two critically injured. Tony Ruggerio himself escaped, but was cut down three blocks from the bathhouse by Harry Wise who waited at Tompkins Square with three men for just such a contingency.

The following day, a twenty-three-year-old gunman named Guido Danza, fanatically loyal to Tony Ruggerio, caught two of Patsy Carbo's best men leaving the funeral home after a mass for one of their slain associates. Guido escaped, but the following day was killed by Albert Fiore. Four days later Albert himself was ambushed and killed in broad daylight outside his hotel. His bodyguard, nineteen-year-old Fred Conti was also killed.

In all, over a period of three months, what came to be known as The Battle of New York claimed twenty-seven lives and decimated the two powerful Italian families. It would be two years before they recovered. Two years in which Leo and Sal absorbed Arnold Steinberger's interests and consolidated them with their own.

By 1927, now unchallenged, Leo Gorodetsky and Salvatore Bracci controlled an organization employing more than six hundred people with an annual gross exceeding $75 million. They were bigger than the phone company.

11

THE roar of the airplane's engine, and the blasting propeller, and the wind rushing past the open cockpit made Leo feel even less safe and more queasy. He gazed below at the green and yellow checkerboard pattern of the Long Island farms and fields, remembering the pilot's warning about heat from the ground creating waves like those of a choppy sea. The pilot was right.

Three-year-old Steven sat in Leo's lap. The safety harness was belted tightly across the little boy's lap, securing them both. "How you doing?" Leo shouted into Steven's ear.

For a moment the boy's eyes were fixed straight ahead on the pilot's white scarf whipping backward into the rear seat's windscreen. Then Steven turned his head toward Leo and smiled. His huge brown eyes shone with pleasure, an expression of total, innocent awe that never ceased to amaze Leo. Nor did the boy himself. Particularly in the past eighteen months, growing and changing, literally as Leo watched, from a squalling, red-faced, pudgy blob into a person. They said he resembled his father. He had the Gorodetsky eyes and thick brown hair, but Leo thought he looked more like Ellie. The high cheek bones and firm jaw; you couldn't be sure yet about the nose, but it seemed Ellie's, which was considered aquiline.

Now Steven shouted, "The sky, Daddy! We're going into the sky!"

Leo nodded glumly. He gazed down, looking for the house. The pilot

said they would see all of Hempstead, but Leo saw only grassy fields and
clusters of buildings at the center of town, and automobiles crawling
along the road in both directions. He should have been able to find the
house. It was big enough. The huge Tudor perched on a gentle knoll,
on five acres with a little pond right in the middle. They bought it six
months ago: $45,000, cash. Ellie was still redecorating, a cool $5,000
itself, but it made her happy and kept her busy. The decorator, Frank
Lanier, a young man whose sometimes patronizing manner annoyed
Leo, was at this very moment at the house. Invited to dinner by Ellie to
see about making the cellar into a playroom.

The pilot racked the little JN-4 biplane around in a tight, descending
turn that made Leo feel his stomach had dropped through the floor.
Not Steven. Steven laughed with delight and banged his fists on the
cockpit padding. He wanted more. The pilot pointed ahead and below
at the airport, Roosevelt Field. The single dirt strip and the four hangars
with dozens of airplanes parked in and around them. Leo strained his
eyes for Ellie. When they took off she was standing near the largest
hangar. They had driven down to Merrick this Sunday July afternoon
to a farm that sold the best sweet corn on the Island. Returning, passing
the airfield, Ellie said, "Look, Steven, that's where Lindy took off from."

Steven knew who Lindy was. Last May, during the Paris flight, he had
insisted on listening to the radio for news of Lindy. So today, the instant
he saw the airplanes lined on the tarmac he asked Leo to take him into
the sky. To Ellie's horror Leo agreed. He had never been in a plane and
was curious. Now, although wishing they were back on the ground, he
was glad he came. The look of wonder and ecstasy on Steven's face was
worth it.

They flew another ten minutes, then landed. Steven immediately
squirmed out of the safety belt and clambered unassisted down from
the cockpit. Leo sat a moment, exhausted. The pilot, a young, pleasant-
looking man, helped Leo down.

Leo swayed momentarily. The pilot gripped his arm to steady him.
Leo said, "I'm okay."

The pilot grinned. "The kid's got you beat a mile, mister."

"I'll say," Leo said. He gave the pilot a ten-dollar bill for the six-dollar
flight. "Keep it."

"Thanks," said the pilot. He grinned again. "Come back anytime."

"Don't hold your breath," Leo said, and started toward the car parked
near the hangar. Steven was already there with Ellie and Hershey. Hershey hoisted Steven on his shoulder and went to meet Leo.

Hershey had decided more than a year ago that the business was
becoming just too big and complicated for him. Everything, all the money,
and George Gerson with his "diversification" and "corporate entities."
The offices had moved twice. Once from the garage to three suites in a
Fourteenth Street hotel, and again to half of the tenth floor of the

Peterson Building on West Thirty-sixth Street. And now it was called IDIC.

IDIC, for International Development and Investment Corporation. Although Gerson was listed as president, Leo explained that IDIC was a holding company whose true owners were Leo, Harry Wise, and Sal Bracci, with Hershey a substantial stockholder with substantial stock dividends, regularly paid.

While Hershey understood all this was merely a method of hiding cash and placing it in banks and legitimate enterprises, he preferred a simpler life. When Leo's regular driver, Howie Tobenkin, was hospitalized two months with a burst appendix, Hershey told Leo he wanted to replace him. No big deal, he didn't need to be a *baleboss*. He had more money now than he could ever spend, and would enjoy keeping an eye on young Steven. And Ellie liked Hershey and trusted him. Hershey loved Steven, and the boy reciprocated. They played together constantly. So now Hershey and Howie shared driving duties, with Hershey spending most of his time at the house. He even had a room over the garage.

"So how was it?" Hershey asked Leo. "The *shtarker* here, he's ready to go again."

"Yes, Daddy!" Steven cried. "Let's do it again!"

"You go with him," Leo said to Hershey. "I think I'll stay on the ground a while."

"You both will," said Ellie, joining them. "I thought I'd die a thousand times with the two of you up there."

"I thought I'd die just once," Leo said. "And for a while I wanted to."

"Can we, Mama?" Steven pleaded. "Can we do it again? Me and Hershey? Can we do it again?"

"Hershey and *I*," Ellie said, annoyed. "And the answer is no."

"Maybe another time," Hershey said. "For your bar mitzvah." He looked at Ellie. "Ain't that right?"

"Please, Hershey," she said. "*Isn't* that right? I spend half the day correcting Steven."

"It's how I learned English, Ellie," Hershey said. He ruffled Steven's hair and lowered him to the ground. "Never say 'ain't,' kid, *die helst*?"

"I want to go into the sky again," Steven said. "Hershey said I could."

"Let him do it, Ellie," Leo said. "How many chances does he get?"

"Not many, Leo," Ellie said brusquely. "Not many at all." She glanced at Steven. "No, you cannot go again!" She strode back to the car.

"I guess she don't like it when I say 'ain't,' " Hershey said wistfully.

Leo said nothing. He knew what bothered Ellie. It was him, always him. Today, when he said he was spending the day at home, she said it was a *mitzvah*. He did not pay enough attention to her, to them. She wanted a house on the Island, so he bought her a house on the Island. She thought it might give them more time together as a family, and be

beneficial for Steven. Better schools, certainly, better friends. And they
might even join a temple, although she should have known better. She
still hadn't forgiven him for their one and only conversation with the
rabbi she invited to tea one Sunday when Leo was home. Leo wrote the
temple a $1,000 check, but made it quite clear that other than Steven's
bar mitzvah, when that time came, he would never participate in any
religious activities. Ellie said she never was so humiliated.

He walked with Hershey and Steven back to the car. A new Pierce-
Arrow, with wire wheels and white sidewall tires, and the spares under
smooth, burnished metal covers in the wheel wells of each front fender.
Not bad for a punk from Delancey Street, he thought, lifting Steven
into the front where he liked to ride with Hershey.

Leo opened the back door. Ellie was just recapping the little silver
flask she carried in her purse. "Again?" he said.

"My nerves, Leo," she said. "It settles me down."

He got in. Hershey put the car in gear and started off. "You've been
having a lot of trouble with your nerves lately," Leo said. She was drinking brandy; he could smell it on her breath. She read his thoughts.

"At least it's good stuff," she said with a brittle little laugh. "It's yours."

Frank Lanier was a tall, Lincolnesquely gaunt man of thirty-two. A
Dartmouth graduate, he had an appreciation for fine furniture and a
talent for decorating he discovered to be more profitable than employ-
ment as a Wall Street customer's man. He was not a good salesman. He
found the very idea of forcing himself on reluctant clients repelling.
The man who hired him, a classmate, said the secret was first learning
to sell yourself, not be so sensitive, and not take initial refusals as a
personal affront.

Decorating people's houses required no self-selling; they came looking
for you. Which had certainly happened with Ellie Gorodetsky, whose
chauffeured Pierce-Arrow was turning into the graveled, curving driveway and rolling to a stop in front of the house.

Frank, cocktail glass in hand, hurried down from the front porch to
the driveway and opened the car's rear door. He assisted Ellie out. "How
are you, Mrs. Gorodetsky?" he asked. He nodded to Leo, "Mr. Gorodetsky."

Leo mumbled "how-are-ya," as Frank continued to Ellie, indicating
the glass, "I helped myself; hope you don't mind?"

"Not at all, Frank," she said. "I'm sorry we kept you waiting. Come
on in." She told Steven and Hershey to carry in the corn and give it to
Mrs. Morton, the cook-housekeeper, and ask her to start dinner.

While Leo went upstairs to change, Ellie and Frank went into the
huge, beamed-ceilinged living room where she immediately fixed another drink at the wheeled cellarette. "Refill?" she asked Frank.

"I'm fine, thanks," Frank said. His glass was still half full.

Ellie sat on the sofa and patted the cushion beside her for Frank to join her. "Tell me what you've decided to do about the playroom," she said.

"Well, I think if we knock out one wall, line it with cork, all four walls, it would make a kind of taproom," he said. "With a wet bar. Be a nice cardroom for Mr. Gorodetsky."

"My husband never gambles," Ellie said. She peered at him innocently over the rim of her glass. He did not smile, as she thought he might. She felt warm and cozy, and quite relaxed. "No," she continued. "He doesn't believe in it."

"What exactly is Mr. Gorodetsky's line of work?" Frank asked.

My God, she thought, he doesn't know. "He's in the delivery business," she said. "He delivers things."

"Oh," said Frank, and then began explaining in detail his ideas for the playroom. He had jotted down some cost figures when Leo and Hershey joined them. Leo's mouth tightened when he noted Ellie's empty glass, but he said nothing.

Hershey said, "Steve, he fell asleep. I guess he ain't hungry."

"I undressed him and put him to bed," Leo said.

"You're a good father," Ellie said. She got up and started to the cellarette. Leo moved to intercept her, but at that instant the phone in the foyer rang.

Leo hesitated in mid-stride. Ellie smiled defiantly at him. He hesitated another moment, then went into the foyer to answer the phone. Ellie poured herself a fresh drink.

When Leo returned he was pale. He looked at Hershey. "They raided Chez When," he said.

Hershey frowned, but before he spoke, Ellie asked, "Who did, darling?" She smiled again, and explained to Frank, "Chez When is a cabaret Mr. Gorodetsky has an interest in."

"We better get right over there," Leo said to Hershey. "You'll have to excuse me, Mr. Lanier. Come on, Hersh."

Hershey had risen but not moved. "Who did it, Leo?"

"I'll tell you about it in the car," Leo said, and to Ellie, "I'll call you later."

"What about dinner?" she asked.

"We'll pick up something in town." Leo nodded good-bye to Frank. "Let's go, Hersh," he said and left.

Hershey hesitated. He knew Ellie liked him to be in the house when Leo was not there.

"He's waiting for you," she said to him.

"Yeah," Hershey said, but remained in the room.

"It's all right," she said.

Hershey hesitated another moment, then joined Leo outside. Leo was waiting in the car, drumming his fingers impatiently on the doorframe.

Hershey did not get into the driver's seat, instead spoke to Leo through Leo's open window.

"Leo, Howie ain't here. I don't like to leave the kid and Ellie too long. You know what I mean?"

"Howie went to the movies in the village," Leo said. "He'll be back anytime. And Mrs. Morton's in the house, and that *fageleh* decorator. They'll all be fine, don't worry."

"Leo, whoever hit Chez When, they maybe are thinking of paying a visit out here, too."

"It was the police," Leo said. "The police raided it."

"Police?"

"Police," Leo said. "Get in."

In the living room Ellie heard the crunch of the Pierce-Arrow's tires on the gravel driveway. She finished her brandy and sank down into the soft sofa cushions. It felt wonderful, like sitting in a feather-lined hole. She giggled remembering once when Leo said she reminded him of that, a feather-lined hole. But that was just after they were married, nearly four years ago. How long now since they had sex? Weeks? A month? She giggled again. She should keep a diary, a log to remind her. A feather-lined log.

"I'm sorry," she said. "I just thought of something my husband said. It was quite funny."

An open, canvas-topped squad car was parked outside Chez When. Four uniformed patrolmen stood casually under the canopied entrance, and a wooden sawhorse, stenciled initials NYPD on the crossbar, blocked the club door. As Hershey pulled up behind the squad car, a patrolman stepped into the street to wave the Pierce-Arrow away. When he saw it was Leo he immediately touched the bill of his cap.

"Oh, Leo, sorry," he said. His name was Kelso. He had been on the payroll since Chez When's gambling room opened.

Another patrolman moved the sawhorse and opened the tufted-leather door for Leo and Hershey. Before they entered, Kelso took Leo aside.

"We couldn't help it, Leo," he said. "The order come from downtown and didn't give us no chance to even call your people."

"Where's Gruber?" Leo asked.

"We had to take him downtown," Kelso said. "Him, and the dealers. We let everybody else go."

"But you closed the restaurant, too?"

"Orders, Leo. I'm sorry."

"Sure," said Leo, and went inside with Hershey. They walked through the darkened restaurant, into the kitchen, and through a stainless-steel door disguised as a refrigerator. In the casino the lights were still on.

"Gottenyu!" Hershey said. "It's like a house I seen once in the *shtetl* after the Cossacks got through!"

The thick wall-to-wall rug looked as though gouged by a lawn mower. The two roulette tables lay overturned, the wheel of one propped against an upended table leg. The craps table, split in two, sagged to the floor like a bridge collapsed in the middle. All three 21 tables were smashed, with broken chairs heaped atop the wreckage. Shredded felt from the baize tabletops, strewn everywhere, resembled green snow.

"Back when we did the game in the garage, nothing like this ever happened," Hershey said quietly. "And all we paid the bastards was a buck a day!"

Leo said nothing. He kept looking around, shaking his head and telling himself he must remain calm. There had to be some logic behind it all. He could not think of any.

Hershey said, "What I want to know is, where was Mullen?"

The answer to this question, "Where was Mullen?," was answered some twenty minutes later in IDIC's office, in George Gerson's conference room.

Walter F. Mullen was an NYPD captain, a veteran of twenty-five years, to whom each and every Thursday afternoon an IDIC messenger delivered an envelope containing $200 in cash. Money Captain Mullen had cannily invested in real estate and blue-chip stocks, and which upon retirement would guarantee him an extremely comfortable old age.

". . . our good and faithful friend, Mr. Jimmy Walker," Mullen was saying, pausing now to tighten the knot on his brown silk tie. He wore a gray tweed suit, with a gold watch chain stretched tight across his big-bellied vest. A large, heavy-fleshed man, his thick brush of silver hair and ruddy face suggested a lifetime of fresh air and sun. Walter Mullen's only exposure to fresh air and sun in the past fifteen years—not including the mayor's annual July Fourth Southampton barbecue—came through the window of his Centre Street office.

Mullen continued, "He came down to the precinct in person, the mayor himself he did. Goddam sick and tired he was, he said, of the newspapers and the church people and all the other reformers calling him crooked. So if we valued our good names, we was to do something about it." Mullen laughed unhumorously. "Him, of all people, talking about 'good names.' Well, he says—he said it, mind you, the mayor did, I heard it with my own ears. He says, 'Those Jews that are running that clip joint up on Forty-seventh Street. Bust it up. Do it good. Axes and hoses, whatever it takes. But close up the goddam place!"

Those Jews, Leo thought, and all at once, for the first time that entire evening, felt anger. He drew in his breath and held it a moment to compose himself. They were all the same. They hated and were jealous of the Jews, but they took your money gladly enough. Just like that Henry Ford, who was forced to apologize in writing for his crazy Jew-hating ranting and raving. But only after the Jews organized a boycott

and refused to buy Ford products. Leo himself had sold every Ford in
the fleet.

He said, "You did a fine job, Captain. I hope you're proud of yourself."

"Leo, it could not be helped," Mullen said. "But I'll have you open as
soon as things quiet down."

"When will that be?" Gerson asked.

"Well, here's the thing," Mullen said. He cleared his throat. "It seems
the mayor has gone and decided to appoint some kind of commissioner
that will, as His Honor says, 'clean up the city.' "

"What, that again?" Gerson said. "Who is it this time?"

"We don't know yet," Mullen said. "But whoever it is, I'm sure he'll
be just another rubber stamp. If you get what I mean."

"Can we at least open the restaurant?" Leo asked.

"Oh, I'm sure of that," Mullen said. "Stay closed one more day, then
open up. I'll keep you informed on the other."

Gerson said, "Captain, you've very carefully not mentioned the other
places." He referred to the three other Manhattan gambling rooms. Two
on the Upper West Side, and one in Harlem in Jules Jefferson's club,
the Aladdin.

Mullen said, "I suggest you might move everything out of them places
for a bit."

"See to it, please, George," Leo said, and to Mullen. "I appreciate this,
Walter, believe me."

They conversed a few more moments. Mullen promised to have Wingy
Gruber and the dealers freed on bail before morning, and then Leo
walked Mullen to the door.

Mullen said, "You're going to be all right, Leo, one hundred percent,
you have my word." He cleared his throat again. "I'll naturally expect
that young fellow at my house Thursday as usual?"

"Naturally," Leo said. "As usual."

Leo returned to the conference room and told Hershey he thought
they might stay in town tonight instead of driving back to Hempstead.
The very prospect of riding an hour over those dark, narrow washboard
roads—even in the Pierce-Arrow—was too oppressive.

Hershey started protesting, but recognized the finality in Leo's voice.
The *boychick* did not want to go home, and Hershey knew why. He had
seen it in Leo's disapproving eyes just before they left the house when
Ellie drank down that last drink. That, though, was the very reason
Hershey wanted to get back. It made him very nervous knowing Steven's
mother was drunk.

Hershey said, "Well, maybe I'll call and see everything's okay." He
had already picked up the phone and asked for Hempstead 80. Hershey's
stomach began tightening when the phone went unanswered after half
a dozen rings. But then Ellie picked it up. She sounded sober, and said
Howie arrived an hour ago, and was in the upstairs guest room. Hershey

was relieved. He explained they were remaining overnight in Manhattan, and to tell Steven that he, Hershey, would be back first thing in the morning. He had promised to take the boy to a carnival over in Mineola. Hershey did not mention to Leo that just before hanging up he heard Ellie giggle and call out to someone, "Turn the record over." Over the phone, from the Victrola in the living room, Hershey heard dance music.

It was a tango, which the record-store salesman had predicted would soon overtake the Charleston in popularity. Ellie loved the lilting rhythm, and loved dancing to it. Leo, of course, never danced a single step in his life. Frank Lanier was a marvelous dancer.

They had finished dinner some time before and took coffee and brandy in the living room. Ellie put on the records. She had twirled about alone a few moments. Then she pulled Frank to his feet.

"Dance, mister?" she asked.

"Sure thing, lady," he said.

When Hershey called, the record had just finished. Frank held her tightly, one hand clasped around her waist, tilting her slightly backward so that for an instant they were frozen, peering at each other. The phone continued ringing. Frank placed his hand in the small of her back and pushed her upright, and suggested she answer the phone. She said she thought Mrs. Morton would get it. He reminded her she had sent the lady off to bed.

After speaking with Hershey, she returned to the living room. Frank had put on another record, and refilled their glasses. Ellie touched her glass to Frank's. "My husband is staying in town tonight," she said, and drank.

Frank said nothing. For a moment they stood looking at each other. "Are you married?" Ellie asked suddenly. "I never thought to ask."

"I'm not married," he said.

"I didn't think so. You don't seem the type."

He removed the glass from her hand and placed it carefully on the fireplace mantel, placing his own glass beside it. Then he kissed her. Tenderly at first, and then with more urgency. She collapsed in his arms and felt herself carried across the room and lowered onto the sofa. She lay on her back gazing up at him, and then grasped his head with both hands and pulled his face down to hers. They kissed again. In her mind she whirled and spun to the tango as his lips caressed her neck, and his fingers groped for her blouse buttons. The same fingers fondled the red, stiffened nipples of her swollen breasts.

She closed her eyes and let it happen. She helped him slide her underpants off, and herself reached down to kick them away. Now, her legs spread wide, she closed her fingers around him, the throbbing hardness. It is wrong, she heard herself telling herself in her mind, rubbing him against her own throbbing, now abruptly moist opening. But why is it wrong? she asked herself, guiding him in, arching her back against him, freeing her hands again to once again grasp his face and bring their mouths together. She felt him slide smoothly into her, and her own muscles contracting, drawing him in.

Vaguely, in the far distance, she heard the tango and imagined they were dancing. And they were, she thought, except that the music was blasting now in her ears and she stood at the rim of a huge, roaring red volcano.

Abruptly, the music stopped. She felt him unexpectedly heavy on top of her, but only for an instant as he rolled over and sat up and stared vacantly down at the carpet.

"I'm sorry," he said.

"It's all right," she said.

"I couldn't help it," he said. "I couldn't hold back."

"It's all right," she said, and it really was because she told herself now that by not coming she had committed a less serious sin. As foolish as that seemed, it made her feel less guilty, less soiled. She lay quietly, waiting for him to move, listening to the click-clack-click of the needle caught in the end grooves. Across the room in the doorway she thought she glimpsed a shadow. She closed her eyes, then opened them. The shadow was gone.

The shadow was Howie Tobenkin's. He had come downstairs for a beer, heard the Victrola spinning, and glanced into the living room. And saw them on the couch. For just an instant he stood transfixed, rooted to the spot through his own curiosity and sense of sudden, frightening power from the knowledge he now held, which in itself was frightening. He hurried away, knowing he had not been seen. His only thought was, Jesus, if Leo ever found out!

2.

Friday night, a week later, Howie was still thinking about it. He sat in the Pierce-Arrow, parked in front of Ellie's parents' Bronx apartment building. Leo, Ellie, and Steven were up there for *Shabbes* dinner.

Howie lit a cigarette and wondered, as he had wondered all week, how he might benefit from what he knew. And realizing, as he had all week, there simply was no way. Not if he cared to stay alive. While he prided himself in keeping the secret, he also would have enjoyed sharing it, but was afraid. All he could do was hope that someday his silence and loyalty would be appreciated.

He laughed aloud. One thing sure, the interior decorator definitely was no *fageleh*. He laughed again.

"Let us in on the joke, huh, Howie?"

The voice, hard and authoritative, came from the shadows behind the car. Howie reached into his jacket for the .38, but saw the glint of steel in the car window, and froze.

The same voice said, "That's right, son, don't go for it."

Two men, both holding guns, stepped into the dim light of the street-lamp. They wore straw hats set squarely on their heads and dark, tight-buttoned double-breasted suits. They were not old, but much older than Howie.

"Put your hands up on the steering wheel," said the second man.

"What do you want?" Howie asked, addressing the first man, who had just opened the door and slid into the seat beside him.

The man grinned. He had white, even teeth that gleamed in the dark and were too perfect to be his own. He removed the pistol from Howie's shoulder holster. The man was unaware that Howie's left hand, dangling between the door and seat cushion, rested on the trigger of a sawed-off shotgun.

"Just sit easy," the first man said. "Where's Gorodetsky?"

Howie gauged his chances. He felt sick being caught this way, drooling about Leo's wife fucking some *shaygets*. He knew he could handle the man who was inside the car, but if he used the shotgun, he could not wheel it around in time on the man outside. He might have a chance if, at the instant he pulled the trigger, he threw himself down on the car floor. And if he missed, if the man at the car window got him, at least Leo upstairs in the house would hear the blast and be warned. Howie would have done his job and perhaps in a small way compensated for his carelessness. It was worth the chance.

He said, "He ain't here. I'm waiting for my girlfriend." His finger curled around the shotgun trigger. "And what's it to you, anyhow?"

The man outside said, "You're under arrest, Howie."

Howie looked at him and knew it was true. They were cops. He read it in their voices, their whole manner. His hand on the shotgun relaxed. He relaxed. He slumped back in the seat and breathed deeply.

"Why didn't you say so?" he asked, and smiled with relief.

"So where's Gorodetsky?" the first man asked again.

Leo at that very instant was in the long narrow apartment foyer but-toning Steven's jacket. Ellie was kissing her mother good-bye. Alfred Baer stood contentedly watching.

"It was a nice dinner, Ma," Leo said to Selma Baer. "Tell your grand-mother, Steve."

"Nice, Nana," Steven said. He clutched Leo's hand. "Let's go home, Daddy."

Selma Baer laughed and picked Steven up, *"Mein schoenes kind!"* She hugged him and put him down. She said to Ellie, "Next Friday, again?" She looked at Leo. "That is, I'm presuming Leo will be away someplace."

Her voice carried such a note of censure that Leo nearly laughed. "You mean 'as usual,' don't you, Ma?"

"You said it," she said. "I didn't."

"I'm not sure yet," he said. "Ellie will let you know." His frequent out-of-town business trips, on behalf of what the Baers referred to as "this investment and development *geschichte*," were a constant source of irritation to his in-laws. Selma Baer constantly admonished Leo for not placing his wife's happiness ahead of his business.

He added now, "But if I am in town, we'll have to go to my mother's."

"Yes, of course," Selma said.

"But why not join us?" Leo said. "You and Al." He smiled at Ellie's father. Leo could just never bring himself to address this man as "Pa."

"We'll see," Alfred said.

Leo smiled again. He knew Selma cringed at the very thought of socializing with Leo's family. His mother, Sarah, had once gotten into it with Selma and Alfred regarding Leo's familial "neglect." Sarah defended her son, reminding Selma that in the old country a woman bore children and the man provided for them. Each did their respective job. Selma replied that this was not the old country, and if "you Russians" only tried to understand and accept that fact, all Jews might be better off.

Leo hoisted Steven on his shoulder and carried him downstairs. He did not immediately see the detectives, one standing outside the car, the other inside. As Leo put Steven down on the sidewalk, the passenger door opened and that detective confronted Leo. Immediately, the other one now also stepped into view.

"Mr. Gorodetsky," the first one said, flashing open his wallet to display the gold badge. "You'll have to come with us."

Ellie clasped her hand over her mouth to stifle a scream. She pulled Steven to her, shielding him. Howie had followed the detective from the car, crying, "They got me from behind, Leo. I didn't have no chance!"

"Do you have a warrant?" Leo asked.

"No, sir," said the detective. "We only want to talk to you a bit."

"My God!" Ellie cried. "In front of the child!"

"It's all right, Ellie," Leo said. Under the shadowy light of the streetlamp he studied the men, wondering if they indeed were police. He knew they were not Italians, although the Italians could have hired outsiders. He looked at their clothes. Cheap, off the rack. And the shoes, those thick-soled, square-toed brogans. If they weren't genuine cops, they deserved a medal for trying.

He said, "What do you want to talk to me about?"

"We'll tell you downtown," said the second detective. He nodded into the darkness of the block. "We're parked over there."

"Call Gerson," Leo said to Ellie. He ruffled Steven's hair. "Howie will take you and Mama home. Okay, let's go," he said to the men, and turned to Ellie again. "Everything's all right. Just call Gerson."

Leo and the detectives started off, but the first detective stopped abruptly and spun around to Howie. He unbottoned Howie's jacket and slipped the .38 back into Howie's holster.

"Don't say I never give you anything," he said. He hurried away and caught up with Leo and the other detective. They vanished into the darkness. A moment later, automobile headlights brightened the street. A black, four-door Packard sedan drove past Ellie and Howie.

"Jesus Christ!" Howie said. He slapped his forehead in sudden chagrin.

"What is it?" Ellie asked, alarmed.

"Nothing," Howie said. He opened the Pierce-Arrow door for Ellie and Steven.

Steven clambered in, but Ellie hesitated. She faced Howie. "Are you sure it's nothing?"

He looked at her. She wore a thin, almost sheer silk dress that even under the dim streetlamp silhouetted her body. It reminded him of the other night. Her, half naked on the sofa, legs practically wrapped around that guy's neck. Howie shook his head as though to erase the memory.

"Honest, it's nothing," he said. "Let's go call the lawyer." He waited for her to get into the car, then closed the door and walked around to the front. He opened the door but stood a moment gazing down the dark road. The Packard. He never heard of any cops driving Packards.

Leo was thinking the same thing. Not about cops driving Packards, but cops not going downtown. In fact, going the opposite direction. They were on Jerome Avenue, heading north, past the reservoir.

He sat in the back with the first detective. For the first time, he felt fear. He said, "Funny way to go downtown."

The first detective ignored the remark, but the driver spoke to Leo over his shoulder. "Look, Mr. Gorodetsky, just sit quiet, huh?"

"What's your name?" Leo asked the one beside him.

"Don't ask questions, okay?"

Don't ask questions, Leo thought, you son of a bitch! Now, anger and remorse dulled the fear. And sadness. They were on top of the world, and this was happening. But he should have known. It was bound to happen. Live by the sword.

Leo thought about Steven. He envisioned the boy grown up. A tall, handsome, charming young man. A law-school graduate, in cap and gown, receiving his college diploma. You should only live so long, he told himself. Yes, he thought.

"Turn left here, Jim," he heard one say to the other. Through the windshield the park loomed ahead. They drove in. Streetlamps positioned every hundred yards or so cast dim patches of light on otherwise total blackness.

"Right here," one of them said. The Packard slowed and pulled up behind another car parked at the roadside. The driver got out and walked to the other car. The man sitting with Leo did not move.

For one split instant Leo considered making a run for it. He could open the door, tumble to the ground, and run. But if they intended to kill him, they would have ordered him from the car. It would have been done by now. But simply sitting and waiting for it was stupid. Yes, he would try it.

He started sliding his left hand along the seat toward the door handle. Just as he was about to reach for it, the door on the opposite side opened. A man stood in the doorway, his body silhouetted in the weak light from the distant streetlamp. This man got into the car, while the detective got out. The man closed the door.

"Good evening," he said. Although Leo could not clearly see him, he immediately recognized the deep, resonant voice.

Robert MacGowan.

"I'm sorry for the dramatics, but the circumstances call for discretion," he said. "I had you brought here for a little chat."

Leo slumped back against the seat cushion, so relieved that for a moment he could not find his voice. "I would have preferred the telephone," he said.

"I find direct communication more satisfying," MacGowan said. "And more effective."

"This was pretty effective," Leo said. He knew MacGowan sensed his helplessness, and resented him for it.

"Isn't this how you people always do it?" MacGowan said. "Take someone for a 'ride'?"

"You're trying to make a point, Colonel. What is it?"

"I've accepted a job as Special Rackets Prosecutor," MacGowan said. "I mean to clean up this city."

"That's why you want a 'little chat' with me?"

"That's why."

Leo said nothing. He brought cigarettes and a lighter from his pocket. He shook a single cigarette from the pack and put it in his mouth. He lit the cigarette, straining to keep his hands steady.

"Little nervous, are you?" MacGowan asked, almost friendly.

"Just a little," Leo said. He looked at him in the dark, and waited.

MacGowan said, "In seventy-two hours, my office will make a sweep of this city. Every important bootlegger, racketeer, and gambler will be brought in. All the police and judiciary you people have bought will be rooted out. I'm not naïve enough to believe I can permanently eliminate all this vermin, but you'll all be on notice that from now on things won't be easy. You're on top of the list, Leo Gorodetsky."

"The vermin list," Leo said. "Thank you."

"I can't think of what else to call you."

"I have a feeling you're about to ask for my 'cooperation,' " Leo said. "In return for information, you'll make a deal."

"I don't need any cooperation," MacGowan said. "Nor do I need information."

"Then what kind of a deal?"

"I'm not making a deal, either."

"Then, Colonel, what the hell do you want?"

"I'm giving you a chance to gather up all your books and records—and get them out of sight. We'll be subpoenaing them. No matter how phony they are, when they're compared against your style of living and tax returns, it could make an interesting case. Oh, yes, you'll probably beat us in court but, Leo, if nothing else, life will be very uncomfortable for you. And, yes, things will cool down after a while. They always do. But you'd be surprised: we'll get lucky with one or two of you, and you'll be put away. I consider you a prime candidate."

Leo said nothing. He drew on his cigarette. He knew IDIC's existing books were not incriminating. Gerson was a genius accountant. And as for comparing them with tax returns and style of living, Leo believed this quite far-fetched. MacGowan's threats were empty.

MacGowan read his mind. "What I'm trying to tell you is that when you're picked up in this sweep, you'll be kept incommunicado for seventy-two hours, roughed up and third-degreed. Extremely unpleasant. And for the next few weeks, if you so much as litter the sidewalk, we'll pull you in. You'll see ordinances from the days of Alexander Hamilton exercised. So my advice to you is take a little vacation for the next month or so. Unless you want to spend most of it in and out of court."

Leo took a last drag of his cigarette and flipped it through the open window on his side. "If I'm such vermin, why are you giving me advance notice?"

"You know perfectly well why."

Leo did know, but had always considered the debt that MacGowan believed he owed was an obligation in MacGowan's mind only. But if the colonel wanted to pay off, let him pay off. It cost Leo nothing.

He said, "No, I don't know why."

"You did me a favor once," MacGowan said. "It spared me much embarrassment and heartache. It was a fine, honorable thing you did." His voice had softened, but again became hard. "But that was before you became what you are."

"Before I became what I am," Leo repeated. "And what am I?"

Again, only briefly, MacGowan's voice was soft, almost reflective. "Once I thought you'd amount to something. I thought you were a man who could make his people proud. Not bring them shame and humiliation. I thought you would contribute to society, not take from it. I thought you could comprehend the difference."

"By your standards," Leo said, hating himself for even responding, but unable not to.

"By any standards," MacGowan said. He shook his head sadly. "But what's truly sad is I think you actually believe you can justify your behavior."

Justify, Leo thought. I do not have to justify anything. The justification is in the bank, and in various safe-deposit boxes in various other banks. So much justification that I cannot even count it. Just the other week Gerson said Leo was worth a million dollars. A bloody millionaire, he thought, and this do-gooder reformer says I have amounted to nothing.

He said, "The last time we saw each other, in Glen Cove, you didn't think my being a bootlegger was so terrible."

"I was wrong," MacGowan said. "We were all wrong back in those days. We were naïve. We didn't understand what it would lead to. The corruption, the killing. But after tonight, Mr. Gorodetsky, we are even. The slate is clean. All bets are off. You're number one on my list."

And without another word, MacGowan opened the door and left the Packard. He walked to the other car. "Take him back," Leo heard him say.

All the way back, the more Leo thought about it, the more he resented it. MacGowan's attitude. So superior, almost smug, as though looking down on him. "Take a vacation." Patronizing, that was the word, as though he felt sorry for Leo and wanted to help him.

Well, Leo Gorodetsky did not need Colonel Robert MacGowan's help. Only when they entered Manhattan, driving past 125th Street, did Leo settle down enough to realize that not following MacGowan's advice could be foolish. Self-defeating. The timely warning could save IDIC considerable grief. Not only from a business standpoint, but personally as well.

A vacation was really not a bad idea. Get away with your family. Get to know your son.

And your wife.

12

IT was a small item on the lower right front page of the March 16, 1928, *New York Times*, with the headline MACGOWAN SWORN IN. Robert MacGowan, after resigning his position as Mayor Walker's Special Rackets Prosecutor, had been appointed assistant New York State attorney general, an office he said would enable him to more efficiently root out the criminal elements of our society.

Ellie knew the story behind the story. MacGowan's frustration with the Walker administration when the erstwhile clean up of the previous year lasted but a few months. The discharged police and politicians were replaced by others equally corrupt. In a Lions Club speech, MacGowan once compared his efforts to that of a child shoveling beach sand into a torn paper bag.

Ellie sat reading the paper in a small cafeteria on West Fifty-eighth Street near Columbus Circle. Each Wednesday afternoon she sat at the same rear table, with an unobstructed view of the cafeteria entrance. Wednesday was the day she came into town for shopping or the theater.

This Wednesday ritual began four months ago, almost immediately after returning from the Caribbean. Leo's "vacation" to Cuba, and the Bahamas. Six weeks of total boredom. Sitting in hotel rooms with little Steven and Hershey Lefkowitz, while Leo was constantly off on business meetings.

Leo certainly was not bored. Especially in Havana where he met with

President Machado to negotiate a gambling license for IDIC. Leo said
it meant paying off half the government, and then taking them in as
thirty-percent partners, but a sensible investment. The potential profits
were enormous, particularly now that Americans could fly to Cuba. Fifty
dollars, Key West to Havana, in little more than an hour. Leo predicted
the airline would be unable to meet the demands of gamblers for seats
on the planes.

This was after the four of them—Ellie, Leo, Steven, and Hershey—
flew to Cuba. At first she had flatly refused to step into an airplane, until
Leo showed her a newspaper story about Amelia Earhart planning to
be the first woman to fly the Atlantic. If Amelia could fly the Atlantic,
then Ellie could fly to Cuba.

She smiled, remembering Steven's excitement at "going into the sky"
again. Not in an open, flimsy little crate, but a giant airliner. A Pan
American Airways Fokker with three motors, and a steward serving hot
and cold beverages. The height of luxury.

The image of the airliner vanished with the quickening of her pulse
as Frank Lanier appeared. He strode toward her, very handsome and
distinguished in a gray-tweed herringbone jacket, blue shirt and white-
and-red-striped tie, dark trousers. It pleased her that he resembled an
English professor or writer more than an interior decorator.

"Hello." He sat opposite her and touched her hand.

"Hello." She entwined her fingers in his.

"You look positively exquisite," he said. "I love that dress."

"Thank you," she said, thinking he damn well should love the dress.
A wide-pleated-skirt Marjan original that cost a hundred dollars at Berg-
dorf's. She knew he would like it; it was quiet and tailored. Leo also
liked tailored clothes, when he bothered to notice.

"Have you had lunch?" Frank asked.

"Hours ago," Ellie said, still thinking of Leo and how little guilt she
felt. Yes, in the beginning, much guilt. But how rapidly it disappeared.
She smiled to herself, thinking that the pleasure from this relationship
—excuse me, she told herself, this *illicit* relationship—really should be
drowning her in guilt. "I have my affair, and he has his," she said
aloud.

"Excuse me?"

She laughed. "I said my husband is busy with his affairs, and I with
mine. Mine, singular," she added.

"He's having affairs?"

"Business affairs." The very notion of Leo having an affair amused
her. She only wished it were so. But the last thing she wanted to talk or
think about was Leo. "Shall we go?" she said.

They walked to the cashier. Frank gave the cashier Ellie's ticket with
a nickel for her coffee, and his own unpunched ticket. They went out
to Fifty-eighth Street, and parted. Frank walked two blocks to the Clin-

ton, a small hotel near Eighth Avenue. He reserved the same room each Wednesday afternoon.

A few minutes after Frank entered the hotel, Ellie followed him in. Neither had noticed a car parked across the street. The same Buick coupe that was parked in the same spot the previous Wednesday, and the Wednesday before that.

Seated in the Buick were Bernie Kopaloff and Harry Wise. This was the first time Harry had been here to personally witness it. He learned of it from Bernie, who learned of it from Howie Tobenkin. Howie, the Gorodetsky chauffeur, always drove Ellie into town, dropping her either at the Russian Tea Room on West Fifty-seventh, or a department store. He picked her up at the same place five hours later.

What aroused Howie's curiosity was that Ellie never purchased more than a few small items, and sometimes none. So a month ago, after dropping her at Sloane's, he parked the car and followed on foot. She went straight to the cafeteria, and then the hotel. This time Howie could not keep it to himself; he told Bernie. And Bernie told Harry.

So now they waited outside the hotel. With the car windows closed against the blustery day and the interior heavy with cigarette smoke, Harry's foul mood increased each minute. He glanced at his wristwatch.

"A fucking hour already," he said.

"Hey, that's rich," Bernie said. "A *fucking* hour!" He nudged Harry playfully. Their shared secret made him feel closer to the boss, more an equal. And he knew that by informing Harry of Ellie Gorodetsky's little Wednesday matinees he, Bernie, had demonstrated his loyalty. It was about time Harry recognized Bernie's real worth.

Harry peered at him icily. "You think it's funny? A wife cheating on her husband? Leo's wife?"

"Jesus, no," Bernie said quickly. "It was just how you said it, that's all. Hey, Harry, don't get me wrong."

Harry turned away to gaze at the hotel. He wanted to kill her. Doing this to a man like Leo. She was nothing but a whore. Worse than a whore. Harry trembled with rage. He had always suspected Ellie. With all her smart college talk and fancy airs, she was nothing more than a fucking *nafke*. No better than the ones that used to sit out on the street selling fifty-cent blowjobs.

But now that he knew, Harry wondered what to do about it. Should he simply confront her? It would scare the shit out of her, yes, but maybe too much. She might run straight to Leo to confess. Not from her own guilt, but to cover herself just in case Leo somehow found out. Harry had to protect Leo from that, from ever finding out.

"Hey!" Bernie pointed through the windshield.

Ellie had emerged from the hotel and immediately flagged a cruising taxi. The cab drove off, east down Fifty-eighth. Harry watched it through the rear window.

Bernie started the Buick's motor. Harry gestured him not to move. Harry had decided exactly how to handle all this. Where Ellie went was unimportant.

"There's the guy," Bernie said.

"Yeah," Harry said, watching Frank Lanier leave the hotel and walk rapidly toward Eighth Avenue. Harry motioned Bernie to follow. Bernie drove slowly, staying close to the curb, ignoring the horns of impatient drivers behind him.

"I think we'll pay this *bocha* a little visit," Harry said. "A social call. One thing," Harry continued quietly as Frank crossed Fifty-eighth at Eighth and walked south now. "You don't say one fucking word about this."

"Who would I say it to?"

Harry said, "And you tell Howie the same. I don't want Leo to ever know about this. The only way he will, is one of you big mouths talking. And that happens, kid, you are in trouble. *Capish?*"

"Aw, come on Harry," Bernie said. "What the hell you think I am?"

"That's a question I keep asking myself," Harry said, the corners of his mouth turned down distastefully as he looked at Bernie. It was a look Bernie often saw directed at him. As if he were a piece of furniture. Sometimes he hated Harry for this.

Frank Lanier entered a brownstone on West Fifty-fifth. Bernie parked on the opposite side of the street. Harry sat silently a moment, studying the building. Then he got out of the car, gesturing Bernie out also. They crossed the street and went into the building foyer.

"Three B," Harry said, tapping the mailbox. They went inside and climbed the stairs to the third floor. Harry glanced at the doors of A and C, and down the stairwell to make sure no one was in sight. Then, very gently, he knocked on 3B, and called out, "Mr. Lanier?"

Frank Lanier opened the door as far as the latch chain would permit. He hardly opened his mouth to say "Yes?" when Harry hurled himself at the door. The force of Harry's weight burst the chain and slammed Frank back into the wall. In an instant Harry and Bernie were inside the apartment. Bernie closed the door and slid the bolt shut.

Frank's eyes were wide with fear. "What do you want?" His eyes darted to Bernie, then back to Harry. "Who are you?"

"You're a prick, you know that?" Harry said quietly.

"Now look here—"

"Shut up!" Bernie said.

Harry stepped past him into the small but elegantly furnished living room. A kidney desk and brocaded-cushioned George III armchair against one wall. Across the room, two Queen Anne chairs, and a velveteen sofa. And a bookcase, one shelf crowded with Dresden figurines, and another with small Wedgwood pieces. And two entire shelves of glass and porcelain cats; all sizes and shapes. On the walls were four ornately framed oils of English countryside scenes. Fresh flowers were in a long slender cut-glass vase on the desk.

"Jesus, what kind of a place is this?" Harry said. He frowned sourly at Frank. "You some kind of queer? You think he's a queer?" he asked Bernie.

"Not from what I heard," Bernie said.

"Yeah, that's right," Harry said. "He's no queer."

"Now, look, please. If you'll tell me what you want," Frank said. "Is it money?"

"Money?" Harry looked at Bernie. "We want money?"

"You got any?" Bernie asked Frank.

"A few dollars perhaps," Frank said. He started toward the bedroom, then stopped abruptly as Bernie blocked his way with an outstretched arm.

"We don't want no money," Harry said, stepping into the bedroom. He regarded the large brass bed with a grim smile, and then opened both doors of a tall, wide armoire opposite the bed. It was filled with suits and jackets, and a tie rack with silk and wool ties. Attached to the inside of the door was a wire shoe caddy holding at least a dozen pair of shoes.

Harry returned to the living room. Frank stood rigidly, clenching and unclenching his fists. Bernie sat slouched in the George III chair, one leg slung casually over an armrest.

"Please, just let me get you the money," Frank said.

"Let me ask you something," Harry said. He sighed wearily. "Don't you know it's dumb to fuck somebody else's wife?"

"Oh, my God!" Frank said in a hoarse whisper. "He sent you! Oh, no!"

" 'Oh, no,' what?" Harry asked. "It's not dumb to do it?"

"I think he means he won't do it no more," Bernie said.

"Yes," Frank said. "I swear to you."

"You swear what?" Harry said. "You haven't been fucking her, or you won't anymore?"

"Please," Frank said. His voice almost broke entirely. "I didn't mean any harm. I just couldn't help myself."

" 'Course not," Harry said. "A good-looking, sexy broad like that. I understand." He smiled. And then, reaching out to the bookcase, in a single sweep of his arm wiped clean the entire shelf of Dresden. The little figurines flew across the room and smashed against the wall. They fell to the floor in a musical tinkle of broken glass.

"No, please!" Frank cried. "Oh, my God, no!" He knelt, fondling the fragments in utter disbelief. He turned, dazed, to Harry. "Why are you doing this!"

"It's called a lesson," Harry said. He looked at Bernie. "What is it? Object lesson?"

"Yeah, that sounds right," Bernie said.

"Oh, no, no, no," Frank said. His eyes were moist now, and he remained on his knees, gathering up the fragments and shards of glass. And then he screamed.

Harry had punched the flat of his hand down onto the center of the shelf of glass and porcelain cats. The shelf split in two, sending the objects cascading to the floor. Then, pulling the bookcase toward him, Harry toppled it to the floor. What was unbroken, Harry ground into the hardwood floor with his shoe. Frank closed his eyes and lowered his head. Harry had stepped across the room to the kidney desk. He kicked the legs, but it was a sturdy piece and remained intact. Harry drew back his foot to try again, but all at once seemed bored. He surveyed the wreckage a satisfied moment, then stepped over to Frank who still knelt amidst the broken china, head bowed, eyes closed. Harry seized Frank's hair and yanked back his head.

"Okay, *bocha*, get the message?"

That same evening Frank Lanier wrote his landlady a check for one hundred dollars and a note instructing her to place the furniture in storage. He packed all his clothes into a steamer truck and two valises, and caught the midnight train to Boston. He said he would send her his new address as soon as he was settled.

2.

The beat cop sauntered over to the Pierce-Arrow that had just swung into the "taxi only" lane at the Lexington Avenue entrance of Grand Central Station. He was perspiring under the early afternoon June sun, and wanted nothing more than to finish the shift, get home, get his clothes off, and drink a cold beer. And listen to the last few innings of the radio play-by-play of the Yankees-Tigers game. In two months the Babe already hit nineteen homers, three more than this same time last year, when he ended up with sixty. Sixty, unbelievable.

The cop had pulled out his citation book when he recognized the driver opening the Pierce-Arrow's rear door. Howie Tobenkin, which meant the car was Leo Gorodetsky's, which meant a five-dollar bill.

Leo stepped from the car behind a well-dressed lady. The cop flipped him a brisk salute. "Mr. Gorodetsky, how are you, sir?"

"Not bad," Leo said, pressing a five into the cop's hand. "The car won't be here long. I'm just seeing my wife off."

"No problem. You take all the time you need." The cop pocketed the money and smiled at Ellie. "Ma'am."

She smiled back, and then turned to Leo. "Don't bother walking me to the train, Leo. Really."

He glanced at his watch: 12:20. He was already late for a meeting at the office with Gerson and a man from the Cuban Interior Ministry.

The casino license was all but sewn up, except that the man from the ministry now required an additional $25,000 for "details." This same man, the president's personal representative, had already been paid $150,000. Leo had no intention of being held up for more.

"Well, all right," he said, and handed her the small overnight bag. "Now you'll be sure to call me if you need anything?"

"What would I need? 'At Grossinger's, we have everything you need.' Isn't that what the ad says?" She kissed his cheek, turned and walked into the station. She was going up to the Catskills' new resort just to get away for a few days. Steven was staying the weekend with her parents, so it was the perfect chance for Ellie to spend a few days at Grossinger's with a Barnard classmate, Leslie Berkovich. They hadn't seen each other in nearly five years.

". . . Ellie forgot her magazine," Howie was saying. He waved a copy of *The New Yorker*.

"Go find her and give it to her," Leo said. He got in the car and closed the door. *The New Yorker*, a new magazine Ellie admired. She was disappointed when he said he thought the magazine's short stories too vague and literarily pretentious. He promised to try them again, but so far had not found time. He was already way behind his goal of a book a week. In two weeks, he had not had a spare minute to even open *Elmer Gantry*, which he was actually anxious to read; he liked the theme. The phony Man of God.

Howie Tobenkin hurried into the station with the magazine, to the Delaware & Hudson window where Ellie would purchase a ticket to Liberty. She was not there. Howie walked around the waiting room looking for her. He saw her at the New York, New Haven & Hartford window.

Buying a ticket to Boston.

Howie darted behind a newsstand and watched. Ellie left the window and glanced at the placard above the ticket booth announcing the train's departure time as 2:30. Then she bought a paper at the newsstand and sat at a bench and began reading. Howie looked at *The New Yorker* in his hand. Boston, he thought. She was supposed to go to Grossinger's, upstate, to Liberty. Not Boston. And all at once Howie knew. It was as clear to him as though printed in giant letters on one of the advertising billboards hanging from the station ceiling.

The sign he was staring at showed a pretty girl at one end, pointing a gloved hand at the center of the billboard, at copy reading:

> "*—because I love nice things—*"
> VAN RAALTON
> SILK GLOVES

Howie imagined the letters to read:

206 *RIDE A TIGER*

> *"—because I cheat on my husband—"*
> ELLIE GORODETSKY
> LEO'S WIFE

This knowledge, as before, frightened Howie. And, as before, too juicy to keep to himself. He went to the nearest phone booth and called Bernie Kopaloff at the garage. Then he dropped Ellie's *New Yorker* into a trash bin and returned to the car. Leo never asked Howie if he saw Ellie, only told him to get going because they were late. Howie drove off, waving to the beat cop and wondering who Ellie's lucky guy was this time.

Harry wondered the same thing. He happened to be in the garage office when Bernie took Howie's call about Ellie going to Boston. That afternoon Harry planned to visit the Union City casino; a craps stickman had been caught switching dice for a friend. Two days ago Harry sent two men to the crook's house in Weehawken. They broke every finger on his right hand, and his left thumb. Now Harry wanted to personally check out each of the other stickmen and the 21 dealers. More accurately, he wanted to make certain they knew of the object lesson taught their former colleague.

But now, after learning of Ellie's Boston trip, Harry changed his plans. He gazed through the office glass partition into the garage. It bustled with activity. Trucks occupied all six service bays and the two new hydraulic lifts. IDIC had thirty trucks on the road night and day. When Repeal came, these same trucks would form the nucleus of a large, profitable, and very legitimate trucking business. Hauling their own legal liquor, from their own legal distilleries.

Harry looked at Bernie. "Where's Leo now?"

"Howie said he was driving him over to the Pete Building to see some spic."

"Yeah, that's right, the guy from Cuba," Harry said, thinking hard, thinking of that bitch of an Ellie. That whore.

"What time's the Boston train leave?"

"Half past two, Howie said."

Harry looked at his watch, then at the clock on the office wall. It was 12:40. "Half past two, huh?" he said. "That gives us almost a two-hour head start. We can be there before the train."

"You mean we drive?" Bernie said. "To Boston?"

"That's where the cunt's going, isn't it?" Harry said.

In New Haven Ellie bought a chicken-salad sandwich from a trackside vendor. She brought it back to the car and ate half, washing it down with the final drops from her brandy flask, which had been full leaving New York. Unfortunately, she felt as sober as when she started. Sometimes, if you were tense and unable to relax, it did not work.

For at least the dozenth time since leaving Grand Central, she removed the little slip of paper from her purse and read aloud the address written in her own hand.

"Seventy-two Marlborough Street." An address that cost her fifty dollars, paid gladly to Frank Lanier's former landlady to whom Ellie concocted a story about desperately requiring Frank's services for a decorating job. She knew the landlady did not for an instant believe the story, making it all the more romantic in the woman's eyes.

In mine, too, Ellie thought now, wondering, for perhaps the hundredth time, why on earth she was doing this. Chasing a man who simply and without a word of explanation had abandoned her when she desperately needed him. Well, more accurately, needed the relationship. A relationship that made her feel wanted and needed. Fulfilled.

Which, she told herself, was reason enough to go chasing after him. And why probe the motive, anyway? Why fill yourself with guilt? Enjoy it. Lie back and enjoy it, as Frank once said.

By the time the train arrived in Boston Ellie was more uncertain than ever, and needed a drink more than ever. Suppose Frank had left because of another woman? What would she do then? Well, then, she would simply take the next train back. At least she would know; she would have gotten it out of her system.

She walked from South Station out to Atlantic Avenue and into a cab. She wanted to ask the driver where she might buy a drink, but was too embarrassed. She never saw the Buick coupe with New York license plates pull out behind the cab and follow it to Marlborough Street. She never saw the Buick edge into a parking space two houses away, or the occupants light cigarettes and then get out to stretch their legs. And then get back into the car to settle down and wait.

It was not at all what Ellie expected. When Frank opened the door for her, he did not sweep her into his arms and carry her into the bedroom. She never saw the bedroom. After gazing at her a long silent, almost grim moment, he invited her in. They exchanged a few awkward amenities. And then he told her why he left New York so hurriedly.

Listening, Ellie felt as though she was being spun in a whirlpool, like a leaf caught in a vortex of water, flushed along a gutter and slammed into a wall. She wanted to run, but was held by a giant vise. She could hardly breathe. She wanted to cry, but could not find the strength.

He talked. She did not hear or understand a single word. Her mind was filled with visions of herself locked in a closet. Windowless, doorless, airless. A rational portion of her brain told her Leo knew nothing of this, was innocent of it all, but at the same time responsible for it all.

She wanted to die. That would be his punishment. But that would also punish their child. No, she must not die. She hardly realized that thirty minutes had passed and she was outside on Marlborough Street, stepping into a taxi Frank called to take her back to South Station. She did not recall saying good-bye to him, and only vaguely remembered agreeing they would never see each other again. But she knew she was glad she came, because it was the right thing to do, the only thing. She would not further jeopardize the man's safety. She lived in a jungle with wild animals, and she now must return to the jungle to resume her life.

Which she fully intended doing. For her own sake, and her son's.

Harry and Bernie watched the taxi drive off. Frank Lanier also stood watching it. After a moment he hurried back into the building.

"That didn't take long," Bernie said.

"It's what they call a quickie," Harry said. He brought his revolver from his jacket pocket and swung open the chamber. He spun the cylinder around, then again, pushing each cartridge snugly into its well. He snapped the chamber shut and dropped the gun back into his pocket.

"Okay," he said. "Let's go pay the *shtarker* another little social call."

3.

Harry missed the old days with him and Leo. The closeness, the friendship, the laughs. While Harry felt they had not exactly drifted apart, things were just not the same anymore. Now a wife and family took up all Leo's spare time. A sad mistake of a wife, Harry thought. But it was up to Leo to learn for himself, to recognize his own mistake; it was the only way to ever properly correct it.

What Harry really wanted to do was kill her. He sometimes imagined himself shoving a gun muzzle into her mouth and pulling the trigger. He would enjoy it. Not only the sheer pleasure of it, but the simple justice. At the same time, he knew this was never to be. As much as he hated her, Harry felt obligated to protect her. For Leo's sake, and for young Steven.

It was for them, then, Leo and Steven, that no one was ever to know. But Harry was sure Ellie's lover had told her that he, Harry, was responsible for the romance ending, and in this he took great satisfaction. He laughed whenever he thought of her dilemma. She could not complain to Leo about Harry interfering in her private life, and she would never confront Harry. She was fucked without the loving, Harry delighted in telling himself.

Nothing would have pleased Harry more than to describe to Ellie his encounter with Frank Lanier that night in Boston. How Frank swore the affair was over, and how Harry told Frank, Yes, it sure as hell was.

Everything, said Harry, is over. They were in the car, Frank squeezed in the front seat between Bernie and Harry. Bernie headed down Marlborough Street, turned on Arlington and continued past the Common. Frank never saw the gun in Harry's hand. Harry leaned forward, then turned slightly and pressed the revolver muzzle into Frank's ribs just under the heart, the barrel positioned so that if any bullets passed through Frank's body they went straight back into the seat cushion. Harry pumped three shells into him. The very first one killed him instantly. The second one to be sure—and the third, as Harry said, for luck.

What disturbed Harry now was a feeling of incompleteness. The book was not closed. Ellie did not know what happened to Frank Lanier. Harry wanted her to know. He wanted her to know even the smallest detail, down to their replacing the Buick's blood-spattered seat cushions in a New Haven upholstery shop that very same night. Only then, when he had the satisfaction of her knowing, would the book be closed.

It became an obsession. In the five years of Leo's marriage, Harry had not seen Ellie a dozen times. But now, in the two weeks since Boston, Harry not only managed to appear at the Hempstead house three times, he even attended one Friday *Shabbes* supper at Leo's mother's.

On each occasion he found something to needle Ellie about. Always, of course, in private. He would ask, How was her weekend at the Catskills; was the food at Grossinger's as good as they said? Or, When Steven got a little older she should think about taking him to Boston, a place loaded with history. Or, Was she still decorating the house?

It was after that Friday supper at Sarah Gorodetsky's when Harry finally achieved his objective. They were on the sidewalk outside Sarah's Amsterdam Avenue apartment building. Esther had walked everyone out, and Leo, Hershey, and Steven were waiting in the Pierce-Arrow for Ellie to finish chatting with her. Harry's Buick coupe was parked behind the Pierce-Arrow. He stepped over to say good night to Esther.

"I got to tell you, you don't move fast, old Georgie'll get away," he said to her. He referred to George Gerson, now in the thick of a hot affair with his secretary.

Esther glanced sourly at Harry and said to Ellie, "He's a real doll, this Harry. He knows goddam well that George and I stopped going out months ago. He also knows—because he made a point of telling me— that I know George and Betty went away for the weekend."

Harry frowned with innocence. "Oh, yeah, I guess I did say something about that, didn't I? Yeah, that's right, Boston. They went up to Boston." He smiled at Ellie. "They tell me that's one great town for making whoopie. You ever been there, Ellie?" He touched the brim of his hat, and walked off.

The next morning, the instant Leo left for Manhattan, Ellie rushed to the phone and asked for Boston information. The number of any telephone at 72 Marlborough Street. There were only two; she called both. One was a first-floor tenant who did not know Frank Lanier. The other was the building's owner, who said Mr. Lanier had not been in his apartment for two weeks. She assumed he was out of town. She would be happy to take a message.

"No message, thank you," Ellie said, and hung up. Just as in Frank's

living room that last night, everything began spinning. Her knees buckled; for an instant she thought she would faint. She sank down on the
telephone-table bench.

She stared unseeingly across the foyer. On the front door, projected
in a huge image as though on a motion-picture screen, was Frank Lanier's
face. So clear she could see the hollow dark circles under his eyes and
the gauntness of his cheeks. This face was almost instantly joined by
another face.

Harry Wise.

Grinning at her, and then at Frank, the same grin that must have
twisted his mouth when he killed Frank. And she knew Harry killed
him. She saw it all quite clearly. She could not have seen it more clearly
had she witnessed it personally.

They killed him. Ended his life as indifferently and callously as though
swatting a fly.

Animals. Wild, insane, bloodthirsty animals.

The jungle.

She forced herself to her feet, and into the living room to the cellarette.
She poured nearly a half glass of bourbon. She carried the glass to the
sofa, sat, and then drank. All of it, in a long, single swallow. She sank
back into the pillows and waited for the relaxation. That warm, floating
sensation that blurred and blunted even the ugliest thoughts.

They killed him.

No, *they* did not kill him. *She* did.

Perhaps not literally, but technically, which was really the same. In
her mind she saw herself strapped to the electric chair, leather mask
concealing her facial agony, writhing in the death throes of thousands
of volts of electricity charging through her body. She had seen such a
sight in that sensational photograph on the front page of the *Daily News*
last year: the New York housewife, Ruth Snyder, electrocuted for the
murder of her husband. Ruth Snyder, like Ellie, was only technically
guilty. She had persuaded her lover to kill the husband.

Ellie drained the glass and thought, Husband. Her husband, Leo. Leo
killed Frank. Harry would never take it upon himself. Harry could not
care less. Harry did it on Leo's order.

She got up and went to the cellarette for another drink. It was working
now, her thoughts coming more slowly, not cascading into her mind as
before. She could consider everything with more care, with more logic
and less emotion.

She drank. Yes, now she knew precisely what to do, and how. She
walked into the foyer and picked up the phone and called Leo's office.
Her voice was surprisingly quiet and calm, and she thought, I am doing
very well, aren't I?

She was saying into the phone, ". . . you will please return home,
Leo. Now."

"Now?" he asked. "What's wrong?"

"Nothing is wrong," she said. "I want to see you."

"Ellie, this is a very busy morning for me."

"Leo, unless you are here in exactly one and one half hours, not one second longer, I will do something quite drastic. Something you will be very sorry for. I know exactly what I am saying, Leo, and I advise you to pay attention."

She hung up. She sat on the telephone bench and waited. Almost immediately, the phone rang. She smiled, pleased. It continued ringing, but she did not answer. She counted the rings, sixteen, until it stopped. She knew he wanted to speak with Hershey, but Hershey was outside with Steven. She knew Leo really did not care about her, but would worry about Steven.

She looked at her wristwatch and smiled again.

The instant Leo saw her, less than an hour later, he sighed with relief; he knew from her very casualness nothing was wrong with Steven. She was on the front porch, leaning back against the metal banister, hands folded loosely across her chest. On the rail was an empty glass. He got out of the car and walked to the bottom porch stair. He looked at her, then at the glass. He picked up the glass and smelled it.

"You just can't leave it alone, can you?"

"Why did you do it, Leo?"

He could not gauge how drunk she was; she seemed fairly controlled. All right, whatever the problem, he would simply have to deal with it.

"Why did I do what, Ellie?"

"Kill him," she said. "Why did you kill him?"

It was a warm, sunny morning and in the distance, near the pond, he heard Steven's high-pitched giggle and Hershey's hoarse voice. They were fishing, he thought. Or swimming. He walked up onto the porch and faced her. "What did you say?"

"Frank Lanier," she said. "You killed him."

"Who in the hell is Frank Lanier?" he asked, and immediately remembered. "The decorator?"

"Yes, Leo, the decorator." She laughed harshly. "The dead decorator."

"What happened to him?"

She laughed again, the same harsh, brittle laugh. "You murdered him."

"I murdered him," he repeated. "Now, Ellie, why would I do that?"

Ellie's eyes narrowed coldly. Her voice was quiet, flat, each word perfectly enunciated. "You murdered him, Leo, because he was my lover."

He knew he heard correctly, and knew she spoke the truth. She repeated it, the same words, but he could not hear them for a sudden roaring in his ears. But he read her lips.

"He was my lover."

She continued talking. He heard nothing. He saw her. Under the man, writhing and heaving, clutching his hair, moaning in ecstasy. And her silk-stockinged legs and garter-belted thighs wrapped around the man's back. And her voice, screaming, "Give it to me! Give it to me!"

He felt sick. He was sure he would vomit. He brushed past her into the house, into the black-tiled powder room inside the entry hall. She followed him in, laughing. Brittle, hollow, taunting. He ran cold water over his hands and face. He looked into the mirror, a face he hardly recognized, a tormented face. The face of a stranger.

". . . that time I went to the Catskills to see my friend Leslie, and I came back the next morning because I said Leslie wasn't there, and I decided the crowd up there was too fast for a married woman?" Ellie was talking to him from the powder-room doorway, her voice no longer flat, but rising shrilly with each word.

"I was in Boston," she continued. "Boston, Leo. At Frank's! With him! But the funny part of it is we didn't do anything. He was frightened out of his wits by your friend Harry Wise!"

He heard clearly now. He lowered the toilet seat and sank down on it. She stepped into the powder room and told him the rest. All, in detail. When and where it started—in this very house, on this very living-room couch. Yes, and while their son slept upstairs!

Listening, he marveled at his own calm, his initial rage replaced with a strange, unfamiliar sadness. He strained to organize it in his mind. Harry, she claimed, killed Frank Lanier. On his, Leo's instructions.

"That is not true," he said.

"You're lying!" she said.

While she talked he had been unable to look at her, but now he did, and again felt anger. The familiar anger that chilled his whole body and sobered him like a cold shower, and allowed him to see each future move in clear, concise detail.

He did not say a single word to her. He left the house, got into the car, and drove straight back to Manhattan. To the garage where he thought he might find Harry.

Harry was not there, but Bernie Kopaloff was. Leo went into the office and removed a .45 from the bottom desk drawer. He slipped the gun into his pocket, then went back out to the garage and ordered Bernie to accompany him upstairs to Hershey's apartment. Hershey seldom used the apartment anymore, but the sink was cluttered with dirty dishes, and the bed unmade as though hastily vacated by its occupants.

"All right, sit down," Leo said, gesturing Bernie into a chair at the kitchen table. He sat opposite him. "You don't have the slightest idea what I want, do you?"

Bernie shook his head. He knew only that something was very wrong.

"Frank Lanier," Leo said.

"Who?" Bernie said.

Leo drew the .45 from his pocket. He cocked it and leveled it at Bernie's head. "Now, Bernie, you tell me everything you and Harry did to this man, Lanier. Very slowly, very thoroughly, Bernie. Everything."

Bernie told him everything. How after Harry shot Frank they drove immediately to a Cambridge funeral home. Harry had arranged it all hours before with Sol Feldman, IDIC's New England representative. The following day the mortician delivered a naked, unidentified cadaver to Boston University Medical School.

Later, telling Harry about it, Bernie said Leo had the craziest look on his face. As though he didn't know whether to laugh, cry, or scream. Or all three. It reminded Bernie of a photograph of a painting he once saw in a magazine. It was called *Revelation*, and showed a man gazing at the sky, the rays of the sun lighting his face. The man had seen a vision. He had seen the truth.

What struck Bernie was that Leo's expression was almost identical to Frank Lanier's. Just before Harry shot him.

Leo was not surprised when he returned to Hempstead that afternoon and found that Hershey had driven Ellie and Steven to her parents'. She planned to remain there. She said Leo would understand.

"Was she sober?" Leo asked.

"Yeah, Leo, she was sober," Hershey said. "I think you really done it this time, *boychick*."

Sure, Hershey, Leo told him in his mind. I really done it. My wife fucked another man, so I guess I really done it, all right. Except she thinks I had the guy who fucked her killed. He wanted to shout this at Hershey, write it on the ceiling for him, but also did not want Hershey to know. He was too ashamed.

He said to Hershey, "Don't worry about it, Hersh. And by the way, Howie won't be driving for me anymore. Find somebody to take his place."

"What happened to Howie?" Hershey asked.

"He said he wanted to go back on the truck," Leo said, which was almost true. After Leo told Howie that if he ever breathed a word of what he knew to a single soul he would wish he were dead, Howie was smart enough to request a transfer.

". . . I'm worried about the kid, Leo," Hershey was saying. "About Stevie."

"Then just go on over to the Bronx and see him." Leo turned and walked out. He did not want to talk anymore. He went up to his bedroom and locked the door. His bedroom, and Ellie's.

He wanted to think. He had to think. About crazy-tempered Harry. Breaking Gorodetsky's Law. Yes, Harry did it out of concern for Leo, but it was so needless, so stupid. Leo felt nothing whatever for Frank Lanier. The poor bastard simply fucked the wrong man's wife. Leo insisted on thinking of it in those terms, "fucking," "fucked." Not making love, or having an affair, or straying. Those phrases were too delicate and honest.

His wife fucked another man.

But why?

He asked himself this question gazing out the bedroom window. At his land, his estate. As far as the eye could see, all his. A large, rolling field sloping down to the pond, and then trees beyond that. The trees and the forest. You cannot see the trees for the forest. That's why you ask "why" she fucked the other man.

A better question, he thought, was Why *not*?

Again, he marveled at his own calm. He should have been in a cold fury, but was calm and composed, thinking rationally. Asking himself once more that question: Why *not*?

Wait a second, he told himself. Wait just one second. Let's try to be fair about this. Let's put the shoe on the other foot. Suppose it was *you* who felt neglected and overlooked. What would *you* do? Wouldn't you look for something to make up for it?

Yes, I suppose I would.

Sure, remember Charlotte Daniels?

Oh, yes, I remember Charlotte. I'll always remember Charlotte.

So why are you in such a rage about Ellie?

I'm not in a rage. In fact, I understand.

When that word, "understand," flashed into his mind he closed his eyes and saw it in large, bright letters blinking across his entire line of sight. "Yes," he said aloud. "I goddam do understand!"

He had forced her into it. Left her with no choice. She wanted love, she needed love and, not receiving it from him, looked elsewhere. And why not? To save herself, her own self-respect.

Suddenly he saw her through new eyes. He saw a woman not totally dependent upon her husband, a woman who refused to feel sorry for herself and instead found the strength and courage to strike out on her own. For her own happiness, self-respect, and well-being. Her own pride.

He admired and respected that. And, as he stood gazing out at the pond, and beyond the pond, the forest whose trees he had been unable to see, he was enveloped by a new, warm feeling for Ellie. A feeling altogether foreign, and therefore slightly frightening, as though he was about to enter some unexplored new land.

But he recognized this strange new feeling.

Love.

A different love than he felt for Steven, which was itself deep and mysterious, and filled with both hope and fear. No, this was the desire to share that feeling with her, to give and take all at the same time. It was all totally new, and so different. He thought he had loved Charlotte Daniels, but now recognized that as simply the desperate need of a desperate man to be accepted for something he was not.

Ellie had accepted him for precisely what he was, and he had turned her away. He would change all that. Now he knew how to.

An hour and a half later he was in Kingsbridge. Asking his wife to
come back to him. Asking her forgiveness, prepared to beg if she refused.
And he would not have hesitated to beg.

It was unnecessary. It was enough he had come for her and Steven.
They held each other, and she wept. He did not weep, but would not
have been ashamed to, in truth wanted to. To share that with her, too.
He had never known such tenderness and love for another human being.

Only once was Frank Lanier mentioned, when Leo convinced her
nothing had happened to him. The man was frightened out of his wits,
yes, but nothing else. She accepted the lie; it relieved her of any guilt.
Guilt she did not truly deserve, anyway.

They went on a second honeymoon, a real honeymoon. To Europe
on the *Mauretania*. They played and laughed, and dined at the captain's
table. Ellie drank only wine, and then not more than a single glass. Leo
said it was all right, but she said she wanted nothing to mask the magnificent feeling of being alive, and certainly nothing to dull those senses.
They made love continually. Every morning, every night, and sometimes
during the day. Each time seemed more exciting and gratifying than
the last.

Ellie called it the Renaissance.

A day from Southampton, at four in the morning, they had just finished making love. They lay in each other's arms and all at once Ellie
laughed. A quiet little laugh of astonishment.

Leo said, "What's so funny?"

She rolled away from him. She leaned up and smiled down at him.
"You just made me pregnant."

"I bet."

"It's true." She kissed him gently on the lips. "I can tell."

"Boy, or girl?"

"Leo, I know. I'm pregnant."

He sat up and faced her. "Now how could you possibly know?"

"I felt the click," she said. "I'm ovulating. Believe me, I felt it connect.
So help me God, I felt a click."

He said nothing a moment. For one terrible instant the thought flashed
through his mind that no woman could really know if she had been
made pregnant, and that Ellie already was pregnant, and from Frank
Lanier. At least two months pregnant. But in that very same instant he
felt immense shame. He remembered that since her return from Boston
she had had two periods.

"A click, I'll be damned!" he said, hating himself for doubting her,
promising himself never to doubt her again.

"Congratulations, Father," she said. "Let's hope Steven will get along
with him or her."

"Them," he said, hugging her. "Maybe it's twins."

"Bite your tongue," she said.

Suddenly both were ravenous. They ordered caviar and roast-beef sandwiches from the steward, which they ate on deck standing at the rail, watching the ship's wake rush foamingly past the hull and vanish in the dark water. Ahead, like a gold curtain being raised, the first glimmer of dawn brightened the night sky. The light lengthened, and widened; soon, from one end of the horizon to the other, the whole sky glowed.

It was a new day.

—— 13 ——

CARLA'S smile reminded Leo of the tinkling of little bells on a bright sunny day. I am getting poetic in my old age, he thought, watching Hershey inexpertly focus the Brownie camera on the little girl. She sat patiently at the table, dwarfed by the gigantic cake with the three candles. Two for her birthday, one for good luck.

"Okay," Hershey said. "Blow them out, darling."

Carla drew in her breath, held it as long as she could, and blew out all three candles in a single breath. Hershey snapped the picture. Everyone applauded. Hershey kissed Carla, then gestured Steven to kiss her. Steven frowned stubbornly, but a firm prod on the shoulder from Hershey convinced Steven to give his sister a quick, reluctant kiss. More applause. Sarah and Esther also kissed the birthday girl, and then Ellie and Leo.

Ellie cut the cake, the first piece for Carla, which she immediately presented to her grandmother, earning another kiss and hug for the pretty little dark-haired girl in the ruffled pink dress and white party shoes. They were in the patio, seated at a big picnic table laden with cake, ice cream, and soda pop. Carla and Steven, Ellie, Leo, Hershey, Esther, Sarah. And George Gerson and his wife, Betty, herself seven months pregnant. The children's maternal grandparents, Selma and Alfred Baer, were at Grossinger's for the Labor Day weekend. Their gift, a gigantic stuffed giraffe, stood toweringly behind Carla.

". . . a fine family, Leo," George Gerson was saying.

"Pretty soon I'll be saying that about you," Leo said, nodding at Betty Gerson's stomach. "Speaking of families, did Sal tell you about Dino Coletti taking over the Ruggerio family?"

"It won't affect us."

"Coletti thinks it will," Leo said. "He wants a meeting."

"He wants a piece of the action," Gerson said. "Especially now that we have the license."

The license.

The gambling permit from the Cuban government, issued only the week before. Construction on the hotel, El Conquistador, had already begun, a condition under which the license was granted. A show of faith, the Cubans said. They wanted to be sure the *Yanquis* were serious. Leo did not blame them; it was only good business.

For them, the Cubans, certainly. One million dollars in cash had passed into various private Havana bank accounts. Another million and a half for the four-story, 250-room hotel, whose lobby Leo had personally designed. A whole new concept, the casino occupying the entire, atrium-like lobby. Three roulette wheels, twelve blackjack tables, four craps tables. Monte Carlo of the Caribbean.

And not a clock visible anywhere. Leo did not want his customers reminded of time. Only money, in the form of glossy chips which deprived the gambler of a sense of reality and encouraged him, if winning, to continue playing; or, if losing, to purchase more in the hope of recouping.

He had worked a year on it. Six trips to Havana, keeping him away from home nearly six full months. He should have been there in Havana himself to receive the license, but he had promised Ellie to be home for Carla's birthday. So Sal went in his place.

El Conquistador was only the beginning. Three more IDIC hotel-casinos were planned for Havana, with the profits funneled to Switzerland, then back to the States. "Washed," as Gerson put it. Clean money to be invested in other, wholly legitimate enterprises.

Gerson said something, but Leo was momentarily distracted. He was gazing at Ellie, who had offered him a large piece of cake, which he declined, thinking "Renaissance." That Renaissance of which Carla was the living product, born almost nine months to the day after Ellie's "click."

But the Renaissance was only a warm, hazy memory. They had slipped back into their old routine. More accurately, he had. Away three or four nights a week, overseeing the casinos in Kentucky and Saratoga Springs, and then absent for longer periods in Arkansas and Florida. Not to mention Cuba.

Leo thought Ellie seemed content and busy enough raising the children. He suspected she was drinking again, although nothing serious, an occasional glass of wine. At least so Hershey vaguely indicated. But then Leo could not be certain; he did not want to confront Hershey directly. Hershey would resent being forced to betray Ellie. It would be like betraying a family member, for that was what Hershey had become. He lived permanently in the house now, the welfare of the children always uppermost in his mind.

". . . take a little walk," Gerson was saying. "Something we have to discuss."

Leo hesitated. It was his daughter's birthday party, but he recognized an urgency in Gerson's voice. He got up and started away, stopping to kiss Carla once more and ask how she liked her present, a miniature, but fully keyed piano. Carla loved music. Her grandmother, Sarah, insisted the child was a prodigy, a talent she believed inherited from Sarah's father, a conscripted flutist in a tsarist army band. Leo ruffled Steven's hair, smiled at Ellie, and joined Gerson. They walked across the yard, and down to the edge of the pond.

"I have word that Brickhill is pressuring the IRS to audit us," Gerson said.

"Closing up Chez When for good gave him a taste of blood," Leo said. "Ours."

Brickhill was Charles Brickhill, formerly Robert MacGowan's deputy. When MacGowan went to Albany as assistant attorney general, Brickhill replaced him. MacGowan had now returned to private practice.

Gerson said, "Yes, and he's more eager than ever to play racket buster. He has ambitions to be New York County D.A."

"The question is, does he have a price?"

"Don't they all?"

"With Brickhill, I'm not so sure," Leo said.

"Well, whether or not he does is only half the problem," Gerson said. He sighed, and Leo realized that now came the bad news. "In fact, that's only the beginning."

Leo said nothing. He waited.

Gerson said, "Bernie Kopaloff."

"George, you have the most annoying habit of stretching—"

"—Brickhill's got Bernie."

"What do you mean, he's 'got him'?"

"Bernie has agreed to testify against Harry Wise for the murder three years ago of a man named Frank Lanier."

A man named Frank Lanier, Leo thought, struck by the irony of that name mentioned on Carla's birthday, she whose conception was the result of the Renaissance for which Frank Lanier had been directly responsible. He glanced sharply at Gerson, wondering if Gerson somehow knew of the connection. No, he was fairly sure Gerson knew nothing, although if the newspapers got it—which they undoubtedly would—then the whole world would know. Most importantly, Ellie. But then

Leo believed she had already secretly suspected. It was just something he would have to deal with.

". . . grand jury meeting right now to bring an indictment," Gerson was saying. "Harry has plenty to answer for."

"Harry always has something to answer for," Leo said, remembering three years ago when Harry, learning that Bernie told Leo about the killing in Boston, went into a blind rage. Not because Leo knew of the killing, but because he now knew of his wife's infidelity. The terrible truth Harry had been so determined to shield from Leo, but which he had failed to do, although never once was it mentioned between them.

So while Harry, for all his fury, was smart enough to control his impulse to put Bernie in the hospital for several months, he had not been smart enough to refrain from humiliating him. He punished Bernie by relegating him to errand boy, the constant butt of Harry's jokes and flunky jobs. Now Bernie was repaying him.

"What other evidence do they have?" Leo asked.

"None I'm aware of."

"If it's only Bernie's word, it's not enough for an indictment."

"Brickhill is bringing Harry in for questioning, anyway."

Leo laughed. "Do they expect him to confess?"

"It's Brickhill's way of applying pressure. He thinks the more he squeezes, the more he'll find a weak spot."

Leo marveled at Gerson's matter-of-factness, simply accepting as an undisputed fact that Harry had indeed murdered a man named Frank Lanier. Discussing it as though exchanging ideas on which stock to purchase. Which, Leo thought dryly, was a poor analogy these days, with all the former so-called legitimate businessmen selling apples on the street, or flinging themselves out of Wall Street windows.

"Let him squeeze," Leo said. "We have nothing to worry about."

Leo was wrong.

Bernie Kopaloff provided Charles Brickhill the name of the Cambridge, Massachusetts, undertaker who had disposed of Frank Lanier's body. In return for immunity this man, Lawrence Cahill, agreed to corroborate Bernie's testimony.

Harry was indicted for first-degree murder, arrested, and held without bail. The arrest of such a high-ranking IDIC principal was unprecedented. A local precinct desk sergeant, witnessing the booking, cried, "Sweet Mary and Joseph, they're human, after all!"

Charles Brickhill was a short, stocky, red-haired man of thirty-four with the fiery temperament of his Irish farmer forebears, and an almost pathological hatred for thieves and hoodlums of any persuasion, size, or shape. His father, a beat cop, in 1912 was gunned down on a Brooklyn street by a purse-snatching punk. Immediately upon graduating from high school, young Brickhill joined the department. Six years of CCNY night school, and three more at Fordham, earned him his law degree. He accepted a job with the Brooklyn district attorney's office, and from there joined Robert MacGowan.

Now, in the autumn of 1931, Special Prosecutor of the City of New York reporting directly to the mayor, Charles Brickhill stood at the threshold of the greatest victory of any peace officer's career.

He was about to bring to trial for first-degree murder a man he devoutly believed one of New York's three most powerful criminals. More important, a conviction would expose and make vulnerable the other two crime bosses.

Brickhill let Harry cool two entire days in a maximum-security cell at the Tombs Detention Center, then had him brought downtown. It was the first time the two had ever seen each other. Brickhill was annoyed, for even in prison denims Harry was almost dapper. And clean-shaven, his thick black hair barbershop trim and neat, even the cheap regulation shoes shined to a high black gloss. They were alone in the office but for a male stenographer seated across the room.

Harry's first words were "Mind if I smoke?" He bit the tip off a huge cigar and dropped the fragment delicately into the brass ashtray on Brickhill's desk. As though waiting for someone to light it, he held the cigar expectantly to his mouth. After a moment, grinning, he lit it himself. He leaned back in the chair and grinned again. "I hear you want to talk to me?"

"I hoped you might want to talk to me," Brickhill said.

"Be glad to," Harry said. "About what?"

"For openers, Frank Lanier."

Harry frowned. "Who's he?"

Brickhill said, "All right, then let's talk about Leo Gorodetsky."

"The little prick that calls himself my friend?"

Brickhill's square-framed face tightened. "That's the game you want to play, eh?"

"I'm not playing no game," Harry said. He pointed the cigar at the stenographer. "Be sure and write all this down. Leo Gorodetsky is a fink." Harry turned to Brickhill again. "A goddam spy, for Christ's sake!"

"Really?" Brickhill said. He leaned forward as if interested. "Tell me more."

"He works for the —" Harry paused, thinking. He had already decided Brickhill was a dunce. "The Latvians," Harry said. "Yeah, Latvia. That's a country near Russia, you know."

"Near Russia? Really?" Brickhill said. "Keep talking."

"Well, they're planning to invade us, those Latvians," Harry said. "Leo's been feeding them secret information for years. They're thinking of making him a governor or something when they take over."

Brickhill laughed good-naturedly. "You're a very funny man, Harry."

Harry smiled, pleased. "I thought you'd get a kick out of it."

"I did," Brickhill said. He pressed a button on his desk intercom box. Immediately, two detectives appeared at the door. "Take him back," Brickhill said, and to Harry, "Thank you for the informative talk, Mr. Wise. We'll do it again tomorrow."

"You bet," said Harry. He rose, exhaling a huge cloud of blue cigar smoke toward Brickhill. He left with the detectives.

"Shall I type that up?" the stenographer asked Brickhill.

"No, Ralph," Brickhill said. "Don't bother."

After the stenographer left, Brickhill sat a moment, thinking. Then he got up and stepped to the window. He looked down at the gray, dreary street, the rooftops of automobiles and trucks. He was not at all disturbed, in fact was quite sanguine. He had not expected anything more from this initial meeting. He would work on Harry Wise the next day, and the day after that, and the one after that, and finally confront him with the mortician's statement. Harry would break.

Brickhill knew the type. Filled with bravado, until the truth suddenly dawned. The truth, meaning the electric chair. In the end, Harry Wise would beg to cooperate. His life for the evidence and testimony that would incriminate the real brains behind IDIC.

Leo Gorodetsky.

Brickhill sat down again. The cigar smoke still hovered above the desk. Brickhill waved his hands through it. He hated the stink.

If Harry was unconcerned, Leo and Sal were more than concerned. They conferred a week later in Gerson's office. Gerson had that very morning talked with Harry in the Tombs attorneys' room.

"He's actually enjoying himself," Gerson said. "Meals sent in, the guards kowtowing to him. He's treated like royalty."

Sal laughed. "Those guards know where their bread's buttered."

"Why does Brickhill let him get away with it?" Gerson wondered aloud.

"Brickhill's smart," Leo said. "He wants Harry relaxed and sure of himself. Then, when he gets him in court, and Harry's sitting there listening to Bernie sing, and then the undertaker, it will all look different."

"Harry'll never crack," Sal said.

Leo said nothing. This was the first time Harry ever really faced the wall. Yes, he had demonstrated his courage and loyalty countless times. But with a gun in his hand, and little time to consider. Him, or them. Now he dealt with a dangerous adversary, Charles Brickhill, a man infinitely smarter than Harry.

Would Harry crack? Leo wondered. Would, given the same circumstances, any of them in this room? Would Leo himself crack? You never knew until it happened.

". . . couldn't believe my ears," Gerson was saying. "He looked me in the eye and said, 'Tell Leo and Sal maybe we should hit Brickhill!' "

"Harry said that?" Sal asked.

"His exact words," Gerson said. " 'Hit Brickhill.' Can you imagine?"

"Yes, I can imagine," Leo said. "That's how his mind works. Kill Charlie Brickhill, our troubles are over. Kill Brickhill, and our troubles just *begin!*" He shook his head tightly. "Our problem is not Charles Brickhill, it's his key witness, Bernie Kopaloff."

"And the undertaker," Sal said.

"Yes, and the undertaker," Leo said.

"They're keeping Bernie in a hotel?" Sal asked quietly, rhetorically.

"Atlantic City, the Breakers," Gerson said. "Guarded round the clock by three detectives."

"And the undertaker?" Sal asked.

"In Boston," Gerson said. "A hotel, too. I'll have the name by tomorrow."

"We can't let Bernie get on the stand, Leo," Sal said. It was a flat, simple statement.

"No, we can't," Leo said.

2.

Roland Sweetzer was not a happy man. He was forty-one, overweight, rapidly balding, and married to a woman who believed sexual intercourse was intended solely for procreation. This same woman, to whom he had been married twelve years, wanted no more children than the five she had already borne, and also believed it a mortal sin to employ any birth-control method save that single one recommended by the Church, abstinence.

The children ranged in age from eleven to six. Each day, returning home from work and seeing them all seated at the kitchen table awaiting his presence before commencing thanks to God for that evening's meal, Roland Sweetzer wondered what it would be like to one day simply not come home to the rented house in Queens, a three-bedroom frame cottage on a street with two dozen nearly identical dwellings.

He was a tough cop who knew his job. He had worked his way up from the beat, cracking more than his share of skulls, and was particularly adept at administering the third degree. He enjoyed forcing punks to talk, and the more they resisted the more he enjoyed it.

He was a detective third grade, working out of the 10th Precinct, Burglary Detail. He earned $2,220 annually, which should have been more than sufficient to adequately feed, clothe, and house his family: $42.60 weekly went a long way, especially in these Depression times.

Ordinarily.

And would have, had Roland Sweetzer not fallen in love.

With a lady he booked on a shoplifting charge. Her name was Letty. She was twenty-four, tall, slender, with bobbed blond hair that framed her face like a gold halo. At the station that day he booked her, he gave her permission to use the bathroom. She was gone more than ten minutes, so he went to investigate. When he opened the lavatory door Letty grasped his hand and pulled him inside. In a motion so smooth and swift it felt like the fluttering of little wings his fly was unbuttoned, and in almost the same instant he was deep within her mouth.

He set her up in a studio apartment on Second Avenue, thirteen dollars monthly, and she was always there when he needed her. Lately, however, she had been demanding a nicer place. He promised to find her one the moment he completed his current, temporary assignment.

This temporary assignment was in Atlantic City.

At the Breakers hotel.

Standing guard over a key witness in a murder trial, Bernard Kopaloff.

On October 12, 1931, Columbus Day, which was the start of his two-day break, Roland Sweetzer drove home from Atlantic City in a NYPD squad car. He spent only enough time there to change clothes and inform the family he had to report downtown and would be unable to join them at supper. He drove immediately to Second Avenue. He had hardly kissed Letty hello when a young neighbor boy knocked at the door.

"A man come to see you," the boy said. "He come in a great big car."

Roland went to the window. From this third-floor angle the vertical sign of a Chinese laundry on the ground floor obscured the street. He could see only the rear fender of a car parked at the curb in front of the laundry.

"He said for you to go talk to him," the boy said.

Roland Sweetzer craned his neck for a better view of the car. He saw only one occupant, a bareheaded man at the wheel. The car was a black Pierce-Arrow sedan.

It occurred to Leo, as he waited for Roland Sweetzer, that he had an intelligence network surely rivaling the famous British MI5. An entire division of paid informers. A single telephone call had obtained the names of the detectives assigned to Atlantic City. Two more calls—and a fifty-dollar payoff to a 10th Precinct civilian clerk—to learn of Roland Sweetzer's Second Avenue love nest.

Only that morning in a conversation with Sal, Leo claimed he was doing this, taking this risk, purely for business. Sal said that was bullshit. Leo was doing it, Sal said, out of friendship, and Sal thought it was admirable. Leo did not debate the point; he was unsure of his own motives. But he remembered what flashed into his mind when he first heard of Bernie Kopaloff's betrayal.

At a trial, Leo's wife's adultery would certainly be an issue. No trial, and not only would Harry be saved, but Leo spared public embarrassment. It was something he preferred not to think about.

When Leo arrived at the Second Avenue tenement, on the seat beside him was a briefcase. The briefcase contained a single object. A plain brown-paper shopping bag. In the bag were one hundred hundred-dollar bills: $10,000. Ten minutes later, when Leo drove away after his chat with Roland Sweetzer, the briefcase was empty.

That evening Roland Sweetzer gave Letty $1,000 cash. He told her he hit a three-horse parlay at Aqueduct. He stayed with her all night and the following day, an exhausting but memorable two days. When he left to report back for duty in Atlantic City he told Letty he did not think the assignment would last much longer.

Roland Sweetzer's partners on this five-day shift were two plainclothes-men from the 13th Precinct. An Irishman named Stine, a twenty-year veteran, and a younger, very eager type named Dworski who had been on the force only four years and whom Roland did not particularly care for. He considered anyone promoted so rapidly an ass-kisser, not to be trusted.

When Roland reported for duty, Stine and Dworski had only one more day to complete their tour. Their replacements would be two uniformed cops Roland did not know. He decided his best chance was to do the job as soon as possible. Now, tonight.

Charles Brickhill had selected Atlantic City because the hotel was nearly empty now at off-season. He put Bernie Kopaloff in a two-bedroom suite on the sixth floor. Bernie slept in one bedroom, the detectives in the other. During the day they listened to the radio, read, played cards. An endless whist game, which Bernie sometimes joined, but always quickly lost interest in. He said the game bored him. The truth was that he could not keep his mind on the cards.

Roland Sweetzer, reporting for duty at 4 P.M., relieved a detective named Ungar. Roland looked into Bernie's bedroom. The room was dark, windows closed, lights out. Bernie lay on the bed, in red and white striped pajamas, staring at the ceiling.

"How you doing?" Roland asked.

"Great," Bernie said, not looking at him.

"That's what I thought," Roland said. "Need anything?"

"Yeah," Bernie said. "A good lawyer."

"You got the best in the business," Roland said. "You got Charlie Brickhill. You got nothing to worry about." He closed the door and stepped back into the living room. Ungar, leaving, suggested Roland take his seat at the game. He said it was lucky. It was. Over the next hour Roland won continually. He was $3.35 ahead when they broke for supper.

"Jesus, maybe I should turn pro," he said.

"Not a bad idea," Dworski said. "Maybe you've found your true niche."

Roland's heart beat faster. The little asshole had given him the perfect excuse. He pretended to be offended, and said, "Now what the hell does that mean!"

Dworski, startled, said, "It means you're a good cardplayer."

"No," said Roland. "You mean something else."

"What, something else?" Dworski said. "I was complimenting you, for Christ's sake!"

"Bullshit," Roland said. "You been needling me with that smart talk ever since we been on duty. I'm fucking sick of it!"

"Hey, Sweetzer, ease up, huh?" Stine said.

Roland hurled the cards to the table. "Fuck you, Stine. Fuck the both of you!" He rose, shoving back his chair with such force it toppled to the floor. "I'll go in and talk to Bernie. He's better company!"

Roland strode across the room to Bernie's bedroom. He flung open the door, entered, and slammed the door shut behind him. Bernie, lying on the bed, turned lazily to him. Roland stood with his back to the door, leaning his full weight against it so he could slide the bolt home noiselessly.

"What's all the commotion?" Bernie asked.

Roland stared at the window and said, "Holy Christ!"

As Bernie whirled to the window, Roland pulled his service revolver from his holster. He flipped the gun around in his hand, grasping it now by the barrel, and smashed the steel-plated handle down on the base of Bernie's skull. The blow was so hard Roland heard the bone crack. The breath rushed from Bernie's lungs like a punctured tire. He lay on the bed on his stomach, limp and still, head hung over the side of the mattress, arms dangling to the floor.

Roland touched his fingertips to Bernie's carotid artery; there was a slight pulse. He considered striking Bernie again, then realized it made no difference, and pulled him from the bed. He dragged the unconscious body to the window, propping it against the wall with one hand while opening the window with his free hand. The courtyard, six stories below, was empty. Roland swung Bernie around onto the windowsill and heaved him out.

The moment the pajama-clad body started falling, Roland saw he had overlooked a protruding ledge just two stories down. Bernie struck the ledge, caromed inward toward the building and for an instant seemed to settle on the ledge. But he teetered another instant and then slipped off. He hurtled downward and struck the cement courtyard with a sharp, cracking sound.

Bernie lay in the courtyard, facedown, his arms somehow tucked into his sides like a fallen bird's folded feathers. A red and white striped bird.

Quickly now, Roland Sweetzer gathered both bed sheets, knotted them end to end, wrapped one end around the radiator pipe and hung the other end out the window. The sheets extended down only one story.

Now, again muffling the sound of the sliding door bolt with his body weight, he opened the door slightly and called out, "For Christ's sake, Bernie, you gonna sit on the can all day? Supper'll be here in a minute!"

Closing the bedroom door behind him, he returned to the living room. Stine was alone. Dworski had gone downstairs for the food trays. Roland said to Stine, "He went and locked himself in the toilet, our prize pigeon."

"So he jerks off a little, he got a right," Stine said. "Listen, why the hell did you take off after Dworski like that?"

"He's a pain in the ass," Roland said. "But if it makes you feel better, I'll apologize when he gets back." He opened the bedroom door again. "Hey, Bernie, how many times you think you can come?"

"Leave him be," Stine said.

"He's been in there too goddam long," Roland said. He opened the door fully. "Bernie . . . ?" He peered into the room. "Shit!" he cried, and ran into the room. Stine rushed to his feet and followed.

Both stood at the open window, gazing incredulously down at the courtyard. Stine started to pull in the knotted sheets. Roland clamped his hand on Stine's. "Don't touch a goddam thing!"

Stine stared at the sheets, then down at the courtyard again. He spoke almost in a whisper. "How in the name of God did he expect to climb out with just two sheets?"

"He didn't," Roland said.

Stine looked at him.

Roland said, "He did it on purpose."

"The poor, dumb bastard," Stine said. He made the sign of the cross.

A few hours later, five hundred miles away in Cambridge, Massachusetts, a sixty-one-year-old woman named Janet Cahill made the same sign of the cross. She had just received a telephone call, a local call by the clearness of the line, from a man. This man very politely suggested she read the morning papers, and further suggested she urge her husband, the undertaker staying with police in a Boston hotel, to also read them. The polite man was sure the Boston papers carried a story about a man in an Atlantic City hotel jumping six floors to his death.

Lawrence Cahill read the papers and recanted his testimony. He claimed never to have been absolutely certain Harry Wise accompanied Bernie Kopaloff the night they delivered the body to him. Such testimony might well condemn an innocent man. His immunity waived, he received a two-year sentence for obstructing justice. The time spent in protective custody was credited to the sentence, which was appealed when the highest-priced criminal attorney in Boston surprisingly agreed to take the case. The appeal was denied, but the court ruled that due to age and failing health the defendant should be placed on probation.

Leo met Harry on the granite stairs outside the Foley Square Courthouse. "So how's it feel to be free?" Leo asked.

Harry stood a stair away and looked at Leo an elated moment. Then he stepped down and embraced him in a fierce bear hug. "You're some fixer, Kleyner!" Harry said. "Someday you got to tell me how you did it. No," he added quickly, "I take it back. Maybe I better not know!"

Leo's new driver, Rich Freedman, waited at the Pierce-Arrow's open rear door. They were taking Harry to Luchow's where Sal had reserved a private room for a celebration. Harry got into the car first, and Leo was just stepping in behind him. From the corner of his eye he saw Rich Freedman pushed roughly aside. He wheeled around to find himself facing Charles Brickhill.

"Don't for one second believe you've gotten away with anything," Brickhill said. His voice was quiet, almost conversational, but conveyed absolute confidence. "One day you'll make a mistake. Scum like you always do. It might not be next month, or even next year, but it'll happen. And when it does, I'll be there. On that, you can bet your life."

Harry leaned past Leo. "Hey, come on, Brickhill, don't be a sore loser!"

"Harry, shut up," Leo said, and to Rich. "Get in the car, Rich."

Brickhill looked at Harry with disdain. "When I put this little man away, you won't have anybody to wipe your ass, will you?"

Harry lunged at Brickhill. Leo needed all his strength to push Harry back into the car. Brickhill had not flinched, only looked coldly at Harry, who was shouting, "You mick cocksucker! Nobody wipes my ass! Nobody!"

"Move, Rich!" Leo said, closing the door in Brickhill's face. Rich put the car in gear and drove off. Harry shook his fist at Brickhill through the rear window.

"That prick!" Harry said. He sat back now and suddenly laughed. "Hey, you see his face when you slammed the door?"

"Harry, you stupid fool!" Leo said.

Harry stopped laughing. "What the hell's with you?"

"You're a fool," Leo said. "You don't know when you're well off. You never did."

"Yeah, well let me tell you something." Harry glanced again through the rear window. "I'm gonna get that Irish bastard. You have my word on it. He is dead!"

"What good will that do?" Leo asked.

Harry seemed astonished. "What good will it do? Are you kidding?"

"Killing Brickhill won't solve the problem," Leo said.

"The hell it won't," Harry said sullenly. But almost immediately he laughed again. He slapped Leo's back. "So tell me, this party. Who are the broads?"

Leo did not hear him. He was gazing out the window. They were on Lafayette Street, just passing Hester. The neighborhood had changed so much you could hardly recognize it. But even with the new clean buildings and a park, the streets three blocks away were clogged with pushcarts and sidewalk stalls, so it still smelled the same. But that, too, would soon change. Everything changed.

Everything but Harry Wise, he thought, sitting back, looking at Harry who had just lit a cigar. "Everything but you, Harry," Leo said aloud, quietly.

"Huh?" Harry said. "What, me?"

"You want to kill Charlie Brickhill, but you don't understand that he'd only be replaced by another reformer. Somebody just like him."

"So we'll get the new guy, too," Harry said. The idea appealed to him.

"Harry, there'll always be Brickhills," Leo said. "Men who refuse to accept the simple truth that since time began, human beings have wanted and needed certain basic pleasures. And they've gotten them, and one way or another always will. And they'll keep getting them, no matter how much Brickhill and his kind keep trying to prevent it. They're hypocrites, these Brickhills. They have false and unrealistic moral standards, and they make false and unrealistic laws to enforce the false and unrealistic standards. And all the time they know these laws beg to be broken! Same thing with religion. Exactly the same. So until the laws are changed, Harry, men will keep lying, cheating, and needlessly harming one another."

Harry said, "Leo, what does all that bullshit have to do with killing Brickhill?"

All that bullshit, Leo thought sadly, and thought that yes, he supposed it was bullshit. But true; he knew it was true. He said, "It has to do with keeping the heat off us, off IDIC. Killing him, or any cop, can only bring them down harder on us. What we have to do is contain him. Neutralize him."

"Yeah, so how do you do that?"

"I don't know, but we better find out."

Leo did not stay long at Luchow's. He wanted to get home and see the children. He was leaving the next day for another swing around the circuit. Newport, Hot Springs, Miami, and then Havana. He was away nearly a month. When he returned he found himself faced with an entirely new problem, one as serious in its own way as Charles Brickhill.

A problem named Dino Coletti.

3.

Harry had to shout to be heard over the brassy orchestra. "They don't look like *shvartzers*! A couple of them, especially the one with the big tits, the one on the end—they look almost white!"

"If you're ready to change your luck, Harry," said Dino Coletti, "I'll have Julie fix you up with her."

"Hey, don't worry about my luck," Harry said. He studied the dancer with the big breasts another moment, then turned to Dino Coletti with a cold, hard grin. "Worry about your own."

They were at a front-row table in the Aladdin, Jules Jefferson's Harlem cabaret. Leo, Harry, Sal, and Dino Coletti. All wore tuxedos, as did the young men accompanying Dino, who sat nearby with Sal's Tom Marizzi, and Leo's Rich Freedman.

Dino said to Leo, "What about you, Leo? Your luck okay, too?"

"So far," Leo said.

"Then it doesn't need changing?"

Leo shook his head and smiled politely. Dino returned the smile, then directed his attention to an intricate marching number the twelve chorus girls were executing on stage. The martial music and military costumes reminded Leo of a story he once read about dragon's teeth. The teeth, planted, grew into soldiers. Like Dino Coletti.

Dino Coletti had been an underboss for Patsy Carbo, one of the few top men to survive the slaughter of five years before. From the remnants of the Carbo and Ruggerio families he formed a new, unified group. He was young, bright, and dangerously ambitious. And patient, for he had bided his time and consolidated his gains, building for the day he would be strong enough to once again challenge the Jews and their Italian ally, Sal Bracci. The five other leading New York families were growing, and learning, and in time would be formidable. But now, in the early winter of 1932, only Dino Coletti's family was ready.

Dino selected the Aladdin for this meeting with Leo and his partners because it was an agreeably neutral site. Dino did a huge narcotics business with Jules Jefferson, an enterprise in which Leo and the others were wholly disinterested. They allowed Dino complete freedom with it, believing he would be satisfied with that and leave well enough alone.

They were wrong.

Dino Coletti wanted no war with IDIC, merely a piece of their New York action.

Twenty percent of it.

In return, he guaranteed peace in the territory. Any hostile move directed toward an IDIC facility or individual would be considered a hostile move toward Dino Coletti. No Italian family or even the boldest Independent would dare challenge that edict.

This was the proposition placed before Leo and his partners in Jules Jefferson's private office later that evening. He was not an unpersonable man, Dino Coletti. He never raised his voice, or gestured with his manicured hands. He dressed well, and conservatively. He was impressive.

"I figured the floor show would soften you guys up," he said. He did not believe in Old World cat-and-mouse semantic games. This was America. The American way was to speak your mind. "I don't think it did, though."

He sat at Jules Jefferson's huge U-shaped desk. Leo and Sal were seated directly opposite him on a dark leather couch, and Harry in a lounge chair. From the club the music, muffled by the thick walls, now and then gently rattled the glassed framed autographed photographs of sports and entertainment personalities on the office wall.

Sal said, "No, Dino, we're not softened up."

"Well, you warned me it wouldn't be easy," Dino said.

Dino had first approached Sal in the vague hope Sal might influence his Jewish partners. Sal only said he would mention Dino's desire to talk business to them. Dino knew better than to even suggest Sal break with the Jews; he remembered the last time all too well.

Sal said, "What I told you, Dino, was I'd go along with whatever Leo and Harry want."

"Maybe they'd do the same for you."

"We act as one," Sal said. "We learned a long time ago it's the only way this business will work."

"Now you're giving me lessons, Sal?"

Harry waved his hands impatiently. "What's all the yakking for? Dino's pulling the old protection racket on us. For Christ's sake, I was doing that with candy stores and pushcart *shmatte* peddlers when I was ten years old!" Harry's voice hardened. "Now we heard your speech, Dino, and we're telling you, no. You want to start a war over it, I got one word of advice: don't."

Dino Coletti's face was absolutely expressionless. "You sure aren't the world's best diplomat, Harry." He turned to Leo. "What about it, Leo?"

"I couldn't agree more," Leo said. "Harry's no diplomat."

"Come on, guys, I didn't ask you to come here to tell jokes," Dino said, still quite composed, which troubled Leo. People like Dino Coletti did not take rejection lightly. Leo glanced at Sal. Their eyes met and held an instant; he knew Sal was equally troubled. Dino continued now to Leo, "I want an answer."

Before Leo could reply, the door opened. Jules Jefferson entered. He was so tall the top of his head brushed the bottom of the Tiffany-shaded lamp hanging from the ceiling. His totally naked scalp gleamed blackly.

"Gentlemen, excuse me just one second, please. . need something." Gesturing Dino to remain seated, Jules opened the middle desk drawer and removed a checkbook. "I won't disturb you again."

"Stay a minute, Jules. I want to ask you a question," Leo said. Jules tucked the checkbook under his arm and looked at Leo, who asked, "How long have you and Dino dealt in drugs up here?"

Jules glanced at Dino. Dino nodded. Jules said, "Three, four years."

"Actually, it's more like five," Leo said. "And each year the take is bigger. Last year it was nearly a million."

Jules smiled. "You keep good tabs, Leo."

Leo did not return the smile, but now looked at Dino. "Last year a million, this year more, and next year at least two million. We don't bother you one bit, do we? We don't interfere, we don't ask for a piece. We don't care."

"So what is that supposed to mean?" Dino asked.

Before Leo replied, he said to Jules Jefferson, "Thanks, Julie."

"You need drinks or anything?"

"I don't think so," Leo said. "Thanks again."

Jules flipped a mock salute and left. Dino said quickly, "Now look, Leo, you're making out like this is some kind of threat from me. It is not. I made you a business proposition. I didn't dream it up sitting on the crapper this morning. I thought it over carefully, and worked it all out. I'm telling you that the other families are getting restless. They're figuring they can take you on. I'm offering a guarantee to sit on them for you."

"Sure, for a fifth of our action," Sal said.

"Sal, you know damn well what's going on with us," Dino said. "The families, I mean. We're growing like crazy. Our guys are young, and smart. There's no more Big Tony Ruggerios or Patsy Carbos. And no more of that small time, secret society shit. The Mafia, or the Unione Siciliano, or whatever. We learned from you. We're businessmen now."

"Yeah, Dino," Harry said. "Like I said, in the protection business!"

Dino was unfazed. "Harry, you don't understand. I'm trying to tell you that pretty soon the families will wake up and see the only way is to get together. Make one big family that'll control everything. When that happens, it's all over for you."

Sal said, "Well, that's where we disagree, Dino. I don't think they'll ever get together. No matter how smart they are, or good at business they are. Don't forget, I know them, too. Don't you think I know Dominic Cranillo? And his ideas about merging with his brother Rocco out in Omaha to form an Empire? An Empire, but they'll slit each other's throats arguing over which one is the Emperor. And that pimp who's running the Brooklyn family, Barbera, Willie Barbera, they tell me not a day goes by he's not plotting some wild scheme to make himself the Boss of Bosses."

"You shouldn't talk down about them like that," Dino said. "They're your own people."

"I'm glad you mentioned that, Dino," Sal said. "Because you seem to forget there's another family bigger and stronger than any of the five." He paused, and then spoke very quietly. "Mine."

Dino's face was bland, but his eyes were hot and angry. Leo could almost read his mind. Yes, Sal did have the most powerful Italian family, but had married it to the Jews, and now made it quite clear he intended to remain married.

They talked a while longer, had drinks sent in, and then Dino Coletti left. Leo, Sal, and Harry returned to the showroom for one more drink. Jules sent over the big-breasted chorus girl for Harry, and a bottle of Dom Pérignon. Sal and Leo donated the bottle to Harry, wished him a pleasant change of luck, and left.

All the way back to Hempstead, Leo thought about Dino Coletti. Sal had agreed with Leo that if Dino was seriously considering starting a war, they dissuaded him. They also agreed that Dino's strategy now almost surely would be to concentrate on uniting the five families into one cohesive group. Which actually pleased both Leo and Sal. It meant Dino would be wholly occupied in a task that if it succeeded at all might take years.

Both of them, Leo especially, underestimated Dino Coletti.

—— *14* ——

THE four milk bottles were still on the service porch in their metal carrying container. It was Thursday, Mrs. Morton's day off, the one morning Ellie made Steven breakfast before he went off to school, and she overslept. Luckily, Hershey fed the boy, although obviously skipping milk. Steven hated milk.

Ellie picked up the container and stood a moment gazing out across the yard. It was warm for January, the sun so bright it had melted much of last week's snow. Even the pond, frozen hard enough for skating, was breaking up in little patches of floating ice.

She wondered if Leo was still asleep. He came home late, and had to be up early for a meeting in town. Another meeting, always a meeting. But then, she thought, I suppose I should be grateful for small favors. This was his third consecutive night at home. A *mitzvah*, as her mother would say. And another *mitzvah*, yet: they made love. A "hurry-up-job," as her mother would *not* say. But not at all unsatisfactory, in fact quite pleasant. She chuckled aloud and went into the kitchen.

Hershey, just returned from driving Steven to school, sat in the breakfast nook opposite Carla. He had lifted the little girl from her high chair and propped her on the bench on several telephone directories and a Sears & Roebuck catalog, and was trying to tempt her with a toasted bagel heaped with cream cheese and lox. Now, pursing his lips in an airplane engine sound, he buzzed the bagel in and around Carla's mouth. Carla snatched the lox from the bagel and popped it into her mouth, promptly clamping her teeth together, preventing Hershey from inserting the bagel.

"You are something else," Hershey said. He sat back, apparently defeated, and began eating his own bagel.

Carla, believing Hershey would not attempt to feed her again, opened her mouth to chew the lox. Hershey's hand flashed out, bagel ready. Carla saw it in time and closed her mouth. It was a game she loved.

Ellie watched, thinking of her good fortune in having Hershey, and doubly fortunate that both children, Carla and Steven, responded to him so well. But then Hershey loved them, so how could they not respond? Leo also loved them, and they responded equally well to him, but never saw enough of him.

Ellie started fixing the coffee, listening to Carla ask Hershey if they were going for a toboggan ride today. Almost daily Hershey bundled Carla into a small toboggan and, holding her snugly, raced the toboggan down the hill to the pond.

Hershey said, "No, *kindeleh*, today I got to go with your father." He explained to Ellie, "Some papers I should sign over at the big office." The "big office" was IDIC's Peterson Building quarters. As opposed to the "little office," the old garage. Hershey continued, "Richie, he'll be here while I'm gone."

"That's good," Ellie said absently. She plugged the electric percolator into the breakfast-nook wall outlet, poured Carla a glass of milk, and went upstairs. Leo was shaved and dressed. "Coffee's almost ready," she said. "Will you be home for dinner?"

"I'm not sure yet. I'll call you." He slapped her affectionately on the behind. "That was very nice last night."

"You thought so, did you?"

"I did."

She held out her hand. "That'll be twenty bucks, then."

He raised an eyebrow. "Is that the going price?"

"It is around here," she said. "This is a high-class house, you know."

"You can say that again." He peeled two twenty-dollar bills from a small, folded sheaf of bills. "A bonus," he said. She slipped the money into her housecoat pocket and kissed him. He glanced at his watch. "Want to go for forty more?"

"Fifty, and it's a deal," she said.

"Hey, for fifty I can buy the whole Latin Quarter chorus line."

"Sure," she said. "But none of them is a Long Island Jewish housewife."

When they came downstairs twenty minutes later, Hershey had driven the car around to the front and sat waiting in the passenger's seat. Leo enjoyed driving the Pierce-Arrow. He settled himself behind the wheel, then noticed Hershey staring tensely into the right-hand side mirror.

Leo turned to the rear window. A green-painted U.S. Post Office truck moved slowly up the street toward the house.

"Too early for the mail," Hershey said, not looking away from the mirror, groping blindly under the dashboard for the .45 attached to a steel spring device just behind the radio panel. He handed the gun to Leo, and at the same time reached under the front seat. He pulled a Browning automatic shotgun up onto his lap and pumped a cartridge into the chamber.

The truck did not swing into the drive. It stopped on the street in front of the house. A uniformed postman got out. A tall, slender man wearing rimless glasses, he tilted his visored cap back on his head and glanced at a delivery pad, then at the white-stenciled street-address number on the sidewalk curb. Then he slid open the vertical rear panel of the truck and brought out a long cardboard carton. He tucked the carton under his arm and walked up the drive toward the Pierce-Arrow.

He waved, calling, "Mr. Gorodetsky?" He was still twenty feet away. Leo gripped the .45 in his right hand and opened the door with his left. The postman, closer now, said, "You him?"

"What've you got?" Leo asked.

The postman tapped the delivery pad against the carton cover. "Need your John Hancock."

Just then Ellie stepped onto the front porch, with Carla directly behind her. Ellie cupped her hands over her mouth and shouted, "Leo, telephone . . . !"

The last syllable was not out of Ellie's mouth when Leo heard Hershey cry "No!" and felt himself pushed violently down into the seat. He knew Hershey had pushed him, and that his forehead struck the steering wheel with such force that he seemed momentarily blinded. In that same instant, almost as one single ear-shattering sound, he heard the sharp rat-rat-rat of a machine gun, the blast of a shotgun, and the shattering of glass. And a scream of terror he knew was Ellie's.

Leo had not seen the postman fling away the delivery pad and flip the cover off the carton, in the same motion discarding the carton which contained a Thompson he leveled point-blank at Leo. But Hershey saw it in time and shoved Leo out of the line of fire.

Hershey fired the shotgun a split second before the postman. The single shotgun blast caught the postman in the shoulder. The impact hurled him backward but not soon enough to deflect his fire. The first burst of three bullets struck Hershey in the throat and face. Falling, the postman's fingers reflexively depressed the Thompson trigger, but the muzzle was tipped upward. The final burst of six rounds slammed into the front door of the house and the sidelight windows on the left side of the door.

Abruptly, all was silent. Entangled under the steering wheel, still stunned from the blow to his forehead, holding the .45, the odor of cordite and gunsmoke nearly choking him, Leo felt paralyzed. Then, again, he heard Ellie scream, followed immediately by the shrill crying of a terrified child. Leo grasped the steering wheel and extricated himself. He threw open the door and tumbled to the ground. The postman lay on his back, eyes wide with shock, the rimless spectacles dangling now from one ear. Near his fallen cap, his outstretched hand still gripped the Thompson.

Leo crawled past the postman to the front bumper of the car. He pulled himself up and saw Ellie on the front porch. She stood frozen, trembling as though convulsed. She clutched Carla, burying the child's face in her skirt. Both stood inches from the bullet-punctured front door, their shoes covered with shards of rose-colored glass from the shot-out sidelight windows. For one terrible moment Leo and Ellie looked at each other.

Rich Freedman, revolver in hand, half dressed, face masked in shaving lather, raced across the drive to the car. "Oh shit!" he cried. "Oh, Jesus Christ!"

Leo pointed to the postman. "You know him?"

Rich shook his head. Leo kicked the Thompson out of the postman's fingers. He said to Rich, "Take Ellie and Carla inside and stay with them!"

Rich strode to the porch, but Ellie had already shouldered Carla back into the house and gestured Rich to stay with the little girl. Ellie remained on the porch, her hand clamped tightly over her mouth as she watched Leo walk around to the passenger's side of the Pierce-Arrow.

Hershey's body was jackknifed, his legs still in the car, his torso extended over the car's running board, the top of his head just touching the graveled driveway. His eyes, open, stared sightlessly. The entire lower half of his face was gone.

"Leo!" Ellie screamed.

Leo whirled. The postman was crawling across the driveway toward the Thompson. Leo was there in a single stride. He picked up the Thompson and lobbed it all the way across the yard.

"Who sent you?" Leo asked.

The postman shook his head. His gray-blue whipcord jacket was soaked with blood that stained the snow on the front lawn.

Leo knelt close to him, a young man, with light hair and fair skin now ash white. Leo jammed the .45 muzzle into the hollow of the man's throat. "Five seconds," Leo said. "You give me a name, you get out of this. You don't, I finish you right here and now."

"Coletti," the postman whispered.

Behind him, Leo heard Ellie say, "They've killed Hershey!" Almost zombielike, she was walking down the stairs toward Hershey.

"Ellie, get inside!" Leo said. "Get inside, and stay there!"

"Hershey's dead," she said.

"I told you to get inside! Stay in there with Rich!"

Ellie hesitated.

"Now!" Leo said.

Ellie ran into the house. When she was inside, Leo knelt to the postman again. Very slowly he raised the .45, cocked it, and pressed the muzzle into the postman's chest.

The postman's lips moved. Leo knew he was trying to say that Leo had promised him his life. Leo answered the unasked question.

"I lied," he said. Then he shot him. He emptied the whole magazine into him.

Hershey was buried the next day. Ellie insisted on a religious ceremony. Leo knew it meant nothing to Hershey whose only wish was to lie next to Edie in the neglected, weed- and brush-overgrown little cemetery in Brooklyn. Ellie wanted the ceremony for Steven. Hershey was Steven's friend. When your friend died, you honored his memory.

She wanted Steven to say Kaddish for Hershey. Steven was after all the closest thing to a son Hershey had. And Carla a daughter, although Ellie agreed that Carla was too young to attend a funeral, and certainly too young to fully comprehend. She accepted as a fact that Hershey had gone away, but might some day return. In later years her only memory of that day was of some "loud popping noises," and that a man fell down.

The rabbi delivered a brief eulogy. Leo endured it, angered at the continual references to God and the deceased going on to a better life. For a crazy instant Leo imagined himself interrupting the service to explain to Steven the utter absurdity of even pretending there was another life. This was it, the only life, period, end. He considered it vitally important Steven understand this truth.

The rabbi led Steven through the Hebrew Kaddish liturgy, and it was over. Almost as fast as it began. Ellie never knew that Leo gave the rabbi half of a torn fifty-dollar bill, promising the other half if the rabbi finished in less than five minutes.

But Leo wept. It came with no warning from deep inside him when Steven all at once threw himself into Leo's arms. He stroked the sobbing boy's hair and mumbled what he hoped were soothing words, but knew were empty, foolish platitudes. And then his own tears came. All this happened at the very end, leaving the grave site.

As he wept, Leo thought of the old days. The garage, and the craps game. And Edie. It was her memory that made him weep. Holding Steven, rocking back and forth with the grief-stricken eight-year-old boy, he suddenly wished Edie knew that he and Hershey had made up. That their friendship was stronger than before, and Hershey had loved Leo's children and taken care of them. And, in truth, saved Leo's life at the cost of his own. Edie would have been proud of Hershey.

They had driven to the cemetery in a veritable convoy. Led by a sedan with four of Harry's men, then Harry's car with Harry, Sal, and George and Betty Gerson. Then Leo's Pierce-Arrow, and Sal's Cadillac with four of his men. They drove back in the same order.

They had just turned on to the new four-lane turnpike when Leo casually said to Ellie, "From now on, for a while at least, three of my men will be at the house all the time."

She said nothing, only looked at him, and for the first time he realized that at the cemetery she had not cried. Her eyes were dry and clear. It would happen later, he thought. She would collapse completely. And he would not be there to help. Immediately after seeing Ellie and Steven safely home he was meeting Harry and Sal in town. To decide exactly how and where to deal with Dino Coletti.

"They're good boys," Leo said. "They won't get in your way."

Ellie remained silent, but he knew what she was thinking. Why weren't those "good boys" there yesterday to avert the tragedy? And as he thought this it occurred to him that not once had Ellie mentioned the danger to her and Carla, those machine-gun slugs tearing into the glass and wood, missing them by scant inches. He felt suddenly chilled and pulled up his coat collar. He glanced at Steven on the jump seat facing him. He smiled at him. More platitudes rose to his lips, but he could not bring himself to say them; it was simply too dishonest. He squeezed Steven's hand, and turned to Ellie again.

"Have Mrs. Morton fix up the room over the garage next to Richie's for the new boys," he said. "And might as well use Hershey's room, too."

Ellie said, "I'm leaving you, Leo." She spoke quietly, but very clearly. "I'm taking the children and leaving."

"To your parents?" he said. "That might not be such a bad idea."

She looked at him, almost surprised. "Yes," she said. "To my parents."

Ellie did not go to her parents. She packed whatever she could in two small bags, and that same evening drove off with the children in her own car, a Nash coupe Leo had given her last year as a thirtieth-birthday gift.

She phoned him the next day from Massachusetts. From Georgetown, a small town north of Boston. She had rented a house there. He did not ask why she chose that particular place, or how. He knew only that he felt enormous relief having her far from New York, and foolish for not having suggested it himself.

He said to her on the phone, "The minute my business here in New York is finished, I'll go to Georgetown, wherever the hell that is, and bring you all home."

"We'll talk about it later, Leo," she said, and hung up.

2.

Shortly after midnight of the day following Hershey's funeral a Buick sedan roared to a brake-screeching stop outside the canopied entrance of the Aladdin. A man in the front passenger's seat rolled down the window and called to the doorman.

"This guy's a friend of Julie's. I don't think he feels too good right now!"

Immediately, the rear car door opened. A body tumbled out into the gutter almost at the doorman's feet. The car raced off. The doorman, terrified, stared at the crumpled form in the gutter—a man, and alive, whimpering like an animal in pain. In the light from the blinking electric sign atop the canopy the doorman saw that the fabric of the man's trousers, at the knees, was shredded and caked with blood.

The doorman rushed into the club for help. The man in the gutter moved slightly, and then rolled over on his side and screamed in unbearable pain. In a moment the six foot six, 275-pound bouncer appeared, and a moment later, Jules Jefferson. Jules recognized the injured man; his first instinct was to walk away, but he forced himself to order the doorman and bouncer to carry the man around to the rear of the club.

Jules stood gazing after them, the man's pain-racked screams still ringing in his ears. Even without the doorman's description, Jules knew who had deposited the injured man on his doorstep, and why.

The man in the Buick was Harry Wise.

The injured man was Dino Coletti. Both of his kneecaps had been shot away.

For nearly a year Sal had had a man planted within the Coletti family. Everything about Dino was known, even his habit of relieving himself before commencing each meal. His routine seldom changed. He enjoyed eating late, and this Friday evening, as each Friday evening, dined promptly at ten at a small Village restaurant on Fourteenth Street, the Bella Vista.

The restaurant's single-stall toilet was located outside the rear of the building. When Dino's bodyguard went out to check the stall for his boss it was occupied. A male voice from within announced he was just finishing. The door opened. The bodyguard stepped aside for the man to leave and found himself looking into the barrel of a .32 automatic. He was instructed to signal Dino that all was clear.

Dino was hustled into a waiting Buick sedan parked in the alley. The car drove uptown to the Twenty-third Street ferry station, closed and deserted this time of night, where Leo and Harry waited. A brief conversation with Dino convinced them that the bogus postman had indeed acted on Dino's orders. Leo and Harry then exchanged a few words, and Leo left. Five minutes later, Harry placed a bullet into each of Dino's kneecaps.

Crippling him for life, a form of punishment uniquely Sicilian, conveying a message not to be lost on Dino's family or the other families. A message of contempt. Dino Coletti was considered so insignificant, he was beneath killing. Treated by his enemies with such disrespect, Dino could hardly demand respect from his own people.

Killing him would only have created a martyr, and a cause. Now, instead, he was a living reminder of the disdain felt for him and his family, and their ability to wage war. If nothing else it would give Dino's successor—and the other four families—pause. It was a bold, calculated risk designed to avoid a war.

And it succeeded. There was no war, or even the slightest hint of reprisal. Dino's successors were too busy fighting among themselves for power. In the end Dino's family once more was split in two, their remnants absorbed by the other four families.

When Harry prodded Dino into the shadows of the deserted ferry station, Dino assumed he was to be killed. But he was no coward, and even slightly contemptuous.

"How come Leo's not doing this himself?" he asked.

"He allowed me the pleasure," Harry said.

"The little bastard's got no balls," Dino said. "He makes you do the dirty work."

Harry laughed. "Don't worry about his balls. I asked to do it."

Harry laughed again when he told Leo about it the next day. He said the dumb guinea just couldn't figure it out. What Dino Coletti did not know was that Leo fully intended to carry out the sentence personally. Harry had not only asked for the privilege, he had pleaded for it.

Leo was thinking about this two days later, driving through Connecticut. The January weather had turned cold again, but the day was clear with no snow forecast. Alone in the car, he had just passed through New Haven, finally out of city traffic and onto the wide, two-lane concrete highway. The road was fairly empty, and bone-dry in the cold, the snow banked in low, crusty piles along the roadside. He was pushing sixty-five, but you would hardly know it. Leo loved the feeling of the power of those twelve cylinders throbbing into his fingertips on the steering wheel. The utter, absolute pleasure.

Pleasure, he thought, which was what had reminded him of Harry and Dino Coletti. Harry said he didn't want to deny Leo his revenge, but wouldn't Leo please consider allowing Harry the pleasure?

This was their brief conversation outside the ferry station after Leo satisfied himself that Coletti ordered the hit. Leo had asked Harry for a gun.

"Leo, this needs a special—" Harry groped for the word. "Touch. A nice delicate touch. You know, like a dentist. A special touch." He grinned in the dark. "Mine."

"I'm not planning to fill his teeth, Harry." Leo held out his hand for the gun.

Harry said, "Hershey was my friend too, don't forget." Before Leo could reply, Harry had continued quickly. "I know you think the only feelings I have are for my *shlong* and what hole I can stick it into. And I'm just a *meshuggener* that you never know what he might do. Well, maybe I am, and maybe I'm not. But this is important to me, Leo."

"Yes," Leo said aloud now, studying the road ahead, two cars approaching in the near distance. One was overtaking the other, both for a moment occupying the entire road, looming larger and larger in the windshield. At the very last instant one car cut sharply back into the proper lane, and then both zoomed past in consecutive whooshes of wind that gently rocked the Pierce-Arrow.

Leo watched them in the rearview mirror. Both were nearly out of sight. He wondered what would have happened if they smashed into him head-on. Well, of course, instant death.

Why in the hell are you so worried about death? he asked himself.

Why? Are you kidding?

You mean, because Dino Coletti almost hit you?

Isn't that a reason to worry?

Sure, but you know good and well it won't be the last time somebody tries to hit you. It will happen again.

That means Ellie and the kids are in danger.

Come on, off the crap. They always were, weren't they?

Always are, present tense, you mean, he corrected himself.

Always will be, he thought, and closed his fist and banged it hard on the wheel. He wanted to erase from his mind that picture of Ellie and Carla standing at the bullet-riddled door and smashed sidelight window.

It was past five and dark when he drove into Georgetown. It was such a small place it would have been easy to drive right through it without realizing. He stopped at a diner and asked directions for the address Ellie gave him.

Only two people were in the diner, but both knew the house the lady from New York had rented. "The old Wicks place, ain't it?" one, a middle-aged, overall-clad man, said.

"Yes," said the other, younger and wearing a frayed railroad brakeman's suit and tie. "Her name's Gordon, somebody said."

"Gordon?" Leo asked.

"Drives a new Nash with New York plates. Has two kids, boy and girl? Name's Gordon. Mrs. Gordon."

Leo found it with no trouble. A neat, ivy-trimmed cottage just off the main street, called Main Street, with a white picket fence and small front yard.

She greeted him cordially, if coldly, but the children hugged and kissed him. Ellie had already given them supper, and despite their protests ordered them to bed. If they quieted down and did as told they could listen to *Amos 'n' Andy*. Leo said he'd see them in the morning when they all would drive home, Steven riding with him, Carla with Ellie.

When both children were in bed, Ellie and Leo returned to the kitchen. Ellie opened a cupboard over the sink and took down a bottle of Jack Daniel's. She poured some into a water tumbler, added water and ice, and set it on the kitchen table, on the back pages of yesterday's *New York Sun*. She placed the glass squarely on a small story on the lower right. The liquid in the glass magnified the column-wide headline: BOGUS POSTMAN SLAIN.

Leo knew the story by heart. An unidentified man was found shot to death in a post-office truck parked on a Brooklyn side street. The truck had earlier been reported stolen by the postal department. Police theorized the vehicle was driven to Brooklyn by the killer or killers.

Ellie said, "Do you want a drink?"

"No thanks."

"Coffee?"

"I stopped in Worcester and had a sandwich," he said. "If we start early tomorrow, we can be home before dark. The weather's supposed to be good."

She picked the glass up from the newspaper and drank. The newsprint was wet and blurred from the bottom of the glass. "We're not going home tomorrow, Leo," she said. "We're not going anywhere."

He said nothing a moment. He got up and stepped to the window over the sink and looked out. He could see the entire length of Main Street, the little single-story business buildings and small homes. Their lighted windows cast a soft yellow glow on the snow, almost like a picture postcard.

"Why are you calling yourself 'Mrs. Gordon'?" he asked.

"Because that's how I want to be known from now on."

He turned to her. "You're ashamed of your name?"

"I'm afraid of my name, Leo."

"There's nothing to be afraid of," he said. "Coletti is through."

"You killed him, too?"

"No, but he's all done. There's no more danger."

Ellie drank down the drink. She rose and carried the empty glass to the sink. She started opening the cupboard, then changed her mind. She stood close to Leo, slightly taller.

"My name is Eleanor Gordon," she said. "Tomorrow morning I'm enrolling Steven in school in a city a few miles from here. It's called Winston. They have a school bus to take him back and forth. I'll find a good nursery school for Carla. And I'll find a job for myself. There's a library in Winston. I'm an experienced librarian."

Leo tried to sound casual. "Just like that?"

"Yes," she said. "Just like that."

"I said there's no more danger."

"I heard you."

"And it makes no difference?"

"Not one damn bit, Leo."

They stood looking at each other another moment. Then he stepped away. He sat at the table. Ellie brought the bottle down from the cupboard shelf and poured another drink.

"I see your nerves are bothering you again," he said. "How many is that today?"

She drank half the glass in a single swallow. "We're staying here, Leo, and there's nothing you can do about it."

Well, there is something I can do, he thought. There is plenty. I can, for example, just send a couple of my people here and simply pack her up and pack her into her car and bring her back.

She read his thoughts. She laughed bitterly. "Of course, you could have me killed. Isn't that how you solve all your problems?"

"You don't understand," he said. "You never did, you never will."

"No, dear sweet Leo, it's *you* who don't understand!" Her voice rose shrilly. "I am finished. *We* are finished! My name is Gordon, my children's names are Gordon. They will grow up as normal, happy children. I will be a normal, happy woman! Now get out of here and leave us alone!"

The swinging door from the dining room opened. Carla stood in the doorway rubbing her eyes. "The noise woke me. Why is everybody talking so loud?"

"Daddy and I are talking," Ellie said. She rushed across the kitchen floor and scooped the little girl up in her arms. "I'll tuck you back in bed."

She carried Carla from the room. Leo sat watching the door wobble on its hinges. His anger had turned to quiet sadness. Because Ellie was right. Now, again, as in the long-ago but never forgotten Renaissance, he admired and respected her. And remembered how only the other day they had enjoyed each other so much. He wanted that again. He needed it.

When she returned to the kitchen, he said, "What will it take to have you come back?"

She stared at him. "Are you serious?"

"Of course I'm serious!"

She raised the half-finished glass to her lips, but put it down without drinking. She came to the table and sat. "Quit," she said. "Quit. Move out of New York, far away. Anywhere. Maine, California. Anywhere. But no more of this." She tapped a finger on the newspaper, the water-stained bogus-postman story.

He felt more confident. He had anticipated precisely such a response and knew how to deal with it. "Now listen, Repeal is coming. No matter who wins next November's election, if it's Hoover, or whoever runs for the Democrats, they'll run on a Repeal ticket. No more bootlegging. We're already getting out of it. It's gone, finished, *kaput*. We're putting everything into the casinos and the racing wire. I didn't tell you about the racing wire. In a year, we'll have it coast to coast. Every bookie in the country will use it. And pay us a weekly fee for it. It's a gold mine."

He paused abruptly. He had never before discussed business with her. What would she know about a race wire? He felt like a salesman selling an unappreciative customer a superior product.

"It's really one hell of an idea," he continued. "It came to me one day at the track. When I saw the telegrapher in the press box tapping the results out to his newspaper. So now we lease this wire from the paper.

It goes over phone lines right into our office, and we have it the same time the track does. Then all we do is relay it on to our own central locations, and they phone it in to the local bookies. Five minutes after the race, the bookies have the prices. Before, they had to wait for somebody to run to a phone booth outside the track, or somebody watching the track through binoculars from a roof. I'm telling you, within a year we'll have it coast to coast."

He stopped. His words echoed back at him. It was like talking to a stone. She looked at him emptily.

"Are you listening to me?" he asked.

"You're not listening to *me*," she said. "You asked what it would take for me to come back, and I said 'Quit.' You want me back, me and the children, you quit."

He said nothing. He did not know what to say. He had said it all.

She said, "How much are you worth now?"

"What are you talking about?"

"How much money do you have? I mean, everything. Your total net worth."

How much? he thought. How the hell do I know? A million? Two? Three? He knew he had very little in his personal bank account, perhaps ten or twenty thousand. But in Switzerland at least $500,000 in cash in a numbered account; and who knew the dollar value of all the companies controlled by IDIC?

He laughed, a gentle, reflective little laugh.

Ellie said, "You find that question funny?"

"In a way, yes," he said. "Because I haven't the slightest idea how much money I have. How much *we* have."

"I do," she said. "Millions."

Millions, he thought. Well, perhaps not millions plural, but certainly singular. At least that much. He remembered the day he asked Joey Epstein for $4,000 to purchase one hundred cases of King's Ransom. Then, he certainly knew how much he had. Zero. And only a few years ago he also knew. To the penny. But now, with millions, not the slightest idea. Relative, that was the word. It was all so beautifully relative.

". . . you don't have to stay in this anymore," Ellie was saying. "You have all the money you'll ever need."

"That's why you want me to quit?"

"Can you think of a better reason?"

Again, he did not know what to say. He had never, not once, thought of quitting. He wanted to answer her with a question: Why would he want to quit? But she had already provided the answer. He had enough money.

". . . not to mention staying alive," she was saying.

A flip reply rose to his lips. The problem of staying alive is an occupational hazard. Comes with the territory. But he knew better than to say it. He expected her to remind him how narrowly she and Carla escaped injury or death, and he desperately groped for a sensible response to that.

"I can't quit," he heard himself say, surprised at his own words.

"The tiger," she said, almost to herself.

He frowned at her.

"Don't you know the story of the tiger?" she said. "The boy riding the tiger? If he doesn't get off, the tiger will carry him into the jungle. If he gets off, the tiger will eat him."

"You don't understand," he said again, but wondering if he himself understood.

She was silent a moment. Her eyes brimmed with sudden tears. She drew in her breath. He could feel her composure cracking. "Leave us alone, Leo! If not for my sake, then for your children! Let them grow up like normal children! Away from you, away from your life!"

She went on, but he hardly heard her. He knew she was right; it was no life for her, or the children. And he knew he must make a choice. He also knew he had already made it.

He did not remain overnight in Georgetown. He drove into Boston and checked into a hotel, registering as Leo Gordon, which at first amused him, but as the night wore on annoyed him for its childishness. He tossed and turned, reviewing in his mind the choice. And why he made it. He could have his family—and very likely die of old age, not gunned down in the street. So why not do as Ellie asked? Quit.

The answer came shockingly as he lay watching the dark sky whiten with drab gray morning light. So simple an answer he realized that it's very simplicity had obscured it.

He did not *want* to quit.

Now that, he told himself scathingly, is very profound. Of course, I don't want to. If I wanted to, I would.

Then the question, more accurately, is *why*? Why don't you want to quit?

Ah, yes, now we're getting to it. You don't want to quit because you have something to prove.

Something to prove? What the hell do I have to prove?

You tell me.

That I can reach the top.

Top? Top of what?

Top of the mountain. The pinnacle, the zenith, the summit.

And that's your ambition? The top?

Well, let me put it another way: I want to see how high the top is.

Why?

That, then, was the real question. He wrestled with it until the room was bright with daylight. When he finally fell asleep, he still did not know the answer.

PART FOUR

THE SPEED OF DREAMS

───── *15* ─────

An hour out of Chicago Harry was $3,500 ahead, on his way to yet another triple *schneid*: 130 points on the first game, 120 on the second, 98 on the third. He waited for Stuart Feigenbaum to finish dealing; he considered it unlucky to look at the cards until all were completely dealt.

"This your second trip to the coast, huh?" Feigenbaum asked, dealing himself the tenth card. He placed the remaining deck on the table and prepared to turn over the knock card.

Harry said, "I already told you that, didn't I?"

"Did you? Yeah, I guess you did." Feigenbaum grinned self-consciously. "You got me so *farblondjet* I don't know if I'm coming or going!" He turned over the knock card. "Jesus!" he said, dismayed. It was the ace of spades. A mandatory gin, with everything doubled.

Harry had his man on the ropes; you could actually smell the fear. "You are in trouble, my friend." He had already sorted his hand. Almost a no-brainer: two melds, and a four-five-seven of hearts.

"I've been in trouble since we started," Feigenbaum said glumly. "Why should this game be any different?" He examined his cards one at a time, placing each into his hand in proper order.

Waiting, Harry turned to the window. The land, flat and barren, whizzed past in a pleasant blur. That, and the musical clickety-clack of the train wheels made him feel relaxed and sleepy.

They had started playing gin rummy in Albany, a friendly little cent-a-point game. It began in the *Twentieth Century Limited*'s club car. Harry was reading an account of the *Hindenburg* disaster in a two-month-old *Time*, the May 17, 1937, issue. He had read it before, and seen it on newsreels, and was only sorry not to have been there to enjoy it in person. The lousy, Jew-hating Nazi bastards should all drop dead. Or burn up, whatever was most painful. Finishing the *Hindenburg* article, he had flipped through the magazine's pages and suddenly laughed aloud. The man in the adjacent lounge chair glanced at him curiously.

"This ad," Harry explained, tapping his finger on the open magazine. A Seagram's gin ad, with a drawing of a glass containing ice cubes. The headline read: ICE—PUBLIC ENEMY NUMBER ONE!

The ad copy went on to claim that melting ice, ruinous to most gins, would not affect Seagram's King Arthur gin. The man, who later introduced himself as Stuart Feigenbaum, a motion-picture producer, did not see the humor. Harry said it was a private joke.

They began chatting casually. Feigenbaum said he had been in New York catching up with Broadway plays. Harry, whose name apparently meant nothing to Feigenbaum, said he was on his way to the Coast to examine some real estate. Then they discussed Joe Louis's knockout of Jim Braddock last week, and how the Brown Bomber was the first colored man since Jack Johnson to win the heavyweight title.

One thing led to another, the Seagram gin ad leading to the gin game. Stu Feigenbaum suggested a new version called Oklahoma, three games played simultaneously. Harry learned fast. By the time they changed to the *Super Chief* in Chicago they moved the game into Harry's private compartment and the stakes to a nickel a point.

Now Feigenbaum said, "You want it?" He indicated the knock card, the ace of spades.

"All yours," Harry said.

Feigenbaum snatched the card and discarded a deuce. Harry wanted to laugh; it was like stealing. On a triple *schneid,* the shmuck was throwing deuces away, totally disregarding the count. Three draws later Harry pulled the six of hearts for gin.

"Hey," he said, straining to keep a poker face. "Remember that ad I showed you? The one about the ice?"

"Yeah, what about it?"

"What did it say ice wouldn't hurt?"

"Gin," Feigenbaum said innocently.

"Well, that's what I got," said Harry. "Gin!" He slapped down his cards and spread them out for Feigenbaum to see.

"You prick!" Feigenbaum said. The moment he spoke he knew it was a mistake. Harry's whole face suddenly hardened.

"Count 'em up," Harry said quietly. "Then figure out what you owe. The game's over."

"Come on, I was only kidding."

"Nobody calls me a prick," Harry said. "Except my friends, of which

THE SPEED OF DREAMS

you are not one. Now count." What he really wanted to do was ram his fist into this bald-headed, ferret-faced little bastard. But he had enough trouble, which was why he was traveling to California.

Feigenbaum's cards consisted of unmatched pictures and tens and nines. A monumental *schneid*. Harry now was ahead more than $5,000.

"You'll give me a chance to get even?" The whine in Feigenbaum's voice was a sound Harry had heard often enough. A man pleading for his life.

"Later, maybe," Harry said. "Right now we'll take a rest."

"I'll buy that," Feigenbaum said. He rose and moved to leave. "I'll catch up with you later."

He had already opened the door when Harry said, "You forgot something, didn't you?"

Feigenbaum frowned, then immediately smiled. "We always settle up at the end."

"I don't."

"Oh, sure," Feigenbaum said quickly. "Check okay?"

"Only if it's good," Harry said, unsmiling.

"Don't worry about that," Feigenbaum said.

"I won't if you won't," Harry said.

Feigenbaum wrote the check. His personal account in the Beverly Hills branch of the Bank of America, he said, assuring Harry that before the trip was over it would be back in Feigenbaum's pocket. With interest. Harry was glad to see Feigenbaum leave. He was bored playing, and wanted to see Nora Thomas again.

Nora Thomas, the actress. Feigenbaum introduced him to her in the club car while they were still playing the friendly game. She was the first movie star Harry had ever seen in the flesh. Tall, blond, with perfect little breasts and a tight ass, and long legs. She had looked him over like a butcher appraising a side of beef. A hungry, horny butcher. Years ago a girl, a singer in an uptown speak, told him it was all chemical. Like jungle animals giving off a scent to attract a mate. And the tip-off was the eyes. Something in the eyes, when they locked and held, sent a message.

Nora Thomas, "The Blond Venus," star of stage, screen, and radio, had sent Harry the message.

Now he rang for the porter. He ordered a drink—straight gin over ice—and sipped it leisurely, gazing out the window. The darkening sky made the passing landscape increasingly hard to see. It reminded him of a curtain slowly lowering, closing off the day, and then rising again on the night. In an hour he would shave, change clothes, and invite Nora Thomas to dinner.

As Harry told Stuart Feigenbaum, this was not his first trip to the Coast. Four months ago he flew out. And swore never to do it again. Queasy the whole way, especially at night, strapped into the little pullman bed, which was like trying to sleep in a hammock on a ship in a stormy sea. Going to L.A. to begin with was Leo's idea. Leo wanted him out of town, fast.

Because of a run-in last November with Charles Brickhill in the Algonquin Hotel lobby. Brickhill, after attending a luncheon celebrating his election to a third consecutive term as New York County D.A., was just leaving. Harry happened to be passing by and stopped in to buy a cigar. The encounter could easily have been avoided, but Harry could not resist the opportunity.

He sarcastically congratulated the newly elected D.A., the only Republican to win important office in the Roosevelt landslide. This led to a brief exchange that quickly turned ugly. Harry told Brickhill to be careful the next time he went out to start his car in the morning. Brickhill called Harry a punk and said that the one thing he was sure of was that someday, and soon, he would see Harry in the electric chair and personally strap him in. And with that, he shoved Harry roughly aside and brushed past him.

Harry, typically, lost his temper. He seized Brickhill's coat lapels and pushed him into the cigar counter. Cigars, cigarettes, candy, newspapers, and glass display case all crashed to the floor—with Brickhill. In the melee Harry nearly punched Brickhill, but was stopped by a plainclothes cop. A newspaper photographer got a shot of Harry leaning over the D.A.

In the end Harry challenged Brickhill to bring charges. A dozen witnesses saw Charles Brickhill instigate the incident. It was all too much for Leo and Sal. They sent Harry to California to cool off.

So when Harry told Stuart Feigenbaum that on this, his second trip west, he was going out to examine real estate, it was technically true.

If a boat was considered real estate.

It was on that first trip Harry saw the boat, an old decrepit collier anchored off Santa Monica Bay. Love at first sight, as he told Leo and Sal. Immediate, passionate love. This old beat-up scow, built at the turn of the century, first hauling coal under one name, then salmon from Alaska under another name, now rotting away. Harry's idea was to strip her down to the frame, rebuild her, and send her back to sea.

With no engines.

Anchored just outside the three-mile limit, served by a fleet of water taxis, the S.S. *Californian*—Harry's new name for her—would be the finest floating casino in the world. Monte Carlo at sea.

Gambling ships had been anchored off the California coast since 1928, so the concept was hardly original. Original, however, was the luxury and service Harry planned, attracting only the best clientele, and therefore the richest. A gold mine. Harry convinced Leo and Sal to put up $350,000 for the boat's purchase and refurbishing. He knew they were investing IDIC's money only to keep him busy, away from New York, but had they refused, he was prepared to risk his own money.

Repeal had changed everything. IDIC had divested itself of all holdings but the hotels and casinos, and the race wire (now an IDIC division called Trans-American News Bureau). Additionally, IDIC held substantial shares in a bank, the First Providence Trust Company. Through First Providence flowed much of IDIC's cash. As George Gerson said, it came in dirty and went out clean. Like a laundry.

Repeal—and the past five years—had also changed Harry Wise. Now thirty-eight, still rakishly handsome, he sometimes seemed almost sedately mature. Until the temper exploded. But he was learning to partially control that, having discovered to his surprise that this could be advantageous—incidents with Charles Brickhill notwithstanding. He was also learning, from Leo's example, to polish himself. Language, manners. He liked to say he had also learned one other lesson from Leo.

Don't get married.

The breakup of Leo's marriage pleased Harry. He could never forgive Ellie for what she did to Leo, although now that they were divorced Harry believed Ellie deserved credit for refusing to take a single cent beyond child support and an educational trust fund.

Harry knew that while Leo missed his children, Leo was the first to admit they were better off without him. He saw them occasionally, but he said not nearly enough. Harry found it hard to believe that in September Steve would be bar-mitzvahed. At thirteen, the kid was already a head taller than his father. And sometimes a little snotty. Or, as Leo said, hostile, meaning a big mouth. For example, when Leo asked him what he'd like for a birthday present Steve said, "A father." Harry would have kicked him right in the ass.

Harry was thinking of this two hours later, lying naked in bed, listening to the quiet, monotonous beat of the train, watching the absolutely flat blackness of the New Mexico desert rush past the window. Last year, when Ellie brought Steve in to Boston to meet his father for lunch, Harry had accompanied Leo. When the kid learned Harry was planning a trip to California, he confessed he had a crush on Deanna Durbin. Harry promised Steve that for his sixteenth birthday Uncle Harry would give him Deanna Durbin. Or, if not Deanna, some other movie star.

Yes, he thought, and old Uncle Harry was now test-driving a movie star to see what they were like. And, for sure, they were pretty good. At least the one asleep in his arms was. He shifted around slightly to relieve the cramp in his shoulder where Nora Thomas's head was nestled. The movement awakened her. She opened her eyes and gazed up at him with a languorous smile, then ran her fingers down his chest and over his stomach and down to his crotch. She closed her fist around him.

"My little Bonzo is dead," she whispered sadly. After dinner, the instant they entered Harry's compartment, she had dropped to her knees and unbuttoned his fly. And whispered, "Come out, Bonzo, come out wherever you are!" And Bonzo came out, all right, springing up at her like a jack-in-the-box.

"Not dead," Harry said now. "Just resting."

"I'll bring him to life," she said, and he felt her hair silkily brushing his chest and stomach, and her lips and tongue fluttering warmly and wetly down on him.

"Jesus!" he groaned, as she swallowed him almost entirely. "Jesus to Jesus!"

In an instant he was hard, and she rolled over under him, on her stomach, raising her buttocks for him to mount her from behind. Doggie style, she called it when they did it before; and never, he thought, never had he experienced anything like it. He felt like an express train rolling through a velvet tunnel. And, he realized with amazement, this was the third time in two hours. He wondered if she was ever satisfied, if she ever had enough.

A day later, at Union Station, watching her drive off in a studio limousine, he still wondered. Stuart Feigenbaum stood with him, amused.

"She showed you something, huh, kid?"

"It was an education," Harry said.

"Some education," Feigenbaum said. "You fuck Nora Thomas, and *I* pay you for it, yet."

"Think of it like you were putting me through college," Harry said. In between bouts with Nora Thomas, Harry and Feigenbaum had resumed their gin game. The final tally was $12,500. Feigenbaum's check rested securely in Harry's wallet.

It was that very same check that made Harry realize Nora Thomas was more than a superior *shtup* with a golden mouth and magic tongue. Her brains were not exclusively between her legs.

The check bounced. The bank informed Harry that Mr. Feigenbaum's present balance was slightly more than $9,000, and he had instructed them not to overdraw. Feigenbaum took Harry's phone call and the position that Harry, whom he had now learned was a notorious professional gambler, had misrepresented himself. Under such circumstances Stuart Feigenbaum considered the gin-rummy debt null and void. Harry could frame the check, keep it as a souvenir, or shove it up his ass. And if Harry had any wild gangster ideas about collecting, Stu Feigenbaum wanted to remind him that this was not New York, but L.A., Feigenbaum's home turf.

Ordinarily, such a declaration was tantamount to a man ordering his own execution. But Stu Feigenbaum's good fortune was that Harry had phoned him from Nora Thomas's patio. She was in the pool and saw Harry slam down the phone in a blind rage. He told her what happened, and what he intended doing about it.

"Harry, for Christ's sake, don't get mad," she said. "Get even."

And she knew precisely how to do it.

At 2:55 that afternoon, five minutes before closing time, Harry was at the main Beverly Hills branch of Bank of America on Beverly Drive. Depositing in cash to the account of Stuart Feigenbaum the sum of $3,500. At ten the following morning Harry was again at the bank, presenting Stuart Feigenbaum's $12,500 check. Yesterday's $3,500 deposit, added to the previous balance of slightly more than $9,000, created a current balance in Mr. Feigenbaum's account of slightly more than $12,500. Sufficient funds now existed to cover the check, which was promptly honored. Harry drew the money in cash.

Don't get mad, get even.

It was like a flash of lightning, a clap of thunder. Harry wondered why he had never thought of that. It made him feel that his whole life up to now had been a waste. He resembled a man who had just seen God.

With commensurate rewards. Everything seemed to all at once work. The ship purchase went off without a hitch, and the refurbishing was less costly than estimated. He leased a huge house on North Roxbury Drive for $500 a month, and bought a sparkling white Cord convertible. Nora Thomas fell madly in love with him, but so had two or three other equally interesting Hollywood ladies. Between Nora and these new acquaintances, Harry met everyone in town. Within a month he was a regular at Sam Goldwyn's Sunday morning bagel brunches and Jack Warner's Thursday poker games. Errol Flynn and Harry formed a mutual-admiration society, and an MCA agent almost sold Howard Hawks the idea of screen-testing Harry. Hawks demurred only because he considered Harry too handsome to play a gangster.

Hollywood and Harry Wise were made for each other.

He was a new man, and if he never saw New York again it would be too soon. The week before Christmas, when Leo phoned asking him to come back for an important meeting, he said it was impossible. The ship was almost ready to be towed to its anchorage. Harry planned to open with a gala New Year's Eve party for two hundred invited guests.

"Why?" Harry asked on the phone. "What the hell's so important?"

In New York, Leo held the phone out at arm's length an exasperated moment before he replied. "Don't you listen to what I've been telling you the past two months? Isn't it in the papers out there?"

"What's in the papers?"

"Sal," Leo said. "Brickhill has nailed Sal. Framed him!"

"Framed him for what, for Christ's sake?"

Leo did not answer immediately. In the brief silence the hum of the long-distance wire in his ear sounded like the echo of rushing wind. It was also like a message of revelation. The last thing Leo needed now was Harry Wise in New York. He must have been crazy to even think of suggesting Harry return. All he needed was for crazy Harry to try to kill Charlie Brickhill. Thankfully, Harry did not want to return.

Leo said, "Well, if you think you should stay there on the Coast, you know best."

"Leo, what the fuck are you talking about?" Harry shouted. "What've they got on Sal?"

"You won't believe this one," Leo said wearily. "White slavery."

Harry laughed into the phone. "Come again?"

"Forget it, Harry," Leo said. "Stay there. Get the ship ready on time. We'll handle everything here fine."

Three thousand miles away, Harry put down the phone and laughed again. In all the years he had known Sal, Sal was death on two things. One was drugs. The other was prostitution.

2.

It was not that Sal disliked whores. Quite the contrary, he respected them. A woman's body was her own, sacred, and if she used it for profit, then she alone should profit. It was the pimps he hated. No lower form of filth existed than a man who made money from a woman's body.

This was the irony of the charge on which Charles Brickhill brought Sal to trial. Too big a story for even Leo's newspaper contacts to play down. A battle of giants. Racket-busting D.A. versus "King of White Slavery." Even more ironic was the fact that Brickhill knew it was a false charge.

A frame.

Made possible, perhaps most ironic of all, by the testimony of a woman Sal once thought he loved.

Life had not gone well for Carol Beech since her return from Texas. She and Sal had resumed their relationship, but the old feeling was gone. She drifted from one man to another; it paid the rent. A man named Sam Shaeffer, a manufacturer of women's gloves, promised to divorce his wife for her. When he finally admitted it was all a lie, Carol threatened to kill herself. In his presence she placed a revolver to her head which he gallantly tried to wrest away. The gun discharged. Sam Shaeffer was killed. Carol was held for murder two.

Charles Brickhill made a deal. He would drop the murder charge if Carol testified that Sal Bracci brought her into New York State for the purposes of prostitution. Convinced by her attorney that no jury would find Sal guilty, Carol reluctantly agreed. No harm would be done, and she would be free. So would Sal.

But Brickhill had a second major witness.

Daisy White, the kindhearted proprietress of the West Seventy-second Street "place of relaxation." Daisy faced not only a five-year sentence for pandering and operating a house of prostitution, but an additional ten on narcotics possession. For testifying that Sal provided her establishment with a constant supply of girls, she was to receive probation.

Despite the indictment, the case was so ridiculously weak that at first

Sal refused to take the matter seriously. In a strange way he felt no animosity toward Carol. He understood her motives. It was a question of survival. At his expense, true, but he felt she had no choice.

As for Daisy White, the unhappy fact was that some years before Sal actually did send her a girl. A hooker he met in a Miami hotel lobby, down on her luck. He gave her Daisy's address and his name for reference. So the charge was absurd, easily refuted.

For these reasons, and perhaps Sal's own conscience, the option of silencing witnesses was never considered. And in any event the whole thing was clearly a publicity stunt, hardly worth the risk involved in any drastic action.

Charles Brickhill was of course unaware of that decision, and this time made certain no harm came to his key witnesses. He sent both out of state to a federal prison, under the personal supervision of his own trusted assistant, Martin Raab.

Martin Raab was twenty-five, two years out of N.Y.U. Law, and as obsessive as Brickhill about smashing the Leo Gorodetsky–Salvatore Bracci–Harry Wise criminal syndicate. He had no idea the women's testimony was blatantly false, and Brickhill had no intention of ever confiding that truth; nor, Brickhill knew, did the women. In Charles Brickhill's book there was no honor among thieves, or those who fought them. Fire with fire. He suffered not the slightest ethical or moral qualms. As far as he was concerned, when they murdered Bernie Kopaloff they provided Charles Brickhill with a blank check.

Leo was unable to attend the eighth and final day of Sal's trial. It was on a Wednesday, the day before Steve's bar mitzvah in Massachusetts. But Leo drove Sal to the courthouse, from where he would proceed immediately to Boston. Sal was jovial this sunny September morning, chatting away about the weeklong American Legion convention in New York, and how the veterans completely tore up the town. In one hotel five Legionnaires dangled a naked girl by her legs out a twelfth-floor window for nearly half an hour. And then, hardly pausing for breath, Sal discussed the Giants' chances in the upcoming series. They were 3 to 1 underdogs against the Yankees, but Sal would lay Leo 2 to 1 right now on Hubbell winning at least two for the Giants. As a matter of fact, he'd take even money DiMaggio wouldn't get more than one hit a game against Hubbell.

"I thought you weren't worried about this?" Leo said when Sal finally ran out of breath.

"I'm not," Sal said. "I took the odds. Five grand."

"I'm talking about the trial, Sal."

"What the hell makes you think I'm worried?"

"It's called being *too* unconcerned," Leo said.

Sal looked at him with a lame smile. "Let's say I'm not so sure anymore."

Leo, noticing they were just turning into Foley Square, leaned forward to tap the massive shoulders of the man at the wheel. "Stop here, Herb."

Herb Seigel, Leo's driver since Rich Freedman went to Miami as a pit boss, swung out of the traffic lane and pulled up at the sidewalk. Behind Leo's car—now a shiny new black LaSalle sedan—a black Cadillac driven by Tom Marizzi also pulled up and parked.

Leo said to Sal, "Ever since this thing started, you were sure you'd have no trouble beating it. It was just a stunt of Brickhill's to get him closer to Albany. You knew it, and he knew it. Now all of a sudden, you're not so sure."

"I had a crazy dream last night," Sal said. "I'm walking down a street. I turn a corner, and can't go any farther. Straight ahead of me is a great big iron gate."

Never, not in all their years together, had Leo known Sal to be superstitious. For an instant he felt the same twinge of disappointment he experienced when he first realized Arnold Steinberger was a different man from the one he once idolized and emulated. He felt disloyal for this even crossing his mind.

"Ralph Levine is probably the finest lawyer in this country," he said, and added wryly, "And the most expensive. He prides himself in his own belief in his clients' innocence. He says you can't possibly be convicted. He even expects the judge to throw out the case on frivolity."

"That was before Judge Cadogan had the heart attack," Sal said. "Before Hollis replaced him. We own Cadogan. Nobody ever even heard of this Hollis. He came out of nowhere. I don't dare to even try to get to him."

"It doesn't matter who the judge is," Leo said. "You won't be convicted."

"Sure, Leo, it's a boat race, that's all it is." Sal slapped Leo's knee and opened the car door. "You better get moving if you want to make Boston for dinner." He stepped out onto the sidewalk. "And congratulate the kid for his bar mitzvah."

"I'll call you tonight," Leo said.

Herb called out, "Good luck, Sal." Sal winked at Herb, then walked quickly to his own car.

Leo moved into the front seat beside Herb. He sat a moment watching Sal through the rear window, then gestured Herb to drive on. A crowd of reporters and photographers was gathered on the courthouse stairs. Leo watched through the rear window again. As the newsmen swarmed around Sal's Cadillac which had just arrived, Herb swung left into Reade Street and Leo could no longer see the courthouse. He felt guilty for not being with Sal, but would feel far more guilt missing Steve's bar mitzvah.

"We'll be in Boston in plenty of time," Herb said.

Leo did not hear him. He was thinking of the iron gate of Sal's dream.

THE SPEED OF DREAMS

* * *

Winston, thirty miles north of Boston, was a shoe-manufacturing center with a population of forty thousand, of whom some two thousand were Jewish. The more affluent Jews had recently broken away from Winston's two Orthodox synagogues to form a Conservative congregation, renovating an old Protestant church in the better part of the city into a modern temple. It was in this new temple, Temple Emanual, Steven was bar-mitzvahed.

The rabbi, a young, aggressive man named Jacobs, had for the past year privately tutored Steve for a small, simple ceremony held in the rabbi's study on a Thursday, rather than the traditional Saturday. It reminded Leo of his own, similarly simple bar mitzvah, except that the father was present, as Leo's father had not been.

My father, he thought, recalling a conversation just last night with his mother and his sister—Sarah and Esther had come up by train the previous day—and Esther said it was a shame the boy's grandfather, Chaim, would not be there. "Shame?" Sarah cried bitterly. "What shame? A blessing!" And she had turned to Leo. "A dead man you would want at your only son's bar mitzvah?"

Leo had thought then, Yes, he is dead. My father is dead. He must be. And all at once he knew it was true. He did not know how he knew, only that he was absolutely certain. He marveled at how little grief or regret he felt. How little feeling, period. You do not feel for a person unknown to you.

All this, now, flowed into his mind watching Steve, listening, remembering his own bar mitzvah. The little boy in the two-dollar secondhand suit. Steve, wearing a new, navy-blue Brooks Brothers suit with a white button-down-collared shirt, red-and-white-striped regimental tie, rich-leathered Cordovan wing-tip shoes. Tall, handsome, flawlessly reciting the Hebrew passages, smiling confidently at his mother, his sister, and his grandparents—Leo's mother, and Ellie's parents—knowing how important this was to them, anxious to please.

Very seldom did Steve glance at Leo, and then almost in defiance. As though snidely aware of Leo's disapproval of such religious nonsense, particularly when the rabbi summoned Leo to stand beside the boy to recite the *Haftarah*, that portion of the Torah allocated to the father in honor of his son's bar mitzvah. Leo, grateful for the little card with the phonetic pronunciation of the Hebrew words, stumbled through it, sensing that Steve, towering over him, enjoyed his father's discomfort.

It angered Leo, but he knew he had only himself to blame.

Rabbi Jacobs congratulated Steve, his parents, and other relatives. His acceptance of Leo's temple donation of a $1,500 check was so matter-of-fact, Leo nearly laughed. Back on Rivington Street that contribution would have guaranteed him a lifetime tenure as synagogue president. The rabbi expressed his hope to see the family at next week's High

Holiday services, graciously declined an invitation to join them at lunch, and bid them all good day. Lunch, at a local restaurant, was pleasant enough. Everyone then returned to Ellie's house in Georgetown.

Leo's suggestion that Steve ride with him upset Carla, who whispered to Leo her desperate desire to go with him. She hated old people, slobbering over her and asking if she was a good girl. And she wanted to know when they were going home, to the big house in Hempstead; she missed it so, especially the pond. Leo tried to explain that he had sold the house, and now lived in a hotel in New York, the Park Central. All right, she pleaded, then let Leo tell her about it in the car. In the end, Ellie ordered Carla to ride with her, like it or not, and Leo solemnly promised Carla the rest of the afternoon back in Georgetown.

Steve and Leo were no sooner settled in the LaSalle, when Steve said, "What I want for a present is flying lessons."

"Flying lessons?" Leo smiled indulgently.

"There's a little airport here," Steve said. "I spoke to the guy. I told him I was sixteen."

Leo said nothing. He lit a cigarette.

Steve said, "That's what I want for a present."

"I don't know, Steve. We'll have to think about that one."

"You said you'd give me anything I want when I got bar-mitzvahed, didn't you?"

What I should give you, Leo thought, is what Harry once suggested. A kick in the ass. But he said, "What about your mother? What does she say?"

"I haven't told her," Steve said. "But she'll do anything I want."

"By the way, how's she been feeling?"

"You mean, is she drinking? Yeah, she is. She never lets us see her do it, but I know where she hides the bottles. She's doing it." Without pausing for breath, Steve continued, "You want to stop in and talk to the airport guy? We pass right by there. It's on Kenoza Avenue." He called out to Herb Seigel, "Take your next left, driver."

Herb glanced narrowly at Steve over his shoulder, then at Leo in the rearview mirror. Leo said to Steve, "You don't talk to people that way, Steve. You want something, you ask in a polite way."

"Oh, sure," Steve said pleasantly. "Driver, take your next left."

Leo's eyes met Herb's in the rearview mirror. Leo shook his head, no. Herb gripped the steering wheel and drove past the street Steve had indicated.

"Hey, you passed it!" Steve said. He turned to Leo. "He went right past it."

"I told him to," Leo said.

"How come?"

Leo drew on the cigarette, then stubbed it out in the ashtray. "You're too young."

"I just told you the guy thinks I'm sixteen."

"*I* know you're not."

"Well, you're not gonna tell him, for crying out loud. So what's the difference?"

"For one thing, it's dangerous," Leo said, thinking that not once had Steve addressed him as "Dad." No address whatever, as though Leo had no name or title.

". . . not dangerous," Steve was saying. "And why should you care, anyway?"

Leo looked at him, startled. "What do you mean, why should I care? I'm your father."

Steve looked him back, his eyes never wavering. "You don't act like it."

Leo slapped him. A hard backhand across the cheek. In the closed car it sounded like a rifle shot. Herb whirled around and peered at Steve, then at Leo. Leo had turned grimly away to the window. Steve slumped back against the seat cushion, his eyes wide with surprise and brimming with tears.

"What'd you do that for?" Steve asked. He was trying not to cry.

Leo did not answer, and did not look at him. He did not know what to say. He wanted to say he was sorry, but did not feel sorry. He did not know what he felt.

Steve said, "I didn't do anything." And then he began crying. Quietly, self-pityingly, huddled against the window.

Leo touched Steve's shoulder, but Steve shuddered and drew even farther away. Leo started to reach out for him, then stopped. A losing proposition, he thought. A bad roll. He would wait for the cards to change.

In the rearview mirror, Herb spoke to him. "Straight back to the house, Leo?"

"That's right, Herb," Leo said. "Straight back."

He had already decided to stay in Georgetown until he resolved matters with Steve. He would book a room in a nearby motor court on Route 1. If it took a week, he would stay.

He did not stay even ten minutes. Five minutes after arriving at Ellie's cottage, he was rushing back to New York. He had received a phone call from George Gerson. Sal's jury brought in a verdict.

Guilty.

Judge Arthur Hollis pronounced sentence a week later. The maximum allowed under the law, and the severest ever meted out for the crime of which Sal had been convicted. It was also the most unusual.

Thirty years in a federal penitentiary.

The prison term to be commuted on condition Sal accept deportation to his place of birth, Italy.

3.

Through his binoculars Mickey Goldfarb watched the launch approach. He had followed it from the pier and now, closer, clearly saw the two passengers. One, in the rear, he recognized as Jimmy Tucculo's body-guard, Pete something-or-other. Jimmy himself, clutching his white Pan-ama against the wind, sat in front with the coxswain.

Mickey watched another moment, then stepped away from the rail and entered the casino. It ran the entire length and width of the main deck, and looked as vast as a football field, which it nearly was: 250 feet long, 40 wide. Except no football fields had rows of crystal chandeliers hanging from the ceiling, mahogany-paneled walls, and half of one wall lined with slot machines.

The metal cleats of Mickey's shoes clacked loud and hollow on the hardwood floor in the deserted casino. The carpeting should have long since been installed, but Harry decided the color he selected was too bright. He wanted a dark brown to match the mahogany paneling. Since the lighter color was cut to order, Harry had to eat it. But no matter. If it was not right, it was no good. Harry knew what he wanted, and what he wanted was the S.S. *Californian* to be perfect.

Mickey paused a moment at a tarpaulin-covered craps table and looked around the huge room, empty but for a couple of cleaning men and a bartender stacking glasses. The emptiness was eerie, almost ghostly. A week before, New Year's Eve, when the *Californian* opened, this room was so crowded you couldn't hear yourself think. And what action! Fifty thousand dollars that very first night, a net profit of nearly three thousand.

The second night was even better, and the third still better. And then, like a truck crashing into a brick wall, it stopped. The city of Santa Monica declared their pier, the only pier within a convenient distance of S.S. *Californian*, unsafe for the water taxis. It was to discuss this unsafe pier that Jimmy Tucculo was visiting the ship.

Mickey resumed his trek across the casino. He turned a sharp left before the bar, knocked at a door marked "Mr. Wise," and entered Harry's office.

Harry stood at the porthole, binoculars in hand, peering out with naked eye. "He's got some balls, I'll say that," Harry said, and added jokingly, "When he comes aboard, ask who he is."

"He knows me, Harry, how many times I have to tell you? But I think everything's under control." Mickey made a circle with his thumb and forefinger.

"It better be, Mickey." Harry placed the binoculars in an open file-cabinet drawer, closed it, and sat down at the desk. It was a huge, glass-topped pine desk built in a semicircle, with Harry's big leather-backed swivel chair in the exact center. Designed personally by Harry, and custom-built by a cabinetmaker recommended by Nora Thomas. The cabinetmaker was too old for even Nora to fuck, so Harry knew the recommendation was genuine and the man a true craftsman.

But then so was Mickey Goldfarb.

Mickey was just twenty-six, and a rare breed: a native-born Californian. His parents, Russian Jews, had settled in Los Angeles and opened a small bakery in Boyle Heights, where Mickey was born. Their American dream was for their son to become a lawyer or doctor. But young Moishe never advanced past the seventh grade; he was expelled for assaulting a teacher who discovered the lad in the act of breaking into a locker not his own.

It was just as well. Mickey was a poor student anyway. And *his* dream was to win the middleweight championship of the world. He loved fighting, any kind, preferably in the street, and particularly with anyone reckless enough to profess a dislike for Jews. Although possessed of sufficient courage and strength for the professional ring, he lacked the grace—or brains—to box. His short-lived career provided an easy transition to a series of nightclub and saloon bouncer jobs, to loan-shark enforcer, extortionist, petty and grand larcenist, bookie runner. If he could act, he would have been perfectly cast. Short, balding, built like a tank, with a perpetually red face and a nose so often broken it looked pasted onto his face.

When Harry met him, Mickey had just been fired from his job as collection agent for a bookie. Mickey, it seemed, occasionally placed bets for nonexistent clients. If the horse won, Mickey collected for the "client." If the horse lost, Mickey informed his boss that the welshing bettor had skipped town.

Harry hired him as a driver and then, when the *Californian* opened, as Floor Boss. With a warning that even the slightest nonsense would land Mickey either in the bay or the Los Angeles River, whichever at the time was closer. Harry had nothing to worry about. To Mickey Goldfarb, Harry Wise was already a legend. Mickey idolized him and would never, ever, cross him.

Outside, the launch had tied up to the gangway.

"Go bring him in," Harry said. "But let him cool a while. Tell him I'm busy." Mickey started away, but Harry called him back. "Aw, fuck that! Why play games? Bring him right in."

A few minutes later when Mickey knocked respectfully at the door, Harry sat leaning back in his chair, feet propped on the glass desk top, carefully rounding the ash of a fresh-lighted cigar. Harry called for them to enter, but remained seated. He waved the cigar at Jimmy.

"Nice to see you again, Jim. You're looking real good."

"I feel good," Jimmy said. Although Sicilian-born, he spoke with no trace of an accent. He was a tall, lean, prematurely gray man of middle years. His long, heavy-boned face was pitted with smallpox scars. His friends referred to him as Jimmy Ice Cube, for the clear, cold blueness of the deep-set eyes that conveyed an immediate sense of strength and authority. He controlled all Southern California bookmaking, and half the Los Angeles Police Department was said to be on his payroll. He was also the man whose permission and indulgence Harry had needed to install the race wire. For a twenty-five percent commission.

Harry grinned. "I think it's true what I heard. You're screwing that movie actor's wife."

"Everybody's screwing some actor's wife," Jimmy said. He walked across the room and placed his Panama on the desk, and sat uninvited in the leather-backed armchair opposite Harry. "You know Pete?" he asked, indicating his companion, a chunky man in his early thirties whose bulk made him appear shorter than he really was. "Pete Donini, Harry Wise."

"Nice to meet you," Harry said, and introduced Mickey.

"We already met," Mickey said. He and Donini stood side by side, inches apart, each with tightly folded arms.

Harry said, "Mick, why don't you show Pete around?"

"That's okay," Donini said. "I was here the other night with Jimmy. Remember?"

"That's right," Harry said pleasantly. "But I'd like for Jimmy and me to talk."

Donini looked at Jimmy, who nodded. Mickey strolled to the door and opened it for Donini. "You need me, just yell," he said to Harry.

Harry made a circle with his thumb and forefinger and waited for the two to leave. Then he offered Jimmy a cigar from a silver-plated humidor, a gift from Nora for one particularly spectacular Palm Springs weekend.

"No, thanks," said Jimmy. "What do you hear from the big guy?"

"Which one?"

"Which one do you think?" Jimmy said. "Sal."

"He figures to be in Havana next month," Harry said.

"He don't like the old country, huh?"

"He hates it," Harry said. "He says all they talk there is Italian."

Jimmy laughed accommodatingly, and Harry thought, Just the idea of Sal Bracci coming back makes this *Talena* nervous. All Sal's appeals of the deportation order were heard and denied in record time. He had been in Italy now less than a month, actually two weeks longer than planned, for even before the final appeal was entered, Leo had secured Cuban agreement for Sal to move to that country. With three casinos operating, and two more under construction—and the Cuban government a full partner—Leo's good friend, Major General Fulgencio Batista, was more than willing to accept Sal. From Havana he would continue his role as Leo's partner, leader of IDIC's Italian faction.

"Be sure and give him my regards next time you talk to him," Jimmy said.

"I will," Harry said. Then, abruptly, cigar clenched in his teeth, he slid his feet off the desk and leaned forward toward Jimmy. "Okay, let's not waste any time with bullshit. The city of Santa Monica said the pier was unsafe for my water taxis. So I'm out of business. What's it cost me to 'fix' the pier?"

"A third of the action," Jimmy said calmly.

"A third?" Harry said. "That's all?"

Jimmy Tucculo smiled. "Yeah, that's all."

"Let me clue you in," Harry said. "This is one of four ships in business here off this coast, but it's the best. It's the classiest. No casino this side of Monte Carlo holds a candle to it. It's *my* baby, Jimmy, and I don't run no clip joint. We don't use mechanics, and we don't roll winners. For every dollar we take in, we pay out ninety-seven cents. I catch one of my guys dealing seconds, he don't deal again. Ever. It's awful hard to deal cards with only your thumbs. So what I'm trying to tell you is, with a three percent margin, there's not enough to give you a third. Or a fourth, or a tenth. Nothing."

Jimmy nodded patiently. "Harry, that three percent is all net. After expenses, salaries, overhead, payoffs, everything. But all you got to do, Harry, is instead of paying off ninety-seven cents on a dollar, pay off ninety-six. You can rig the slots alone to do that." He raised his hand to silence Harry's protest. "Please, Harry, like you said, no bullshit. Don't shit the troops. I let you put your race wire in, that was okay—"

"—yeah, it ought to be," Harry said. "For twenty-five points."

"—but this is too much," Jimmy continued. "What if *I* came to New York and pulled this? I can just see you guys sitting still for it. Come on, now, let's do business like businessmen."

Harry said nothing a moment. He got up and stood at the porthole. The early spring day was so overcast you could not see the beach. He opened the porthole. The air was chilly, but crisp with the fresh smell of the sea. Far in the distance an unseen foghorn sounded a low, mournful cry.

"I'll have to talk it over with Leo," he said, looking out at the ocean.

"Sure," Jimmy said. "And believe me, he'll understand."

"I hope so," Harry said, facing Jimmy now, shaking hands with him, amazed at himself, at how well he controlled his temper. Of course, much of this calm was the result of having long before decided exactly how to deal with Mr. Jimmy Ice Cube Tucculo.

Don't get mad, get even.

At three that same afternoon, Harry sat in his regular booth at Jack's at the Beach, a restaurant on the pier adjoining the amusement park. The restaurant, one of Nora Thomas's favorites, had become Harry's second home. When he was not on the *Californian*, of course. The booth, facing the ocean, was permanently reserved for him. From here on a clear day he could gaze out over the water and see the ship.

He ordered a beer and asked for the phone. After the waiter plugged it in and discreetly backed away, Harry made two phone calls.

The first was to Mickey Goldfarb at a downtown hotel. Mickey had gone ashore earlier, rushing to the hotel for a previously made appointment. Over the phone, Mickey's hoarse voice sounded even more grating.

"Hey, you won't believe this, Harry, but while I'm waiting in the bar downstairs for him, I get to talking with one of the girls. She tells me the son of a bitch goes there to get himself beat up. Honest to God! He likes this special girl that slaps him around. Sometimes, she says, with a wire coat hanger! A coat hanger, for Christ's sake!"

"Mickey," Harry said patiently. "Will he do it?"

"Yeah, he'll do it."

"You trust him?"

"Listen, it took me two hours to talk him into it. He's scared shitless. But he'll do it."

"Where is he now?"

"Back where he's supposed to be, I hope."

"Ambitious little wop, ain't he?" Harry said, and hung up. He waited until the rattle of the amusement park's roller coaster faded, then dialed another number. Jimmy Tucculo's. "An hour ago, I spoke to Leo," Harry said into the phone, which was true. "And he agreed." Which was also true.

"Hey, what'd I tell you?" Jimmy said. "Okay, you can run the taxis starting tonight."

"Appreciate it, Jim," Harry said, and almost as a casual afterthought, added, "Listen, how about coming out tonight for a little celebration dinner?"

"Well, I don't know," Jimmy said warily.

"Best food in town. I brought this chef down from San Francisco, you know. A *paisano*. Makes an *osso buco* that'll have you creaming all over yourself. As my guest, naturally."

"Hold on a second," Jimmy said, and Harry heard him muffle the mouthpiece with his hand as he spoke to someone else. Then he was back on the phone. "I'll have to bring a couple of my guys. And my own man to drive the boat, you don't mind. The same boat I was in this afternoon, not one of your water taxis." He laughed unhumorously. "I don't trust them fucking things."

"No problem," said Harry. "I'll have Mickey wait for you at the pier. He'll hold a parking spot for your car. Then he'll come out to the ship with you so your people can get aboard without the guards bothering you."

He hung up and turned to the window to see if the day had cleared enough to see the ship. Not yet. When the waiter brought his beer, Harry ordered a sandwich. He had not been hungry all day, but now for the first time had an appetite.

That evening the pier bustled with activity. Water taxis shuttled back and forth to the *Californian*. Between the skywriter Harry hired to advertise the reopening, and the front-page ads in the late-afternoon papers, word traveled fast.

At eight-thirty Jimmy Tucculo drove onto Santa Monica pier with Pete Donini and two other men. Mickey met them and guided Jimmy's car into a reserved slot. Jimmy's boat, with the same coxswain, was tied up and waiting under the pier stairway. Mickey gestured Jimmy and the others down the stairway to the landing. Jimmy and the three men got into the launch, Jimmy in front with the coxswain. Mickey remained on the landing and removed the tie line. He tossed it into the launch, then cupped his hands over his mouth and called to them.

"You guys go on ahead," he shouted. "I got to wait for a customer!" He grinned. "A big movie star!"

Jimmy peered narrowly at Mickey, but Mickey was already climbing the stairs back to the pier. After a moment, Jimmy signaled the coxswain to start the engines. The launch headed out to sea and rapidly passed the breakwater. Far in the distance, as though rising up out of the ocean, the night sky was brightened by huge illuminated letters: S. S. CALIFORNIAN.

Mickey Goldfarb raced to the harbor master's station at the head of the pier and down the rickety wooden stairs to a landing below. There, waiting, engine idling, was a water taxi. Mickey boarded the taxi and gestured the coxswain to move. The coxswain jammed the throttle forward and steered the taxi toward the breakwater.

Mickey scanned the water through his binoculars. It was a dark night and he could not immediately find the launch's riding lights. Over the taxi's engine, he heard music from the pavilion in the center of the pier. A local band trying to sound like Benny Goodman. The hundreds of bobby-soxers jitterbugging to the music enjoyed it, applauding enthusiastically to the number just finished. Immediately, another number started, one Mickey liked, "Bei Mir Bist Du Schoen."

All at once, ahead, the entire sky was bright. It was like a flash of lightning. And then a boom of thunder. Mickey needed no binoculars now. A half mile away, flickers of yellow flame danced on the water. Mickey looked through the binoculars again. He saw no launch, only the flames.

Just fifteen seconds before, a mile from shore, Jimmy Tucculo's launch bore steadily for the *Californian*. Jimmy sat up front beside the coxswain. Behind him were Pete Donini and the other two men. Pete, crouched low below the gunwale, lit a match and cupped his hands over it to peer at his watch. The fourth time he did this since leaving the pier.

"Hey, Pete," one man laughed. "What's the matter, you got a hot date?"

Pete did not reply. He stared at the watch. He was counting the seconds. Just as the second hand reached 50 Pete stood upright in the boat and hurled himself overboard.

"Jesus Christ!" someone shouted.

Jimmy Tucculo whirled around. In the water, Pete swam frantically away from the launch. For an instant Jimmy was paralyzed. It was in that instant he knew. Then he, too, tried to fling himself over the side. Too late.

The launch exploded in a mass of bright orange flame and black oily smoke. On the space of ocean it had occupied, now there was nothing, only fragments of shattered, burning wood showering down on the water. The fiery embers struck the surface with a loud, abrupt hiss, followed immediately by the sound of soft crackling flames from those few pieces remaining afloat.

Five hundred yards away, Mickey Goldfarb's water taxi approached the swimming Pete Donini. Mickey pulled him aboard and at full throttle the water taxi sped toward the *Californian*.

Behind them, where the launch had been, was only a small pool of burning debris. And silence, but for the drone of the water taxi, and "Bei Mir Bist Du Schoen" from the pavilion on the pier. The music ended. Applause rippled quietly across the water.

─── *16* ───

FULGENCIO Batista was not much taller than Leo Gorodetsky, but enough to enjoy standing close to him and looking down at him. Leo did not mind; it meant he had the general's undivided attention. At this particular time, however, Batista's attention was directed to the briefcase in Leo's hand.

In civilian clothes, a blue pinstripe double-breasted suit, Batista seemed almost drab and out of place beside the impeccably uniformed young captain at his side. The captain, in khaki blouse, gray whipcord jodhpurs and cavalry boots so highly glossed they reflected the late afternoon sun, functioned as both the general's aide and translator.

"The general says that he notices you brought your artwork," said the captain, whose name was Alvarez and who spoke flawless English. He smiled, as had Batista when he made the remark, and indicated Leo's briefcase.

"Artwork" was a private joke. Years before, before Batista promoted himself from sergeant to major general—but just after he led the coup that overthrew the government and installed his own man as president—Leo had brought him a gift, a small token of gratitude, in a large manila envelope, which Leo explained to Batista's guards contained "works of art."

"All masterpieces, General," Leo said. He displayed the briefcase, but did not present it. Instead, he said, "May I introduce my good friend and business partner, Mr. Salvatore Bracci."

Sal, standing beside Leo, nodded politely at Batista.

Batista returned the nod, then spoke in Spanish, translated by the captain. "Any friend of Leo's, Señor Bracci, is a friend of mine."

"The same goes for me, General," Sal said. "And I have to tell you, I've been in your country less than four hours, but already I love it." He waved his hand around. "Especially your beautiful house."

They were on the terrace of that house, which was indeed beautiful, in the Miramar section of Havana in the hills overlooking the harbor. A rambling, gracious, three-story Colonial on an estate once owned by a Chief of Staff of the Cuban army. He was dead now, executed at Batista's order. As a sergeant, Batista had greatly admired this particular property.

Sal had arrived in Havana from his brief Italian exile only that morning. He was met at the pier by Leo who had flown in from Miami the previous day, and both went directly to General Batista's residence to pay their respects.

Captain Alvarez continued translating the conversation. He was very efficient, his English version only a few words behind the general's Spanish. ". . . from what I understand," he was saying to Sal, "Leo has arranged a dinner party that will make you love the country even more." Batista smiled down at Leo as Alvarez went on, "I've heard about those girls in the chorus line at El Conquistador."

"You should come and see them yourself," Leo said.

Batista rolled his eyes in dismay. "Not if I care to keep peace within my family—and my *cojones*. You've met my wife, Leo."

"A most charming lady," Leo said.

"Thank you," Batista said glumly in English. He spoke the language well enough but preferred a translator. It reduced the possibilities of mistakes or misunderstandings, and also allowed him time to organize his thoughts. Now he snapped his fingers at a group of mess-jacketed soldiers waiting attentively near the terrace doors. Immediately, one moved forward with a silver tray of filled champagne glasses. He offered the tray first to Batista, who gestured the soldier to serve the guests. Leo and Sal took glasses, then Batista.

"To continued success," said the general, raising his glass in a toast. All clicked glasses and drank. Batista exchanged his empty glass for a fresh one and said, "Now, this matter of Mr. Bracci's visa . . ."

Leo said, "We believe it is to the benefit of all concerned for Mr. Bracci to remain here in Havana. He will be in complete charge of the casinos, accountable of course to you personally."

Batista nodded impatiently, and through Alvarez said, "The problem, Leo, is your country. Already, I've had several requests from the American Embassy not to issue the visa. They are, to put it mildly, agitated."

Leo said, "We understand the diplomatic problems involved, and we appreciate your assistance."

"And I," said the general, "appreciate the pain and suffering endured when a man is exiled from his own country. I also appreciate what you have done for my country."

Not to mention, Leo thought, what we have done for you, personally, sir. Plus an additional $100,000 in cash, in $500 and $1,000 bills, in the briefcase. The "artwork," which he now presented to the general, and which he knew would shortly be deposited into one of the general's several numbered Swiss bank accounts.

"Mr. Bracci and I ask that you please accept this small token of gratitude," Leo said.

"It is not necessary," Batista said in English, hefting the briefcase.

"We insist," Sal said.

"In that case, you leave me no choice." Batista handed the briefcase to Alvarez and spoke to him in rapid Spanish.

"General Batista says Mr. Bracci is a welcome guest in Cuba," Alvarez translated. "He will be issued a nonresident visa, allowing him to remain here indefinitely."

"Thank you, General," Sal said.

Batista smiled his acknowledgment, and then excused himself, unless of course there was further business to discuss. Leo did have a problem concerning an impounded shipment of cement cinder blocks, but decided to take it up with the deputy interior minister, Raúl Sandoval. The blocks were consigned to the third hotel, the Caribe, still under construction. In fact, he would have Sal deal with Sandoval; it was a good opportunity for Sal and this particular minister, whose cooperation was vital, to establish a personal relationship. In Interior Minister Sandoval's case, it meant extending a casino credit line. Leo made a mental note to suggest Sal limit the line to $50,000, and to forgive the man's outstanding markers, which totaled nearly that amount.

"So what do you think of our 'partner'?" Leo asked, when they were in the limousine returning to the city.

"A great man," Sal said loudly, for the benefit of the chauffeur, a Cuban army sergeant. And then, under his breath, added, "The biggest fucking crook I ever saw!"

"That's right," Leo said. "But he's our crook."

"Yeah," Sal said, and sat back to enjoy the view. Below, beyond the narrow twisting road, was the whole city, and the blue of the water, the ships anchored in the bay, and Morro Castle. Sal was impressed. "It ever occur to you we're the only company in the world that's in partnership with a government?"

"I'm more concerned with our partnership," Leo said.

"What the hell does that mean?"

"This came in just before I went to meet you." Leo removed a cablegram from his pocket and handed it to Sal.

MCKAY RADIO, NEW YORK. 10 MAY, 1938.
LEO GORODETSKY, EL CONQUISTADOR HOTEL,
HAVANA, CUBA

URGENT BRACCI CONTACT THE AMBITIOUS ONE
IMMEDIATELY UPON ARRIVAL HAVANA STOP
SERIOUS FAMILY ARGUMENT TO BE SETTLED
STOP SIGNED GERSON

Sal read it, then reread it. "The ambitious one?" He folded the cable-gram and returned it to Leo.

"Dominic Cranillo," Leo said. "He's been sniping at your guys ever since you left. I think he's making his move now, before you get settled back in and can take over from here."

"He's not ambitious, he's crazy," Sal said. "Besides, Tommy has every-thing under control."

"Tommy's a good boy, and loyal to you," Leo said. "But, Sal, even while you were on the ship coming here, Tommy lost three men to Cranillo. They simply told Tommy it was better they went with Cranillo. Tommy says at least four others are on the fence. They don't believe you can run things from Cuba."

"Seven men won't change anything, Leo."

"If seven go, seven more are ready to. If Dominic Cranillo brings a dozen of your people over, he'll be the biggest man in New York. Or think he is, which is just as bad. It won't be live and let live anymore. They'll want everything."

"Tommy can hold things together for me."

"I think you should do as Gerson suggests," Leo said. "Phone Dominic. Just hearing your voice might sober him up."

"I'll phone Tommy first," Sal said, after a moment. "Then I'll talk to Dominic. I know how to handle him."

But Sal never did complete the phone call to Tom Marizzi. Even as Leo and Sal entered the huge, atriumlike El Conquistador lobby, thirteen hundred miles away in New York, on a sidewalk in Queens a few houses away from his own modest home, Tom Marizzi lay bleeding to death.

It happened shortly after lunch. Tom, recently married, enjoyed com-ing home at noon for lunch. Tom's two bodyguards always dropped him off at the corner of his street, remaining parked there in the dark-brown Chrysler sedan until he returned. He did not want them ever to be seen in front of the house. At 12:45, lunch finished, Tom strolled back along the sidewalk toward the waiting car.

A police squad car appeared, momentarily blocking Tom from the view of the two young men in the parked Chrysler. The policeman on the passenger's side leveled a .12-gauge shotgun through the open window and at point-blank range fired both barrels into Tom Marizzi.

Simultaneously, the policeman driving the squad car opened his door, stepped out into the street, and fired exactly fifteen rounds from a Thompson into the Chrysler's windshield. From start to finish the entire operation consumed less than ten seconds. The squad car was a quarter mile away before the first neighbor, reacting to the sound of gunfire, rushed hysterically from her house.

The men in the Chrysler were killed instantly. Tom Marizzi lingered nearly two hours. But even before Tom Marizzi was pronounced dead, Dominic Cranillo had contacted Tom's key people. They could maintain their positions by bringing themselves and their men into Dominic's family.

Leo returned to New York two days after Tom Marizzi's death. Gerson met him at Newark Airport. Leo had no sooner settled in the backseat of the car than Gerson said, "He wants a meeting."

"Cranillo?"

"In the next twenty-four hours, he said."

Leo said, "Which one of us is supposed to be crazy? Him, for suggesting it, or me for even considering it?"

"He says he'll meet any neutral place you want."

Leo glanced out the rear window. Another IDIC car with three other men was close behind. "You're not taking any chances, I see."

"Leo, the coup of the century is for Dominic Cranillo to kill you. With Sal in Cuba, it makes him undisputed Boss of Bosses. In three months the Cranillos swallow up IDIC whole."

"If he kills me," said Leo.

"It makes it a lot easier for him," said Gerson.

"That's what Sal said, too. He cried like a baby when he heard about Tom. He smashed his fist into a wall, and cried. I don't think I ever saw him lose his composure that way. And he looked at me, George, and he said, 'You know what, Leo? Charlie Brickhill did to me what we used to talk about doing to him. Neutralize him. He did it to me. I go back to New York, they arrest me. I'm helpless! I can't lift a finger for my people.'"

"It's even worse than that," Gerson said. "This so-called neutralizing has made you vulnerable to the Italians. That's why Cranillo is moving."

Leo said nothing, but was thinking, Yes, that is exactly what has happened. And none of it should have happened. Sal should still have been in New York, still boss of the most powerful family, the family married to the Jews, both parties continuing to grow and prosper. But Sal was careless, complacent, perhaps even arrogant. Not taking Brickhill's frame seriously until it was too late. Now they were paying the price.

Leo said, "Sal predicted Dominic would ask for a meeting."

"Did he also predict what Dominic would want?"

Everything, Dominic wants everything, Leo thought. But he said nothing, only smiled dryly and then, aware they were turning onto the Jersey City turnpike, spoke to the driver. "You taking the tunnel?"

"Yeah," said the driver, a tall, slender man of thirty, whose name was Benny Roth. He wore loud clothes and a wide-brimmed gray fedora with both front and back brim snapped down in a style long out of fashion. He considered himself a natty dresser.

"How about trying the new tunnel instead?" Leo said. "The Lincoln, the one they just opened and that goes right into midtown."

"Jesus, Leo, it's all the way up to Weehawken," Benny said. "You want to go that far out of the way?"

"I don't mind if you don't," Leo said. "It's a nice day for a ride."

"Sure thing, Leo."

"Besides, I want to talk to George."

"You're the boss," Benny said.

"Thanks," Leo said.

"My pleasure," said Benny, and swung the wheel hard to drive back onto the Union City road.

Leo rolled up the partition window and looked at his watch. "Ten after five," he said. "Ten after two on the coast. First thing we get into the office, call Harry. If he's not in, leave word it's urgent. If you happen to talk to him, tell him he's to charter a plane for Omaha."

"Omaha?" Gerson said. "Nebraska?"

"That's right, George. Where they pack all the meat. I'll explain it in a minute." He leaned forward again, making sure the partition window was closed tightly. "Yes, Sal knows what Dominic wants. He wants everything."

"So why even bother meeting him?"

"For one thing, we have no choice. For another, though, I just might be able to make him change his mind."

"You won't, Leo. He's sure he can move in on us now. Once he makes up his mind he believes it's a sign of weakness to change it."

"Arrange the meeting, George."

George Gerson knew Leo well enough not to argue and not to ask questions. "All right, but I'll tell him the meeting has to be at a place we set."

"No," Leo said. "Let him name the place."

"For God's sake, Leo, it could be a trap!"

"Arrange it, George."

2.

The Cranillo brothers, Dominic and Rocco, were born in Chicago. Dominic in 1894, Rocco in 1901. Shortly after Rocco's birth their father, a day laborer, died of a heart attack. Dominic, then seven, went to live with an aunt in New York. Rocco remained with his mother until her death in 1905. A bored mortuary clerk misspelled the mother's name, and instead of being sent to his aunt, Rocco was placed in a county orphanage. Not until 1917 were the brothers reunited.

By the time he finally located Rocco and brought him to New York, Dominic had been arrested twelve times and served one three-year term for manslaughter, and two fourteen-month sentences for armed robbery. This last armed robbery was committed in the service of Anthony Ruggerio who had already earmarked Dominic as a potential future boss.

After the dissolution of the Ruggerio family in 1925, Dominic formed a new family from it remnants. Although not as ruthless or cunning as Dominic, under the older brother's aegis Rocco became a sub-boss. In 1928 he married a young woman from Omaha and moved to that city. Using his brother's power and influence he established an organization that eventually controlled nearly all midwestern independent bootlegging and gambling.

Now, ten years later, Dominic Cranillo was ready to merge the two groups into one gigantic entity that would surpass Sal Bracci's and Leo Gorodetsky's. This achievement would acknowledge him as Boss of Bosses of the four other New York families. To succeed, however, he had to first absorb Sal's people entirely, a task now under way and made easier with the death of Tom Marizzi.

There remained, then, only Sal's Jewish partner. Dominic Cranillo did not intend repeating Dino Coletti's mistake of employing outsiders. It would be done by Dominic personally, and this time properly.

The park was uncrowded this May late afternoon. From where he sat Leo could see the top floors of the Riverside Drive apartment building he and Ellie lived in when first married, the apartment with the bathroom he liked so much. He smiled with the memory; those were not bad days.

He shifted around, facing the river and the warm sun now low across the river. On the river, boats moved up and down. One, a large cabin cruiser anchored near the New York side, was close enough for Leo to see several men sitting at a table on the fantail. They were playing cards, drinking, obviously having a good time. He envied them.

Riverside Park was a strange place to meet a man who wanted to kill you. In the open, with a clear field of vision for blocks in all directions. But then again, perhaps not so strange. Leo assumed a car or two of Dominic Cranillo's was parked up on the Drive behind the bluff. But he felt sure nothing untoward would be attempted—if, indeed, Dominic planned anything. Not in full view of dozens of people.

As arranged, they had picked Leo up outside the Park Central Hotel, searched him (with appropriate apologies), and proceeded downtown. On Thirty-eighth Street, satisfied he was not followed, the driver entered a garage. Leo was transferred to another car. This one drove uptown to the park, to this particular spot where Leo would await Dominic Cranillo. Also, for what it was worth, the driver assured Leo that Dominic would come unarmed.

"Not even with a fountain pen?" Leo had asked.

The driver, a grim, narrow-eyed young fellow, did not see the humor. "Hey, Mr. G, didn't I just say Dom give his word?" Leo had smiled coolly, but his heart beat rapidly, and he felt flushed, his throat bone-dry. The dryness of fear.

He looked at his watch: 4:35. Dominic was five minutes late. Leo wondered what would happen if he simply got up and walked away. Nothing, probably, unless someone from one of those cars parked up on the Drive suddenly showed up to stop him. He doubted it. Dominic might be crazy, but certainly not clumsy, or stupid.

A middle-aged nanny wheeling a stroller passed. Ellie had walked Steve in this same park. And now Steve was nearly fourteen. Leo had not seen him since the bar mitzvah, the day he slapped him, a day hard to forget. He had written the boy, sending along a gift of a huge model airplane, a Stinson Reliant. He should write again, and to Carla also. No, better to see them in person, perhaps this very weekend. He would drive up.

That is, he told himself wryly, if I am still alive. What brought this to mind was the sight of Dominic Cranillo briskly approaching. Dominic removed his hat and waved it at Leo.

"Hey, Leo," he shouted. "How the hell are you?"

Leo did not rise, or shake Dominic's extended hand. He said, "You're late, Dominic."

Dominic seemed unoffended. He smiled and sat on the bench beside Leo. He was a man of medium height, solidly built, with only the slightest hint of flab. "Yeah, the traffic, you know. Hey, what's happening out on the coast with that ship of yours? I heard you had some trouble?"

"None I know of."

Dominic's smile broadened. "You couldn't prove that by poor old Jimmy Tucculo."

Leo was sure Dominic did not know all the details of Jimmy Tucculo's boating accident. It might not hurt to enlighten him a little. "You'll have to ask Pete Donini about it," Leo said.

"Oh, yeah, the guy that took over for Jimmy."

"Only with our blessing," Leo said, deciding not to add that Pete Donini's price for the "blessing" was a five percent cut of the *Californian*'s take. Leo wondered how long Pete would wait before demanding a larger cut.

"Your 'blessing,' huh?" Dominic said. "I'm glad we don't have to worry about that no more here. Your blessing, I mean."

Leo said nothing. Dominic's deep-set dark eyes were narrow and cold. Leo glanced past him. Still no indication of anyone in the park but the regulars.

"Okay, might as well get straight to the point," Dominic said. He put on his hat, adjusting it so it lay square on his head with the brim shading his eyes. He peered out at the anchored cruiser. The card game seemed to have broken up; the players milled about the rail. He faced Leo. "I want you to retire, Leo. That means you walk away from everything you got here in New York. The books, the clubs, everything. You just pack up and get out."

"Jimmy Tucculo only asked for a third," Leo said mildly.

"I'm not Jimmy Tucculo," Dominic said. "And Jimmy Tucculo didn't have a hundred men ready to hit the mattresses and stay there until every last one of you Jews is dead."

"You don't like Jews, do you, Dominic?"

"Don't take it personal, Leo. This is business."

"Then keep it on business, Dominic."

"What's it to be, Leo? Easy, or hard?"

"I'm willing to negotiate," Leo said.

"There's nothing to negotiate," Dominic said. "You're out. Period."

"Unless I want a war, is that it?"

"Which I know goddam well you don't want," Dominic said. He glanced at the anchored cruiser again. "Unless you got a thing for suicide, and just want to kill a lot of your guys for nothing. Come on, Leo, it's over. Face it."

"You could have written all this in a letter, Dominic. Or sent one of your boys to tell me. You didn't have to go through all the razzle-dazzle of meeting in the park."

"Yeah," Dominic said. "But I wouldn't have a guy in that boat over there, with a thirty-thirty with a telescopic sight aimed right at your heart."

Leo's eyes flashed to the anchored cruiser. The men on the rail were gone, the deck deserted. Leo saw no rifle, but knew it was there.

". . . water's so calm that deck's like a cement sidewalk," Dominic was saying. "I just take off my hat and wave it in front of my face, and you're dead, Jew man."

Leo laughed, which surprised Dominic. "I don't doubt there's a gun pointed at me, Dominic, but I thought you were smarter than that."

"The more I think about it, Jew man, the more I think it's better we kill you anyway," Dominic said. He sounded reflective, as though the idea had just occurred to him.

Leo was himself reflective, somewhat amazed at his own calm. I am only inches away from death, he thought, and behaving as though it is happening to somebody else. And almost as though the experience is so interesting I want to stretch it out as long as possible to examine it more closely.

He said, "Why do Sicilians like to complicate things so much? Why not just send three guns over one day when I'm walking out my front door?"

"It's a thing we have, Leo," Dominic said. "We call it style. We like to do things with style."

"So do I, Dominic," Leo said. "That's why what you should do right now is have one of your men—I'm sure they're back up there on the Drive—have one of them call Rocco."

"Rocco . . . ?"

"Your brother, Dominic. In Omaha. Omaha, Nebraska."

3.

To his Hummel Park neighbors Rocco Cranillo was a businessman, with interests ranging from real estate to meat-packing. His Protestant neighbors were well aware of his devout Catholicism, and that his four children attended church schools. If they did not quite accept him, they certainly tolerated him, and enjoyed his monthly Sunday-afternoon backyard barbecues. To be sure, none of Rocco's business associates were ever present at these affairs, and indeed were seldom at the house itself.

Life in Omaha was so easygoing Rocco never bothered with bodyguards or chauffeurs. Each morning promptly at eight he left the house in his maroon Lincoln Zephyr convertible coupe. Alone, he drove to work. At eight-thirty he was at his desk in the offices of the Crane Realty Corporation on the twelfth floor of the Omaha National Bank Building. His workday consisted of supervising the operations of some half dozen sub-bosses, auditing accounts, settling disputes, personally deciding the merits of any transaction over $2,000—and the fate of the individuals involved in those transactions. In general, then, he functioned as chief executive officer of an enterprise doing an annual gross business of well over $4 million.

The morning of the day his brother and Leo Gorodetsky met in New York, Rocco did not appear in his office at the usual time. He phoned to say he had decided to drive over to Council Bluffs to inspect a parcel of land. He would phone in later.

Rocco made this call from a public telephone in the men's room of the Council Bluffs Inn, a roadhouse with an adjoining motor court twelve miles outside Omaha on Highway 30.

With, quite literally, a gun to his head.

Harry Wise and Mickey Goldfarb had arrived in Omaha three days earlier. They had checked into a downtown hotel, the Fontenelle, then rented a car and driven to Hummel Park. For two days they observed Rocco Cranillo's routine. Mickey said they were almost too lucky; it was almost too easy. The man driving his own car, no protection. Harry said it was because God favored the right side, and since God was one of our boys, He was inclined to maybe make the odds a little better for His own kind.

When Rocco drove away from his big brick mansion on the hill that morning he never noticed the gray Plymouth coupe pull out of a side street and follow close behind. Then, at a rail crossing—another piece of luck—Rocco stopped behind a line of other cars. Suddenly the Zephyr's passenger door opened and Mickey slid into the seat beside Rocco.

"Hi, there," Mickey said pleasantly. In his hand was a .45, the muzzle leveled at Rocco's belly.

Twenty minutes later, in the Council Bluffs Inn men's room, looking into the muzzle of that same .45, Rocco made the phone call to his office. He was then escorted from the roadhouse and into a cabin. Two cars were parked outside the cabin, the maroon Lincoln Zephyr and the Plymouth coupe. An hour later, Rocco called his office again, leaving word he would not return until after lunch. He had run into some old friends, and in fact might take the whole day off. He did, however, expect a call from his brother Dominic in New York. Dominic was to call back on the roadhouse number.

"You did good, Rocco," Harry said when they were back in the cabin.

"Yeah, Rocco, you make a good actor," Mickey said. Then he laughed and unbuttoned his fly. "Hey, you want to make out like you're a queer?" He pulled the tail of his shirt through the open fly and flapped it at Rocco. "When we signed up for the cabin, I bet that's what the old woman in the office thought. 'Three fairies out for a little afternoon blowjob!' "

"Jesus, Mickey," Harry said. "Even if Rocco was a fairy, he'd never go for you."

"Yeah, why not?" Mickey asked. He chucked Rocco under the chin and spoke in a high falsetto. "That true, big boy . . . ?"

"Go fuck yourself, Jew," said Rocco.

Harry slapped him across the mouth. Rocco fell back against the bed. Harry glared down at him. "From now on, you call him *Mister* Jew."

Two hours after they arrived at the motor-court cabin, Dominic phoned. The call came in to the motor-court office. Harry gave the old woman who managed the place a five-dollar bill for privacy. He allowed Rocco to say hello to his brother, then snatched the phone away.

"Okay, Dominic," Harry said into the phone. "Now this is how it goes. You got Leo, and I got Rocco. Until I hear from Leo he's safe, Rocco stays with me. Anything happens to Leo—I mean anything, even he cuts a finger, you get little brother back in little pieces. *Capish, paisano?*"

The New York end of the conversation took place in the lobby of a small Seventy-second Street residential hotel. "You prick!" Dominic said quietly to Leo when he hung up. They were standing at the single public telephone, surrounded by four of Dominic's men whose glowering glances had twice already discouraged people from approaching the phone.

Leo said, "Do you want to waste time calling me names, Dominic, or do you want to do business?"

"What about Rocco?" Dominic asked.

"That's up to you," Leo said. "You behave yourself, he'll be home with his wife and kids for supper tonight."

Dominic peered angrily down at Leo, then at the four men surrounding them. Leo could actually feel Dominic's rage and humiliation. For an instant he thought Dominic might lose his temper entirely. Then all at once Dominic sighed. A long, heavy sigh of resignation, of defeat.

"What kind of business you talking about?" he asked.

Leo always thought of that day as the day that changed everything. It was like the First Day, the Day of Genesis. And whenever he thought of the unseen rifle in the boat anchored in the river opposite the park, he had to admit that for a man who claimed not to rely on luck he had certainly enjoyed more than his share that day.

Truly a Day of Genesis.

The first day of the Alliance.

This, the Alliance, was the business Leo wished to conduct with Dominic Cranillo. And with three other men. Two from New York, Vincent Tomasino and Paul Calvelli; one from Providence, Rhode Island, Nicola Franzone. Collectively, they controlled directly, or influenced, every important Italian family on the eastern seaboard. Their interests ranged from blatantly criminal activity to primly legitimate commercial enterprises. Loan sharking to laundry, whorehouses to brokerage houses, with several large labor unions for good measure. Only in big-time gambling and bookmaking were they not represented.

Leo faced these men the very next afternoon in the living room of a suite in the McAlpin Hotel especially booked for the occasion. All, with the exception of Nicola Franzone, were American-born, and all might easily have passed for typical American business executives.

Leo knew Dominic Cranillo was much too embarrassed and humiliated to reveal to his colleagues the true circumstances behind this important meeting. He had simply informed them that Leo Gorodetsky wished to submit a proposal. A proposal whose substance Dominic personally knew nothing about, but out of respect for Leo should at least be heard.

Leo also knew he was in no immediate personal jeopardy. He had secured Dominic Cranillo's word of honor. Rocco had been released, unharmed, and Harry Wise and Mickey Goldfarb were already back in California.

"Dominic was good enough to ask you to come here," Leo began, after some brief amenities and small talk. "And I appreciate the inconvenience." He nodded deferentially at Nicola Franzone. "Especially you, Don Nicola. I know it wasn't easy to drive all the way down here."

Nicola Franzone acknowledged with a limp wave of his hand. He was considerably older than the others, and reputedly in ill health. Leo continued now, "I think the time has come for us all to sit down and very carefully plan for the future. We're all businessmen, and we're all interested in profit. Not power, not personal ego, but profit. The balance sheets. That's our prime objective: money. But our interests have begun to overlap. This results in conflict. One tries to take something belonging to the other. But this only decreases the profit, and helps our mutual enemies—"

"—I have no enemies, Leo," Nicola Franzone said in his thick accent. "Not even the police."

"Excuse me, Don Nicola, but you have many enemies," Leo said. "The government, the newspapers, the reformers. And sometimes even the public. Now none of that will ever stop, which is why I say that every time we fight each other, we only weaken each other. We strengthen those who oppose us."

Vincent Tomasino said, "None of us four are fighting with each other, Leo."

"Only with you, Leo," Dominic said.

"Why?" Leo asked.

"Why what?"

"Why are you fighting with me?" Leo asked, and immediately answered his own question. "Because I have something you want. An operation you believe you can run. But you're wrong. You couldn't run it a tenth as well."

"Leo, are we here to listen to a proposition?" Vincent Tomasino asked. "Or get a lecture?"

"Let the man talk," Nicola Franzone said.

Leo nodded his thanks at Nicola, and continued, "You're not fighting with each other right now. But for how long?" He looked at Paul Calvelli. "Until Vinnie here decides he wants a little piece of your loan business, Paul?" He looked at Vincent Tomasino. "Or until Paul decides he wants some of your longshoreman action?" He looked at Dominic. "Or my race wire?"

Nicola Franzone laughed. "I'm gratified to be living in a place where no one bothers me too much."

"Is that why that man in New Hampshire, what was his name—?" Leo asked, and immediately remembered. "Digarmo, Louis Digarmo. Is that why he started his car one morning and it blew up in his face? Because he wasn't bothering you?"

Nicola Franzone sighed heavily. "He was a wise guy. I tried to reason with him, but he refused to listen."

"Nicola, there'll always be wise guys who won't listen," Leo said. "But they would, if they knew that if they got out of line, they're finished. And they'd know this for sure if there was one central organization they had to answer to."

Nicola Franzone said, "Central organization? What central organization?"

"An Alliance," Leo said. "Every important family in the country, the whole country, tied together, working together. You work together, you can all survive. And profit. You can build an organization as powerful as any government. With your own police, your own army." He smiled dryly. "Even your own taxes."

"And who would run this organization?" Nicola Franzone asked. "This 'Alliance'?"

"A Grand Council," Leo said. "A governing body with the final word on any and all decisions affecting the Alliance as a whole. The Council would also settle disputes among the members, and no Council member could be punished or receive disciplinary action without a unanimous vote."

Nicola Franzone, mildly curious now, asked, "And who would sit on this Council?"

"Yourself," Leo said. "Vincent, Dominic, and Paul, the heads of five or six other important families from throughout the country—and me."

"You?" Vinnie Tomasino said. "Where do you come in with the families?"

"I throw my people into the Alliance," Leo said. "Mine, and Sal's. That means the casinos, the books, the wire." He spoke fast now, feeling their skepticism and suspicion. "The five of us in this room—combined with those other families, Philadelphia, Chicago, Miami, Omaha, and the Coast—are big enough right now to control this whole country! East to west, north to south. Just think about it a minute. Instead of killing each other, we can make each other rich!"

"This idea come to you in a dream, Leo?" Vincent Tomasino asked, smiling at the others. "Because that's all it is, a dream."

"Why?" Leo asked.

Before Vinnie could reply, Nicola Franzone said, "I run my own businesess, Leo, my own way. To do this thing that you suggest means that in some cases I would be required to place my own interests behind those of another." He shook his head. "I, personally, would not care for that."

"Don Nicola, Vincent said my idea was a dream," Leo said. "But so was General Motors, and U.S. Steel, and Standard Oil. Think of the Alliance as any big company. The phone company, or the railroads. They all began as small companies, competing with each other, cutting each other's throats. Nobody made any real money, or had any real control. Not until they plugged the leaks. Like a paper bag with a hole in the bottom—"

"—yes," said Dominic Cranillo. "Filled with shit!"

"Be quiet, Dominic," Nicola Franzone said quietly. "Let him talk."

"A paper bag filled with money," Leo said to Dominic, and then addressed the others. "They plugged the leaks by pooling all their resources so where one operation might be weak or nonprofitable, the strength of another compensated for it. They took the best parts of all those separate companies and combined them into one company for the greatest efficiency. Five or six companies became separate divisions of one giant corporation. No division interferes with the other, but all share their main resources. So now they're the biggest, best, and richest in the world. Nobody can compete with them. We can do the same."

He continued, encouraged by his own enthusiasm. He quoted potential profit figures that astounded them, but which he supported with logic no one could refute. He talked for thirty minutes, and then all at once stopped. He had said it all, or most of it.

Paul Calvelli said, "I like the sound of it, Leo. It's the 'we' part of it I don't see. With all due respect, what've you got that we need?"

"You mean what've I got that you think you can't eventually take?" Leo said.

"Whatever," Paul said.

"Paul, do you honestly believe you can knock on, say, a federal judge's door—one of my judges—and introduce yourself and tell him that from now on he'll be doing business with you instead of me? Do you know how long it took me to build those contacts? Those people trust me, Paul. They wouldn't even talk to you."

"We have contacts, too, Leo," Vincent Tomasino said. "We get along okay."

"Sure," Leo said. "You have contacts, and Paul has, and Dominic. And Nicola. But just think how much more juice you'd have if you added *my* judges and policemen and the people I have in Albany and L.A., Miami. And Washington, too." He smiled. "My 'division.' I share my resources with you, we'd practically have our own House of Representatives. Think what it would mean." He looked at Vincent Tomasino. "What's the matter, Vinnie, don't you think you could use my bank? All that cash you don't know how to hide? Just think what you could do with it if you funneled it through a dozen different legitimate corporations, all with tax write-offs and investment credits."

"What good is it to us if you own the bank?" Dominic Cranillo asked.

"What is this bank, Leo?" Nicola Franzone asked, interested.

"The First Providence Trust," Leo said. "We bought into it during the Depression. It's a gold mine. But gentlemen—" he paused. He had planned to say it almost casually, but the enormity of it tightened his voice. For an instant he wondered if it was necessary. Did he have to give up that much? Yes, he did. There was no other way.

He continued, "I'll give the Alliance a fifty percent share of all our casinos. With the understanding," he said, watching their astonished faces and again wondering if he had given too much, but again knowing there was no choice. "With the understanding that Harry and I run them with no interference."

For a moment no one spoke. The men looked at each other, bemused and still suspicious, and then at Leo. He said, "That's my proposition."

"You said 'give,' Leo?" Nicola Franzone asked. "You will give those shares away, not sell them?"

"Give, Don Nicola," said Leo. "Give, not sell."

"You're giving away a lot, Leo," Paul Calvelli said. "What do you want back for it?"

"I'm not giving away a damn thing, Paul," Leo said. "I'm investing. In a magic formula that changes salt water into oil. There'll be so much money we'll need a dozen banks just to hold it!"

"You did not answer his question, Leo," Nicola Franzone said. "What does this Alliance thing do for you?"

Leo said nothing a moment. He was thinking, All right, here it comes. This is where they see I'm admitting my own weakness, my desperate need for their cooperation. But he also knew they were intelligent men who could not fail to perceive the benefits that would accrue to them through an Alliance.

"It guarantees me freedom of movement," Leo said. "I can concentrate on building casinos, not worrying about who might take a shot at me next." This last was directed at Dominic Cranillo, who reddened but said nothing. Leo smiled narrowly at him and continued, "It allows me freedom to expand my 'division,' and make more money for all of us. Money, remember? That's why we're in business. To make money."

"I want to hear more, Leo," Nicola Franzone said, and Leo knew they had bought the idea.

They haggled over details for hours, well into the evening. One detail was Sal Bracci, whom Leo insisted be included on the Council. Dominic Cranillo claimed, accurately, that Sal's family was seriously fragmented; Sal no longer commanded his former prestige and power.

This discussion, concerning Sal, commenced at nine P.M., nearly five hours after they started. Everyone was tired and irritable. Nicola Franzone dozed on the couch; he had fallen asleep over dinner that was brought in. On his lap was a paper plate containing an unfinished steak sandwich. Nicola had ordered it well done, and Leo remembered wondering how anyone could enjoy burnt steak. For a fanciful instant, gazing at the plate, Leo considered asking Nicola if the taste for well-done meat stemmed from his younger years when, as a means of obtaining information, it was said that he sometimes applied a blowtorch to the bottoms of naked feet.

Instead, Leo said to Dominic Cranillo, "I'll make a compromise with you. You give Sal a seat on the Council, I'll convince him to release his family to you."

"Now just how will you get him to do that?" Dominic asked.

"Sal is no fool," Leo said. "He knows he can't hold his family together from Cuba. But he also knows that unless he gives them his approval, you'll have one hell of a time getting them all. Half, maybe. Not all, never. Not without his okay."

Paul Calvelli said, "You talk him into it, Leo, and I'll go along. Somebody like Sal on the Council will get the respect of a lot of people. In the long run, maybe save us big grief." He glanced at Vincent Tomasino. "How about it?"

Vinnie nodded, yes.

"Okay," Dominic said. "But only if Sal sends word personally." He said this to Leo, his eyes cold and narrow as that day in Riverside Park when a wave of his hat would have sent a bullet into Leo's heart.

"I think I can get him to do it," Leo said, knowing full well he could since he and Sal had already discussed it. He did not, however, consider it advisable to reveal that, or certain other of Sal's plans whose disclosure at this time was equally inadvisable.

"All right," Vincent Tomasino said. "What else?"

"That's it, I guess," said Leo. He still faced Dominic, knowing Dominic suspected a trick. I know you will never forgive or forget my finessing you, Dominic, Leo told him in his mind. And I know that right now your brain is filled with ideas for revenge. And you are probably composing words for my funeral wreath: "From Dom and the Boys." But I hope I am wrong, Mr. Big Man. For your sake.

"Okay, then," said Paul Calvelli, and it was done.

The Alliance was formed.

4.

The penthouse atop El Conquistador faced east so that the rising sun shone blindingly bright off the glassed penthouse wall. When Dominic Cranillo, driving in from the airport, saw this radiance in the distance he recognized it as an omen. A beacon guiding him toward his destiny.

He knew Sal Bracci occupied that particular penthouse, but also knew similar penthouses were available in other hotels. Three, to be exact, and all IDIC-owned, which now meant fifty percent Alliance-owned.

This was Dominic's first visit to Havana, and long before the hotel limousine reached the hotel he made two important decisions. One, he would occupy a Havana hotel penthouse. Two, he would own the hotel it was in. He, personally, not the Alliance.

He had come to Havana to discuss with Sal the amalgamation of Sal's family into Dominic's. The personalities involved, Sal's recommendations for sub-bosses, the various enterprises concerned. The thousand and one details.

And some other, far more important details.

No details, however, important or unimportant were immediately discussed. Dominic was tired from the long train ride from New York and the dawn flight from Miami. But not too tired to enjoy the sumptuous breakfast in Sal's own penthouse dining room. Served by white-jacketed waiters, and joined by two of the prettiest girls Dominic had ever seen. Dancers in the hotel's chorus line.

After breakfast Dominic went to his suite on a lower floor, accompanied by both girls who promptly introduced him to a Cuban game they translated as "sandwich." Each girl was a slice of bread; he was the meat between the bread.

After the game he slept for six full hours. Rested and refreshed, he called Sal and was invited back to the penthouse. They went out to the terrace for coffee. Dominic thought the view overwhelming. One side of the terrace faced the mountains in the near distance; the other side faced the harbor, and the water beyond.

"You sure know how to live," he said to Sal.

"I knew you'd appreciate it, Dominic."

"And them two girls," Dominic said. "What's their names? Lita . . . ? Rosarita . . . ?"

"Estrellita," said Sal. "And Ramona. Ramona's the big one. They took good care of you, I see."

Dominic made a circle of his thumb and forefinger, then kissed the encircled fingers. The gesture of the connoisseur. "Sal, all this here—" Dominic waved his hand toward the harbor, then at the hills. "It could all be ours. Yours and mine."

"I'm not so sure General Batista would like that."

"You know what I mean," Dominic said. "I'm talking about the hotels."

"Then I don't think my partner, Leo, would like it."

"That's what I want to talk about, Sal. Him, you partner."

"I thought you wanted to talk about my guys," Sal said. "About who takes Tommy Marizzi's place."

"You know I didn't have no choice about that, don't you?" Dominic said. "Tommy, I mean. He practically declared war on me."

"Spare me the bullshit, Dominic," Sal said. "Please."

"It was business, Sal."

"All right," said Sal. "Now what about Leo?"

Dominic cleared his throat. He knew precisely what he wanted to say and had rehearsed it at length. Suddenly, he was not so sure. The image of Sal in exile had transformed him in Dominic's mind to a weak, pitiful figure. But face to face, it was the same old Sal, a figure of power and strength. Not a man to be underestimated.

Ever since the meeting four months before that formed the Alliance, Dominic had brooded about Leo Gorodetsky's presence on the Council. Leo's fancy talk had suckered them all in. Dominic seemed to be the only one who realized Leo was no longer needed. Every IDIC operation could have been smoothly taken over.

A few days after the meeting, in conference with Vincent Tomasino and Paul Calvelli, Dominic suggested they merely move in and take over. He was shouted down. Vinnie Tomasino said the Jew was a genius with money, leave him alone. So Dominic realized his only choice was to bide his time. He also realized he had committed a grave error not killing Leo. But that would have cost Rocco's life. Whenever Dominic thought of that, the blood pounded in his temples, and he felt the same flush of shame and humiliation as that day in New York.

". . . you said you wanted to talk about Leo?" Sal was saying. "What's the matter? The two broads cop your joint so much you're too weak to remember what you want to say?"

"Hey, Sal, take it easy," Dominic said. "I don't like to be talked to that way."

Sal said nothing, only studied Dominic coldly. After a moment, Dominic said, "His idea on the Alliance thing was good. I got to admit that. But, Sal, we don't need no Jews. We can do it all ourselves."

"The Council doesn't agree," Sal said.

"He's got no more use, Sal," Dominic said. "How do they say it—? Outlived his usefulness? He's outlived his usefulness, Sal."

For just an instant Sal wondered if his ears deceived him. Could this man, Dominic Cranillo, sitting opposite him and just now drinking down half a cuba libre in a single swallow possibly be so stupid?

Sal said gently, "You'd defy the Council?"

"For their own good," Dominic said. "For all our own good." He spoke with quiet earnestness. "I know he's your friend, Sal, but he's outlived his usefulness. We don't need him anymore. You and I, we can take over everything. You down here, me in the States. Even on the Coast, I'll move on Harry Wise. I talked with Donini out there. He'll do it in a second."

"And what do we tell the Council?"

"Goddamit, Sal, they'll thank us!" Dominic rose. He pointed his glass at Sal. "Come back to your own people, Sal!"

Sal shook his head slowly. "You're asking me to okay a hit on Leo?"

"I want you to back me up with the Council on it."

"You just said you know he's my friend."

"Sal, this is business," Dominic said.

Sal rose and stepped over to him. He was several inches taller, and for a long moment stood glaring down at him. Then he said, "I don't want to hear any more of that, Dominic. You understand? Not another fucking word!"

Dominic's whole body tensed. He glared back at Sal, but then almost immediately relaxed. He smiled. He gestured with his hands, palms down like an umpire signaling safe. "Hey, forget it. I respect your loyalty." He drank the rest of his drink and shook the empty glass. "Can I get a refill?"

Sal fixed him a fresh drink, and then they discussed Dominic's takeover of Sal's family. They talked nearly an hour, interrupted only for a snack of sandwiches and beer. They resolved the important points of the amalgamation, settled on personnel, and concluded with each reasonably satisfied.

Sal walked him to the door. "I'll see you tonight at dinner," Sal said. He winked. "You want Estrellita and Ramona again, or you want to try something new?"

"You decide," Dominic said.

"Leave it to me," Sal said.

The instant Dominic was gone, Sal made two telephone calls. Both to New York. One to Vincent Tomasino, and one to Paul Calvelli. The same two subjects were discussed in each call. The first subject was the fabulous success of the Alliance in its brief existence, which Sal said could be credited to Leo Gorodetsky. Vinnie and Paul both agreed, and on the second subject also.

Although the content of this second subject technically should have been brought before the full Council, the men decided that the rule could be waived in this one instance. Sal phoned Leo later that same evening with the unhappy news that less than one hour before, near El Conquistador's main entrance, a taxi struck and killed Dominic Cranillo.

The accident occurred in full view of a traffic policeman who determined that the taxi's brakes had failed. The Havana police had ruled the death an unfortunate accident, but promised to investigate the possibility of charging the taxi driver with negligence.

Sal did not bother mentioning to Leo that when he identified the body, he whispered to the dead man, "Dominic, this is business."

Leo did not attend Dominic Cranillo's funeral later that same week in New York, but he did attend a funeral some six months afterward, in the spring of 1939. This second funeral was far less ostentatious than Dominic Cranillo's, conducted with Episcopalian stolidity, and little publicized. While the funerals were unrelated, both in a sense were at least indirectly attributable to the same source.

Leo Gorodetsky.

Or so Charles Brickhill and his young deputy, Martin Raab, believed, although their quoted accusations referred to the source as "organized crime."

The man laid to rest in the second funeral was the president of the First Providence Trust Company. He had been in a meeting with Martin Raab, discussing certain bank difficulties. Ten minutes after the meeting started the bank president excused himself and stepped into the bathroom adjoining his office. There, standing at the mirror, he inserted the barrel of a small pearl-handled .22 automatic into his mouth and pulled the trigger.

His name was Clark Daniels.

Charlotte Daniels's father.

—— *17* ——

F ROM where he watched Leo could not hear the minister, but knew
it was the usual, useless litany. Much cleaner, however, than Jewish or
Catholic ceremonies, with none of the wailing hysteria, the breast-beating.
You had to admire these proper Protestants for that at least.

It was a pleasant day, the sun warm and comfortable, with a gentle
breeze rustling the new spring leaves of the cemetery maple and elm
trees. Three funeral-parlor limousines were parked near the burial site,
a small hillock overlooking the entire grounds, which themselves appeared to slope gently down into the flatlands of Flushing Meadows. Far
in the distance, the two-hundred-foot-tall Trylon symbol of the New
York World's Fair rose up out of the Meadows like a needle outlined
against the sky.

Charlotte stood with her mother, a tall, sturdy woman; both women
in black, veiled. With some dozen other men and women, they faced the
flower-covered bronze casket. Nearby, three gravediggers waited with
bored respect.

Charlotte's mother reminded Leo of Sarah, and of his visit with her
the previous evening, and his promise to see her again this evening. To
meet her neighbor, one Samuel Stern, a widower, a druggist constantly
harassed in his small Yorkville pharmacy by antisemitic hooligans. The
police refused to help, so Sarah suggested the druggist speak with her
son, Leo, who she knew had important friends on the police force.

Leo said he wasn't sure he could meet the druggist; he had to attend a funeral, and did not know what his day looked like after that. Whose funeral? Sarah asked. A business associate, Leo said, a *shaygets* banker who had committed suicide. Sure, Sarah said, they were still jumping out of windows, these *goyisher* bankers. Leo said that in this case the man did it to spare himself the pain of a lingering illness.

Leo came to the funeral only from curiosity. Curiosity to see what Charlotte looked like after all these years. Six years. He had considered speaking to her, offering ironic condolences, but decided it was better this way. Watching from a distance, keeping his distance. You never knew. Even with her Gentile composure, the sight of him might easily trigger some embarrassing outburst.

You killed him! she might cry.

Which in a technical sense was not untrue. Clark Daniels had committed suicide to spare himself and his family the humiliation of public exposure as the banker-partner of prominent organized-crime figures.

More realistically, a junior partner. Clark Daniels had sold his bank to the organized-crime figures. *Mortgaged* it to them, actually. One thing sure, that rainy day in 1923 when Clark "interviewed" Leo at the Union League Club, he never dreamed of someday finding himself in debt to the little Jew.

After their 1923 meeting Leo did not see Clark Daniels again until 1933, six years ago, the second morning of FDR's bank holiday. Leo arrived at his office to find Clark waiting. A business call. And Clark was businesslike about it. He needed money: $250,000. It was a familiar story. Respectable businessmen, attempting to cover losses, naïvely believing the Depression would soon end, borrowing from their own declining assets, plunging deeper and deeper into debt.

Most vulnerable were small banks unable to collect their own loans. Banks such as Clark Daniels's First Providence Trust. Clark had borrowed from his customer deposits and then, desperate, came to Leo. For collateral, he pledged twenty-five percent of his shares in First Providence Trust Company. In time there would be further loans, more shares pledged. In the end, IDIC controlled fifty-one percent of a recognized, licensed, legitimate banking institution, the "laundry" through which IDIC's undeclared, untaxed cash—the vast sums earned from the bootlegging years, and now the casinos and race wire—was channeled.

Leo was gracious and understanding, even sympathetic. He wanted to be; he knew it made it all the harder for Clark. He told him he would take the loan request under consideration, but from the very instant he saw Clark waiting in the anteroom he knew he would grant the loan.

Because he knew, too, precisely what would happen next.

He would receive either a phone call or visit from a former friend, a lady. He was so sure of this he canceled a dinner date that very same evening with a woman he had been occasionally seeing. A buyer for a department store, an attractive lady he met in Saratoga shortly after Ellie left him. He enjoyed this lady's company, but wanted to wait for the other woman.

He did not have to wait long, only until the following Sunday evening. He was in the living room of his Park Central Hotel apartment, reading Walter Winchell's column in the *Mirror*,—and at the same time listening to Winchell's new weekly radio show. *"Good evening, Mr. and Mrs. America, and all the ships at sea . . ."*

The phone rang. The familiar voice. Soft, husky, each word clearly enunciated as though a priceless gem reluctantly parted with.

"Leo, this is Charlotte."

Now, all these years later, watching her approach her father's grave and place a flower atop the already lowered casket, he remembered that night. Not that he ever forgot, or ever could. He even remembered what she wore. It was chiseled into his memory as vividly as the letters and numbers on Clark Daniels's tombstone.

He had opened the door for her and she stepped into the room. He closed the door. Neither of them wasted words, not even hello. Leo said, "Quite a comedown, isn't it?"

"Shall I beg you?" she asked. "Is that what you want?"

"Isn't that what you came to do?"

"I came to ask a favor."

"From me?" he asked innocently. "What possible favor could I do for *you*?"

"To start with, you might act decently."

"All right," he said. "Tell me again why you're here?"

"To ask a favor."

"Oh, yes," he said. "A favor from an old friend, excuse me. All right, 'old friend,' take off your clothes."

"You bastard!"

"Don't you mean 'Jew bastard'?"

"Perhaps I'd better leave." She moved toward the door.

"For Christ's sake, Charlotte, cut the crap. Do what you came here to do."

"Will you give him the money?"

"I don't know. Let me see first if it's worth it."

She hesitated a moment, then strode past him and walked into the bedroom. He did not turn to watch her but remained in the living room, his back to her. He had planned this for two days, even to the exact words spoken, although she had not yet given him the opening for "pound of flesh." Pound of flesh, he planned to say, that's what us Jews charge!

"I'd like a drink, please."

She stood in the bedroom doorway, naked but for shoes and stockings. He had never seen her naked. The size of her breasts surprised him.

Very large, but firm with taut, dark nipples. Then he remembered having seen her breasts once before, the last time he was with her, when he had hit her and knocked her down. He wanted to say, "For a woman pushing forty, you don't have a bad body." Instead, he said, "Get on the bed."

"I need a drink first."

He wanted to hit her. Like that last time when it seemed to arouse her so. But now he found the very thought of even touching her revolting. Without a word, he turned and walked into the kitchen. He poured two glasses of Scotch from a bottle of Chivas Regal and carried them back to the bedroom. He gave her a glass and watched her drink it down in a single swallow.

"You still like the booze, I see," he said.

"I need it," she said.

"That's right, so you can fuck a Jew," he said. "Everybody needs a drink for that, I suppose."

"I'm trying to be nice to you."

"Like any good whore."

"Whatever you say," she said. She put the empty glass on the dresser top and sat on the edge of the bed. "Well?"

He drank down his drink. It burned his throat.

"I'm ready," she said.

He had that feeling of being an observer, part of an audience watching a stage play, a tableau. He did not understand why he had allowed things to go this far, why he had allowed them to start at all.

He said, "I'm sorry. Get dressed."

She was genuinely surprised. "Get dressed?" She cupped her breasts, nestling each one on an open hand, extending them to him. "I thought this is what you wanted? What you've always wanted."

"I changed my mind," he said. He put his empty glass on the dresser next to hers. "Get dressed."

Her eyes fell to his crotch and narrowed with sudden, almost amused enlightenment. She got up and stood facing him. "You don't understand, Leo. I *want* you to do it."

He nearly laughed in her face. He stepped past her to the bed and gathered up her clothes. He tossed them at her and walked into the living room. He stood at the window. It faced north, softening the glare of midtown lights, with a clear view of the lights of the windows of Central Park West hotels and apartment buildings. The letters of the huge sign atop the General Motors Building cast a hazy red glow in the night sky. He had switched on the radio before she came, and vaguely remembered moving the dial from station to station, searching for music, and finally finding the Stromberg-Carlson hour on WJZ. He listened absently to the music, a ballad he recognized from a recent movie, but whose name he could not immediately recall, or the name of the movie.

"I tried, Leo." She was in the living room, but he did not move. He did not want to look at her.

"I'll give him the money," he said. "You did your job."

"You hate me, don't you?"

He faced her. She was fully dressed, purse in hand. For a moment he imagined her naked again. "I pity you," he said.

Those three words, "I pity you," gave him more satisfaction than a dozen pounds of flesh. The rigidity of her face when he said it, the indignance in her eyes. And then, almost at once, the face relaxed and sagged. The eyes softened. She looked away in humiliation and defeat.

His gratification had been nearly sexual; no, transcended sexuality. It was utter and complete, but at the same time he remembered Hershey's adage. "Swatting flies with a cannon." No percentage. So now, six years later, watching her link her arm through her mother's and leave the grave site, he felt nothing. His victory was total, but he felt nothing.

At this very instant, at that same cemetery, another man observed the funeral unseen—and Leo.

Martin Raab, who himself could technically have been accused of killing Clark Daniels. Martin Raab was in conference with Clark when the tragedy occurred. The conference concerned a tax-evasion case against IDIC in general and Leo in particular, all dependent upon Clark Daniels's testimony.

Once again, a witness was silenced.

Martin Raab watched Leo descend the sloping flagstoned pathway toward his car and hurried to intercept him.

Benny Roth waited at the parked LaSalle. His attention seemed focused not on Leo, but on a man approaching from another direction. Leo, alerted, turned to face the man.

Young, not yet thirty, medium height but quite stocky. With his red, full cheeks, thick black curly hair and deep, dark eyes, he was the picture of a nice Jewish boy. Leo had seen him once before, at Sal Bracci's sentencing.

". . . like to talk to you a second," he said. "I'm Martin Raab."

"Raab, formerly Rabinowitz," Leo said. "Your father was a *shochet*. I know all about you. It has to be important for you to chase me out here."

"I wasn't chasing you," Raab said. "I was here for the funeral." He glanced at Benny. "You have something to do?"

"It's okay," Leo said to Benny, who did not know Martin Raab and was looking at Leo for any signal. Benny hesitated, then walked around to the other side of the car and lit a cigarette.

Raab strained to keep his voice steady. "I was with Clark Daniels when he died."

"I guess that's what's called being an eyewitness," Leo said. He knew of Raab's experience, down to the last detail. Even how Raab had to kick open the bathroom door that had been wedged closed by Clark's head.

"Do you know why I was there?"

"I have a good idea."

"I just bet you do," said Raab. "I was questioning him about his relationship with you."

Leo said nothing. He knew all that, of course, and knew Raab knew. He wondered what the kid's point was, what he was trying to prove. At the same time, he had to admire him. It took guts for a young deputy D.A. to confront a man this way.

"We hadn't even talked five minutes when he did it," Raab said. "He just said, 'Excuse me, please.' And he went into the bathroom. A second later I heard the shot."

Leo remained silent. He waited for the rest, but there was no more. Raab said, "All I want to tell you is that one day I hope to attend another funeral. Yours."

"I'll see that you're invited," Leo said. "What else?"

"That's all." Raab started away.

"Hold it!" Leo seized Raab's arm and swung him around, in the same motion gesturing to Benny Roth that it was all right, to stay where he was. Leo said to Raab, "I just love the way hypocritical little smartasses like you try to transfer their own guilt!"

Raab laughed. "Talk about transferring guilt—"

"—no, no," Leo said. "It won't work. This man, this man you've decided is a martyr, killed himself because of you! *You*, Mr. Deputy D.A., who does Charlie Brickhill's shit work. You killed the poor, dumb, yellow bastard! You told him what a bad person he was, and how he'd spend the rest of his life in jail because he sold his bank to me. So he decided he was too old and too proud to let anybody know about that. About how he had to stoop so low to try and save his business that he totally messed it up. You killed him, Mr. Raab, but you don't have the guts to admit it!"

"Fine speech," Raab said. "You through?"

"Yeah, I'm through," Leo said. He almost wanted to laugh himself; it was almost funny. This little *pisha* trying to outstare him. And the *pisha* did not outstare Leo. He turned and walked away. Leo watched until he was out of sight.

Leo returned to the car. Benny opened the front door for him. "Who the fuck was that, Leo?"

"A Jewish boy, Benny," Leo said. "A nice Jewish boy."

Benny put the car in gear and drove off. Out of the cemetery and onto the highway. He glanced at Leo from the corner of his eye. Leo stared broodily, unseeingly, out the window.

"Back to the hotel?" Benny asked.

Leo heard the question, but did not answer. He was thinking about Martin Raab, and that they would meet again. Yes, of course, he told himself. Of course, you'll meet him again. The little bastard will never get off your back. Especially now that he thinks he got to you.

Thinks he got to me? Leo asked himself, and replied, He did. Leo cringed inwardly hearing in his mind his own voice protesting any responsibility for Clark Daniels, and then he heard another voice.

"Leo?" It was Benny. "You feel okay?"

"Why?"

"I don't know, you look kind of funny."

"Like what?"

"I don't know," Benny said. "Just funny."

"I'm fine, Benny," Leo said. "I just feel a little sorry for myself."

"Are you kidding? You? Feel sorry for yourself?"

"What's the matter, Benny, you don't think it's possible?"

"You want the truth?" Benny said. "No."

Leo said nothing a moment. Then, "Get over on the Parkway, Benny. I'll go up and see my mother."

"Right," said Benny. He swung the big car around to pass a truck and then cut sharply into the right lane for the Parkway exit. "Hey, I didn't say nothing to make you mad, did I?"

"No, kid, don't worry about it," Leo said. He sat back and watched the passing landscape. He had decided he might as well see why Sarah wanted him to meet the old druggist, Samuel Stern. If he did not at least talk to the man he knew that Sarah, too, would never get off his back. He could not have known it then, of course, but the seeds of his next encounter with Martin Raab were sown that very night when he met Samuel Stern and heard his story.

2.

The Highgate Pharmacy, on Third Avenue halfway between Eighty-fifth and Eighty-sixth streets, offered none of the conveniences of a modern drugstore. No soda fountain, candy, or sundries. An old-fashioned pharmacy, down to the mortar and pestle in the show window.

Tonight, waxed onto the glass of that show window, was a crudely drawn Star of David. And the words:

JEW, GET OUT!

"It's like the newsreels of Germany," Leo said.

"Of course," said Samuel Stern. "From the same people, isn't it?"

"But how do you know it's them?"

"Mr. Gorodetsky, I saw those—" he groped angrily for the word. "Animals. Those animals. I saw them and talked to them. They act like Yorkville is part of Berlin. They even wear uniforms. With the polished leather belts yet, and the armbands."

"Did you see them write that on the window?"

"I didn't have to see it, Mr. Gorodetsky, to know who did it. The only other Jew left in the whole neighborhood beside me was Gofstein, the tailor. They smashed the windows of his place and tried to set it on fire. *That,* I saw!"

"Why didn't they break your windows?" Leo asked.

"They told me I'd be next," said Stern. "They enjoy that, the little *shtick dreck!* They like you to sweat some before they do anything. So you can think about it, and worry."

Leo said nothing. They were sitting in the back of his car, parked near the pharmacy. Samuel Stern was a small, frail, bespectacled man of seventy who had arrived in New York twelve years earlier. A longtime widower, a successful pharmacist and chemist in his native Germany, he was wiped out in the postwar inflation. A distant cousin lent him enough money to open the Yorkville pharmacy. Until a year ago he had lived comfortably in a two-room flat above the pharmacy which, patronized by the area's German-speaking residents, had been modestly successful. Then, increasing harassment from German-American Bund thugs forced him to seek new quarters. He moved into the same Amsterdam Avenue apartment building occupied by Leo's mother.

Now Sam Stern said, "Listen, I only brought you to see it because your dear mother insisted. I didn't expect you to do anything about it. Nobody can."

Leo gazed at the pharmacy window, the Jewish star. He had seen this before, but not for years. Not since the old days when roving Irish gangs sometimes daubed *shul* windows with black paint and Jew-hating epithets. Now it was Nazis.

". . . and it's of no matter anymore, anyway," Stern was saying. "I told you, I got an offer to sell the place. Maybe it's about time, anyway. I'll make a few dollars. I can't complain."

"Where did you say these Nazis meet?" Leo asked.

"Up on Eighty-ninth, near Second," Stern said. "In a lodge hall. An Elks lodge, I think."

"Go over to Eighty-ninth and Second," Leo said to Benny Roth. They drove off.

The white letters JEW, GET OUT! glowed in the dark.

The building at Eighty-ninth and Second was a three-story tenement. The ground floor, once a grocery store and more recently an Elks Lodge, had been converted into a German-American Bund meeting hall. The plate-glass display windows were covered with heavy brown paper from the inside. On the paper was a large painted replica of an American flag crisscrossed with a Nazi flag.

The LaSalle drove past. Cars were parked bumper to bumper on both sides of the street, and even half a block away shouts and applause could be heard from the building. Two burly jackbooted, brown-uniformed young men stood in the open doorway. They wore Sam Browne belts, storm-trooper caps, and swastika armbands. Leo ordered Benny to park around the corner and remain in the car with Samuel Stern. He got out and walked to the meeting hall.

"Good evening," he said to the guards.

"Good evening," one replied, his voice drowned out in a chorus of voices from inside shouting, "*Sieg heil! Sieg heil!*"

Leo peered past them into the hall. A brown-uniformed man stood at a lectern on the podium, speaking into a microphone. On the wall behind the podium was a huge portrait of Adolf Hitler. Leo smiled at the guards and started in.

"Excuse me." The second guard blocked his entrance. "I don't think I know you."

"No, this is my first time," Leo said. "May I go in?"

The first guard, worried, asked, "Are you a reporter?"

"No, sir, I am not," Leo said. "I'm a man who believes in the cause, and would like to contribute to it." Both men instantly stepped aside. Leo entered the hall, thinking these American Nazis were not very smart. And probably not too dangerous, either. Break a few windows, scare a few old Jews.

The hall was crowded with enthusiastic men and women sitting on folding chairs, their attention riveted on the speaker, a tall, slender, balding man of fifty whom Leo recognized from newspaper photos. The German-American Bund co-chairman, Kurt Baumer.

". . . only when this scourge is rooted from our society, only then can we truly call ourselves 'civilized'!" Baumer was saying. On either side of the podium two large portable loudspeakers amplified Baumer's voice reverberatingly through the room. "In Germany, the adored Führer, Adolf Hitler, long ago recognized the danger and alerted our people, so that now, after casting aside its Bolshevik Jewish slavemasters and warmongers, Germany has regained its rightful place among the nations! And we will do it here in our own country. We will purify the race. We will do it! We will do it! We will do it!"

The audience applauded and cheered, and then rose, fists clenched, eyes shining with evangelistic fervor, screaming "We will do it! We will do it!" The words echoed through the hall like the beating of a drum. Finally, almost reluctantly, they quieted as Baumer motioned for silence.

"The homeland needs your help," Baumer continued. "I am preparing a book to be signed by every loyal German-American citizen. I want six thousand signatures, each signature to be accompanied by ten dollars. I shall go to Berlin, and personally present the money and the book of signatures to the Führer. He needs this gesture of support and solidarity from his American friends. He needs to know that in a time of crisis America will not desert him! He needs to know that the enemies of Germany are our enemies! Germany's enemies are America's enemies!"

Leo had heard enough. He left. "When is the next meeting?" he asked the guards.

"Friday," said the first guard.

"I'll be here," said Leo.

He returned to the car. He got in and for a moment leaned wearily back against the seat cushion. Samuel Stern remained silent.

"Go on back to Amsterdam Avenue, Ben," Leo said finally, to Benny. He looked at Samuel Stern. "I read about this in the papers. But I never believed it."

"Now you do?"

"Now I do," said Leo.

"And you see, Mr. Gorodetsky, everything is legal. They commit no crimes the police can arrest them for. All the window breaking and beating up of people, nobody can prove."

Leo looked at Stern a moment. "Mr. Stern, do you know what I do for a living? What my business is? I'm a gambler, Mr. Stern. A profession illegal in this state. I could be put in jail for the way I make my living, and there are people who would like nothing better than to do that." He jerked his thumb behind him. "But what these Jew-hating bastards do is not illegal. Does that make sense?"

He was really thinking aloud, but Samuel Stern did not realize that and said, "That's what I been trying to tell you, Mr. Gorodetsky!"

Leo was only half listening. He was recalling the stories he had heard and that Samuel Stern confirmed from his own experiences. The Nazis were confiscating everything the German Jews owned, then kicking them out of the country. There were even stories that Jews unable to bribe their way out were placed into hard-labor camps. Work, or starve.

"Why don't they fight?" he said to Stern, thinking aloud again.

"Excuse me?"

"The Jews," Leo said. "Why don't they fight back? That's the trouble. That's always been the trouble. Jews won't fight back."

"The German Jews?"

"Any Jews, all Jews," Leo said. "Why don't they fight back?"

"Fight back with what?" Stern asked. "Their intellect? Their disbelief such a thing could happen? It's been happening for two thousand years, hasn't it?"

"Then they should expect it, and plan for it."

"No one expects it, Mr. Gorodetsky. Do you expect it? Do you expect it to happen to you here? Are you planning for it?"

Leo said nothing a moment, thinking, then spoke to Benny. "That kid brother of yours, what's his name?"

"Doug," Benny said. "Good kid." He glanced over his shoulder at Leo. "Some name for a Jewboy, huh? Douglas." He continued talking as he looked away to turn left on Eighty-sixth Street. "My mother was nuts about that actor, Douglas Fairbanks." He caught Leo's eye in the rearview mirror. "What about Doug, Leo?"

"He's eighteen, nineteen?" Leo asked.

"Seventeen," Benny said. "Looks older, don't he?"

"Tell him I have a job for him."

"Hey, no shit!" Benny turned to grin at Leo. "That's great."

"Does he have a lot of friends?"

"The kid?" Benny said. "Yeah, he's very popular."

"Tell him I have jobs for some of his friends, too," Leo said. "Maybe half a dozen of them. I'm forming a club." Leo looked at Samuel Stern. "For young Jewish boys. I even thought of a name for it. 'HDA.' "

"HDA?" Stern said. "What is that, please?"

"HDA," Leo said. "Hebrew Defense Association."

Sarah Gorodetsky was pleased Leo took such an interest in her friend Samuel Stern. And more than delighted when Leo asked her to invite Mr. Stern for Friday *Shabbes* dinner.

It was a pleasant meal, although Leo irritated Sarah by continually looking at his watch. "What's the matter, Laibel," she asked. "You in such a big hurry to go someplace?"

"Yeah, Ma," he said. "Mr. Stern and I have an appointment."

"We do?" Stern asked.

"I forgot to mention it," Leo said. "I want you to meet some people."

"What people?" Sarah asked suspiciously.

"Some people who don't like what the Nazis are doing in Yorkville." Sarah beamed proudly at Samuel Stern. "Didn't I tell you my Laibel would help?"

After dinner, Benny drove Leo and Samuel Stern to the Bund hall on Eighty-ninth Street. The meeting had already started, but people were still entering. Benny double-parked near the hall entrance.

"You just stay in the car with Benny," Leo said to Stern. "I'll be right back."

He got out of the car, opened the trunk, and withdrew a large paper sack. He carried the sack down the street and around the corner. A small Dodge pickup truck was parked in the shadows between street-lamps. Three young men sat in the truck cab, and four others in the open truck bed. This truck, an hour before, had been parked with twelve identical vehicles in the yard of a Queens construction company. Its theft would not be noticed until morning, if then.

"Okay," Leo called to the group in the truck bed. The four boys scrambled out; all carried baseball bats. Immediately, they vanished into the darkness of the alley.

The day before, at three in the morning, Leo had taken these same seven boys to the Bund hall. Reconnoitering, they discovered the building had only one rear entrance into the adjoining alley. It was ideal for Leo's plan.

Now Leo struck a match to glance at his watch. He spoke to the three in the cab. "All set?"

"You bet," said the driver, Doug Roth, a tall, lean young man wearing a heavy denim work jacket and Brooklyn Dodger baseball cap.

"Nervous?" Leo asked.

"Naaw," said the one in the middle. "Don't worry about us, Mr. Gorodetsky."

"Hey, you give us twenty bucks each for this," said the third boy. "We'd of done it for nothing!"

"Okay, give it back then," Leo said. He smiled to show he was only kidding. "It's nine-thirty. I'll go in now—" he rustled the paper sack. "Give me ten minutes, then move!"

He started back toward the Bund hall, stopping briefly at the corner to transfer the contents of the paper sack—small tubelike cylindrical objects—into his jacket pockets. Making sure the pockets did not bulge, he strode to the hall entrance.

The same two uniformed men guarded the door. "I was here the other night," Leo said. He removed a bill from his wallet and handed it to the first guard. "I told you I wanted to contribute."

The guard looked at the bill and whistled. "A hundred!"

"See it gets to Baumer," Leo said.

"Of course, sir," said the guard. "What is your name?"

"Bradford Peabody," Leo said. "I'm a great admirer of the Bund."

"Well, we thank you, Mr. Peabody," said the other guard.

"Call me Brad," Leo said, and walked into the hall.

Nothing had changed. The same people, the same hypnotic intentness. And Kurt Baumer ranting into the microphone, now on the "Jewish Conspiracy."

". . . outright, blatant lies being promulgated in this country by the Jewish-owned press!" he shouted. "They did not tell you how innocent boys and girls of German descent were savagely beaten by Jews—and, yes, sometimes murdered! They did not tell you how these German citizens desired only to be reunited with the Fatherland! Our Führer had no choice, then, but to rescue his people from the barbarous Czechoslovakians . . . !"

The hall rang with applause. Leo sidled around to the front and leaned against the wall a moment. Then he bent as though to retrieve something from the floor. He straightened up and moved on. Behind him, on the floor, was one of the cylindrical objects which he had snapped in two with his fingers before carefully placing it on the floor. He was so close to the podium he could see Kurt Baumer's beard stubble and the reflection of the overhead lights in Baumer's rimless spectacles.

Leo placed another cylinder under some cigarette butts in a sand-filled ash stand. He continued around to the other side, sliding one cylinder under a chair, one under a radiator, and two more on a table atop a pile of hats and coats.

". . . there will be no war!" Baumer was saying. "Germany wants peace. Germany needs peace! But Germany will never again be victimized by the Jewish bankers and their followers. No more! No more! No more!" The crowd chanted wildly with him, "No more! No more! No more!"

All at once Kurt Baumer frowned. His nostrils crinkled. He removed his glasses and lowered his head, sniffing. Others on the podium and in the audience stirred uncomfortably. Throughout the hall people began whispering, ". . . what is that smell?" ". . . it's terrible!" "It smells like gas!" "Rotten eggs!" "Stink bombs!" "It's stink bombs!"

In the front row a woman clutched her throat and began coughing uncontrollably. A man beside her shot to his feet and started pushing past others in a desperate dash to the aisle. Everyone in the hall seemed to be choking, coughing, gasping for breath in the acrid, sulfuric stench suddenly enveloping the entire room.

Leo was already outside. He smiled to the guards. "When's the next meeting?" he asked.

The guard did not answer. He and the other guard brushed past Leo, racing into the hall where people were climbing over each other to escape, screaming and shouting in panic.

At that instant the pickup truck appeared. It was on the sidewalk, which was just wide enough to accommodate the truck's width. Doug Roth brought the truck to an abrupt stop on the sidewalk at the hall's main entrance. The whole right side of the truck cab was jammed against the hall threshold, completely blocking any exit.

Leo opened the left-hand door and helped Doug out. They locked the truck door and hurried away down the block toward the alley.

Across the street in Leo's LaSalle, Benny Roth and Samuel Stern watched. The old pharmacist was bewildered. "What is happening?"

"Blitzkrieg, Mr. Stern," Benny said. "A goddam Blitzkrieg!" He slammed the car into gear and sped away toward the alley entrance.

In the meantime, unable to squeeze past the truck, people fleeing from the hall turned and charged back inside to the only other exit, the rear.

There, in the alley on each side of the narrow door, Doug Roth's friends waited with baseball bats. The Bundists streaming from the building were swatted with the bats. Only the uniformed ones; Leo's orders were clear. And only the first few. Leo knew that after the initial confusion the Nazis would quickly regroup.

After knocking down half a dozen storm troopers, Leo's young men retreated through the alley to the waiting LaSalle. The big car raced off, packed with laughing boys, all talking at once, all congratulating each other. Samuel Stern was overwhelmed. Never had he seen such a sight, or even imagined it. Jews beating up on Nazis. The old man wept with joy.

From his apartment that same evening, Leo made an anonymous call to the City News Bureau. Every New York newspaper the next day carried the story:

BUND MEETING DISRUPTED BY
"HEBREW DEFENSE ASSOCIATION"

What Leo did not know was that several Bundists had been seriously injured, one critically. He also did not know that a passerby, not a Bundist but an off-duty policeman, had noted the LaSalle's license plate when it was outside the meeting hall.

"Close the door," Charles Brickhill said to Martin Raab. Brickhill, legs propped up on his file-folder-laden desk, sat gazing out the window. His office on the seventh floor of the Federal Building faced east, overlooking Chinatown and the bridge. Brickhill did not look up at Raab, but continued watching late-afternoon traffic crawl toward Brooklyn. Blindly, he indicated a newspaper atop the stack of file folders.

Raab sat opposite Brickhill and slid the newspaper onto his lap. It was the morning *Times*. The headlines read:

CHAMBERLAIN TO MAKE PERSONAL PLEA TO HITLER

Below this was a smaller story: AFTER 2,130 GAMES, GEHRIG ASKS TO BE BENCHED. Raab glanced quizzically at Brickhill.

"Lower left," Brickhill said. It was the story of HDA's attack on the Bund meeting.

"I saw it," Raab said.

Brickhill eased his legs off the desk top and swung around to face Raab. "The Hebrew Defense Association is Leo Gorodetsky," he said, and told him of the license-plate identification.

Raab smiled reluctantly. "I kind of admire him."

Brickhill said, "Baumer won't press charges."

"Of course not," Raab said. "The scumbag wouldn't admit that Jews are capable of interrupting his admirable activities."

"I want Gorodetsky nailed for this," Brickhill said.

"Jesus, Charlie, is that what we're down to? Charging Leo Gorodetsky with planting stink bombs in a public place?"

"One of the men they attacked has a fractured skull. I want you to get Baumer to swear out a complaint."

Raab started to laugh, then stopped. "You're serious."

"Once we have the complaint, I'll get a warrant to search Leo Gorodetsky's offices and living quarters," Brickhill said. "We're looking for a suspected cache of weapons intended for use against future Bund gatherings."

Raab said nothing. It was so ridiculous he knew Brickhill had another motive. But when he heard it, he was astounded. It, too, was ridiculous.

". . . in the process, we'll seize all the little man's books and records," Brickhill was saying. "If we're lucky, perhaps even the names of judges and policemen on his payroll."

Martin Raab knew Charles Brickhill as a particularly unhumorous man, so this was no perverted humor, not even whimsy. He said, "Charlie, you know very well they don't keep records or books. Or names. They keep it all in their heads. The important stuff, anyway."

"I want the bank records, Marty," Brickhill said. "The information Clark Daniels would have given us. The real books, not the phony ones available on subpoena."

"Come on, Charlie. They're not hidden under Leo Gorodetsky's bed!"

"They're not all in his head either," Brickhill said. "They're on paper. Somewhere. All we need, goddamit, is a start. Even the slightest hint of a transaction that doesn't match the auditor's report or the declared tax returns."

He really was serious, Raab thought with dismay, and said, "You're reaching. We'll end up looking like asses."

Brickhill peered at him a cold instant. "Can we look more like asses than we do already? The Keystone Kops look smarter!"

"This won't help, Charlie."

"I can't sit around and wait for another Bernie Kopaloff."

This, Raab knew, was what drove the D.A. so obsessively. He had had Harry Wise practically strapped into the electric chair, which would have opened the way to finish Leo Gorodetsky, but they outsmarted and outmaneuvered him. He would never rest until that special score was evened.

Martin Raab also knew Brickhill would stop at nothing to achieve this, even taking the law into his own hands. Or distorting it to suit his own purposes. Raab had long suspected Brickhill of somehow rigging Sal Bracci's trial. This, however, was only supposition, an instinct, and in truth he never wanted to know what actually happened.

He said, "Charlie, it's a waste of time."

"We sent one of them into exile," Brickhill said. "Another is out in California, apparently to stay. But the one we want is still here. The more we push, the more we make life so miserable for him, the more he's liable to make a mistake. Marty, if I can't put the son of a bitch in the death house, the least I can do is put him behind bars. Even if it's a lousy tax-evasion count, at least we get him out of circulation!"

Martin Raab, too, certainly wanted Leo behind bars. Not a day passed since Clark Daniels's suicide that he did not relive that terrible scene. His compulsion to smash Leo Gorodetsky nearly matched Brickhill's. So in his mind when he criticized Brickhill, he rationalized it by assuring himself that he, Martin Raab, would never, ever, bend the law to achieve his objective. Nor compromise his principles.

"Go talk to Baumer, Marty. Get him to press charges."

Raab said, "I'm not going to ask Kurt Baumer for anything. I wouldn't lower myself to talk to that filth."

"He won't do it for anyone else."

"Then why would he do it for me?" Raab asked, and instantly wanted the words back. He knew the answer even before Brickhill spoke.

"You're Jewish," Brickhill said. "Baumer will love the irony of one Jew using him, the Nazi, to get at another Jew." Brickhill leaned forward, his finger pointed at Martin Raab's chest. "You talk to him, and you get him to swear out the complaint."

"Forget it," said Raab.

"I'm not asking you," said Brickhill. "I'm telling you."

"Tell somebody else."

Brickhill's face was impassive as he said, "When you sit in this chair —and chances are good that someday you will—when that day comes, you run the office your way. Until then, Marty, you do it my way."

Raab hated himself for not simply turning and walking out. But he knew it was true. Someday he would be D.A. But not without Brickhill's endorsement. So it was a price to be paid, in the end perhaps worthwhile.

He released his breath in a long, grim sigh. "I'll think about it," he said, and started for the door.

"Marty," Brickhill called when Raab opened the door. "Don't come back without Baumer's signed complaint."

Kurt Baumer was forty-five years old, the only child of a Bremen hotel night clerk and a chambermaid mother who emigrated to America before his birth. Ironically, he had once admired Jews and attempted to emulate their business prowess, their familial dedication, their determination to succeed in the new land.

But his first visit to Germany in 1933 showed him a new way to reawaken in a defeated people their own pride and self-respect, not to mention wealth and power for their leaders. He was convinced that Americans would quickly adopt the Nazi formula to recover from their own economic chaos. Blame the Jews.

It all rapidly transcended mere Jew-baiting. Response, particularly in German Yorkville, was so immediate and sincere he became a convert to his own proselytizing. The Aryan race was the master race. He even established camps in upstate New York for the express purpose of breeding pure Nordic stock. He enjoyed an occasional personal contribution.

The stink-bomb incident hardly disturbed him. He relished the publicity. At the same time he had no intention of providing these Jewish thugs any further satisfaction by pressing assault charges. Why allow them a courtroom forum to air their absurd accusations of Nazi brutality in the Fatherland? It was a trap he refused to fall into.

Until his mind was changed by the deputy district attorney, Martin Raab, a Jew.

3.

The instant Kurt Baumer left the office, Martin Raab opened all the windows, wide. The room stank of Kurt Baumer. Worse than the stink bombs thrown at the Nazi and his Jew-hating maniacs.

Raab picked up the phone to call Brickhill but immediately put it down. He wanted to sit a moment, think, regain his composure. He also did not want to allow Brickhill the moment of triumph. On his desk was Baumer's signed complaint.

Of all the loathsome creatures Martin Raab ever encountered, none compared to Kurt Baumer. Sitting there, smiling, nodding as Raab explained how the German-American Bund could be instrumental in bringing this notorious gangster to justice. It was Kurt Baumer's patriotic duty.

Raab clenched his teeth now, remembering the final, convincing argument. "I'm Jewish, Mr. Baumer," he had said.

"So I presumed," Baumer had replied.

Raab wanted to ask him the basis of that presumption. Raab's Jewish nose? His name? The horns in his head? Instead he said, "I am more than ashamed that Leo Gorodetsky is also a Jew. I'm not speaking now as an officer of the law, Mr. Baumer, but as a citizen, a human being. An American. I want this man put where he belongs. You can help us. In fact, sir, you are the only one who can help us. I'll be that honest."

Baumer's response could have come straight from Charles Brickhill's mouth. "A Jew using a Nazi to bring another Jew to justice? How ironic."

"Yes, sir," Raab said, hating himself for "sir," realizing it was the second time he used it, and vowing not to do it again.

Baumer finally signed the complaint. Raab felt no particular sense of achievement; it really had been simple. And why not, for you were dealing with simpletons. Fools. You merely fed their egos, their prejudices. The swine ate from your hand.

He phoned Brickhill now. "I got it," he said. "He signed."

"I'll have the search warrants within twenty-four hours," Brickhill said. "We'll hit those offices with a dozen men. I guarantee you, Marty, we'll find something!"

"Yeah, sure," Raab said wearily. He started putting the phone down, but Brickhill was still talking.

". . . great job, kid. I'm proud of you."

"Thanks, Charlie," Raab said, and hung up. "Fuck you, Charlie," he said to the dead phone.

Later, reflecting, Raab knew he should have urged Brickhill to move faster. Brickhill should have had the warrants already issued. They should have realized Leo had contacts everywhere.

Leo knew of Baumer's complaint the same hour it was entered. A typist at the D.A.'s office secretarial pool, the widow of a slain policeman, a lady on a twenty-five-dollar weekly retainer, informed George Gerson.

Three hours later, accompanied by an attorney, Douglas Roth and six other young men walked into the 19th Precinct station house. All seven signed statements admitting their participation in the stink-bomb incident and the theft of a Chevrolet pickup truck from the Wordsworth & Carnes Construction Company in Queens. And the theft of the LaSalle sedan, registered to the company employing Douglas Roth's older brother.

The seven were arraigned and brought before a night court that very day. All were sentenced to six months at the Children's Village juvenile detention center in Westchester. The court, however, noting the defendants' youth, the compelling motive behind their act—although certainly no excuse for breaking the law—and the defendants' obvious remorse, suspended the sentence.

The judge's name was Herbert Jennings, Jr. At thirty-three, he was the city's youngest municipal-court judge. He was also the protégé of a New York State senator whose reelection the previous November was made possible, in part at least, by a generous IDIC campaign contribution.

Judge Jennings's sentence effectively nullified the complaint against Leo signed by Kurt Baumer and obviated any reason for the D.A. to raid IDIC offices or Leo's living quarters. But it embarrassed Kurt Baumer. He was sure the German Legation had reported the story to Berlin. He planned to leave shortly for the Fatherland to present the Führer the beautiful book, bound in gold, containing the six thousand signatures of loyal German-Americans. But now how could he even face the Führer knowing the guilty young Jewish monsters were unpunished?

One evening a week later Kurt Baumer sent six uniformed storm troopers to Broadway and Seventy-second Street. They burst into a dairy restaurant and in the space of sixty seconds smashed countertops and dishes, some furniture—beat several elderly diners with their fists—and daubed the plate-glass display windows with a Star of David and the message: ACHTUNG, JUDEN!

That same week the door of a small Seventy-sixth street *shul* was desecrated with a similar white painted message. And then another synagogue on West End Avenue.

Sarah Gorodetsky phoned Leo that Samuel Stern wished to see him urgently. They met the following morning for breakfast at Sarah's. Samuel Stern had reconsidered his initial enthusiasm for Leo's HDA. He thought now maybe it was too much.

"I know you now, Mr. Gorodetsky," Stern said. "I know already you are planning something new against them."

"Not with the same boys," Leo said. "I'm recruiting a different bunch."

"You must not do it."

"Why not?"

"Why not?" Stern said. "Did you see the Ansche Grodlicz?" He referred to the West Seventy-sixth Street *shul*.

"Yes, I saw it," Leo said. "That's why something has to be done."

"Mr. Gorodetsky, excuse me, but you already did it."

Sarah said, "Laibel, what Mr. Stern is trying to tell you is—"

"—I know what he's trying to tell me, Ma, and he's wrong." Leo looked at Stern. "Is this how it happened in Germany, Mr. Stern? Nobody did anything? Because they were afraid? Look what it got them!"

"They didn't want us in Germany," Stern said.

"It looks like they don't want you here, either," Leo said.

"Please, Mr. Gorodetsky, this is not Germany."

"The other night you said the same thing could happen here," Leo said.

"It's different," Stern said lamely.

"Why are you afraid?" Leo asked.

Sarah said, "All right, Leo, that's enough. It's going round and round. You heard what he said. No more of it."

Stern said, "Please, Mr. Gorodetsky, don't think we don't appreciate your effort. But it only makes them angrier at us. And don't forget, please, it's not you that suffers. It's us, here. Please, okay?"

Leo said nothing a moment. Then he shrugged. "Okay," he said. He lit a cigarette and got up and went into the kitchen. He poured a glass of water and drank it down. In the dining room he heard his mother and Samuel Stern talking. He smiled suddenly.

"Absolutely," he said aloud, quietly. "Exactly what we need." Into his mind had flashed a picture of Harry Wise. He could just imagine Harry and the Nazis. A bloodbath. Nazi blood. One look at Kurt Baumer, and the closest Harry would allow him to get to Berlin with his golden book of six thousand signatures would be the Hamburg-America Steamship Line pier. Driving past it in a hearse.

"What's wrong?" Sarah asked. She stood in the doorway, Samuel Stern just behind her.

Sam Stern said, "I think he's thinking, Mrs. Gorodetsky. And I think I know what he's thinking about."

"I'm thinking about you, Mr. Stern," Leo said.

"That's what I mean. And you must do what I ask, Mr. Gorodetsky."

"Nothing, you mean."

"Yes, nothing."

"What about your pride, Mr. Stern?" Leo asked. "Your self-respect as a Jew? What about mine?"

"Yours?" Stern said. "You are young and strong. You can fight them back. We can't."

"You don't have to," Leo said. "I'll do it for you "

"No, Mr. Gorodetsky. Thank you, but no," Stern said. "They'll take it out on us. When your back is turned, Mr. Gorodetsky, they'll come down on us like Cossacks. And so then you'll take revenge. It will never end. Let it go, please."

"Do what he wants, Laibel," Sarah said. It was an order.

"Okay," Leo said after a moment.

"Thank you," Stern said.

Leo did not hear the old man. He was staring at him, but through him. It alarmed Sarah. "Leo, are you sick?"

"No," he said.

"Such a funny look on your face," she said.

He had been thinking, again, of Harry and Kurt Baumer. He moved toward the doorway. "I have to go. I want to get to bed early. I think I'll drive up to Boston tomorrow and see the kids."

"Oh, that's nice," Sarah said. "I told you about my grandchildren, didn't I?" she asked Stern, and continued in the same breath to Leo, "Your sister, she should only get married and have children. But who would marry her now? A forty-one-year-old woman. It's a tragedy."

"Don't let her hear you say that, Ma," Leo said.

"Why, her feelings might be hurt?" Sarah said. "It's too late for that, too." She stepped aside for Leo to enter the dining room. He picked up his topcoat and prepared to leave. "No hat, Leo?"

"Ma, I haven't worn a hat for three years." He kissed her cheek, then extended his hand to Stern. "The Hebrew Defense Association is finished, Mr. Stern."

"I'm sorry for that," Stern said, shaking hands. "Honest. You explain to them, yes? You make them understand."

"I will," Leo said. "I know just how to handle it."

Leo drove to Massachusetts the following Wednesday, which happened to be the day Kurt Baumer dined at Hans Jaeger's on West Eighty-sixth Street. The restaurant, forty years at the same location, was Baumer's favorite. Each Sunday and Wednesday evening, he occupied the same booth at the far end of the room and was served the same meal, *Casseler Rippenspeer*, roasted smoked pork loin. Since the HDA incident, Baumer was constantly accompanied by at least two bodyguards. He had also demanded, and received, limited police protection. This Wednesday evening two uniformed policemen stood outside the restaurant. Nearby, in civilian clothes, was a storm-trooper bodyguard. Another patrolled the rear of the building. Any unrecognized customer was politely requested to identify himself.

Kurt Baumer was enjoying dessert, a *Schwarzwalde Kirschtorte*, when the newspaper reporter and a photographer arrived. Immediately, they were confronted by the bodyguard. The two policemen watched alertly.

The reporter was a tall, slender, very clean-cut young man wearing horn-rimmed glasses, porkpie hat, and rumpled tweed suit; he felt slightly out of place in this garb, being more accustomed to loud clothes and snap-brimmed fedoras. The photographer, a short pudgy man in his late twenties, wore a double-breasted light-brown gabardine suit. A press badge was stuck in the band of his white fedora whose brim sat levelly just above his eyes and partially shadowed his muscular face and crooked nose. His camera and flash equipment were in a large leather case slung over his shoulder.

"*Sun*," he said briskly. "We want a few snaps of Baumer."

"No interviews without an appointment," the guard said.

"Hey, come on," said the photographer. "This fucking guy ain't the fucking pope, you know." Such reference to Kurt Baumer was certainly no way to charm a bodyguard, but the photographer had arrived from California only a few hours before and was tired and irritable after the long trip. And Mickey Goldfarb never was the world's fastest thinker.

The reporter glanced impatiently at his watch. "Listen, we don't have all night. We're supposed to cover a DAR convention at the Statler, and we can't get the pictures developed and processed in time for the morning edition unless we're back at the office by ten." He looked at Mickey. "Forget this one, Joe. They get enough publicity, anyway."

"Yeah, Tom, you're right," Mickey said. "Let the fucks hire a publicity agent!" He and the reporter started away.

The guard, reconsidering, called them back. "All right, but just a single picture. No statements." He blocked the reporter. "Only you," he said to Mickey. "Only the photographer."

"You wait, I'll be right out," Mickey said to the reporter.

"You be sure and tell the city desk what happened, Joe," the reporter said to Mickey. "They wouldn't let me in."

"Hey, why can't he come in?" Mickey asked the guard.

"I said just you," the guard said. "Now do it and get it over with!"

"Go ahead, Joe," the reporter said to Mickey. "Get at least one good shot."

"Do my best, kid," Mickey said. He shifted his heavy camera-equipment case to the other shoulder and entered the restaurant.

The reporter strolled back to his car, a Chevrolet coupe with a large PRESS sign taped on the inside front windshield, and a *N.Y. Sun* logo decaled on both doors. Behind the wheel was another man, also with a press badge in his hatband.

"Tell our buddy we'll be right back," the reporter with the porkpie hat called to the guard. He got in the car. The driver started the motor and they drove off.

In the crowded restaurant, Baumer sat chatting with another man. He did not notice the approaching photographer until Mickey was almost at the booth, opening the leather case.

"Mr. Baumer?" Mickey said. "*New York Sun*, Mr. Baumer.*" Mickey removed a Graflex camera from the case and placed it on the table, then reached into the case again.

"If you want a statement, you'll—" Baumer never completed the sentence. Mickey pumped three bullets from a snub-nosed .38 Smith &

Wesson squarely into Baumer's chest, swiveled the gun on the other man who had reached into his inside jacket pocket, and shot him in the face just below the left cheekbone. The impact of the bullets had driven Baumer's body backward into the wall, then bounced it forward again. His head crashed down into the plate of *Schwarzwald Kirschtorte*. The weight of his head squashed the cake and shattered a full cup of coffee. Cherry syrup oozed from the plate and merged with the coffee in a pool of brown-and-red-streaked liquid on the white tablecloth under Kurt Baumer's open, lifeless eyes. It looked like blood, and was almost the same color as the actual blood pouring onto the floor at Baumer's feet.

A split instant after he shot the second man, even before he heard the first scream from the first terrified female, Mickey had whirled and rushed toward the kitchen. He charged through the swinging door, dodging startled cooks and waiters, to the rear service entrance. In four seconds flat he was in the alley, stepping past a large trash-collection bin where the unconscious body of another storm-trooper guard lay curled in a fetal position, and into the waiting Chevrolet coupe.

Forty minutes from the minute he walked into Hans Jaeger's, Mickey was on his way to Chicago in the club car of the *George Washington*. He immediately struck up a conversation with a mining engineer also traveling to the coast. Mickey declined the engineer's offer of a drink, explaining that he never drank hard liquor because in his business you had to be on your toes every second, and you never knew when you might be assigned a job. His business, he further explained, was demolition. He, too, he said, in a way could be called an engineer. A demolition engineer.

At the precise instant Kurt Baumer's dinner was so lethally interrupted, Leo also was at dinner. At the Towne Lyne House in Lynnfield, Massachusetts, with his former wife, his son, and daughter. A pleasant enough dinner, although perhaps slightly too late an hour for Carla. Tired and cranky, she had picked at her food, then leaned her head on Leo's shoulder and fallen asleep.

Steven, however, was lively and animated. He reminded Leo of his sixteenth birthday next year, and Leo's promise of flying lessons. Leo did not recall any specific promise, but said he thought it depended on Steve's school marks. Steve was a high school sophomore, taking a college course—and not doing well.

". . . you promised me a trip to California, too," Steve was saying. "For my sixteenth birthday. Why do you keep looking at your watch?"

Leo was startled. "Am I doing that?"

Steve said to Ellie, "Isn't he, Mother?"

"I hadn't noticed," she said, looking levelly at Leo. He thought she looked exceptionally pretty tonight; and the little gray streak in her black hair gave her a certain matronly appearance he liked.

Leo said, "All I'm thinking about is how nice it is being here with all of you."

"There, you see," Ellie said. She was addressing Steve, but still facing Leo, and he knew she realized his mind was elsewhere. He also knew she resented it.

She said, "I think we should be getting back."

"You haven't told me about your new job," Leo said. She had just been promoted to head librarian at the public library in Winston.

"It's the same job, only with more responsibility," she said. "Leo, we really should go."

Carla, stirring in her sleep, had shifted positions so now her head was almost in Leo's lap. "I hate to wake her up," he said. "Would you like a drink? A brandy?"

She smiled wanly. "Are you testing me, Leo?"

Steve said, "Mom hasn't had a drink in six months!"

Leo wanted to slap him. At the very least tell him he had a big mouth. Instead, he said, "I know, son." He called for the check, woke Carla, and in a few minutes all were in the car driving back to Georgetown. He had driven from New York alone. Benny Roth was on special assignment—at a German restaurant—and Leo wanted to be alone with his family anyway.

It was only a thirty-minute drive on the new highway, the Newburyport Turnpike, and no one spoke much. Leo tried to keep his mind on New York, but his thoughts kept focusing on Ellie. He wondered if she had any men friends, wondering why he couched it so delicately. Men friends. Boyfriends. Lovers. Bedmates. Sex partners. She was an attractive, intelligent woman. He would have to ask her. But then, what difference did it make? None, he told himself. None whatever.

Ellie put Carla to bed while Steve showed Leo his latest model airplanes. The Deanna Durbin photographs were long since replaced by airplanes. Dozens, hanging from strings attached to the ceiling of his room, lined up on the bookshelves. And again, Steve pressed the flying lessons. The matter was left unresolved by Ellie coming in and ordering Steve to bed.

"You promised," Steve reminded Leo.

"You want flying lessons, or the trip to California?"

"You promised both."

"Get the marks first," Leo said. "Then we'll see."

"Shake on that," Steve said.

They shook hands on it. "See you tomorrow after school," Leo said. He started out.

"He staying overnight?" Steve said to Ellie, as though Leo was not even there. Leo wanted to slap him again.

"I'm at the motor court," Leo said.

"Oh," said Steve. "Well, good night, then."

"Good night, Steve."

Ellie and Leo went into the living room. She did not invite him to sit down. "He's a handful," she said. "I'm sorry."

"He has a big mouth," Leo said.

"Yes, I know."

"Carla seems fine."

"She's doing very well with her music."

"That's great," Leo said. "And you're doing well, too, I see. Money okay?"

"Fine, thank you." She had refused to accept any money other than for the children. Leo wished she would take more. She needed a new car, and women always needed clothes. But he knew this was her way of reminding him that she did not need him.

"Leo, I'm tired myself," she said. "And I have to be at work early."

"In that case, I guess I won't ask to be your overnight guest." He tried to make it sound light, a joke, just in case she turned him down.

"Sleep with me, you mean?"

"That was the general idea," he said, and added wryly, "That is, if Steve doesn't object."

"No," she said, after a moment. "It's not a good idea."

"It's not a bad one, either."

"We haven't . . . been together since the divorce. No, since we stopped living together. Why the sudden interest?"

A good question, he thought. A marvelous question. The idea had simply popped into his mind at the restaurant. She looked so good, better than he remembered ever seeing her. And he hadn't been with a woman in weeks, longer.

He said, "Strictly physical."

"I suppose I should be flattered."

"You're a good-looking woman, Ellie."

"With all the normal needs and desires, eh? That isn't why you came up here, Leo."

"I came up here to see the kids."

"I watched you at dinner, Leo," she said. "Looking at the time every five minutes. You came up here because for some reason you don't want to be in New York. You forget, I lived through all that once. I know the signs."

"What does that have to do with my staying with you?"

She smiled suddenly, a thin, knowing smile. "What is it Hershey used to say? No percentage? Yes, that was it. No percentage."

He started denying it, then realized she was right. Why start something that would end nowhere? He was actually relieved. "You're right, no percentage." He moved to leave. "I'll see you tomorrow."

"In the afternoon," she said. "I won't be here until after three."

"Three o'clock," he said, and left.

He heard about Kurt Baumer on the car radio, a news flash on WNAC. ". . . Kurt Baumer, self-styled American Nazi Führer, was shot to death early this evening in a New York restaurant. Reports are sketchy, but eyewitnesses state that the lone assailant escaped. More details as they become available."

He snapped off the radio. Now he could relax and enjoy the drive on this warm, clear night. Tomorrow he would return to Georgetown and deal with his son. Already, it was obvious the boy needed a father's firm hand. But even as he thought this, he wondered how an absentee father applied a firm hand.

In bed, in his cabin at the motor court, he continued thinking of Steve. And Carla, growing so fast, now all arms and legs, but soon—too soon—a young woman. It would be nice to be there to see it.

He fell asleep with this on his mind, but woke less than an hour later from a dream. Of Hitler and Nazis. Uniformed, jackbooted men marching into a huge hall, proceeding to the front of the hall where Hitler stood waiting. Seated near Hitler was Leo's sister, Rivka, and he remembered thinking in the dream that Rivka was dead.

Awake, he knew the dream related to Kurt Baumer, and he struggled to reconstruct it. Fragments of it drifted across his vision, none complete enough to form a picture.

He lay staring at the ceiling. The window curtain was too narrow to entirely block light from the streetlamp outside the cabin. The uncovered spaces on each side of the curtain were projected onto the ceiling as long thin white lines. Pointing to New York, he thought, where a man lay dead because he, Leo Gorodetsky, had decided the man should die.

And who are you, he asked himself, to make such decisions?

Somebody has to make them, he answered himself.

But you are not disturbed about it.

No, not in the slightest. Why should it disturb me? That man deserved to die.

Yes, he did, didn't he? he told himself, and fell back to sleep.

When asked what his father did, Steve's ready reply was that he was in business, something to do with investments. Not even Steve's best friend, Billy Colton, knew the family's real name was not Gordon, but Gorodetsky. Ever since Steve could remember, Ellie cautioned him never to reveal this. When he asked why she angrily told him to please just do as she asked. In time it became less important to him. He assumed it was because of the divorce.

In the years Ellie drank, Steve hated his father. It was he, Leo, who made his mother drink. Leo had abandoned them. Steve often imagined himself simply walking up to his father and smashing him in the jaw. That's for doing what you did to my mother! he would say, and spit on the figure cowering at his feet.

Long ago, Steve realized he could hurt Leo with jokes about height. "Hey, I can eat peanuts off your head!" Or "How's the weather down there?" Leo always pretended to laugh it off, but Steve knew it made him angry; it also gave Steve a sense of power.

Once, when Ellie scolded him and said he had no respect, Steve had replied, "Why should I respect him?"

"Because he's your father," she said.

"If he was my father, he'd live with us, wouldn't he?"

But that was long ago. Now he was glad Leo did not live with them. All he wanted was what Leo could give him, which he knew was almost anything he asked. The flying lessons, for one thing. Just act nice to the guy.

Steve was thinking all this that afternoon when he got off the school bus at Cowan's Drug Store. He had decided to discuss airplanes with Leo. A subject Steve knew did not particularly interest his father but in which he, like all adults, would pretend interest just to carry on a conversation. From there, it was easy to bring up the flying lessons.

Leo's LaSalle was parked in front of the house. Across the street, outside the drugstore, was another car with New York plates, an Oldsmobile sedan. One of Leo's business friends, Steve thought. And then it suddenly occurred to him that here, now, he might learn more about his father's business. Instead of entering the house from the front, he went around back. Ellie's car was not in the garage, and he knew Carla was at her piano lesson.

He stole into the kitchen. From the living room, he heard loud, arguing voices. He tiptoed around to the swinging door separating the dining and living rooms. Through the partition he could see and hear unseen.

The man in the living room with Leo was Martin Raab. He had driven to Georgetown that morning, the morning after Kurt Baumer's murder. He parked across the street near the drugstore and waited two hours for Leo to arrive. He watched Leo enter the house—it was never locked—then walked over and knocked on the door. He had been there only a few minutes when Steve got home.

". . . and where the hell do you get off coming here to question me in front of my wife and children?" Leo was asking.

"Frankly, Mr. Gorodetsky, I couldn't wait for you to get back to New York to do it."

"That's too bad, then," Leo said. "You could have saved five hours of driving. Not to mention the gasoline."

Raab said, "All night I lay awake thinking about you. About your arrogance, your absolute contempt for the law. You snap your fingers, and a man is dead!"

Listening, Steve wondered what they were talking about. A man dead? He watched through the crack in the door partition as his father, seated on the divan, looked at the other man and shook his head sadly.

"What's bothering you, son, is you can't pin Baumer on me," Leo said. "It's driving you crazy."

"That's what I mean about arrogance."

"I suppose it never occurred to you that Kurt Baumer's death is a *mitzvah* to the whole Jewish race? Instead of wasting taxpayers' time and money expressing your personal outrage, you should be dancing in the streets! Whoever did kill that vermin deserves a medal."

"I knew that's how you'd try to justify it," Raab said. He stepped over to the divan, momentarily obscuring Leo from Steve's view. "You embarrass me as a Jew!"

"Why? Because I have the guts not to turn the other cheek?"

"Sure, you have so much 'guts,' you make certain you're four hundred miles away when your orders are carried out."

"I can't believe it," Leo said. "You come all this way just to say that to me?"

"I came all this way so you'd know there's someone you can't frighten away. Or buy off."

"Charlie Brickhill put you up to this, didn't he?"

"He doesn't know a thing about it. I'm here on my own."

Just then Steve heard Ellie's car tires crunching on the gravel drive. He hurried away from the dining-room door and went outside to help her in with groceries.

"He's inside with somebody," Steve said.

Ellie said nothing. She handed Steve the two largest bags and started into the kitchen.

"I think it's a policeman," Steve said, opening the door for Ellie. His voice fell to a whisper. "And you should hear how he talks to him!"

"How who talks to who?" Ellie said. Steve stood facing her, preventing her from entering. She shifted the grocery bag in her arms.

"My father," Steve said after a moment. It was as though the two words were foreign and had to be translated into English in his mind. "The way he's talking to the other guy, the policeman. I mean, he's not afraid of him or anything. He says . . . my father . . . ordered a man killed!"

Ellie brushed past Steve into the kitchen. Now she heard the men's voices. She walked into the living room. Martin Raab, in mid-sentence, stopped speaking and clamped his mouth shut.

"This is my wife," Leo said, rising. "Mr. Raab is with the D.A.'s office, New York."

Ellie ignored Raab completely. "Nothing ever changes, does it, Leo?" she said.

"No," Leo said. "Never." He glanced behind her at Steve. "My son, Steven," Leo said. He was beginning to feel slightly flustered.

Ellie spoke sharply to Steve. "Steven, go to your room!" Then she said to Leo, "I'd like both of you"—for the first time she looked directly at

Raab—"I'd like both of you to leave. Now, please."

Steven had not moved. He said, "Mother, I want to talk to my . . . to him." He pointed at Leo.

Ellie glared at the boy a moment. "Talk to him, then!" She pushed him out of her way and returned to the kitchen.

Martin Raab said, "I'll wait for you outside, Mr. Gorodetsky."

Leo said, "If you want to question me, do it where you have jurisdiction. And when you have it. And right now, Mr. Raab, you have neither. You're trespassing."

Raab hesitated, but then turned abruptly and stepped to the front door, and out. Steve rushed to the living-room window and peered through the curtains.

"He's going," Steve said. After a moment he backed away from the window. He studied Leo's face, his clothes. It was as though he had never before seen him.

"I heard what you and that cop were saying," Steve said. "We talked about Kurt Baumer in current events at school today. I'm glad he's dead."

"You shouldn't be glad anybody's dead, no matter who they are," Leo said.

"I am about him," Steve said. "You were right. He deserved to die. I read how he talks about Jews. I know all about the Nazis, too. They're bastards!"

"Would you fight them?" Leo asked. "If you were old enough?"

"You bet I would!" Steve said. "And I'm glad you're fighting them now. What kind of business are you in?"

"Steven, you've been told a dozen times! Your father is in the real-estate business!" It was Ellie, in the living-room doorway, tying on an apron.

"I thought it was investments," Steve said.

"It's the same thing," Ellie said. "Go over to Mrs. Marston's and walk Carla home. She'll be finished with her lesson by the time you get there."

"I want to talk some more to . . . my father," Steve said. He addressed Leo. "I think it was swell how you told that cop off. Did you really order him bumped off? The Nazi guy, I mean?"

"Steven!" Ellie shouted.

"Did you?" Steve asked Leo.

"Do what your mother says," Leo said. "We'll talk when you get back."

"Okay," said Steve. He started leaving, then stopped. "I was proud of you!" he said, and ran off.

Ellie whirled and strode into the kitchen. Leo followed her in. She sat at the table peeling potatoes. Without looking up, she said, "He's proud of you. That's marvelous."

"What's wrong with it?" he asked.

"Get out of here, Leo," she said. She looked up at him. "Get out of my house!"

"My son said he wanted to talk to me."

"What do you think he wants to talk to you about, Leo? What do you want to talk to him about? Bringing him into the family business?" She slammed the vegetable peeler on the table, sending it skidding through the pile of potato peelings, scattering them over the table and onto the floor. She stared, surprised, at the mess and began sweeping the peelings together with the flat of her hand. Quietly, she said, "Your son has nothing to say to you. You have nothing to say to him."

But I do, Leo thought. I have much to say to him. I want to tell him I love him. I want to tell him I would like to watch him grow up. I want to help him. I want to share his troubles, and his pleasures.

"Now, will you please leave?" she said, in the same quiet voice.

Leo knew suddenly he could have what he wanted. The words were already moving from his brain to his tongue. Familiar words, used once before, seven years ago in the same room. *What will it take to get you and the kids to come back?* He almost spoke them, but did not because he knew the answer would be the same.

Quit. Get out. Retire.

Well, why not? He was thirty-nine years old, and a millionaire. A multimillionaire. He owned a bank, and a dozen casinos and hotels. Men lived and died on his very whim. So he had it all, and had done it all. So why not stop? He could have his family. He could watch his son and daughter grow up. They needed him. He needed them.

"Please, Leo. Before Steve and Carla get back."

He felt very tired, so tired he did not think he could walk to the door. "Tell Steve I'll send a check for the flying lessons," he said. "If it's all right with you."

"Yes, it's all right, Leo," she said. "It's fine." She looked at him a moment, then resumed peeling the potatoes. She did not glance up even when she heard the door close quietly behind him.

He drove to the turnpike, pondering whether or not to stop overnight at a motor court. His head ached, and he wanted to sleep, but knew he would not. His mind was filled with those questions.

Why not quit? Why not retire? Why not stop?

Marvelous questions, he thought, and of course there was always that marvelous answer. The Tiger. You cannot get off without being devoured. But he did not believe that. He believed the answers were much simpler. Very simple.

He could not stop until he reached the top. Until he had beaten them all, and won it all. Until nothing remained to be won. Then, and only then could he stop. At the top.

But even as he thought this, he wondered where the top was, or even if a top existed. Suppose there was none? No top, and no end. He had to find out.

He drove back to New York. He drove very fast. He made it in under five hours.

18

TAKING off from Grand Central Air Terminal in the small charter plane, Leo felt fine. And the scenery was spectacular. You could see Los Angeles spread out behind you, all the way to the ocean. But soon, over the desert in the summer heat, the air became bumpy. By the time they reached Las Vegas, he did not care if they landed or crashed.

The flight made him appreciate Steven's accomplishment all the more. How the hell could anybody fly in these flimsy little crates? He wondered if Steve had earned his license yet; they hadn't talked since Steve's jubilant phone call a few weeks before. He could still hear the boy's voice. "Dad, I did it! I flew my first solo! I did it!" Only after they hung up did Leo realize Steve called him "Dad." The first time since Steve was a child, and then it was "Daddy." Leo sent him a $1,000 check for the solo. Ellie deposited the money in a special account for Steven's college education.

Now, far in the distance, Leo saw Las Vegas. A few ramshackle buildings in the middle of a vast desert, surrounded on all sides by mountains. What in this godforsaken place could Harry possibly consider so important for Leo to see? Harry assured him he was in no trouble. Far from it, he said, he was on to the biggest thing in his life.

Leo probably would not have made the trip if he weren't already traveling. He had been in Havana for the opening of the fourth casino, the Caribe, on June 13, 1940, the day before the Nazis marched into Paris; bad luck for the French, not the Caribe. War or no war, the most successful opening yet. An Argentine cattle tycoon dropped $125,000 at roulette, and an American oilman lost $100,000 at baccarat. When the figures were transmitted to the Alliance Council each member was assessed ten percent of his next dividend payment—to be presented as a gift of appreciation to Sal Bracci.

Leo remained in Havana an extra week. Sal was ill with a nagging, persistent cough. Sal's Cuban physician suggested the possibility of a lung tumor. He was seeing more and more of it in smokers; even, he ruefully admitted, cigar smokers. Sal had never smoked in his life. Leo arranged for a prominent New York specialist to examine Sal. He diagnosed Sal's condition as chronic bronchitis, prescribed some bronchial dilators, collected his fee of $2,500 plus transportation, and left. He was a magician.

Now, literally before Leo's eyes, Sal's health improved. The coughing stopped. Sal's complexion, white and pasty, regained its normal color. He regained his strength; he was himself again.

Leo paid his respects to General Batista, and then flew to Los Angeles to see what Harry's new *mishegoss* was all about. Mickey Goldfarb met Leo at the airport and drove him to the other side of the field where he boarded the charter plane waiting to fly him to Las Vegas.

The Las Vegas airport, called Western Air Field, consisted of a single dirt strip with two small wooden hangars and another under construction. Surprisingly, two U.S. Army bombers, Martin B-10s, were parked off to the side. The charter pilot said the army was considering the site for an air base. He also said there was a word for it, "boondoggle," meaning political payoff. Leo said it was hard to believe some of the things they got away with nowadays.

Harry impatiently awaited him at the airport. He was anxious to share his great new discovery. They drove in Harry's Cord over the rutty, dusty dirt road, through the blowing sand and tumbleweed to the main highway, Highway 90, and then to an area in the desert fronting the highway. Harry got out of the car and ran around to open Leo's door.

"This is it!" Harry shouted, shielding his eyes to ward off a gust of sand.

"What is 'it'?" Leo saw nothing but desert. Sand, as far as the eye could see, swirling and blowing in all directions.

Harry pulled Leo from the car and waved his arm in a circle. "This," said Harry. "The Barclay!"

"Barclay?"

"That's what we're gonna name it, Kleyner, the Barclay!" Harry began pacing in the sand. He stepped off twenty paces. "Right here, it's the main entrance!" He clambered over a sand dune. "And over here, right by the driveway that'll curve up from the highway, a fountain. A fucking fountain, Leo!"

Leo walked over to join Harry atop the dune. He sank into the sand past his ankles. "Harry, what the hell are you talking about?"

"Our new hotel, that's what the hell I'm talking about. The Barclay!" Harry closed his eyes against the sand blowing into his face, opened them, then grinned. "Like the Barclay in New York. You know how I always thought the name was so classy. Well, this is the *Vegas Barclay!*"

Leo said nothing. He did not know what to say.

"Four floors," Harry said. "The biggest casino in the world. The casino's the whole lobby, like in Havana. And a show room, and three different bars. Two hundred rooms, each one with a marble bathroom. For Christ's sake, Leo, can't you *see* it?"

"All I see is sand," Leo said. "In the middle of nowhere."

Harry took Leo's arm and pulled him farther along the desert. "I bought it," he said. "Forty acres. One hundred bucks an acre." He stopped and pointed ahead. "The parking lot, and behind it maybe an annex for employees to live. The whole shmear, Leo, I can build for under two million. In a year, less maybe, we make it back. I mean, can't you see it? Jesus Christ!"

Leo looked around again, then started back to the car. Harry trotted alongside, excitedly describing the complex he would build. A gigantic swimming pool, where they might even hire Billy Rose to stage one of his Aquacades. And in the showroom, the biggest Hollywood names. Harry knew them all. For opening night, chartered transport planes would bring in high rollers. The Barclay would offer its customers the finest food, drink, and entertainment available. The most beautiful women.

". . . and it's all goddam *legal!*" Harry was saying as Leo got into the car and sat down. "Gambling is legal in Nevada!"

"Yes, Harry, since 1931," Leo said wearily. He removed one shoe and shook out the sand. "And it's all miles away from here, downtown. Sawdust-floored grind joints with whorehouses upstairs. Truck drivers and busted-out prospectors for customers. A five-dollar bettor is a high roller."

"Leo, I was right about the boat, wasn't I?"

Leo removed sand from his other shoe. He sat facing Harry who stood outside the open door. "Harry, one reason the boat worked was location. Location, Harry, close to the city. A traffic generating area. A million people living within thirty minutes away."

"Jesus Christ, Leo!" Harry said. He strode out to the center of the asphalt road. "This, Leo," he shouted, "is a road. The main road, the only road, between here and L.A. Straight as an arrow, Leo! Straight to L.A.!" He came back to the car and waved a finger in Leo's face. "They'll come here by the fucking droves! To the oasis in the desert." He rolled the words around on his tongue. "Hey, that's not a bad slogan. 'Oasis in the Desert'!"

"How did you ever find this 'Oasis'?"

Harry was too wound up to notice the sarcasm. "Well, I guess for that you can thank Nora. I drove out here one weekend with her and this little French number that does her hair. Jackie, they call her. Some quiff, let me tell you! We stopped overnight in Barstow and they both worked me over good." He sighed with the delightful memory. "Next day, we get here to Vegas and we all stay at this dude ranch—" he pointed into the distance. "Something something El Vegas, I think. Anyway, after we get there, I take a walk around and I come back to the room, and what do I find? The two of them in bed. Going down on each other, for Christ's sake!"

Harry shook his head in mock disapproval, and went on, "I'm telling you, Kleyner, the things that go on in this town!" He shook his head again. "Anyway, I see I'm like a fifth wheel, so I decide I'll go into town and look the place over. I'm driving, and all of a sudden there's this sign: ACREAGE FOR SALE. And, Leo, on my mother's grave I swear I saw the whole thing. Like one of them . . . what do you call it when you're dying of thirst in the desert and you see a sign that says 'ice-cold beer'?"

"Mirage," said Leo.

"Yeah, a mirage. There it was, right in front of my eyes, on this very spot—" he swept his hand over the area. "Even the fucking neon sign with the name in big red lights, BARCLAY! Rising right up out of the desert, this hotel. The Barclay."

"One question," Leo said, wondering why he even humored him, but remembering he considered Harry's gambling-ship idea a harebrained scheme at first. He laughed suddenly.

"What's so funny?"

"I was just thinking about Elmira," Leo said. "When we wanted to pay the guards a buck apiece to let us run a penny craps game."

Harry was in no mood for nostalgia. "Yeah, sure. Now what's your question?"

"Two questions," Leo said. "First, what about Pete Donini? We all agreed Nevada is West Coast territory. Pete has to be consulted."

Harry drew in his breath angrily. "I don't consult with that greaseball prick! I don't interfere with him, he don't interfere with me. That's the deal."

"The Alliance might not see it that way. They'll want to protect an Italian."

"Fuck the Alliance!" Harry slammed his fist on the car doorframe. "Goddamit, Leo, this is my operation, my baby! Nobody gets cut in!"

"Where do you think the money comes from?"

"From us, Leo. You and me."

"Two million?"

"Sure, our own money. We don't need their money, and we don't need them."

"Harry, without their blessing, you wouldn't stay open five minutes. In fact, you wouldn't even get to open. Whether we like it or not we're in bed with them," he said, and added dryly, "Till death do us part."

"Bullshit," Harry said, but his voice suddenly lacked confidence.

"We need the Alliance, Harry, and they need us. They'll put up the money if I say so. And I say so."

"But I don't deal with Pete Donini," Harry said. "That, you make them understand."

"Can you handle him?"

"What, handle him? I'll just tell him I'm building a hotel in the desert." Harry laughed. "The stupid shit will wish me luck."

"He has to tell the Alliance it's okay with him if you operate here."

"Believe me, he'll do it."

"Well, that brings up the second question," Leo said. "Why the desert? Because that's the question they'll consider even more important than Donini. Why dump two million into a palace in the desert?"

Harry smiled. "In the desert, Kleyner, after you eat, drink, and fuck, there's only one thing left to do, ain't there?"

"What's that?" Leo asked patiently.

Harry smiled again. "Gamble," he said.

What Harry neglected to tell Leo was that he and Peter Donini had already been in protracted negotiation concerning Las Vegas. Donini indeed, as Harry said, "wished him luck," but only in return for a larger cut of the *Californian*'s take. Harry had no intention of meeting this demand, or of seeking Leo's assistance. Or the Council's. The ship, just as he intended Las Vegas to be, was his province. His responsibility.

So when Harry assured Leo he could handle Pete Donini, he had already determined how, and where. The only question was when. And this all depended on Donini, and how hard he pushed.

It did not happen for six months, not until January of 1941. Leo was not present to witness the event but, quite coincidentally, his son was.

Steve, failing a third check ride for his student pilot license, ran away from home. An unfamiliar telephone number on his desk was identified as American Airlines' East Boston Airport reservation office. A ticket had been purchased to San Francisco. Ellie immediately notified Leo. Within twenty-four hours Steve was traced to an Alameda, California, hotel. Four hours later he was in Harry Wise's custody.

The two instantly hit it off. Over the phone Steve begged Leo to allow him to stay a few weeks in California, reminding Leo of his previous promise. Leo obtained Ellie's approval. She reluctantly agreed Steve was probably safer with Harry than in his own bed.

Harry was informed of this at the Oakland Airport coffee shop in a second phone conversation with Leo. ". . . sure, I'll take care of him, what do you think?" Harry said. "But listen, you sure this kid is only sixteen? He looks and acts thirty, for Christ's sake!" Harry paused for breath. He was in a phone booth, watching Steve at the counter drinking a Coke. "He's almost as tall as me. He must be a foot taller than you!"

"Did he tell you why he ran away?"

"Something about he couldn't recover from a stall, whatever that means," Harry said.

"Stall a plane," Leo said. "That's why he failed the test. He has trouble making the plane come out of a stall. He just can't seem to do it."

"Yeah, well, I'll tell you, he's not having any trouble with the ladies. He's sure not stalling with *them!*" Harry spoke, watching Steve just then strike up an animated conversation with two U.S. Navy nurses. "Leo, is he still cherry?"

"I don't know," said Leo. "Just take care of him, okay?"

"I think he can do that pretty good himself," Harry said. One of the nurses was writing her phone number on the back of a matchbook cover for Steve.

On the plane returning to Los Angeles Steve showed Harry the matchbook cover. "That's the redhead," Steve said. "She was prettier than the other. Although maybe not so much."

"You like redheads?" Harry asked.

"You bet," Steve said. "And blondes, and brunettes, too."

"You know something, kid? You and me, we think the same. We're gonna get along great."

They did. And Harry doubled his long ago promise to fix Steve up with a movie actress. He fixed him up with two. Starlets, recommended personally by a Warner Brothers production VP. Harry gave them fifty dollars each, with instructions to show the kid the time of his life. Whatever he wanted. They were in Harry's house, and Harry found it hard to believe that Steve and the starlets ventured from the guest bedroom only twice in twenty-four hours. To eat. So the question of Steve being cherry was now academic.

Harry finally sent the girls home. Steve then slept twelve full hours, awoke famished, devoured a steak, and informed Harry he was now ready to see the sights. Starting with the S.S. *Californian.*

Steve found the ship interesting, but not especially exciting. Not until he and Mickey Goldfarb climbed to the main deck from the engine room, the final stop on the grand tour. Steve innocently asked, "What are those two boats out there? They're not water taxis."

"Oh, those lousy bastards!" Mickey cried. "Kid, you stay here. I got to get Harry!" He dashed into the casino.

"Who are they?" Steve called after him.

"Cops!" Mickey shouted over his shoulder, and was gone.

Steve, wondering why what appeared to be a routine police visit would agitate Mickey so much, watched the approaching boats. Two launches, crowded with policemen, a combined force of Santa Monica police and L.A. County sheriff officers. Steve did not know it was a raid, and the first on the ship in its three years of operation.

"So they finally decided to do it!" It was Harry, rushing to the rail with Mickey. He seemed surprisingly calm, almost pleased. He shouted to Mickey, "Okay! Lower it!"

Mickey hurried away toward the bow. A moment later, like a portcullis descending over a moat, a grated iron gate was lowered over the *Californian*'s forward loading ramp. Harry waved cheerily to the police launches as the gate clanked shut.

From the nearest launch a deputy sheriff shouted through a megaphone. "This a police operation! You must allow us to board!"

A voice from the forward area shouted back, "Up your ass!" It sounded like Mickey Goldfarb.

Steve stood with Harry at the rail watching the police launches cruise back and forth along the ship's starboard side. Harry had explained the three-mile limit, and that the police had no jurisdiction, but suppose they had guns? Just thinking of it, Steve's heart pounded with excitement. He wanted to ask Harry about the possibility of gunfire, but did not want Harry to think him that unsophisticated.

"This'll give you something to tell the guys about back in—where is it?" Harry asked. "Provincetown?"

"Georgetown," Steve said. "You really won't let them get on?"

"Let 'em on? Listen, I'll sink the bastards!"

"Harry, they're *cops*!"

"Hey, is there a better reason?"

Both police vessels edged closer. Again the deputy bellowed through the megaphone: ". . . you are in violation of city and county ordinances prohibiting the establishment of gaming devices within city and county limits! We wish to board your vessel to serve notice of closure, and confiscation of equipment!"

Harry laughed. He nudged Steve hard in the ribs, then cupped his hands over his mouth and shouted back. "Go fuck yourself!" To Steve he said, "Excuse the language, kid, but that's all these guys understand."

"We are prepared to use force!" the deputy called.

"Watch this," Harry said to Steve, and raised a finger at Mickey waiting with some sailors on the service deck below. This deck, more like a narrow fenced platform extending the entire length of the ship, was used to take on supplies and stow the lifeboats and two fire hoses. Each hose, now unrolled and ready, was held by three crewmen, each hose nozzle trained on a police launch. A seventh crewman crouched at the circular water turn-on valve.

The launches moved to within thirty yards. "This is your final warning!" the deputy called. "You will be charged with resisting arrest!"

Harry dropped his hand. Mickey signaled the crewman at the valve. The crewman spun the valve wheel. The hoses wiggled and flopped on the deck; then, inflated with surging water, stiffened and straightened. The policemen, helpless, could only fling themselves down behind the gunwales. The water hit them, arcing from the nozzles in heavy, steady streams that smashed into the launches and instantly scattered all eight policemen along the floor of each launch like minnows trapped in a net.

Aboard S.S. *Californian* the sailors laughed and howled, yelling all manner of catcalls and obscenities. The force of the water finally pushed the police boats back out of range. Harry gestured the crewman to shut the hoses off.

"Next time, bring rubbers!" Harry shouted. He pulled Steve close to him in an elated hug. "What do they think, they're playing with babies?"

Steve thought it was the funniest thing he ever saw. He could not stop laughing, nor could Harry. But, in truth, Harry was relieved. The suspense was over. Peter Donini, in arranging the raid with police and sheriff on his payroll, had at last made his move. It was his message to Harry: Increase Pete's percentage, or take the heat.

Well, Harry had a message for Mr. Donini.

2.

From Los Angeles to San Diego, Peter Donini controlled Southern California. The police, the bookies, the whores, the loan sharks, even some trade unions. He had a piece of IDIC's race wire and five points of the gambling ship. He was forty-two years old, with a wife and four children, the oldest, Peter junior, just entering USC. A long way from the little two-room San Francisco flat in the rear of Pete Donini's father's barbershop.

He had never feared Harry Wise, not even three years ago when he did the job for Harry on Jimmy Tucculo. He used Harry and the Jews not only to make himself top man on the Coast, but a respected Alliance member as well. He had great expectations of soon being appointed to the Council.

Pete was purposely vague about the precise figure of the increased percentage he demanded from Harry's action; he knew Harry would refuse any figure. He also knew the attempted police raid on the S.S. *Californian* would provoke Harry into some retaliation. All this was all part of a minutely planned strategy.

He knew Harry could not move against him without Alliance approval, but also knew that would not deter Harry. Harry was crazy. So Harry would try something, and fail—because Pete would be careful—leaving Harry in the untenable position of having defied the Alliance. Harry, then, just might be pushed aside, with the Council probably rewarding Pete if not with the ship itself, then surely a much bigger cut of the take.

Pete knew his customer. Harry was determined once and for all to teach Peter Donini a lesson. Besides, there was not enough room on the Coast for them both now. Harry never discussed any of this with Leo; he knew Leo would disapprove. What really concerned Harry was the certainty that once the Las Vegas hotel was established, Pete would demand in on that, too.

Las Vegas was Harry's, all his, only his.

* * *

Harry sent Steve to Palm Springs for the weekend with the two starlets. He wanted him out of harm's way while he dealt with Pete Donini. Although, as Mickey Goldfarb said, the only harm that might come to that kid would be his pecker falling off.

Mickey had just returned to Beverly Hills from driving Steve and the girls to the desert. Harry was waiting for him in the living room of the North Roxbury Drive house. Harry wore a new hundred-dollar Sy Devore blazer; he looked ready for a party. He ran his comb through his hair and grinned.

He said to Mickey, "I got a call from Mrs. Watson. Our friend will be there in an hour." He looked at his watch. "At six on the dot."

Mickey shook his head, perplexed. "I can't figure a guy that gets his jollies from whores slapping him around with coat hangers."

"Hey, each to his own," Harry said.

"Tell that to the man from Seattle," Mickey said.

The man from Seattle was a twenty-seven-year-old former professional hockey player who at that very instant occupied an attic room of a three-story Spanish Colonial house on a quiet Santa Monica street. He had been in this room nearly three days, alternately dozing and reading Carl Sandberg's new book, *Abraham Lincoln: The War Years.*

It was a few minutes past five in the afternoon. In slightly less than an hour, a stout, middle-aged lady named Doris Watson would knock at the man's door and whisper, "He's here." This was what the man from Seattle had waited three days to hear.

Mrs. Watson, as everyone addressed her, owned the house, which was also home to six talented and attractive young women, each a specialist in her own field. Mrs. Watson, like all L.A. madams, was in business only through Peter Donini's sufferance. He never examined Mrs. Watson's accounts too closely; her establishment was a special favorite of his.

Twice each month, on varying days, Pete visited Mrs. Watson's. Always to see the same girl, a petite brunette named Jan weighing hardly more than one hundred pounds, but an unsurpassed expert in administering spankings to naughty boys. Her clientele consisted of motion-picture executives, businessmen, two army generals, several police chiefs, any man (and an occasional woman) who could afford twenty-five dollars for a half hour's "disciplining"—and Pete Donini.

Since the raid on the ship Pete took no chances. Four men accompanied him everywhere. When he visited Mrs. Watson's the entire building was sealed off. Knowing this, but not knowing exactly when Pete would visit, Harry planted the man from Seattle in the house three days before.

For such cooperation, Harry paid Mrs. Watson $2,000, $500 of which Jan would receive for following a few simple instructions.

Satisfied the house was secure, Pete relaxed a few moments in the parlor over a drink with the two women. Under her diaphanous red negligee Jan wore a black, tasseled brassiere and garter belt with fishnet stockings, and black, six-inch stiletto-heeled pumps. They discussed the probability of a German invasion of England, an event Jan feared imminent. Jan was of English extraction; and, although a second-generation American, spoke with a most distinct Oxford accent. She claimed it reminded her clients of English public schools. She could administer a dozen smart blows with a cane to a man's buttocks, making him scream with pain and beg for mercy, without ever drawing blood.

". . . you know, of course, no one has invaded England for nearly a thousand years," Jan was saying.

"Records are made to be broken," Pete said. "Right?"

"Oh, quite," Jan said. She glanced at her watch: 6:15. Pete seldom took more than a half hour. If she could get him upstairs now, he and his bodyguards would be gone before 7:00. The house could reopen for normal business. She patted Pete's knee. "What do you say we go up and see how you've been behaving?"

Pete grinned at Mrs. Watson. "How come she's so nice to me?"

"You're a nice man," Mrs. Watson said.

"The best," Jan said, and then whispered into Pete's ear, "He's really a rotten son of a bitch who, if he doesn't come to my room this instant, will get the living shit beat out of him!"

"Okay, okay," Pete said, playing the game. "I'll do it; whatever you say."

"Then come on," Jan said. She grasped Pete's arm and pulled him to the stairs.

"The Red Room, dear," Mrs. Watson called after them.

The room was indeed red, bathed in a dull red glow from the single, crimson-shaded Tiffany chandelier. One wall contained several sets of metal shackles. On a table, lined up like surgical instruments, were various quirts, riding crops, canes, handcuffs. Everything else was red. Bed, veloured walls, carpet, red-bordered ceiling mirror. Even a red-leather gymnastic horse. And the window drapes, heavy red brocade, billowing gently in the summer breeze from the open window.

Jan removed her negligee and stood a moment confronting Pete. She placed her hands firmly on her hips and spread her legs slightly apart. She glared sternly at Pete, a pose she knew he enjoyed.

"Well?" she asked.

"What do you want me to do?"

"Well, first, you son of a bitch, you call me mistress!"

"Yes, mistress."

"Take off your clothes!"

He started removing his clothes. She watched him, wondering why a man with the power over other men's lives and deaths felt the need to be humbled in such fashion. It never ceased to amaze her. She had read somewhere it was their own guilt, their own peculiar, sick way of compensating. Doing penance. She never understood it.

"Don't look at me!" she shouted. He averted his eyes as he finished undressing. Now, naked, he stood before her. She looked him up and down, then grabbed his penis. She squeezed it until he gasped.

"Nothing!" she said disdainfully. She squeezed him once more, then disgustedly swept her hand away. "What a miserable excuse for a man you are! Get down on your hands and knees!"

He fell to his knees. She raised one foot toward his mouth, offering him the toe of her shoe. Immediately, he began licking the leather. After a moment she jabbed the shoe into his chin, toppling him backward. She seized a bamboo walking cane from the table and stepped after him, prodding the tip of the cane into his chest.

"Did I give you permission to stand?"

"I'm sorry, mistress. Forgive me."

"Forgive you, shit! I'll teach you a lesson, that's what I'll do!"

"Oh, please, don't hurt me!"

"Get on the bed!"

He started rising but she pushed him down again.

"Crawl!"

He crawled to the bed and clambered up on it, lying on his back atop the red coverlet, watching her. His eyes glittered excitedly. She stood disdainfully above him, for a moment tapping the cane against her thigh, and then hooking the tip of the cane into the elastic band of a red velvet sleep mask on the end table. She swept the mask off the table and dangled it before him.

"You know what to do!"

He snatched the mask from the cane tip, slipped the elastic band over the back of his head and the mask over his eyes, and almost in the same motion spread-eagled his hands and legs. He loved this game; it was his favorite.

"Mistress, what are you doing to me?" he asked in a quavering voice.

"Shut up!" she said. She was shackling his wrists and ankles with metal cuffs attached to leather straps fixed into the bed headboard and sides. She pulled the straps tight, leaving him only enough slack to partially lie on his side.

"Mistress, please don't punish me!" he whimpered.

"I'll do whatever the fuck I want, you worm!" she said, noticing from the corner of her eye the window drapes opening ever so slightly.

"Mistress, I'll be good!" Pete said. "I swear it!"

"I told you to shut up!" she said, her eyes fixed on the window. A man, a tall, very muscular man, had just climbed over the windowsill and into the room. His hair, thick and black, slicked down on his head, gleamed in the room's roseate light.

Suddenly she regretted agreeing to participate in this practical joke.

Mrs. Watson had assured her Pete would not object, but now Jan had a bad feeling about it. Mrs. Watson said the man, an old friend of Pete's, would win a sizable bet by laying a few strokes on Pete's behind. He would do it and be gone before Pete even realized he had been there.

"Be good to me, mistress," Pete whispered. He rolled over on his side as far as the shackles allowed, presenting his buttocks and widening his thighs to accommodate his huge, sudden erection.

The man placed a finger to his lips, pointed to Pete, and nodded. Jan hesitated, then smashed the cane down on Pete's naked buttocks. He screamed with pain.

"Shut up!" she said.

The man gestured her to step aside. As she did, she saw that he had picked up a pillow from the bed and was holding it against his chest, patting it to flatten it down. He nodded at her once more. She felt paralyzed. Her heart raced, and her temples throbbed.

"Mistress, I've been bad!" Pete moaned. "Punish me!"

The man nudged Jan with his fist. She shuddered at his touch, but she knew now what was happening, and that her own life was in jeopardy. She struck Pete again with the cane.

"Oh, Jesus!" he cried ecstatically. "Do it! Do it!" He tried to turn further on his side and raise his buttocks higher. "Do it some—" the words ended abruptly, muffled, as the man stepped forward and covered Pete's masked face with the pillow. He placed both hands on the pillow and leaned all his weight on it.

Jan turned away. She heard the flopping and thrashing of Pete's body against the mattress as the pillow smothered his life. He was strong, and it was not easy, but the man with the pillow was stronger. Jan heard the soft sag of Pete's body collapsing. Then she heard the sound of the metal shackles being unfastened.

Jan forced herself to look. The man was unfastening the shackles; he had already removed the mask. Pete's bulging eyes stared sightlessly. His arms and legs, relaxed now, remained in the same spread-eagle position. The red coverlet under him, between his thighs, was white with a small pool of viscous liquid. In his death throes he had ejaculated. The ultimate orgasm.

The man slid the pillow under Pete's head and, without even a second glance at him or Jan, strode to the window, climbed out, and was gone. She gazed at the window, wondering if she had somehow imagined it all, knowing she had not, realizing that other than the slicked-down hair she had not the slightest recollection of the man's appearance; in her memory he was faceless.

She looked at Pete. She knew she must never reveal the truth. And she knew exactly what to do. She flung the door open and stepped out into the hall. And screamed.

"He's dead! Somebody help! He's dead!"

* * *

The attending physician, aware that such sexual abberations sometimes proved fatal, genuinely believed the cause of death cardiac arrest,
and Pete's bodyguards had no reason to suspect otherwise. They knew
no one had entered or even come near the house.

Everyone cooperated. For her discretion, Mrs. Watson received a generous bonus from Pete's people, and the coroner allowed the circumstances of the tragedy to be altered. Pete's body was driven to the parking
lot of a Beverly Hills restaurant. There, out of respect for his wife and
children, the charade was replayed. Pete's driver and bodyguards stated
that when they opened the car door he all at once slumped over, dead.
It made sense, and spared Pete's family needless embarrassment.

Danny Esposito, Peter Donini's number-two man, did not learn of his
boss's heart attack until shortly afterward. Harry Wise broke the news.
Danny was at a Sunset Boulevard nightclub, the Mocambo. Harry was
there at the same time, at the bar, when Mickey Goldfarb phoned him
at 6:55.

"You sound real happy," Harry said into the phone. "Something tells
me Pete had the time of his life."

"Ask the man from Seattle," Mickey said. "Everything under control
where you are?"

Harry peered across the room at a booth where Danny Esposito sat
with a beautiful young blond woman. "I'll know in a few minutes," Harry
said. "Come join the party."

Harry returned the phone to the bartender and walked over to Danny's booth. He asked Danny if he would mind sending the blonde over
to the bar for a drink, on him of course. He wanted a few minutes alone
with Danny.

"What about?" Danny asked.

"Pete," Harry said.

"Go have the drink," Danny said to the blonde, whose name was Mary
Lou Carter and who was an MGM contract bit player, and a former
friend of Harry's.

"Just whistle when you're ready," Mary Lou said, and left.

"Nice girl," Danny said, gazing after her. He was thirty-six and, like
Pete Donini, a San Franciscan. He was big and tough, and quite hand-
some with his dark wavy hair and strong face. He was also very ambitious.
"So what about Pete?"

"He's dead," Harry said.

Danny knew Harry was not being figurative. For an instant he was
too shocked to speak. Harry wasted no time. "Heart attack," he said.
"Can you fucking believe it? A heart attack! In the Harlequin parking
lot of all places. Mickey just phoned to tell me. It happened less than a
half hour ago."

"You get the news fast, I see."

"My sources of information, kid," Harry said. He smiled sourly. "But you don't sound too broken up about it, or surprised either."

Danny said nothing.

"I guess you'll be number one now," Harry said.

"That depends on the Council," Danny said.

"Yeah, Danny, that's just what I was thinking," Harry said. "How'd you like me to use my influence?"

Danny said nothing.

"I sit on the Council," Harry said. "I might just be able to swing it for you, for Pete's sake." He smiled suddenly. "Hey, get it? For *Pete's* sake!"

Danny, unamused, sat back and lit a cigarette. "Just like that? You'll speak up for me because you like my looks?"

"Because you're not dumb, and because I know you didn't exactly love Pete like a brother," Harry said. "Now listen good, Danny. You don't get greedy like Pete, and you keep the same five percent arrangement with me, I'll go to the Council for you."

"That all I have to do, Harry?" Danny asked. "Nothing else?"

Harry glanced past Danny's shoulder, at the bar, at Mary Lou, and at Mickey Goldfarb who had just arrived. Harry gestured Mickey to stay at the bar. "There is something else," Harry said. "I want your word you won't interfere in my Las Vegas plans."

"Las Vegas?" Danny asked. "Where's that?"

"Smart boy," Harry said. He rose and clasped Danny's shoulder lightly. "I'll send Mary Lou back."

"I still can't get over Pete," Danny said. "Young guy like that having a bad heart."

"You never know," Harry said. "Can happen to any of us. Kind of like a message from God. Like a warning to the rest of us that it could happen any time, you know?"

"Yeah it could," Danny said. He was too smart to openly accuse Harry, but he could guess the truth, or knew. Which was precisely what Harry wanted.

He said, "I don't mean to sound like I got no heart, but this might turn out to be the luckiest thing that ever happened to you."

"Maybe for you, too."

Harry extended his hand. They shook, and Harry glanced at the bar where Mary Lou was laughing at something Mickey said. Harry gestured her to return to the table.

"Great little piece," Harry said. "Later on tonight, when you're sticking it to her, think of me." He started away, then quickly returned. "No rough stuff. She hates it."

Not twelve hours later, shortly after eight the next morning, Harry was sure Danny double-crossed him. He was in the shower when Mickey pulled open the stall door.

"Phone, Harry . . . ! One of them bimbos from Palm Springs. The kid's gone! Steve, he took off from the hotel!"

Harry nearly knocked Mickey down rushing into the bedroom for the

phone. One of the starlets said Steve left the hotel sometime early in the
morning. He had scribbled a note. ". . . don't tell Harry I've gone. I'll
call him and explain."

"For Christ's sake!" Harry shouted into the phone. "You were supposed to take care of him!" With each word, Harry envisioned the conversation with Leo. *Leo, I don't know how to tell you this, but—*

"Last night, at the bar, he was talking with some English flyers," the
girl said. "From the war, I mean. Royal Air Force guys. We couldn't get
him to stay away from them. So finally we left him down there at the
bar. We both fell asleep and didn't wake up till just now. Honest, Harry,
we didn't know he was gone!"

"Shit!" Harry said, and hung up.

"He likes to run away a lot, don't he?" Mickey said.

Danny Esposito swore he knew nothing, but Harry gave him twelve
hours to produce the boy. If one fucking hair of that kid's head was
harmed, what happened to Pete would be paradise compared to what
Harry would do to Danny.

Harry decided not to inform Leo immediately. They had spoken only
the night before when Harry phoned him about Pete Donini. Leo didn't
buy the heart-attack story; he knew Harry too well, and was furious. If
the Council ever learned the truth, Harry would be in trouble not even
Leo could fix.

Just as Harry reached for the phone to call Palm Springs again, it
rang. It was Leo.

"I just heard from Steve," he said. He paused. Harry gripped the
phone and felt his stomach turn over. "He's in Canada."

"Canada? What Canada?"

"Vancouver," Leo said. "And will you get this: he joined the Canadian
Air Force!"

"Come on, Leo, no jokes," Harry said. "I been tearing my hair out all
morning looking for that kid. So where is he?"

Leo said patiently, "He joined the Royal Canadian Air Force. He's
only sixteen, but they took him. I'm on my way up there now."

Harry hung up. He sat on the bed edge. He was still wet from the
shower. The water soaked the bedspread where he sat. "Canada," he
said aloud. "He went to fucking Canada!"

3.

The adjutant hated this duty. A stout, graying man of forty-five, with
the two and one half stripes of an RCAF senior officer on his sleeve
cuffs and a silver "O" half wing embroidered over his left breast pocket,
he served in the first war as an aerial gunner-observer. He had hoped
for an overseas assignment in this one, but was told his work here at
home was just as important. Some work, he thought now, glancing at

the glum, nervous boy seated beside him. Some war, nursemaiding young Americans who lied about their age to get into the scrap.

Generally, you simply took them to the nearest U.S. border crossing with their mustering-out papers. Good-bye, thank you for your interest, come back and see us when you're of age. This one, though, was the son of someone important. The adjutant's orders were to deliver the lad personally.

"Well, we're here," he said. The staff car had pulled up outside the Victoria Hotel. "Your dad's inside, I guess."

Steve stared blankly at the RCAF lance corporal driver who opened the rear car door and stood waiting at smart attention. He felt sick, and empty. His war was over before it even started.

"We have to go, son," the adjutant said gently. Steve got out. The adjutant got out behind him. Steve stood hesitantly. The adjutant touched Steve's shoulder. "I'm obliged to escort you in," the adjutant said.

Steve walked with the adjutant into the crowded, bustling hotel lobby. A short, slender, well-dressed civilian the adjutant immediately recognized as the boy's father made his way anxiously toward them through the dozens of blue and khaki uniforms. But for the height difference the resemblance was remarkable.

The adjutant touched the bill of his cap in a casual salute. "Mr. Gordon?"

"Gorodetsky," said Leo, looking at Steve. "Hello, Steve." He glanced at the adjutant. "Thank you . . . Commander?"

"Squadron Leader," said the adjutant. He removed an envelope from his inside blouse pocket and handed it to Leo. "His papers. They're all in order."

"Thank you," Leo said.

The adjutant said to Steve, "We appreciate your interest, son. I'm sorry it couldn't work out."

"So am I," said Steve.

The adjutant patted Steve's shoulder, saluted Leo again, and left. Steve and Leo both watched the adjutant vanish through the revolving doors. Then Leo asked, "Hungry?"

Steve glared down at Leo. He was so much taller Leo had to step back to face him fully without arching his neck. Steve said, "Why'd you do it?"

They were in the center of the lobby, constantly jostled by people coming and going. "Let's get a bite to eat and talk it over," Leo said.

"I don't want anything." Steve smoothed his rumpled seersucker jacket over his chino slacks and stared down at his scuffed white-buck shoes. He shifted the little canvas bag containing his things from one hand to the other. "I'm not hungry."

"How about sitting with me while I have something?"

Steve shrugged and said, "I don't care."

"I do," Leo said, and guided Steve into the hotel coffee shop, to a corner table. "I booked a compartment on the train to Montreal," he said when they were seated. "We'll change from there to Boston."

"How come you didn't charter a plane?" Steve said. "That's what you always do, isn't it?"

"I thought the train was better," Leo said. "We can spend some time together."

"I'd rather fly," Steve said.

"We'll take the train," Leo said.

"How long will it take?"

"To Boston? Three days."

"We can get there in less than a day if we fly."

"I said we're taking the train."

"What'll we do for three days?" Steve asked.

"Talk," Leo said.

"I don't want to talk," Steve said. "There's nothing to talk about."

"Then you can look out the window," Leo said.

Steve changed his mind about eating when the waitress took Leo's order. He decided to have a hamburger and french fries. The food relaxed him enough to talk about his journey. He was quite proud of the achievement. He had ridden to Vancouver with the RAF pilots he met in Palm Springs. They dropped him at the RCAF recruiting-station door.

Steve had a second hamburger and dessert, and then they went to the railway station. Not until they were in their compartment on the train did Leo directly address the issue. He had evaded Steve's "why'd you do it" questions simply because now, face to face with Steve, the long logical speech he composed sounded pompous and foolish in his mind.

"You didn't have to do it, you know," Steve said.

The train was speeding across the darkened Canadian plains. The steel-against-steel of the wheels rolling on the track and the occasional wail of the locomotive whistle made Leo feel more sure of himself.

"But I did have to do it," he said. "Your mother—"

"—in eight months I'd have graduated," Steve said. "I'd be an officer, flying Spitfires. Just like those pilots I met in Palm Springs. They were in the Battle of Britain. One of them shot down three Germans. Three! And you know how old he is? Nineteen!"

"I'm trying to tell you about your mother," Leo said patiently.

"You already told me," Steve said. "A hundred times. How she wants me to go to college—"

"—which is exactly what you're going to do."

Steve looked at him, then away. He was slouched in a chair facing Leo who sat on the bed edge. "I don't want to miss the war," he said. He looked at Leo again. "Don't you understand, this is my big chance! I don't want to miss it!"

"Miss what?" Leo said. "What the hell do you think is so much fun about a war? Don't forget, I was in the last one." But even as he spoke, he was thinking that the war, at least his war, was not so bad. He was remembering only the good parts. Paris, and Coblenz. Even Charlotte Daniels, an education in itself. Herself.

". . . you were in the last one," Steve was saying. "You weren't much older than me."

"I was seventeen."

"I'll try it again," Steve said. "I'll try it a hundred times until I get in."

"When you're old enough, we'll talk about it."

"It might be over before I'm old enough!"

Leo started to say Steve had no worries on that account, this was a war that would not so soon be over, not with the Germans occupying nearly all of Europe except Vichy France. Instead, he said, "But it's not your war. Not ours," he corrected himself.

"It will be! And I'll miss the whole thing!"

"I'll make a deal with you," Leo said. He paused, wondering if what he was about to say was only being said to avoid further arguing. He decided to say it; it was not a bad gamble. "You go back home and stay there. Finish high school. When you're eighteen, if you still want to, I'll sign the papers for you to join the U.S. Army. Believe me, by then, we'll probably be in it, anyway."

"The Air Corps?" Steve said. "Flying cadets?"

"Sure."

Steve studied him a suspicious moment. "You'll sign," he said. "What about Mom?"

"You only need one parent's signature," Leo said.

"Hold it," Steve said quickly. "You need at least two years college for flying cadets. I won't even finish high school for another year. I can't wait three years!"

"That's the deal," Leo said. "Take it or leave it."

"Suppose I want to join up anyway when I'm eighteen," Steve said. "I mean, like the regular Air Corps. Will you still do it?"

"Yes."

Steve studied Leo again. Then, unexpectedly, he grinned. He offered his hand. "Shake."

They shook hands. Leo marveled at the boy's firm, confident grip, the eager, alert brightness of his eyes and healthy glow of his skin. The strength of his face. Looking at him, Leo heard the little five-year-old boy shouting, "Daddy, we're going into the sky!"

Steve said, "We have a deal."

"A deal," Leo said, sad and glad at the same time. He knew Steve would keep his word and finish school. No longer a child, Steve had made an adult decision and commitment. Leo was very proud of his son.

He liked to say that when they reached Boston three days later they had gotten to know each other. In truth, Leo came to know Steve better, but not the other way around. For one thing, Steve did not appear too interested in learning more about his father. He seemed to accept without question that Leo was in the "hotel business," and the gambling ship on which he had such an exciting adventure was owned jointly by Leo and Harry.

Leo was relieved. He had anticipated certain probing questions, and was unsure how to answer. He did not want to be placed in a position of having to justify his own existence. Which he would refuse to do anyway, for he felt no obligation to justify himself to anyone.

So the three days with his son actually provided Leo his first real relaxation in months. He was sorry when it was over, and promised himself to do it more often.

All the good feelings were ruined by Ellie.

The instant they walked into the Georgetown house she began scolding Steve. The misery he had caused her, the heartache. Had he no consideration at all? She wondered if he wasn't mentally disturbed; perhaps she should send him to a doctor. Leo defended Steve, angering Ellie more. Finally Leo told Steve to go to bed. He, Leo, would straighten things out.

"You!" she cried, as soon as Steve's door closed. "You're trying to take him away from me!"

He knew she was drinking; he had seen an empty Scotch bottle in the kitchen trash barrel. "Come on, Ellie, I went up to Canada and got him, didn't I? I brought him home."

"Then why is he talking about joining the army when he's eighteen?"

"If he wants to, you should let him."

They were in the kitchen, Leo seated uncomfortably at the table, Ellie lighting a cigarette from the stove gas jet. She waved the cigarette at him. "You put that idea in his head, didn't you? I know you did."

"I thought you quit drinking?"

"Why have you done this to me, Leo? He's all I have. He's my whole life, him and Carla!"

"Where is Carla?"

"Staying overnight at a friend's," Ellie said. "I have nothing else but them, you know that!" She sat at the table opposite him. "Why are you doing this to me?"

"Ellie, I'm not doing anything to you."

"You're stealing my son."

He lit a cigarette. He wanted desperately to leave, but also wanted her to realize Steve was his son, too. She read his mind.

She said, "I don't want you to see him again."

"You're crazy. Or drunk," he said. "Or both."

"I'm not afraid of you, Leo. I'll get a lawyer and have a court order forbidding you any contact. I can do that, you know. All I have to do is remind the court of who and what you are." She laughed harshly. "They won't even let you write him a letter!"

He stubbed out his cigarette in the huge clamshell ashtray. He marveled at his calmness. He felt no anger, only sorrow. For her, for himself, for the children. "Don't do that, Ellie," he said quietly. "Don't even think it."

She laughed again. "What will you do, Leo? Have me killed?"

He remembered her asking that same question years ago when she first left him. He answered the question now, still feeling no anger. "I might, Ellie," he said. He got up and looked down at her. "I just might."

He walked into the dining room, and then to the front hall, and out. When she heard the car drive off, she opened the cupboard and reached behind a stack of canned goods for a bottle of Scotch. She brought it and a water glass to the table. Just then, in robe and pajamas, Steve entered the kitchen.

"I wanted to say good-bye to Dad," he said. "Why'd he go without saying good-bye?"

"He wanted to catch the midnight train."

"He drove, Mom. He rented a car to drive back to New York."

"I thought he said something about the train."

"No, he's driving," Steve said. "You still mad?"

"No. Go to bed."

Steve glanced at the empty glass on the table, and the bottle in her hand. He stepped over to her and kissed her cheek. "Good night, Mom," he said, and left.

Ellie sat staring at the dining room door until it stopped swinging. Then she poured three fingers of Scotch into the glass and drank it down.

19

THE great ship lay capsized at the pier with her three stacks nearly flat on the water. The exposed starboard side was charred and blackened, and the wooden decks still smoldered. Wisps of greasy, gray smoke swirled into the damp early April air.

"Not very pretty, is it?" MacGowan asked.

They were in MacGowan's U.S. Army staff car, high above the pier on the West Side Highway. Leo had seen the *Bristol Queen* from his hotel window when she started burning three days before, a day before she was to sail for England. The disaster crowded the war news off the front pages, even the German invasion of Greece and Yugoslavia. A spark from a welder's acetylene torch had set off the conflagration.

The fire broke out on her promenade deck. In minutes, the entire top deck was a mass of flames. Fire crews poured tons of water into her, making it impossible to unload cargo and fight the fire at the same time. A day later, the fire still out of control, swamped by the weight of the water, the *Bristol Queen* began listing. With the incoming tide, her stern rose up from the shallow pier bottom and she rolled over on her side like some giant stricken animal waiting to die.

"Among other supplies desperately needed by the British, it carried two hundred jeeps and seventy-five Studebaker heavy-duty trucks," MacGowan said. "And twenty-five Lockheed Hudson bombers."

Through the rear window Leo gazed at the *Bristol Queen*. It reminded him of a toy boat Carla once "sank" in the pond at the Hempstead house. He watched until the car swung off the highway at Seventy-second Street. Then he turned to MacGowan. Even in the army uniform, with the two silver stars on his shoulders and a chestful of ribbons, MacGowan looked old. But then he was old, Leo thought. Pushing sixty, at least.

"All right," Leo said. "What's the point?"

MacGowan leaned forward and spoke to the army corporal driving. "Stop anywhere, son." The corporal pulled up at the corner of Riverside Drive and Eightieth Street and immediately scrambled from his front seat to open the door for the general.

"Let's take a walk," MacGowan said to Leo. He got out of the car. Leo followed. "Wait for us here, please," MacGowan said to the corporal. He acknowledged the corporal's brisk salute with a casual wave of his gloved hand and started walking. Leo plunged his hands into his coat pockets and walked along with him. MacGowan looked at him from the corner of his eye. "Almost like old times, eh?"

"I'm surprised you didn't send a couple of MPs for me."

"You have a hell of a memory," MacGowan said. "That was ten years ago."

"Fourteen," said Leo.

For a moment both walked silently, as though thinking of that last meeting, when the detectives arrested Leo and brought him to see MacGowan in the dark of night. This time MacGowan had politely, almost diffidently, requested a meeting. On a matter of extreme urgency, he said. He sent the army staff car for Leo, then took him on the drive past the burning *Bristol Queen*.

MacGowan smiled thinly. "I damn well might have used MPs," he said. "If you hadn't agreed to meet."

"I was curious," Leo said. "I couldn't imagine why the chief of Army Intelligence wanted to see me."

"Deputy chief," MacGowan said. "And it's not Army Intelligence. It's Office of Strategic Services. O.S.S." He stopped abruptly and faced Leo. They were on the sidewalk adjacent to the park, which was deserted in the chilly, rain-threatened day. "That ship, the *Bristol Queen*, the fire was no accident."

Leo said nothing. He buttoned his coat collar; it was very cold for April.

MacGowan said, "I need your help."

"That's a new twist," Leo said. "Your protégé, Charlie Brickhill, can't sleep at night scheming up ways to put me in jail, and his protégé, Marty Raab, spends half of each working day building a new tax evasion case against me—and you come to me for help."

"We can't afford another *Bristol Queen* incident," MacGowan said. "The British rely on us for supplies. We're their only source. The German and Italian sympathizers have to be flushed out. And the Irish nationalists. And the labor agitators. We can't afford dock slowdowns, or strikes, or even threats of strikes. The docks have to be cleaned up, Leo."

"I don't control the docks, General."

"The Longshoremen's Union does," MaGowan said. "And Vincent Tomasino controls the union."

"So I've heard."

"And I've heard he's on the Council."

"What Council is that?" Leo asked.

"The same Council you're a member of," MacGowan said. "The Council that runs the Syndicate. The Alliance, the Combination, whatever it's called. The group that runs organized crime on the East Coast, and probably the entire country as well."

"Oh, that one," Leo said. "The one Brickhill and Raab are always trying to break? The one that's a figment of their imagination—and yours, too, I'm afraid, General."

"Come on, Leo, neither of us has time to play word games." MacGowan tightened his coat collar against a cold gust of wind sweeping in from the trees in the park. "This country is shipping England everything it possibly can, even depriving our own forces of vital material at a time we're rearming. We'll be in it, don't worry. Sooner than you think. But we're not ready, and won't be for at least two years—1943, the earliest. The English are holding them off for us. For Christ's sake, man, must I give you a patriotic speech?"

"You're doing it anyway, General."

MacGowan nodded. "Yeah. Well, then suppose I tell you I have solid intelligence that the Nazis are systematically murdering the Jews of Europe. Does *that* make a difference?"

You bastard, Leo told him in his mind. What you mean is, if I won't help my own country, then I should do it for my fellow Jews. He strained to keep his voice steady. "I just read that the U.S. government has no documentation of those reports."

"They have plenty of documentation," MacGowan said. "But certain State Department elements consider it politically inexpedient to acknowledge the truth. Even if they did, beyond delivering 'strong protests,' there's no action we could take. And no amount of protests would cow the Nazis anyway. They know we're preparing for war. They're gambling on defeating the British before we're ready."

"So what do you want me to do?"

"Have Tomasino order the Longshoremen to cooperate," MacGowan said. "Help secure those docks, goddamit!"

Leo started speaking, then stopped. He looked at MacGowan. The general seemed older than before. His face, wrinkled and gray-pallored, sagged.

MacGowan said, "Don't you understand what I'm saying?"

"You must be really desperate to have to come to me," Leo said. " 'A gangster,' 'thug,' and what did Brickhill call me: 'Crime Czar'?"

"It is untrue?"

Leo laughed unhumorously. "All in the eye of the beholder, General. But you know what's really funny? You, representing the so-called forces of law and order, can't keep law and order. So who do you come running to for help? The very people you're sworn to put away. Now that should tell you something about the human condition."

"Believe me, I have no illusions about the 'human condition,'" MacGowan said. "I never had."

"That's right," Leo said. "You're only trying to do a job."

"A long time ago, I saw something in you," MacGowan said. "A potential for . . . well, good, I suppose. A potential for good. You wanted to make something of yourself—"

"—I have."

"That, too, is in the eye of the beholder."

"I don't have to justify myself to you," Leo said, wondering why he was saying this, realizing the very words were themselves an attempt to justify.

"No one asked you to," MacGowan said. "And I couldn't care less right now why you are what you are, or what you've become. All I'm interested in are those docks. And all I want is a straight answer. Now, will you or won't you help?"

Leo looked at him, then away, at the staff car parked on the corner. In place of a license plate was a red plaque with two white stars. He remembered seeing Pershing's car once in Chaumont; attached to each front fender was a little blue flag with four white stars. He looked at MacGowan again.

"Suppose, if by chance, I just do have these contacts you think I have," Leo said. "If by chance, I could help clean up the docks. The labor problems—"

"—and the sabotage," said MacGowan.

"Suppose I could. What's in it for me?"

MacGowan's eyes all at once hardened, filled with such cold disdain Leo had to force himself not to look away. MacGowan said, "What's in it for you is stopping the Germans. Isn't that enough?"

"No," said Leo.

"What is, then?"

"You're asking me to use my influence," Leo said. "All right, then I'll ask you to use yours."

"How?"

"Quash the income-tax evasion case Brickhill and Raab are building against me."

"That's your price for helping your own people?"

"That's the price, General."

Leo hated himself for saying it, and hated MacGowan for finessing

him into saying it. But MacGowan was naïve. It was like playing poker
with an amateur. It reminded Leo suddenly of the poker game so many
years ago when Arnie Steinberger stood pat with two small pair against
three kings.

MacGowan said slowly, "I don't think I can do it."

"Try," said Leo. He almost wanted to laugh, it was that funny. Surely,
MacGowan realized Leo would help with the docks—at least do what he
could—for no price. How could you demand a payoff for assisting people who fought Jew-killers? But MacGowan did not have the guts to call
the bluff. He was old and tired. Leo felt sorry for him.

"All right," MacGowan said after a moment. His face sagged again,
but his eyes held their cold disdain. "I'll try."

They regarded each other a long, silent moment now, and Leo wondered if perhaps MacGowan actually did believe him that mercenary,
that callous. The possibility filled him with shame.

"I can't guarantee results," MacGowan said.

"Neither can I, then."

MacGowan drew in his breath in a long, exasperated sigh and shook
his head tightly, and Leo thought, Why the hell should I care what
MacGowan believes. MacGowan was a man unable to do a job, forced
to come to another, more capable man.

He said, "You know what they say, General: Deal with the Devil, pay
the Devil."

"I'll drop you at your office," MacGowan said. He turned and started
walking toward the car.

"Don't bother," Leo said, "I'll find a cab."

MacGowan continued walking. He did not look back.

It never occurred to Leo that perhaps MacGowan was not so naïve,
not at all duped; that all the time Leo believed he was manipulating
MacGowan, it was he, Leo, being manipulated.

Leo convinced Vincent Tomasino to secure the docks. An astute business procedure, if nothing else, because the United States would eventually be in the war. A cooperative Longshoremen's Union could enjoy
the fruits of cost-plus government military contracts. A cooperative union
would receive generous fringe benefits. A cooperative union was a patriotic union. Patriotic unions stood no danger of government scrutiny.

Martin Raab personally delivered the government files on Leo's in-
come-tax-evasion case. Leo and George Gerson were in Leo's office when
Raab arrived, unannounced. He had brushed past the IDIC receptionist
and simply barged into the office. He dumped two large, file-crammed
envelopes on the desk.

"As per agreement," Raab said.

"Thank you," Leo said. "And thank Mr. Brickhill for me. Look these
over, George, would you please?" As Gerson gathered up the envelopes,

Leo continued, "You know Mr. Raab, don't you, George? He's with the D.A.'s office."

"We've met," Gerson said. He nodded at Raab and left.

Leo expected Raab to leave also, but the deputy D.A. clearly had something on his mind. He waited until the door closed behind Gerson. Then he said, "I want to give you a piece of information—"

"—sit down," Leo said.

Surprisingly, Raab sat. He placed his hat on the desk and said, "When General MacGowan came to us with this proposition, Brickhill turned him down cold. *I* convinced Charlie to do it."

"Well, I appreciate it," Leo said. "But I have to ask why."

"I told Charlie we had to be realistic. The objective is to secure the Port of New York. If giving up the case against you is the price, then it's worth it."

"That's what I said all along."

"We'll build another case. You're a marked man."

Leo nodded. "What else?"

"That's it." Raab picked up his hat and rose to leave. "I just wanted you to know it."

"Now I want you to know something." Leo also rose. He faced Raab across the desk. "I would have done it even if you hadn't given up the case."

"Yes," said Raab. "You're a patriot."

Leo said, "I did it for our fellow Jews."

"Yes, I know."

"What do you mean, you 'know'?"

"I know you did it to help the Jews. MacGowan knows it. Brickhill knows it. You're a credit to the race."

Leo refused to dignify the sarcasm. He said, "At least I don't try to protect Nazis. You didn't believe me when I told you what they were doing."

"You're wrong, Mr. Gorodetsky. I did believe you. In fact, what they were doing then is only kid stuff to what's happening now. The bastards are setting up death camps all over Europe. Nobody here pays much attention and the papers don't play it up much, but we know it's happening."

"That's why I would have helped with the docks even if I didn't get the files," Leo said. He knew he was repeating himself, but felt his point was not made; he had finessed Martin Raab and Charles Brickhill, and wanted them to know it. It was very important to him that Raab understand this. And petty, he knew that, too. But he could not help himself. "You could have gotten what you wanted, and still had the tax case."

"I've already told you," Raab said. "We're aware of all that."

"Sure," said Leo. "That's why you let me bluff you out."

"You didn't bluff anybody."

"You flushed your tax case against me down the toilet, didn't you?"

"The case is for your 1937 returns. This is 1941. We have to bring you to trial within the year, before the statute of limitations runs out. Leo Gorodetsky in prison won't have much influence on the Longshoremen's Union." Raab smiled. "Get it?"

Leo stared at him. He felt foolish, trapped, and he had a crazy image of himself, naked, leaping over a tennis net to congratulate the fully-clothed opponent who had just defeated him.

"Yeah," he said. "I get it."

"Good," said Raab. He turned and moved to the door.

Leo, to have the last word, called after him, "You know what the Nazis are doing to Jews, but you'd still like to nail me for Kurt Baumer."

"Kurt Baumer was not murdering Jews, Mr. Gorodetsky. He may have wanted to, but he never did."

"Because he was stopped, Mr. Raab."

"Maybe I'll suggest to General MacGowan that he send you to Germany. To assassinate Hitler. Would you accept the assignment?"

"That's really not in my line," Leo said. "But I could recommend some good men."

"I'll just bet you could," Raab said. He put on his hat and straightened the brim. "See you around."

Leo watched him open the door and leave. A moment later George Gerson appeared. He hefted the two envelopes in the palms of both hands.

"They kept their word. You're free and clear."

Leo gazed down the hallway a moment. "Not while Marty Raab is in business, George." He stepped back into the office and closed the door in Gerson's face.

Gerson stared at the closed door and wondered why Leo displayed no elation. Not even a congratulatory handshake. But this did not trouble him as much as Leo's remark, "Not while Marty Raab is in business." George Gerson was well acquainted with Gorodetsky's Law: *Violence committed for its own sake is stupid.* The other side of that was, of course, *Violence is to be committed only when it achieves a purpose.*

2.

Gerson need not have worried. Leo had no intention of invoking the Law. It had never entered his mind, but only because he knew there would always be a Martin Raab or a Charles Brickhill. At least they were enemies he recognized.

Just as he recognized the Nazis—and then, in December of that year, the Japanese. Leo was in Havana when Pearl Harbor was attacked. He and Sal remained in Sal's penthouse living room all day, listening to the news from the Miami clear-channel station, WIOD.

"Jesus . . . !" Sal said for at least the dozenth time. It was almost all he had said since the first news flash. But now, in his unfamiliarly hoarse voice, he was more eloquent. "I guess with us in the war, coming here from Miami won't be like taking the BMT to Coney Island anymore."

"No," Leo agreed. "It'll hurt us like hell."

Sal grinned. It seemed almost an effort, heightening the already skull-like outline of his face, the deep-sunk eyes and protruding jaw. "So I guess I won't have to worry so much about a new general manager for this place. It won't be so important with no business."

In addition to his duties as IDIC vice-president in charge of the corporation's Havana hotels, Sal functioned as El Conquistador's general manager. That morning they had reviewed names of possible replacements. Because Sal would not be on the job much longer.

"Sal—" Leo said, feeling helpless.

"—hey, it's okay, Leo. No big deal." Sal pushed himself up from the chair and went out to the terrace. Leo dialed the radio tuning knob to another Miami station, WQAM. Singapore had been bombed, Thailand and Malaya invaded. All a rehash of previous bulletins. Leo turned the radio off.

From the living room he watched Sal on the terrace gazing out at the harbor. It was a lovely day, warm, with the sun low over Morro Castle now in the late afternoon. A beautiful day, Leo thought, although not so beautiful a day in Hawaii or the Philippines.

And certainly not for Sal Bracci. On the other hand, any day he was alive certainly could not be called unpleasant. Sal would not, as once predicted, live to be a hundred. Sal would not live to be forty-four.

Cancer.

Adenocarcinoma, the worst kind. Inoperable. All they could do was try to keep him comfortable. There would be some pain, but not as severe as with other cancers. So he had lucked out with that at least.

Leo watched him, remembering Sal's phone call two days before. "Well, kid, I bought the farm it looks like." Leo had marveled at the calm, even voice. It showed style. Style, and grace. Leo only hoped that when his time came he behaved half as well.

"Why don't you lie down?" he said as Sal, restless, returned to the living room.

"I was just thinking," Sal said. He lowered himself back into the same chair. "It's so fucking—" he groped for the word. "Ironic. Yeah, ironic. We spend our whole lives figuring to go out with a bullet in the head, and never knowing when. So here I am, knowing how—and almost when. Shit."

Leo tried to sound light. "How many people do you think would give everything they own for that information?"

"Like knowing you'll toss ten sevens in a row, huh?" Sal's grin tightened. "Or boxcars."

Leo looked at him, at the skin drawn so parchment tight over the haggard face it resembled a transparent lampshade. The face of death. A thousand platitudes flooded Leo's mind. Death was nothing. Another phase of living. The Big Sleep. You'll never know the difference. Take it in stride. We all die. Fuck 'em all but six, and save them for pallbearers.

Sal read his thoughts. "Come on, don't take it so hard." Another skull-like grin. "Think of all the guys we're disappointing, who won't get the chance to do the job themselves."

Leo laughed accommodatingly, and turned the radio on again. Miami, a Glenn Miller recording, "In the Mood." In the mood for what? Leo thought absently. He lit a cigarette and they sat silently, listening to the music, thinking.

The phone rang. Sal answered. He listened. "Okay," he grunted, and hung up. "Our friend the minister of labor has just dropped thirty-five thousand," he said. "He wants an additional twenty-five thousand in credit."

"When I looked at the books yesterday he was in to us for two hundred thousand," Leo said. "All in markers."

Sal shrugged. "So it'll be two-sixty. What's the difference?"

"Does he ever win?"

"Never," said Sal. "And he never pays, either."

"Great customer."

"Shall I shut him off?"

"Never," Leo said, and they smiled at each other.

Sal died six months later. A comfortable death, if any death can be called comfortable. Wingy Gruber was with him. Wingy, who had worked for Leo and Sal since the Chez When days, had been brought in to take over for Sal as El Conquistador manager. Wingy said it was late afternoon, an hour Sal enjoyed, the time between day and night. The day over, the night to look forward to. He was on the terrace watching the ships in the harbor. He claimed he could predict within ten percent the number of passengers from the cruise ships who would gamble in the casinos. He claimed he knew from their clothes. But that was before the war.

Sal, Wingy said, had just decided to close El Conquistador. With the war cutting so sharply into business, only the Caribe and another, smaller hotel, the Windward, would remain open. They were discussing the details when Wingy realized he was talking to himself. Sal had simply closed his eyes and died.

Leo was at home when Wingy called from Havana. It was almost seven, and he had already been on the phone two hours. First with Ellie. She was unable to deal with Steven. After graduating from high school the previous week, he now, instead of applying for college, demanded that Ellie release some of his savings for a two-year college-equivalency-test tutorial.

"And do you know why?" she had shouted shrilly. "So he can join the army! Because you said you'd sign the consent papers!"

Leo reminded her that in September, at eighteen, Steve would be drafted. An Air Corps aviation-cadet appointment required a minimum of two-years college or the equivalent. Better to join the branch of his choice than be drafted into the infantry.

The instant Leo hung up from Ellie, Harry called from Los Angeles. More bad news. As if postponing the Las Vegas project for the duration of the war hadn't been bad enough, now the *Californian* was closed down. And this time for real. The navy had declared the vessel a navigational hazard and towed her back to port for reasons of national security.

And then the call from Havana.

Leo asked Wingy to notify Harry; he did not want to talk to anyone anymore, especially Harry. Leo left his private-line telephone off the receiver and ordered the hotel operator to plug in the switchboard phone. He fixed himself a drink and gazed out the window at the buildings outlined against the cloudless June twilight sky. Sal's favorite hour. A nice time to be alive, he thought, picturing in his mind Sal's ashes scattered at sea. Sal's instructions were cremation, ashes scattered at sea.

Leo laughed aloud remembering that conversation. "Leo, you could do one thing so it all wouldn't be a total waste," Sal said. "You could toss the ashes in Charlie Brickhill's face!"

Yes, Leo thought, that would have been good indeed. He drank down his drink, made another, and went to bed. It was far too early to sleep, but he was very tired.

3.

When he saw him in the restaurant foyer, Leo's heart beat faster. A tall, brown-haired boy in an olive-green uniform removing his cap, the leather-billed garrison cap with the large brass winged-propeller medallion of a United States Army Air Corps aviation cadet. A boy bearing such a striking resemblance to his father that for years his paternal grandmother called him "Little Leo." "Big Leo" now, Leo thought, watching Steve tuck the cap militarily under his arm and follow the maître d' through the crowded dining room.

Leo rose to greet him, immediately struck by the thought that even in the few months since their last meeting, Steve was taller.

Steve's whole face brightened. "Hi, Dad."

For an instant the words seemed clogged in Leo's throat, but as they shook hands he managed to say, "Hi," and gestured Steve to sit. He snapped his finger at a waiter. "What are you drinking?" he asked Steve, and to the waiter, "Give him whatever he wants."

"Sir—" the waiter began hesitantly.

"Dad, I'm not old enough," Steve said. "Coca-Cola," he said to the waiter.

"Yes, sir," said the waiter, relieved.

"They all know most of the Barksdale cadets are under twenty-one," Steve said as the waiter left. "No sense trying to snow them." He looked around the room, the Grille Room of the Hotel Shreveport. It buzzed with laughter and talk from Air Corps officers and enlisted men occupying almost every table. "First time I've ever been here," Steve continued. "Everybody says it's the only decent restaurant in town."

Leo said, "From what I saw, it's the only restaurant."

"The only real one, I guess," Steve said. He smiled at Leo. "I couldn't believe it when they called me into the orderly room and told me I had a pass for town. What are you doing in these parts, anyway?"

"I had to go to Miami on business," Leo said. "So I figured why not take a little detour?"

"That's some 'little detour'," Steve said. "A thousand miles. And how'd you figure to get me a pass? We're not supposed to have any leave for three more weeks."

"I made a phone call," Leo said.

"A phone call," Steve said wryly. "To who? FDR? It'd take almost him to get me off the base."

"Don't worry about it," Leo said, thinking he almost did need FDR for Steve's pass. Two Washington calls, one to a senator who himself had to make two calls. Well, if you had the juice, why not use it? The senator owed Leo more than a small favor of arranging a visit to his aviation cadet son.

". . . can't use the car," Steve was saying. "And please, Dad," he added quickly, "don't pull any strings for that. I'll just have to get along without a car like everybody else. But thanks, anyway."

The car was a brand-new lime-green 1941 Mercury convertible, with a "C" gasoline-ration sticker. Leo purchased it in New Orleans and had it driven to Shreveport, only to learn cadets were not allowed their own cars. So the car was in a local garage for six months until Steve graduated.

"How's the dough?" Leo asked.

"Come on, Dad, I can't spend it!" Steve said. He reached over and touched Leo's hand. "I appreciate it, though. Everything, honest. Thanks," he said to the waiter who had just served the Coca-Cola and was impatiently awaiting their dinner order.

"I guess I'll have the frog's legs," Steve said. "Can you just sautée them in a little lemon butter?"

"Certainly, sir," said the waiter, and turned to Leo. But Leo was staring unseeingly at Steve, and thinking, "Can you just sautée them in a little lemon butter?" And hearing, "Daddy, we're going into the sky!" How was it possible the little brown-haired brown-eyed boy had grown into a brown-haired brown-eyed six-foot-tall young man? And so fast. Why, he wondered, so fast?

"Dad . . ." Steve was saying, with the waiter clearing his throat at the same time.

Leo glanced up, startled. "I'm sorry," he said. "I'll have the same."

"Also sautéed in lemon butter?"

"Of course."

Steve talked all through dinner, his voice now almost a deep baritone, occasionally shaded with a New England twang. Leo loved the sound of it. He was working harder, Steve said, harder than he ever believed imaginable. Academics were a breeze compared to flight training. The same old problem: recovering from a stall. Something seemed to paralyze him the instant he pulled the control stick into his stomach and felt the airplane mush out, and then roll over in a slow, sickening spin. Recovering was a simple enough maneuver. Dive, and apply power. But each time the airplane went into the spin, Steve became so disoriented he froze on the controls. But he would master it; he was determined. Everbody said it was mind over matter.

"What happens if you can't do it?" Leo asked.

Steve's face tightened. "I wash out."

"You won't," Leo said. "I know it. I can feel it, just like I can feel when a shooter's about to get hot. You know it's going to happen. It's something in the air, something electric."

"That's not good for business," Steve said. He smiled wanly; he welcomed the chance to change the subject. "What do you do when that happens?"

"When somebody gets hot? Nothing."

"You just sit and take it?"

"There's nothing else you can do."

"I've heard of places that don't let you win," Steve said. "They bring in shaved dice, or they mark the cards."

"Not a real casino," Leo said. "It's stupid to cheat. The percentages eventually grind the player down. There's no way the house can lose."

"What about the man who broke the bank at Monte Carlo?"

"That's why we have a limit. No matter how hot the player is, if the bank is big enough, and there's a limit, he can't break you."

"You never take the limit off?"

"Never."

"A sucker play, huh?"

"The worst kind."

"Then how does anybody win?" Steve asked. "You say a winner is good for business. If you won't let them play over the limit, they can't win."

"Sure they can," Leo said. "And they do. The smart gamblers. They take us for plenty sometimes. And once in a while, even with a limit, we get nervous. But we always have enough in the bank to ride out the percentage. The smart ones, though, know when to push their luck, and have the guts to do it. And the guts to walk away when they're ahead, or when they know they're on a losing streak. The brains to quit. Leave the table. They're dangerous." He winked. "But good for business."

"How do they know when to quit?"

Steve's voice contained such a note of resignation it startled Leo into momentary silence. This was the first time he had ever openly discussed business with Steve, and the first time Steve ever openly acknowledged an awareness of Leo's business. It gave him an abrupt, almost embarrassing sensation of a son indicating his reluctance to enter the family business. But this son, Leo told himself, had nothing to worry about. This son had a father who did not want him following in his footsteps. Not in a million years.

Leo said, "Why are you so interested?"

"I'm wondering if it's not time for me to quit."

Leo felt foolish. He had misread Steve entirely. The boy was in trouble, seeking his father's help.

"You're talking about this thing with flying the plane?"

Steve's lips were pursed tightly. He looked down at his plate a moment, then straight at Leo. "I don't think I can cut it. I don't know whether I should just . . . leave the table. Or keep playing."

"Maybe you're not playing the cards properly. You can't win unless you do. That's why you're playing, isn't it? To win? Isn't that what you want, to win?"

"More than anything."

"Then you figure out what you're doing wrong, and change it," Leo said. "You can do it."

"I don't know if I'm good enough," Steve said. "That's what I meant about knowing when to get out, when to quit."

"You're worried about losing? About failing?"

"Yes."

"Let me tell you something," Leo said. "Winners never think about losing. They only have a single idea in their heads: to win. They play to win, period."

"They have to be lucky, too."

"Listen to me," said Leo. "Luck is a word. Nothing more than a word, with a thousand different meanings to a thousand different people. It has nothing to do with winning. Nothing. People believe that it does, which makes them suckers because luck is only a combination of totally unknown and unconnected factors that all come together at the same place and time."

"But these factors?" Steve said. "What are they?"

"Anything and everything," Leo said. "From the temperature outside, to whether the dealer had a fight with his girlfriend the night before."

"Or whether my instructor did," Steve said ruefully.

"Steve, the instructor isn't having trouble recovering from spins. You are."

Leo felt foolish again, and a little pompous, as Steve studied him intently. But then Steve relaxed. He grinned. "Winners never think about losing," he repeated. "I like that."

"Remember it," Leo said.

It was only later, sitting in the taxi watching Steve walk through the air-base gate, that Leo wondered if he had not made a mistake equating winning with flying. Flying required certain skills, mental and physical coordination. Winning—whether gambling, business, or merely living —was a matter of instinct, determination, courage, and timing.

And he had forgotten to tell Steve more about those "factors" that composed luck, that the trick was to research them, learn what and where they were. And then accept or reject them to your advantage at the right time and place. That was what brought the percentage around to your favor.

He cringed now, remembering how he said to Steve, "Good luck." He hated the word.

Two weeks later the percentage went the wrong way.

4.

Leo was in his office when Gerson announced a visitor. "A soldier," Gerson said, hardly able to repress a grin. But no laughing matter when, over dinner at the Stork Club, Steve explained his presence in New York.

"I'm AWOL."

Leo had just raised his coffee cup to his mouth. He replaced it carefully in the saucer; his hand trembled. "Say that again?"

"I'm AWOL," Steve said. "Over the hill."

"You said you caught a ride on a bomber that was flying up here."

"I did."

"Why didn't you tell me you were AWOL?" Leo said.

"You didn't ask me," Steve said.

"Goddam you!" Leo said quietly. "Don't get smart with me!"

"I'm sorry."

Leo glanced around the room. They were in a rear booth in the Cub Room, which was crowded with uniforms. Leo felt suddenly trapped and helpless. He lit a cigarette and signaled for the check. This was too public a place; his Park Central Hotel apartment was safer.

In the taxi, Steve blew on his hands for warmth. "Feels like snow," he said.

"Where the hell are your gloves?"

"I left in a hurry, Dad."

That was their total conversation until they were in Leo's living room, and he had poured himself a small brandy, and lit another cigarette.

"All right," Leo said finally. "So why did you go AWOL?"

"I wanted to talk to you."

"About what?"

"Winning," said Steve, and told him how he had been scheduled for a check ride yesterday, Friday, but reported sick. The check ride was rescheduled for the following Monday. Steve arranged for a classmate to cover for him at roll call and simply strolled over to Operations and hitched a ride on a B-25 being ferried to Mitchel Field. As Steve correctly assumed, it never occurred to the B-25 pilot to question the cadet's travel authority.

". . . I'll wash out," Steve said now. "I'll never fly. All my life I wanted to be an army pilot. Now it'll never happen."

"So you come crying to me?"

"I'm not crying."

"You're running away."

"I thought you might help."

"Steve, this is something you have to work out for yourself."

"I know that. But I thought we could talk."

Leo looked at the boy sitting rigidly on the divan opposite him and saw an eighteen-year-old frightened child, and remembered himself at eighteen, equally frightened. Lugging a Springfield .30-.30 through Saint-Mihiel. Lying in a French field hospital. Frightened, yes, but he never ran crying about it to anyone. He never had anyone to run to.

"All right, we'll talk," Leo said. He was unable to keep the anger and disappointment from his voice.

Steve said, "Maybe I made a mistake coming up here." He rose, reaching for his greatcoat.

"Sit down!" Leo said. "Act your age, for Christ's sake!"

"No!" Steve said. "You don't want to talk, I understand. It's okay. I'll go." He looked around for his cap.

"Steven, sit down," Leo said. He realized that despite his fear, his need for help, Steve honestly intended leaving. He was playing no game. Leo respected that. "Please," Leo said. "I know what you're going through."

Steve sank down onto the divan again. "In Shreveport, what you said about winning, I kept thinking about it—"

"—so did I," Leo said, suddenly aware of the untouched brandy snifter on the coffee table. He had lost his taste for it. "And I think I was talking through my hat."

"No, you were right," Steve said. "At least when you said winners never think about losing." His eyes met Leo's. "Teach me how to be a winner."

Jesus, Leo thought, how do you answer *that*? And in the same thought, with crystal clearness, he envisioned himself talking with his own father. Except that his father's face was blank, so he wondered how he knew it was his father. He also did not recall, when in trouble, ever talking to his father.

". . . but did I ever try?" he said aloud, for an instant completely lost.

"Excuse me?" Steve said, bemused.

"Nothing," Leo said. He had the answer. "I'll tell you the difference between a winner and a loser. The loser is the person who's afraid to fail. He's not big enough to take a failure. He doesn't understand that there's no shame in failing—as long as you give whatever it is an honest try. But the winner, Steve, the winner is never afraid of failing. And he keeps coming back, and back, and back. Until he wins."

Steve said nothing, and Leo thought again, Jesus! The philosopher philosophizing. You can buy better advice in Woolworth's for a dime. All right, he told himself, so maybe it was a little pompous, and no doubt naïvely oversimplistic. But it made sense, goddamit.

Leo smiled self-consciously. He said, "Want me to write that down?"

Steve returned the smile. "I'll remember it."

"And remember, too, a man can do anything he wants if he wants it badly enough."

Steve smiled again. "Got it."

"Good," Leo said. "Now you go back there, and you get into that plane, and you try. That's all, just try. You fail, you fail. But not because you didn't try. Okay?"

"Okay."

"How will you get back to Shreveport?"

"Same way I left," Steve said. "Hitch a ride from Mitchel. I've got my cadet I.D. No one'll ask for travel orders. I'll be back before Sunday roll call."

Leo had to look away. He did not want Steve to see the tears suddenly welling in his eyes. From pride, and admiration. He had fully expected Steve to suggest Leo make another of those "phone calls" on his behalf. But Steve intended getting himself out of the predicament he had gotten himself into. He was accepting responsibility for his own actions.

Leo took Steve to Penn Station for the Hempstead train. He could not drive him to Mitchel Field; his car was in the garage for repairs, and no taxi driver would make the sixty-mile round trip. Not even for a fifty-dollar bonus. Gasoline was too precious. After the third taxi turned them down, Leo decided to waste no more time.

Penn Station bustled with hundreds of civilians and servicemen and civilians. One of them was Major General Robert MacGowan. He and Leo nearly collided in the entrance. MacGowan, accompanied by several officers, said nothing, only glanced at Leo, then at Steve. His eyes lingered on Steve an extra, almost curious moment. He nodded curtly and continued on his way.

"A general!" Steve whispered, awed. "And I forgot to salute!"

"I don't think it bothered him," Leo said. He left Steve at a Union News Company kiosk near the LIRR track while he went to purchase the ticket. When he returned Steve was gone.

For a moment Leo saw only the same profusion of khaki and blue. Then, halfway across the station floor, he saw him. Just the back of his coat, but Leo recognized the winged-propeller patch on Steve's sleeve. And the MP brassards worn by the two soldiers escorting him.

Leo hurried after them. "Hold it!" he called. "Where are you taking him?"

The first MP, a burly, freckled-faced redhead, said, "You know this soldier?"

"I'm his father."

The MP's fingers dropped to his white-washed webbed gun belt and rested on the holstered .45. "He's got no travel orders."

"He's an aviation cadet from Barksdale Field," Leo said. "He's on his way back there."

"He claims he lost his papers," said the second MP. He was almost as big as the first, but less officious. "You know how many times a day we hear that? We'll see what the provost marshal says." He prodded Steve gently. "Let's go."

Leo plunged his hand into his inside jacket pocket for his wallet and then suddenly froze. You are crazy, he told himself. It will only make things worse. He stood a helpless moment watching the MPs guide Steve toward a door marked U.S. ARMY TRANSPORTATION OFFICER. Then he whirled around and searched desperately through the crowd.

He was looking for a certain soldier, a certain familiar face. And then, past the shoulder of a young sailor embracing an older woman in a mink coat, Leo found him.

MacGowan.

Far across the station with his officers, entering the gate for the Washington, D.C., train. Leo rushed after him and onto the platform. MacGowan, a distance ahead, walked briskly, his eyes fixed on the numbers on the stainless-steel sides of the passenger cars.

"General!" Leo shouted.

MacGowan turned. He regarded Leo unhappily.

"I have to see you," Leo said. He paused to catch his breath. "It's important."

MacGowan peered at him an instant, then at a bespectacled major beside him, then back at Leo. "My train's leaving."

"Please, it's important."

MacGowan peered at him again, annoyed now, but then addressed the major. "I'll be with you in a second." The major and the others boarded the train. MacGowan faced Leo.

"That boy I was with," Leo said. "That's my son. He's an aviation cadet—"

"—nice-looking boy," MacGowan said impatiently.

"—he's in trouble," Leo said, and explained. MacGowan listened impassively.

"Yes, I would say he most decidedly is in trouble," MacGowan said when Leo finished. Behind them a conductor called, "All aboard!"

"I need your help," Leo said.

"I can't help," MacGowan said. "He's AWOL."

The major appeared in the car doorway. He tapped his wristwatch. "General . . . !"

"Listen to me," Leo said. He strained for control. Part of him wanted to threaten, part wanted to plead. "This is his whole life. It'll be ruined. They'll wash him out for sure."

"They should," said MacGowan. The corners of his mouth turned sardonically down; he seemed almost amused. "This is one situation you can't buy your way out of, Mr. Gorodetsky."

Leo said, "I once did you a favor. For your son. I need one now for mine."

MacGowan's eyes hardened. Leo knew he resented being reminded on an old debt, but also knew MacGowan considered that particular marker paid long ago.

"Do you want me to get down on my hands and knees and beg?" Leo said. "Is that what you want!"

MacGowan said nothing. The conductor climbed up into the car doorway, ready to give the signal to move.

"He's lived with his mother since he was eight," Leo said. "I only see him occasionally. He came to me for help."

"I can't do anything for you, Gorodetsky," MacGowan said. "You should know better than to even ask."

"General, please," Leo said. "Help me. Please!" He did not want to say this, and had promised himself not to, but now could not stop himself. While all this rushed through his mind, he and MacGowan were looking at each other, both in that moment back in Paris, in the hotel room where Leo delivered the pathetic young lieutenant to his father.

MacGowan walked over to the conductor. He spoke tersely, pointing to his watch. The conductor shook his head in exasperation, but stepped down from the car. MacGowan returned to Leo.

"Come with me," he said.

They hurried through the station to the provost marshal's office. At the door, MacGowan stopped. "I'm not sure I can get him off," he said. "You understand that? I'll have to pull rank, and I don't know if it'll work with these people. I don't even know who they are."

"Whether you do it or not," Leo said, "I appreciate it. Now, for sure, we're even."

Once more Leo saw that hard, cold look in MacGowan's eyes. "I'm not doing it to repay a favor," MacGowan said levelly. "And I'm not doing it for you. I'm doing it for your boy, because I think you're right: this will ruin his life." The eyes softened suddenly. "I know what that means. Wait here."

Leo waited. Two minutes, then five. I have lost, he thought. He recognized the feeling, the helplessness of losing. The sure knowledge of it deep in your stomach and chest, and up into your head. Your brain filled with visions of revenge and vindication.

And, worse, he had groveled. Begged for mercy.

The door opened. Leo could not see Steve or MacGowan, only the two MPs, standing at parade rest before an officer seated at a desk. Then MacGowan appeared. He did not say a word, merely looked at Leo and strode past him into the station.

Leo stared after him, his mind for an uncontrollable instant flashing back to a crap game in an Orchard Street alley when he was so confident the dice would fall in his favor. He had lost then, just as he knew he lost now.

"It's okay." Steve's voice. Leo turned. Steve stood in the doorway. "It's okay," Steve said again. He waved a slip of paper. "The general vouched for me." Steve exhaled in a loud sigh of relief. "He said you and he were old friends. You soldiered together in France."

Leo savored the words, hearing them clearly over the booming, amplified voice of the station announcer reporting arrivals, departures, and track numbers.

"He's a nice guy," Steve said.

"Yes," Leo said. "Yes, he is."

And the following Monday, just as clearly as Leo had heard the train announcer's voice, Steve heard Leo's voice. Loud and clear in his earphones . . . *you can do anything you want, if you want it badly enough.*

Steve had just yanked the Stearman's stick into his belly. The little yellow biplane's nose rose. She shuddered with the loss of airspeed and airflow, and then rolled over on one wing and began spinning. That sickening spin that sent Steve's brain and stomach also spinning.

"All right!" the instructor in the front cockpit bellowed into the gosport tube. "Now pull her out!"

Steve heard nothing, not even the wind screaming through the guy wires, or the ear-shattering blast of the engine. He was paralyzed. The ground whirled before his eyes in a blurred green and white checkerboard pattern. His arms were leaden. His feet clamped to the rudder pedals were encased in steel vises.

The spin tightened.

"Jesus Christ, boy, pull out! Pull out, or I'll have to take her!"

Steve did not hear that voice. He heard Leo's voice. "You want to win, don't you?" And his own voice replying, Yes, he wanted to win. Yes, he could do it. Yes, he was a winner. Steve's right hand pushed the stick forward. His left hand moved the throttle ahead. The airplane continued spinning. Steve applied more power. She continued in a dive, but now her wings slowly straightened. Steve eased back on the stick. The airplane's nose rose. In an instant they were flying straight and level.

The instructor turned and looked at him. He saw a youngster with a wide, triumphant grin and, even through the goggles, the eyes shining with elation. The gosport intercom allowed one-way conversation only, instructor to student. But the instructor had no difficulty reading this student's lips as Steve shouted, "Can I try it again?"

The instructor replied with a thumbs-up. Steve pulled the stick back. The Stearman's nose rose. She began mushing. Steve allowed her to stall and then wing over in the spin. He counted the revolutions, two, three, four. He pushed the stick forward. The airplane straightened, nose down in a power dive. In full control now, Steve dove a moment more, then leveled out.

The instructor spoke into his mouthpiece. "Not bad, Gordon. Not bad at all."

"It's easy," Steve said.

The rest was easy, too. Steve sailed through basic, and then primary. In the top third of his class, he was allowed to select advanced training of his choice. Heavy bombers. In September of 1943, a week after his nineteenth birthday, Steve received his wings and commission as second lieutenant in the Army of the United States. He was assigned to the USAAF base at Smyrna, Tennessee, for B-24 transition.

The very first week in Smyrna Steve had a surprise visitor.

Harry.

In the vicinity on a business trip, on his way back to California from Arkansas after closing the Biltmore, the IDIC casino in Hot Springs. Local authorities pressured by the army finally forced the move. The posh casino was simply too conspicuous. So Leo sent Harry in from the Coast to supervise the job.

Harry was accompanied by the most beautiful woman Steve had ever seen.

Her name was Elizabeth DiFalco.

They took Steve to dinner in Nashville. As Steve told Leo in a phone call, Harry behaved like a love-stricken kid. All through dinner they held hands and called each other "darling," "honey," "sweetheart." Frankly, said Steve, it made him a little nauseated.

Over the phone Leo sounded incredulous. "She was *with* him?"

"I'll say," said Steve. "And, Dad, is she ever a knockout!" Leo did not reply. Steve heard him sigh wearily; it sounded almost like a groan. "Dad . . . ?"

"I know," Leo said. He sounded very tired. "I know all about it. You say they're on their way back to California?"

"On the train," Steve said. "Harry said he was glad he couldn't get a plane. He said a couple of days on a train with Liz was like a year on a desert island."

"He's going back to L.A. with her?" Leo asked again.

"Yes, Dad, L.A. What's the matter?"

"Nothing, kid," Leo said. "Nothing at all. How're the B-24s?"

"Great. I honest to God love it. I love those big airplanes."

"Keep 'em flying," Leo said.

After they hung up, and Steve was back in his room at the BOQ, he thought about Liz DiFalco and Harry. He really envied Harry. But he wondered why Leo sounded so surprised learning Liz was with Harry, and so concerned about their returning to California.

Steve would have been surprised himself had he known that the instant he finished speaking with his father, Leo booked a flight to California. He wanted to be there before Harry and Liz arrived. He wanted to be there to meet them.

— 20 —

THE last person Harry expected to see at Union Station—and the first he did see—was Leo. A stolid, solitary figure in the midst of soldiers and sailors streaming off the *El Capitán*, all hurrying past him down the tunneled concrete ramp to the depot. One look at Leo's face, Harry knew he was in trouble.

"We got a welcoming committee," he said to Liz.

She tensed. "Danny?"

"Just as bad," Harry said. "Leo."

She relaxed. She smiled. "The big man?"

"The big little man," Harry said. "And with a hair across his ass. I can tell."

"What's he doing in L.A.?" Liz asked.

"What the hell do you think?" Harry said. "To read me the riot act. I told you everybody's in a uproar about us."

"Fuck them," she said.

"In spades," Harry agreed. He gazed at her; she was so tall they were almost at eye level. "Jesus, I love that suit!"

"So do I, sweet." It was a tailored, white-linen suit that heightened the rich blackness of her hair. "All right, so let's go see what's on the big little man's mind."

Harry placed his arm protectively around Liz's shoulder; holding her close, they went, as one, to meet Leo.

When Leo sent Harry to Hot Springs to close the casino, he never dreamed Harry would be foolish enough to take Liz DiFalco with him. She was Danny Esposito's girl. Danny, for the past three years Boss of Bosses in Southern California, cooperating with Harry fully and peaceably. And they actually were good friends; after all, Harry had endorsed him with the Council for the L.A. top job.

But now, in the late spring of 1944, the friendship suddenly ruptured, and Los Angeles was in turmoil.

Because of the lady named Liz.

Even in a town where Walter Winchell said beautiful women outnumbered the palm trees, Elizabeth DiFalco was outstanding. Tall, proud of her tallness, that lustrous black hair in a pageboy style deliberately defying popular fashion, with wide-set, huge dark eyes in a strong, angular, perfectly contoured face. Her poise and presence were almost regal. She knew who she was, and where she was going; and, at twenty-seven, she had been everywhere and done everything.

The illegitimate daughter of a Flint, Michigan, housemaid, her childhood was spent in various Catholic foster homes on the upper Michigan peninsula. Her earliest recollection was the dank, acrid, cabbagelike odor of light housekeeping. As a young girl she constantly yearned for the clothes and cars and good life she read about in magazines or saw in motion pictures.

She was a fifteen-year-old child in the body of a twenty-five-year-old woman when she ran away with a traveling shoe salesman who turned out to be a bank robber. His name was George Duval. Liz liked the name, certainly more than her own. Liz Duval sounded far more interesting than Elizabeth Rademacher. And her life, too, was far more interesting. She loved the excitement, the action, the danger.

George Duval became part of her past one afternoon outside a bank in a small Kansas town. Waiting for him in a parked Chevrolet sedan, Liz saw two police cars drive up behind her. Policemen scrambled out, some blocking the bank exits, others rushing inside. They completely ignored the Chevrolet and the grim young woman at the wheel. So she calmly drove off. By the time George Duval decided five years in prison preferable to a morgue slab and surrendered, Liz was ten miles away.

She immediately took up with another gang, and then another, and then a man who brought her to Chicago. Soon she was the girlfriend of a former Capone sub-boss, Edward Bonaventura, who fell desperately in love with her. Although Bonaventura would have gladly abandoned his wife and family for her, home or family was not what Liz wanted. What she wanted, in addition to the good life, was an education. Bonaventura financed a series of expensive tutors and two years of night extension courses at the University of Chicago, along with elocution lessons to enhance her naturally low, throaty voice, and a luxurious five-room lakefront apartment.

Under the canopied entrance of this apartment building, early one cold windy November morning in 1940, Edward Bonaventura was gunned down.

Liz turned up in California that same year, with a new name, DiFalco, and a new boyfriend. Danny Esposito. For nearly two years they were a happy couple. Until Danny brought her to the S.S. *Californian* for the gala party celebrating the ship's wartime retirement. Harry described the first instant he and Liz saw each other as an explosion. As though all the stars in the sky suddenly glowed, and bands played, and thousands cheered. Harry managed to somehow control himself then, and for a long time afterward. It was at another party, hosted by Harry at the Ambassador Hotel, that it all began in earnest.

Mickey Goldfarb's welcome-home party.

Corporal Mickey Goldfarb, U.S. Marine Corps. More accurately, *ex*-corporal. Always welcoming a fight, Mickey enlisted as a marine before the draft board caught up with him. Wounded at Guadalcanal—and awarded a Bronze Star for meritorious service—he was separated from the service early in 1944 with a medical discharge and a lifelong limp.

Five minutes after they were reintroduced at this party, and once again looked into each other's eyes, Harry whispered into Liz's ear a single, succinct question.

"You ever been fucked in an elevator?"

Three minutes later, Harry paid an elevator boy twenty dollars to stop his car between floors and climb the hell out. Ten seconds after that, in the elevator car, he and Liz were ripping off each other's clothes.

The following evening Liz broke a date with Danny. She had dinner with Harry that night, and the next two nights as well. Danny at first asked Harry politely, and in all friendship, to back off. Harry politely refused. He had never known such a woman. She was all his dreams and fantasies come true. All rolled into one gorgeous creature just wild about Harry.

Danny Esposito had no intention of losing her. Forsaking pride, Danny warned Harry that unless he dropped Liz, IDIC could expect no further cooperation from Danny's people and contacts.

Harry did not take him seriously. Leo did.

At Union Station, watching them approach, Leo cursed himself for allowing Harry too much credit for brains. At the same time, however, he certainly could understand Harry's interest in this woman.

She was absolutely charming. And intelligent. Well-read, well-informed. All the way back to Beverly Hills, her remarks mainly directed at Leo, she discussed the war. An Allied invasion of France this year probably depended on the Italian campaign; if we remained bogged down there, Eisenhower would surely send his soldiers to France. Much depended on the Russians as well. If they continued pushing west, then we had to move before they overran the entire continent.

Harry's proud eyes were fixed on Liz. "Tell him about the Japs, baby," Harry said to her; and to Leo, "She knows her stuff, huh?"

Leo said, "You should join the army, Miss DiFalco. You'd be a great asset."

"I'm more valuable on the home front, Mr. Gorodetsky," she said. She touched Harry's cheek. "Keeping up civilian morale."

Harry said, "Hey, Leo, you know what else she found out? In the army, every single month, the GIs gamble over two hundred and fifty million dollars! Every month! Two hundred and fifty *million*!" He shook his head sadly. "And we don't see a goddam cent of it."

"Where did you get that figure?" Leo asked her.

"It's in the *Congressional Record*," Liz said.

"It's wrong," Leo said. "A hundred million. If that much."

Liz bowed her head in acknowledgment. "I defer to the expert."

Harry wrapped his arm around her shoulders and pulled her close. "She's something, huh, Kleyner?"

"She sure is," Leo said, looking straight at her. Their eyes met, and held. Hers were cold, hard, with a message that she recognized the enemy and was prepared for battle.

"I hope we'll be friends, Mr. Gorodetsky," she said.

"I'm sure we will be, Miss DiFalco," he said.

"Call me Liz," she said.

Mickey awaited them at the Roxbury Drive house with drinks and appetizers. Here, another small surprise awaited Leo, although on reflection it really was not that surprising. Shortly before leaving for Hot Springs, Liz had moved out of her Hollywood apartment and in with Harry.

After a few minutes of small talk and inside jokes about the home-front difficulty of obtaining genuine blended whiskey, Liz excused herself to change for dinner.

"Give you and Harry a chance to talk business," she said. "I'm sure that's what you came to see him about."

"That's exactly why," said Leo.

She smiled confidently. "Be my guest, Mr. Gorodetsky."

"Call me Leo," he said.

"Something, ain't she?" Harry said, as she swept up the stairs. "Okay, Leo, let's get it over with."

"Let's go outside," Leo said.

They went out to the patio. Harry sprawled in a thickly upholstered recliner while Leo drew up a straight-backed lawn chair. Leo started speaking, then glanced sourly at Mickey who hovered nearby. Mickey mumbled something about fixing dinner and hurried back into the house.

Abruptly, Leo said, "Did you know she lived with Eddie Bonaventura?"

"She didn't live with him," Harry said calmly.

"All right, he kept her," Leo said. "You like that better?"

"You did some research, I think."

"I did a lot of it," Leo said. "She met Danny in Chicago, when she was still with Bonaventura. There's even talk she set Bonaventura up."

Harry's eyes flashed with anger. "That's bullshit!"

"She was cheating on Bonaventura with Danny," Leo said. "And he didn't like it."

"Leo, did you come all the way out here just to tell me that? You wasted a trip."

I am going about this the wrong way, Leo thought. But then, what is the right way? Is there a right way? He said, "I came here to tell you it has to stop."

Harry drank down his drink and studied Leo over the rim of the glass. "That an order, Leo?"

"A request," said Leo. "Maybe even a plea."

"Then I got to tell you, Leo," Harry said in the same quiet voice, "I got to ask you . . . to please mind your own business."

"Well, Harry, that's the word. Business."

"Yeah, I know. It's bad for business."

"You knew that going in, goddamit!"

Harry regarded him indignantly a moment, then all at once smiled. Leo, too, had to smile. The same thought had occurred to them simultaneously. Harry said, "All I knew 'going in,' Kleyner, was I never wanted to come out."

"You're going to have to come out, Harry," Leo said. "You've made a fool of Danny Esposito. He'll go after you. There'll be blood and bodies all over the place."

"Maybe that's a good thing. Maybe it's time we did a little spring cleaning out here."

"Now I know your brains are all in your *shlong*! You and Danny start a war, it brings in the police, and everything gets closed up. Then we have to answer to the Council. And Harry, have no illusions about us and the Alliance. They want all our operations, all IDIC, under total Alliance control. Only the other day Vinnie Tomasino said it was like some independent army working inside the United States Army. It's under the army's protection, but not subject to its orders. He says 'How the hell can you run a war that way?' So we're walking on razor blades, Harry. You keep this up, you fall off. We both do."

Harry looked at him a moment, then shouted, "Mickey!" Immediately, Mickey appeared at the patio door. "Get me another drink," Harry said to him. "What about you?" he asked Leo.

"I'm fine," Leo said, and Mickey vanished inside. Leo said to Harry, "Do I have to say more?"

"You already said enough, Leo."

Leo fell silent now, wondering how to get through to him, and wondering how a grown man became so love struck. A kid, yes, not a mature, experienced adult. Sure, he told himself, but who ever accused Harry Wise of maturity? I see, he answered himself, Harry is immature because he falls in love, while you are mature because you do not fall in love. And could not now, not in a million years. But even as he thought this, he realized he envied Harry.

He hardly heard Harry's voice. ". . . okay."

"Okay, what?" Leo asked.

"Okay, it'll stop."

"Just like that?"

"Yeah, Leo, just like that."

"Why?"

"Why?" Harry repeated, almost offended. "Because she's just another cunt. The town's full of 'em, ain't it? If it's bad for business, then fuck her." He laughed once more. "Without the loving, I mean."

Leo knew Harry was sincere. The unexpected turnabout was not merely to get Leo off his back. Even for his own selfish motives, Harry's pride and ego prohibited him from allowing anyone even the momentary belief they had cowed, conned, or subdued him.

Leo suspected another motive.

Las Vegas.

Problems with the Council might spell problems with Las Vegas. Harry was determined to build the Barclay. Nothing would interfere, certainly not a woman.

Now, as Mickey brought Harry's fresh drink, Leo said, "Don't lie to me, Harry. Please."

Harry was grim. "How long we known each other?"

"Okay," Leo said. "But don't waste any time."

"You ready for dinner, Leo?" Mickey asked.

Leo rose. "I think I can make a plane if I get out there and wait."

"We're barbecuing steaks," Mickey said. "I got this butcher that's in to me for a fortune." He rolled his eyes. "Unluckiest horseplayer I ever seen."

"Drive him to the airport, Mick!" Harry said.

The anger in Harry's voice startled Mickey. "Jesus, Harry, what's all the panic?"

"Just do it," Harry said, quieter. He rose and shook Leo's hand. "Have a good flight." He turned and walked into the house.

"What'd I say?" Mickey asked.

"You didn't say anything," Leo said. "I did."

"Oh."

They entered the garage directly from the patio. As Mickey backed the Cord into the driveway, he said, "Hey, you didn't say good-bye to Liz."

"Harry will say good-bye for me," Leo said.

Harry fixed a tall gin fizz for Liz and brought it upstairs. She was in the bathtub, reading, lounging under a layer of thick white suds. The room smelled of the lavender bath salts and Liz's perfume—and Liz.

He glanced into the mirror over the sink and carefully ruffled his hair to cover the widening area of scalp in front. He did not care about getting gray, but baldness terrified him. "Honey, I got something to tell you," he said.

"I'll just bet," she said, not looking up.

He removed the book from her hand and placed it atop the bamboo bathtub caddy. He placed the gin-fizz glass atop the book. "*A Bell for Adano*. I knew a guy named Adano once. Used to work for Sal."

"This Adano is a town," she said. "In Italy." Her soaped hand drew a foamy line of suds down the side of his cheek. Her very touch excited him. "I heard a car drive off."

"Mickey drove Leo to the airport."

"He wouldn't stay for dinner?"

"He couldn't. Hey, you're getting me all wet!"

"Do you mind?" She placed her other hand around his neck and pulled him down to her. They kissed. Her lips were soft, and firm, and filled with her fragrance. "I don't think he likes me," she said when they broke away.

"Leo? Are you kidding? He's crazy about you. Honest."

"I just bet." She began unbuttoning his fly. "You wanted to tell me something?"

Harry closed his eyes and drew in his breath. He was nestled in her palm, her soapy fingers sliding up and down, around the tip, lingering, then smoothly down the entire length of the shaft to the base, lingering, then back up again. And down, up, down. He decided to wait until Mickey returned from the airport before telling her. They would have dinner. After dinner, over a brandy, he would tell her.

An hour later Mickey returned. He said Leo had a seat on a TWA plane at least as far as Kansas City. The flight would not leave until ten, nearly three hours, but Leo said he didn't mind waiting at the airport, and sent Mickey back. He said he thought Harry might need Mickey around.

"What'd he mean by that?" Mickey asked.

"He thought maybe I'd be lonely," Harry said. They had finished dinner and were in the living room in front of the fire. Liz was in the kitchen making coffee. Harry had prepared his speech. Short and sweet. He loved her, and always would, but for a lot of good reasons it simply wasn't to be. She'd understand. Okay, let's get it over with.

From the kitchen, Liz called, "Black, darling, or cream and sugar tonight?"

The sound of her voice inspired a new thought. "Listen, let's go to the Troc for coffee," he said. "You and me, and Mick." In the nick of time he had realized that a nightclub provided the proper atmosphere. It just happened that Liz felt like going out that night. Leo's visit had unnerved her. She wanted to relax.

At 8:30, still daylight, Mickey pulled the Cord up behind a Chrysler limousine and a LaSalle convertible in the Trocadero parking lot. It was a large parking lot, in back of the building with a concrete stairway leading directly to the Troc's rear entrance. Liz and Harry got out of the Cord and followed several couples in formal dress toward the stairway. Mickey remained behind to give the valet a ten-dollar bill and instructions to wash and gas up the car. He peeled a "C" ration stamp from an inch-thick filled booklet. These were counterfeit stamps, obtained from the same butcher of the meat points, and of such quality that in six months none had been questioned.

"And keep one for yourself," Mickey added, presenting the boy a stamp. At that instant a car raced into parking lot and came to a brake-screeching stop.

Danny Esposito jumped from the front seat. "Liz!" he called, and strode across the lot toward Harry and Liz at the foot of the stairway. Two of Danny's men scrambled from the car after him. At the very top of the stairs, both of the formally attired couples stopped to watch the commotion.

Mickey hurried to the scene, arriving as Danny brushed Harry aside to face Liz. "I have to talk to you, Liz," Danny said.

Harry said, "Fuck off, Danny."

Danny ignored him. "Liz, we have to talk."

"Honey, there's nothing to talk about," she said. "It's over."

"Liz . . ." Danny said. He reached for her.

Harry blocked Danny's hand. "You don't hear so good, Danny. Tell him again," he said to Liz.

"Danny, please," said Liz. "We're finished."

"I only want to talk to you," Danny said.

"Go home, Danny," Harry said quietly, almost in a whisper.

Now the two faced each other. Danny's men were positioned slightly behind him, themselves facing Mickey whose hand rested just inside his jacket. Another couple had driven into the parking lot and gotten out of their car, but now stood uncertainly a few feet away. The valet was writing their license-plate number on a claim ticket.

Liz said, "We'd like to go upstairs and enjoy the show, Danny." She tucked her hand under Harry's arm and both started away.

"I never knew you went for seconds, Harry," Danny said.

Harry stopped. Liz seized his arm, but he shrugged her off. Danny waited smugly for Harry's response; he felt quite secure with his men present.

"You didn't mean that, did you?" Harry asked him.

"About seconds?" Danny said. "Yeah, I meant it. It was always so wet in there, I always used to wonder myself. You know, if maybe somebody wasn't there just ahead of me. But I've heard of guys that go for that. I guess you do, too, huh?"

Harry hit him flush in the mouth. It almost resembled a ballet. Danny staggered backward. Harry stepped after him. Liz screamed, "Harry, no!" Danny's men stepped sideways, each reaching into his jacket. Mickey's hand flushed out with a .38 trained on the two men. "Don't none of you cocksuckers move!"

The men froze. Harry said to Danny, "I want you to apologize to Liz for what you said."

"Apologize to a whore?" Danny said. "Fuck you, and her, too!"

Very calmly, almost delicately, Harry plucked the .38 from Mickey's fingers, leveled it at Danny's stomach and fired. Two shots, so rapid, so smooth, both sounded as one. The impact hurtled Danny backward, but even before his body struck the metal stairway banister, Harry had swiveled the .38 around on the two bodyguards.

"Freeze!" he said, and already Mickey had moved forward to disarm them. Mickey hurled the weapons into the parking lot. Both couples at the top of the stairs stood petrified, one woman's hand clamped to her mouth. The other couple, still standing with the valet near their car in the parking lot, also watched, awed. The claim ticket slipped from the valet's fingers and fluttered to the ground.

Danny lay on the concrete stairway landing, one hand clutching the banister rail, the other outstretched. His open eyes stared unseeingly. His mouth was also open, jaw slack as though awaiting a dentist's probe. The front of his beige jacket was soaked with blood. In the twilight, under the diffused glare of the single parking-lot floodlight, it gleamed dully black.

"Nobody saw nothing!" Mickey shouted. "Blow!" He shouted up to the couple at the door. "You didn't see a thing! Harry, get the hell out of here!" he continued in the same breath, taking the gun from Harry and leveling it on the bodyguards.

Harry grasped Liz's hand and rushed across the parking lot toward the white Cord. They got in and drove off. The Cord's retractable headlights swept up and out from the fenders. When Mickey saw the headlights swinging west on Sunset, he waved the gun at Danny's body, and said to the men, "Get him the fuck out of here!"

It was too late.

Two siren-screaming, light-flashing police cars rolled into the parking lot. Six uniformed policemen rushed out with drawn guns. Already, Mickey's hands were raised, the .38 dangling harmlessly from one finger crooked into the trigger guard.

"Jesus!" said one policeman. "It's Danny Esposito!" He took the gun from Mickey. "What the hell happened?"

"I really ain't sure," Mickey said. "Am I under arrest?"

At Lockheed Air Terminal Leo's flight, delayed twice in the past four hours, was scheduled for a midnight departure. He had passed the time reading and watching airplanes—night fighters from the Lockheed factory—landing and taking off. He also phoned Steve in Smyrna. Steve expected to be checked out shortly as a B-24 copilot and assigned to an active squadron.

Just after midnight Leo's flight was finally called. Through the terminal's glassed doors, beyond the canopied walkway to the departure gate, he saw the big airliner parked on the ramp. A TWA DC-3, with red scripted letters above the fuselage windows: *The Lindberg Line*. Baggage was being loaded into the little cargo door behind the cockpit.

Diagonally opposite the terminal door was the airport newsstand. As Leo approached, a stocky young woman wearing blue coveralls crossed the terminal floor with a stack of newspapers on her shoulder. They all looked like stevedores these days, Leo thought idly, watching her slam the bundle down at the newsstand.

It was the morning edition of the *Los Angeles Times*. The headline read:

MOBSTER ESPOSITO SLAIN!

Leo did not even break stride. He wheeled around and walked back to the ticket counter and canceled his seat. Two hours later, at the Beverly Hills jail, he posted a $5,000 bond for Mickey Goldfarb.

Mickey was charged as an accessory. His gun had killed Danny Esposito. Mickey insisted Harry shot Danny accidentally and in self defense. Danny's men swore it was cold-blooded murder. The recollections of the half-dozen other witnesses were all somewhat vague. The only point of agreement was that Harry had indeed pulled the trigger.

Harry and Liz, despite a statewide APB, had simply vanished. Leo suspected them holed up at some nearby beach, probably a friend's house, but he knew Harry would eventually attempt to contact either him or Mickey.

It happened sooner than Leo expected, the very next afternoon. A call from Ensenada. Harry and Liz were staying at a charming little hotel, with a view of the ocean like a painting in a museum, and marvelous food. As far as Harry was concerned, he might stay there forever,

"... and, Kleyner," he said to Leo on the phone, "I got to tell you something. I ain't going to lose her. No matter what you say, or the Council, or the fucking President of the United States! Leo, she means more to me than money, than friends, than even life. *Die helst?* Leo? You hear me?"

"I hear you," Leo said.

"What are we gonna do?" Mickey asked when Leo hung up.

"Nothing," Leo said. "We let him rot there!"

"No, Leo, you got to do something. Danny's guys'll figure out where he is. I bet even right now they're down there trying to find him. Two Anglos can't stay stashed forever. They stand out like a sore thumb, for Christ's sake!"

Leo said nothing. He hated Harry for his stupidity, his cupidity, his arrogance, and Leo's mind reeled with the problems all this had created. But he knew he would save him, and he hated himself, too, for that weakness.

". . . and them greaseball cops," Mickey was saying. "They'll suck him dry for payoff money because the cops up here'll be squeezing for extra—what do they call it when they want somebody back? Extra-something?"

"Extradition," Leo said.

"Yeah, that's it." He shook his head mournfully. "I should have stayed in the fucking Marines."

Leo said nothing. In his mind he saw Mickey in Marine uniform, and then Steve in his Air Force uniform. And then Martin Raab, now an officer on Eisenhower's staff, who could do everybody a favor by going over to France in the invasion Liz DiFalco said was sure to come soon. In the first wave, Leo hoped, perplexed that his mind wandered this way. He knew why. To keep from thinking about crazy Harry and his crazy love affair.

". . . go down there and help him," Mickey was saying. "He needs me."

"What?"

"I said maybe I should get my ass down to Ensenada."

"Sure," Leo said. "And jump your bail. That's all we need." He got up and looked around for his coat. "Drive me back to the airport, Mick."

Mickey was shocked. "Leo, you can't leave at a time like this!"

"I'll give you odds that right now, in New York, Vinnie Tomasino is talking to everybody on that Council about putting out a contract on Harry," Leo said. "You just sit tight until you hear from me."

Leo was right. Two days later in New York, he was summoned to Vincent Tomasino's Long Beach home. The Council had given Vinnie carte blanche to deal with Harry. Out of courtesy, Vinnie delayed issuing the order until he spoke with Leo. Leo reminded him that disciplinary action could not be taken without unanimous approval.

"It doesn't hold in this case, Leo. I'm sorry."

"Because an Italian was hit?"

Vinnie turned away and gazed at the French doors at the far end of the living room. The doors faced the garden and were open on this warm day. In the distance Leo saw Vinnie's seventeen-year-old daughter, a tiny, frail thing, bearing little resemblance to Vinnie, who was tall and heavy-framed. But then Leo recalled Vinnie's wife, also petite. Quite the opposite in Leo's case. Carla, now fourteen, was very tall, like Ellie.

"That's her boyfriend," Vinnie said, as a young soldier stepped into view with the girl. Vinnie shook his head, as though his daughter having a boyfriend displeased him. Or at least this particular boy.

They were holding hands, laughing. A strange sight, Leo thought, remembering the cars in the driveway and the three or four grim young men standing watch. Leo wondered idly why they were not in uniform. And then thought they *were* in uniform: the same wide-brimmed fedoras and unbuttoned topcoats.

"Wouldn't matter what Harry was," Vinnie said now. "Italian, Jew, what." He turned to Leo again. "Wouldn't make any difference."

"Who's taking over in L.A.?" Leo asked. He knew, but wanted to sound surprised at the reply.

"Vito Mancuso," Vinnie said. "He's on his way out there right now."

"Vito, your Vito?" Vito Mancuso was Vinnie's son-in-law, married to the elder Tomasino daughter. Leo had attended their wedding three years before and given them a thousand-dollar check as a gift.

"Yeah, Leo, my Vito. It's his chance. He earned it."

"I don't have to remind you, Vinnie, it was me who arranged his draft exemption," Leo said. "My judge, remember?"

"One thing got nothing to do with the other, Leo."

Not much, Leo thought, and decided he had no choice but play the hole card. He said, "I'll give Vito twenty percent of the wire."

Vinnie studied him narrowly. "Thirty," he said.

Leo felt all the tension and worry of the past days drain away. "You Sicilian bastard!" he said good-naturedly. "You never were serious about a hit. You only wanted to *hondle* some more points out of us!"

"Hey, I learned from you, Leo."

Leo thought, I'll say you learned from me. You learned well, too. He had suddenly realized that nothing could have been more to Vincent Tomasino's advantage than Harry killing Danny Esposito. It opened the way for Vinnie's son-in-law.

He said, "Twenty-five percent, Vinnie, that's all we can afford."

Vinnie nodded. "Deal."

They shook hands, and Leo said, "You're a good father-in law."

"You're a good friend," Vinnie said. "To go to the wall for that nutty, cunt-crazy wild man." Vinnie spoke with the same, friendly smile, but now it faded. "But Leo, next time it won't be so easy. Harry never won no popularity contest with us, you know that. From here on he better watch his step. He slips again, he gets the families pissed off at him again, you won't be able to save him, Leo."

Leo said nothing. He knew Vinnie was serious.

"All right, so you squared it with us, but how do you square it with the West Coast cops?" Vinnie asked. "How do you get them off his back?"

That, Leo thought, was a real sixty-four-dollar question. As Mickey Goldfarb said, Harry could not stay stashed in Mexico forever. Sooner or later the Beverly Hills police would find and extradite him. He had to get away, far away, and stay away until it all blew over.

". . . kind of a problem, huh?" Vinnie was saying. Clearly, a problem he found not displeasing.

Leo glanced out at the garden at Angelica Tomasino and her young soldier. A nice-looking boy, Leo thought, as the soldier just then looked at him with a shy smile. Leo returned the smile. He did not know it, and realized it only weeks later in Havana, but the answer to the question, the solution to Harry's problem, was staring him in the face.

2.

The olive-drab paint of the big airplane parked near the end of the runway blended in with the brown foliage of the Havana hills in the background. It was a C-87, the transport version of a B-24, which, as Leo told the young American pilot, was the same plane his son flew.

"They're cranky old ladies," the pilot had said. He was a captain who did not look much older than Steve. But then they were all so damned young.

"That's just what my son says."

"They get you there, though, and they get you back," said the pilot, and dryly added, "Most of the time."

It better be all the time, Leo thought, as the embassy station wagon drove through the airport gate and swung onto the highway. He glanced out the station wagon's rear window for a final glimpse of the airplane. The side of a hangar slowly obscured the block letters decaled atop the fuselage, AIR TRANSPORT COMMAND, and the ATC emblem, a pylon superimposed on a lineal projection of a world globe.

The station-wagon driver was a middle-aged, well-dressed Cuban in suit and tie. Like the C-87 pilot, he presumed Leo to be a high official on an important mission. As the pilot said, ". . . you have to be somebody important to rate being flown down here on an ATC airplane."

"All in the eye of the beholder," Leo had modestly replied.

Eye of the beholder, he thought, remembering smiling to himself when he said it, a phrase borrowed from MacGowan, the person responsible for Leo's being here in the first place.

On a diplomatic mission.

Leo Gorodetsky, diplomat.

More accurately, Leo Gorodetsky, trusted friend, confidant, and business associate of Cuban President Fulgencio Batista. It was this convenient relationship that just five days before had inspired General MacGowan to once more seek Leo Gorodetsky's assistance. It was becoming a series of quid pro quos between them, which amused Leo. Quid pro quo, also MacGowan's phrase. The quid, as he said, or pro, being a certain service recently rendered Leo by the general. Of course, the particular assistance he presently required—this "diplomatic mission"—would also serve Leo's interests, which was why he believed Leo most qualified to carry it out.

It was on the flight from Washington's Bolling Field to Havana, chatting with the flight engineer, that Leo realized he had the answer to Harry's problem. The flight engineer was a grizzled old master sergeant with a chestful of World War I ribbons and hashmark-filled sleeve, and

Leo had casually remarked on having served in the first war himself.

"I was with the Seventy-seventh," he said, suddenly regretting not wearing the little enameled Croix de Guerre lapel ribbon, mislaid years ago in the confusion of moving from the Hempstead house. "We were at the Aisne, and Saint-Mihiel."

"How about that?" said the master sergeant. "I was with the One hundred thirty-fifth Aero Squadron. They flew the old DH-4s, the ones they called Flying Coffins. And I guess they were."

"I'll bet our paths crossed more than once," Leo said. "You stayed in?"

"No, I got out in '18. Went back to Minneapolis and opened my own garage for a while. When it went bust I took a mechanic's job with an airline. I came back in right after Pearl Harbor. They were glad to have me, I'll tell you."

Leo fully expected the master sergeant to ask why he, Leo, had not volunteered to serve again—although he had certainly registered for the draft—and he was composing replies in his mind when he realized the master sergeant considered him a civilian VIP, far more valuable than a retread doughboy.

It was at that moment the idea struck him. The way to get Harry off the hook. And, in Major General Robert MacGowan, the means to make it possible.

Quid pro quo.

But before Leo negotiated that, he wanted to succeed with his mission here in Cuba. Then he would have bargaining strength. He said to the driver now, "You're taking me straight to the palace?"

"Yes, sir," said the driver. "Those are my instructions."

"Good," said Leo, and sat back to enjoy the drive. The usual cooling late-afternoon breeze was blowing in from the ocean, which reminded him of Sal's fondness for this time of day. Thinking of Sal, he laughed to himself. Sal would never believe this one.

Leo Gorodetsky, diplomat.

For years Leo had urged Fulgencio Batista to assume his rightful place as president of the republic. Not only was it the general's destiny, it would also once and for all secure IDIC's position as a full—if silent—partner of the Cuban government.

In 1940, with the assistance of an IDIC lump-sum $500,000 campaign contribution, Batista arranged to have himself elected president.

Now, four years later, his term up, Batista faced a new election. Serious opposition was anticipated, but Batista had formed a coalition with the Cuban communists that would defeat the opposition. The United States government strongly disapproved of this coalition. MacGowan had selected Leo to convey that message to Batista, and offer an alternative strategy.

Leo, maker of presidents.

Batista, expansive this lovely early summer afternoon, was delighted to see his old friend and business associate. His eye of course immediately fell to Leo's hand, the hand usually carrying the briefcase but empty today.

"So," Batista said, when they were seated comfortably on the palace patio with drinks. "What is this urgent message you carry? And why is it so confidential you wish me to be without my translator?" He smiled, displaying his white, even teeth, another contribution from Leo (via Leo's own Park Avenue dentist, at $2,500 per visit, not including transportation, living expenses, and a $10,000 casino line of credit).

"As you know, Your Excellency, I am here on behalf of the United States government," Leo said, deciding to get straight to the heart of it. "Frankly, General, they are very concerned about the election."

"They sent *you* to tell me this?"

"Yes, I suppose it is a little like sending the Devil."

"I meant no offense," Batista said. "But I'm sure you'll agree that your function as an official emissary does appear somewhat peculiar."

Which, Leo remembered, was also his impression when MacGowan first proposed the mission. The United States government was indeed desperate, Leo had wryly commented, asking the "Devil" to perform a service for his country. If the Devil suits my purpose, MacGowan said, I use him.

"My position is unofficial," Leo said to Batista, emphasizing the word. "They sent me because they know I enjoy your friendship and trust. And because our personal interests here in Cuba, yours and mine, coincide."

"What has that to do with the election?"

"If your government falls, then my hotels are endangered," Leo said. "That's an investment of perhaps twenty million dollars."

"You have little to worry about, then," Batista said. His teeth flashed again, in a smile of self-confidence that dismayed Leo; it would not make the task any easier.

Leo said, "General, the United States government wishes you to renounce the Cuban Communist party."

Batista's smile faded. "That is the message?"

"Yes, sir."

"You can't be serious?"

"Yes, sir, I'm afraid I am."

Batista, studying Leo's impassive face, realized Leo was indeed serious. "How can it not be obvious to the Americans that only by allowing the communists to participate in my government, only in this manner, have I kept them in check?"

"The United States believes that once the election is won, the communists will attempt a coup," Leo said. "The people in Washington say you have ignored their repeated warnings about this."

Batista's mouth hardened. "Those so called 'warnings' are composed of nothing more than imagination and misinformation."

But the voice lacked conviction. It reminded Leo of bust-out gamblers requesting additional credit. A certain quaver, an almost imperceptible change of pitch. It told Leo what he wanted to know. He said, "As improbable as you may believe it to be, if the communists did try to take over, the United States government would have no choice but to exercise certain wartime prerogatives." He paused, then continued flatly, "They will be forced to occupy Cuba."

For a moment Batista seemed stunned. Then he rose and walked across the marble patio floor to the balcony rail. He stood, hands clasped behind him, his back to Leo. He said, "With troops. They would send soldiers."

Leo said, "The only way to prevent that is to renounce the communists."

Batista turned. His voice echoed weakly across the patio. "You realize I have made considerable accommodations with the communists. Cash, and patronage. Should I renounce them, they will abandon the coalition."

"And you'll lose the election," Leo said. He got up and walked over to join Batista.

Batista, looking down at Leo, said, "You are suggesting, then, that the Americans want me to lose the election? They want me out of office?"

"If you won't renounce the communists, there won't be an election," Leo said. "The Americans won't allow one."

Batista walked back to the table and sank into a lawn chair. Leo watched him, thinking, Heads you win, tails I lose. Which also meant *he*, Leo, lost. Which was why MacGowan, cleverly and cynically, dispatched Leo to deliver the message. A communist takeover, or American occupation, either one jeopardized Leo's financial interests.

Leo rejoined Batista at the table, saying, "The United States is determined to neutralize the communists here."

"Even at my expense?" Batista asked.

Leo shrugged, and said nothing, but was thinking, I must ask Liz DiFalco, who seems to know everything, about communists. But then, he thought, she probably knew no more than he did, which was that they were our allies, fighting Hitler, and that if they took over in Cuba they would almost surely close the casinos.

"The Americans want me out." Batista spoke with no anger; he sounded almost hurt.

"Yes, General, they want you out," Leo said, and added carefully, "At least until the war is over."

"Until the war is over?" Batista's voice contained a hopeful note. He had taken the bait.

Leo steeled himself for the next move, for now he had to present the plan devised by himself and MacGowan. The plan, acceptable to the

United States, that would permit the IDIC casinos to remain open. A plan MacGowan believed acceptable to Batista only if proposed by a friend standing to lose as much.

Leo said, "Step down, General. Step down, and name a replacement. Someone prominent enough to satisfy *all* parties." He took a deep breath. "Ramón Grau San Martín."

"Grau San Martín?" Batista said, pronouncing the name almost as an epithet. "The communists will never accept him!"

"The other parties will," Leo said. "The Social Democrats and every other opposition party. They'll all support Grau San Martín. He'll win easily. Without communist support."

"If I endorse him."

"He's your man," Leo said. "You own him."

"I will own him no longer if he becomes president."

"You would," said Leo. "If he understood that he sits in this palace only with American blessing, and is president in name only. Answerable to you, General. And you will be ninety miles away, General, in Florida. As soon as the war is over, you'll return to Cuba."

And, Leo said to himself, new casinos will be built, and we'll all get rich. Richer, he corrected himself. Especially you, Your Excellency, who already cannot even begin to count all your money, most of it deposited safely in Switzerland. But Leo knew—and was heavily depending on— Batista's endless greed.

Batista said, "If, as you say, Leo, you are here unofficially, what guarantee have I that when the war is over, the Americans will support my return?"

Leo cursed himself for not having raised that question with Mac-Gowan, and cursed MacGowan for not raising it. "General, you have my personal guarantee," he said, aware this was as good as no guarantee, but not knowing what else to offer. He wondered if the general understood the word *chutzpah*. He felt a sudden urge to turn and run.

". . . I must think about this, and discuss it with Mr. Braden," Batista was saying. Spruille Braden, U.S. ambassador, had never bothered to conceal his contempt and distaste for General Batista. He would guarantee Batista nothing, but Leo knew the general had already accepted the inevitable.

Batista continued talking. Leo only half heard, thinking, Diplomat. Leo Gorodetsky, diplomat. The little Delancey Street Jew. Only the cutaway and top hat were missing. Maybe, with the cutaway, he could wear a yarmulke and *tallis*.

He was abruptly aware of Batista shaking his hand and snapping a finger at a servant for champagne. Clicking the congratulatory glasses, Leo wondered how he could deliver the guarantee if the United States reneged. Well, worry about that when the time comes, he thought, and said, "Your good health, General."

"And our good fortune, Leo."

"To both, then," Leo said, and drank.

Leo's diplomatic work was not entirely finished. From the presidential palace he went, not as per instructions directly to the embassy to report to Mr. Braden, but instead to Wingy Gruber's private office at the Caribe.

To make a phone call.

To another general. MacGowan.

The call was put through immediately. "Where are you?" MacGowan asked. "What's happened?"

"Nothing yet," Leo lied. "Before I go to see Batista, there's something we have to discuss."

"Make it fast."

"Quid pro quo."

"What?"

"Quid pro quo," Leo said, and quickly, carefully, outlined his proposal: MacGowan was to pull the necessary strings for an over-age volunteer to be inducted as an enlisted man into the United States Army. Leo had toyed with the notion of insisting upon a commission for the over-age volunteer, but decided that was asking too much.

"His name," said Leo, "is Weisenfeld. Harry Weisenfeld."

For a long moment Leo heard only the hollow, static hum of the long-distance telephone cable. He regretted the coyness of using Harry's real name, which had never legally been changed. MacGowan, of all people, knew Harry Weisenfeld was Harry Wise. He would resent Leo trying to make a fool of him.

MacGowan's voice came loud and brusque in Leo's ear. "Why does he want to get into the army? I know damn well it's not out of patriotism."

"I want to get him out of sight a while," Leo said, deciding to be totally honest, although not so honest as to tell MacGowan why. And it was then—the picture of Harry and Liz popping into his mind, remembering Liz's remark about soldiers gambling $250 million monthly—that all at once he had the absolutely brilliant, second idea.

Leo continued, "Believe me, General, he can be a great asset. He can tour the camps lecturing the GIs about gambling. How to spot professionals and cheats. Have you any idea, General, of the money those boys would save? The money they'd otherwise be giving away? My God, think of the public-relations value alone!"

Another silence, and Leo thought, I must be crazy. Or stupid. Or both. For a moment he considered informing MacGowan that the Batista mission was successful, accomplished, so forget about Harry Wise's induction into the army. Forget it. Let Harry stay in Mexico a while longer; we'll figure out what to do with him somehow.

". . . isn't that like the fox guarding the chicken coop?" MacGowan was saying. But he sounded amused. Before Leo could answer, Mac-

Gowan said, "You do what you're supposed to do with your friend El Presidente, and I'll see what I can do about your other friend ... Mr. Weisenfeld."

"I'll do my best," Leo said.

"I'm sure you will," MacGowan said. "So will I."

Quid pro quo.

3.

If not the oldest private soldier in the United States Army, Private Harry I. Weisenfeld, ASN 12116683, was close to it. But, at forty-five—and, in truth, looking more like thirty-five—he was an inspiration to all soldiers. A man who served his country in the first war, volunteering once again to save the world for democracy.

". . . and the boys from card sharks!" said the young Air Force first lieutenant, completing the toast. Everyone laughed, clicked glasses, and drank.

It was the fourth toast offered by the lieutenant in the past five minutes. The first having been to Dr. Ramón Grau San Martín, the newly elected president of Cuba. The second to the newly reelected president of the United States, Franklin Delano Roosevelt, who, eleven days earlier on November 7, 1944, had won an unprecedented fourth term. The third to himself, First Lieutenant Steven Gordon, departing the very next morning to join his squadron for the flight to England.

And this fourth toast to his good friend and comrade in arms, Private Weisenfeld, was immediately followed by two more. To Liz DiFalco, whom he considered the most beautiful woman he ever knew, and the kindest: she was fixing him up that evening with a chorus-girl acquaintance.

". . . and, finally, to my father."

Steve raised his glass to Leo. The silent gesture contained more meaning and love than a ten-minute speech. Everyone raised glasses to Leo and drank.

They were at the Latin Quarter, Leo, Steve, Harry, and Liz. Harry in town on a five-day furlough, Steve en route to Presque Isle, Maine. Leo had taken them all to the nightclub to celebrate.

Six months ago when Harry was informed by Leo that only by joining the army could he beat the rap, Harry laughed and told him to get lost. He certainly did not laugh when Leo additionally informed him the price of quashing the Danny Esposito murder charge would be at least $150,000 cash, every dime to be paid from Harry's own pocket. Harry said forget that one, too: He and Liz would stay in Mexico until things cooled off. But Liz agreed with Leo. Harry in the army was the perfect solution. Harry listened to her. He always listened to her.

And it all worked out beautifully.

Even to Harry's earning a commendation from General MacGowan, who himself received a War Department commendation for his innovative suggestion to teach naïve young American soldiers how to spot cardsharps and cheaters. And what better teacher than a major-league professional gambler?

Private Weisenfeld's work was considered so vital he was designated Special Consultant to the Chief of Special Services, and not required to report for duty to any specific command or station. Each week he visited at least three army posts or air bases, his lectures so popular he was booked solid the entire year. The army generously provided him a modest per diem living allowance, which hardly covered Harry's basic expenses, and certainly not Liz's. She accompanied him from camp to camp like any faithful wife or girlfriend. As far as the Pentagon was concerned, Private Harry I. Weisenfeld contributed more to the war effort than an armored division.

Two divisions.

". . . oh, and one last thought," Steve said, offering yet another toast. "To Harry's promotion. May he be the oldest PFC in the United States Army!"

Everyone seconded the toast, then settled down for the show. When it was over Liz introduced Steve to his date for the evening, a tall red-headed showgirl named Beverly Foster.

"Chip off the old block, huh, Kleyner?" Harry said, as Steve and the redhead moved onto the dance floor. "I taught him good, just like I taught the old man."

"I think you taught him too good," Leo said. The redhead and Steve, dancing, seemed engrossed in each other.

Liz said, "He certainly doesn't waste any time."

"He doesn't have much time," Leo said.

"I taught him that, too," Harry said. "Time is money. Hey, I think I'll use that in the next lecture: Time is money. Not bad, huh?"

"Yes, darling, that's very original," Liz said. "He's one of a kind, our Harry, isn't he?" she said to Leo.

Leo nodded absently. He was thinking about his earlier conversation with Steve. Steve had spent two days with Ellie and Carla before coming to New York. He said Ellie was not feeling well, and seemed remote, detached. Steve thought she might be drinking again. Leo said he would go down and see her. He wanted to see Carla, anyway.

". . . we're pushing off, Leo," Harry was saying. He was on his feet. "I'll get your coat, baby," he said to Liz and hurried away.

Liz gazed after him a moment, then turned to Leo. "I want to thank you again."

"For what?"

"For being his friend."

Just then Steve and the redhead returned to the table. "Dad, if it's okay, we're leaving. Bev's taking me to a party at some guy's penthouse. What is he?" he asked her. "A writer?"

"A composer," she said. "Very famous. There'll be lots of celebrities."

Steve grinned. "The big time. My father always said I'd get there."

Leo rose to say good-bye. He almost said, Don't come home too late, but instead said, "See you later, kid." He shook Steve's hand and nodded politely to the girl.

"Breakfast?" Steve asked Leo.

"Sure thing," Leo said. "What time's your train?"

"Ten."

"Talk to you later, then."

Leo watched Steve and the redhead make their way past the crowded tables and the matchbox sized floor with couples dancing to "I Don't Want to Walk Without You, Baby."

"They make a nice-looking couple," Liz said.

"They're nice-looking kids," Leo said, and looked at Liz now. " 'Thank you for being his friend.' What are you trying to say?"

"I'm trying to say, Leo, that I appreciate your not interfering. I know you're not crazy about me."

Leo started to say, That's not true, but the words sounded false in his mind. He said instead, "You've been good for him."

"I love him," she said.

"I know," he said, thinking there it was again, that word *love*. That word so alien. "And you certainly don't need my approval."

"I don't," she said. "He does."

Leo said nothing. He was relieved to see Harry approach with Liz's coat. Harry draped the coat over her shoulders, a camel's hair polo coat whose style and simplicity made other women, wearing furs, garish.

Liz rose. She said to Leo, who had remained seated, "Aren't you going back to the hotel?"

"Not right away," Leo said. "I'll have another drink, I think."

"*I* think maybe you got something lined up, huh?" Harry said. He jabbed Leo's shoulder playfully.

"No such luck," Leo said. He waved his hand at the dancers. "Besides, I'm not in uniform."

"Hey, join up, then!" Harry said. "It ain't bad at all. Not like the las. time, believe me. Oh, Leo, you took care of that option?"

"Gerson sent it off," Leo said. The option was on the Las Vegas property, which had to be renewed. Leo had signed the check only that morning.

"Great," Harry said. "Leo, you should hear this little lady's plans for Vegas!" He drew Liz to him. "In the driveway, colored fountains! And a eighteen-hole golf course, and tennis courts. And a health spa!"

As Harry spoke, Liz's eyes were fixed on Leo almost challengingly. A statement of defiance. She had insinuated herself into their lives, his life, and knew he resented it.

"With a special section for women only," Liz said. "Keep the wives and girlfriends busy while their men are dropping millions."

"She's got some great ideas, Leo," Harry said. "We come a long way from the old floating crap games."

Liz said, "The Barclay will be the most luxurious casino in the world."

"In the middle of nowhere," Leo answered wryly, but with a smile.

Liz clasped Leo's hand. "Thank you," she said.

"Yeah, we had a great time," Harry said. He jabbed Leo's shoulder once more, and guided Liz away. Liz glanced back at Leo. He nodded, a message that he understood, and that it was all right.

He sat a while studying the dancers. Most of the men were in uniform, and most were officers. He tried to note the ribbons, wondering how many had seen combat. Not many, he was sure. He decided to go the bar; he did not want to sit alone at a front-row table, but did not want to go home yet, either. He felt too good The war would soon be over, and Havana would reopen. And Vegas. Harry's enthusiasm was infectious. Leo could actually see the Barclay. The bright colored lights glittering in the desert night, the fountains, the droves of well-dressed players filling the casino. Then and there he decided to concentrate only on Cuba and Las Vegas, where it was legal, ending once and for all the problems of payoffs, police, and politicians. He thought he might also sell off half the race wire to the Alliance and use the money for still another Las Vegas hotel.

He slept soundly that night, waking early with the anemic winter sun brightening the room. He turned on the radio for the news, which was very good, especially for the U.S. Army. In Germany, Patton had captured Aachen; and at West Point, Army beat Notre Dame. Leo had bet George Gerson ten dollars Army would score at least thirty-five points, a bet Gerson gleefully accepted. A real sucker bet, Gerson said, because Leo was ignoring the percentages. In five years Army had not scored a single touchdown against Notre Dame. Yesterday's score was Army 59, Notre Dame 0. Gerson should have known Leo did not make sucker bets.

At breakfast with Steve, they discussed "after the war." Steve said he had decided aviation was what he wanted.

". . . you'd pass up the family business?" Leo said, kidding. That notion was now a comfortable standing joke between them.

"I'm too chickenhearted to be a gambler," Steve said. "I'd give everybody credit. Seriously, Dad, I already spoke to some ATC guys. Civilians, on a war contract. They're with Pan Am. They said the airlines'll really open up after the war. You can't believe some of the airplanes on the drawing boards! Bigger than DC-4s, or Connies. A hundred and fifty passengers! And cruise better than three fifty. New York to L.A., nonstop, nine hours!"

"What about college?"

"What about it?"

"Ever think of law school?"

"No, never."

"Would you consider it?"

"I told you: aviation."

"I'll buy you an airline," Leo said, and asked, "How'd you make out last night?"

"Dad . . . !" Steve blushed.

"Okay," Leo said. "You answered the question."

"Listen, she's a very patriotic girl. After all, a soldier on his way overseas—"

"Harry used to pull that," Leo said. "He said it worked every time."

"Like a charm," said Steve. "A charm."

"Okay, let's charm your way to Grand Central," Leo said, looking at his watch. "If you get lucky, maybe you'll find an empty seat next to another patriotic girl."

Steve did get lucky. An attractive WAC corporal, going home on furlough, but unhappily not all that patriotic. But then again, how patriotic can you be on a crowded train? It reminded Steve of Leo's definition of luck: the combination of unrelated factors all merging at the same time and place.

He thought about this again the next morning at final briefing for the transatlantic flight. They were taking off ahead of schedule to outrace a storm front moving in from the west. He had a sudden, bad feeling about it and wanted to talk it over with Leo. But all the long-distance circuits were busy.

It was still on his mind when he wheeled the big airplane down the long runway. They were heavy with a full fuel load. Steve wanted all the takeoff run possible. On the ground she was like a truck, the B-24, with no nosewheel steering control, only the twin rudders. It required constant, heavy pedal pressure to keep her on the center line. He had used less than half the runway when she reached flying speed. He rolled back elevator trim and felt her break ground. Much more responsive now, she flew into the air.

"Gear up!" Steve called, jerking his thumb upward at the copilot, a fuzzy-cheeked second lieutenant even younger than Steve.

The copilot grinned. "Hey, she flies!"

"Don't let her hear you say it!" Steve shouted back, relieved, for he had almost convinced himself that the bad feeling at briefing presaged a takeoff accident. He had actually seen himself burning up at the end of the runway.

He felt infinitely better. He did not know how he knew, but knew he had been very close to the accident he envisioned, and that he had somehow lucked out and the danger was over.

Those luck factors.

He called for climb power, then radio-checked the navigator and radio operator on the flight deck behind him, and the bombardier in the nose compartment. He glanced out his side window at the Maine coast slipping away below and behind. They were in an easy climb, the airplane performing flawlessly. He called for another power reduction and considered putting her on autopilot but decided to hand-fly her awhile.

Steve loved this moment. The immense power of the engines throbbing through the hard-rubber handles of the yoke, pulsating into him, through his entire body. He was part of the airplane, it was part of him.

He felt the impact, and heard it, but did not know what caused it. One instant they were climbing smoothly, the next instant the entire flight deck behind him was disintegrating in a grinding, shuddering crunch of metal on metal. The yoke was torn from his fingers and hurled into his stomach. The airplane's nose rose almost vertically. She began falling off to the right.

"Full power, three and four!" he shouted, fighting the yoke, pushing it forward with all his strength. And he could not see; he was blinded by a viscous red haze.

"For Christ's sake, give me full power on three and four!" He wiped the red haze from his eyes. His hands were wet and sticky. Hydraulic fluid, he thought. The overhead lines had ruptured, spewing the red fluid over the instrument panel and windshield. And then he remembered the B-24's lines were below the cockpit, not overhead.

It was blood. His face was covered with blood. But not his own, he realized, and for the first time saw the thing in the copilot's seat. Slumped sideways against the control pedestal, a thing lacking face and chest, only a torso, blood gushing upward from serrated flesh and a mass of quivering, gray-red intestine spilling down from the torso onto the cockpit floor.

Steve stared at it. The dank fecal odor flooded his nostrils and penetrated his throat. He wanted to vomit and wondered why he did not, and wondered also why his earphones were so silent. All he heard was the roar of the two left engines and the scream of rushing wind. And now he glanced behind him and did not believe what he saw.

A gaping, jagged hole in the flight deck through which the blue early-morning sky and white puffy clouds were clearly visible. And a section of wing, its shredded fabric flapping against a mangled wing strut, and the splintered hub of a single-bladed laminated-wood propeller.

It was a dream, he thought. It never happened. A midair collision. They had not been hit by another, smaller airplane. The small airplane's wing had not struck the B-24's right wing, plowed through both engines and into the flight deck. It had not sliced the fuzzy-cheeked copilot's body in half.

He struggled to wake from the dream as the B-24, out of control, stalled out, rolled over on her back and plummeted toward the ocean.

A power-on stall, Steve knew, from which he could not recover. He nearly laughed at the irony. His nemesis, the stall. He did not even try to leave his seat. The wreckage trapped him in the cockpit. He knew the intercom was out so he could not warn the crew. He hoped they had bailed out. He faced forward, staring down at the ocean rushing up at him. Closer, closer, closer. He reached for his microphone, but the centrifugal force of the dive pinned his arms. He imagined himself speaking into the microphone: ". . . we're going in," he said calmly. "Sorry about that!"

Before his eyes as the water sprang up at him he saw the little WAC from the train. He talked to her in his mind. A perfect stranger, but he knew she would understand. "I want to apologize for making that pass before," he said. "I think it was because I was afraid I'd never see you again. After the war I'm going to start an airline." He smiled. "My father doesn't know it yet, but he's the guy that'll finance it. He'll do it, because he knows a good business proposition when he sees it—"

The B-24 struck the water and exploded.

Harry took the call. He was at Leo's apartment waiting for Leo to return from the barbershop. Liz was shopping, buying up Bergdorf-Goodman, Harry supposed. Why the hell not? Harry, Leo, and George Gerson were to meet in an hour to wrap up some business before Harry left for his next lecture at a camp in Pennsylvania. Harry really wasn't that much interested in the business anymore; he cared only about Vegas and Liz, and he had both. The goddam war would be over soon. Everything was working, going their way.

Then Ellie phoned. He told her Leo wasn't there but should be back any minute.

". . . you say Leo isn't there?"

"He's downstairs getting a haircut. How are you?"

Harry would never forget her voice. Flat, quiet, as though telling him a ball game was canceled for rain. "The Red Cross has just notified me that Steven was killed in an accident this morning."

Harry wanted to run. He wanted to rush from this room and race down the corridor. He felt as though the floor had opened up to swallow him. He could hear his heart pounding, and he could not breathe. For minutes after Ellie hung up he stood frozen, his hand still clutching the dead phone.

He heard the key in the lock, and the doorknob turning, and the door opening. "Hey, how do I look?" Leo asked, circling around for Harry to see the haircut. "I told him, just a trim. Not like the last time when he made me look like a German butcher!"

Harry said nothing. He placed the receiver back into the cradle. He remembered noticing the gray at Leo's temples and wondering why it always seemed to show up after a haircut.

"Gerson call?" Leo asked, and saw Harry's face. "What the hell's the matter with you?"

And then Leo knew. He saw it in Harry's eyes, and the tears streaming down Harry's cheeks. He knew, but pretended not to. He pretended Harry was not speaking.

". . . midair collision. Don't know all the details yet."

Leo shook his head. He really could not hear for the roaring in his ears, but recognized the words, although did not understand them.

"Sit down, Kleyner," Harry was saying. "Please, Leo. Please." He placed his arm around Leo.

"No!" Leo said. He pushed Harry away. "What're you, crazy? You tell me things like that! You son of a bitch! No!"

Leo remembered little of those first hours. He knew he had to compose himself, and managed to make several telephone calls. One to Ellie. She repeated the Red Cross message. He told her not to believe it, not until it was confirmed. So he called a man in Washington, who called Presque Isle.

Confirmed.

Regret to inform you . . .

Confirmed.

Before he knew it, some hours had passed, and several drinks, and he was relatively calm. He was also alone. He had asked Harry to please leave him alone. He loved Harry but wanted to be by himself. It was very important to be alone. He had to think, to work it out, to face it.

To find the answer to some questions.

Why?

Yes, why? That was the first and most important question. Why did it happen?

Why?

In the darkened living room the phone rang; it had been ringing most of the day. He did not know which line, private line or hotel phone, and did not care. He did not bother to take it off the hook or ask the switchboard for a plug. Several people came to the door, but he told them to go away. "I'm all right," he said. "I'm fine."

He was sure Ellie had called, or was calling, which was one reason he had not answered a phone. He just did not want to speak to her, to hear her say he had killed his own son. Another murder for you, Leo! And then there was his mother. Somebody had to tell her. He poured another drink but pushed it away. He had had too much. The room would begin spinning, and he would have to lie down. He would sleep. He did not want to sleep. He had to think.

He needed to find the answer to the question, Why?

Ah, yes, of course. Retribution! That was the answer. The son punished for the father's sins. And as this possibility swept through his mind, he remembered his mother after Rivka's death.

". . . no more Rivka."

No more Steve.

Why?

The retribution made no sense simply because no one could exact such punishment. So, okay, he told himself, so we drop that theory. So what does that leave us? Oh, wait, hold it! There *is* someone who can order retribution.

God.

What? he asked himself. Are you crazy? God?

No, I am not crazy, he answered himself. Somebody did it, didn't they? Act of God, they call it. All right, so let's for a second say it was God. Now what do you do?

Pray, of course.

Pray for what?

Pray that maybe it was a mistake. Mistaken identity. It could happen. They haven't even found the plane yet. They just said it was seen going down.

All right, I will do it. I will pray. I will even do better than just pray. I will go to a synagogue and pray. I will do anything.

He never knew how he got out to the street, or to the synagogue on Seventy-sixth Street, or how he even knew a synagogue was there. He stood on the sidewalk, coatless in the wet, light snow that had begun falling, gazing at the Star of David sculpted into the rose window just above the entrance of the darkened building. After a moment, he climbed the stone stairs.

The doors were locked.

He went around the back to a small porch. A screen door protected a windowed inner door. The screen door was open, but the inner door was locked. He removed his handkerchief, wound it around his fist, and smashed a windowpane. He groped for the slide bolt and opened the door, and entered.

It was so dark he stumbled into the wall. He stepped back and carefully felt his away along the wall. He reached another door. A heavy oak door that opened with a sound like chalk grating on a blackboard. He was in the vestry. Ahead, he saw a dim, flickering light and a series of partially ajar doors resembling a theater entrance.

The light came from the sanctuary, from a canister of burning oil of the *Ner Tamid,* the eternal light above the ark. He did not remember where he had learned this, or when, but thought it must be from the Hebrew-school lessons of so many years ago. He stood in the doorway, peering into the shadows of the vast empty room, the rows of pews, the pulpit, and behind the pulpit the ark that contained the Torah. And the flame of the *Ner Tamid.*

He stepped inside, sliding his hand along the back of a pew in the last row of the sanctuary until he reached the aisle and sat down. His mind raced with a thousand different thoughts and at the same time was totally blank. He was vaguely aware that his hand throbbed, and knew it was from breaking the glass. He wondered if he had cut himself, but felt no blood, and also wondered why the door was not wired for a burglar alarm, and why he had not considered that when he broke in. But then why would a synagogue need a burglar alarm? Who would be crazy enough to break into a synagogue?

Well, all right, he told himself, so you're here. So do what you came to do.

Which is what? he asked himself.

Pray.

To who? For what?

He did not want to answer those questions. He knew the answers, of course. Pray to God. To change what had happened. That it was all a crazy mistake. But it was not a mistake, and will not change. It cannot change, and no one or nothing can change it. Then what in the hell are you doing here?

He felt a sudden urge to get up and walk to the altar, and kneel as he had seen Catholics do. They crossed themselves and prayed to Jesus Christ. Maybe you should pray to Jesus, he told himself. Don't they say faith can move mountains?

Maybe that's why all this happened. Because you don't believe in God. Jewish, Christian, Buddhist, any. God is the greatest con game ever devised by man. Gorodetsky's Law number six hundred and twenty. Maybe that's why you are being punished.

So why would praying to Jesus make things different?

It would show you believe in some God.

But I don't. I do not believe, and never will.

So please tell me why you came here?

"I don't know," he said aloud. "I don't know!"

The words echoed through the room and reverberated back into his head. He smashed his fist against the prayer book receptacle, the little slatted wooden box built into the back of the pew in front of him.

"You fucking hypocrite!" he cried aloud, the words directed at himself. "You don't have the fucking guts to face the truth!"

What truth?

The truth that there is no God! He smashed the box again, and felt the slats crumble and the pain in his knuckles and hand. You fool! he told himself. Of course, there is no God! And do you know why there is no God? Because if there were such a thing he would never kill a marvelous boy like Steve.

Yes, you so-called God, answer me that, will you! Why kill the kid? What the hell did he ever do to you? He was only twenty years old, for Christ's sake! Twenty!

Leo suddenly remembered a belated gift for Steve's twentieth birthday last September. The jeweler said it would be ready sometime next week. A set of white-gold USAAF pilot's wings. Now what would he do with the wings?

He shouted aloud, "I'll give them to you, God! You can put them with the rest of your medals and give them to all the fools who believe in you!" Now Leo began trembling. He rose and placed both hands on the back of the pew to stop trembling. He pressed down on the polished wood with all his strength.

He imagined himself rushing to the altar, climbing up to the ark doors, flinging them open and pulling out the Torah and tearing it into pieces. But he could not seem to move, and wondered why, but knew why.

Because it was useless. Just as God is useless.

All right, God, he told him in his mind. If there is such a thing. If there is, then you are a phony, a fake, and I insult you! I challenge you! I always knew you did not exist, and now you have proved it!

Why did you do it? Why? To get even with me, is that why? Yes, of course that's why you did it. That's how you do business, the only way you know how to do business, the only way you can do business! You are a fraud!

But as all this rushed through his mind he was also wondering why, if he believed what he said, why had he come here at all? To rail at a nonexistent Diety? To make a fool of himself before something that was not real?

So it was not God who was the fraud, it was he himself. He, Leo Gorodetsky, aged forty-four, father of a dead boy. A boy who might have been everything that he, Leo Gorodetsky, was not and could not be, and who certainly would never enter a synagogue—or any house of worship—to insult a God he knew did not exist.

"A fraud," he said aloud, quietly, his legs so suddenly weak they began to buckle. He lowered himself down into the seat and slumped back. Staring at the flame far across the room, he realized his eyes were blurred, that tears clouded his vision. He was surprised to be crying. He had not cried since Hershey's funeral, and then only because of Steve's weeping.

"Poor Steve," he said aloud. "You ran out of luck, I guess. Just plain out." But the instant the word *luck* was out of his mouth, he felt foolish again. All the pompous, fatuous lecturing about luck, those factors he had so pretentiously contrived in his mind as the difference between good and bad luck.

He had just plain run out of it.

November 21, 1944, he thought. The day the luck ran out.

And then he began weeping. He sat staring at the *Ner Tamid* flame, and the ark, and the silhouetted menorahs on each side of the ark, and he wept.

PART FIVE

THE PROMISED LAND

21

BEN Sylbert was a Columbia Law graduate who liked to say the only bar he ever passed was a B-girl joint called La Ronde, on the Marseilles waterfront, and only because it was off limits to U.S. naval personnel. He was thirty-one, a solidly framed man of medium height with sandy hair thinning so rapidly it was cause for occasional, self-conscious alarm, although he had little time to worry about it now in the early winter of 1947. He was far too preoccupied with his new career, the career he considered infinitely more interesting and exciting than law.

Publicity director for a Las Vegas hotel called the Barclay. He knew absolutely nothing about publicity and public relations, or the hotel business, but the concept of a luxury casino in the desert intrigued him. Besides, he liked Harry Wise, especially Harry's straightforwardness.

"That's okay, kid," Harry had said. "I don't know nothing much about it, either. We'll learn together."

Harry was more impressed with Ben's salary demands: twenty-five dollars weekly for expenses, plus two points of Barclay ownership. Which at present was two points of nothing. Any man with that much faith in the project was a man Harry wanted.

And for this project, faith was needed. The Barclay, only half completed, rose up out of the desert like some abandoned ruin crumbling in the sand. It had already consumed all of the Alliance's $2 million investment, plus $1 million of Harry's. Everything he had. If he intended to open within a year, or at all, he needed more money. Another $2 million.

Ben had accompanied Harry to New York to plead his case before a group of men Ben believed existed only in the imagination of frustrated law-enforcement officials and politicians running on reform tickets. All Harry said was "they" controlled things. To Ben, "they" resembled any group of pragmatic businessmen. If you overlooked the Italian names and some ungrammatical speech.

Harry had explained the problems. Union intransigence, material shortages, water. "They"—with the exception of Harry's partner, Leo Gorodetsky—were prepared to walk away. Only fools throw good money after bad. But Leo convinced "them" to give Harry more time. Harry promised a gala opening within one year, no later than New Year's Eve, 1949. He got his $2 million, and rushed back to Nevada.

Ben remained in New York, to confer with Leo Gorodetsky on a matter of importance. Nothing behind Harry's back, for Ben had explained his reasons for wanting to see Leo.

Harry had laughed and said, "And they call me crazy!" But he added, "If anybody can help you with this *meshuggeneh* idea, it'll be Leo. He's maybe the only one."

A *meshuggeneh* idea called Israel.

The motorcycle cop hiding behind the bridge abutment near the Milford cutoff of the Merritt Parkway watched the shiny new sandstone-brown convertible with the wood station-wagon sides flash past. He had just decided to chase a battered Plymouth coupe traveling a good ten miles an hour faster than the convertible, which itself was doing at least seventy.

The Plymouth probably was driven by some kid, the cop thought, gunning the bike out onto the road. So he'd write the ticket, and that would be the end of it. The convertible could be a whole other story. Anybody driving that much car was sure to be ready to hand over a twenty-dollar bill to forget the whole thing. The cop did not realize how almost correct he was.

Leo Gorodetsky drove the convertible, a brand-new 1948 Chrysler Town and Country, built like a tank, with a semiautomatic transmission called "Fluid Drive" that really worked. You could shift gears without depressing the clutch. Leo knew the car should not be pushed for the first thousand miles, until properly broken in, but he could not resist. There was little traffic this cold November morning, and the highway, scraped clean of last week's snow, stretched dry and inviting.

"How fast do you think we're going?" he asked Carla. She sat close beside him on the plush leather seat.

"Fifty?" she said.

"Try seventy-two," he said, pointing smugly to the speedometer. He felt a little foolish driving so fast, like a kid with a new toy. But then that's what it was, he supposed. A new toy. He had bought himself a new toy. And why not? Why the hell not? "The reason you think you're not going fast is because of the weight and the way she's put together."

"Daddy, it's a car you're talking about," Carla said. "Not a woman."

He looked at her. That smile. Tinkling bells. And now she was eighteen. How could it be? The little chestnut-haired girl had become a big chestnut-haired girl. A grown woman at least a head taller than her father, whom everyone said she resembled, with his brown eyes, heavy eyebrows, and stern chin. She had her mother's patrician nose and mouth.

"I love you," she said.

"Does that mean no more arguments about school?"

"Are you kidding? You're damn right we'll argue. I'm going to the New England Conservatory. Not Barnard, Hunter, or Middlebury. Boston!"

"I really want you closer to home."

"Boston," she said.

"We'll compromise, then," he said. "Juilliard."

"Boston." She glanced behind her and tapped his arm. "Daddy, I believe somebody wants a word with you."

He heard the siren, and saw in the rearview mirror the motor cop's flashing red lights. Now he truly felt foolish. He slowed and pulled off the road.

The cop stopped his bike behind them and fussed with his gloves and citation book. In the car Carla watched with interest through the rear window. "He's going to give you a ticket."

"Naturally," Leo said. He had removed a ten-dollar bill from his wallet, then decided to make it a twenty. He folded and palmed the bill, careful for Carla not to notice.

"Why didn't he catch the car that passed us before?" she asked. "He was going faster than you."

"It's more of a challenge to catch a new car," Leo said. He watched the cop approach in the side mirror. Swaggering, self-important. Leo knew immediately he had a price.

Carla, eyes fixed on the window, said, "Offer him something to fix it." Leo was startled. "What?"

"Give him some money," she said. "A bribe."

Leo felt himself redden. "Where did you ever get an idea like that?"

"Come on, everyone does it."

In the mirror the cop was almost abeam the rear of the Chrysler. Leo closed his fist around the palmed twenty-dollar bill. He tucked it down between the seat and the door. He touched the button lowering the electric window and faced the cop.

"License and registration, please?"

Leo handed him the documents. The cop studied them, then eyed Leo. "Gorodetsky . . . ?" he said. "Don't I know you?"

"I don't think so," Leo said. "Listen, would you mind telling me why you stopped me?"

"Do you know how fast you were going?"

"Sixty, I think."

"I clocked you at seventy-three. The limit is sixty-five."

"I'm sorry, Officer. It's a new car, and—" he glanced at Carla who had just then nudged him. She was rubbing her thumb and forefinger together in a "money" gesture. "A new car, and sometimes you just forget."

"Yeah," said the cop. He had unscrewed his fountain-pen cap and poised the pen over the citation pad. "I'll have to write you up." He waited an expectant moment.

Leo said nothing.

"I'll have to give you a ticket," the cop said.

Again, Carla nudged him. Leo pushed her firmly away. "You have to do your duty," he said to the cop.

The cop wrote the ticket, asked Leo to sign it, returned the license and registration, and hurried back to his motorcycle. Leo waited until the cop roared away. Then he started the car and swung back onto the highway.

"Why didn't you pay him off?" Carla asked.

"I've heard they let you offer them something and then arrest you for attempted bribery," he said. "That would be real dumb, don't you think?"

"But everybody does it. Once in Boston, Mom gave a cop a five-dollar bill. He tore up the ticket."

"I don't do it, Carla. And I don't want you to do it."

"You know something, Leo?" she said. "You are one hell of a terrific guy."

"Why? Because I wouldn't pay off a two-bit cop?"

"Because you have the integrity not to."

Her words, as they often did, left him momentarily speechless. He had not paid the cop, quite simply, because he was ashamed to do it in her presence. And she thought it was integrity. He did not know what, if anything, Ellie had told Carla about his business. Despite the money and favors dispensed to keep his name out of the newspapers, occasionally it was mentioned in connection with "organized crime," or "gambling enterprises." But Carla seemed to unquestioningly accept it as "hotels and real estate," and he was certainly willing to let it go at that. Someday the issue would have to be faced directly. He would deal with it when it happened.

He said, "I think you're a terrific guy, too. I mean, gal."

"You hate that word *gal*, you said."

"But I love you."

"I love you, too."

"I'm glad," he said, and felt the corners of his eyes smart with tears. God, he did love her; she was the best thing that ever happened to him.

She sat up and looked at him. "Daddy, are you okay?"

"Absolutely," he said, but was thinking, How okay can you be after a visit to the mother of your child, your ex-wife, a forty-five-year-old woman who looked seventy?

In a sanatorium.

It happened shortly after Steve's death. At first Ellie behaved quite rationally. Our country was fighting for its very survival; its children were expected to defend the freedoms generations of Americans before them had fought and died for. She continued her work at the Winston Public Library and tried to comfort Carla, who for months was totally inconsolable. Her brother had been part of her life. She could not reconcile herself to his death.

But as Carla gradually accepted the reality, Ellie slipped further and further into fantasy. She began referring to Steve in the present tense. "Oh, yes, my son is in the Air Corps." "God, how I pray each night he survives those bombing missions. They need twenty-five before they can come home, you know." "Sometimes I see those Gold Stars in windows, and how my heart goes out to those poor mothers!"

And then one day Carla phoned Leo to say she had found Ellie seated at the kitchen table, lighting a cigarette, drawing on it, mashing it out, immediately lighting a fresh one, all the while staring at the front page of *The Winston Gazette*. A photograph of MacArthur receiving the Japanese surrender, and the headline:

ONE YEAR AGO TODAY!

When Carla spoke to her, Ellie said, "Yes." No matter what the question, she answered, "Yes."

Ellie was admitted to Baldpate, a private psychiatric hospital not far from her home in Georgetown. After several months she was sent to the Hartford House, in Hartford, Connecticut, for electroshock and insulin therapy. Briefly, after each treatment, she appeared improved, but always slipped back into a catatonic state. Leo had little faith in any of this, but they said it was her only hope, so he allowed it to continue.

He brought Carla to live with him in New York and moved into a spacious Central Park West apartment. For a time she brooded, but Leo encouraged her not to conceal her deep grief for Steve and Ellie, to openly discuss her feelings. He also spent as much time with her as possible. They dined together almost nightly, attended the theater, museums, concerts. And with this, and new friends, and a new school—and the whole new world of New York—she was soon herself again.

Now, speeding along the Merritt Parkway, he thought—a little guiltily—how much she had compensated for his loss of Steve and failure with Ellie. She read his thoughts. She had an amazing facility for this.

"You were thinking about Steve, weren't you?" she said. "I can tell."

"How?" he asked. "How can you tell?"

"Your eyes. They turned very sad. When you're angry, they're almost icy. When you're unhappy, they get sad. It's like watching a light go off and on."

"I'm not unhappy."

"But you were thinking about Steve?"

"Yes."

"And Mom."

"Yes, her, too."

"You don't feel responsible for what happened to her?"

He gripped the wheel and concentrated on the road. "Carla, we've talked about this before. I feel responsible for the marriage breaking up, but not for her illness. Yes, she's sick because of Steve, and yes, I encouraged him to fly. I've told you before, and I'll tell you again: I'm glad I encouraged him, and I'm glad he did what he wanted." He put his arm around her and pulled her close to him. "Can you understand that, honey?"

"Of course I can."

"Good," he said, noticing a billboard advertising a diner a quarter mile ahead. "Hungry?"

"We'll be home in an hour, won't we?"

"Yes, but I'm having dinner with somebody."

"Oh."

"It's not business. You can come if you like."

"Who is it?"

"The man who does publicity for the Barclay,' he said. "Ben Sylbert."

"The Barclay," Carla said dryly. "The hotel that's taking ten years to build?"

"Seems like it, doesn't it?" Leo said, and thought, The way it is going it just might take ten years. Crazy Harry, who only yesterday rushed back to Las Vegas with a $2 million transfusion, this morning scrapped more than $100,000 worth of plumbing fixtures simply because he didn't like the color. Black toilets, he wanted. Black, can you believe it? No wonder the original $2 million estimate had more than doubled.

"... I'll just grab a sandwich at home," Carla was saying. "I'm pretty tired, anyway."

"Okay," he said. "I won't be out too late."

"What did you say his name was? The man you're having dinner with?"

"Ben Sylbert. He has some *meshuggeneh* idea he wants to talk about."

2.

In 1941, on the day he received his law degree, Ben Sylbert was called to active duty in the U.S. Naval Reserve. He served as a gunnery officer on various combat vessels throughout the South Pacific in the early, hard days. In 1945, by then a Lieutenant commander, and reassigned to the Western Naval Task Force in the Mediterranean as a SHAEF liaison officer, he was one of the first Americans to liberate the Nazi concentration camp at Dachau.

He, the son of Polish Jews who had settled in Baltimore in 1912, never forgot what he saw in Dachau, or the single, driving desire of the survivors for their own nation. A Jewish state. He also never forgot his own shame and guilt. Shame for not having believed this actually was happening, guilt that as a Jew he had not shared their suffering.

Returning to America early in 1946, a civilian, he married a lady he met at an art-gallery opening. Her family owned a small soft-drink bottling plant in Los Angeles. Ben was made sales director. He hated it. He considered the product inferior, poorly merchandised, and overpriced. His father-in-law disagreed. Several arguments later, the lady Ben married suggested he either shape up or ship out. He shipped out.

He held six different jobs in one year. From short order cook at the coffee shop of the Hotel Del Coronado in San Diego to San Francisco taxi driver, where one evening he picked up a fare he vaguely recognized. A man he had met at Dachau.

At Dachau this man, weighing all of ninety pounds, who could have been any age from twenty-one to sixty, had immediately vomited the C-ration dinner Ben naïvely gave him. Food far too rich for a starving body. He had noted Ben's horrified expression.

"You are surprised?" he asked. "Why?"

"Why?" Ben replied. "This is unbelievable. Human beings treating other human beings like this!"

"We are not human beings," the man said. "We are Jews."

Two years later in Ben's taxi they met again. The man, Aaron Cahane, now living in British-mandated Palestine, was in America seeking money to purchase munitions for a Jewish underground army. He gave Ben a New York address where he could be reached for the next four months, until the end of November, when the United Nations was expected to vote on the partitioning of Palestine into separate Arab and Jewish states.

One day at lunch months later, as the Barclay's director of publicity, Ben heard Harry casually relate the story of Leo and the Nazi Bund leader, Kurt Baumer. (Although omitting the end result.) In an instant Ben knew Leo was the man for Aaron Cahane.

So now, this freezing November night, Ben Sylbert met with Leo at a Lexington Avenue restaurant, Sazarac. Ben was so certain of Leo's cooperation, he had invited Aaron Cahane to join them.

"I'll get right to the point, Mr. Gorodetsky," Ben said after some brief amenities. "Aaron Cahane here is—" he paused abruptly. Cahane was staring at Leo with a deep, bemused frown.

Leo said to Cahane, "Is something wrong?"

Cahane, a small, slight man, entirely bald but for a few wisps of stringy gray hair, studied Leo another moment, then almost rudely turned to Ben. "Mr. Gorodetsky is nothing like I pictured him as."

Ben glanced uneasily at Leo and laughed. "I'd say he's the picture of health."

"Sure," Leo said, amused. "I walk three miles every morning. I watch what I eat and drink. I don't chase women; well, not all the time. I feel fine."

Cahane said to Leo, "I pictured you bigger, more of a *shtarker*. A man in your business."

"Abe—" Ben flushed with embarrassment.

Cahane turned to Ben again. "You said Mr. Gorodetsky was a gambler." In his guttural, singsong Yiddish accent he pronounced it *gembeler*. "The biggest gambler in the whole world, maybe."

Ben wanted to sink through the floor. Leo looked at him coolly, then spoke to Cahane. "Well, I suppose there's some truth to that—"

"—I said Mr. Gorodetsky's contacts were what you needed," Ben said, clearing his throat; the words sounded as though he had swallowed them. "I said in his business—" he cleared his throat again. "In his business, he meets people all over the world."

"I'm glad you straightened that out," Leo said to Ben, and then to Cahane, "Mr. Cahane, just what is it you want of me?"

"Planes."

Leo was not sure he heard correctly. "Planes?"

"Yes, sir. And guns."

"Planes?" Leo said. "Airplanes?"

"For an airlift," said Cahane, and explained that after the hopefully favorable UN vote, the British would abandon their mandate. The armies of six Arab nations would then attack the new Jewish state.

". . . the problem, sir," Cahane continued, "is not only to obtain the matériel, but to *deliver* it. The English navy already blockades the coast so no more refugees get in. Every day you read here about ships getting caught. So if we are stopped from bringing it in by sea, we got to *fly* it in!"

As he spoke, Cahane gestured to a man seated alone at the bar. A young man, quite tense and nearly stern in appearance whom Leo had noticed occasionally watching them. Immediately, the man rose and came to the table.

"Mr. Newman, please meet Mr. Gorodetsky," said Cahane.

Ben Sylbert, more embarrassed than ever, said, "Aaron, you didn't tell me somebody else would be—"

"—he is a flyer," Cahane continued, grasping Newman's arm possessively. "An American. He has a plan."

Raymond Newman not only had a plan, he was the most self-assured young man Leo had ever seen. His first words to Leo were, "Mr. Gorodetsky, I need money, as much and as often as I can get it. I also need to utilize your contacts in the Caribbean."

"Have you had dinner, Mr. Newman?" Leo asked.

"No, sir. I can't afford a place like this."

"I'll buy," said Leo.

Ray Newman talked all through dinner. A USAAF veteran of fifty B-17 missions over Europe, a pilot, he had raised $30,000 from various Jewish philanthropies to purchase three war-surplus airplanes, PBYs, long-range twin-engined amphibians. The plan was to pick up refugees in Europe, fly them to Palestine in the PBYs—*over* the British blockade—and parachute them into the country.

When Newman paused to order coffee, Ben Sylbert asked, "How many refugees can these planes take?"

"Twenty, maybe thirty."

"That's ninety at a time," Ben said. "Christ, every week you'll bring in hundreds!"

Aaron Cahane, pleased, said, "All new soldiers for the new Jewish army. So, Mr. Gorodetsky, what do you think?"

What do I think? Leo thought. I think you are all crazy, that's what I think. But I love it. The whole idea. He especially liked the young pilot, Ray Newman. While there was no physical similarity, Newman reminded Leo of Steve. Leo was sure that had Steve survived the war he would be one of the American volunteers flying the Jewish airlift. In Leo's mind, therefore, Ray Newman became Steve.

He said to Newman. "Where are you from?"

"Connecticut," Newman said. "Bridgeport."

Leo said, "Would you believe: I got a speeding ticket there just this afternoon. You're a Jew?"

"You think I'd be doing this if I wasn't?" Newman asked. "But if you want to know *why* I'm doing it, I can't tell you."

"What do you mean, you can't tell me?"

"I mean, I don't know myself," Newman said. "All I know is that men like Aaron"—he leaned over and pulled Aaron Cahane's jacket sleeve up, revealing Cahane's forearm, the blue tattooed numbers D-13345—"maybe this is why. Maybe it's because if my grandfather hadn't left the old country when he did, that number might be on my arm, not Aaron's."

The waiter just then arrived with the coffee. Leo and Ben Sylbert lit cigarettes. Newman filled a battered meerschaum pipe and lit it. Newman waited until the waiter left, then went on, "I have to tell you, nobody ever called me 'dirty kike,' or 'Christ killer,' or whatever. I never even knew what an antisemite was until I read it in the paper. My father's a dentist who never denied being a Jew but liked to call himself a 'free-thinker,' and the closest we ever came to a synagogue—after my bar mitzvah—was at my grandfather's funeral." He paused to taste the coffee, then continued, "In the army, I learned a trade. Now I can put it to use to help my own people."

Leo heard his own voice saying quietly, "I had a son in the air force."

Ben Sylbert said, "Yes, Harry told me."

"He flew B-24s," Leo said. "He was killed back in '44."

"I'm sorry," Newman said.

Leo said to Ben, "Didn't you tell Mr. Cahane about my boy?" He realized why he was telling them this. It made him feel more their equal.

"Yes, he told me," Cahane said. He touched Leo's arm gently. "I simply had no chance to express my condolences. Your son, *alavhasholom*, was a hero."

"No, just a kid doing his duty," Leo said. Aware he had made himself an object of their pity, he wanted to stop, but felt obliged to continue. "His plane was hit by another one when they were taking off for England."

"That's a rough go," Newman said. "He was a pilot?"

"Top third of his cadet class. Forty-three-G. He was a first lieutenant," he said, thinking, Jesus Christ, enough already, the next thing you'll be telling them is all about the white-gold wings. "All right, so you need money. We'll get it for you, all you need. But what's it have to do with my Caribbean contacts?"

Aaron Cahane said, "Mr. Gorodetsky, at this moment the entire Jewish arsenal consists of maybe nine thousand rifles, some so old they won't even fire. A few thousand Sten guns, a couple hundred light machine guns, and six hundred two-inch mortars. And no more than three days' ammunition for all of it. Newman here knows where there are two hundred .50-caliber machine guns. In Mexico."

"I don't have any contacts in Mexico," Leo said.

"But you do in Cuba," Newman said. "Now, I can get my hands on the guns all right. If I could move them by boat to Cuba, one of the PBYs can pick them up there and take them on over."

Ben Sylbert said, "But we need Cuban permission."

"That's it, Mr. Gorodetsky," Newman said. He removed the pipe from his mouth and pointed the stem at Leo. "That's where you come in."

Leo said, "Why does everybody think I own the goddam island?"

"Don't you?" Ben asked.

3.

The instant he heard the phone ring, even in a sound sleep, Leo knew it was trouble. No one used the private line unless it was trouble. He let it ring twice. The green-glowing phosphorescent hands on the night-table clock read 4:30. Trouble, all right.

Kingston, Jamaica, calling. Collect, no less.

Ben Sylbert.

". . . a little problem," said Ben, and over the phone Leo heard him sigh. "We're in jail."

Leo sat up in bed and switched on the lamp. The last he heard from Ben and Ray Newman, yesterday, they were in Camagüey, Cuba, the PBY loaded with two hundred machine guns—packed in twenty crates marked "agricultural implements"—about to take off for Paramaribo, Dutch Guiana. The first leg of a flight across the South Atlantic that would eventually take them to Palestine.

"Leo, did you hear me . . . ?"

"I heard you," Leo said. He pushed the early edition of *The New York Times* off the bed; he had fallen asleep reading it. He glanced at the headline:

U.S. WARNS CITIZENS IN PALESTINE FIGHT!

Ben Sylbert's voice was loud and clear. "Well, I'm afraid we need some help."

The newspaper story, datelined April 10, 1948, quoted the State Department's warning of possible loss of U.S. citizenship to individuals entering the service of either Jewish or Arab armies. On May 15, when the British left Palestine, the war would begin. Already, it was rumored, many Americans had enlisted in the Jewish cause. The State Department should only know, Leo thought. They should only know.

He said into the phone, "What the hell are you doing in Jamaica anyway?"

"We lost an engine an hour out of—" he lowered his voice. "Our point of departure. It was either land here or put everything into the drink. Leo, listen, I think the only way we'll ever get out is if you get somebody in Washington to push."

"You mean it's that complicated?"

"I'm afraid so."

"Have you contacted the U.S. consul?"

"That son of a bitch is the one that got us in here!" Ben drew a deep breath. "They've impounded the plane and cargo, Leo."

"Impounded?" Leo repeated helplessly.

"They opened one of the crates. They resealed it and took the whole kit and caboodle off the plane. They're waiting further instructions from London now."

"You're some public-relations man."

"Hey, give me a break, huh?"

"Sorry, bad joke," Leo said.

"Make all the jokes you like, Leo, but just get us the hell out of here!"

"All right, stay put," Leo said, and could not help laughing at that bad joke. Even Ben laughed; in jail, he had no choice but to "stay put."

After they hung up, Leo lay in bed watching the first glimmer of dawn outline the window drapes. He felt as though he had been sucked into an ever-widening and racing whirlpool. A few months ago, immediately after the UN voted the partitioning of Palestine into separate Arab and Jewish states, it seemed simple enough. Some airplanes to fly refugees to Palestine. Then, almost daily it grew more complicated.

And expensive.

$25,000 to Ray Newman to purchase the Mexican machine guns. Another $10,000 for bribes to Mexican customs authorities and rental of a creaky old boat to take the guns to Cuba.

And then $100,000 for Fulgencio Batista, still in exile in Florida, to convince his latest Cuban presidential surrogate, Carlos Prío Socarrás, to grant permission for the creaky old boat to dock at a southern Cuban port, Manzanillo. And permission to bring the cargo on this vessel, undisturbed, to an airfield outside Camagüey. To be loaded onto a certain airplane, a PBY, which would be allowed to take off, undisturbed.

That, however, was only the beginning. Crews to fly the airplanes had to be found. Preferably Jewish boys with wartime experience. The various Zionist organizations were flooded with inquiries from young Americans and Canadians volunteering their services, but the more qualified pilots, navigators, and radio operators were attracted to another, far more glamorous Haganah aviation project. A bona fide airline called Líneas Aéreas de Panamá, flying the Panamanian flag, and operating with some dozen large war-surplus American transport aircraft.

Ray Newman had to settle for the castoffs and adventurers.

To make matters worse, two of the three original PBYs crashed. Thankfully with no injuries, but the accidents effectively destroyed the plan to parachute in refugees. Ray Newman's only goal now was to bring the remaining PBY—with the machine guns—to Palestine.

Ray Newman and Ben Sylbert had purchased the guns in Mexico and smuggled them out by sea. A saga in and of itself. Once their boat nearly foundered in a storm, and then the Mexican navy fired on it. Finally, miraculously, they reached Manzanillo. The "agricultural implements" were promptly cleared through customs, trucked to Camagüey, loaded onto the waiting PBY, and flown out.

Only to lose an engine over the water, forcing them to land in Jamaica, a British Commonwealth nation. Jewish guns in British hands.

Three hours after speaking with Ben Sylbert, Leo was in a mini-suite of a small East Sixtieth Street hotel, Hotel Fourteen, having coffee with an assertive, black-haired, chain-smoking woman named Golda Myerson.

Ben Sylbert had introduced Leo to her some months before. She had appeared surprisingly cool to the PBY plan, but grateful for Leo's help, grateful for any help. She was in America raising money for the Haganah. Her goal was $50 million, of which $12 million already was pledged. She showed Leo the names of the largest individual contributors, all well-known Jewish industrialists and entertainment figures. None exceeded $50,000. Leo wrote a personal check for $100,000.

"How can I thank you?" Mrs. Myerson had asked.

"By winning," he said.

So now, weeks later, he came to her for help. He explained the Jamaican predicament—which she gently suggested was a fiasco rather than a predicament—and when he finished she studied him intently. Her face, framed by the tight black hair, was deeply wrinkled. He idly wondered how old she was; middle-aged, he thought, like him. At forty-eight, with hardly a gray hair on his head, he had never thought of himself as middle-aged.

Her words were equally surprising. ". . . not sure I want to do anything."

"I beg your pardon?"

"I said, I am not certain we should do anything. It might be best to simply leave the plane and guns where they are."

"Those are fifty-caliber guns!" Leo said. "Aaron Cahane said you had no heavy machine guns!"

"They happen to be eight-millimeter caliber," Mrs. Myerson said calmly. "Of Italian manufacture. Fiat, I believe—Fiat Reville is the model—complete with tripods. You don't know who Aaron Cahane is, do you?"

"Of course I know who he is—"

"—he's an Irgunist," said Mrs. Myerson.

Leo reached in his jacket pocket for cigarettes, then remembered he had left in such a rush he forgot them. Mrs. Myerson slid her leather cigarette case across the table to him. He took a cigarette and leaned over for her to light it. He wanted these few seconds to think. Irgunist, how could that be more important than a planeload of machine guns?

He said, "You'll excuse me, Mrs. Myerson, but I don't want to get involved in your politics. Irgun, Haganah, Stern. What's the difference? You're all Jews, aren't you? You're all fighting for the same thing."

"Yes, definitely," she said. "But we consider the political objectives of the Irgun not only prejudicial to the establishment of the state, but to its continuance. These guns, for example. We believe some of them may be consigned to Mr. Begin's private cache of arms. We know he's stockpiling weapons of his own."

"What does that have to do with the establishment of the state?"

"Quite simply, Mr. Gorodetsky, Irgun policies—and I won't bore you with details, since I'm sure you'll believe them all subjective—are directly inimical to those of the government that will take over the country on May fifteenth."

"The Irgun wants to take over instead?"

"It's a distinct possibility."

Leo had heard of this: the infighting, the dizzying labyrinth of Zionist politics. Put two Jews together, you'll have an argument. Three of them, you'll have four political parties. But not now, not when everyone should be working together.

He said, "I can't believe you're willing to sacrifice those guns."

"Are you willing to?" she asked. "Are you willing to sacrifice them?"

"The guns? Of course not!"

"I mean, are you willing to give them up to me?" she said. "Remove them from Irgun possession. Turn them over to me."

"I don't care who gets them!" Leo said. "As long as they end up where they're supposed to. With Jews."

Mrs. Myerson spoke, lighting a fresh cigarette from the stub of the old one. "I think we might be able to save them, then." She pointed the cigarette at him. "But you'll have to go down there yourself, Mr. Gorodetsky. To see that the cargo is released."

"Released to who?"

"The crew of another plane that will arrive in Kingston. A Panamanian airline plane."

"Líneas Aéreas de Panamá?"

She smiled grimly. "Not the world's best kept secret, is it? And I'll let you in on another secret, one I pray to God the Panamanians never find out about. Those Líneas Aéreas de Panamá airplanes, which at the moment are engaged in actual transport operations in Panama, are destined to one day soon fly away en masse—to Palestine. In the time required for the aircraft's Panamanian insignia to be replaced by a Star of David, Líneas Aéreas de Panamá will cease to exist."

Leo was impressed. "I hope the Panamanians have a sense of humor."

"Yes, I'm afraid they'll need one," she said. "So, you will instruct those boys to release the cargo? Yes?"

"I'm sure they'll be only too happy to," Leo said. "But how do you get the Jamaicans to release it?"

"You've been incredibly generous with your money, Mr. Gorodetsky, and your influence." She mashed out her cigarette. "Now we require your brain."

Twenty-four hours later Leo sat in the cabin of a BOAC DC-4 staring down at Jamaica Bay and the runway extending out into the water of the bay like a long, thin concrete finger. Landing, taxiing toward the terminal, the DC-4 passed a hangar marked TRANSIENT AIRCRAFT. Parked near the hangar, lonely and forlorn, was a battered old PBY. She resembled some useless machine abandoned on a roadside.

Not far from the PBY in the same transient-aircraft area was another airplane. A C-46, a huge, chunky twin-engine transport bearing blue scripted letters on its fuselage: LÍNEAS AÉREAS DE PANAMÁ.

In the customs shed the black customs officer regarded Leo with cold suspicion. "Nothing to declare?"

"Nothing," said Leo. He carried only a poplin topcoat, a small bag, and a briefcase.

"Traveling light, aren't you, sir?"

"I'll only be here a few days."

"Welcome to Jamaica," said the customs officer in his hard, clipped, Calypso-accented voice, and stamped Leo's passport.

Leo got into a waiting taxi and asked to be taken to Portsmouth House. The driver, a young man, twisted around with a puzzled grin. His fine-featured face shone like an ebony sculpture.

"Man, that's the jail," he said. "You a lawyer or something?"

Leo was not listening. He was wondering, as he had wondered throughout the flight to Miami, and then on to Kingston, why he had agreed to come here. That woman, he thought, that Golda Myerson. She had hypnotized him. Sold him a bill of goods.

Go to Kingston, arrange for the machine guns to be released, placed on the Panamanian C-46, and flown to Panama. The crippled PBY would be left behind.

"Arrange." Golda Myerson believed anything could be "arranged." He could still hear her throaty reply when he asked just how she thought "arrangements" might be made.

"Mr. Gorodetsky, do I tell you how to run your business?"

The perfect answer, and what amazed him was her absolute confidence that not only would he go on the mission, but succeed.

". . . you all right, man?" the taxi driver was saying.

"What?"

"You had this dreamy look, man, like you are in a trance." He grinned again. "Or in love."

"I didn't think it showed," Leo said. He sat back and cradled the briefcase in his lap. Inside the case, tucked between the linings, were the arrangements.

Five hundred $100 bills.

On their word of honor not to attempt to leave the island until their hearing, plus a $5,000 cash bond, Ben Sylbert and Ray Newman were released from jail. They sat now with Leo in the Britannia Hotel dining room, enjoying their first full meal in three days.

On the opposite side of the room, flirting with two Pan Am stewardesses at a nearby table, were the three C-46 crew members. Young Americans, Jews, who reminded Leo once more of Steve. They pretended not to know Ben and Newman, although one, the youngest—he looked no older than Carla, and probably was not—made Leo nervous by continually glancing their way. They were in the same hotel because all the airline crews stayed here; a different hotel would have been conspicuous.

It was a game with them, Leo thought enviously. Cloak-and-dagger stuff. And the plot would thicken in a few hours when the C-46 crew went out to the airport and filed their departure flight plan. They had arrived from Panama City that morning on a "training mission," and were returning to Panama City at night.

The C-46, which had arrived with a crew of three, would depart with a crew of five. The two additional crew members, listed only as flight engineer and third officer, were to be Ben Sylbert and Ray Newman. The departure manifest would also indicate no cargo, but this was a slight bookkeeping error, for there would be cargo.

Cargo Leo had convinced Ray Newman to turn over to the Panamanian crew. Cargo that otherwise might end up in a British impound yard—and very likely sold to parties sympathetic to the Arab cause. Four thousand pounds of unmanifested cargo. Twenty large wooden crates, bound with iron strapping, marked AGRICULTURAL IMPLEMENTS.

Prior to its expansion Kingston airport consisted only of a short dirt strip and a small corrugated-metal hangar. In time the hangar, now three miles from the new installation, became a bonded warehouse for various items of cargo in transit. The loading dock was located at the rear of the building, facing the old runway. The front entrance was just off the highway.

The building was neither fenced nor gated. Security generally consisted of two members of the Jamaican Constabulary sharing watchman duty, each working a twelve-hour shift. It was a good job. The watchman spent most of the night sleeping in the little office inside the warehouse. In the unlikely event anything did happen, the airport police were no farther than the telephone.

Present circumstances, however—the presence of two hundred contraband machine guns—temporarily demanded more stringent security measures. For this reason the regular watchmen had been replaced by military policemen from the Kingston RAF detachment.

The man with the night duty this shift was a sergeant, a short, tough Welshman named Charles Warfield. He was thirty-three and had transferred to the RAF after fifteen years in the British army, including five years with the Eighth Army in North Africa, and three years of postwar police duty in Palestine.

For certain personal reasons he did not at all object to guarding the contraband in the warehouse. To the contrary. For those same personal reasons, he relished the duty.

He was relaxing on his bunk in the darkened warehouse office, listening to Radio Jamaica's all-night program of popular reggae music. He loathed the music but it was the only clear-channel station he could tune in on the small table radio. Through the uncurtained window he saw automobile headlights sweep up from the road and stop outside. From the car, a horn blasted impatiently.

Sergeant Warfield rose, slipped into his uniform blouse and blue cap, strapped on his Webley service revolver, and stepped outside. The car, a large DeSoto sedan, was driven by an RAF flight officer; he had turned the car's engine off but left the lights on. Warfield had never seen this flight officer, nor the civilian seated beside him.

Warfield saluted and said, "Yes, sir?"

The flight officer stared at Warfield. He seemed momentarily speechless, but the civilian spoke up fast. "Yes," he said, clearing his throat. "I'm Mr. Blankenfort. Why isn't the constable on duty here?"

"We've taken over for a time," Warfield said. "Now how may I help you, sir?" He stepped around to the car's passenger side. The civilian rolled down his window. He was an older man, with a crisp, authoritative edge in his voice. He sounded American, or Canadian.

.   "Peter Blankenfort," he said. "I just arrived from London. The airport manager telephoned you."

"Nobody has telephoned me, sir," Warfield said. "Not since I've come on duty."

"I spoke to him not thirty minutes ago," the man said. "I'm to examine an impounded shipment."

Warfield's hand dropped to his whitened gun belt and rested on the holstered revolver. "Excuse me, sir?"

"We removed cargo from a plane the other day," the civilian said. "It's sitting in your warehouse. I want to see it."

"I'm sorry, sir," Warfield said. "I can't allow you in without proper authority."

"Look, Sergeant, I don't have time to argue. It's nearly eleven o'clock, and I've been on a plane for the last ten hours, and I've not been to bed for the past twenty-four! Now kindly show me into the building!" He opened the car door to get out, but Warfield pushed it closed.

Warfield had no intention of allowing entrance to any unauthorized person, which the civilian in the DeSoto knew very well. This civilian had expected to be greeted not by an armed RAF sergeant but by a black Jamaican Constabulary officer whom he was prepared to bribe if necessary. All at once, the entire situation was changed. The definite possibility of having to resort to violence existed, and this the man in the car, who of course was Leo Gorodetsky, wished to avoid. For any number of reasons, not the least of which were the repercussions such an action was sure to bring.

". . . need to see some identification," Warfield was saying.

"Sergeant, you'd better phone your superior, or you'll be in more trouble than you ever dreamed possible!" The RAF flight officer had found his voice. He shifted around awkwardly and unbuttoned his top jacket button. The uniform, purchased in a downtown Kingston usedclothing shop, was far too tight in the shoulders and crotch for Ben Sylbert. Military attire was his idea; it would impress and confuse the warehouse night watchman. Clearly, now, facing this genuine RAF person, a bad idea.

"Sir, I must ask you to remain in the car," Warfield said. He unsnapped the canvas flap over his holster.

"Goddam you, Sergeant!" Ben said. "I'll have you on report for insubordination so fast you'll have to sign up for an extra twenty years to get those stripes back! Open that door!"

"That's all right, Peabody," Leo said. "The sergeant's only doing his duty."

"Then let him keep a civil tongue in his head!" Ben said, amazed he could keep his own tongue steady; his eyes were fixed on Warfield's revolver hand.

But Warfield, recognizing an officer's commanding tone, decided to be more prudent. "Sir, you say you've just come in from London?"

"That's right, Sergeant. London."

"All right, sir, I'll make the call. Please stay here." Warfield wheeled around and strode back toward the warehouse.

"Jesus!" Ben whispered. "What the hell do we do now?"

"Exactly what we planned to do," Leo said, watching Warfield enter the building. An instant later the office light went on.

"Leo, that guy means business!"

"Come on, Ben, move it!"

Ben hesitated a moment, but then got out of the car and hurried to the side of the building near the office window. He pulled a pair of shears and a flashlight from his pocket, trained the light on the telephone junction box, and cut the wires.

In the car, Leo removed another flashlight from the glove compartment. He pointed it out the window, flicked it on, then off again. A moment later a large six-by-six truck trundled up from the highway. The truck's headlights were off, and it was on the far side of the hangar where its motor could not be heard. It rolled up to the crest of a gently descending slope and, motor off now, coasted off the highway and onto the road behind the warehouse.

The truck, driven by Ray Newman, had been purchased outright earlier in the day from the same agency that supplied the DeSoto. The agency manager was given a $500 cash bonus, leaving him with the assumption the vehicles were employed in some smuggling enterprise, which was precisely the desired effect. He would ask no questions.

In the truck cab with Newman was a young American named Phillip Skaff, the C-46 radio operator. The other two C-46 crewmen, the pilot and copilot, were at the airport filing their flight plan for the late-night departure to Panama.

Newman steered the truck close to the warehouse loading dock. Both men got out. Newman went to the back of the truck for a small rubber-tired cargo dolly, while Skaff scampered up onto the loading dock and peered into the building through the tiny window on the hangar access door. He could see all the way across the floor to the office. The RAF sergeant was still there.

"He's talking on the phone," Skaff whispered.

In the office, Charles Warfield held the telephone in one hand, the cylindrical earpiece in the other hand. He jiggled the cradle with the earpiece. "Operator . . . ? Hello . . . ?"

The phone was dead. He glanced out the window at the car. The two men in the front seat were lighting cigarettes. Warfield knew someone from London was en route to inspect the impounded cargo but not scheduled to arrive until next week. He put the phone down and went back outside.

In the rear of the building, the instant they saw the RAF sergeant leave the office, Ray Newman and Phillip Skaff jimmied open the access door with a screwdriver. The lock was a simple dead bolt; the screwdriver hardly scratched the doorframe. They entered, swept their flashlights across the concrete floor, and immediately located a number of crates stacked against the opposite wall. The black stenciled letters in the top left corner of each crate shone under the light.

From: BROCKHEIMER EXPORT CORP.
Des Moines, Iowa, U.S.A.

And larger stenciled letters across the center.

AGRICULTURAL IMPLEMENTS

The metal strapping of one box was broken, with a large white tag attached to each separated end. Each tag bore a Jamaican customs-office stamp and red printed block letters: OPENED BY CUSTOMS.

"Jackpot!" Skaff whispered. He pushed the crate slightly to the side, positioning it by itself a few feet in front of the other crates. "Okay?" he asked Newman.

"Perfect," said Newman. He grasped one end of a different crate. Skaff hoisted the other end and they loaded it onto the dolly.

"Christ, it's heavy!" Skaff said.

"Listen, if you think this first one is heavy, just wait till we get to number nineteen!" Newman said, and they began wheeling the dolly across the floor toward the truck outside.

In front, in the car, Ben had lit Leo's cigarette, then his own. In the match flare they studied each other. Ben's hand was shaking. Leo suddenly laughed. Ben said, "Instead of a nice, gentlemanly colored civil servant, we have to deal with a tough RAF sergeant with a gun. That's funny?"

"I was remembering once when Harry and I did something like this. In the old bootlegging days. It worked quite nicely."

"Can I ask a question?"

"Only if it's not personal," Leo said breezily. He felt good. The memory of the old days, the adrenaline pumping through his body, the excitement of a challenge. Pitting your wits against a system. Winning.

Ben said, "Instead of this complicated little maneuver, wouldn't it be simpler to just shove a gun in that guy's stomach?" He slid a .45 from the glove compartment and placed it on the dashboard. "Lock him in a closet, drive the truck in, get the guns—and get out."

"No," said Leo. "Because that would create another international incident." He put the gun back in the glove compartment. "This way, when the British finally realize what happened they'll be much too embarrassed to ever admit it."

"Leo, the whole thing hinges on whether or not he goes with us to make the phone call," Ben said. "We have to get him away from here long enough for the truck to load up and clear out!"

"It'll work," Leo said. The plan had been to drive the watchman—in this case, now the RAF sergeant—to a telephone to call his superior, and at the last minute to decide not to bother the poor man, the superior. So they would take the watchman back to the warehouse. By then the crates would have been removed. "Believe me, it'll work."

"If it doesn't, we may have to end up using muscle anyway."

"Be sure to remind the sergeant of that before he shoots us," Leo said.

Ben had no chance to reply, for just then Charles Warfield returned. "The telephone is out," he said. In the glare of the DeSoto's headlights his face was opaque. "I can't let you in without proper authority."

"That is absurd!" Leo said. "Who is your superior?"

"Wing Commander Helmsley."

"Then you come with us. We'll drive you to the airport where you can find a phone that does work!" Leo opened the DeSoto rear door for the sergeant.

"Sir, I am not leaving my post." Warfield's hand fell to his holster again.

Ben said crisply, "What is your name, Sergeant?"

"Warfield—"

"—do you know anything about those machine guns?" Ben asked, gentler. "Do you know where they were going?"

"Yes, sir, I do," Warfield said. "They were being smuggled to the Jews! And I guarantee you no Jew will ever see a single one of those guns! I was in Jerusalem when the bloody bastards blew up the King David Hotel. They killed two of my mates!"

Ben gasped in dismay, but Leo spoke up fast, almost soothingly. "Our job is to identify those weapons. And then to see that the people who tried to smuggle them are brought to justice. And punished so they'll never dare to try it again—"

"—sir, I'm sorry, but—"

"—I could wait until morning for your Commander Helmsley to give me proper authority," Leo said, thinking that if they could keep the sergeant interested, keep him outside, Ray Newman and Phil Skaff could complete their task. They should be halfway finished by now. "But I'd like to do it now and get back into town and get on a phone and report to Whitehall," he continued quickly. "And then interrogate the people we arrested. I feel the same way you do about the Jews, and believe me, they'll get all they deserve. Everything, Sergeant. I give you my word on that."

Warfield's heavy-fleshed face was still set stubbornly, but his voice betrayed a slight uncertainty. "Sir, I have my orders—"

"—all I want is a look at the boxes," Leo said. "Just let me drive you to a phone to call your officer. I'll have you back here in five minutes. It's important, Sergeant."

"Sergeant, there are serial numbers on the guns," Ben said. "They'll make it possible to identify the people who sold them to the Jews!"

Leo said, "And help put them into prison that much sooner."

"All right, but only you, sir," Warfield said to Leo. "And you'll have to sign the log."

Leo had opened the car door again for Warfield. Now, abruptly, shockingly, he realized he was being invited into the warehouse. "I beg your pardon?" he said.

"You can come in and examine the guns," Warfield said.

"Oh, yes, of course," Leo said. He opened his door. "You stay here, Peabody."

"Yes, yes, by all means," Ben said, carefully regarding Warfield who had stepped away from the car for Leo to get out. Ben reached into the glove compartment for the .45. He dropped the gun in Leo's lap.

Leo pushed the .45 onto the seat between them. He did not want to be even tempted. He got out of the car. "Lead the way, Sergeant," he said, and followed Warfield to the warehouse door.

Ben watched, knowing that the truck in the rear, which now should be loaded with the crates, could not leave without Warfield hearing or seeing it. As the lights flashed on in the warehouse interior, Ben envisioned Leo standing with hands raised, looking into the muzzle of the RAF sergeant's revolver. He fought an overwhelming urge to turn the car around and drive off.

And at that instant, from the rear of the building, he heard the chugging wheeze of the truck engine starting and roaring throatily into life.

Inside the warehouse they also heard it. "What the bloody hell is that?" Warfield shouted, and ran to the rear access door.

"Sounds like my car!" Leo called after him, cursing the two boys in the truck for not keeping their heads when the warehouse lights went on. He glanced around for the crowbar he had noticed propped against the wall, cursing himself now for not making some contingency plan and for refusing Ben's .45. He reached for the crowbar.

Warfield hurled open the access door and stepped out on the loading platform. Leo gripped the crowbar and approached Warfield. The rumble of the truck engine was fading but still clearly audible.

"That's not your car!" Warfield said. He stood gazing into the darkness. Leo moved back a step for better leverage with the crowbar. Warfield said, bewildered, "Who the hell was it?"

Just as Leo prepared to raise the crowbar, trying to gauge the force of the blow to only stun, not kill, Warfield stepped farther out on the platform. "One of them kaffirs, I'll bet. Out with his girl trying to wet his wick. The boys say this is one of their favorite places for it."

Warfield turned to Leo, but slowly, just slowly enough for Leo to relax his grip on the crowbar. He dangled it in his hand and smiled lamely. "The human instinct, Sergeant. Been going on a few million years."

"The way they go about it here, you'd think they just discovered it,"

Warfield said. He glanced at the crowbar. "All right, so let's take a look at these guns of yours."

"Yes," Leo said. "Yes, let's do that."

For the first time now he had a clear view of the warehouse floor. Quite barren but for some tarpaulin-covered boxes in one corner, and several dozen smaller, cardboard parcels. And—against the wall—twenty wooden crates. All stacked neatly but for a single one a few feet in front of the stack. This was the same, previously opened, Jamaican Customs–tagged crate Ray Newman and Phil Skaff had earlier pushed to the side.

All the crates bore the same Brockheimer Export Corp. black stenciled letters.

Immediately, Leo inserted the crowbar under the top slat of that first crate and pried it up. He pulled it entirely open. "Yes," he said. "Yes, everything seems in order."

Warfield peered into the crate over Leo's shoulder. Lined neatly in the top row, packed in Cosmoline that gleamed dully under the overhead lights, were five machine-gun barrels. Leo poked the crowbar deeper into the crate, spreading aside the top layer of gun barrels. Underneath was another layer, five more barrels.

"Well, that's what I wanted to see," Leo said. "There are your Jewish guns, Sergeant. And there they'll stay!" He slammed the lid down and banged the top nail into the wood with the crowbar.

"What about the others?" Warfield said. "Don't you want to examine them?" He prodded a crate with the toe of his shoe, then bent to pick it up. It was very heavy.

"I see no reason to," Leo said, prodding the crate also. "No sense upsetting the customs boys. I have what I want." He pushed the heavy crate back into its original position, and walked away, hoping Warfield would follow. Hoping Warfield would not notice the grain of the wood of the other nineteen crates was markedly different from the one they inspected.

"Whatever you say," Warfield said, and started away.

Leo, walking just ahead, suddenly was aware that his fingers felt wet and sticky. From where he had touched the crate, the fresh stenciled letters. They had done a good job with the phony stencils—cutting the letters on a shirt cardboard donated by Phil Skaff.

"Does everything in here look correct to you?" Leo asked, stopping, facing Warfield.

"As far as I can make out, yes, sir."

"Good." Leo gestured Warfield to go ahead of him now. He followed, glancing at his fingers; they were black with paint. He wiped his hands with his handkerchief. He hoped the smudge on the crate was not too noticeable.

"You've been very helpful, Sergeant. What did you say your name was?"

"Warfield, sir. Charles Warfield."

"I'll mention you to the director."

"Thank you, sir. Very kind of you."

"My pleasure," Leo said, wondering if there was not some conceivable way to salvage that one remaining genuine crate. He hated leaving it behind.

Two hours later the Panamanian C-46 took off. On board, in addition to the original three-man crew, were Ray Newman, Ben Sylbert, and nineteen wooden crates containing one hundred and ninety Fiat 8-mm machine guns complete with tripod. Three weeks later, on the night of May 16, that same C-46, with the same cargo, landed at an airfield twelve miles north of Tel Aviv. One day after the State of Israel was proclaimed.

But that night in Kingston Leo watched the departing airplane until the red glow of its engine-exhaust flames vanished into the dark sky. Then he went into the airport terminal and waited for the morning BOAC flight to Miami.

At seven A.M., seated in the forward cabin of a Pan Am Constellation climbing out on takeoff, Leo saw the warehouse below the airplane's left wing. There seemed to be no unusual activity, so he presumed Sergeant Charles Warfield was off duty and enjoying breakfast at the NCO club. It might be weeks before the crates were reexamined. One crate would contain ten Fiat 8-mm machine guns. The other nineteen, a variety of bricks and boulders, including one with a half-empty can of black paint, a brush, and several cardboard stencils. Thinking about it, Leo could not help laughing.

"Let me in on the joke," said the man sitting beside him, a silver-haired Catholic priest.

Leo leaned back in the plush leather seat. "I guess that's what it was all right, Father. A joke." He rubbed the thumb of his right hand against the forefinger and felt the rough texture of the few remaining flecks of black paint. It was good quality; it would not easily wash away.

22

ON Valentine's Day, February 14, 1949, three days after Leo Goro-detsky's forty-ninth birthday, the Barclay opened. More than a year behind schedule, and still not entirely ready. But this was the day Harry said he would open, and open he did. Miraculously, only a few things went wrong.

First, the battery of eight klieg lights, placed for their beams to intersect in a brilliant octagonal burst of light above the highway, broke down. All eight. Then the water pressure for the multicolored fountain in the center of the driveway failed. Harry said it reminded him of an old man peeing. The beautiful black tile on some bathroom walls kept falling to the tiled floor, and not all the showers had hot water. But the toilets flushed, and the electricity was on, and the elevators worked. February in the desert, fortunately, obviated the need for the air conditioning, which did not work. Unfortunately, neither did the heat.

Other than that it was a fabulous opening.

Ben Sylbert had done his job well. The Los Angeles and San Francisco papers were filled with stories of the spectacular new Las Vegas hotel. Jimmy Durante and the Andrews Sisters in the main showroom; in the big lounge, the Lexington Room, Larry Clinton and his band. The smaller lounge, the hideaway, featured a popular Negro trio, Richard, Lewis, and Alex King, "The Brothers Kay."

Three restaurants, the Concord Grille, a twenty-four-hour coffee shop, the Bella Vista ("for the finest Italian cuisine this side of Rome!"), and the Monaco, the hotel's gourmet room. Only the coffee shop anticipated a profit; the other two restaurants were loss leaders. The Monaco's chef was imported from Paris where he had been *sous-chef* at Maxim's. His salary alone was $25,000. Under construction was a fully equipped health club with a sauna rivaling any top European spa. And Harry had plans for yet another restaurant: the Control Tower, atop the fourth-story roof.

Chartered plane after chartered plane arrived from Los Angeles, Houston, Detroit, and New York. Harry Wise's guests for this once-in-a lifetime opening night ranged from Hollywood celebrities to Texas high rollers, politicians, war heroes, important Alliance figures, labor leaders. Guests, quite literally: fully comped, all expenses paid. The estimated cost of this alone exceeded $100,000.

Extravagant, yes, but the publicity and goodwill could never be measured in dollars. Besides, the expenditure would be recouped in the first week's play from the casino's three craps tables, nine blackjack tables, and two roulette wheels. Not to mention the slots, located in their own area away from the main casino. Harry hated the idea of slots in the main casino. The constant clanging of the levers and wheels. Too much like a downtown grind joint. He actually had considered eliminating slots entirely, but could not ignore the figures. Slots produced more win than any other game.

Harry and Liz personally greeted each celebrity and high roller, Ben Sylbert the smaller fry. After settling in their rooms—each containing a huge basket of fresh fruit, with a personal card from Harry—everyone trooped downstairs to a buffet in the lobby. Two tables heaped end to end with beluga caviar, Louisiana shrimp, Maine and Pacific lobster, crab, abalone, roast beef, turkey. Dom Pérignon champagne, 1935 Lafite, California Chardonnay.

Then, the guests comfortably mellow and overfed, Liz cut a ceremonial yellow ribbon officially opening the casino. As the people flowed past him to the tables, Mickey Goldfarb, functioning as executive casino host, said, "Jeeze, I never seen so many shmucks so anxious to dump their dough!" Over the years he had put on weight. In his tuxedo he resembled a plump penguin.

Leo watched all this from the bar of the Hideaway Lounge. When everyone appeared settled at the tables he went outside to the darkened, deserted pool. He wanted to be alone awhile, to think, to relax. He had been in Las Vegas nearly a week, helping organize the cashier's cage, the accounting department, the counting room, and key personnel. Barclay pit bosses, floormen, and dealers were recruited from IDIC hotels in Havana and the recently closed casinos in Covington and Hot Springs. The best of the best. And paid accordingly. Dealers guaranteed seventy-five dollars weekly, plus tips.

He sank into an upholstered deck chair, wrapping his heavy wool tweed jacket tight against the cold. He was glad now he forgot to pack his tuxedo. For a moment he debated going back inside, but decided it was not that cold and the fresh air would clear his head. And it was warmer here than in Washington, where he might have been now, perhaps should have been.

At a victory party at the Israeli Embassy.

If he had been invited.

He would have been more than pleased to attend that victory celebration. He was proud of his role in Israel's creation; he wanted it recognized. But they did not invite him, and he believed he knew why.

They feared his presence at such a function—he, the "Underworld Gambling Czar"—a Jew, might embarrass Israel.

Embarrass.

The word reminded him of the time Martin Raab, now in Washington himself as a Justice Department assistant attorney general, said Leo embarrassed him as a Jew. Leo wanted such people to acknowledge what he did for Israel. Oddly enough, only a few weeks ago, Golda Myerson had phoned him from Tel Aviv. At first he thought her call was to invite him to the victory party, but it was merely to once again express her gratitude for his services to the new nation. She did, however, invite him to Israel.

She said, "Mr. Gorodetsky, I hope you will visit us soon in Israel. No, not 'visit'! Come to stay. Come home, where you belong."

"I thank you for that," he had said. "But I'm an American, and intend to remain one."

"You are also a Jew."

"A Jew, yes. An Israeli, no."

"Well, should the day ever arrive, you'll be more than welcome," she said. "Israel does not forget her friends."

Even if they do embarrass her.

But Golda Myerson certainly was not embarrassed nine months before, in a different telephone call from Tel Aviv. To Leo, in Mexico City. He could still hear her deep, resonant voice booming into his ear.

"Mr. Gorodetsky, the packages have arrived. We thank you!"

The "packages," of course, the machine guns. And then she had asked, "And how goes the new project?"

"Slow," he had replied, which was the understatement of the century. The "new project": purchase of twenty-five P-47 fighter airplanes from the Mexican air force, requiring endless, agonizing negotiation with brokers, cabinet ministers, middlemen, cousins, and brothers-in-law. In the end U.S. State Department pressure canceled the entire sale. But by then Leo was deeply involved in other equally complicated and vital purchasing missions. Israel, attacked by five Arab armies, was in a state of war, besieged, and denied assistance by the entire world. For nearly nine months Leo traveled constantly. Europe, South America, even Formosa. Although, ironically, never to Israel. There never seemed to be enough time.

He bought, or supervised the buying of, entire stocks of war surplus matériel. From guns and ammunition to food and clothing. Even an aircraft carrier, a former U.S. Navy escort carrier, the *Attu*, a project regretfully abandoned, but only because of the impossibility of obtaining carrier aircraft. Sometimes, when matériel could not be purchased, it was "borrowed." Not much different from the old bootlegging days.

Including the bootlegging of people.

He chartered a ship to carry 731 displaced persons from Marseilles to Haifa. Payment from his own pocket. These efforts, along with personally raising more than $3 million, consumed him, leaving little time for his own affairs. But IDIC, under George Gerson's management, showed more profit than ever, and paid more taxes. So Leo devoted himself to the new Jewish state, working harder than he had ever worked at anything, but never with more gratification. He knew that if to the rest of the world Leo Gorodetsky was a gangster, to Israel he was a savior.

By January 1949, it was over. The Jews had won. His finest hour came with a personal message from David Ben Gurion. Two simple words.

"Thank you."

So now, in Las Vegas, huddled against the cold in a deck chair, staring unseeingly at the blue-green chlorine sparkle of the pool water in the sunken pool lights, he remembered, and told himself that he understood and felt no bitterness. Disappointed, perhaps, but not bitter.

After all, it was all only a question of business.

And that, of all things, he understood.

"Hey, you in a trance, or something?"

A short, wiry, youngish, curly haired man stood grinning down at him. A beautiful girl clung to the man's sleeve, a blonde in a satinlike dinner gown, shivering in the cold. Even in the shaded patio lights Leo saw the goose bumps on the girl's bare shoulders and arms. A hooker, one of dozens of "high-class types" Harry had imported from Los Angeles and San Francisco. Leo did not know her, but knew the man.

Tom Stohlmeyer.

President of UATW, Union of American Transport Workers. Tom Stohlmeyer's muscle had enabled Harry to overcome the labor problems and finally open the Barclay. The price for persuading various union locals to cooperate was $35,000, which Leo knew went into Stohlmeyer's pocket. But, as Harry said, You get nothing for nothing.

So, as Harry also said, Thomas Stohlmeyer was an honored guest. Greeted, feted, fed, and fucked—that "comp" of course provided by the blond young woman now trembling with the cold.

Leo looked at him. "Tom, how are you?"

"Not bad, Leo. Not bad at all."

"Enjoying yourself?"

"Every minute," Stohlmeyer said. He fondled the blond girl's firm buttocks. "*Every* minute, believe me. Honey, you know Mr. Gorodetsky?"

"I don't believe I've had the pleasure," she said.

"I doubt it's much of a pleasure for you," Leo said. "You're freezing out here."

She smiled bravely. "Oh, I enjoy this weather. I find it real refreshing."

Stohlmeyer said to her, "Yeah, well, why don't you go inside and refresh yourself with a hot toddy or something?" He jangled his room key in front of her, then slipped it into the front of her gown. "Then go up and wait for me."

"Sure," she said. She retrieved the key. "Nice meeting you, Mr. G.," she said to Leo, and hurried away, her high heels clattering hollowly on the patio tile.

Stohlmeyer snapped his tuxedo jacket collar up around his neck and pulled a straight-backed patio chair up beside Leo's deck chair. He sat, rubbing his hands together and blowing on them for warmth. "Jesus, it really is cold!"

"I find it real refreshing," Leo said, poker-faced.

"For Eskimos, maybe," Stohlmeyer said. "I thought maybe we could have a little chat. Get to know each other a little."

All Leo knew about Tom Stohlmeyer was that he was a former Toledo, Ohio, truck driver whose fists and guts had carried him to the top. Leo also knew he was about to know Stohlmeyer better. The man wanted to talk, and not about the weather or pretty blond hookers.

"Sure," Leo said. "Good idea."

"I like the hotel," said Stohlmeyer. "I think it'll do real fine. Make you guys some money."

"We certainly hope so."

"Listen, you sure you don't want to go inside? Be a hell of a lot more comfortable."

Leo was not all that uncomfortable in his wool jacket and did not feel inclined to accommodate Stohlmeyer. He knew a proposition was forthcoming. The idea of it being presented by a man in a thin tuxedo shivering with cold amused him. He decided it was because of the crude way Stohlmeyer treated the girl.

He said, "You want to talk, we'll do it out here."

If Stohlmeyer was offended, he gave no indication. "Okay," he said easily. He drew a single cigarette from his inside pocket. He lit it, exhaled, and said, "If this place makes it, within two years there'll be half a dozen other ones. You'll need money to build them. I control a pension fund worth more than thirty million. We're always interested in sound investments."

Leo said, "I have a feeling the Nevada licensing authorities, and the

NLRB—not to mention the Federal Trade Commission—might not look too favorably on a labor union as a casino partner."

"I'm talking about a loan."

Ah, yes, of course, Leo thought. A loan. "At what interest?"

"It's negotiable," Stohlmeyer said. "Depending on the principal amount, but I guarantee not over four percent."

"Very generous," Leo said. He smiled blandly at Stohlmeyer, whose cigarette was clenched in clattering teeth. "I'll keep it in mind if we do build another hotel."

"I'm willing to commit right now."

"How much?"

"Say, two million."

"At four percent?"

"Yes, four."

Leo faced him another moment, then got up. He had suddenly begun feeling the chill. A $2 million loan at four percent should have felt warm, but he knew it was too good to be true; there had to be a catch. There was.

Stohlmeyer, rising with him, flipped his cigarette butt into the pool. Nothing Leo's disapproving glance, he said, "Nobody's swimming in this weather, huh?"

"I hope not," Leo said.

"Naturally, there'll be a slight finder's fee."

"Naturally," said Leo. "How 'slight'?"

"Well, since the face value of the loan probably will be more than half of what you'll need, I think a fee of, say, five percent is fair."

"A hundred thousand," Leo said. "Whose pocket does this finder's fee go into? Or is that a foolish question?"

Stohlmeyer smiled.

If Leo Gorodetsky's finest hour was Ben Gurion's message, Harry Wise's finest hour was now, here in Las Vegas, fulfilling the Dream. A dream that, four hours after the official casino opening, Leo discovered was turning into a nightmare.

After his talk with Tom Stohlmeyer, Leo went into the Concord Grille for coffee. He was tired enough now to sleep. He would have the coffee and go to bed. It was good coffee, hot and strong, so he had a second cup, glancing over the front page of the *Los Angeles Times*, the next day's early edition, which the hotel had contracted to be regularly flown in. Another small, loss-leader service of Harry's; he said it added one more touch of class.

The paper contained nothing particularly important or interesting, other than an AP squib with a New York dateline: Congressman Charles Brickhill's announcement of his candidacy in next year's U.S. senatorial election. The story referred to Brickhill as a one-time protégé of the late

Major General Robert MacGowan, which reminded Leo of MacGowan's death a year ago. Heart attack, although Leo thought "broken heart" more accurate. Truman had dissolved O.S.S., creating in its place the CIA, whose new director fired MacGowan. A grateful government's gratitude. Leo reminded himself to make a generous contribution to Brickhill's opponent.

He put the paper aside and considered ordering a corned-beef sandwich. Harry claimed Concord Grille corned beef the finest outside of the Stage Delicatessen, unarguably the world's finest. But Leo felt conspicuous alone at a table in the fairly crowded restaurant. He regretted not bringing Carla with him. She wanted to come, but the new semester was just starting. She was in Boston, at the New England Conservatory, living in a Back Bay apartment with her aunt Esther, whom Leo had sent to look after her.

He mulled the corned-beef sandwich another moment and decided it was too late, nearly 2:30. No matter how good the sandwich, it would lie like a brick in his stomach. He signed the check and left a five-dollar bill for a tip or, in Vegas parlance, a "toke."

The instant he stepped from the coffee shop, even before entering the casino proper, he knew there was trouble. He knew even before he heard the shrill, elated cries of winning players. A hot streak. It enveloped you, and swept through the whole casino like a searing gust of wind.

The first craps table.

An excited crowd gathered three and four deep around the table. A tall, stout, middle-aged man wearing a pearl-gray ten-gallon hat and tuxedo stood at the end of the table. Dice rattled in his closed fist as he prepared to roll.

". . . once more, you little darlin's!" the man shouted in a Texas drawl. "One more natural!" He hurled the dice. A moment of utter silence. And then screams of triumph.

"Seven!"

Leo recognized the shooter. Leroy Conners, a Dallas oil wildcatter, a longtime good customer in Covington and Hot Springs. With a $50,000 A-1 credit line. A degenerate gambler who had won and lost several oil fortunes. Casino gambling was simply an extension of his life. He had flown to Vegas in his own private plane, with three "secretaries," tall, leggy Texas girls now clustered around him at the crap table.

Leo, hurrying toward the table, saw Mickey Goldfarb break out of the crowd and start toward the cage. Leo stopped him. Mickey's face was ashen.

"That fucking Conners!" said Mickey. "I got to get more chips."

"How much is he ahead?" Leo asked.

"Not much," Mickey said wryly. "Only ninety grand! 'Scuse me," he muttered, and brushed past Leo. Leo seized his sleeve and pulled him around.

"How can he be ninety ahead?" Leo asked. "With a five-hundred-dollar limit?"

"Harry raised the limit to two thousand," Mickey said, and rushed off again.

"Where is Harry?" Leo called after him.

Mickey pointed to the gold and silver chandeliered ceiling, the pinpoints of lights trained on the tables. Harry was up inside the partitions above the casino, the Eye in the Sky, the observation ports where you watched casino action.

Leo went into the cashiers' cage, then turned left and through a door marked "Authorized Personnel Only." This opened into a narrow corridor, the walls still damp with unset plaster. A rickety ladder led to a trapdoor in the ceiling. Leo clambered up the ladder and onto a catwalk under the roof that extended the entire circumference of the casino. Here, amid a maze of wiring and steel beams, at locations directly above the two blackjack pits, two men lay on their stomachs peering into the padded eyepieces of binoculars set into a ceiling porthole. Harry was at the far end of the catwalk above the first craps table. He was also peering through binoculars, but kneeling, not lying down. He looked very cramped and uncomfortable.

Harry heard Leo's heels on the wooden catwalk and glanced up from the glasses. His somber face brightened. He swept his hand about in a 360-degree circle. "So what do you think, Kleyner, finest casino in the world, right?"

"Leroy Conners sure must think so," Leo said. He gestured Harry to step away from the binoculars; he wanted to see for himself. The binoculars, which could observe the entire table, or zoom in on any individual player or dealer, were focused on Leroy Conners's hands flinging the dice. Leo watched the dice carom against the padded table sides, then fall and settle. A pair of threes. The stickman's voice was clearly heard:

". . . six, the winner! Pay the line, pay the number!"

Leo zoomed the glasses in on the fingers of a dealer deftly stacking black chips, sliding them across the table to match an equal stack on the line.

"Fourth pass this roll," Harry said.

"Why did you raise the limit?"

"Why not?"

Leo pointed to the floor, the unseen craps table below. "That's why. But, all right, we'll catch him." He pushed himself up from the viewing position. "What's the rest of the action look like, Harry?"

Harry's face was somber again. "I had Mickey run an early audit on every table. We got a very low drop." The drop was the amount of cash or markers dropped into the table boxes during play, balanced against the table's chips to determine the win. Harry tapped the binoculars. "And I'm not even including *that*. I mean, all the tables."

"Play's only just started," Leo said. "It'll change. Besides, Harry, it's good for business."

"Leo, ever since I know you, it's the same story. 'A winner is good for business, good publicity.'" Harry shook his head and pointed again to the craps table below. "That kind of winning, Leo, is not good for business!"

"Roy Conners won't leave this place with our money," Leo said. "The percentages will catch up with him and grind him away. He's a steamer. He won't quit."

Harry said nothing a moment. From the casino below, more triumphant shouts. Then, quietly, Harry said, "I'm having Johnny Fingers take over the stick."

Johnny Fingers, otherwise known as Jacob Feinberg, was an expert in detecting, and foiling, cheats. Sixty years old, he knew every trick ever devised to rig a slot machine, manipulate a deck of cards, rig a roulette wheel—or switch dice. He had worked for Leo and Harry since the Chez When days, his services obviously invaluable.

Johnny Fingers's skills were employed against players only if the player was a high roller bent on cheating the house. Small-timers—after their photos were taken and placed in a black book—were merely shown the door and thereafter barred. Dealers caught cheating were summarily discharged, their names and photos also placed in the book. Sometimes, depending on the magnitude of the offense and the inclination of the individual casino manager, the punishment was more severe.

Leo said, "Johnny Fingers isn't a good idea, Harry."

"I got a bad feeling about this one, Leo."

"Forget it."

"Leo, you know we're running a short bankroll. Vinnie Tomasino's out there watching. And Calvelli, too. They see a big loss like this, I'll look like a horse's ass!"

"I don't care what you look like," Leo said. "In my casino, we don't cheat!"

"*Your* casino?" Harry said. "What am I, Leo, the towel boy?"

Leo understood Harry's anxiety, but a temporary losing streak was no excuse for a ringer in the game. He had never done it, and would not start now. "Harry, if I see Johnny Fingers at that table, I'll close this place down so fast you won't know what happened!"

The refracted glow of the casino chandeliers in the ceiling under their feet shadowed Harry's face, all but his eyes, hard and cold. Leo could feel Harry's temper; almost hear it, like the clanging of a steel door.

"Harry, listen to me. Please."

"I didn't work all my life to get here, Leo—to have some shit-kicker jump on a roll that'll wipe me out. It's not right!"

"The older you get the dumber you get."

"He's into us now for over a hundred grand."

"You *are* a horse's ass!" Leo said. "Don't you realize that the second Roy Conners sees a new stickman, he'll know what's happening? Not only will he cash in, and walk out with all your money, but he'll pass the word! 'Harry Wise tried to slip shaved dice into the game!' "

In the dark Harry peered at him.

"It's no good, Harry. It's a sucker play."

Harry was silent another moment, and then all at once he relaxed. His whole body seemed to sag. "Yeah," he said. "Okay. Okay."

Leo patted Harry gently on the shoulder. "Believe me, I know Roy Conners. I know how he plays. He hasn't a chance of leaving here a winner. He's not smart enough to quit ahead."

Leo was wrong.

At 4:00 A.M., Leroy Conners was $250,000 ahead. It was then that the dice changed. The percentages started catching up. At 4:30, Conners had dropped $38,000 of his winnings. He asked to see Harry, who had remained upstairs watching. Leo, no longer sleepy, was in the Concord Grille. He had instructed Mickey to keep him informed. Mickey rushed in to tell Leo that Leroy Conners wanted the limit raised to $5,000.

". . . you know what he said, the cocksucker?" Mickey said to Leo. He tried to imitate Conners's drawl. " 'Ah'm a gonna break you smartass Jewboys! Ah've bin waitin' maybe fifteen fuckin' years for it. Now ah'm a gonna do it!' " Mickey paused for breath. He had unloosened his tie, a premade bow, but not the collar. A layer of fat drooping over Mickey's collar button jiggled as he continued, "So Harry said okay, he'd raise the limit again. Five thousand—"

"—five thousand?" Leo nearly shouted the word. The few people in the restaurant glanced at him curiously.

Mickey held up his hand like a traffic cop. "Wait. When Harry said okay, then the *goy* prick, he smiles. The greasiest smile I ever seen, Leo. He smiles, and he says, 'I figured that's what you'd do. So I also figured I'd best take my money and go home!' And Leo, that's just what he did. He cashed in and left!"

"Left?" Leo asked numbly.

"With two hundred and twelve big ones. Honest to Jesus, I thought Harry was about to have a stroke right there. He looked like somebody whacked him with a shovel."

"Where is he?" Leo asked. "Harry?"

"I don't know," Mickey said. "Nobody's seen him. Liz don't know where he is, neither."

Leo glanced at his watch: 4:45. "How long ago did Conners leave?"

"Fifteen, twenty minutes."

"Get a car," Leo said. He got up and started to leave. Mickey remained standing, confused. Leo said, "A car, Mickey! Now!"

"Where we going?"

"The airport!"

* * *

The new airport, McCarran Field, was only five minu:es from the hotel, another "feature" Ben Sylbert's press releases emphasized. It consisted of two 6,500-foot asphalt runways, several hangars, and a prefabricated building serving as a terminal and operations office. Night facilities were not yet operational, so Leo knew Conners was still on the ground. He also knew this was where he would find Harry.

Mickey raced the hotel station wagon onto the ramp and pulled up near Harry's Cord, which was parked almost under the wing of a Beechcraft AT-11, a small twin-engined passenger airplane. The Cord's headlights shone on the airplane's door, on the word DALCOL, overlaid in blue letters across a brilliant yellow sunflower, decaled on the airplane's door. In the glare of the automobile headlights, Harry and Conners stood arguing. Both stopped as Leo got out of the station wagon and strode toward them.

Conners said, "Your partner here's got a big hair acrost his ass, Leo. You better quiet him down 'fore he does something foolish!"

Harry said, "I'm trying to explain to this man, politely—" he paused, and untied his tux bow tie and unbuttoned his collar. "I'm explaining, politely, that when you gamble, you're supposed to give the other guy a chance to get even!"

Leo closed his eyes, exasperated. He heard Conners laugh harshly and say, "Jesus, now I heard everything!"

So have I, Leo thought, and opened his eyes and said to Harry, "Could I talk to you just a second? In private." He said to Conners, "Roy, will you give us just a second?"

Conners laughed again. He glanced at the sky beyond the hills to the east, brightening yellowly with the rising sun. "Five minutes," he said. "Then we're taking off."

Leo grasped Harry's arm and led him back to the automobiles, where Mickey waited anxiously.

"Jesus, Harry, what the hell are you doing?" Mickey asked.

"I'm trying to get my money back!" Harry said. "What the hell do you think I'm doing? That answers your question, too!" he said to Leo.

"The man won," Leo said. "He has a right to quit."

Harry said, "The only way he quits is if he's a corpse!"

"You're crazy," Leo said. He strained for control. He knew losing his temper would only make Harry more determined. "You'll blow everything we worked for. Everything!"

"*We*," Harry said, almost spitting the word. "There it goes again: we. It's *me*, Leo. *I* worked for it. It's mine!"

Leo, remembering a hundred similar experiences with Harry and the constant struggle to keep him in line, wondered why he had bothered, and why he bothered now.

". . . now just fuck off, Leo!" Harry was saying. He moved to leave.

Leo seized Harry's wrist and said, "Harry, the man is not going back to play. Even if he wanted to, he wouldn't now. Why can't you get that through your head?"

"He's not leaving here with two hundred thousand of my money, Leo. Now that's all there is to it!" Harry wrenched himself free, and started away.

Leo felt momentarily unable to move, as though trapped in a dream. Harry walked toward Conners who stood casually at the airplane's door, his thick gray hair cushioning the ten-gallon hat tipped back on his head. Leo realized Conners was unafraid, making him as stupid as Harry. Stupider.

It was still like a dream, as though watching himself from a distance, as Leo plunged his hand into Mickey Goldfarb's jacket, into Mickey's shoulder holster, and withdrew Mickey's little .32 Colt automatic.

"Harry!" Leo called. He stepped forward, his arm stretched straight out, the gun trained on Harry's heart. "You're my oldest and best friend," Leo said quietly. "But I swear to you, Harry, if you don't back off, I'll pull this trigger." The sound of his own voice was strange and frightened him as nothing before ever frightened him because he knew he meant every word he said.

Harry knew it, too, and so did Mickey. Mickey stood gazing in openmouthed, almost glazed bewilderment at the gun in Leo's hand aimed at Harry. Leo wondered if Mickey would move, and wondered what he would do about that.

He knew he had only a split-instant to resolve the issue. He had opened the bottle and freed the genie. The genie was his own finger squeezing the gun's trigger. He spoke quietly, but fast and deliberately.

"You took a loss, all right. But you'll make it up. Believe me, Harry, this two hundred thousand will come back a thousand times in profit! You know why, Harry? Because you—" Leo was very careful not to say *we;* he would indulge Harry that much. "You'll turn it to your advantage. Ben Sylbert will flood the gossip columns with stories about Roy Conners's big strike. The high rollers will come begging for a chance at some of that easy money. Harry, think, please! Please, Harry!"

Leo wanted to say more but felt too drained, empty. He held the gun so tight his fingers ached, but his hand was so soaked with sweat he dared not relax his grip for fear the gun would slip to the ground.

Then he felt the gun pushed almost gently away, and saw Harry's lips moving, and heard, ". . . Kleyner, you are something else. Relax." Harry turned and walked to his car. He got in, slammed the door, gunned the engine, and drove off. Off the ramp, through the airport gate, and back onto the highway.

Leo heard Mickey release his breath in a deep, heavy sigh. Leo handed him the gun and walked over to Conners. "Sorry about all this, Roy. Harry gets a little excited sometimes."

Conners replied, but Leo was not listening. He was gazing at the Cord's
red taillights receding in the distance, and thinking it had all been just
a little too easy. Harry Wise never gave up that easily. He thought about
this until he no longer saw the taillights, or heard the low, throaty hum
of the car's engine.

2.

Leo's prediction that the Barclay would turn a profit was correct. Eleven
months after opening, the casino was in the black. Twelve months later
it showed a net profit of $2 million, and construction began on another,
larger hotel, the Oasis.

Financed by a $4 million UATW Pension Fund loan.

Groundbreaking ceremonies for the new hotel, located diagonally across
Highway 91 from the Barclay, were held New Year's Eve, 1951. A black-
tie, invitation-only, celebrity-studded party with the New York City Ballet
performing *Swan Lake*, the first ballet company ever to play Las Vegas.
Liz DiFalco's idea. and a rousing success. Proceeds for the $100 per
person event were donated to the Las Vegas General Hospital Fund.

Harry Wise presented a $10,000 check to the Hospital Fund chairman
the elderly widow of a pioneer Vegas casino operator and real-estate
speculator. In his presentation speech Harry paraphrased the remarks
written for him by Ben Sylbert.

"Folks, this is only the beginning. Someday Vegas'll be a big city, with
more hospitals and more schools, churches, paved streets. Even a country
club. You wait and see. Highway Ninety-one, from here all the way to
downtown, it'll be a single strip of hotels from one end to the other!"

Harry sat down to genuine, enthusiastic applause, for not a single
person in the audience doubted his prophecy. Embracing Liz, he said,
"Goddamit, why wasn't the Kleyner here! He'd be real proud of me!"

Liz said, "*I'm* proud of you. Doesn't that count?"

He looked into her eyes. God, how he loved her! "More than anything,
babe, you know that."

"And, Harry, darling," she whispered coolly into his ear. "Don't be so
sorry Leo isn't here. He might want to see the books."

"Yeah, he might," Harry said after a moment.

The last thing on Leo's mind was the Barclay, or its books. He was in
Florida, where it was a few minutes past midnight of the new year, a
guest of Major General Fulgencio Batista at the general's palatial Daytona
Beach home. There were a dozen other guests, including three former
Cuban government cabinet ministers and their wives, a U.S. State Department undersecretary and his wife, and a Wisconsin congressman
and his wife.

And Carla Gordon.

Leo and Carla sat at one of a number of small tables set up on the tennis court, which had temporarily been converted into a dance floor. Their tablemates were the Wisconsin congressman and his wife. Carla thought the lady an insufferable bore, and her husband only slightly less so. And even worse, a six-piece very American orchestra had replaced the four-piece Cuban band that had entertained them so satisfactorily the first two days of their visit.

"Daddy, do you think we can leave soon?" Carla asked, after the Wisconsin congressman and his wife got up to dance.

Leo studied her a moment. "You know, I ordinarily would never suggest it, but just this once I think it might not hurt you to get drunk."

"The time-honored cure, eh?"

"It works sometimes. For some people," he added quickly, thinking of Ellie, hoping Carla would not pick up on it. She did not; she was too preoccupied with her own troubles.

"I certainly made a fool of myself over that bastard, didn't I?" she said.

"We all make fools of ourselves sometime, honey," he said. "Forget it."

"That bastard!" she said. "That rotten bastard!"

An aide of General Batista's approached. "Mr. Gorodetsky, the general would appreciate you joining him in the library." The aide, a cold-eyed former Cuban army captain whose expensive Italian silk suit was itself a uniform, smiled apologetically at Carla.

Carla returned the smile. The captain clicked his heels and left. "Happy New Year," she called after him.

"Walk me to the house," Leo said to Carla, who, grateful for any excuse to leave, joined him immediately. "Wait for me out here. I'm sure I won't be long," he said when they reached the veranda. "And please do me a favor: forget about the rotten bastard."

The rotten bastard was a forty-three-year-old Boston University tenured professor named Tibor Matona. He was the reason for Carla's being here in Florida with Leo.

She had fallen in love with Tibor Matona.

They had met at a cocktail party given by Carla's musical-theory professor. They liked each other immediately. He was tall, muscular, with a face resembling a block of finely chiseled granite. His quiet, easygoing manner exuded confidence and reminded her, she said, of her brother. She, he said, reminded him of a beautiful young woman in a Gibson painting. A beautiful young woman impatient to begin living her life. A lunch date led to dinner and, within the week, bed. It was not Carla's first sexual experience, but the first she truly enjoyed.

Carla's aunt Esther, with whom she lived, approved of her occasionally dating. Normal and healthy for a girl that age. Esther had no idea Carla's new date was a forty-three-year-old man of the world. Esther's prime concern was making a good home for Carla, and seeing that she wrote her mother regularly and visited her at least once each month.

Carla drove to Hartford House in her own car, a Ford convertible, a twenty-first birthday gift from Leo. She was an honors student, a happy young woman, and that pleased Leo, which in turn pleased Esther. She adored her young niece, and was herself quite content. Especially four hundred miles and five hours away from her own mother, whose very existence was a constant reminder to Esther of her own empty life.

Over coffee one morning, Carla casually announced that she and Tibor were driving up to New Hampshire for the weekend.

"New Hampshire?" Esther said. "Weekend? What New Hampshire? What weekend? Where will you stay?"

"Oh, we'll find something," Carla said. "Tibor says there are cabins everywhere up there."

Esther instantly notified Leo. He was not upset. "She's twenty-one, Esther," he said. "She's a grown woman."

"Leo, are you crazy?" Esther screamed into the phone. "They're going to *sleep* together!"

"It happens all the time," Leo said.

"Leo, I think he's a *shaygets!*"

"Esther, don't worry about it. She'll be fine." Actually, Carla's having an affair did not displease him; it was about time.

"That's all you can say, Leo? 'She'll be fine'?"

"What do you want me to say, Esther? Shall I tell her not to do it? Or shall I tell her it's okay only if it's a Jewish boy?"

"Leo, you're her father!"

He knew nothing he said would ease Esther's mind; and he suspected, too, she was jealous. She, to his knowledge, had never slept with a man. And now, a fifty-four-year-old spinster, probably never would. Of course, he was curious about the man his daughter slept with—he assumed it was a college classmate, her own age—but not at all concerned. He trusted Carla's judgment. He said to Esther on the phone, "Don't worry so much about it. Believe me, it's healthy."

"Vay iz mir!" she said, and hung up.

A week later, while at his mother's Amsterdam Avenue apartment for Friday evening *Shabbes* dinner, Leo received another call from Esther. Luckily, Sarah was busy in the kitchen and asked him to answer the phone.

"Leo!" Esther shrieked into the phone. "She's in jail! They took her away to jail, Leo!"

"Jail? Is she hurt? Is she all right?"

"She's in jail, I said! How can she be all right?"

"Please, calm down. Please. Tell me what happened?"

"Don't you hear what I'm saying, Leo? She's in jail!"

"Esther!" he shouted. "Is she all right?"

"Yes, she's fine. But she's in jail. *Gottenyu!* Oy, I'll die! Leo. Jail!"

Leo nearly laughed with relief. "What happened?"

"Leo, when I tell you, you won't believe it! She tried to run somebody over in her car! Leo, *die helst*? She tried to run somebody over! A teacher, yet! A college professor!"

"She 'tried'?" Leo said. "She didn't do it?"

"No, thank God. He ran away where the car couldn't get him. Leo, she drove up on the sidewalk! On the sidewalk!"

Leo said nothing. A few months ago on a Cambridge newsstand, Carla saw a newspaper headline about a U.S. Senate Crime Committee investigating Leo Gorodetsky. He had explained to her then, for the first time, that he was in the gambling business and precisely what that meant. Now, he imagined another headline: DAUGHTER OF GANGLAND FIGURE HELD IN MURDER ATTEMPT!

"Leo!" Esther screamed. "Do you hear me?"

"Yes, I hear you," he said, glancing at his mother who had entered the living room and was watching him curiously. He put his hand over the telephone mouthpiece and said to Sarah, "It's Esther, Ma. She wants to come down to New York with Carla next week."

"So tell her yes," Sarah said.

"I already did," Leo said, and into the phone said to Esther, "All right, I'll take care of everything." He hung up and asked his mother to fix him some coffee, waiting for her to leave so he could place a call to his Boston attorney.

When he returned to the dining room his mother asked, "So they'll be here next week, Laibel?"

"I think so, Ma, yes."

"A lovely girl, that daughter of yours. She should only meet a nice boy."

"Yes, Ma," Leo said. "That would be very nice."

"God should only make it happen," Sarah said, and then frowned. "Leo, do you know your hair is getting gray?"

By the time Leo had arrived in Boston the following afternoon, Carla was free on bail on charges of reckless driving and attempted manslaughter. It seemed that in broad daylight, on Commonwealth Avenue, she had deliberately driven her car up onto the sidewalk, clearly intending to run her alleged victim down. The man, a Boston University professor, escaped injury only by darting into a doorway. Passersby reported her license-plate number to the police.

The professor of course was her lover, Tibor Matona, whom she accidentally had discovered to be married, with four young children. She went to Tibor's Brookline house and met and talked with the wife, a very nice woman whose very first words to Carla were "Oh dear, not again?"

Carla sped back to Boston and waited outside the university for Tibor.

She originally planned merely to confront him, tell him what she thought of him, perhaps slap his face, and let it go at that. But when she saw him, his handsome, chiseled-in-granite face and steel-gray hair, she remembered the gentle fingers caressing her skin, and the impeccably middle-European accent uttering all those declarations of undying love and passion. Before she knew it, she had raced the Ford convertible up onto the sidewalk after him, in the process knocking over a hydrant that flooded the nearby sidewalk and storefronts and blocked traffic nearly thirty minutes in that busy intersection.

Tibor Matona understandably refused to press charges, and Leo's Boston attorney got the charges of attempted manslaughter and destruction of public property reduced to simple reckless driving. But Leo decided, temporarily at least, to remove Carla from the scene of the crime. Christmas and New Year's in Florida would be a good change for her, and then she would accompany him to Cuba.

They had been in Daytona three days as General Batista's honored guests. During the day, while Leo engaged in intense discussion with grim men who drank and ate constantly, Carla basked on the sand or romped in the surf with the two friendly Batista Great Danes. Each night, at dinner in the huge dining room adjoining the patio, the four-piece band played tango and rhumba music. After dinner Carla usually sat on the veranda while Leo, the general, and several of the men went to the library for brandy and cigars. And more talk, smatterings of it sometime drifting through the balmy night to the veranda.

Words like "coup," or "political exigencies," "loyal officers." Carla asked Leo about it, but he said it was too complicated to explain at the present time. He said she would understand everything soon, in Havana.

Happy New Year, she told herself now, sitting in the glider on the veranda, waiting for Leo to finish his meeting inside. She was gazing at the full yellow moon hovering low over the ocean, and listening to the wind rustle warmly through the palm trees fronting the beach, and the sound of the surf foaming up on the sand. Yes, Happy New Year, she thought again, wishing she had someone other than her father to talk to. The only person close to her age was Batista's seventeen-year-old son, the dark complexioned boy everyone called Little Sergeant. He enjoyed dancing with Carla because his head, which hardly reached her chin, could rest on her bosom. He was a bore.

But she could handle him. After Tibor Matona, she could handle anything. Anyone. She bristled whenever she thought of him, that bastard, and her little excursion to his home in Brookline. But when she thought of afterward, when she tried to run him down with the car, she shuddered at her stupidity. And at her father's anger. Leo really had her pegged. An actress, he had called her, feeling sorry for herself and making a damn fool of herself.

Making a damn fool of herself seemed par for the course in her relationship with Tibor. Such as when she told him he reminded her of her brother. What a totally ignorant, stupid thing to say! But then, in truth, the man was attractive, handsome really. Like Steve. She missed Steve so much. Far more than she missed her mother, she thought sadly, recalling her visit with Ellie last week. Seeing Ellie made Carla realize that she, Carla, was not sick, and never would be. Leo said he was sure she had used up all her illnesses—mental ones, that is—chasing poor old Tibor along the Commonwealth Avenue sidewalk.

Thinking of Leo, she decided to go into the house and walk casually past the library. Perhaps they might invite her in, or at least hurry up the meeting. She started into the house and nearly walked straight into him. Nearly into his cigar.

"My God!" she said. "How long have you been here?"

"A few minutes," he said. The cigar ash glowed red in the dark. "I was watching you."

"I had no idea."

He sat on the glider and patted the cushion for her to join him. "I know. You were in some kind of trance."

"I was thinking of you," she said. She sat beside him and kissed his cheek. "Is your meeting over?"

"All finished. Tomorrow we drive to Miami. We catch a two o'clock plane for Havana."

"And what happens in Havana? More of the same?"

"Probably," he said. "But there'll be more for you to do. You'll have more fun."

"I'm having fun here, Daddy. How many nice Jewish girls can say they had an ex-president of Cuba's son trying to feel them up?"

"Carla, do you have to talk that way?"

She laughed and kissed him again. "I'm sorry, Daddy. I forgot your Puritanical upbringing."

"It's a matter of good taste," he said. "Where is the little bastard, anyway? I haven't seen him all day."

"He went into town." She imitated the junior Batista's Spanish accent. "To find for myself a *real* woomun . . . ! Daddy, speaking of bastards, did you have to pay Tibor off?"

Even in the shadowed veranda Carla saw Leo's eyes turn abruptly cold, an expression she recognized as far back as a child. It always made her feel he was a different person. Sometimes, in a dream, she saw him with that expression. Always the same dream, which she had dreamed often as a child, but now infrequently; and always with the sharp, popping sound which was explained to her as a gun shooting when someone named Hershey was killed. A hunting accident, they said, in the woods near the pond behind the big house they lived in.

"Let me tell you something about your friend Tibor," Leo said. "He is the luckiest man alive. And not because you're such a clumsy driver.

Now, Carla, that's all I have to say about it. I don't want to ever hear his name mentioned again. Okay?"

"Okay," she said.

"Good," he said. In the dark his eyes were still cold.

They arrived in Havana the next afternoon. While other passengers stood in line for customs and passport inspections, Leo and Carla were greeted by two handsome young army officers who snapped their fingers at the officials and whisked them into a limousine.

"You really rate," Carla said as they drove out of the airport.

"I should," he said. "I'm half the gross national product of this country." He placed the two briefcases he had carried from the plane on the seat between them. He had not allowed them out of his sight on the airplane, and refused to permit the young officers to carry them. They seemed very heavy. She suspected they contained money.

"I can't wait to see all those wicked floor shows," she said. "Do the girls really dance naked?"

"Never mind the floor shows," he said.

"Sure, Dad, sure," she said. She felt good, alive. It was exciting to be in a foreign country, although strange to see this wide, concrete highway crowded with horse- or donkey-drawn carts. The limousine chauffeur, a soldier, constantly sounded his horn to pass, shaking his fist and swearing in Spanish at the drivers of the carts.

She heard Leo sigh quietly. She looked at him. He said, "I was just remembering when your mother and I came here once. With Steve. He was only a baby. We drove into the city on this same road, only then it was hardly more than a dirt path. And the hotel we're going to, the Caribe, wasn't even built."

"You said you're building two new ones?"

"Planning to build them," he said carefully. "The Cubana Royale, and El Presidente. Both of them twelve stories higher than anything in town now. Except the Presidente won't actually be in the city. It'll be at the racetrack. Every gambler's fantasy: afternoon at the races, then walk fifty yards to the biggest casino you ever saw." He paused to light a cigarette and realized Carla was not listening. She was staring out the limousine window at the tin-roofed shacks on each side of the highway. People loitering outside the shacks, children playing listlessly in the dirt, chickens fluttering in and out of the buildings.

"They're all so poor!" Carla said. "I never realized."

"It's a poor country," Leo said.

"A poor country?" she said. "And you're putting up million-dollar hotels?"

"A little more than a million, I'm afraid," he said. "Try *six* million."

"For each?"

"For each," he said, recalling the artist's depiction of El Presidente.

Two twelve-story towers atop a block-long casino, a quarter mile from the racetrack. Rooms facing south overlooked the track, with a clear view of the tote board. You could phone in a bet to the sports-book desk downstairs, watch the race from your private terrace, and then come downstairs to either pay or collect. Of course, to reach the sports-book desk, you had to walk through the casino.

"Captive audience," he said, thinking aloud, and pointed out the window at more shacks, the families clustered in and around the doorways. "You see all these people? They can't find work. It wasn't like this before the war. A lot of them worked either in the hotels, or in jobs connected to the hotels. Construction work, cooks, waiters, taxi drivers. Thousands of jobs, and all providing money to buy food and clothes, pay rent. The economy was good. Everybody profited. But since Batista's been in exile, the whole thing's gone to hell."

"You said he was coming back."

Leo glanced at the back of the chauffeur's neck through the glass partition. He reached out for the handle to make sure it was closed. "That's the problem, honey," he said. "We can't build the new hotels—or even refurbish the old ones—until he does come back. The people who took over for him just don't have his—" Leo groped for the word; it was not easy to find a word describing a Batista virtue. "Vision. They don't have his vision."

Which, he thought, was an odd word for graft. More accurately, the *degree* of graft. The difference between Batista and his successors was that they were too greedy. Batista knew exactly how much to take without jeopardizing the hotel-casino business as a whole. His successors, fools, had bled it dry.

"That's why we're here, isn't it?" Carla asked. "You're trying to fix it for Batista to come back."

"That's why," he said.

"But the elections aren't for two more years," she said. "Until 1953."

Again, Leo studied the driver's neck. He wondered if they had rigged a microphone in the backseat. That would be nice, he thought wryly. Real nice. But then what could they learn they didn't already know?

He said to Carla, "The man who now is president, Carlos Prío Socarrás, made an agreement with Batista to resign this year, to step down in favor of Batista. The trouble is that Señor Prío has decided he likes being president of Cuba. He wants to serve out his elected term."

"Oh, I see," said Carla. But she really did not see, and only understood it months later, back in Boston, reading about Fulgencio Batista's triumphant return to Cuba. A coup, it was said, but quite bloodless and with the full support of the Cuban people.

Her suspicion that the two briefcases Leo carried that day contained money was correct: $150,000 in cash in each, one for the commander of the Cuban National Police, the other for the general commanding the army. Tokens of Batista's appreciation, in return for which they assured him their loyalty. This, plus a guarantee to Prío Socarrás of an annual $75,000 pension, his price for a radio address to his countrymen, informing them that in the national interest he had requested Fulgencio Batista to return from exile. Batista, said Prío, would guide Cuba to a greater and more prosperous future.

Three weeks after Batista's assumption of office, construction commenced on the two new hotels.

Eighteen months later, El Presidente opened, and on March 10, 1953, the Cubana Royale. Both were instant successes. Now, Cuba secured, the way to the Bahamas was cleared.

Immediately after the Cubana Royale opening, Leo went to Nassau. Here, too, he was successful. Far more than he anticipated, for not only did he obtain a casino license, he met Renata Koval.

3.

She was on the beach in front of the Grand Bahamian Hotel when he first saw her, her face shadowed by a large umbrella. He was nearly fifty feet away, on the hotel terrace. She had removed her sunglasses, holding them at an angle that reflected the sun's glare back into his eyes. Annoyed, he moved his head to avoid the glare. Simultaneously, she lowered the glasses and rose.

He was so startled he sat straight up, tumbling the book on his lap to the floor, and then his reading glasses. He thought he was hallucinating. He thought he was looking at Edie.

Edith Lefkowitz, Hershey's wife, Edie of his boyhood. Edie, dead all these years. Then she turned fully, and he realized that other than being a tall, full-bodied, attractive blond woman in her mid- or late thirties, she bore no resemblance.

She sat again, leaning far back in the deck chair, her face to the sun. He peered at her another moment, then retrieved the reading glasses and book. *The Girl on the Via Flaminia*, Alfred Hayes's 1949 novel, which he had been enjoying, but now was unable to concentrate on.

You are tired, he told himself.

Well, I should be, he answered himself, continually on the go for nearly a month. From Carla's graduation in Boston, to the hotel opening in Havana, to the negotiations here in Nassau. Three days of endless meetings with Sir Sidney Coleman, and with Gregory Peters.

Sir Sidney Coleman, Her Majesty's High Commissioner to the Bahamas, who reminded Leo of Ronald Colman, although Leo doubted that Ronald Colman would ever request a twenty percent share—in his own name—in the Bank of the Caribbean, Ltd., a Nassau corporation, which was a division of the First Providence Bank & Trust Company, a New York corporation.

Not to mention an additional cash payment of $50,000 for services rendered in convincing the Bahamian Parliament to draft legislation for the issuance of a casino license to certain acceptable parties."

Gregory Peters, a black man, once a busboy in the dining room of this very hotel, was now secretary general of the Freedom Party, an organization dedicated to an independent Bahamas, and not above employing terrorist tactics to attain that objective; or, at the very least, status as an independent member of the British Commonwealth.

Leo thought of his business with Gregory Peters as securing the flank. Hedging the bet. When he first proposed this to the Alliance they rejected the idea. The blacks did not have the intelligence to run their own country. "Since when do you need intelligence to run a country?" Leo asked. In the end they agreed on a $25,000 "contribution."

Gregory Peters's courage and determination impressed Leo. And the man was far from unintelligent. He knew exactly what he wanted and how to get it. Leo admired that, too. Not to mention eliciting from Leo a promise that when and if IDIC hotels were built, they would be built solely with native Bahamian labor. Not only the structures, but all the ancillary construction: roads, bridges, even parking lots.

Thousands of jobs.

So now, after all that, Leo was relaxing. Easier said than done, especially after a confidential, disquieting report from George Gerson. While Harry and Liz were away on a brief European vacation, Gerson ran a routine, cursory audit at the Barclay. Cash on hand and accounts receivable were uncomfortably unbalanced. A discrepancy of slightly more than $100,000.

There was a name for it.

Skimming.

Like skimming the cream off the top of the milk. Before entering the figures, remove a little cash. Cash not on the books could not be declared as taxable income.

Gerson confided this to Leo in a telephone conversation from New York. The word *skimming* was never mentioned, or the fact, known to each of them, that only one person at the Barclay had enough real access to skim.

Leo said he would have a talk with Harry sometime soon. He did not want even to think about it now. What he wanted to think about was Renata Koval. He saw her again that same evening in the dining room, alone, her back to him, at a small table in center of the room. Reading a book. He wondered if the book might be something he had read. A long shot but certainly not impossible, and a convenient excuse to meet. He toyed with the idea of tipping a waiter to find out. Of course, he could always send over a drink.

He liked the way she dressed. A tasteful, conservative, white knit dress, with the long blond hair falling over her shoulders. She had those high cheekbones he admired, and a full firm mouth and strong chin. Her eyes, whose color he could not see but which he thought must be blue, were wide-set, and large. Her nose seemed at first a little too angular, but then he decided that perhaps it was a good nose for that large-boned face. Yes, absolutely.

Suddenly she gestured the waiter for her check. Dismayed, he realized he had only half finished his own dinner. Dover sole, grilled to perfection, but he hardly remembered touching it. He had planned to finish dinner when she did, then note where she went, and perhaps strike up a conversation. He watched her sign the check, tuck the book under her arm, shoulder her purse, and leave. She had to pass his table. She walked confidently, eyes straight ahead. Good legs, long, tapering nicely up into her hips. She was not as tall as he first believed. Five six, he estimated, which of course was tall enough, and nearly two inches taller than he.

Watching her, he felt himself hardening. The first time in months he felt any sexual stirring, any need. Now it welled up in him all the way from his groin, and flowed back down through his whole body. He forced himself to keep looking at her as she approached. She really was attractive and now, close, he saw her eyes. Blue, as he guessed, very clear, almost azure. She glanced at him and smiled politely. His heart raced. In his mind he saw himself getting up, saying, Excuse me, but I couldn't help noticing you—

It was too late. She walked past. He had to force himself not to turn and gaze after her.

Five minutes later, his dinner still unfinished, he left the dining room. He went directly to the lobby house phones and called the hotel manager. Leo apologized for disturbing him, but he needed a favor. Some information about another guest. The manager, a tall, taciturn Scot named Colin Beckworth, was only too delighted to be of assistance. He knew Leo by reputation, and his connection with Sir Sidney.

Waiting for Colin Beckworth to obtain the information from the front desk, it suddenly occurred to Leo that she might be a hooker. He hoped so. It would certainly simplify everything. And he would not risk making a fool of himself. But then, if a hooker, she would have gone immediately to the bar, which was empty but for a few young American couples. And even if she was in the bar, that hardly made her a hooker. Probably married, waiting for her husband to join her. Leo pondered the odds on that.

Renata Koval's registration card listed a London address. She had arrived two days ago, booking a small single room for a week. Colin Beckworth was only too delighted to arrange an introduction.

The dining room was crowded with the first breakfast service. Leo had ordered a window table, with a vase of fresh white roses. He sat nervously watching the entrance. She arrived precisely at eight, as arranged. The hostess escorted her to the table. She wore white tennis shorts and a white oxford-cloth shirt, sleeves rolled halfway to the elbows. And tennis shoes, which for this initial meeting made Leo feel more comfortable: she would not be that much taller. He rose to greet her.

"Mr. Gorodetsky . . . ?"

"Miss Koval?"

She smiled. It seemed to brighten her whole face. "Renata," she said.

"I'm Leo. Please sit down."

"I must ask you one question," she said, nodding for the waiter to pour coffee. "What did Mr. Beckworth mean when he asked if your name meant anything to me?"

Leo said, "I hope you weren't offended at how I went about this . . . ?"

"Offended?" she said. "I'm incredibly flattered. You're the first man in three days who's paid me any attention."

"They're all blind, then."

"All attached." She pointed her coffee cup at him. "You haven't answered my question. What did Mr. Beckworth mean about the importance of your name?"

"I haven't the slightest idea," Leo said, embarrassed, and promising himself to have a word with that fool Beckworth. He would have the fool fired if, as he suspected, the idiot had told Renata Leo was a big American racketeer. "What exactly did he say?"

"That's all. Did your name mean anything?"

"Does it?"

"No. Should it?"

Leo loved the sound of her voice, low and husky, with that marvelous British accent. He thought he could listen to her talk all day. He thought he would like to.

He said, "No, I don't think my name should mean anything. I'm in the hotel business, maybe that's what he meant."

"Well, then it's not important, is it?"

"Not at all," he said. "Now, I have a question for you. What was the book you were reading at dinner?"

"I just lost a bet with myself," she said. "I bet that your question was 'Are you married'?"

"A bet?" he asked lightly. "You mean you gamble?"

"Good heavens, no. I think gambling is silly."

"I couldn't have said it better myself," he said. "But are you married?"

"No."

He could not repress a little grin of relief. "What was the book?"

"*The Horse's Mouth.*"

"The Horse's what?"

She laughed. "*The Horse's Mouth.* Joyce Cary. An Englishman. He's quite good."

"I'll read it."

"Yes, but before you do, could we order breakfast? I'm starved."

They talked easily. She was on holiday from her job as a BOAC ticket-office supervisor in London. The airline had arranged a special rate for her at the Grand Bahamian. How else could she afford such deluxe accommodations? No, she had never been married, although once was engaged. The classic story of the handsome young RAF pilot who never came back.

They explained their names. Koval was Polish, changed from Kova-leski by her father upon his arrival in England shortly after the first war. He held a University of London chair, a professor of medieval literature. A longtime widower, he shared with Renata the Chelsea house they had lived in since 1919.

Leo said, "Gorodetsky is spelled with a *y*." He smiled. "A Jewish *y*."

"As opposed to the Gentile *i*," she said.

"Some of my best friends are Gentile," he said.

"Mine, too," she said, and laughed again. "Seriously, I don't care what a person's religion is, and I don't want them to care about mine. I don't believe in it, anyway."

"In religion, you mean?"

"I have none," she said. "Does that disturb you?"

"It not only doesn't disturb me, it tells me we must have dinner to-gether."

"On one condition."

"Name it."

"Neither of us brings a book to the table."

Renata saw in him a rather shy, gentle, quite charming middle-aged man. An attractive man, with warm, deep brown eyes and thick brown hair speckled gray, which she suspected would soon be all gray, making him even more attractive. He dressed well, expensively, but with no ostentation. He appeared clearly accustomed to money, so she assumed him wealthy. And while they had shared confidences—he told her of his divorce—she had no idea, other than the vague reference to the hotel business, how he earned his living, and he had not volunteered the information. But then she had not asked.

She also saw a lonely man. She wondered about his friends. He must have friends. But then again, maybe not, at least no close friends. Successful men were usually lonely men. Perhaps, though, that was the formula for success. Depending, of course, upon your definition of success.

For all his self-assurance, she knew he was sensitive about their height difference. She dealt directly with it that very night at dinner. She wore high heels. She not only liked them, she knew they did wonders for her legs.

"Look, I hope the fact I'm a few inches taller doesn't bother you," she said. "Because it does not bother me. Not at all."

"Then it certainly doesn't bother me," he said.

"And you wouldn't have it any other way, would you?"

"Never," he said.

She knew they would sleep together. She decided if he did not ask, she would. She wanted to be made love to. She needed love. She had gone without it almost a year, since breaking off an affair with a married pilot. A nice man, but beset with guilt continually inhibiting the relationship. Besides, as she told him in the end, she was tired of being his between-planes lay.

It happened with her and Leo sooner than she expected, and far more gratifying than either expected. On the second night. After dinner they walked along the promenade from the hotel to the beach, both a little giddy with wine and good food and good talk. They sat on a wooden bench on the terrace at the edge of the stone wall separating the beach area from the hotel's grass lawn.

"They seem to having a nice time," she said, pointing to a large yacht anchored a quarter mile out in the harbor. The main deck blazed with light, and every stateroom was lighted. Dozens of people were visible on deck, and even at this distance sounds of laughter and chatter floated loud across the water.

"I think that's Hartford's boat," Leo said. "I heard he was here."

"Who, might I ask, is 'Hartford'?"

"A very wealthy young man who inherited a chain of grocery stores. He owns an island nearby."

"His own island?"

"His very own."

Renata thought about that a moment. Then she said, "I'll settle for the boat."

"I think I might prefer the island."

"Why?"

"My own island," he said. "King of all I survey."

She looked at him in the dark. His face was very serious. She said, "Something tells me, Mr. Gorodetsky with the 'Jewish *y*'—that you are king-of-all-you-survey now."

He laughed quietly, but said nothing. He shifted about to reach for cigarettes. Their shoulders touched. She liked the strong warmth of his body against hers. He held the cigarettes out to her. She removed the entire pack from his hand, placed it very carefully on the bench beside her, then cupped his face with both hands and drew him to her.

They kissed. Tenderly at first, then with more passion, but a certain restraint. As though each was unsure of himself, reluctant to proceed further for fear of offending the other. After another moment she broke away. She handed him a cigarette from the pack and took one for herself. He lit her cigarette, then his own. They smoked silently a moment.

"That was nice," she said.

"Should we leave it at that?" he said. "Or go on to the next chapter?"

"We don't have to even open the book," she said. "We know what happens in that chapter."

Ten minutes later they were in her room making love. His gentleness and thoughtfulness did not at all surprise her, or his patience. He was a sexually considerate man whose own pleasure clearly was derived from giving pleasure. They both fell into an exhausted, deep sleep, only to wake a few hours later for more love. And, in the morning, more.

They joked about his amazing stamina. At fifty-three, how the hell could he manage three times in a single evening? Three? she exclaimed. Mister, you haven't even *begun*!

Five delightful days. For the last two he chartered a yacht, complete with skipper, crew, and a cordon bleu chef. She shuddered when she thought of the cost. They sailed the islands, stopping at little cays for picnic lunches, then boarding the yacht again for more island-hopping. During the last day, the final afternoon and evening, she began counting the hours. She knew that for both of them it was a brief, wonderful interlude. Ships passing in the night.

He drove her to the airport. Her London flight was leaving an hour before his Washington flight. He explained he had some people to see in Washington before he went home to New York. So they parted at the BOAC gate. He wrote his telephone number and address on a business card.

"Write me," he said. They were standing near the ticket counter, constantly jostled by people. It was difficult to hear, or concentrate. "Better, call me. Collect," he added. "Be sure it's collect."

"Once a week," she said, joking. "You have my number. You do the same."

"Collect?"

"Only from a coin box," she said. "And if a man answers, introduce yourself and say it's Gorodetsky with an *i*. He'll think you're Polish, and he'll accept the call!" She kissed him and hurried away.

From the window of her airplane she saw him at the gate, waving. She waved back, although she knew he could not see her. She took his business card from her purse and looked at it for the first time. A simple card, engraved letters:

INTERNATIONAL DEVELOPMENT & INVESTMENT CORPORATION
Leo Gorodetsky

On the back were two phone numbers: his office, and home. And a Central Park West address. She studied the card, recalling how she had learned only that morning the purpose of his trip to Washington. When she checked out of the hotel, the manager, Colin Beckworth, had snidely asked if she enjoyed her stay.

"Quite," she had said, hating him, and then really not caring. Why be bothered with such trash?

"I suppose you heard about his row with that committee?"

"I beg your pardon?"

Colin Beckworth brought a week-old copy of *The New York Times* out from under the desk. He tapped a manicured fingernail on a small story on the lower right front page.

KEFAUVER COMMITTEE SUBPOENAS
GAMBLER GORODETSKY

A brief, two-paragraph story. Leo Gorodetsky, whose gambling interests ranged from Las Vegas to Cuba, had been subpoenaed to appear before a senate committee investigating organized crime in the United States.

She felt no shock, and very little surprise, and instantly realized why. Because it made not the slightest difference to her. It did not change him in her eyes. He could have been a doctor, or a shoe salesman. It had no bearing on their relationship.

The surprise came ten minutes after takeoff. The DC-6's seat belt sign had gone off and the stewardess was taking cocktail requests. Renata ordered a vermouth cassis. The stewardess started away, then stopped. She gave Renata an envelope.

"I nearly forgot. A gentleman asked me to give you this once we were airborne."

It was Grand Bahamanian Hotel stationery. Renata opened the envelope. Inside was a folded note. Inside the note were five one-thousand-dollar bills. The bills fluttered onto the armrest separating the two seats, and then onto the empty seat beside Renata. She reached blindly for the bills and gathered them in her hand while she read the note.

No salutation or signature. *I agonized for hours trying to decide whether or not to do this. I am terrified you might be insulted, or feel degraded. You know this is not my intention. Please don't be angry with me. Please accept it. I will be the one who is insulted if you don't.*

She stared at the money now. She had never seen a thousand-dollar bill. She never knew there was a thousand-dollar bill. She had never seen so much money at one time. She read the note again, then reread it. She could actually see him writing it. "Agonizing," as he said. She understood him. She thought she knew, or was beginning to know, how his mind worked. And she knew exactly why he had decided to risk her anger. Any woman, he probably reasoned, angered at such a gift had to be crazy.

She still clutched the bills when the stewardess brought the drink. "There you are—" the stewardess stared at the money, then at Renata, then at the envelope on the seat.

Renata smiled at her. "It was a bet."

"Must have been some bet," the stewardess said. She was Irish, pronouncing bet as "bat."

"Yes, we bet whether or not I'm crazy." Renata tucked the bills back into the envelope, and the envelope into her purse. She took the glass of vermouth from the stewardess. "I won."

— 23 —

> **GORODETSKY**—Sarah Rachel, aged 78. On Sept. 23, 1953, in New York City. Devoted mother of Esther and Leo. Beloved grandmother of Carla. Interment in Tel Aviv, Israel.

NOT even the sharpest-eyed reporter caught the item in that day's *New York Times* obituaries. So the irony went unnoticed. The irony was not Sarah's death—she had died peacefully in her sleep—but that the front and inside pages of the same newspaper carried in-depth stories of her son's appearance before the Senate committee probing organized crime in the United States.

Leo had returned to New York immediately after completing his testimony. He was exhausted after nearly a week in Washington, three full days of it testifying. Grueling days, with the committee's special counsel, Martin Raab, sparing no effort to link Leo to what Raab termed "the scourge of this nation." The organization known as the Alliance, which he claimed more of a threat to our way of life than a dozen Nazi armies.

Unlike previous witnesses—Vincent Tomasino and Paul Calvelli among others—not once did Leo take the Fifth. Eyes smarting under the lights of television and newsreel cameras, he faced the six U.S. senators of the committee. And a seventh man, a "special consultant," the junior senator from New York, Charles Brickhill.

". . . now, Mr. Gorodetsky, would you please inform this committee precisely how you make your living?"

"I am executive vice-president of International Development and Investment Corporation."

"This is a company that ostensibly owns and manages various hotels in the United States and in Cuba?"

"Ostensibly?"

Raab sighed. "Strike the word *ostensibly*," he said to the stenotypist, and to Leo, "Please answer the question, Mr. Gorodetsky."

"That is correct," Leo said. "The company owns and manages hotels. We also have interests in the Bahamas."

"Thank you for the additional information," Raab said dryly. "These are all gambling casinos, are they not?"

"Yes, sir."

"This is your sole means of livelihood?"

"Yes, sir."

"How long have you been, ah, involved with this company? IDIC, I believe it's called."

"Since its incorporation in 1926."

"And before that?"

"I beg your pardon?"

"Before 1926, Mr. Gorodetsky, how did you make your living?"

"Gambling, Mr. Raab. I made my living gambling."

Raab's eyebrows arched dramatically. "Illegal gambling?"

"Sometimes, yes."

"Isn't it true, Mr. Gorodetsky, that IDIC was created as a front for the channeling of illegal bootlegging profits into various legitimate enterprises?"

Leo placed his hand on the microphone to muffle his voice while he conferred with George Gerson seated beside him. Then he said into the microphone, "No, sir, that is not true."

"But you were heavily involved in bootlegging during Prohibition?"

"I was involved, Mr. Raab. How 'heavily' is a matter of interpretation. Thousands of people in those days were involved in bootlegging. Hundreds of thousands."

"To be sure, Mr. Gorodetsky," said Raab. "And some of those . . . thousands and hundreds of thousands associated with you, some were notorious criminal figures, isn't that true? People such as Salvatore Bracci, Arnold Steinberger, Harry Weisenfeld––otherwise known as Harry Wise. Along with other such heroic individuals whose names are too numerous to mention at this time."

"I knew those people, yes."

"You did business with them, Mr. Gorodetsky."

"Yes, I did."

"And are you not, now, in partnership with individuals calling themselves the Alliance? Or, as it is sometimes known, the Syndicate?"

"I have no knowledge, Mr. Raab, of any such organizations."

Martin Raab glanced dryly at Brickhill, then said to Leo, "No knowledge?"

"Well, if you mean have I heard those terms used—Alliance, Syndicate—yes, I've heard of them. Hasn't everyone?"

This drew some laughs and guffaws from the audience, silenced immediately by the chairman's gavel and an admonition for order and decorum in the hearing chamber. Raab went on, "You are stating, then, you have no knowledge of the existence of any such criminal groups?"

"No firsthand knowledge," Leo said. "No, sir."

"None whatever?"

"No, sir."

Raab sighed, almost as though amused. After a moment, he consulted his notes. "Mr. Gorodetsky, what can you tell us about Harry Wise?"

"Harry Wise is a boyhood friend," Leo said. "As a matter of fact, we enlisted in the army together in 1917. He, as you know, is an officer and stockholder of IDIC."

"Yes, we're aware of that," Raab said. He turned to the chairman. "Although presently under subpoena, Mr. Wise seems to be on extended vacation in Europe."

Another humorous reaction from the audience, silenced again by the chairman's impatient gavel. Raab continued, "Let's move forward just briefly. Are you acquainted with Mr. Thomas Stohlmeyer, president of the Union of American Transport Workers?"

"I know Mr. Stohlmeyer, yes."

Before Raab could pose the next question, Brickhill rose from his seat and hurried over to him. He whispered tersely into Raab's ear. Raab listened carefully. Then he nodded, placed the notes he was consulting on the bottom of the file, and confronted Leo again.

"I call your attention to the name Bernard Kopaloff. Does that name conjure up any memories?"

Leo replied carefully, and Raab led him through the events leading to Bernie Kopaloff's death. George Gerson continually objected to that line of questioning: Leo Gorodetsky had no direct knowledge of the case and therefore could, at best, offer only hearsay evidence. The chairman finally requested Raab to pursue another line.

It went on for three days, on national television, radio, the newspapers and magazines. In the end Leo was dismissed without citation. And during the final day he managed to have the last, gratifying word. He had stated that IDIC's acquisition of the controlling shares of the First Providence Bank & Trust Company was a transaction of public record, approved by all appropriate agencies, and no criminal or civil complaints had ever been lodged against the bank.

Before Raab could challenge Leo's testimony, Brickhill suddenly spoke into his microphone.

"Mr. Gorodetsky, is it not true that you are the Czar, the head man—

well, one of them at least—of organized crime in the United States—?"

"—no, sir, it is not true—"

"—if not the world?" Brickhill finished.

"Senator, I would like to respectfully remind you that for a number of years you personally have sought to have me charged with these crimes, and as yet have produced not one shred of evidence to substantiate them. I want to say now, again, I deny all these—"

The chairman interrupted. "—you're making a speech, Mr. Gorodetsky. Please refrain." He nodded at Brickhill. "Does the senator wish to question the witness?"

"Not at this time," Brickhill said. "I doubt my stomach could stand it."

"Nor your conscience, Senator," Leo said crisply.

Immediately, the gallery exploded in more laughter. The hearing adjourned shortly thereafter, and Leo and Gerson returned to New York in the club car of the Baltimore & Ohio *Bullet*. Leo had more than his customary one Scotch and soda; he had three. He desperately needed to relax, unwind. Halfway through the third drink he noticed that Gerson had lowered his newspaper and was gazing broodily at the drawn shades of the windows on the opposite side of the car.

Leo said, "What's the matter, George? You should be celebrating, but you look like you just came from a funeral."

"I keep thinking about when Raab started questioning you on the UATW connection," Gerson said, still facing the window. He looked at Leo now. "When Brickhill rushed over to him, and all of a sudden Raab put the file away, and changed the whole line of questioning."

"I remember that, yes."

"Leo, we know they've been gathering evidence about the loans. They're trying to nail Stohlmeyer with a conspiracy-to-defraud. I think Brickhill told Raab to table that matter so as not to give anything away."

"They don't have anything," Leo said. "Stohlmeyer's fees were paid in cash. The loans are legitimate."

"Suppose somehow they indict Stohlmeyer, and he says you offered him those fees in return for his help in getting the loans? That makes you a party to the conspiracy."

"They have to prove it," Leo said. "It's his word against mine."

Gerson said nothing, but Leo wondered why the attorney had raised the Stohlmeyer issue; it was so flimsy it hardly merited discussion. He knew something else was on Gerson's mind. Over the years it had become a near ritual with them: Gerson invariably prefaced a topic of vital interest with a different, unimportant matter. As though providing Leo time to prepare himself for the real thing.

Leo accommodated him. "All right, George, spill it."

Gerson swiveled his club chair around to to face Leo. He said, "Harry." Leo waited.

"Two million dollars," Gerson said. "Maybe more."

Leo's whole body went cold. He drank down his drink and started to signal the porter for a refill, then changed his mind. The last thing he needed now was another drink.

"Are you sure?"

Gerson nodded slowly, tightly.

"Go back out there and do another audit!"

"Leo, this is the third one I've done this year. Each one, the handle goes down a half point or so. What I can't figure out is why he doesn't seem even to try to doctor the books. Anybody can read the numbers."

"Well, doesn't that tell you something?" Leo asked, relieved. "If Harry was skimming, he'd never be that clumsy."

"Leo, Harry is in Geneva right now," Gerson said. "Supposedly, he went there to duck the Senate subpoena. Supposedly, he'll be back some-time next week—"

"—supposedly?" Leo said. "Are you trying to say he won't come back?"

"—he's with Liz," Gerson continued patiently. "This is the fourth time, the *fourth*, Liz has been in Geneva this year. Now, Leo, what does she do in Geneva?"

"She buys watches," Leo said. "How the hell do I know?"

"She carries money," Gerson said. "Money Harry skims from the Barclay."

Leo strained to remain calm. He concentrated on the metallic clack of the train's wheels. He looked at the others in the club car. A few businessmen, two army officers with embroidered KOREA flashes on their shoulders, and one gray-haired woman sitting alone, reading *Time*, a full-length mink coat folded casually across her lap. He envied every one of those people. They were traveling to or from their homes or offices, would greet their families, enjoy dinner, go to bed, awaken in the morning concerned only with that day's routine problems.

Which he was certain did not include your oldest and best friend cheating you. Thinking of that, cheating, Leo heard Hershey's gravel voice in his mind: "*. . . you don't steal off your friends.*"

". . . don't have to tell you what'll happen if the Council ever finds out," Gerson said, his voice fading in momentary exasperation as he realized Leo was not paying full attention. "Leo, I said that one of these days Vinnie Tomasino will send his own accountant to Vegas to look over the books. He'll see the same figures I did."

"And he'll come to the same conclusion I did," Leo said. "If Harry was skimming, he'd be clever enough not to advertise it. But I'll talk to him about it when he comes back."

Gerson said nothing. He recognized the stubborn, final note in Leo's voice. No point in pushing further. He, Gerson, had done what he had to do. Let Leo worry about it from here.

Harry returned from Europe the following week, after the Senate committee had dissolved and the subpoena became invalid. But Leo had no opportunity to discuss the matter with him. Leo was himself out of the country then, in Israel.

Burying his mother.

2.

". . . look, let's just say the machinery simply stopped," the doctor had said. He was a young man with brown Brillo hair and an acne-scarred face. His name was Burton Rosenthal. He had treated Sarah for several years, and only last month when examining her complaint of chest pains found nothing wrong. She was remarkably healthy for a woman her age.

"She was seventy-eight," Leo said. He knew he was repeating himself, but did not know what else to say.

Dr. Rosenthal said, "Listen, I'll settle for seventy-eight right now. If it's any consolation, Mr. Gorodetsky, she never knew what happened. She just went to sleep and didn't wake up. It's not a bad way to go."

"I didn't know there was a good way," Leo said.

They were in Sarah's Amsterdam Avenue apartment. It was nearly noon. Leo had been here since ten, since being awakened by a telephone call from Sarah's longtime neighbor Mrs. Goldbaum, who each morning for the past six years had shared with Sarah coffee and a *putter kuchen*. Each morning they alternated kitchens. Today was Sarah's turn. When she did not answer the door, Mrs. Goldbaum knew something terrible had happened. She did not know how she knew; God sent her a message, probably. She called the super. He opened the back door and they found Sarah in bed. Ice-cold, the poor darling. You never felt such cold flesh.

Mrs. Goldbaum notified Leo who, thank God, was home. Mrs. Goldbaum discreetly did not mention the newspapers strewn over Sarah's bed, and on the floor. All with photographs of Leo, and those headlines about the Senate crime committee. But when Leo arrived he of course saw the papers, and when he angrily crumpled them into the trash bin, Mrs. Goldbaum thought it best not to tell him how Sarah's only comment on the stories had been a bitter expletive: "Lies . . . ! *Goyisher* lies!"

He asked Mrs. Goldbaum to please leave him alone. He phoned the doctor first, then Esther in Boston. Talking to Esther, listening to her anguished wails, he felt his eyes moisten. But he did not cry. He had not cried since Steven and wondered why he did not now. Later, he thought. Later, when it became real.

He sat on a chair beside the bed and gazed at her until the doctor arrived. She looked so peaceful, almost happy. He could not believe she would not awaken. He remembered Harry telling him how he sat with his mother at her hospital bed after she died, and talked to her. Leo could not recall what Harry told him he said to his dead mother.

What could Harry have said? What could Leo say now? Ma, I loved you. She knew that. Ma, I'm sorry I didn't become a lawyer, or a doctor.

Or a salesman. He could not say that because he was not sorry. I am what I am, Ma. You'll just have to live with it. I'm a millionaire, Ma, and that's not so bad for a kid from Delancey Street. I have so much money, I can't count it. And I did okay for you, we both know that. I gave you a pretty good life.

But even as he thought this, he wondered. She never once told him how she felt about his life, his business. Not once. My Laibel, she used to tell her friends, he's in real estate. He builds hotels and things.

And things.

A week later, in Israel, standing with Carla at the grave site, watching dirt shoveled onto the plain pine box, listening to the four old men on the opposite side of the grave recite the Kaddish, he talked to Sarah again. And don't forget, Ma, I did what you wanted. I buried you in Israel.

Her request for this years ago had surprised him. He had assumed she wanted to be buried beside Rivka. At the time, however, trying not to be serious about it, he said, "Ma, when you came to the new world, it was supposed to be for good." She replied, "Laibel, Israel *is* the new world!"

An interesting idea, he thought, as the rabbi gestured him to read his portion of the Kaddish. The strange letters crowded the page and swam before his eyes. He moved his lips, pretending to be reading to himself. The four professional mourners continued the dirge, swaying back and forth on their heels, one noisily moistening his fingers with his tongue to flip a page. Leo glanced at Carla. She was looking at him with a gentle smile of understanding.

He loved Carla for that, for not considering him hypocritical. His participation in these services merely complied with his mother's wishes. This, whether or not you believed in any of it, was a simple matter of respect. No more, no less.

Had his sister Esther been standing there watching him, it would have been with a scowl of disapproval for his "blasphemy." She was unable to accompany them to Israel. She had taken ill at the last minute, hospitalized with pneumonia. She was better now and would be discharged in a few days. Leo was glad she was not here; he did not want to deal with her histrionics.

He tried to concentrate on the book, but finally looked away. The land beyond the cemetery, which was on the outskirts of Tel Aviv, was green with the tops of citrus trees. In the far distance the high-rise hotels on the beach outlined the sky. It was quite serene and beautiful. His mother would have approved.

He continued "reading," thinking he might like to end up in this same place. Not a bad place. In the past, with the possibility—no, the probability—of death always real, he never cared where they might put him. Or how. Bury him, burn him, what difference? Who cared? But now, suddenly, he decided that here, Israel, was where he wanted to be.

You are getting old, he told himself.

Why? he asked himself. Because I want to be buried in the land of the Jews? That is not getting old, that is getting smart.

". . . Daddy." Carla nudged his sleeve. "It's over."

He looked at her a moment. "Yes," he said. "It's over."

Golda Myerson, now Golda Meir and now minister of labor in the Israeli government, had smoothed the way for Leo to bring his mother here. Following the funeral, she arranged a grand tour of the country for Leo and Carla. They saw it all, from the Galilee to the Negev, Tel Aviv to Tiberias.

The country fascinated Carla. She said it throbbed with energy. You saw it in people's faces and eyes, and heard it in their voices. They walked with pride and confidence. They were determined to build a nation and nothing could stop them.

Now, seeing it, walking the streets, breathing the air, Leo felt rewarded for his efforts five years before. But he also sensed a strange coolness, or formality, from some of those he had worked with in 1948.

Twice in his three weeks in Israel, official receptions in Leo's honor were canceled on short notice. Once, with Aaron Cahane, who had joined the ruling Labor Party, and once with Ben Gurion himself. Leo thought Golda Meir a little too anxious to explain these cancellations, which he believed required no explanation. The men were busy running a country.

Golda Meir, however, invited Leo and Carla to dinner at her Tel Aviv apartment, and personally prepared the food: *humus tahini*, an Arab dish consisting of crushed chick peas, garlic, and olive oil spread over *pita*, the flat, yeastless Arab bread. Then, thick veal loin chops, fried in *shmaltz* with potatoes and onions.

"Just like my mother used to make," Leo said with a wan smile.

"Mine, too," said Golda Meir. "Good, old-fashioned, Jewish heart-attack food!" She leveled her cigarette at Carla. "And you, young lady, I hope your unfortunate experience at Beersheba hasn't diminished your enthusiasm for our country."

Carla wore a small cast on her left wrist. Two days before, attending a concert of the Israeli Chamber Ensemble at a kibbutz near Beersheba, she tripped over a tent guy wire and fractured the wrist. A hairline fracture, but the young Hadassah Hospital physician insisted on a cast.

"My enthusiasm remains undiminished," Carla said. "As a matter of fact, the doctor wants to see me again before I leave. I'm meeting him in an hour."

Golda's eyebrows rose in a thick, dark inverted V. "In an hour? To-night? At the hospital?"

"At the bar of the Kaete Dan."

Golda's eyebrows rose even further. "That's where they see patients now? At the Kaete Dan bar?" She nodded wryly at Leo. "Yes, I think your daughter will fit in beautifully here! Who is this nocturnal physician?" she asked Carla.

"His name is Avi Schiff."

"I think I know him," Golda said. "Tall, very slender. Dark hair that he'll probably always have. And very handsome?"

"That's him," said Carla.

"A sabra," Golda said to Leo. "I know the family."

"When did all this happen?" Leo asked Carla.

"This afternoon when he put on a new cast."

"Of course!" said Golda. "That's why he must see her tonight. To see if the cast is comfortable. Yes?"

Carla was unflustered. "He wants to know about the States. He's going to the Peter Bent Brigham for a year's surgical residency."

"Peter Bent Brigham?" Leo asked. "In Boston?"

"By coincidence, it happens to be in Boston, yes," Carla said.

"That's quite a coincidence," Leo said, and explained to Golda Meir. "My daughter goes to graduate school in Boston."

Golda said, "I hope they both pay attention to their studies."

Leo met Dr. Avi Schiff later that evening. He was twenty-seven, South African educated, and clearly infatuated with Carla. And, clearly, the feeling was mutual. The instant she arrived at the hotel and saw him standing impatiently at the bar entrance, her whole face brightened. She introduced Leo, anxiously studying him for the smallest hint of an impression. She need not have worried. Leo liked him immediately.

They obviously wanted to be alone, and Leo found an opportunity to excuse himself gracefully a few minutes after the three had settled at a table in the lounge.

A man at the bar, staring at them in the bar-length mirror, suddenly called out, "I don't believe it!" He whirled around. "Leo . . . !"

It was Ray Newman, he of the ill-fated PBY venture, Leo's partner in the retrieval of the machine guns from Jamaica. After introductions, Leo suggested he and Ray go off by themselves to talk over old times. Leo reminded Carla they were leaving in the morning, so please not get to bed too late.

"To her, that will mean five in the morning," Leo said quietly to Ray as they left the Kaete Dan and started out to Hyarkon Street. But Leo was not at all displeased; he had a good feeling about Avi Schiff. He smiled to himself, thinking how his mother would say, ". . . don't knock horses with gifts, Laibel. He's a Jewish boy, isn't he? And a doctor, yet!"

Ray Newman was now an El Al captain, flying Connies on the Tel Aviv–London run. He expected transatlantic duty soon and would most certainly look Leo up in New York. They walked along the Esplanade, talking—Ray doing most of the talking—bringing Leo up-to-date on mutual acquaintances. They made a wide circle, then headed back toward Leo's hotel, the Gat Rimmon. Ray asked if Leo had seen Aaron Cahane.

"No, I haven't," Leo said. "And I'll tell you, I almost have the feeling he's ducking me."

They were just starting into the lobby. Ray stopped and looked at Leo. "I'm sorry to hear that."

Ray's very tone told Leo he had been correct. Leo said, "Do you mind telling me why?"

Ray studied Leo a moment, thinking, then sat on the stone steps of the hotel entrance. He gestured Leo to sit beside him. "Guys like Cahane are businessmen, Leo. Just like you. They're tough, pragmatic people who learned survival the hard way. When they need you, they'll kiss your ass and even wipe it if it'll get them what they want—" he paused to light his pipe.

"The same beat-up old Kaywoodie," Leo said. "I'll have to send you a new one."

"It's a Dunhill," Ray said. "Look, Leo, I'm not apologizing for them, but you have to understand why sometimes their behavior might seem strange."

"Like ducking me?"

"Yeah," Ray said. "And the reason, Leo, is a man like Aaron, who is now a respected member of the government of a respected nation, is afraid you might embarrass him."

"Embarrass him?" Leo repeated hollowly. "Because of all the publicity of the past weeks? That Washington business?"

"That did not help, believe me," said Ray. He spoke fast, as though anxious to say it and get it over with. "The fact of it, Leo, is that you're a notorious American gangster—"

"—thank you," Leo said. It reminded him of not being invited to the victory celebration five years before, although, then, as hard as it was to accept, he certainly understood their "embarrassment." He had expected it to be different now, here.

"I'm simply stating facts," Ray said.

"It's all right, I've been called worse," Leo said.

Ray said, "Israel is a respected nation. The presence of someone like yourself might—to some people, Leo, not all—might be embarrassing. Politically, that is. Diplomatically, whatever you want to call it."

"I don't know what to call it, frankly," Leo said. He knew why he could not so easily understand their so-called embarrassment here. There might easily be no "here" had he not given so much of his time, money, and effort. But even as he thought this, he knew it was not true. The nation would have been created without him. Someone else would have done the work. Nothing, no one, could have stopped it.

Small consolation.

"But, look, that's only Aaron Cahane," Ray Newman said. "Golda doesn't feel that way. You just had dinner at her house That's not chopped liver."

"No, veal chops fried in *shmaltz*," Leo said. "A consolation prize."

"Look, Leo, don't make a federal case out of it." Ray paused abruptly and laughed at the inadvertent pun. Even Leo could not help smiling. Ray went on, "You ever decide to settle here, you'll be more than welcome. The Law of Return is one of the few things in this country that's so uncomplicated and straightforward even a politician understands it. Any Jew, no matter what his nationality, is automatically and irrevocably granted Israeli citizenship."

"As long as he doesn't open a casino," Leo said.

"Hey, the place can use one!" Ray said. He rose. "I got to go. I have a whole day of ground school tomorrow."

Leo insisted on buying Ray Newman a nightcap. After Ray left, he sat alone at the Gat Rimmon bar a long while. He was tired, but knew he would not sleep well. He knew he would spend hours analyzing and brooding about his "embarrassing presence." Suddenly he began looking forward to going back to America, back home. And then he decided to make a brief en route stop. In London.

London, where Renata Koval lived.

Just thinking of her, he felt better, and two days later, seeing her, he felt even better. Carla appeared to like Renata, which pleased Leo immensely. He had booked a suite at the Dorchester, planning to stay at least a week. During the day Carla and Leo went off sightseeing, then were joined by Renata at dinner. After dinner, a West End theater, or the Albert Hall, and once a Curzon Street private gambling club which reminded Leo of the old Chez When days. A special password, followed by a close once-over from two burly young men whose tuxedos bulged conspicuously. But inside the club all was very sedate and dignified. The women played roulette, Leo, 21. They won, he lost.

Leo and Renata had little chance to be alone until Carla insisted on returning to Boston. By herself. She claimed she had missed too many classes already, and knew Leo had "important business" in London, and she was only in the way.

"Don't be such a wise guy," he said.

"I'm not a wise guy, Daddy," she said, and kissed him. "I love you."

"And you're treating me like some love-sick old fool."

"Yes, I am," she said. "Because I think it's about time, and because you deserve it. And because I think she's terrific. When's the wedding?"

"Hey, come on. She's only a friend."

"Sure. Dad. Sure."

Leo stayed on four days. Four marvelous days and nights that ended abruptly early one evening in the Dorchester lobby. Renata had arrived from her Piccadilly Road office and was waiting for him outside in a taxi. They were going to Simpson's for dinner. Leo had just stepped into the revolving door when the porter called to him.

"Telephone, Mr. Gorodetsky. New York. You can take it in the private cabinet, if you wish."

Leo entered the small enclosed phone booth adjacent the hotel cloak-room and picked up the phone.

It was Vincent Tomasino. "Leo, you there?" He sounded skeptical, as if unwilling to believe he could hear Leo's voice so clearly from London.

"What's up, Vinnie?"

There was no immediate reply. The phone was loud with a hollow, wind-rushing sound, broken finally by Vinnie's voice. "Leo, we got big trouble."

Leo said nothing.

"Leo?"

"I'm here, Vinnie. What kind of trouble?"

"I called a meeting of the Council, Leo. For tomorrow morning. Can you get here?"

"A meeting about what?"

"Harry," said Vinnie. "Our partner, Harry."

"What's Harry done this time?" Leo knew what Harry had done and suspected Vinnie knew he knew. But he wanted to hear Vinnie say it; it was almost as though he hoped he might hear something different. Perhaps Harry had done something crazy like insulting Vinnie's son-in-law.

"Two million four hundred and sixty-five thousand dollars," Vinnie said. "He's a thief, Leo, a fucking thief."

3.

Mickey Goldfarb met Leo at McCarran Field. Bald head gleaming in the afternoon sun, Mickey stood behind the meshed-wire cyclone fence waving his hat. He wore a suit and tie, sweatstained in the October desert heat and sadly rumpled. Leo wore an open-collared knit sport shirt, his jacket slung over his shoulder.

"Hey, how you doing?" Mickey said.

"Where's Harry?"

"He had to meet the restaurant-union guy," Mickey said. "They been giving us an awful hard time, screaming for salary hikes and their god-dam medical plan! Jesus, can you imagine? A bunch of waiters and drink hustlers that say they won't work unless we pay their fucking doctor bills!"

Mickey blurted it all out in a single, breathless sentence, so Leo knew he had rehearsed it carefully. It meant Harry sent Mickey to the airport in his place because he was not yet ready for Leo's questions.

Mickey continued, "See, when you called yesterday and said you was flying out today, he already told the union guy he'd meet him." They were walking through the terminal, dodging ladders and platforms and dozens of workmen. Whenever Leo came to Vegas it seemed the airport was undergoing some new expansion.

"Where's Liz?" Leo asked.

"Liz?" Mickey said. "Oh, she's here. Over at the Desert Inn today, I think. She plays golf a lot, you know. Harry says he might put one in at the Oasis. A golf links."

"When is she going to Europe again?"

"Europe?"

"Yes, Mickey, Europe. The place on the other side of the Atlantic Ocean."

"Oh, Europe, yeah. Jeeze, Leo, I don't know."

They stepped out of the terminal, and Mickey gestured toward a waiting limousine. The driver, who had already retrieved Leo's Valpak from the baggage counter, opened the back door for them. Leo stopped and faced Mickey.

"What the hell are you so nervous about?"

"Huh?"

"I asked why you're so nervous?"

"I ain't nervous, Leo. What should I be nervous for?"

"Your future, Mickey, that's what you should be nervous for," Leo said. "Your future."

"My future? What's the matter with my future?"

"Forget it," Leo said, and got into the car. They rode to the hotel, Mickey keeping up a constant chatter, commenting on the warm weather, and how they were already talking about a new airport terminal on the other side of the field in a few years, and a new paved highway from the airport into town that they would call Paradise Road. Pretty clever name for a street, huh? Come to Vegas, it's like coming to Paradise. Mickey thought the guy who dreamed up the name was Ben Sylbert. Leo knew, didn't he, that Ben had quit as the Barclay's publicity director to start his own newspaper? Comes out once a week, *The Las Vegas Record*. Mickey was sure Ben got most of the money to start it from Harry. Five grand, Mickey heard. They made a deal for Ben to give the Barclay and the Oasis free advertising for a year.

Leo hardly listened; he knew Mickey was talking so much because he was under instructions to answer no questions concerning Harry or Liz. He gazed out the window. Like the airport, new buildings seemed to have sprung up overnight. A motel here, a car-rental agency there. Even a ramshackle little movie house. Behind these structures the desert extended endlessly, miles to the north, all the way into the hills. But even there, far out, you could see an occasional wooden frame of yet another building under construction. And still, as though protesting the relentless growth, tumbleweed and sand sometimes skittered across the highway from the desert.

A whole continent removed from Vincent Tomasino's Long Beach house where Leo had been only a day before. A whole different world. There, in Vinnie's living room, the Council met. Vinnie, Paul Calvelli, the heads of the three other leading New York families, and Anthony Curcio who had replaced Nicola Franzone in New England. And, of course, Leo.

Six Italians, one Jew.

Collectively, the six Italians represented business interests grossing well over $2 billion annually. Every phase of American commercial endeavor, from automobile agencies to fast-food franchises. Racetracks to restaurants. Trucking companies to chemical plants.

A virtual empire, and quite legitimate.

But the Jew—more accurately, two Jews—represented the empire's most precious possession. The casinos in Nevada and Cuba, over which the Italians lacked complete ownership and control. The Italians had tolerated the two Jews, and would continue to as long as it remained in their best interests. But one Jew was a thief, which most assuredly was in no one's best interests. Furthermore, they were all of them businessmen, Italians *and* Jews. A business where one partner stole from another was not a sound business, and could not long prosper.

They had Harry Wise cold. With his hand jammed in the cash drawer. They had awaited Leo's return from Israel before dealing with the matter. A matter of more than $2 million, deposited in several Swiss bank accounts. The money must be returned, and Harry punished. The precise form of such punishment to be determined when the Council heard Leo's report of Harry's side of it.

Everyone understood Harry had no side. The facts—the figures in the account ledgers—were on paper, made worse by his arrogance in not even attempting to disguise those figures, in blatantly challenging the rules and authority he had agreed to obey. He could not have shown more disrespect had he urinated on their shoes. But he was, after all, a Council member and therefore privileged to defend himself.

All this flashed through Leo's mind on the short ride from the airport to the Barclay. And all with the constant, nagging feeling of a missing piece. A jigsaw puzzle with one missing piece. Harry was not stupid. Why had he not at least doctored the books? Why, with the money safely in Swiss banks, and knowing his scam was discovered, why had he not remained in Europe? Why return?

Leo did not have the answer to those questions, but believed he knew the answer to why Harry stole the money in the first place.

Liz DiFalco.

She had cast a spell over Harry. He was entirely under her influence. Leo still could not comprehend a man loving a woman enough to sacrifice everything for her, although the very idea of falling in love that once was so alien to him now seemed not so impossible. Renata Koval had proved that, even if he thought "love" perhaps too strong an image.

". . . hey, Kleyner!" Leo was suddenly aware the limousine had stopped, and they were under the shade of the Barclay's huge, mirror-ceilinged portico. Harry had thrown open the car door and stood with open arms to embrace Leo.

They went inside and directly to Leo's top floor suite. A huge basket of fruit—fresh from L.A., flown in that very morning—was on the living-room coffee table. The wet bar was stocked with liquor and soft drinks. As soon as the bellhop deposited Leo's bag in the bedroom and was tipped by Mickey, Harry said to Leo, "Want to talk now, or after dinner?"

"Now," said Leo, looking at Mickey, who understood his cue to leave. Harry opened a bottle of beer. He held the bottle out to Leo.

Leo declined with a wave of his hand, and asked, "Where's Liz?"

"Golfing," Harry said. "She's getting real good at it, too." He drank the beer straight from the bottle. "Broke a hundred last week for the first time."

"Congratulations." Leo walked over to the bar and sat on a stool facing Harry. "I'm trying to save your life," he said quietly.

Leo expected a typical outburst of temper. He expected to hear Harry screaming, Save my life? From who? Them dago pricks! Fuck them! Who the fuck do they think they are? It's my money, I earned it! I got a right to do what I want with it!

Instead, Harry merely nodded, a polite little nod of acknowledgment.

"Did you hear what I just said?" Leo asked.

"Yeah, I heard."

"And you have nothing to say?"

"What do you want me to say, Leo? You want me to ask how you'll do it? How you'll save my life? Okay, how?"

"First, I want you to tell me why you did it."

Harry put down the beer bottle. He brought a comb from his pocket and ran it through his hair. Leo had not seen him do that in a long time. Harry said, "Leo, that's a dumb question."

Yes, Leo thought, it certainly was. Not even worth repeating. Two million dollars spoke for itself. He said, "All right, then here's one maybe not so dumb. Why didn't you stay where you were in Geneva, or wherever it was? Why come back knowing what would happen?"

"You're wrong, Kleyner," Harry said. "That's also a dumb one. I knew they'd find me no matter where I was. I figured my chances were better coming back and making a deal."

"A deal?" Leo nearly spat the word. "What kind of a deal? Fifty cents on the dollar? A dime? What?"

Unexpectedly, Harry grinned. "I figured you'd handle all that for me."

Leo said nothing. He looked at Harry, then away at the wall-length living-room window. The distant snow-capped hills that formed the basin ringing Las Vegas were splashed with shades of gold from the late afternoon sun. A sight so beautiful was somehow out of place here, now, he thought. It was wrong, just as everything Harry was saying was wrong.

"... you'd figure something, I knew it," Harry was saying. Leo heard the words, thinking not only were the words wrong, but a little too pat. Too smooth, too calm. Harry was reciting a speech. The puzzle with the missing piece. A man steals money, leaving a Boy Scout trail straight to his door and then looks you in the eye and says he knew you'd bail him out.

But then—and the very thought of it made Leo wince with chagrin—Harry happened to be correct. Leo had indeed bailed him out. He said, "I guaranteed the money, Harry. I guaranteed you'd return it. I vouched for it."

Harry grinned again and spread his hands in an elaborate shrug. "So there you are."

Leo wanted to hit him. For a crazy instant he actually considered it. He had felt anger at Harry before, a thousand times, but not with hate. The hate frightened him. He struggled for composure. "Then you will return it?"

"Yeah."

"Just like that?" Leo's own voice sounded hollow in his ears. He felt himself, like Harry, an actor in some well-rehearsed play. No, a puppet. He was being manipulated. Now he expected to learn what the missing puzzle piece was.

"I don't have a choice, do I?" Harry said.

No, that was not the piece; it still was missing. Leo said, "You'll have to return the money, and you'll have to get out of Vegas. Out of the Barclay, and the Oasis." And out of my life, he thought, but did not say it. That would come later.

"That's the price for my ass?"

"That's the price."

"How do you know the Council'll buy it?"

"I don't." Leo had no intention of making it easy for him. Let him sweat.

But Harry knew that answer, too. "They don't gain a thing from hitting me. All they want is their money back. 'Their' money, which is really mine, but what the fuck!" He threw up his hands in a shrug of helplessness.

Leo said, "You're finished with the Alliance, you realize that?"

"Yeah," Harry said. "Good riddance."

"Good riddance?" Leo repeated quietly. "Everything you worked for all your life is finished, and that's all you can say? Good riddance?"

Harry said, "Yeah, good riddance. So I'll retire. I'll get a job someplace as a dealer. Cuba, maybe, huh?"

"Harry, if you're thinking you can liquidate your points in the hotels, forget it. That's part of the price: turning them over."

"What am I supposed to live on? My good looks?"

"That's your problem."

Harry brought the comb from his pocket and ran it through his hair again, the second time in the past few minutes. This time Leo realized Harry's hair was noticeably thinning.

Leo said, "You're losing your hair."

"Tell me about it," Harry said glumly. He held the comb to the light, searching for stray hair strands. There were none. He smiled over that small victory and put the comb away.

"I'm having George Gerson come out here to take charge until we find somebody to replace you," Leo said.

"I'll have to go back to Geneva to get the money."

"No stupid tricks, Harry. You said it yourself: there's nowhere you can go they can't find you."

"Don't worry, Leo. No tricks." Harry picked up his beer bottle; it was empty. He lobbed the bottle expertly into the wastebasket behind the bar. "No tricks."

Leo knew Harry had considerable money stashed away. Not the millions he wanted, and he had lost a potential fortune in his hotel points, but enough for him and Liz to live quite well.

Live, the operative word.

He was alive. His life had been saved.

But still, that missing puzzle piece. It preyed on Leo's mind that whole week, and even when Vinnie Tomasino's courier returned to New York from Geneva with every cent of the skimmed $2,456,000, Leo still wondered. Harry and Liz were in France now, Menton, a small town on the Riviera near the Italian border. They had rented a house on the beach.

". . . the good life, Kleyner," Harry had said to Leo in a phone call just that morning.

"Harry, do you want to tell me now what the scam was?"

"Scam? Jesus, Leo, you got a suspicious mind! Listen, I'm out of the thing, I'm a solid citizen. *Die herst,* Leo? I got my woman, and I'm happy."

"Okay," Leo said.

"Leo, thanks."

"For what?"

"For saving my ass."

"Don't mention it."

Twelve hours later, Leo found the missing puzzle piece. George Gerson arrived from Las Vegas and drove straight to Leo's apartment. One look at Gerson's grim face, Leo knew it concerned Harry. Up all night on the airplane, George was bone-tired, but this was too important to wait.

They sat at Leo's kitchen table, Gerson sipping a cup of instant coffee, silent a long moment assembling his thoughts. Then, with a long, weary sigh, "Leo, the figure was not two million four. It's *four* million four."

"Four?" Leo repeated, not immediately comprehending.

"He skimmed four million, Leo."

"Four?" Leo said again, sounding foolish, feeling foolish, as though the butt of some practical joke.

Gerson drew in another deep, heavy breath. "What he did was rig the books so they'd show two million missing. He *wanted* it to be found. He *knew* he'd be caught." Unexpectedly, Gerson began chuckling; it was as though he had just thought of something so hilarious he could not control himself.

Leo peered at him. Gerson continued chuckling, then all at once stopped and was as somber as when he arrived. "What's so funny, Leo, is that Harry's had the last laugh! Right now, I guarantee you, he and Liz DiFalco are laughing themselves silly. What they did was so simple, it was absolutely brilliant!"

"Explain it to me, please, George," Leo said quietly. He felt more foolish than ever, and totally helpless.

Gerson said, "He knew you'd argue the Council into letting him off the hook if he returned the money and resigned all his interests. I'm not sure exactly what accounting tricks he used, other than some plain common sense: when an audit shows a glaring discrepancy like two million, four hundred thousand dollars, the accountant usually doesn't delve deeper. That's enough right there. Listen, I only caught it by accident. And Vinnie's man certainly didn't. He bought the original figure. Do you understand, Leo?"

Leo said nothing.

Gerson said, "I think you understand, Leo. You just don't want to."

Leo said, "Is anybody liable to pick it up later? In another audit?"

"Doubtful," Gerson said. "With the money re-entered, the books balance. Everybody's satisfied, even the tax man."

"If it's that easy, anyone can do it," Leo said. He wanted to concentrate on this, the possibility of it happening again. He did not want to think about Harry. His oldest, closest, and best friend who had stolen from him. Who had used him.

"I'm going to set up a new system," Gerson said. "A table-by-table, pit-by-pit, hourly check on the drop and hold. Then shift-by-shift. We'll know to the penny at the end of every shift how much cash went in, how much went out. The figures will be locked in, signed, countersigned, and signed again. It will take a gigantic conspiracy to skim so much as ten cents. Half the people in the whole casino would have to be involved."

Leo only vaguely listened. He was thinking of Harry, and the old days, and how he, Leo, always knew Harry would someday pull something like this. He was thinking quite calmly, rationally, which surprised him. He should have been enraged, but instead was only mildly annoyed. He thought it was because all the anger was drained out of him, replaced with disappointment. Hurt, that was the word. He felt hurt, not anger. It was worse.

". . . but you know who's idea this was, don't you?" Gerson was saying. "Harry just isn't that smart. It had to be Liz."

'Yes," Leo said. "She's one smart lady, all right." He got up and went into the living room and turned on the television. Leo sank into a chair. He stared at the blank screen, waiting for it to warm up.

"What's so important on TV?" Gerson asked.

"Milton Berle," Leo said. "He makes me laugh." He looked at Gerson. "I need a laugh."

4.

Milton Berle's *Texaco Star Theater* came on at eight P.M., Eastern Daylight Time. In Menton, France, where it was two A.M., Harry and Liz were just leaving the little beachfront casino. After a fine dinner at the casino restaurant, they had played chemin de fer for several hours. Liz liked the game, which Harry once considered installing at the Barclay but decided was too slow for American tastes. Tonight, Liz enjoyed a spectacular run of luck. Twelve straight coups.

They stepped onto the Promenade, and stood a moment gazing out at the beach, at the surf splashing up on the sand. It was a cool night. A brisk ocean breeze filled the air with a strong smell of the sea.

Harry said, "You know, if you'd have bet the limit in there, you could have killed them."

"I felt sorry for the croupier," Liz said. "He seemed to take it so personally."

"Are you kidding? Never feel sorry for the house."

"They have a thirty-five-thousand franc limit," Liz said. "So how much could we win, anyway?"

"Thirty-five thousand francs is a hundred bucks," Harry said. "You could have won over a grand."

"I had more fun this way," she said. She shivered suddenly. "I didn't realize it was so cold at night here. Maybe we'd better forget walking on the beach for tonight."

"Yeah, let's go home and go to bed," he said. He removed his jacket and placed it over her shoulders. "That more comfortable?"

"Darling, you're so gallant!"

"No, horny," he said. He grinned at her, and placed her hand on his crotch. "See what I mean?"

"You'll have to do better than that, dear boy."

He pulled her to him and kissed her. A long, lingering kiss. He loved the soft warmth of her lips on his, the full firmness of her breasts flattened into his chest, the feel of her heart pounding against his. He loved her so much that sometimes when he thought about it he felt dizzy.

The Promenade was an arbor-covered concrete walk extending a quarter

mile along the beachfront, dimly lit and deserted at this time of night.
In Menton, but for the casino, which closed at two, everything was shut-
tered. And so quiet the only sound was an occasional automobile, and
the surf crashing up on the beach.

The town itself was small and very old, with narrow winding cobble-
stone streets fronted by ancient, sagging three- and four-story villas. A
single main street, Boulevard Des Angleterres, was lined with tall eu-
calyptus trees. Menton was a resort town, bustling in season, but now in
October almost ghostly. A kind of solitude giving one a sense of strange
security.

They walked to the end of the Promenade and turned onto the boulevard. They were staying at the Hôtel Ambassadeurs until their rented
house was available. They walked silently, Harry's arm draped tightly
around her. He loved walking with her that way, feeling her close
to him.

Liz saw the car first. Parked on the boulevard outside the *pharmacie*,
shadowed by the sidewalk trees, hardly visible even under the streetlamp.
But Liz glimpsed the flicker of light from the car interior when the door
opened.

"Harry!" she screamed.

He had time only to push her away from him and turn to face the
figure looming up in the dark. Time only to regret not carrying a gun,
and also to realize that even if he had a gun it was too late to draw it.
The muzzle flash of the shotgun reflected off the pharmacy plate-glass
window and brightened the whole sidewalk. The blast of the gunshot
reverberated like a clap of thunder.

Liz did not see Harry's face disintegrate, or the entire top of his skull
fly off and splatter redly against the whitewashed stone side of the pharmacy. The instant Harry pushed her away she had started running. It
resembled her worst nightmare, her legs mired in thick mud, unable to
place one foot ahead of the other. But she knew she must run. Somehow,
she must.

Ahead was another street, a narrow twisting street she remembered
led back to the beach. She turned into it, stumbling on the cobblestones,
flailing her arms for balance. In the distance, she heard the car start.
She glanced back. The car's lights were not on, but in the diffused light
of the corner streetlamp she saw it clearly. A black Citroën, very similar
to the car Harry had rented, but that one was real, and at the hotel.
This one was in the nightmare.

And a man walking behind her—she wondered if it was the same man,
and tried to remember if he wore a hat; this man did not. She ran faster.
The clatter of her heels on the cobblestones echoed into her ears as a
drum pounding out a message over and over: *run faster, run faster, run
faster.* Behind her, the man was walking slowly, not at all in a hurry,
which she thought very strange. He should be chasing her. And then,

shockingly—so shockingly she drew in her breath to scream but could not find the strength and felt only a dryness in her mouth and throat, and a tightness over her whole body as though a blazing hot steel strap had been clamped over her and was being pulled tight—she realized why the man walked slowly.

The street was a dead end, closed off by a grated gate. Now she remembered. The street led into a short section of the Promenade containing a series of shops that was closed off at night at both ends.

Dead end.

The words danced before her eyes and rang mockingly back at her with the loud rattle of the steel bars of the gate as she tugged them with all her strength. She turned now to face the man. She could not see his face, only his form, larger and larger before her eyes. He approached, holding an object in his hands which he slowly raised. She was paralyzed. A thousand sentences flashed into her mind, all blurred, like the illuminated sign in Times Square running wild.

She felt the circular coldness of the gun barrels against her cheek. Her lovely, smooth skin. It was the last thing she ever felt. Her last thought was of that lovely, smooth skin. It would never look the same.

This happened precisely at 2:12 A.M. Menton time. In Las Vegas, where it was nine hours earlier, Mickey Goldfarb had just rolled his new Caddy El Dorado convertible into a "Reserved" slot in the Oasis executive parking area. He opened the door, squinting against the glare of the still-bright sun sinking behind the western hills. An outside force slammed the door shut, pushing him back into the seat. A young man, jet-black hair neatly cropped in a crewcut, wearing a bright red and yellow Hawaiian sport shirt, stood smiling down at him.

"Stay in the car, Mickey," the man said. "Slide over."

At the same moment, the passenger door opened. Another man, also wearing a colorful sport shirt, slipped into the right-hand seat. This man, older, with weather-wrinkled skin, also smiled. The smile never left his face as he quickly, deftly, removed the .32 from Mickey's shoulder holster.

Mickey, now seated between these two men whom he had never before seen, said, "What the fuck is this?"

"We're going for a little drive, partner," said the crewcut. He started the car and backed out of the slot. They turned onto Las Vegas Boulevard and in an instant were swallowed up in the heavy late-afternoon traffic.

Eighteen minutes later, 8:30 in New York, Leo sat watching Milton Berle. He had not moved from the chair since George Gerson left twenty minutes earlier. Berle had done a skit about a Hollywood writer pleading for a job with a producer. Leo did not recall a single scene. He had thought of nothing but Harry, and how he wanted to hate him but did not, and in fact somewhat grudgingly admired Harry's *chutzpah*.

On the television screen, four men in Texaco service-station uniforms sang a barbershop-quartet song extolling the gasoline. The door buzzer sounded. Leo thought if he did not answer they would go away. The second buzz was more insistent. Leo got up and opened the door.

Vincent Tomasino stood solemnly in the doorway, both hands gripping the brim of his hat, sliding it around in an endless circle. Just behind him stood two men Leo vaguely recognized as Vinnie's bodyguards. Both in uniform: double-breasted suits, floral-patterned ties, wide-brimmed, gray fedoras.

"Can we talk a minute?"

Leo stepped aside for Vinnie to enter. The bodyguards followed Vinnie in, but remained near the door. They avoided Leo's eyes, and kept their own eyes fixed on the television screen.

"Leo, I wanted you to hear this from me personally," Vinnie said. He seemed suddenly aware of the hat in his hand. He placed it carefully on the sofa armrest. "Sit down, huh?"

"Maybe I better hear this standing," Leo said. He tried to sound light, but Vinnie did not smile.

"A half hour ago, in France, we hit Harry."

Leo heard the words through a sudden roaring in his ears. He felt his legs weaken. He reached out to steady himself. The whole room became hazy, as though seen through a red filter. The roaring was louder. Vinnie continued talking. Leo heard some of the words.

". . . had to be done . . . Liz, too . . . Mickey Goldfarb . . . no sense taking a chance on that maniac doing something crazy, you know . . . no choice, Leo . . . don't have to explain . . . guy fucked us, think of the example it'll set . . . didn't expect you to order it, so wouldn't even ask you . . . did it fast and good, Leo. Believe me, he didn't feel a thing . . ."

Vinnie talked on and on. Leo heard some of it, but his mind was composing his own words. Himself talking to Vinnie. Harsh angry words. *What the hell is going on? Don't we follow our own rules anymore? Nobody gets hit without a unanimous Council vote!*

But those words were never spoken, for even while they came to his mind, he knew how meaningless they were. And how naïve he was to even imagine he could have saved Harry. Harry deserved to die.

Leo never knew how long Vinnie stayed, or when he left. He knew only that he sat in his own living room, gazing at a television screen at a man in a Texaco uniform speaking to him. Words that, like Vinnie's, Leo simply did not understand. But all at once the man in the Texaco uniform was Harry, pointing a finger at Leo, accusing him of ordering the hit.

"No," Leo said aloud, quietly, to the screen. "No, Harry, no. I'd never do that. You know better!"

He shook his head, almost violently. The man on the screen was Milton

Berle again. Leo went to the window and opened the curtains. He stared out at the park, the twin trails of lights from vehicle headlamps, and the naked light bulbs on the trellis of the Tavern On The Green.

The scene blurred before his eyes, and he realized he was crying. He wiped his eyes. Everything remained blurred. He thought if only he had someone to talk to about it, tell them about it, make them understand he loved Harry and would never harm him. Yes, he must tell someone.

Tell them what? That you are a coward?

Coward? Where'd you ever get that bright idea?

If you are not a coward, then why didn't you tell that greasy-faced dago son of a bitch about the two million four Harry *did* make off with?

Listen, don't even waste your breath answering, because I'll tell you why.

The fact that you even knew about it would have meant to Vinnie that you were in on it with Harry. So old Vinnie and his Alliance would have made a real clean sweep. Another Holocaust, for Christ's sake!

He had to laugh suddenly. Through his tears he laughed. Because Harry really did have the last laugh. With Liz also dead, the money, Harry's money, would rot forever in some Swiss bank vault. Collecting interest. In a hundred years, compounded, it would be worth a hundred million.

But I would just like to talk to somebody. Tell them about this, and me, and how I feel, and what's going on in my head.

Why? You think that would make you feel better?

It might.

So go talk to somebody.

But who? he asked himself.

A friend, he told himself.

Friend? What friend? I have no friends.

Carla?

Don't be silly.

George Gerson?

No, why drag George into it?

The concept of no friends left him feeling empty, and almost frightened. Alone, that was the word. All alone. And a man must not be alone. Being alone is death in and of itself. These thoughts raced faster and faster through his mind until all were jumbled and unintelligible.

And then, like the bursting of a star shell, with the whirling fragments forming gigantic glittering silver letters across the night sky, he had the answer.

He did have a friend! A fine, loyal, honest person he trusted and could talk to. Just talk to and tell her how he felt. How all alone he felt and needed her to talk to.

He stepped away from the window and sat at the big oak desk facing the other window. He switched on the lamp, slid the locator arrow on the address pad to "K," and punched the button. The cover sprang open. He ran his finger down the names, stopped at KOVAL, RENATA. 72 ALBANY STREET, LONDON, NW1. TEL: EUS 3023.

He picked up the phone and asked for the overseas operator. He gave her the number, then listened impatiently to the bland voices of the various relay operators; and then, with anticipation, to the chimelike sound of the phone ringing in London.

Now, his mind crystal clear, he knew exactly what to say, and did. After apologizing for the late hour—nearly two in the morning in England—he wasted no more time.

". . . I want you to come to New York," he said into the phone.

"New York?" she said. "My God, Leo, are you drunk?"

"I'm stone sober," he said. "And it's very important to me. I need you."

"You can't possibly be serious."

"Please, Renata, don't argue. Just do it."

She was silent a moment. The hum of the transatlantic wire echoed shrilly in his ears. Then, "I have a job, Leo—"

"—quit the job," he said. "Please, I need you."

Another silent moment. Then, "All right. I'll come."

"Thank you," he said. "Thank you very much."

They discussed details. She had to give notice, of course, at least a month. A month? No, that was far too long to wait. In that case, she suggested, he had just better go to Idlewild Airport tomorrow, get on the first plane to London, and come over and get her. That, he said, was exactly what he would do.

When he hung up, he sat a long while, his hand still gripping the phone. He tried to keep his mind on her, not on Harry. Finally, he got up and stepped to the window again. On the street, and in the park, it seemed busier. More cars, more people. He wondered how many were alone, how many had friends. He had envied some of them before, those who had friends and were not alone. He had no reason to envy them now. He was no longer alone.

PART SIX

RIDE THE TIGER

——— 24 ———

At night, in the clear desert air, the city glowed like a cluster of sparkling gems. From the Control Tower restaurant high atop the Barclay you had an unobstructed, 360-degree view. Looking north, Highway 91—now called Las Vegas Boulevard and lined with one shiny new hotel after another—stretched all the way to the downtown area, where blocks of glaring neon turned night into perpetual, garish day. South, the highway rolled into darkness, broken only with a brief carpet of light from McCarran Field, then dark again. To the east and west, the desert, and then the hills.

As Harry Wise promised, Las Vegas had become a real city. With schools, churches, two full-service hospitals, supermarkets and department stores. There were four golf courses, two Little League ball fields, five automobile agencies, three newspapers, a television station, and three radio stations, one an FM station featuring classical music. A good police and fire department, and a Chamber of Commerce. Paved roads, sidewalks, and sewers. Municipal services, from trash collection to property-tax collection. And now, in the spring of 1956, fifty thousand people.

The two and one half mile section of Las Vegas Boulevard north of the Barclay, known as The Strip, glittered with nine other large hotels. The Oasis, the New Frontier, the Desert Inn, the Stardust, the Thunderbird, Flamingo, Sands, El Rancho Vegas, Silver Slipper, Sahara. Each with a bigger, brighter, more colorful marquee, each blazing with the names of big-time entertainers. Frank Sinatra to Sophie Tucker. Salaries paid some performers were said to exceed $25,000 weekly.

The ten Strip casinos that year reported gross revenues of more than $100 million. These ten, plus some twenty smaller, far less lavish downtown establishments, employed seventy-five hundred men and women, whose basic living requirements—from automobile mechanics to cosmetologists—provided jobs for twelve thousand others. Under construction were three new Strip hotels, the Riveria, Royal Nevada, and the Dunes.

And a racetrack, Thunderbird Downs.

These proud facts and figures were the basis of Ben Sylbert's lead editorial in tomorrow's *Las Vegas Record*, which two months ago went daily. To be sure, certain information pertinent to those facts and figures would be discreetly omitted. For example, the Barclay and the Oasis were ostensibly owned outright by a New York corporation, IDIC. In reality, through a series of ingeniously convoluted lease and leaseback arrangements, IDIC shared ownership of those two hotels with elements the newly created Nevada Gaming Commission deemed undesirable and who would have otherwise been denied participation.

Also omitted, with equal discretion, was the fact that substantial points in five other Strip hotels were held personally by Leo Gorodetsky.

Ben, seated at one end of the long table at the east window of the Control Tower Restaurant, was thinking about this now. About discretion. He gazed another moment at the dazzling red and white moving letters of the Oasis marquee across the street, then turned from the window and peered down the length of the table at Leo sitting at the opposite end. This was the only occupied table in the room. The entire restaurant had been reserved for a small private function, a wedding reception, whose announcement Ben had already written for publication in tomorrow's paper.

... services were performed by Rabbi Harry Fleet of Temple Beth-El of Las Vegas. The bride, Carla Gordon, is a graduate of the New England Conservatory of Music. The groom, Dr. Avi Schiff, of Herzliya, Israel, has recently completed his surgical residency at the Peter Bent Brigham Hospital in Boston. The couple plan to make their home in Tel Aviv, Israel, where Dr. Schiff has accepted a position in the surgical department at Hadassah Hospital in that city.

The four-piece orchestra had started playing "Mood Indigo," and Ben's wife was gesturing him to get up and dance with her. He rose, whispering into her ear, ". . . and the bride's father, Mr. Leo Gorodetsky of New York City, owns half of Las Vegas."

"What are you talking about?"

"About my newspaperman's obsession with truth," he said as they began dancing. "And my own obsession not to bite the hand that fed me."

"As usual, darling, you make no sense." Ruth Sylbert was a petite, attractive woman in her late thirties. Two years ago, in Nevada to divorce her philandering husband, she met and married Ben. He had never been happier.

"Not making sense is a hangover from my legal background," he said. If Ben had never been happier, he never recalled seeing Leo so happy. The charming English lady seated between Leo and his sister was responsible for that. Ben was glad for Leo. And for Carla and Avi, who were also dancing.

"They look so pleased with each other," Ruth Sylbert said.

"Nice kids," he agreed absently, smiling at George Gerson and his wife. The Gersons and the Sylberts were the only other nonfamily guests.

"I can't imagine why he wouldn't want to practice here in the States," Ruth said.

"Because he's an Israeli," Ben said, watching Carla abruptly stop dancing and pull Avi over to Leo and Renata.

Ben heard Carla say, "All right, Avi, now give my new mother a treat and dance with her."

"New mother," Ben thought. Interesting. Which was also Renata's reaction: interesting. She liked it. Perhaps because she knew she would never have children of her own. Perhaps, too, because she knew it pleased Leo.

"We haven't had much chance to talk," Avi said, guiding Renata onto the floor. "I want to thank you for being so kind to Carla."

Renata drew away an instant and looked at him. "I'm not 'kind' to her, Avi. I love her like my own."

"More reason for my gratitude," Avi said. "You were there to help her through that terrible time. I'll never forget it."

Nor I, Renata thought, remembering that cold, gray evening last December. Carla, home on Christmas holiday, had just returned from visiting Ellie in Connecticut. Carla said she told Ellie of the handsome young Israeli doctor she was dating, who would be coming down to New York for a few days over Christmas. Carla said Ellie appeared not to understand, but she wondered if this was not Ellie's way of punishing her for having skipped last month's visit. The visits were becoming too depressing. They were at dinner that evening when the phone rang. Carla answered. She listened, and then screamed. A shrill, ear-piercing cry of pain.

Ellie had walked into the hospital driveway and thrown herself under the wheels of a glazier's truck. The hospital director later told Leo he believed that Ellie, experiencing a moment of sudden, total lucidity, had chosen that moment to assume responsibility for her life.

And ended it.

Leo had tried to comfort Carla, but Renata motioned him away. She would take care of her. And she did. That whole night, simply allowing Carla to weep and to talk. In the morning, it was over. Carla was a strong young woman.

". . . and we'll expect you both to visit us soon," Avi was saying now.

"Absolutely," Renata replied, with no idea of what he said. She had been thinking about Leo, and how he had confided to her his own feelings of guilt for Ellie's death—and life. He had told Renata the whole story of his marriage to Ellie, the childish rebound from the childish infatuation with Charlotte Daniels. If not for him, Ellie's life might have turned out entirely different; it sometimes made him feel he had stolen her life. He said he wished he could have given it back to her. That was the one and only time he ever discussed it with Renata.

She returned with Avi to the table now and said to Carla, "Thank you for letting me borrow him. I may do it again."

"You'd better do it soon, then," Carla said. "When I'm finished with him I doubt there'll be much left to borrow." She kissed Avi. "Yes, darling?"

"I'm a strong young man," he said.

"And you'll need every bit of it," she said.

Esther said, "My God, how they talk these days!"

"Come on, Aunt Esther, get with it!" Carla moved back on the floor with Avi. The orchestra had started a new number.

"Listen, young lady, I'm 'with it' all I want to be," said Esther. She aimed a finger at George Gerson, "So how about you having a dance with me? I'm sure Betty won't mind."

"Are you kidding?" Betty Gerson said. She pushed George to his feet.

Esther and George Gerson stepped onto the floor. Ben and Ruth Sylbert remained at the table with Leo and Renata. Renata listened to the others chat, but the words did not register. She was gazing at Leo and thinking that not for a single instant had she regretted her decision to come to America. A wholly impulsive decision, a hunch, a feeling. He needed her, she needed to be needed. Love? Well, the word required a definition. If it meant two people wildly and continually intrigued with each other, unable to keep their thoughts, or hands, off each other, no. If it meant mutual pleasure, respect, and consideration, yes. If it meant sharing and caring, again yes.

". . . let me in on it," Leo was saying to her.

"Let you in on what?"

"You were smiling," he said. "As though you had some marvelous secret."

She had not realized that her eyes had wandered to Esther and George Gerson on the dance floor. "How old is Esther?" she asked.

"Fifty-eight, two years older than me," he said. "Why?"

"I just wondered," she said. She had no intention of confessing that it suddenly occurred to her that both she and Esther were old maids, spinsters, and likely to remain so. Marriage was a term never once mentioned by Leo or herself. A word forbidden as though by some unspoken, implied contract. Their relationship was an "arrangement." In truth, Renata did not believe she wanted it any other way.

In a recent conversation Carla had suggested Renata demand marriage. Leo, Carla said, would do it. Demand, said Renata, as Carla should well know, was a most imprudent method of approach to her father. But that aside, other than perhaps an occasional snide reference to her as his mistress—and those people petty enough for that were unimportant, anyway—she had all the advantages of marriage with none of the responsibilities.

And some quite practical considerations as well. Leo not only had established a trust fund, an enormous sum of stocks and bonds, in her own name, but was also negotiating the purchase of a travel agency for her.

He wanted her to be independent, he said, so if she ever tired of the arrangement, she would have lost nothing. Suppose *he* tired of it? she had asked. He looked at her as though she had said something so foolish it did not merit response.

Now everyone was toasting the bridal couple's departure. A chartered plane awaited them at the airport to fly them to New York. From there, the *France* to Europe, and a six-week Grand Tour of the continent before settling down in Israel.

Downstairs, Renata hung back while Leo said good-bye to Carla and Avi. "Listen, Doctor, you take good care of her, understand?" Leo said. He knew the words were trite, but did not care. He meant them.

"You know I will," Avi said.

Leo nodded. "I'll hear from you soon?" he asked Carla.

"I'll call you from Paris."

"I'll be in Havana," Leo said.

"I'm sure they have phones there, Daddy," she said. "That is, if the terrible old Generalissimo will allow you to use one."

"Listen, he has a serious problem," Leo said. "And when he has a problem, so do I."

Ben Sylbert said, "The trouble is that Batista won't admit there's a problem. He says it's nothing more than a nuisance. Believe me, Fidel Castro is more than a nuisance."

"That remains to be seen," Leo said. He did not consider it advisable to add that with a $60 million plus investment in Cuba he wanted to see for himself and, through Wingy Gruber's contacts, had arranged to meet Castro.

"If there's a problem, I'm sure you'll solve it," Carla said. "You always do."

"You bet," said Leo, and kissed her, shook Avi's hand, kissed Carla once more, then walked quickly into the hotel.

Leo did not see the photographer. He had appeared like a *paparrazo*, snapping pictures of everyone in the hotel driveway. George Gerson motioned to Ben, who confronted the photographer.

"Who do you work for?" he asked.

"*Review Journal*," said the photographer.

"You must be new," Ben said. "I've never seen you."

"First week on the job."

Ben held out his hand. "Let me have the film."

"Hey, come on, give me a break." The photographer glanced at the two plainclothes Barclay security men who materialized. He grinned lamely, popped open the camera, and gave Ben the roll. "I'm only trying to do my job."

Ben did not know it, and never would, but he had just been victimized by a photographer's version of the old shell game. The surrendered film cartridge was blank. The genuine film was preserved on another roll.

The photographer was an FBI agent temporarily assigned to the Nevada Gaming Commission. The commission was cooperating with Martin Raab's special Justice Department task force in its investigation of the links between Nevada casinos and organized crime. They had hoped to find evidence of Leo in Las Vegas in the company of known Alliance figures.

The photos, on Raab's Washington desk twelve hours later, were disappointing. Raab was not surprised. Leo seldom, if ever, socialized with his Alliance associates. Such evidence would have strengthened the government's pending case against Leo, but Raab believed they were strong enough anyway to go to trial.

Raab had already obtained a sealed grand-jury indictment naming Leo Gorodetsky and Thomas Stohlmeyer co-conspirators in the misappropriation of monies from Stohlmeyer's UATW pension fund. Stohlmeyer, in return for immunity from prosecution and his promise to resign all union offices, had agreed to testify against Leo.

A warrant for Leo's arrest had been issued, and would have been served within the week had Leo not gone to Cuba. He would be served immediately upon his return.

2.

The room stank. Chickens, dogs, goats, and a pig wandered in and out. It was the front room of a small adobe farmhouse at the junction of two dirt roads leading up into the Sierra Maestra hills from Santiago de Cuba. Parked outside was an old Chevrolet sedan with a faded checkerboard strip along both front doors and "taxi" in sloppily handpainted white letters on each side of the hood. The taxi driver, an old man with a thick, scruffy mustache, sat dozing on the running board.

Parked near the Chevrolet, with a commanding view of the terrain below, was a battered 1932 Ford pickup truck. Four men were in the vehicle, two in the cab and two in the truck bed. All wore food- and grass-stained fatigues, and all carried Czechoslovakian-manufactured submachine guns with open safety releases. All were bearded, all at first glance resembling their leader, the bearded young man inside the house, engaged in conversation with Leo Gorodetsky.

What struck Leo first about twenty-nine-year-old Fidel Castro was his long, straggly, jet-black beard, not unlike an Orthodox rabbi's. Fidel Castro exuded the same religious intensity, his deep, penetrating eyes shining with an evangelistic gleam as he reviled the fascist dictator enslaving his country.

Castro, like his enemy Fulgencio Batista, spoke passable English but preferred an interpreter. The interpreter, whose long black hair was bundled tightly under her forage cap, and who wore a U.S. Army issue Colt .45 in a polished leather holster, was a young girl, certainly no older than ninteen. Her translation, although in heavily accented English, was literate and accurate.

Leo had flown to Santiago de Cuba and, as arranged, contacted a certain bartender in the city's best hotel, El Oriente. A few minutes later he was in a taxi driving through the center of town, which was under martial law and crowded with Cuban soldiers. General Batista had declared Oriente Province in a state of emergency. All this for the "mere nuisance" he claimed the rebels to be.

When Leo had entered the taxi, the driver never said a word. He started the motor and drove off, through the city, and out into the hills. Twice they were stopped at Cuban army checkpoints. Soldiers, rifles slung casually, sauntered into the middle of the road. At each checkpoint the taxi driver turned to Leo with outstretched palm. Leo placed an American ten-dollar bill into the palm. The soldier, into whose palm the money was in turn placed, immediately waved them through.

Soon, on a continually ascending road, they were deep in the hills. It was midday. The air inside the taxi was thick with road dust and oven-hot from the high, bright sun. Eventually they reached another checkpoint. This one was manned by bearded guerrillas with leveled rifles. More terse conversation, but now no exchange of money. They were waved through. On up into the mountains, higher and higher. Leo began wondering if they would ever reach their destination, and why he had come even this far.

I am fifty-six years old, he thought. I know I look forty-six, and have more brown hair than gray, but fifty-six is too old to be playing Hemingway-in-the-mountains-with-the-rebels. I am also tired, battered, hungry, and thirsty. I am also, I think, crazy. I must be crazy to do this.

At the farmhouse, Leo waited nearly an hour for Castro. When Castro and the young girl interpreter, whose name was Elena, finally arrived, Elena said, "Mr. Gorodetsky, Fidel wishes to apologize for keeping you waiting, but some government aircraft were observed and we could not move until they were gone."

Leo nodded at Castro, who was lighting a long fat cigar. Leo said, "In that case, I'm glad you kept me waiting. It's far preferable to being caught in crossfire between you and the government troops."

As Elena translated, another young man entered the house. Clean-shaven, shorter than Castro, and heavier, he also wore fatigues and a holstered .45. When Elena finished, Castro introduced the young man.

"This is Rafael," Castro said in English.

Rafael shook Leo's hand and in accentless English said, "I am Fidel's Chief of Staff." He smiled as though the title were some private joke, and spoke in Spanish to Castro.

Castro looked at his watch and spoke to Elena. She said to Leo, "Fidel must leave in five minutes, but Rafael is authorized to act in his behalf. Now, to answer your previous question, Fidel says it is always possible to be caught in a crossfire between us and the government, but unlikely."

"Why is it unlikely?" Leo asked.

Before replying, Castro offered Leo a cigar from a tooled-leather case. Leo accepted it, and a light from Castro's gold Dunhill lighter. While Castro answered the question in Spanish, Leo drew on the cigar. It was surprisingly mild.

Elena translated, "There will be no government attack because they believe they have us trapped here in the Sierra Maestra, and eventually will starve us out."

"Will you be starved out?" Leo asked.

Castro laughed; it was unnecessary for Elena to relay the question. In Spanish, he said, "I don't even think Batista believes it. He's only hoping someone will kill me, or my own soldiers will rebel against me. Batista knows his days are numbered and he's stealing as much money as he can before he turns and runs. You'll see, one of these days the country will wake up to find that bastard back on his estate in Florida. Or somewhere in Spain, safe and sound, leaving his friends and subordinates to answer for his crimes."

Before Elena could finish translating, Rafael spoke quietly to Castro, pointing to his wristwatch.

Castro rose and shook Leo's hand. "You must excuse me." He nodded at the others, and left, vaulting into a jeep packed with bearded guerrillas. Horn blasting, the jeep raced off.

Rafael said, "In an hour, if you look to the south and see a huge cloud of smoke, it will be all that remains of a government barracks and gasoline storage dump. Now, please, how may we serve you?"

Elena spoke first. She said to Leo, "I am curious to hear how you could come to Oriente without Batista knowing?"

"He does know," Leo said. "I told him I would report back on your strength and on your positions."

Both guerrillas thought Leo was joking. They were wrong; he was quite serious. At the last minute, realizing the improbability of meeting Castro without Batista learning of it, he had told the general—not untruthfully—that his approach to Castro would be as a businessman concerned with the future of his own interests. While thus engaged, he might do a little spying for Batista. As Leo anticipated, the president was more than agreeable.

Leo said to Rafael and Elena, "It's true. I told Batista I would report what I saw."

Rafael knew Leo could not possibly have seen anything of genuine military importance. He laughed, amused. "And what have you seen?"

"A strong band of dedicated young people," Leo said. "Prepared to fight a long time. Years, if necessary."

It was precisely the right thing to say. The two young people beamed with pleasure. Elena said, "We *will* succeed, Mr. Gorodetsky! There is no way we can be stopped."

"Yes, and please be sure to tell this to that fascist son of a bitch!" Rafael said, and in the same breath, continued, "So now, sir, what exactly is it you wish from us?"

Leo looked at him and the girl, and then through the open door to the men outside with the Czech submachine guns. They reminded him of the young Israeli soldiers patrolling the streets near the demarcation line of East and West Jerusalem. The same unique calm and deadly determination.

He said to Rafael, "If you overthrow Batista, what happens to the casinos?"

Rafael said, 'What happens to them? Nothing happens to them. We don't kill the golden goose."

Golden goose, Leo thought, the understatement of the year. Of the century. Sixty million dollars' worth of goose. "Then we speak the same language?"

"To the letter," said Rafael. "Our objective is to reestablish democracy in Cuba, not destroy its economy."

The same language, all right, Leo thought. Dollars. And why not? He felt much better, in control again. Money always put you in control.

He said, "I would like to donate a certain amount to your cause." He paused, wondering if perhaps he should reduce the figure. He decided no. Go all the way. "Two hundred and fifty thousand," he said. The girl's eyebrows rose, but Rafael merely nodded, expressionless. A cool customer, Leo thought. I would not mind having him on my side. "The money can be delivered to one of your representatives in Miami. Would that be acceptable?"

"Two hundred and fifty thousand dollars is always acceptable," Rafael said.

Leo wondered how much Fidel Castro would salt away in *his* Swiss bank account.

* * *

That same evening, in Havana, Leo enjoyed a leisurely private dinner at the presidential palace. *Paella*, which Batista knew Leo liked, and a three-inch-thick filet mignon for the general.

". . . this man calling himself Rafael," Batista said. "He is an Argentinian whose true name is Ramón Sandoval. He has personally executed no less than a dozen of my soldiers unlucky enough to be captured. He is a communist, and a terrorist of the worst kind. You know, Leo, they are all communists."

"Whatever they are, they need money," said Leo, who doubted they were communists and knew that to justify his brutality toward the rebels, Batista had to label them communist. He looked Batista straight in the eye and said, "They asked me for two hundred and fifty thousand."

"They don't think small, do they?"

"It costs nothing to ask, Your Excellency."

"And your answer?"

"I said when they were sitting here, in this room, in your chair, that would be the time to open financial negotiations."

Batista laughed. He sliced a huge square of beef from the filet and popped it into his mouth. Chewing noisily, he said, "At least you were honest with the scum."

"I always find it wise to cover all bases, General," Leo said, thinking this at least was true, and that he was becoming quite an accomplished diplomat. Or liar, which is the same.

". . . and what is your opinion of these rebels?" Batista asked.

Leo decided to answer with complete honesty. "In my opinion, General, for what it's worth, I think you have a serious situation on your hands."

"After we sent them back into the hills with over a hundred dead and wounded? They are trapped up there, Leo. In three months, they will be starved out."

"I must disagree, General," Leo said. "And I must also confess I'm worried."

"No need for worry," Batista said. "I give you my word."

"All the same, I'd like to offer some modest financial assistance in your valiant struggle against these people," Leo paused to examine a lobster claw he had just extracted from the *paella*. "One hundred thousand dollars."

Batista was impressed. "Very generous, I must say."

"It's an expression of my concern."

"I understand," said Batista. "And you may be sure the money will be well spent."

"To combat the rebels," Leo said. "The money must be used only for that."

"You have my word."

Leo did not for an instant believe him, but thought that this $100,000 plus the $250,000 to Castro constituted an ironclad insurance policy. No matter which side won, IDIC was covered. And $350,000 to protect $60 million was a fire-sale bargain. He ate the lobster claw meat now. It was delicious.

After dinner Leo was ushered into a presidential car for the short ride to El Conquistador. An army major hurried down the palace stairs to stop the car. He was Batista's legal adviser.

"His Excellency forgot to mention that he has been approached by an American for a gambling license," the major said. "This individual is prepared to offer a large amount of money for it."

"Who is he?" Leo asked.

The major consulted a small notebook. "Agnessi," he said. "Frederick Agnessi."

"Agnessi," Leo repeated. The name was vaguely familiar.

"His Excellency informed Mr. Agnessi that he would discuss the matter with you."

This was Leo's agreement with Batista. No casino licenses granted without IDIC approval. Leo said, "Please tell Mr. Agnessi that I do not approve."

Leo wondered why the man had not checked with him first, instead of contacting the Cubans directly. He remembered Fred Agnessi now. A small-time Miami enforcer and loan shark with big ambitions. He worked for the Alliance, which was disturbing, for no soldier—especially an Italian—would ever make such a request without addressing it through Council channels. Then why did the Council not refer Agnessi to Leo?

The more he thought about this, the more it bothered him. He forgot it only when he arrived in Miami and was met at the airport by federal marshals with a warrant for his arrest on a charge of conspiracy to misappropriate labor-union pension funds.

3.

The cioppino broth, ladled carelessly, had spilled onto the white linen tablecloth, and the front page of the *The New York Daily Mirror*. Almost prophetically, the headlines appeared bloodstained.

MOST IMPORTANT VICTORY OVER
ORGANIZED CRIME IN QUARTER
CENTURY, SAYS BRICKHILL

"They got Stohlmeyer locked up in the stockade at Fort Dix," Vincent Tomasino said. "This time, there won't be any 'accidents.'" He was paraphrasing Senator Brickhill at the previous day's press conference. Leo Gorodetsky's conspiracy trial would commence September 10, 1956. Until then, co-defendant Thomas Stohlmeyer was safe and secure.

"Leo says they don't have a chance," Paul Calvelli said. "There's not a shred of evidence he bribed Stohlmeyer for the loans."

"Come on, Paul. Brickhill and his guy, there, the Jew, what's his name—?" Vinnie snapped his fingers recollectingly.

"Raab," Paul Calvelli said. "Marty Raab."

"Yeah, Raab. Him and Brickhill, they're not amateurs. They don't go to trial without good evidence."

"The money to Stohlmeyer was paid in cash, Vinnie. It came right off the top of the loan proceeds, disbursed from a dozen different construction accounts. Impossible to trace. Remember how we all congratulated Leo on him using union money to build the Oasis? You yourself said how you admired him for his business rule: 'Never use your own money when you can use other people's.' "

"There's always a chance for a conviction, Paul," Vinnie said "With a jury, you never know."

"It's Stohlmeyer's word against Leo's," Paul said. "I think we're okay.'

The waiter came over just then to mop up the spilled cioppino sauce. Vinnie waited impatiently for him to finish. They were at Tosca's, a small Bronx restaurant Vinnie believed served the best cioppino in town. He had invited Paul Calvelli to lunch to discuss Leo's arrest and impending trial. A matter of great concern that would be placed before the full Council. Vinnie needed Paul's support in the action he intended rec ommending.

It was a warm July day, and both men were in good spirits. Vincent Tomasino not only had settled a threatened Longshoremen's strike that week, but did it with a huge increase in medical benefits and featherbedding concessions.

Paul Calvelli that very morning learned that his oldest son was accepted to Harvard Medical School. The same boy who at eighteen had been arrested eleven times on charges ranging from check forging to auto theft. It cost Paul a small fortune to keep him out of jail, and for that he had Leo Gorodetsky to thank. More accurately, Leo's judges and police officials. But Leo refused to use his connections to keep the boy out of the draft. He told Paul it was the best thing that could happen. And it was. Nothing short of a miracle. Ralph Calvelli returned from Korea a different person, a wounded and decorated hero. He studied diligently to complete his high school courses, then compressed four years of college into three, the final year at Columbia. And now Harvard Medical.

To this day, Paul did not know what happened to his son in Korea, but credited, indirectly or not, Leo Gorodetsky for the transformation. He was very grateful.

During lunch, as though it might be an improper subject with good food, the main issue, Leo, had not been seriously addressed. Now, over coffee, no more time was wasted.

Vincent Tomasino lit a cigarette and said, "Look, Paul, this is the first time any Council member has ever been brought to trial. We don't know how he'll act, or what he'll say, or what else the feds might have on him to spring as a nice surprise. Leo Gorodetsky is no superman, even though I know you might think different."

"If you're suggesting, Vincent, that Leo might talk at this trial, forget it. You're wrong."

"To save his own neck?"

"Make a deal, you mean?" Paul said. "Give us over to save himself? Not Leo, Vinnie, never."

"You can't rule it out, Paul."

"Why?"

"He's a Jew," said Vinnie. "He's got no special loyalty to us."

"That's bullshit," Paul Calvelli said quietly. "You know better."

"Now listen," Vinnie said in an equally quiet voice. "I'm talking to you like a . . . a realist, a practical man. Charlie Brickhill has had a hard-on for Leo ever since Leo and Harry Wise did that Bernie Kopaloff thing. The other guy, too, the lawyer, the Jew that'll try the case."

"Raab," said Paul Calvelli. "Martin Raab."

"Yeah," Vinnie said, annoyed. "Why do I keep forgetting that name? I think because the son of a bitch worries me. Him and Brickhill, they'll pull any rotten trick they can dream up to nail Leo. And they might just do it. They have to figure on at least a fifty-fifty shot for conviction, so it's only common sense they know Leo might be figuring that, too. That's why I think they'll offer him a deal."

"What do you want to do, Vinnie?" Paul asked. "Make sure Leo isn't tempted?" He spoke in sarcasm and was genuinely surprised at Vincent Tomasino's response.

"Yes."

"You can't be serious!"

Although they were in a secluded corner of the room, Vinnie glanced around carefully. "I don't mean he should get hit. Not exactly."

" 'Not exactly'?"

"I want to test him."

"Test him," Paul repeated. "Leo?"

Vinnie cleared his throat and glanced around once more. "There's a kid in Miami, Fred Agnessi. He's been up here a few times; you met him. He could be big someday, maybe even be Council. I say 'maybe,' because sometimes he can be stupid. He's got a short fuse. Like Harry Wise, remember?" Vinnie smiled almost nostalgically. "Well, he asked me how to get in on the Cuban action, open his own place down there. I told him the only way was if the little man said okay. Well, the little man said no."

"That shouldn't surprise you," Paul said. "I'd say no, too."

Vinnie said, "I told Agnessi to ask Leo to reconsider."

"Why?" Paul asked. "Leo will only turn him down again."

"That's right," Vinnie said. "He will."

Paul said nothing. He realized that Fred Agnessi was part of a plan Vinnie was ready to set in motion. Vinnie would reveal it, but slowly, tantalizingly. A childish game he enjoyed playing.

Vinnie said, "That's the test, Paul. The test of Leo's loyalty." He paused, expecting Paul to urge an explanation, but Paul refused to play the game. Vinnie seemed almost offended. "All right, Leo turns him down again. So this kid Agnessi, he blows his stack. He's just nutty enough to try to hit Leo. Because, being that I recommended he ask Leo to reconsider, the kid thinks Leo's turning *me* down, turning the Council down. He'll think he's doing us all a favor. And maybe he is."

"I think you're nuttier than the kid," Paul said quietly.

"Like a fox," Vinnie said. "Look, Leo Gorodetsky isn't standing around waiting to get hit. Yeah, I know all about how he doesn't believe in bodyguards because if somebody means to hit you, they'll damn well do it. But it still wouldn't be easy, even for the best of us. And a headstrong kid's not even close to the best. So I figure he'll miss. When that happens, that's when the test begins."

Once again Vinnie paused, waiting to be urged on; and, again, Paul remained silent. Vinnie impatiently brushed back the sides of his thick white hair. Paul idly speculated about Vinnie's exact age; he claimed fifty, but Paul, who was forty-seven, was sure Vinnie was at least ten years older.

Vinnie said, "Agnessi misses, so what does Leo do? He has to figure we ordered the hit, that Agnessi would never do it on his own. I know the little man. He'll be so pissed off he'll do one of two things. Come after us himself, which would be okay because we could handle it and it might solve all our problems. Or, he might decide the smart move is to turn against us. He does that, we know where we stand with him, and we have him hit. But by our own people, that don't miss."

"Now I know you're crazy," Paul said.

Vinnie sat back and mashed out his cigarette, waiting for Paul to ask the obvious question. This time Paul accommodated him.

Paul said, "And if Leo does none of those things, we know he's loyal?"

"You got it."

"What makes you so sure this Agnessi will hit him?"

Vinnie smiled smugly. "A hunch, Paul. How do you say it? An educated guess."

Paul knew then that Vinnie had already arranged it with Agnessi. If Leo refused Agnessi's second request for a Havana license, Agnessi would make the hit. He said, "Did it ever occur to you that Agnessi wouldn't be stupid enough to make the hit himself? That he might hire somebody that wouldn't miss? That they might kill Leo?"

Vinnie's eyes widened innocently. "In that case, well, maybe it'll all be for the best. Hey, Paul, like they say, nobody's indispensable."

Paul Calvelli gestured for the waiter. He wanted a drink. A small Amaretto. He was thinking, Nobody is indispensable, except some people are more indispensable than other people.

Vincent Tomasino personally conveyed to Leo Fred Agnessi's request for reconsideration. He neither approved nor disapproved Leo's denial. He merely told Leo he respected the decision and would relay it to Agnessi.

Later that same week Leo and Renata had dinner at Grenado's, a Basque restaurant in the Village. Simple food, but exquisitely prepared, Leo particularly fond of a thin veal steak sautéed in a garlic and caper sauce, and wafer-thin potatoes fried in olive oil with onions and red peppers.

They were on their way out when the maître, telephone in hand, called to Leo from the foyer, "Long-distance, Mr. G."

The call was from Miami, Fred Agnessi. Brief, succinct. "Leo, I have to ask you one last time. The license . . ."

"Fred, I'll tell you one last time. No," Leo said into the phone, and hung up. He thanked the maître and joined Renata outside. She was already waiting in a taxi.

"Some kid who's been bothering me," he explained. "Nothing important."

"How did he know where to find you?"

"Vinnie Tomasino must have told him. I think I mentioned to him we were having dinner in the Village. He knows when I go to the Village, I usually eat at Grenado's."

And with that, he put it out of his mind. He reached into his pocket for cigarettes, pulled out the pack and a slip of paper clinging to the cellophane wrapper. As the taxi moved uptown on Sixth Avenue, Leo unfolded the paper and tried to read it in the intermittent light of the streetlamps and oncoming car headlights. It contained a figure representing the month's win at the Oasis: $647,050. Gerson had given him the paper earlier that day.

The Oasis figure reminded him that next morning's *Times* business section was to carry a story on the Hilton Hotel corporation's bid to purchase a Vegas hotel. He had forgotten to buy the newspaper at the kiosk outside the restaurant. He debated asking the cabbie to stop at the next newsstand, but the taxi, swinging into Central Park West, made every light to eightieth. It U-turned smoothly and pulled up at the canopied entrance of 151. The doorman went off duty at nine, so Leo opened the cab door for Renata.

"You go on up," he said to her. "I'll drive down to Columbus Avenue and get the paper."

"Get some coffee, too, Leo," she said. "I think we're almost out."

He waited until he saw her in the lobby at the elevators, then motioned the cabbie to drive off. He bought the newspaper and coffee, and returned in the cab to the apartment. He tipped the driver five dollars and started into the building.

A figure stepped from the shadow of the potted ficus trees under the canopy. Even in the dim, refracted lobby light, Leo saw him clearly. A man in his early twenty's, heavyset, with close cropped light hair, and the round jowly face of an athlete long out of condition. He wore a bright red sweater and khaki slacks. He held a gun which resembled a Colt .45, but turned out to be a Smith & Wesson 9-mm Parabellum.

"This is for you, Leo . . . !"

The first shot hurled him backward into the door, his own weight and momentum shattering the plate glass and forcing open the door. The second shot, fired almost simultaneously, spun him sideways against the door and facedown onto the marbled lobby floor. He lay on the broken glass, feeling no pain, only the smooth coolness of the marble against his cheek. His ears still rang with the blast of the gunshots, and his eyes burned from the glare of the muzzle flash.

He could not move. He remembered the last time he was shot, in France, in the rain at Saint-Mihiel. He remembered the pain, concerned now because there was no pain. He thought he must be paralyzed and wondered if he would die. He preferred death to being paralyzed. If you were unable to move, you were paralyzed. He moved his legs; good, they moved. Now the arms, the left one first. It felt very heavy. The whole left side of his body felt heavy, but he could move the arm. He dragged it along the floor toward his face, determined to touch his face with his fingers. He waggled the fingers.

And then he felt the pain. Surging through him like an electric shock knifing into his body just below the ribs, zigzagging its way up to his shoulder. He thought he screamed. The voice sounded strange.

It was not his voice. It was a woman living on the first floor who had heard the shots and rushed out to the lobby. Then he heard other voices, male and female. He closed his eyes and listened. He could not understand a word. All the voices blended into a single voice, all with the same words. Over and over. Just before everything went black he heard the words clearly.

"This is for you, Leo . . . !"

He was not paralyzed, and not seriously injured. One slug creased his left shoulder, the other burrowed into the fleshy area just below the shoulder blade.

Leo the Lucky.

Lucky, even with the police officers responding to the emergency call. One, years on the IDIC payroll, had the presence of mind to report the name of the gunshot victim admitted to Lenox Hill Hospital as Leonard Ross. So the newspapers never played the story, although one columnist heard of the shooting and suggested that a big-time racket figure was the target of an assassin's bullet.

Senator Charles Brickhill and Deputy Attorney General Martin Raab, however, knew of the incident three hours after it happened. They were in New York the very next morning. Leo, who had already returned from surgery, deliberately kept them waiting that entire day, and then agreed to see them only on their solemn promise not to reveal to the newspapers the identity of the patient in Room 201.

But Brickhill and Raab, like the NYPD detectives stubbornly interrogating Leo, wasted their time. Leo had no intention of providing even the vaguest information.

". . . how many times do I have to say it? I did not—repeat, not—see the gunman!" ". . . the paper with the figures on it? I haven't the slightest idea, sorry." ". . . I can't imagine why I'd be 'set up.' That's your phrase, not mine." ". . . I've told you all I know." ". . . why can't you people accept the fact that it was nothing but a common burglary? Why are you so stubborn?" ". . . sure, my wallet wasn't touched, so what? The man was frightened away by the people in the building!"

After an uncomfortable first day, he recovered rapidly. Renata insisted on taking an adjoining room. She was with him constantly. They read, or talked, and sometimes merely enjoyed each other's silent presence. He fretted over her neglecting the travel agency, open now only a few months and struggling for business. She said the business could wait.

Leo knew that for all her outward calm, she was very frightened. Finally, she had come face to face with the reality of who and what he was, a reality he knew would soon overwhelm the calm she pretended. He wondered how he would handle it.

It happened on the fifth day. He felt well enough to go home. He was restless, bored with the Yankee–Red Sox game on television. She was at the window; she had been standing there for some time, silent, thinking.

He said, "I'm going to ask the doctor to discharge me. He says he wants me to stay another few days, but I feel fine."

She said nothing.

"I really feel okay," he said.

Still facing the window, she said, "Don't you think it's time you considered having someone to drive you? A chauffeur?"

"A bodyguard, you mean? I discovered long ago that they attract, instead of detract. In a strange way it makes you even more of a target."

She turned now. She looked at him a moment, then turned back to the window. He switched off the television. "Would you get me a cigarette, please?"

She said nothing. She remained at the window.

"Did you hear me?"

When she turned again, he noticed the redness under her eyes. She said, "The doctor said it would be better if you didn't smoke for a while."

"You were crying," he said. "Why?"

"Fatigue, I suppose. I often cry when I'm tired."

"Or when you're frightened?"

She said nothing. She removed a single cigarette from the Chesterfield package on the bed table and gave it to him. She did not offer to light it. "Now look, I know you're frightened," he said. "But believe me, you never were in any danger. It was me he was after. You wouldn't have been harmed, no matter what." He smiled lamely. "As my friend Harry Wise used to say, 'We only kill each other.' "

But even as he spoke, he wondered. He had been telling himself that botched job or not, the gunman was a professional who would not have been panicked into killing her as well. But if she had gotten a clean look at him, he might have had no choice. Surely, she realized this.

". . . you fool!" she said. He had never seen her so angry; it startled him. "Don't you understand that my fright is not for myself? It's for you, Leo! For you!" She sat on the bed edge and grasped the top bar of the metal headboard, squeezing it with all her strength. "I could not bear losing you! Don't you understand? I don't want to lose you!"

She leaned sideways, resting her head and shoulders against the headboard, and began weeping. He did not know what to do, or say, or even think. He was not even sure it was all happening to him. It was not him, then, who sat up in bed and pulled the weeping blond woman to him. And held her, stroking her hair, caressing her tear-streaked face, kissing her. She lay her head on his shoulder now, and continued weeping. She could not stop.

"Nothing will happen to me," he said, rocking her in his arms, cradling her. They held each other that way a long while, and he never wanted it to end. He loved the silken feel of her hair brushing his cheeks, and the warmth of her body, and the feeling of being wanted, and needed, and loved.

To thwart any newsmen who might have guessed the truth, three detectives escorted Leo and Renata through the hospital's rear exit. The detectives drove them back to the apartment where all were given a drink and ringside tickets to next month's Archie Moore—Floyd Patterson fight, and sent on their way.

The moment they were gone, Leo went into his den and locked the door. He placed a call to Miami. To a man named Jack Maynard, a young, ruggedly handsome man with blond hair so sun-bleached it was almost white, and who several days before had come to Florida from San Diego.

After he completed this call, Leo joined Renata for coffee and then at her insistence took a long nap. He awoke refreshed, alert, and prepared to deal with the first order of business. A visit from Vincent Tomasino. He had phoned Vinnie from the hospital and asked him to come to the apartment at five that afternoon.

Vinnie brought a huge basket of fruit and a case of B & G Margaux '45. Renata ushered Vinnie into the den, a spare bedroom that over the years Leo had converted into a library-office with built-in bookshelves, a small TV set, and the same faded-wood, battered and splintered rolltop desk from the office in Hershey Lefkowitz's garage. Leo said he kept it to remind him of Delancey Street.

He sat at the desk in bathrobe and slippers, feet propped on a nearby chair, and waved Vinnie into the deep-cushioned leather couch. "Thanks for the wine. It's my favorite."

"Yeah, I remembered," Vinnie said. "Me, my taste goes more for dago red. But each to his own, like they say. Hey, let me tell you something." He pointed a finger at Leo. "I never saw you looking so good. Honest to God."

"Maybe I should get shot more often," Leo said. He smiled narrowly. Vinnie replied with a quick smile of his own. "Listen, a week in the hospital is almost like a vacation. A Florida vacation." He smiled again. "Miami, Vinnie, that's a nice place for a vacation. Miami. You know some people down there, don't you? Kid named Agnessi?"

Vinnie nodded gravely. "Leo, I know what you think—"

"—please, Vinnie, don't insult my intelligence," Leo said. "Or your own. Don't goddam deny you had a hand in it. The whole thing stinks of you!"

Vinnie reddened, but kept his voice calm and flat. "I want you to know, Leo, how much all of us, the whole Council, how much we appreciate how you clammed up. Like Paul said, it shows style."

"A hell of a lot more style than your clumsy little plan," Leo said. "Manipulating that moron Agnessi like that!"

"If you'll cool down, Leo, I'll try to explain."

"Vinnie, you're an asshole."

"Hey, now just take it easy—"

"—shut up!" Leo said. He got up and walked over to Vinnie's chair. "It was stupid, Vinnie. You're stupid! You have to be, to even think I'd betray the Alliance. What the hell for? What good would it do me? Where would I run?"

"Leo, I don't like to be talked to that way!"

"Switzerland?" Leo said. "I'd run there, like Harry? Come on, Vinnie, there's no place I could hide even if I wanted to! But why would I want to in the first place? Just answer that."

"For Christ's sake, Leo, we made a mistake!" Vinnie looked at him defiantly. "I'm sorry. I apologize!"

"You apologize. That, and a nickel gets me a cup of coffee," Leo said. "And if I hadn't been alone, if I was with that lady you were just so charming to, telling her she's better-looking every time you see her? If I was with her, and the shooter decided he had to take her out, too? You'd have still apologized, I suppose?"

Vinnie started speaking, then shook his head in exasperation. Leo returned to the desk and sat again. "I accept your apology, Vinnie," he said quietly.

"From now on, Leo, you have my sacred word," Vinnie said. "I protect your life with my own."

Leo said nothing. He was thinking, Sure, you prick, until the next time you try it.

Vinnie said, "I'll take care of Agnessi."

"Sure," Leo said. "You'll take away his golf clubs. He's a golf nut, I hear."

"Leo, I said he'll be taken care of."

Leo said, "What time is it?"

Vinnie glanced at his watch. "Ten past five."

Leo said, "Vinnie, I feel kind of tired . . ."

"Oh, sure, sure," Vinnie said. He rose. "I'll get going and let you rest." He extended his hand. "No hard feelings?"

"Don't be silly," Leo said as they shook hands. He smiled narrowly. "As long as it never happens again."

"Don't *you* be silly," said Vincent Tomasino.

Not until later that evening, when he arrived at his Long Beach home, did Vincent Tomasino learn about Fred Agnessi. Two hours earlier, at approximately the same time Vinnie walked into Leo's apartment with the fruit and wine, Fred Agnessi was addressing his ball on the twelfth tee of the Indian River Country Club in Hallandale, Florida. It was a long, dogleg par four with thick rough on one side of the fairway and a monstrous bunker on the other. It was also the most distracting hole on the course. The wire-fenced, ivy-covered golf-course boundary here paralleled a busy boulevard. On the other side of the boulevard were rows of expensive high-rise apartment buildings.

Fred Agnessi settled himself over the ball, wiggled his toes to relax, brought the club up in his backswing, and collapsed face down in the grass. From his ear oozed a trickle of blood.

Even if anyone had paid attention, which they had not, it was unlikely they would have seen the muzzle of a high-powered rifle protruding from the closed drapes of a window on the topmost floor of the apartment building directly across the street. They would certainly not have seen the young, ruggedly handsome blond man holding the rifle, for he had carefully positioned himself behind the drapes. An instant after the single shot was fired, the rifle muzzle vanished inside and the window was closed.

The irony of it was that Fred Agnessi, who had never broken 80 but was steadily improving, that day played the finest round of his life. At the fatal twelfth hole, he was only two strokes over par. He could have bogied all seven remaining holes and still shot 79.

——— *25* ———

THESE were difficult times for Albert Collins. An honorable man, he willingly and unfailingly paid the stipulated monthly child support on each of his seven children from three ex-wives. It meant scrimping and denying himself even the most basic pleasures, and perpetual debt. To friends, credit unions, loan sharks. An unenviable situation for a forty-four-year-old man with chronic asthma, but he would not have it otherwise. He had incurred those obligations and intended to discharge them.

He was therefore understandably dismayed when summoned for jury duty on a criminal case of national importance. The five-dollar daily juror's fee was less than half his salary as a janitor in the New York City school system.

The trial was that of *United States* v. *Gorodetsky*. A trial originally scheduled for September 10, 1956, but delayed more than a year with endless and ingenious defense continuances. And then an additional six months while the government's key witness, Thomas Stohlmeyer, recuperated from a near-fatal heart attack.

Selecting the jury consumed more time and resembled a chess game, a battle of wits and strategy between Martin Raab and Leo's chief counsel, a flamboyant Washington attorney named Robert Lewis Peyton. Finally, at 4:30 P.M, Friday, October 3, 1958, all plaintiff and defense challenges were exhausted. Peyton outmaneuvered Raab for the last venireman, a slight, slender man with sharply defined facial features, a hairline receding with alarming rapidity, and an honest desire to harm no one. And the only black.

Albert Collins.

Sunday, October 5, the day before the trial began, as he had each Sunday for fourteen consecutive years, Albert Collins attended early services at the Abyssinian Baptist Church on Seventh Avenue. Inspired by the Reverend Adam Clayton Powell's pulpit-pounding sermon demanding public-school desegregation, Albert Collins had pledged ten dollars to Congressman Powell's reelection fund.

He was thinking about this walking home, about the difference equal educational opportunities might make in his children's lives, and what it might have done for his own life. He did not immediately notice the long, fire-engine red Lincoln convertible sedan sidle up beside him. The driver grinned at him through the open window.

"Hey, Al, how you doin'?"

It was Jules Jefferson. Albert was both perturbed and flattered; Jules Jefferson had never once so much as looked at him, let alone called him by name. Not in the twenty years Albert purchased numbers tickets from Jules's runners, placed horse bets with his bookies, or borrowed money from his shylocks.

And now Jules Jefferson was inviting Albert Collins to ride with him in his car, to discuss a matter of utmost delicacy. A matter concerning Albert's jury duty. It seemed the man on trial, Leo Gorodetsky, was a good friend and business associate of Jules Jefferson. Jules feared that his friend might not receive a fair trial.

Jules explained all this as they drove. Then, abruptly, he pulled the car over to the curb. He brought a large manila envelope from under the seat and gave it to Albert.

"Little something for you," Jules said. "A surprise." Albert looked at the envelope, then at Jules. "Open it," Jules said.

Albert felt his lungs fill and his chest tighten. He drew in a heaving, wheezing breath. He really did not want to open the envelope, but when Jules Jefferson asked you to do something, you did it. Albert unfastened the clasp and peered inside. It was filled with bills, crisp, green, hundred-dollar bills.

"Jesus!" Albert said.

"Twenty-five thousand dollars," Jules said. He reached into the envelope and brought out five thick packets of bills, each tightly wrapped with a narrow dark-green paper binder on which was printed: $5,000. He dealt out the packets like cards, lining them neatly on the red leather seat between himself and Albert Collins. "All yours, Al."

"Jesus," Albert said again. "What do you mean, all mine?"

"Like I'm saying, just see my friend gets a fair trial."

Albert stared at the money. More than he ever saw in his life, or was likely to see—250 one-hundred dollar bills. The only time he had seen a bill that size was once at a 128th Street horse parlor when a man bet a hundred dollars on a horse. He still remembered the horse's name, and the race. Float Me, in the sixth at Belmont Park. He did not remember if Float Me won or lost.

Jules Jefferson stuffed the packets back into the envelope. He refastened the cover and placed the envelope on Albert's lap. "It's important to me, Al," he said.

Albert said nothing. He was afraid to say anything.

Jules patted Albert's shoulder. "Why don't you just hold on to it a while? No obligation, honest. You want to keep it, keep it. You don't, just give it back. What do you say?"

"Jesus," Albert said.

Approximately ten minutes after he left Albert Collins clutching a manila envelope on a Harlem street corner, Jules Jefferson phoned Leo with a terse, one-word message.

"Fixed."

Leo took the call in his den, then returned to the dining room to rejoin his guests, George Gerson and Robert Lewis Peyton. Leo looked at Gerson and nodded, then said to Peyton, "I'm sorry for interrupting. You were telling us about the judge. What's his name, Kimberly? Unfortunately, not one of ours."

"Not one of anybody's," Peyton said. He was a tall and lanky man, with snow-white hair falling almost to his collar. The skin of his bony face resembled coarse, wrinkled parchment, but his eyes were a striking blue-green, and crystal clear. "But then sometimes it's better that way. The case is tried strictly on its own merit. If the case is good," he added. "If the defendant is truly innocent."

"How many truly innocent clients do you have?" Leo asked.

"Most of the truly innocent ones can't afford me." Peyton liked to say he specialized in "defense law," rather than criminal law, and was proud of his reputation as the most expensive defense attorney in America. His seventy-five percent acquittal score justified the expense.

"I'm not truly innocent," Leo said. "But neither am I truly guilty."

"You don't appear truly worried, either," Peyton said.

Leo and Gerson exchanged glances, and Leo knew they were thinking the same thing. The juror they had just bought. It reminded Leo of a mouthwash ad, "Even your best friends won't tell you." In this instance—more literally, case—even your clients won't tell you. But in this case what your attorney does not know will not hurt him. Or you.

"With you defending him," Gerson said to Peyton, "Leo feels he has nothing to worry about."

"I'm flattered," Peyton said. "Not all my clients express so much confidence in me."

Leo tasted his coffee, then put it down. He hated tepid coffee. "I'm worried," he said. "I'm plenty worried. I wasn't at first, not for a long time. I think I never believed it would ever come to trial. But now it has, and I can see many things about the case that I wasn't able to, or didn't want to." He sipped the coffee. "I think it's like our certainty of immortality when we're young. It can't happen to me. Well, your logical brain tells you, yes, it can happen, but your emotional one refuses to believe it."

He paused abruptly, thinking, Leo the Philosopher. But it was true: In the beginning, just like Sal so many years ago, he had not taken it at all seriously, but now he was worried, very worried. Because anything could happen—even with a fixed juror—and everything could come tumbling down. All at once, and all on top of him.

". . . actually, strange as it sounds, my only genuinely unworried clients are those facing the chair," Peyton was saying, unsmiling. "I don't know why, but they always seem so calm. Maybe it's me, though. My own imagination."

"Maybe it's because they're resigned to it," Leo said. "They've accepted it. I haven't."

"Well, you're not facing the chair," Peyton said. "Only ten to twenty." Now he smiled, pleased at his own joke. "No, I agree there's nothing highly substantive to the government's case, and that it's only more of their continuing program of harassment. But we both know what they're capable of, and to what lengths they'll go. And while the whole thing certainly appears to border on the capricious, let's just proceed on the premise that it's not."

"Let's hope Judge Kimberly thinks it is," Gerson said.

William Everson Kimberly was forty-two years old. A 1939 Yale Law School graduate, he passed the New York State bar that same year, and joined a prestigious Wall Street firm. In 1941, called to active duty with the U.S. Navy, he served throughout the war as both a legal officer and defense counsel at stateside bases. After the war he opened a private practice in Albany. In 1955 he was appointed to the federal bench, one of the youngest judges in the court's history. He was considered a bright, no-nonsense, scrupulously fair judge.

He was also a confirmed, almost pathological antisemite.

Martin Raab knew this, and found it ironically amusing. Judge Kimberly presiding at a trial where a Jewish defendant faced a Jewish prosecutor. It never occurred to Raab that this alone might neutralize the judge's antisemitism.

Judge Kimberly overruled Raab's every attempt to connect Leo to various known criminal figures. Irrelevant to the issue at hand. Eleven government witnesses were called. Union officials, construction-firm executives, bank officers, even restaurant suppliers. Much of their testimony was hearsay and the evidence presented circumstantial, but Raab was unconcerned. He had designed his case like a pyramid: the broad base, narrowing with each witness until the peak, the only witness whose testimony truly mattered.

· Thomas Stohlmeyer.

". . . now, sir," Raab began, "let's immediately clear the air and dispense with some matters that have recently received considerable public note. First, is it correct that you have been granted immunity from prosecution in return for your testimony as a government witness?"

"Yes, sir," said Stohlmeyer. He looked wan and haggard, and seemed unable to face Raab directly.

"Is it also correct that as an additional facet of this . . . uh, plea bargaining, you have agreed to resign all your union offices?" Raab asked.

"Yes, that is correct."

"Now, as president of the Union of American Transport Workers, you approved a series of loans from the union's pension fund to a company controlled by Mr. Gorodetsky, did you not?"

"Yes, sir."

Raab asked a few more pertinent questions, then addressed the main issue, the fees allegedly paid Stohlmeyer by Leo to obtain more than $8 million in loans.

"What was the total amount of these fees?"

"Four hundred thousand dollars," Stohlmeyer said.

"Four hundred thousand dollars," Raab repeated. "Paid in cash?"

"Yes, sir."

"Exactly where and when did this occur?"

"Excuse me?"

"When did Mr. Gorodetsky give you the money, and where?"

At the defendant's table, Leo listened carefully and made occasional notes on a large legal pad. Each time he glanced up over his reading glasses he caught Albert Collins looking at him. It gave him a bad feeling about Albert Collins; he wished they had tried reaching someone else. But then, studying the stolid, middle-class white faces of the other jurors, seven men and four women, he decided the black man was their best chance.

". . . now you state the first of these payoffs occurred sometime in the spring or summer of 1955 . . ." Raab was saying.

"Objection!" Peyton called quietly.

Raab acknowledged the objection with a thin smile. He said to the stenotypist, "Strike the last question, please." He faced Stohlmeyer. "You state that the first of these alleged fees was paid you in 1955?"

"Yes, sir," Stohlmeyer said.

"Where?"

"Here, in New York."

"How?"

"I beg your pardon?"

"Was payment made in cash, check, what?"

"Cash."

"By Mr. Gorodetsky personally?"

"By messenger," said Stohlmeyer. "A man came to my home one evening with the money in a small briefcase." He glanced at a ragged sheaf of notepaper cupped in his palm. "One hundred and seventy-five thousand dollars."

"Did you know this messenger?"

"No, sir."

"Then how did you know the money came from Mr. Gorodetsky?" Raab peered over his shoulder at Leo. "It could have been a gift from any admirer, could it not?"

This brought a smattering of laughs from the spectators, immediately silenced by Judge Kimberly tapping the cap of a fountain pen on his desk. "We can do without the sarcasm, Mr. Raab."

"Excuse me, Your Honor," Raab said, and faced Stohlmeyer again.

"We had arranged for the delivery in a phone call that morning," Stohlmeyer said.

"The five percent fee for the first installment of what was ultimately an eight-million-dollar loan?"

"Yes, sir."

"Now, of the other investments made by the UATW Pension Fund, how many involved these so-called finder's fees?"

"None."

"None," Raab repeated. "Had you in previous transactions ever suggested payment of a fee? Transactions other than with Mr. Gorodetsky?"

"No, sir."

"Were you aware that accepting money from Mr. Gorodetsky constituted a criminal conspiracy?"

"Yes, sir."

"Was this ever discussed between you?"

"Yes, sir, it was—"

"—objection!" Robert Peyton called quietly.

"Withdraw the question," Raab said. He stood contemplatively before the witness box a moment. Then he sighed, as though having reached some difficult decision. He addressed the judge. "I think we can once more cut through much of this. Mr. Stohlmeyer's personal bank statements, in three different accounts, reflect deposits of the amounts claimed to have been paid. Totaling, eventually, four hundred thousand dollars. All this evidence, plus considerable corroborative evidence, has or will have been presented. Your witness," he said to Peyton and strode back to his seat.

Robert Peyton approached Stohlmeyer like a jungle cat circling a helpless prey. "How did you manage to convince the pension fund trustees to grant the loans? No, wait," he added quickly. "Let me revise that.

How did your union become involved in this business in the first place?"

"I made a proposal to Mr. Gorodetsky," Stohlmeyer said. "I saw an opportunity for a good investment for the pension fund."

"Not to mention for yourself," Peyton said, and in the same breath said to the stenotypist, "Strike that last remark, please," and to Stohlmeyer, "Was it a good investment?"

"So far, yes."

"The loans have been repaid?"

"Not yet. They're straight fifteen-year notes."

"Principal and interest paid promptly?"

"Yes."

"Secured how?"

"With trust deeds."

"At what rate of interest?"

"Objection!" Raab shouted.

"Where is this going, Mr. Peyton?" the judge asked.

"Your Honor, I am attempting to establish—" he paused with a shy, almost self-effacing smile. "Well, I guess I'm only trying to understand just what it is that my client is accused of. The complaint says conspiracy to misappropriate union monies. However, the issue of whether or not he paid a finder's fee notwithstanding, it seems to me that getting a loan at a low rate of interest is nothing less than plain good business. By the same token, from Mr. Stohlmeyer's position, granting a loan at a lower rate of interest than ordinarily might be earned is poor business. Very poor business, indeed. Well, isn't that essentially what my client is charged with? Obtaining a loan at a low rate of interest? Since when is good business a crime?"

"We're not concerned with your client's business prowess, Mr. Peyton," Judge Kimberly said. "Only whether or not in concert with his co-defendant a crime was committed. The objection is sustained. The jury will disregard Mr. Peyton's remarks. Please proceed, Mr. Peyton."

"Yes, Your Honor," Peyton said. He glanced at Leo blandly, but his eyes danced with satisfaction. The jury had been instructed to disregard, which they would. But the judge would remember Peyton's point: his client was on trial for having made an advantageous business deal.

The weeklong trial was front-page news throughout the country and a nightly item on national television. In Las Vegas, Ben Sylbert ran an editorial accusing Charles Brickhill of conducting a witch hunt, comparing it to the McCarthy days. Ben also wrote that no one ever denied the presence of certain organized-crime figures in the casinos, but these elements were systematically being rooted out. The day after the editorial appeared, both the Barclay and the Oasis awarded Ben's *Las Vegas Record* new advertising contracts.

Leo was the one and only defense witness. When they swore him in, with his right hand on the Bible—and, later, as Raab cross-examined, and as he categorically denied bribing Stohlmeyer—the thought occurred to him that since he, Leo, had sworn by Almighty God to tell the truth, with not the slightest intention of keeping that vow, he was really challenging this so called Almighty to do something about it.

God was equal to the challenge. The jury believed Stohlmeyer. After the first day's deliberation, the vote was 11 to 1 for conviction. The eight men and four women were sequestered in the Windom, a small hotel on East Eighth Street. The evening of that first day, a bellhop appeared at Albert Collins's door with a sandwich and soft drink. A burly marshal stood in the corridor watching every move, listening to every word.

"Evening," said the bellhop. "You ordered sliced chicken, but the kitchen's all out. So they sent up chicken salad instead." Before Albert Collins could say he had not ordered any food, the bellhop continued, "It's real good here. They call it a 'Big Jules.' "

The next morning, Albert Collins stubbornly resisted all pressure to reverse his vote. Leo Gorodetsky was innocent, and nothing could change Albert's mind. Two days later, they were hopelessly deadlocked at the same 11 to 1 for conviction.

On the third day, realizing Albert Collins might keep them sequestered indefinitely, three other jurors voted not guilty. Now it was 8 to 4, and when Judge Kimberly sent word they would remain in the jury room all day and all night until reaching a verdict, one more juror voted for acquittal.

And then God surrendered.

Judge Kimberly ruled the evidence—as indicated by a jury deadlocked at 7 to 5 for conviction—clearly insufficient to convict. He could have dismissed the case, but the government most certainly would have appealed. The appellate court would send the case straight back to Judge Kimberly for retrial. He wanted no more of it. Let the two Jews insult each other in someone else's court. And while he did not doubt Leo had committed perjury, he considered Stohlmeyer's crime, in this instance at least, far more heinous. Furthermore, the government's rationale in granting Stohlmeyer immunity not only smacked of personal vendetta but was itself a shameful and flagrant disregard of due process. He ordered a judgment of acquittal.

Leo, George Gerson, and Robert Peyton were on the sidewalk outside Foley Square courthouse. They had been discussing Stohlmeyer, also acquitted but a very sick man whose union career was finished and posed no further threat to Leo or IDIC. Leo paid little attention to the conversation. He was watching the courthouse doors. He wanted to see Raab emerge. He was glad he had insisted Renata not attend the trial; he did not want her subjected to the scene he anticipated.

A scene he wanted, for he could easily have left sooner, avoiding Raab. He had planned his response to Raab's diatribe carefully. He would not respond at all, but merely say in a quiet, polite voice, "I'm sorry you feel so bitterly toward me, Mr. Raab. Very sorry." He knew that such civility, not rubbing Raab's face in the defeat, would truly humiliate him. A moment as gratifying as the verdict itself.

Facing the courthouse entrance, waiting, for an instant Leo was hurled back in time to another confrontation. On these same Foley Square courthouse stairs, when Charles Brickhill and Harry Wise nearly came to blows. The place was becoming a regular boxing arena.

Martin Raab appeared. Alone, grim, hefting his briefcase, he started down the stone stairs. Leo moved away from the others and walked to the center of the stairs. He stood waiting.

Raab approached. He headed directly toward Leo. When they were almost almost close enough to touch, Leo said, "My condolences, Counselor."

Raab never stopped moving. He glanced at Leo, shook his head sadly, and continued past. Leo whirled to see a chauffeured sedan with U.S. government plates pull up at the sidewalk. Raab got in. The sedan drove off. Raab never gave Leo a second glance.

"Cool customer, eh?" It was Gerson, coming up beside Leo and following Leo's gaze at the departing sedan. He waved good-bye to Peyton who was entering a cab, and said to Leo, "But you can be sure he knows something happened in that jury room."

"Probably," Leo said. He felt like a child denied a tantrum. He forced himself to smile at Gerson. "And he'll never give up on me. So what else is new?"

"You're on a roll, Leo. I think it's great."

A roll, Leo thought. Yes, it was a roll. First, escaping the attempt to kill him, then finding an Albert Collins, and then an impatient judge. It was a streak. But the percentage had to catch up with a streak, even the house's. Especially the house's.

And it did.

Four months, two weeks, four days and seven hours later. In Havana, at 11:36 P.M. on the thirty-first day of December, 1958. New Year's Eve.

2.

El Conquistador, festooned with balloons and gaily colored paper streamers, for this one night was closed to the public. President Batista had reserved the entire hotel for his own gala party. Even the casino was closed, its tarpaulin-covered tables laden with platters of caviar, lobster, shrimp, crab, and various Cuban delicacies. For house wine, the hotel's three bars offered Dom Pérignon champagne, and Château Lafite '36. In the main showroom the most beautiful showgirls in Cuba performed on stage in a continuous, lavish spectacle created especially as a tribute to the president.

There was even a party within the party in the Morro Castle Room, a small lounge with its own orchestra and buffets. Girls from the city's best brothels entertained a group of bachelor army officers and selected civilians. The doors of the lounge were closed so as not to offend the wives and daughters of the more than five hundred other invited guests. By ten P.M. they said the Morro Castle Room resembled a Roman orgy.

All this was President Batista's reply to those accusing him of preparing to flee the country. True, after capturing Oriente Province, Fidel Castro's army now threatened Havana itself, but the government was confident it could hold the city and defeat the rebels in the decisive battle that once and for all would finish Castro.

Leo sat at President Batista's table in the main showroom. He had eaten too much and was light-headed from too much champagne, and not at all enjoying himself. He felt bloated, and bored.

And alone. Renata was in England, visiting her gravely ill father. Leo came to Havana not to celebrate the New Year, but to meet with casino managers and inspect the newest hotel, the Miramar, construction nearly completed and scheduled to open September 1, 1959.

He had planned to return to New York on the evening plane. He had no desire to celebrate New Year's Eve in Havana, alone. But President Batista insisted Leo attend the party and even offered to provide him company. The most beautiful girl in Cuba. Or, if such was his preference, girls. Plural. Leo had declined with thanks. The only woman he wanted was three thousand miles away.

Shortly after eleven, when the party was in full swing, a grim, road-dusty army major burst into the room and strode straight to Batista. The two conversed tersely as Batista's face wrinkled in ever-increasing incredulity. For an instant, he swayed, as though losing his balance, and gripped the major's arm for support. Then he stood erect and nodded at the major who walked over to Señora Batista. A moment later, the major escorted Señora Batista from the room. The president, with his cabinet ministers and their wives, followed. Everyone noticed the departure and stopped dancing or talking to watch. The music stopped.

Batista halted in the doorway and waved to the crowd. "Enjoy yourself, my friends," he shouted in Spanish. "Happy New Year!"

A staff colonel shouted back, "Viva Batista!" Others repeated the cry, and now all began applauding. Batista waved once more and left. The orchestra resumed playing. The dancers stepped back to the floor. The party continued.

At 11:30, Leo decided he had enough. He would return to his suite at the Caribe, and go to bed. Or perhaps wait up another hour, if he could stay awake, to phone Renata in London.

Outside, only the doorman was at his station under the hotel portico. No bellmen or valets, and not a taxi in sight. Parked off the hotel driveway were some army staff cars, their chauffeurs grouped around one car, smoking and gossiping quietly. But for muffled music and laughter from the hotel, the entire Vedado district was so silent you could not even hear the grind of the electric trolleys on Avenida Malecón.

New Year's Eve. The streets should have been alive, vibrant with celebrating crowds, not ominously silent. Leo stood a moment, listening, thinking, seeing in his mind General Batista leaving his own party and saying good-bye. Saying good-bye with the sad, almost resigned look of a man saying it for the last time.

Leo rushed back into the hotel. He ran through the casino, darting in and out of small groups of people chatting and drinking. He bumped the corner of a craps table, knocking to the floor a platter of shrimp, spraying a blob of red cocktail sauce on the white trousers of a man talking with two women. The man cursed Leo in Spanish as Leo raced past and continued across the casino to the cashier's cage. The only occupant was a Cuban security guard who unhesitatingly opened the door for Leo.

He hurried across the cage to the counting-room door. He pressed the buzzer with that day's signal, two longs, one short. A viewing aperture in the door slid open, and Leo was immediately admitted into the room by two more guards. Both, like the cage guard, wearing white linen double-breasted jackets and holding Thompson submachine guns.

"Go in the other room, please," Leo said in English. "I'll call you when I'm ready."

When the door clicked shut behind the guards, Leo opened the vault built into the wall at the far end of the room. A large, walk-in vault, with bills stacked in neat piles on the shelves. He estimated at least $500,000, all U.S. currency, the only paper negotiable in the casino. On the floor in wooden crates was perhaps $5,000 in coins.

At the rear of the vault were three leather suitcases. These suitcases contained $10 million in $1,000, $500, and $100 denominations, money held as a reserve backup for all five casinos. Quickly he dragged each heavy suitcase across the counting-room floor to the opposite wall. He laid the flat of his hand on the wainscoting and pushed downward. An entire section of the wall opened. Behind it was only wood stripping and the bricks of the exterior wall—and a platform that had been built into the wall, just wide enough to accommodate the suitcases. Leo placed the suitcases on the platform and pushed upward on the wainscoting. The wall closed tight. Not even the casino manager knew of this compartment. Only Leo, and Sal Bracci.

He left the counting room and hurried back through the casino, and outside again. He heard the gunfire before he reached the sidewalk. At first it sounded like the popping of distant firecrackers. Small arms, pistols and rifles, louder and louder, from the boulevard. And then, louder than the gunfire, like an oncoming wave. The roar of a maddened crowd.

Now, far down the boulevard, dozens of vehicle lights. Trucks, jeeps, private cars. At the hotel the chauffeurs had gathered on the sidewalk to peer curiously at the approaching procession. They watched for a frozen moment and then, as though at a signal, all rushed back up the driveway and into the hotel. The vehicles, moving in from both sides, were very close now.

Through the cheers, words were discernible. "*¡Revolución!*" "*¡Castro!*" "*¡Viva la revolución!*" "*¡Viva Fidel!*"

A line of jeeps and trucks wheeled into both sides of the driveway, blocking any exit, their headlights trained on the hotel entrance. Rebel soldiers swarmed onto the hotel grounds. Most were young, many women, all wearing tricolored armbands on uniforms varying from the familiar fatigues to shabby suit jackets or thin cotton dresses, and all carried rifles or automatic weapons. They charged past Leo into the lobby.

Shouts and screams mingled with gunfire and the shatter of smashed glass from the lobby's crystal chandeliers and mirrored walls. Party guests stampeded from the hotel, mess-jacketed officers and tuxedoed civilians, women in evening gowns, half-naked show girls. The rebel soldiers seemed to almost disdainfully ignore them. But that was because the rebels sought Batista whom they had believed was here.

But Batista had escaped them, so in a frenzy of revenge the rebels destroyed everything in sight. They overturned tables and slot machines, hurled platters of buffet food against the walls, and shot away the ceiling light fixtures and two army officers foolish enough to draw pistols. The casino reverberated with gunfire, and the screams of terrified women and shouts of panicked men.

Outside, the boulevard, which only a few minutes before had been so deserted and silent, was clogged with people. Rebel soldiers, civilians, children. Dancing on the pavement, jumping from vehicle roof to vehicle roof, shooting rifles and pistols in the air, a single mass of humanity proceeding toward the plaza—and, along the way, tearing from the concrete pavement every single parking meter.

Leo watched it all from the portico, cursing Batista for deserting his friends, cursing himself for having made Batista too rich, so rich he had lost his will to fight. But Leo also congratulated himself for having secured IDIC's $10 million. He would simply wait for the situation to stabilize, then negotiate with Castro for the return of the money he had left for the rebels to find. The $500,000 here in the El Conquistador vault, and whatever other amounts might be seized from the other casinos.

A bright light shone directly in his eyes. He threw his arm protectively across his face. Behind the glare a female voice shouted, "Mr. Gorodetsky!"

It was the young girl, Elena, Castro's translator. When she lowered the powerful flashlight, Leo saw she was with two other rebels. They were all so young that for a whimsical moment Leo imagined them schoolchildren playing soldier. He knew better, of course.

He relaxed. He smiled. "Well, you did it, I see. Congratulations." This last word trailed off as Leo saw that in Elena's other hand was her U.S. Army issue Colt .45—leveled at his stomach.

The girl said, "In the name of the provisional government of Cuba, you are under arrest!"

Leo was held one full week in the same El Conquistador penthouse suite once occupied by Sal Bracci. They treated him well enough, with adequate food and drink, although an armed guard was constantly outside the door. On the second day they allowed him a single telephone call to George Gerson in New York. He told George he was all right, and to please inform Renata in London. He knew she would relay the news to Carla in Tel Aviv.

Either deliberately or through oversight, they had not removed the television and radio, so he learned officially what he already knew. Batista had fled into exile, and Castro had proclaimed himself president. The Cuban army no longer existed. Round-the-clock military courts-martial were trying former army officers and government officials on treason charges, their sentences a foregone conclusion. Already, in the first week, more than one thousand had been summarily executed.

Among the names were many known to Leo, men he had done business with, or helped. Jaime Delgado, deputy commander of the air force. Daniel Salazar, assistant interior minister. Raúl Gómez, director general of the post office. The thought crossed his mind that his own name might be added to that list. It was possible; anything with these fanatics was possible.

At two A.M. of the seventh day Leo was awakened by three bearded rebels. They took him to the palace, finally, to see Castro. The palace resembled the set of some disaster movie. Glass from smashed windows everywhere, and from chandeliers and picture frames. Tapestries were torn from the walls, lighting sconces hung from naked wires. The entire length of the corridor leading to the dining room rang with the echo of combat boots and was littered with empty food cans, beef and chicken bones, chunks of bread, empty wine and beer bottles.

Soldiers moved endlessly in and out of the dining room, their boots crunching over the broken crockery that covered the terrazzo floor like another layer of tile. The huge, high-ceilinged room, the scene of formal state dinners, was filled with dozens of fatigue-attired, gun-toting rebels. Some were curled up in a corner sleeping, others lounged about drinking vintage French and Spanish wine directly from the bottle, or eating from platters and bowls heaped high with chicken, beef, shrimp. There was so much shrimp it spilled from one bowl in a pink trail all the way to the head of the table where Castro sat.

Muddy boots propped up on the once-crisp white Irish-linen tablecloth, fat cigar clenched in his teeth, he leaned far back in his chair, folded his arms tightly across his chest, and regarded Leo. Seated beside him, pouring champagne into a fluted glass, was the only clean-shaven man in the room, the man Batista said was the Argentine communist, Ramón Sandoval, known as Rafael.

"Good evening," Rafael said.

Leo nodded wryly. "What the hell is good about it?"

Castro laughed, so did Rafael. No one else in the room paid the slightest attention. Castro gestured Leo into a chair and spoke to him in Spanish. Rafael translated.

"Fidel apologizes if you have been inconvenienced."

Leo did not immediately reply. He glanced past the two men to the open service entrance of the kitchen. He could see the doors of the two big restaurant refrigerators hanging open, shelves stripped bare. The victor's spoils: two hundred pounds of Batista's favorite three-inch-thick filets mignons, Leo thought, and said, "I'd like to know why I was held incommunicado."

"Again, our apologies," said Rafael. "We've been busy, you know, and Fidel has only now arrived in the city." He listened as Castro spoke rapidly, then said to Leo, "There is a small matter of some twenty million dollars."

"Money from your casinos," Castro said in English.

Rafael said, "Please, Mr. Gorodetsky, spare us the futility of a denial. A great sum of money, twenty million at the very least, is missing from the vaults. It belongs to the Cuban people."

"Whatever is in the vaults is all there was," Leo said. He addressed Castro. "And what of your promise to keep the casinos open?" He forced himself to smile. "Not to kill the golden goose?"

Castro required no translation. He pointed the cigar at Leo and spoke flatly in Spanish, which Rafael translated. "For this to be possible, there must be serious negotiation. Many conditions must be changed."

"I'm sure we can reach an understanding," Leo said.

Rafael translated Castro's reply. "Yes, I'm sure we can. But first we require the twenty million dollars."

"I'm sorry," Leo said. "There is no such amount."

"Mr. Gorodetsky, we know large sums are kept on hand," Rafael said. "We also know no money was taken out of the country." He smiled almost gently. "So it must still be here."

Before Leo's eyes flashed an image of a bonfire, fueled by a mound of hundred-dollar bills. Sixty million dollars' worth. The value of IDIC's Cuban assets. At least sixty, probably closer to seventy. A pile of ashes.

Golden goose, Leo thought. Golden sucker was more like it. They had him, and they knew it. If he continued denying the existence of the money they would simply send him back to the States. They would reopen the casinos, which they now owned by right of simple possession, under new management. IDIC would be out on the street.

All at once he laughed. He could not help it. "I just remembered something funny," he said. "Pay no attention to me." He decided not to explain that what he remembered that was so humorous was the story he had concocted for Batista about his initial meeting with Fidel Castro. When he said that he told Castro the time to negotiate finances with the rebels would be when Castro sat in this very dining room. Talk about prophecies.

Leo said, "The figure is not twenty million, it's ten." And he told them where to find it.

He was driven back to El Conquistador where he waited nearly two hours. Then, flanked by three soldiers, Rafael appeared. "All right, Mr. Gorodetsky, if you will accompany us, please."

"I presume you found the money?"

"We did," said Rafael. "There was slightly more than ten million in that very ingenious hiding place. Thank you." He barked an order in Spanish for the soldiers to take Leo's luggage.

"Where are we going?" Leo asked.

"You are going. Only you," Rafael said, and for a stomach-loosening instant Leo wondered if they did not after all intend shooting him. But then Rafael continued, "You are leaving Cuba, sir. By order of the president himself."

Anger replaced the fear. "We had an agreement!" Leo said. "Are you trying to tell me that after I gave you ten million dollars, Castro will not keep his word?"

"Excuse me, Mr. Gorodetsky, but Fidel never gave his word to you on anything."

"He said he'd keep the casinos open!"

"No," said Rafael quietly. "I am afraid you misunderstood. The casinos are closed permanently. The hotels are to be nationalized."

Rafael gestured Leo to leave the room. Leo stepped into the corridor, then stopped. He said, "In the Sierra Maestra, when I gave you the two hundred and fifty thousand dollars, and Castro said he had no intention of closing the casinos, he was lying. And you knew it, too."

Rafael's eyes never left Leo's. "The casinos are closed."

"I trusted you, and you lied to me," Leo said. The words sounded banal even as he framed them, and more so when he actually heard them from his own lips. He felt like a child to whom a promise had been broken.

"Your plane leaves in forty minutes," Rafael said.

Leo never remembered hating anyone as much as he hated these people. He could taste it bitter in his throat, driving up from deep inside him, enveloping him in alternating waves of heat and cold. He entered the elevator car, which was crowded now with the presence of the four large men and himself, and rank with the strong, sour odor of their sweat and the almost aromatic odor of the cottonseed oil from the polished wooden stocks of the U.S. Army M-1 carbines slung over their shoulders.

It was at that moment, riding in the elevator car of his own hotel that by presidential decree no longer was his, boxed in by four hard-eyed young men who made him feel not only small and old, but helpless, it was at that moment he knew he had to kill Fidel Castro.

3.

The entire block was cordoned off. From 126th Street to 127th, Lenox Avenue to Seventh, with police barricades fifty feet in all directions from the Hotel Theresa. No one without an authorized permit could approach the hotel, and then only with a police escort.

"They're sure not taking any chances," Jules Jefferson said. He put down the binoculars and looked at Leo. "Killing a man ain't easy, is it?"

"It's the easiest thing in the world," Leo said, wondering why he said it, knowing that in this particular case it was far from easy. He had been trying to do it now for eighteen months.

He picked up the binoculars and focused them on the hotel. It was a six-story shabby brownstone building in the center of a block of other brownstones, tenements, storefronts, and one abandoned theater. Not much different from the Lower East Side, with the kids playing in the street, and the bedding airing on the fire escapes. It smelled the same, too.

Leo closed his eyes against the sudden glare of the late-morning sun on the naked light bulbs of the hotel's vertical sign. He lowered the glasses and glanced at his watch: 10:26.

"They'll be moving soon," he said.

"I hope so," said Jules. His face, framed in the open window, resembled a black marble sculpture. "This sure ain't the most comfortable place in the world."

They were at a window in a room on the eighth floor of a building on 128th Street, two blocks away but overlooking the Hotel Theresa. Jules had disapproved of Leo's coming here; he wanted to handle it alone. Leo would not hear of it. It was his project; he wanted to be sure all went as planned. Another reason was that he suspected Jules considered him too old for such action. Some action, he thought. Sitting at a window, watching a fleabag hotel two blocks away.

Fidel Castro's temporary residence.

Fidel, in New York to address the United Nations, had initially checked into the midtown Hotel Shelburne, but moved out when the management demanded payment in advance. Now he and his entourage were settled in this small Harlem hotel, the Theresa. Already, Leo heard, the Cubans had made a pigsty of the Theresa. It did not surprise him.

"Leo!" Jules Jefferson nudged Leo's shoulder and pointed out the window at the hotel. Two Chrysler limousines and a Plymouth Valiant sedan had driven up behind a police car and three motorcycle policemen. Four more motorcycles were lined up behind the limousines. Other policemen prevented spectators from crossing the barricade. From the hotel, accompanied by a half dozen men and women wearing fatigues and forage caps, Castro appeared.

Castro and three others entered the first limousine, the rest got into the second car. Behind this second limousine was the Plymouth Valiant. It contained three U.S. Secret Service agents. Sirens screaming, the vehicles started down 126th Street, turned left on Seventh Avenue and headed south.

"Make the call!" Leo said to Jules.

But Jules already was speaking into the telephone near the door of the unfurnished room. "On the way," he said quietly, and hung up.

The call was received in a telephone booth in a cafeteria on the corner of 110th Street and Seventh Avenue by a man who had waited at a nearby table nearly an hour for the phone to ring. A tall, lean black man wearing white coveralls with red scripted letters embroidered above the left breast pocket: NYSD. His name was Edward Brodnax. He was one of Jules Jefferson's most reliable lieutenants. He was twenty-seven years old, a man with little or no fear, and boundless courage. He was also an occasional Alliance contract killer.

He strode from the cafeteria, out to the street, and around the corner to a parked New York City Sanitation Department garbage hauler. Two other black men were in the truck cab, both wearing similar coveralls.

"Let's go," Edward Brodnax said. The truck's big diesel rumbled into life and the driver pulled away from the curb. Brodnax, settling himself in the cab, reached under the seat and brought out a small, collapsible-stocked AR-15 semiautomatic rifle fitted with a flash suppressor. He handed the gun to the man in the middle. Then Brodnax slid two more AR-15s from under the seat, and three twenty-round ammunition clips. One for each man. These were weapons stolen from an upstate New York National Guard armory, modified personally by Brodnax to fire .22-caliber ammunition at a rate of nine hundred rounds per minute.

The three men rode in grim silence down Seventh to 105th, then turned east. Halfway up the block was a parked sedan, a green 1958 Oldsmobile 98. A lone black man sat at the wheel. He wore a frayed GI-issue field jacket and dark corduroy work cap. The garbage truck drove past. Edward Brodnax nodded at the man in the sedan, who touched his foot to the car's accelerator starter pedal and was momentarily alarmed when it did not immediately engage. But then it caught, and he gunned the engine, watching the garbage truck in his rearview mirror. When it reached the end of the block and turned left, south again, the man pulled the Olds away from the curb and drove casually toward Seventh Avenue.

Six blocks away, Fidel Castro's motorcade sped south on Seventh Avenue, passing 120th Street. The garbage truck, after backtracking one block, was on 105th Street once more, trundling west toward Seventh Avenue. Edward Brodnax drew back the AR-15's charger handle and cranked a shell into the chamber, then flipped the firing selector switch forward to "auto." He raised his dust mask so it fit snugly over his nose and mouth and adjusted his sunglasses. The two other men fixed their dust masks also. In the distance Brodnax could hear the motorcycle sirens. He gestured the driver to slow slightly; they were approaching the intersection too fast.

At this same moment, the green Oldsmobile 98 arrived at the corner of 106th and Seventh. The driver stopped outside a variety store, double-parking next to a small pickup truck. Directly across the street was a Chock Full o'Nuts restaurant. The Olds driver let the engine idle, now and then gently depressing the accelerator to keep the plugs from fouling. He estimated the speed of the approaching motorcade at thirty-five to forty miles per hour. At that rate the first motorcycle would reach the intersection in two minutes. Time enough for a cigarette.

Back in the empty eighth-floor room on 128th Street, Leo Gorodetsky also lit a cigarette, although not limiting himself to two minutes for it. In truth, however, those two minutes were the culmination of eighteen months of frustration and disappointment.

Not to mention money. A cool $600,000. At least that much, every dime his own. He was paying Edward Brodnax $25,000 for services rendered this day, plus $10,000 to each of his two helpers, and $15,000 to the Oldsmobile driver. A grand total of $50,000 for this operation alone.

But less than one tenth the amount already invested in similar projects, ridiculous to sublime. From exotic science-fiction schemes like blowing up the presidential palace with long-distance rockets launched from a Goodyear blimp, to poisoning Fidel's cigars.

George Gerson said it had become an obsession. But, as Leo pointed out, losing a $60 million investment was reason for obsessiveness. And Leo had to answer to the Council for all that. It was their money lost in Cuba, too. So it had been a bad eighteen months, made worse by Martin Raab, himself obsessed, relentlessly attempting to indict Leo on another tax-evasion charge.

But then, in the spring of 1960, the cycle swung back in Leo's favor. The United Nations accepted Fidel's request to address the body in New York. The instant Leo heard of it, he knew he had him. And, making it all so much better, in the home park!

When Fidel Castro indignantly moved from the Hotel Shelburne to a Harlem hotel, it was like finding a word or thought that had naggingly eluded you. All at once everything fell into place. Leo went immediately to Jules Jefferson, who provided Edward Brodnax, who worked out the final plan.

A plan which at 10:33 on this morning of September 18, 1960, the day before Fidel Castro's scheduled United Nations appearance, as he rode off to attend a reception in his honor at the Soviet consulate, was twelve seconds from being implemented. With Castro dead, Cuba—with the blessings and assistance of the United States government—would quickly return to democracy, and the casinos would reopen.

And Leo's nightmare would be over.

But even now, gazing out at the half-broken crossbar of the "T" on the sign atop the Hotel Theresa's weather-battered marquee, he wondered—as he had been wondering ever since he started this vendetta, which was every bit as fanatic and fanciful as any Sicilian's—what he was trying to prove. At this stage of his life, what difference did it make? So Castro made a fool of him, so what?

". . . should be going down just about now," Jules Jefferson was saying. Jules was staring at his watch, his hand on the telephone, ready to pick it up at the first ring.

Leo was not listening. The thought had just occurred to him that this plan, too, might fail. And if so, he would have made a still bigger fool of himself. The worst kind of fool, an old fool.

The phone rang.

"Yeah!" Jules shouted into it. He listened, then slammed down the receiver and said to Leo, "They're there."

The call came from another public phone. In the Chock Full o' Nuts restaurant on 106th Street, the caller a policeman, a black patrolman assigned to crowd control. He was also on Jules Jefferson's payroll and would make certain the Olds 98 was not interfered with. From the restaurant he watched the motorcade's lead motorcycles roar past the intersection.

A block south, at 105th, the big garbage hauler crossed the intersection and stopped directly in the path of the oncoming motorcade. The first motorcycle cop squeezed both hand brakes and simultaneously swung his handlebars to the right. He skidded sideways, followed by the motorcycle just behind him. The police squad car fishtailed around and skidded to a halt behind the limousine carrying Castro, which now also stopped. At the same instant the three NYSD coveralled men scrambled out of the garbage hauler, Brodnax in the center, the other two fanning right and left.

All three trained their AR-15s on the limousine and fired. Brodnax's bullets smashed the windshield. The men on the right and left emptied their magazines into each side of the car. In an instant the windows burst, and the doors flew open. Two bearded, fatigue-clad bodies tumbled to the ground. Brodnax hurled his empty gun toward the car, whirled, and ran toward the Olds, which was parked facing east, away from the action. The Olds driver threw the gear-shift selector into reverse and raced the car backward to meet Brodnax. Brodnax heard, but did not turn to see, the gunfire from the police and Secret Service men.

The door of the Olds was open. Brodnax placed one foot inside. The car was stalled. The driver desperately pumped the accelerator pedal; the engine wheezed sluggishly, sickeningly.

"The fucking battery!" the driver cried.

Instantly, Brodnax pushed himself away from the door and started running down the street. He never saw the U.S. Secret Service agent behind him, and never felt the bullets that thudded into his back and neck, or himself falling face first onto the pavement. He also had never seen his two associates shot dead moments before, although he heard the gunshots and had anticipated all that anyway. The plan, of course unknown to the two, was that they unwittingly would provide enough diversion for Brodnax to escape. And he might have, had not the engine of a car with a bad battery inexplicably stalled.

And if Fidel Castro's two bodyguards had not thrown him to the limousine floor and shielded him with their own bodies, the plan might have succeeded in any case.

As the NYPD Public Affairs spokesman commented on NBC's *Huntley-Brinkley Report* that same evening, it was as botched a job as he'd seen in years. Even the driver of the getaway car was killed, cut down by a policeman assigned to crowd control. The NYPD spokesman refrained from mentioning that the crowd-control policeman, a black, had stepped over to the car and calmly shot the driver while the man was still attempting to start the stalled engine.

The one fortunate aspect of the entire fiasco was that the only casualties were two Cubans, and the three black assassins, and the driver of the getaway car. Of the four, only Edward Brodnax was known to the police.

An Alliance hitman.

The following morning, September 19, in Washington, D.C., at approximately the same hour Fidel Castro addressed the United Nations in New York, Charles Brickhill and Martin Raab sat at a rear booth in the Hotel Mayflower coffee shop. They had just returned from an unpleasant meeting with the FBI director in the pleasant garden of the director's Georgetown home. Mr. Hoover had greeted the two men by displaying, like a towel covering his chest, the front page of *The Washington Post*.

GANGLAND CONTRACT ON CASTRO!

The same newspaper now lay front page up on the table between Raab and Brickhill. Raab could still hear Hoover's words. "That's some task force you have, Mr. Raab." Task force sounded like an obscenity. "We look like idiots. Incapable of protecting the head of a foreign state. You know, they're hinting we may even have had a hand in it." His jowls tightened. "In concert with the CIA! Can you damn well imagine it? The CIA!" CIA sounded like an obscenity, too.

There was more of the same, but thankfully brief. After ten minutes, Hoover thanked them for coming and said he expected a full report from Raab on "Operation Roma," the code name for Hoover's plan to once and for all break the Mafia.

"He's convinced there is still such a thing as Mafia," Raab said now. "When I try to explain it's been dead for years in this country—if it ever really existed here, other than a few old Moustache Petes, now long gone, with some small-time extortion and strong-arm rackets—he points out the Italian names of the big Alliance families. 'You call it Alliance,' he says, 'I call it Mafia. It's one and the same, isn't it?' "

"Maybe you'll get lucky, Marty, and if Kennedy wins, he'll fire J. Edgar," Brickhill said. He smiled sourly. "Maybe he'll make you attorney general, and then you can fire the old bastard."

Raab resisted a temptation to suggest the possibility of Brickhill's losing his reelection bid in November, in which case Raab might offer him a Justice Department job. Martin Raab, confident that his appointment was secure in any administration, would enjoy being Charlie Brickhill's boss.

Raab said, "Now he'll activate 'Operation Roma.' Every two-bit hoodlum named Tony, or Patsy, or Guido will be hauled in. A couple of months of that, and then there'll be a press conference where the director announces meaningful progress in the battle against organized crime in the United States. I can't even get him to read my memo detailing the evidence that the money behind the Castro assassination attempt came from Leo Gorodetsky. Jesus, my four-year-old grandson can figure that one out!"

"How are you doing with the jury-tampering thing?" Brickhill asked.

"Doing good," Raab said, then added, "I think. It's the black man, Collins. Albert Collins. It has to be. We finally located him in Detroit. We'll have the name he's using any day now."

"He was smart to move," Brickhill said. "They would have killed him sure."

"Only because he tried holding them up for more," Raab said. "So he wasn't so smart. In the meantime I have a phone tap on him, and a twenty-four-hour surveillance. He can't even take a pee without a Justice Department agent knowing it."

"Who, the juror?"

"Gorodetsky," Raab said. "My 'fellow-Jew,' as you once referred to him."

"Correction," Brickhill said. "That was how you referred to him. Don't confuse me, please, with the antisemites. I don't give a damn what they are, Jews, Italians, or moon worshipers." He paused to sip his coffee, and made a face. "God, what swill! Worst coffee in town. Now let me ask you something. With all the pressure on Gorodetsky, you'll have him racing around pulling injunctions out of every pocket. Why alert him like that?"

Raab suddenly felt very superior and wanted to tell Brickhill that he was only emulating Brickhill's own tactics. But he did not care to give the senator any kudos.

He said, "The real pressure on Mr. Gorodetsky will come from this" —he flicked his fingers on the newspaper—"from his Alliance associates. One gets you ten that right now they're leaning all over him." Raab sat back and folded his hands comfortably behind his neck. "He's become a problem for them, Charlie. A public relations problem. A detriment. He fucked up good this time, my fellow Jew did. He might be in big trouble. Maybe even terminal trouble."

Charles Brickhill said, "You've really become quite bloodthirsty, Marty."

"I learned from you, Charlie," Raab said.

26

MARTIN Raab had sound reason for suggesting Leo might be in trouble with the Alliance. He had inside information. Raab's agents had learned through their telephone tap of a meeting Leo would attend the afternoon of that same day.

The meeting was held in a new, glass-walled high-rise in Jackson Heights, in the conference room of Hamilton Associates Inc., a real-estate firm specializing in the development of shopping malls. Hamilton Associates was a division of Intracorp, itself a branch of yet another holding company whose stock, while public, was controlled by a consortium of other corporations, some of which owned shares in IDIC. Each man attending the meeting that day was listed as an officer or board member of one or the other of all these various corporations.

In addition to Leo and Vincent Tomasino, those present were Paul Calvelli, Anthony Curcio, Carlo Miranda, and Santo Lomanni. At Leo's specific request, George Gerson was also here, and even allowed a chair at the table next to Leo.

After a cordial exchange of a few bad jokes and some gossip, Vincent Tomasino said, "Leo, I guess you must know why we're all here today. I mean it can't come as any big surprise."

Leo smiled accommodatingly. He said, "No, Vinnie, it's no surprise."

Anthony Curcio, who had flown in from Boston just that morning, said, "Why didn't you clear it with the Council before you tried that—?"

he groped for the word. "Stunt. That stunt, Leo. It was not a smart thing to do. Not at all."

"It was a personal matter, Tony," Leo said. He had anticipated all their questions, and was well prepared. "Something I had to handle by myself. I didn't want to involve the Council."

"But you did involve us," Paul Calvelli said. He rose and stepped to the window. He raised one louver of the venetian blind and nodded toward the street below. "Right now, that Buick parked down there. Two government agents that you know've been on your tail!" He let the louver snap back into place and returned to his seat. "We don't need that kind of heat, Leo!"

"There's no heat, Paul. Except what's in your imagination," Leo said. "We're too big to be affected by 'heat.'"

"That's why you tried to hit Castro?" Paul Calvelli said. "Because we're too big?"

"Look, even if somehow they did manage to pin the Castro thing on me, you think it would matter? It wouldn't matter if every one of us in this room went to prison. The machine we built wouldn't stop. It can run by itself. It's too big and too well organized. And it really would run by itself, too. It's an integral part of this whole society now. As a matter of fact, I think we're an integral part of the government. The United States government, I'm talking about."

"That's a fine speech, Leo," Vincent Tomasino said dryly. "I think the older you get, the crazier you get."

"In all the news stories about it, were any of our names mentioned?" Leo asked. "Have any charges been brought?"

"That's not the point, Leo," Santo Lomanni said. He was the youngest Council member, having recently succeeded his father, Gerardo Lomanni, as head of their powerful Jersey City family. Their interests ranged from automobile agencies whose origins lay in the sale of stolen automobile parts, to a nationwide chain of loan companies that had evolved from waterfront loan sharking.

Leo remembered Santo as a gangly, smart-mouthed adolescent chauffeuring old Gerardo around. Hard to believe the boy was now thirty-five. And a college graduate, an attorney no less. He thought of Steve as an attorney, although certainly not an attorney in his father's company. No, Steve would have done what he wanted, fly. An airline pilot. That would have been nice.

"Leo . . . ?"

They were all staring curiously at him. "Sorry," he said, thinking that he should stop brooding about Steve, but realizing—a little guiltily—it was becoming less painful all the time. Time, he thought. Time heals everything. Almost. He said to Santo Lomanni, "Well, what is the point, then?"

Santo Lomanni did not reply. He looked at Vinnie, who said, "The point, Leo, is we want you to take a vacation. I mean, a long one, far away. Enough is enough. We just can't afford to let you keep doing this crazy stuff."

"A vacation," Leo said. He smiled thinly. "Like the one Fred Agnessi once tried to send me on?"

"Oh, come on, Leo!" It was Carlo Miranda; he seemed almost insulted at Leo's implication. Carlo Miranda was now Boss of Bosses in Philadelphia. Middle-aged, short, stout, white haired, he had made his mark as an enforcer, but had become such an astute business executive it was said he ran his organization more efficiently than IBM. "That Agnessi thing, that's ancient history!"

"Excuse me, Carlo," Leo said sarcastically. "I forgot. We don't do that anymore."

"What are you making this so hard on everybody for?" Vincent Tomasino asked. He pointed a finger at George Gerson. "Can't you talk sense to him?" He looked at Leo. "Can't anybody?"

Leo glanced at Gerson, almost pleased. He had told Gerson nearly verbatim what these eminent Councilmen—the "steering committee" of the full Council—would say, even down to tones of voice and facial expressions.

He said, "I haven't forgotten that 'ancient history,' and I think all this hysterical moaning and groaning about Fidel Castro is just a continuation of it. You tried to ease me out once, but failed. So now this is a perfect excuse to try again. Some gratitude! Every one of you sitting here is a multimillionaire today, thanks to me! I made the money for you."

"Leo, nobody is trying to ease you out," Paul Calvelli said.

"Let him talk, Paul," Vincent Tomasino said. "I want to hear this. Go ahead, Leo, tell us about all you did for us. I'm really curious to know."

Leo was angry now, but in a cool, controlled way. He liked the feeling, and enjoyed making them uncomfortable. He said, "Please, if not for me you'd all still be rolling drunks somewhere, or holding up gas stations. Do I have to remind you how I had to beg for the money to build the Barclay? And before that, when we formed this Alliance?" He paused abruptly.

The word WHY, with a huge question mark, had suddenly flashed into his mind. *Why?* The word glittered before his eyes and obscured the features of the men seated opposite him. Why was he arguing? Why was he reminding them of their debt to him? Did he truly expect an acknowledgment? What did he expect from them? And what would be proved?

". . . didn't do it by yourself," Vincent Tomasino was saying. His voice had taken on a hard, almost raspy edge. "You had plenty of help from us! In fact, you couldn't have done it without us. No way. You've been selling that line of bullshit for twenty-five years, and I got to tell you, I'm pretty fucking tired of hearing it!"

And I'm just as tired of saying it, Leo said to himself. Aloud, he said to Vinnie, "Do you want the Cuban casinos back, or not?"

"Cuba is dead!" Vinnie said. "Now forget it. We lost it, and there's no way we'll get it back. Write it off, Leo!"

Tony Curcio said, "What we want, Leo, is for you to lay low a while—"

"—you don't mean 'lay low,' Tony," Leo said. "You mean step aside. You want me out."

Vincent Tomasino slammed his fist on the table. The glass ashtrays and coffee cups clattered. "Goddam you, Leo, if we wanted you out, you'd be out! We want you, like Tony just said, to lay low." He addressed Paul Calvelli. "Talk to him. I heard him say once you're the only one of us that has any class. Maybe if you talk, he'll understand."

"He understands," Paul said. "He understands that what we want is for him to keep out of the limelight until things quiet down."

Leo really did not hear him, and was only vaguely aware of other voices at the table exhorting Gerson to convince Leo of the necessity of absenting himself from New York. His cool anger had been replaced by chagrin. He had just discovered the answer to WHY? He was playing a childish game of make-believe in a foolish attempt to salvage self-respect. He knew they had already passed judgment, and all this was a formality, a protocol to be observed. But he had deluded himself into thinking he might change their minds.

He had wanted their approval. An expression of appreciation for the initiative he took on their behalf to recover what was stolen from them by the thief and liar now governing Cuba. But he had botched the job, and how or why was unimportant. The truth was that the fault was his. And now he groveled before them, blurting, You want me out. He cringed, remembering those words.

He hardly recognized his own voice. "All right, I'll do it. I'll take a vacation. It's about time, anyway."

For a moment no one spoke. Everyone seemed startled, almost disappointed. He wanted to laugh in their faces. "What's the matter?" he asked. "Don't you believe me?"

"Sure, Leo," Paul Calvelli said. "We believe you."

Now Leo did laugh. "I have a feeling you didn't expect me to make it so easy for you."

"I hope you're serious about this, Leo," Anthony Curcio said. "Because we are."

"You want it in writing, Tony?" Leo said. "I said you're right. When you're right, you're right."

Anthony Curcio started replying, then stopped. He looked at Vincent Tomasino, who was studying Leo suspiciously. "No more bullshit about Cuba?" Vinnie asked.

Leo grinned. "Where's Cuba?"

* * *

The Buick sedan stayed behind them all the way back to Manhattan, and not because the government agents were clumsy. Clearly, they wanted the occupants of the chauffeured Chrysler Imperial to know they were followed. But as Gerson pointed out, there was a certain irony to it.

". . . it's like having your own police escort," he said to Leo. "Extra protection."

The chauffeured Imperial was Gerson's. The chauffeur was Joseph, a big black man who once ran numbers for Jules Jefferson and who, if necessary, could drive the Imperial like a Formula One race car. He could also, if necessary, break a man's neck with a single blow of the flat of his hand.

"Listen, they're only doing their job," Leo said.

"So is the Council," Gerson said. "And they did it pretty well this afternoon, getting you to all of a sudden fold up and tell them yes, you'll take a vacation. Except that I'm waiting for you to tell me the real reason."

"Why I said I'd go?"

"Yes, Leo. Why you said you'd go."

"You want the truth?"

"Please."

"I was tired of arguing. I think I'm tired, period."

"No, Leo, I don't buy that. Try something else."

Leo gazed at the Queensborough Bridge towers outlining the distant sky and thought, but did not say it, Old. I am getting old. I look at the face in the mirror and see little wrinkles and blotches that yesterday were not there. And then he did say it.

"I'm getting old, George. We both are."

"Speak for yourself, please. I don't feel old."

"Wait till you hit sixty," Leo said. "A magic number."

"Three years," Gerson said. "I can wait."

Leo said nothing. He glanced again through the rear window. A cream-white Thunderbird convertible, top down, had just passed the Buick and slipped in behind the Imperial. A young boy was at the wheel, snuggled close to a girl with long blond hair flowing backward in the wind. Talk about young, he thought enviously, watching the T-bird from the corner of his eye until it roared past, and the Buick resumed its position behind them.

The sun, glinting off the Buick's windshield, obscured the agents' faces. Leo wondered idly what they looked like, and wondered if he needed distance glasses. Lately it seemed distant objects were slightly blurred. Age, he thought. Something else you never believed could happen to you.

". . . should stop at the office to sign those estimated-income tax forms," Gerson was saying. He jerked his thumb at the Buick. "We can thank them for reminding me."

Leo turned front again. He lit a cigarette. "George, you're always telling me how rich I am. How rich am I?"

The question seemed to surprise Gerson. He studied Leo a moment, then looked away, out the window at the midtown skyline. "I would say, with the real estate, the stocks and bonds, casino points—" he turned again, removing his glasses now to face Leo directly. "I would say, conservatively, fifty million."

"I like the way the number rolls off your tongue," Leo said.

"I like the way it looks on paper."

"How much of it is liquid?"

"As much as you want."

Leo thought about this a moment. Then he said, "My father once gave me a quarter to buy the Friday night *cholent.*" He spoke quietly, really thinking aloud, remembering, studying the thick, rippling black muscles of the chauffeur's neck. "Or was it more? Forty cents?" He looked at Gerson. "I blew it in a crap game. And now you tell me I'm worth fifty million!"

"For a man who's supposed to be the wizard of the ages with figures, you surprise me," Gerson said. "I'd have thought you knew how much to the penny."

Leo smiled. "I stopped counting back when it got to twenty."

Gerson did not return the smile. "I want you to live to be able to enjoy it, Leo. I hope you really are taking them seriously."

Leo said, "I started thinking, So Castro made a sucker out of me. So I lost some self-respect. Big deal. I thought, Who the hell cares about my self-respect, and why should they? And at the same time I was thinking this, I was also thinking that if I step back now, I'll live to fight another day." He looked away, out the window. They were crossing the Queensborough Bridge. "That's the smart thing, isn't it? Live to fight another day?"

"A minute ago you said you were tired, and old."

"George, I said I was only thinking that, about living to fight another day. The truth is that I'm looking forward to a little rest. And Renata will appreciate it."

"I'm sure she will," Gerson said.

Leo remembered yet another time when someone advised a vacation. Robert MacGowan. That night they "arrested" him at Ellie's parents' house and took him for a ride to see MacGowan.

Poor old MacGowan. Poor Ellie. Poor Ellie's parents. Both dead years ago, within months of each other, the mother first. Leo had been away somewhere and unable to attend Selma Baer's funeral, but he did pay Alfred Baer's hospital expenses, and for the funeral. And this with the old man refusing to allow Leo to visit him in the hospital. An intern told Leo that Alfred Baer said Leo had murdered his daughter. The ravings of a dying man, the intern had explained with clinical arrogance. Deathbed statements were often quite bizarre.

"Not so bizarre," Leo said aloud now.

"Excuse me?"

"Nothing," Leo said. "I was daydreaming. George, do you think Renata would like a cruise? A real luxury cruise. Say, the *Queen Elizabeth*? One of those first-class penthouses. I think I read somewhere that on a round-the-world trip they go for about ten thousand dollars. Check it out for me, will you?"

Gerson said, "Leo, like Vinnie Tomasino said, no bullshit?"

"No bullshit, George."

"I'm not sure I believe you, Leo."

"Well, George, then that's your problem."

At Leo's apartment building the Buick pulled up only a car's length from the entrance. Leo got out of the Imperial and waited for Gerson to drive off. Then he stepped over to the Buick. The man behind the wheel was young, rather chubby, with a crewcut. The other looked only slightly older, also with close-cropped hair. Both seemed embarrassed.

"Gentlemen," Leo said through the open window. "I suggest you ask Mr. Raab to buy you two tickets on the *Queen Elizabeth*." He flipped them a brisk salute and walked away.

2.

Renata was surprised Leo endured the round-the-world cruise as long as he did, although he appeared to genuinely enjoy the first leg, New York to Rio. Up early, a brisk two-mile walk-jog around the boat deck, then a huge, leisurely breakfast. A daily golf lesson, skeet shooting, an hour of swimming, then lunch. Followed by at least three hours of reading, a short nap—occasionally featuring some delightful lovemaking ("matinees," as both referred to it), forcing Leo to agree that you are only as old as you feel. Tea in the main lounge, then dinner at the first serving; formal dress, which Leo liked, but not the gain of four pounds from the rich, constantly tempting food. A movie, or just sitting listening to the dance band, and then bed. A full, splendid night's sleep.

Total relaxation.

Impossible, of course, for him to tolerate long. At the end of the second week, just after Rio, he began spending considerable time in the radio room. Transatlantic calls to George Gerson in New York and Ben Sylbert in Las Vegas. More and more of them to Ben. By the time they reached Capetown he had run up a telephone bill of more than $2,000.

There, at Capetown, the *QE* nearly sailed minus one passenger, Leo, who had been in the hotel talking on the phone with Ben. Leo made it with less than five minutes to spare. Over dinner—and he did not wear his tuxedo, a clear sign he was getting bored—Renata finally asked what on earth he and Ben talked about so much.

"You know, I really like that gown," he said. It was a sedately simple chemise-styled black taffeta with a deep V bodice. He had seen it in the ship's boutique the first day out and bought it for her. The price was outrageous. She had reminded him that her steamer trunk already contained exactly half a dozen evening gowns, but he said the black highlighted her blond hair to perfection. "You're a beautiful woman."

"Thank you," she said. "Does that mean you don't care to answer my question?"

"What question?"

"My question about why you and Ben talk so much."

"Oh," he said. "Well, you know I'm worried about Esther." Shortly before they left New York, Esther had slipped and fractured her hip. She said she did not look where she was walking. She was more and more forgetful lately.

"Leo, what does Ben Sylbert have to do with Esther?"

"Oh, did I say Ben?"

"No, darling, I did. I asked why you and Ben are on the phone so often."

"I thought you meant George," Leo said.

Renata nodded dryly. "Okay," she said. "I won't ask again."

Leo grinned. "Thanks."

"You're welcome."

But while it lasted, it was a marvelous trip. They kept mostly to themselves, which did not displease Renata. It was the first time in years she had his exclusive attention. But then the phone calls started, and the old tenseness returned. Soon he could not seem to sit still. He was also unusually interested in the world news, hardly able to wait for the posting of the daily bulletins. He said it was the Eichmann trial soon to begin in Israel, but she overheard him asking the purser to inform him the instant the ship's radio received any further details concerning the U.S. threat to break diplomatic relations with Cuba.

The diplomatic break was officially announced the day they docked in Hong Kong. A drab, blustery January morning. Four hours later Leo and Renata were in a Pan American Airways Boeing 707 flying to Los Angeles.

Leo said it was vital he see Ben in Las Vegas. Ben had worked hard and effectively for John F. Kennedy's election and made important contacts in the new administration. He was also a close friend of the president-elect's brother, Robert, the attorney general-designate. Ben might exert some influence on the Democrats to ease Justice Department pressure in Las Vegas.

Renata really did not regret leaving the cruise. She was getting bored with the ship herself. And she did look forward to flying in the huge, shiny new jets. Everybody said they cut the flying time nearly in half, while doubling the comfort.

True enough.

Sixteen hours after leaving Hong Kong, they arrived in Los Angeles, and an hour later in Las Vegas. The miracle of speed. Which delighted

Leo, but only increased Renata's anxiety. Leo's explanation about Ben and the Justice Department made sense, but Renata knew it was events in Cuba that had motivated the impromptu departure from the *Queen Elizabeth*. She could not understand how Justice Department pressure on Las Vegas was related to Cuba.

Three days later Renata was no better informed. Leo and Ben Sylbert spent hours together, Leo continually jotting figures on yellow note-paper, revising, discussing. And then there were smatterings of conversations over lunch or dinner.

". . . I'll let you know as soon as I hear," Ben said in one of those conversations.

"But how long will that be?" Leo asked.

Ben shrugged. "I haven't a clue. Maybe a day, maybe a week. I'll go to Washington in the morning and talk to him. That's all I can tell you."

"Can't you push?"

"Yes, Leo, I'll push."

"Hard, kid," Leo said. "You have to push hard."

"I'll push, I'll push."

This was at the Barclay pool one afternoon after they had returned from visiting Ben's new plant downtown. *The Las Vegas Record* now occupied its own imposing four-story building. The paper, with a guaranteed circulation of thirty thousand, had made Ben a power in Nevada politics. A "mover," as he wryly said. A kingmaker.

During the tour of the new facilities, Ben mentioned a series of editorials he planned that might win him a Pulitzer. These editorials concerned "mob influence" in Las Vegas.

"What the hell does that mean?" Leo asked.

"Leo, do you know what the population of Vegas is today?" Ben asked. "One hundred and fifty thousand! Ten years ago, it was forty thousand. Ten years from now it'll be three hundred thousand. That means more and bigger hotels. The owners of these new casinos will have to be so clean, they'll be denied a license if they've ever so much as picked up a parking ticket. It means, Leo, the old days are over, and the old people are out."

"The people who made this city," Leo said.

"I'm afraid so," Ben said.

"Since when have you been such a reformer, Ben?"

"Since I came to love this place, Leo. I even like it in the summer. I want it to grow and flourish. I want it to be what Harry dreamed: an oasis in the desert. But it won't happen unless we clean it up once and for all."

"Clean up what?" Leo asked. "There's nothing to clean up."

"Come on, Leo, you know better. Pretty soon casino revenues will hit more than a billion dollars a year. Billion, with a *B*, Leo! No state earning taxes from that kind of industry will sit still for what they call 'organized crime elements' to share those profits." Ben's mouth tightened. "I'm naming names: Tomasino, Calvelli, Curcio. It'll sound like the cast of an Italian opera."

Leo said nothing a moment. Then, "Where's 'Gorodetsky'? Or would that make it too much like Yiddish theater?"

Ben looked at him. "I'll have to, Leo. Sooner or later."

Leo's eyes turned cold, but almost immediately he relaxed. "You're sure you don't want me to go with you to Washington?"

"Let me handle it my way, Leo."

"Okay, kid, you handle it."

Ben phoned from Washington the following evening while Leo and Renata were at dinner in their suite. Renata heard only Leo's end of the conversation, but he seemed suddenly more alert and energetic than in months.

"I see," Leo said. "When?"

". . . . ."

"Remember, Ben, if he goes for it, there's a price. He gets something, he has to give something for it."

". . . . ."

"Where are you now?"

". . . . ."

"A bar?" Leo laughed nervously. "What'd you have to do? Get him drunk?"

". . . . ."

Leo laughed again. "Okay, I'll see you when you get back. And, Ben—" he paused and glanced almost pensively at Renata. Then he continued into the phone, "Thank you."

He hung up and rejoined Renata at the table. He measured a quarter teaspoon of sugar into a spoon, dropped it into his coffee cup, and said, "How do you feel about moving away from New York?"

The question startled her. "What do you mean?"

"Moving," he said. "Permanently."

"I've never thought about it," she said, knowing his question was not a question, but a statement of a decision already made, and obviously motivated by Ben's phone call.

"I have," he said. "Especially about the travel agency. I've worked out a way you can lease it to the employees, with their option to buy. So if they work hard, it'll be worth their while—and yours." He started drinking the coffee, but put the cup down untouched. "So where would you like to move to?"

"May I ask the reason for all this?"

"I've decided to retire," he said. "And since there's no way I could stay in New York, retired, we'll have to go somewhere else. Right?"

"Right," she said, knowing it was what he wanted to hear.

"So where do you think you'd like to go?"

"Wherever you'd like."

"Well, I've been thinking of—"

"—what about California?" She was damned if she'd be hustled about like a piece of luggage. He asked her, so she'd tell him.

"California?"

"Yes, darling, you've heard of California. On the Pacific side of the continent. I think I'd like living there."

It was not what he wanted to hear. Now he did sip some coffee. He put the cup carefully back into the saucer. "I was thinking more of Florida," he said. "Miami, maybe."

"Oh," she said. "I see. Florida."

"Florida has everything California has," he said.

"I'm sure," she said. "And of course you'll just sit around on the beach? And play gin rummy with the other retirees? Or perhaps after all those golf lessons, you'll join a country club—"

"—the sarcasm is unnecessary. I just thought you'd like Florida."

"More than California?"

"I think it's a nicer place, yes."

She studied him, those determined eyes she had learned to read so well. She said, "You know, I do believe I would like Florida." She smiled. "When do we move?"

He smiled back. "Right away."

Coincidentally, ten minutes earlier, twenty-six hundred miles east in McLean, Virginia, in the bar of a Holiday Inn just off Interstate 495, Ben Sylbert made the identical reply to a similar question put to him by Robert F. Kennedy.

"When does Mr. Gorodetsky plan to move to Florida?"

"Right away," Ben said.

Kennedy poured the remainder of a bottle of LeBatt's Canadian Ale into his glass. He truly had little time for this meeting, and considered Ben Sylbert's errand somewhat frivolous, if not outright foolish. But when you thought about it, you almost had to ask yourself, Why not? What can we lose?

He said, "Run through it again."

Ben said, "He says he can recruit thousands of anti-Castro Cubans. He's in constant contact with them in Miami, and has been assured of their willingness to do this."

"When he says 'thousands,' is he exaggerating?"

"I've never known Leo Gorodetsky to exaggerate," Ben said. "Numbers are the one thing he respects and understands best. If he says thousands, plural, I believe him."

"Who would train this . . . invasion force?"

"For that, Bob, you'll need U.S. Army personnel."

Kennedy shook his head. "Jesus, Ben, overthrowing a foreign government? The United States can't be involved in anything like that!"

"Since when?"

Kennedy peered at Ben over the rim of his glass, then swallowed down the rest of the beer. "I suppose if the training cadre were CIA, we might get away with it." He placed the glass precisely on the cardboard coaster on the table. "What assurances have we that once we're involved, he won't renege on his guarantee to personally fund this operation? Leaving us with a battalion of anxious and angry Cubans, and shit all over our faces for having started the thing in the first place?"

"He said he would fund the initial stages," Ben said. "He's willing to commit ten million dollars. Now where the hell else will you find a man ready to partner in with you to overthrow a communist country?"

"For purely self-serving reasons," Kennedy said. "So he can get those casinos reopened."

"What difference does it make? You're getting what you want. With not a drop of American blood spilled."

Kennedy laughed unhumorously. "Only Marty Raab's, when he hears Gorodetsky's price for this little fantasy."

"It's worth it," Ben said. "At twice the price."

"Marty won't think so."

"I'll say it once more, Bob. What've you got to lose?"

Kennedy said nothing a moment. He stared into the empty glass. "I'll have to talk to the President."

"Order another round," Ben said, rising. "I promised Leo I'd call him with your answer."

Robert Kennedy watched Ben walk across the room to the telephones. The attorney general was already composing his explanation to Martin Raab.

Martin Raab knew of Leo's Florida move almost before the supervisor of Leo's Central Park West apartment building. That Leo had rented a small house in South Miami Beach was slightly surprising, but nothing compared to what awaited Raab three weeks later in the attorney general's office.

Kennedy gestured Raab into a chair and came straight to the point. "What's the status of the Leo Gorodetsky case?"

"It's ready to go to the grand jury."

"I'm taking you off the case."

Raab thought he was joking, but Kennedy did not laugh. "You're serious," Raab said.

Kennedy said, "I'd like the file, if you don't mind."

"Excuse me, Mr. Attorney General, but I do mind. I've got this man cold. On jury tampering, with my key witness safe and sound on a military base, guarded round the clock. There is no way I can lose!"

"Marty, please, bear with me," Kennedy said. "I can't tell you why yet, but the case can't go to the jury—"

"—you'll have to tell me why. I goddam insist!"

"I can't."

"Then I can't cooperate. No one, nothing, will stop me this time."

Robert Kennedy looked at Martin Raab a long, hard moment, then said coldly, "I'm sorry, Mr. Raab, something will stop you. Me. Your direct superior. And I'm ordering you to surrender the file."

"Sir, I must insist on an explanation."

"Damn it, Marty! It's in the national interest! Isn't that good enough for you?"

"I'm supposed to just forget it, is that it?"

"That's it, yes."

"For how long?"

"For the time being, Mr. Raab, Leo Gorodetsky is an untouchable," Kennedy said. "All surveillance and wiretaps are to be immediately removed. Is that understood?"

"What does 'for the time being' mean?"

Kennedy looked away at the desk top and shuffled some papers aimlessly. "I'm appointing you head of a strike force in Las Vegas." He looked up again. "To clean the city of Mafia influence."

" 'Mafia!' " The word exploded disdainfully from Raab's lips. "You know very well the 'Mafia' is nothing but a catchall phrase, an all-purpose villain. The real criminal power in this country has as much to do with the Mafia as I do with the Women's Christian Temperance Union! Now what in the hell is this all about?"

"I can't tell you yet," Kennedy said. "I'm sorry."

Words he dared not utter flowed into Raab's mind. You've been bought, you son of a bitch, just like your father! The whole corruptible lot of you!

Kennedy read his thoughts. "I will say this just once more, Mr. Raab. The order I have issued is in the interests of national security. It has the President's approval. If you don't choose to cooperate, I'll regretfully accept your resignation." Kennedy rose. "Good day, sir."

Martin Raab returned to his office where a report awaited him of the latest surveillance on Leo Gorodetsky. It contained little of real significance, a routine review of Leo's movements in Florida, including the not too surprising information of the subject's daily contact with former high-ranking officials of the deposed Batista government.

The report was so thorough it mentioned Esther Gorodetsky's hospitalization with a tentative diagnosis of Alzheimer's syndrome, even providing an explanation of that illness: ". . . a sometimes debilitating condition known to hasten the aging process." Also noted was Leo's purchase of a yacht, the *Meredith II*, for a cash price of $175,000.

Martin Raab inserted the report into the bulging file labeled u.s. v.

GORODETSKY, then summoned his secretary to hand-deliver the package to the attorney general. Then he switched on his dictaphone and dictated a memo ordering the immediate cessation of all surveillance and telephone taps on subject Leo Gorodetsky.

3.

They first saw the schooner at a West Palm Beach yacht broker's slip. They were on an innocent Sunday-afternoon drive, one of the infrequent days Leo was not off on a mysterious errand with former Cuban friends and business associates. By now of course Renata knew that the men training so hard on the beaches of nearby Coconut Grove, and its marshy interior, were preparing an invasion of Cuba.

That Sunday, he said he wanted just to ride around and think. And talk. He had returned only that morning from a hurried trip to New York to put Esther into a nursing home. He wanted to sort out his feelings. He had neglected Esther, sometimes actually ignored her. And now her life was over. Renata let him talk; it made him feel better. After all, what he could he really have done to improve Esther's life? That the woman never married was now perhaps a blessing. And she did have the pleasure of helping raise Carla. Although almost surely she would never share the pleasure of Carla's child, whose birth was expected any day. When Leo mentioned Carla's pregnancy, Esther had said, "Leo, does Ellie know?"

Leo was relating this to Renata when he saw the ship. More accurately, at first, the masts. Three, riding majestically above the roofs of the buildings on the pier. For a moment he was back on the Long Island beach on the day he saw Arnold Steinberger's *Westwind*. When he envisioned her wind billowed sails pulling her serenely through the blue water, and himself straddling the deck, the fresh clean air whipping into his face with a fine mist of salt spray he could even now taste on his lips.

Meredith II, 120-feet long, was a three-masted, twin-dieseled staysail schooner. Built in 1915, a Herreshoff-designed craft, she could accommodate ten passengers in her four main cabins, and a crew of four, including a cook. Under full sail she made twenty knots, twelve on the diesels.

The yacht broker, a middle-aged man with the glib tongue and eager eyes of a securities salesman who had just spotted a live one, said *Meredith II* was owned by the scion of an oil family. The man had squandered his inheritance and needed fast cash.

"I happen to know he's in deep to the gamblers," said the yacht broker to whom Leo was obviously a total stranger. "You wouldn't believe how much he's dumped. Horses, cards, you name it."

"It's a terrible curse," Leo said. "I never gamble myself."

"Oh, come now, darling," Renata said. "What about those church bingo games?"

"That's for charity," Leo said. "That doesn't count."

The asking price was $175,000, but for cash ten or fifteen percent might be discounted. Leo said he felt charitable; he'd pay the asking price. What the hell, anybody who blew that much money gambling couldn't be all bad.

Driving away from the boatyard, Renata was aghast. What on earth did he intend to do with a boat?

"Sail on it," he said. "What do you think?"

"I thought you had enough of boats."

"This one's different," he said. "It's my own."

Later that same evening she asked him why, if he wanted a boat of his own, why a yacht? Let alone a luxury yacht, not to mention a yacht requiring a permanent crew.

"A whim," he said.

"A whim?" The word amused her. "My God, Leo, I'm surprised you didn't buy the *Queen Elizabeth*!"

"To tell the truth, I thought it might make up for that," he said. "I mean, dragging you off the cruise that way."

"Really, Leo, I told you I didn't mind."

"But you like the boat, don't you?"

"I think when it's that big it's called 'ship,'" she said. "Or is it? But, of course, I like it. I love it. How could anyone not?"

"I'm renaming her the *Renata*."

"Because she's so broad in the beam?"

He looked at her, then took a deep breath and said, "Because it's your wedding present."

"I beg your pardon?"

"I suppose this is a hell of a way to propose—" he reached for her hand. "I . . . well, that's it."

"Is this a whim, too?"

"No!"

They were in the dining room of the little South Miami Beach house, holding hands awkwardly across the table. For a moment each studied the other, then Renata looked away. She shook her head, bewildered.

"Will you?" he asked.

She turned to him. Her eyes were moist. She clasped his hand to her cheek. And then she began laughing and crying all at the same time.

"What's wrong?" he asked, alarmed.

The tears streamed down her cheeks. "I thought you'd never ask," she said.

Marrying Renata was no whim, nor sudden. The idea had been lodged in Leo's mind for years, probably since the first moment he saw her. But he had always told himself that exposing her to his kind of life was unfair. Never mind the stigma, the physical danger alone. And yet, obviously, married or not, the same danger existed, which invalidated that argument. But certainly did not invalidate the very real history of his former marriage, and the memories of Ellie asking him to quit the business, get out, live a normal life.

A normal life, whatever that meant.

They were married by a justice of the peace in Boca Raton, waiting period waived and license provided through the good offices of a Broward County commissioner whose career had begun as an IDIC casino bouncer.

Leo promised Renata a real honeymoon. In Havana, which he was confident would soon be in friendly hands. They would sail there on the *Renata* when the yacht was ready. She was up on the ways in a West Palm Beach boatyard having her hull recaulked and keel repainted.

Renata had hardly tried on the ring—a huge, five-carat emerald surrounded by diamond baguettes in a platinum frame, whose cost she refused even to begin to imagine—when Leo asked her if she objected to driving home alone. He had been invited to Coconut Grove to observe a full-scale exercise of the planned landing on the Cuban beaches. He would be taken to the beach by the man who was sole witness to the wedding, a Brooks-Brothered attired, crewcutted thirty-two-year-old former U.S. State Department employee named Carleton Embry.

"Please try to be home early, sweetheart," she said teasing, mostly for the benefit of Carl Embry, who was a little too pompous and patronizing for her taste. "You will get him home early, Mr. Embry?"

"Do my best, Mrs. Gorodetsky," Embry said. He spoke with the slightest hint of a southern drawl Renata was sure was affected. He smiled back at her. "I sure hate taking him away just after you two went and got married. Snatching him out of your arms, you might say."

"Really?" she said. "Is that what I might say?"

Carleton Embry was an All-American tackle at the University of Wisconsin, a Green Bay Packer second-round draft choice until he suffered a shoulder separation in the 1949 Ohio State game. Of course, had he played pro football, he never would have joined the CIA.

She watched them drive off in Embry's white Jaguar coupe, waving good-bye with a pleased smile that vanished immediately the car turned the corner. She resented Carl Embry's smugness. She resented him, period, but also knew he was an integral part of this project that consumed so much of Leo's time and, she knew, money.

She was mentally composing the cable to her father announcing the marriage when it occurred to her that she had been left standing on the City Hall stairs. Proverbially, of course, it was the bride-to-be left standing here. In Renata's case, the bride herself.

The "Blues," identified by blue bandannas tied to their fatigue sleeves, were the defending force. The "Whites," sporting white bandannas, stormed the beach. First, the assault boats hove into sight around the curve of the bay. Six LCIs, their U.S. Navy numbers still fadingly visible on the hulls, crammed with White troops. Immediately, the beach defenders began firing. Machine guns and mortars.

Live ammunition, carefully calibrated to fall short, but close enough to send continual geysers of water splashing into the approaching landing craft. On the beach, officers designated as referees dashed back and forth indicating shore batteries that would be knocked out by the promised U.S. Air Force and Navy air cover.

This air support, however, was what Carl Embry termed a "worst case scenario," necessary only if the invasion force somehow lost its advantage of surprise, a contingency not anticipated. The invaders would come ashore shortly before dawn, quickly securing the beachhead and moving inland with their jeeps and APCs. They would join up with counter-revolutionary units already rolling to meet them, driving Castro's defenders into a pincers that would squeeze them like a nutcracker.

A piece of cake.

With Embry and several insurgent staff officers, Leo observed the exercise from a promontory two hundred yards away. One officer elatedly pounded Leo's shoulder.

"Soon, Leo, we are back at El Conquistador! And the girls will dance again, and the wheels spin, and we all live like human beings again!"

His name was Esteban Machado. A former major of the National Police, he had narrowly evaded capture and certain execution. In Havana, he was notorious for his high living, much of it subsidized by various casino managers. Just prior to the revolution he fell madly in love with a beautiful show girl. She was still in Cuba, at a special camp for the rehabilitation of prostitutes.

Machado swore undying gratitude and loyalty to Leo for his support of the anti-Castro movement. It embarrassed Leo because he never particularly liked the man. He knew him as a pimp and thief, and not the only one here. Many, despite now willingly risking their lives, in Havana had lived off the stupidity and cupidity of others.

But these were really only a handful. Most of the Brigade—and Leo found this quite revealing—had been workers, ordinary laborers whose living conditions under Castro certainly could be no worse than under Batista. Taxi drivers, waiters, house painters, gardeners, store clerks. Few had actual military experience. Two months ago when training began they were flabby from a year of inactivity and soft Miami living. Now they were tough and hard, determined to liberate their country, absolutely convinced that once on Cuban soil they would be joined by thousands, and then tens of thousands of other patriots. Castro's revolution was finished.

After the exercise everyone returned to the camp for midday chow. Leo watched them line up at the mess tent. Beside him, Major Machado struck a match for Carl Embry's cigarette.

Embry inhaled luxuriously, then waved the cigarette at the men in the chow line. He said to Leo, "My guys say they're almost ready."

Leo disliked Embry even more than Renata did, especially the man's occasional comparisons of this operation with Leo's Israeli involvement. Leo appeared to be a perennial backer of the underdog, said Embry, a trait he claimed to admire in Jews. The difference between Jews and Cubans, said Embry, was Jews really stuck together. With these Cubans, you couldn't be sure half weren't communist spies.

Leo, knowing Embry was baiting him, had so far resisted taking the bait. But later, when their objective was attained, he might indulge himself in a little baiting of his own. Mr. Carleton Embry might well find himself sitting in a CIA office somewhere in the Alaskan tundra. Or the Arabian desert.

Leo said to Embry, "They look more than almost ready. They look like they could go right now."

"Man, you can say that again!" Machado said. He jabbed Embry's arm. "Listen, you put us on the beach tonight, I guarantee that in twelve hours we're marching down the Prado!" He jabbed Leo's arm. "If only the general could see them, eh, Leo!"

The general, Batista, was in Spain. Rumor said he did not wish to return. Leo was undisturbed; he had others in mind for the presidency, men less greedy and more amenable to the reforms needed for a truly stable Cuban government. The casinos could function far more efficiently and profitably under a liberal, less corruptible regime.

Leo said, "Yes, the general would be proud of them."

So was Leo. Every time he saw them, he could not help thinking, My army. My own personal army! Bought and paid for from his own pocket. He felt like an old-time emperor or warlord. He did not dislike the feeling.

He said to Embry now, "When do you think they'll go?"

Embry regarded him narrowly. "Now, Mr. Gorodetsky, that ain't exactly a question you should be asking. Nor one I'd be answering. When it's time for you to know, you'll be told."

Leo glanced at Machado, who looked away, embarrassed, as Embry went on, ". . . you know how they say, loose lips sink ships!"

Leo felt himself redden. He gestured Embry aside so they could talk privately. He knew he was being manipulated, and hated himself for allowing it, but could not help himself.

He said, "You know something? I'm tired of you acting like you're doing me a favor even letting me come here to see these people! You know goddam good and well that without my money, my hard cash, none of this would be happening!"

Embry stared incredulously at Leo; it was almost as though Leo had committed some breach of ethics. Leo continued, "You don't want to reveal operative information, I can understand it. I shouldn't have asked, you're right. But just say it like a gentleman, not some two-bit, asshole, self-important bureaucrat!"

" 'Your money'!" Embry hurled away his cigarette. "You know how long 'your money' lasts in this thing?" The southern drawl was tinged with disdain. "A month, maybe. Maybe! We're dumping five times what you put into it! And if we need air cover, there's no by God way to compute the cost. So wise up, mister, huh?"

"I said," Leo said quietly, "if I hadn't started it, it wouldn't have happened."

"Mr. Gorodetsky, sir"—Embry deliberately slurred the "sir"—"the United States government would have mounted an operation such as this with or without you. You just happen to provide the perfect front. If it succeeds, it'll officially be credited to some privately financed, anti-communist Cuban superpatriots. Your name won't be mentioned, because we assume you wouldn't want it known that you paid men to lose their lives so you could get your casinos reopened. But if it fails, now that's a whole other bag of worms. Then, you can be damn sure we'll put out the word loud and clear of you being behind it! You'll make a perfect fall guy, Mr. Gorodetsky, sir!"

Leo could not believe the man so stupid as to be goaded into such an admission. Only long afterward did he realize Carleton Embry was far from stupid, and had not been goaded. He wanted Leo to know all this, to know how he was being used. It was their way of putting the rich little kike in his place.

But all Leo knew then, and truly cared about, was that with the U.S. government behind the operation it could not fail. So his $10 million was well spent. It was about to generate a return of at least six times the investment, the $60 million value of the stolen Cuban properties.

Leo and Carl Embry might have both reconsidered their positions had they followed Esteban Machado into Miami Beach later that same night, to the crowded bar of the Eden Roc Hotel. The major, now in a dapper white-linen suit, ordered a cuba libre and made conversation with a couple of American girls, hookers, who indignantly refused his offer of twenty dollars each. He bought them a drink and excused himself to go to the men's room.

There, while urinating, he lit a cigarette. The last one in the pack, which he crumpled and tossed into the sand-filled ash receptacle adjoining the shoeshine stand. The men's-room attendant, a handsome young black man, himself a recent Cuban refugee, handed Machado a towel. The major washed, flipped the attendant a quarter tip, and left.

The attendant waited until another patron left and the room was empty. Then he retrieved the crumpled cigarette pack from the ash stand. He smoothed it out, separated the glued seams, and peeled away the silver foil. On the reverse, blank side of the wrapper was a hand-written Spanish notation. The attendant read it, then ripped the paper in two, and then again. He stepped into the nearest toilet stall and flushed the pieces down the bowl. What it said was *Bahía de Cochinos. 18/4.*

Bay of Pigs. April 18.

4.

On the morning of Tuesday, April 18, the *Renata* was anchored just off Sand Key, outside the Key West bight. Leo sat on the sun bright deck listening to three different radios, all reporting the invasion. The force had sailed the previous evening and, as per plan, landed in the dark shortly before dawn.

At the Bay of Pigs.

And was being decimated.

Embry had phoned thirty minutes earlier from Key West after returning from an aerial reconnaissance of the landing area. ". . . fucking disaster! They were waiting for us!"

"What do you mean, 'waiting'?" Leo shouted into the phone. "How could they have been waiting?"

"Can't you understand plain English, Leo?" Embry's voice was hoarse and weary. "They knew exactly where we were going! When, and how!"

Leo said nothing a moment. From the radio at that same moment a somber commentator's report of "extremely high casualties among the invading force." Over the phone, Embry heard the commentator's voice and confirmed the statement. "They've been cut to pieces," he said. "It's all fucking over!"

"Where's the air support?" Leo asked.

"Canceled!" Embry said.

They spoke a few more moments, then Leo hung up and gave the marine operator Ben Sylbert's telephone number in Las Vegas. The connection was surprisingly fast. Ben, also listening to the reports, was equally dismayed. Leo asked him to call his contact in Washington and demand air support. They had promised it if needed. It was needed.

Ben was back to him in less than thirty minutes. "It's no go, Leo. The President himself canceled it. What I think happened is he got cold feet."

"Ben, those poor bastards were promised air support! We've double-crossed them!"

What he meant to say, but could not bring himself to, was *I* double-crossed them. He, Leo. But his mind refused to accept this, no more than it accepted the fact that he had once again been beaten by Fidel Castro.

After that, it was like a row of dominoes. Within a week, he was talking with Ben again, only now face to face. In Nassau, where Leo had ordered the *Renata* to sail directly from Key West. The boat was moored at her slip in Nassau Harbor when Ben arrived. He had flown in from Las Vegas.

With information too sensitive for the telephone. ". . . they're preparing an indictment," Ben said. "Jury tampering. The Stohlmeyer case."

Ben and Leo were seated at a garden table on the canvas-covered fantail. Renata had entered with a tray of drinks just in time to hear Ben say it. She gasped, and seemed to falter. Both men jumped up to steady her. Ben took the tray and placed it on the table. Leo helped her into a chair.

"Does that mean they'll arrest him?"

"They'll issue a warrant the moment the indictment is handed down," Ben said.

Leo's eyes were cold. "Your friend double-crossed you."

"Leo, he never promised to kill the case," Ben said. "Yes, I'm sure he'd have done it if the invasion came off. But now with the papers filled with those headlines—" Ben swung his attaché case up onto the table and opened it. He brought out a week-old copy of the *Las Vegas Review-Journal*. He spread it on the table in front of Leo.

CUBAN INVASION FINANCED
BY GAMBLING KINGPIN?

Leo glanced at the headline. "The one in your paper must have been in red, in twenty-point type."

"I didn't run the story," Ben said.

"You're compromising your journalistic integrity."

"Just the opposite," said Ben. "I'd have compromised it if I had run the goddam thing. Because it's a half-truth, and I can't tell the story as I happen to know it. The whole, true story."

"But you are compromising," Renata said. "By not telling the real story. That the United States government sanctioned the invasion, and then backed out."

"I gave my word," Ben said. "Them breaking their word gives me no license to do the same."

Leo measured a quarter teaspoonful of sugar and stirred it into the iced-tea glass. "Leaving me the patsy," he said quietly, almost sadly.

"Leo, why do you think my—" Ben paused, searching for the proper phrase. "My source. Why do you think my source tipped me about the indictment?"

"I'm asking myself the same question," Leo said. "I know it's not because he's so fond of me."

"He's giving you a chance to leave the country before the warrant can be served," Ben said.

Leo could not help smiling. "Everybody wants me to take a vacation. Now even the attorney general of United States."

"Listen, it was decent of him to give me advance notice," Ben said.

"Oh, yes, these are real decent people," Leo said. "Salt of the earth." He shook his head sadly. "And they call me a criminal. They don't even think twice about condemning a couple of hundred good men. You know how many got killed in the invasion, Ben? More than three hundred, I'm told! And the ones captured, another few hundred. Right now they're probably facing firing squads." He slammed his fist on the table, nearly upsetting the tea glass. "All because they wouldn't send the airplanes they promised. The rotten pricks!" He glanced apologetically at Renata. "I'm sorry."

"That's all right," she said. "I quite agree."

For a moment the three sat silently. Beyond the pier, over the roofs of the smaller whitewashed buildings, the windows of the top floors of the big hotels glinted in the sun. Soon, hopefully within the year, replacing the lost Cuban properties, two new IDIC hotels would be built. Construction to commence the instant the Bahamas was granted Commonwealth status. Sir Sidney Coleman would be the first governor. IDIC and Sir Sidney were partners.

Ben read Leo's thoughts. He said, "Leo, if you tried to duck the indictment by staying here, the publicity might kill your chances for a casino license. You have to wait somewhere else until things cool down."

"It seems I spend half my life waiting for things to cool down," Leo said. "Is that your best advice, Ben?"

"It's good advice," Ben said.

Leo nodded. He looked at Renata. "You know what I think we might do?" He looked at Ben again. "I have a granddaughter I'd like to see. In Israel. She's six weeks old."

"Five weeks," Renata corrected. She smiled. "And three days."

"Her name is Sari," Leo said to Ben. "Sari, Hebrew for Sarah. After my mother. Yes, I think that's what we'll do." The decision, now made, pleased him. "When Avi phoned about the child, I was listening to him and I suddenly realized that we attain immortality through our progeny. Generation after generation."

"Like a relay race," Ben said.

Leo said nothing. He was thinking of the men slaughtered on the Cuban beaches and wondering if they died content knowing their immortality was perpetuated through their children and grandchildren. He doubted it.

Leo also wondered who betrayed the landings. He never did learn, and had he been in the United States a few weeks later almost surely would have been unaware of a small item in the *Miami Herald*. The body of an unidentified man, a Latin thought to be a Cuban refugee, was discovered in a downtown alley. Although robbery was suspected as a motive, the means of death—a single bullet in the back of the head— suggested political assassination.

The dead man was Esteban Machado, whom Leo had assumed was killed or captured in the landing. But even if Leo had somehow known of Machado's Miami death, he could not possibly have known that the execution was carried out by Carleton Embry. Or that a year later, on a New Orleans street, Embry himself would be murdered by agents of Fidel Castro.

A relay race.

* * *

They left the *Renata* in Nassau and flew to Tel Aviv. The instant Leo looked into Sari Schiff's brown eyes—Gorodetsky eyes—he knew his theory of immortality was correct. The little girl had his strong mouth, and Carla's firm chin. She was the most beautiful creature he had ever seen. He could recall no such overwhelming feelings about his own children, but realized that in those day he had been much too preoccupied with himself and his survival. Now he could afford the luxury of enjoying a small child of his own flesh and blood.

He and Renata rented a small house outside Tel Aviv, in Herzliya, supposedly the Malibu of the city. A lovely stucco house on the beach, just off the coastal highway, with a garden and a cluster of orange trees.

He liked Tel Aviv. The museums, the sidewalk cafés, the symphony concerts, the beach where he walked daily—accompanied by a handsome golden retriever pup he purchased for Sari. Because she was much too young to appreciate such a dog, the dog, named Zahav, "gold" in Hebrew, became Leo's.

They had been in Israel three months when George Gerson phoned from New York to say the indictment was finally handed down. But Leo was safely out of their jurisdiction. They could whistle. That very evening he took Renata into Tel Aviv to celebrate. They had dinner at a little restaurant in Jaffa, owned by Arabs who really knew how to broil lamb and prepare mouth-watering *humus tahini* (every bit as good as Golda Meir's, whom he had not yet contacted, but planned to shortly).

After dinner they went to the new Sheraton on the beach for a glass of champagne. Everything was going well now. The dominoes were once again upright. Gerson had discovered where the government held their witness, Albert Collins. On a military base, exact location soon to be determined, as would a method of successfully resolving the problem.

You do not question the morality of dealing harshly with a blackmailer, which was precisely what Albert Collins was. After accepting money for a service, he had demanded further payment for silence. He was a fool. You do not suffer fools—or blackmailers. They suffer.

Yes, all was good. Even the Cuban fiasco was a fast-fading memory. So he lost. Not the first time, undoubtedly not the last. You take the good with the bad. And Nassau would replace Havana. There was also Tahoe. He had always considered that northern Nevada mountain resort unattractive to high rollers, but now thought he might study it more carefully

They left the Sheraton and walked along the Esplanade. Directly below, a line of automobile headlights snaked around the roadway toward the Hayarkon Street exit ramp. It was a lovely evening, warm and clear for December. So clear you could see the mirrored reflection on the surface of the water from the lights of ships anchored far offshore.

He stopped and leaned against the concrete rail to gaze out at the distant lights. "Reminds you of the *Renata*, doesn't it?" he said. "We should have brought her over here."

"And taught Franco to cook kosher," Renata said. Franco was the *Renata*'s black cook; his specialty was Cajun fare, and he was continually dismayed at Leo's insistence on milder food.

"Listen, why don't we do that? Bring the boat here?" Leo said, and at that instant felt the pain.

A gigantic vise squeezing his chest. The exact center of his chest. He could not breathe, and saw the sky roll around as the vise crushed his chest and ribs. He had never known such pain and opened his mouth to scream but could not scream because the vise had now clamped his throat.

There was a scream. Renata's. But he never heard it. He heard only a roaring in his ears like an approaching express train, louder, louder, louder. It drowned out all other sound, and then all sight.

And then the roaring decreased, and the sight returned. He saw the sky, but blurred, as though through a rain streaked window. Now, too, voices. He could not understand a single word. The pain had lessened; now it was only a constant dull throb through his whole body. He felt himself being lifted, and his jacket being removed and his sleeve rolled up. He knew he was in an ambulance because he heard the tires rumbling on the road surface and felt the plastic object, which he knew was an oxygen mask, placed over his mouth and nose.

He felt very sleepy. He wondered where Renata was, and then saw her bending over him. She seemed so far away he thought he was looking at her through the wrong end of binoculars. His last thought before falling asleep was that he was in the relay race, rushing to hand the baton to the next runner, who was nowhere in sight.

27

GERSON was not immediately aware of the big Lincoln sedan parked in front of the house; he had hardly realized they were off the Parkway and already in Riverdale, let alone on Whitney Lane. Joseph, from the Imperial's front seat, quietly called his attention to it.

Although the streetlights were on, enough daylight remained to see the white picket fence of the Cape Cod cottage at the far end of the street. He knew Betty was home; her Olds convertible was in the driveway. For one shameful instant he seriously considered ordering Joseph to turn around and drive off, telling himself that whatever Vincent Tomasino's reason for coming here, certainly no harm would come to Betty.

But he said nothing. He sat up and peered through the windshield as Joseph leaned to the right and opened the Imperial's glove compartment. A shaft of light from the glove compartment gleamed off the long-barreled .357 Magnum Joseph slid onto his lap. Joseph's eyes remained on the parked Lincoln now, and the young man standing casually at the Lincoln's right front fender.

"What do you want me to do?" Joseph asked.

Gerson wanted to say, "I'm too tired to think." And he truly was exhausted. All day at the office, continually at the telephone. Four calls alone to Avi Schiff in Tel Aviv. Leo had a fifty-fifty chance. Myocardial infarction. A gigantic heart attack that should have killed him, probably would have killed an ordinary man. The next seventy-two hours would tell the story.

Gerson said to Joseph, "Just pull up as though nothing is wrong." His hands were wet and clammy. He wiped them on the leather seat, which did not help, then on his trousers. "Stay in the car, I'll let myself out."

Joseph pulled the Imperial in behind Betty's Olds. Gerson opened the door and got out. He gazed across the Imperial's hood at the young man standing outside the Lincoln. The young man nodded politely. Gerson wiped his palms on his trousers again and started up the walk to the front door.

Opening the door, he thought of the day's other phone calls. From Vegas, the Barclay's manager, Art Lewis, informing him of the arrival of three New York men. Vincent Tomasino's people. What the hell were they doing there, and what should Lewis do about it? Gerson told him to sit tight, and then almost immediately took another call. From the Oasis. Same situation.

Betty met him in the hall. She was pale and rigid. "We have a visitor," she said.

Gerson put his arm around her. "It's all right," he said, and started into the library.

Betty grasped his wrist. "George, any change with Leo?"

"No," he said. "I'll talk to you later about it."

The library was his favorite room, and the one that twenty years ago sold him on the house. Mahogany-paneled, with built-in bookshelves on three walls. The most pleasant hours of his life were spent in this room.

Vincent Tomasino sat almost primly on the oversized, tufted leather divan. He rose, hand extended. "George," he said somberly.

"Vinnie, how are you?"

"What do you hear from Leo?"

"He's the same," Gerson said, shaking hands, embarrassed because his own hand was so moist and Vinnie's hand, withdrawn quickly, was cool and dry. He knew Vinnie sensed his fear. It made him feel all the more helpless. "Sit down."

"Sorry to barge in on you like this," Vinnie said, sitting again. "But it's important."

Gerson sank into a leather lounge chair and forced himself to look directly at Vinnie. The face he loathed, the thick red mottled skin, the tiny glittering eyes behind the horn-rimmed glasses.

"We have to talk," Vinnie said.

Gerson nodded.

Vinnie cleared his throat. "The Council has decided that under the circumstances—I mean, after what's happened with Leo, there's no choice but make sure our interests are protected—"

"—your interests *are* protected, Vinnie."

"—so there'll have to be a change of management in the casinos."

"That's why your men are in Vegas now?"

"Yeah." Vinnie rose once more and stood looking down at Gerson. 'I hope there won't be no trouble."

Which, Gerson thought, was certainly putting it straight on the line. He strained to keep his voice level. "What about Leo's interests? He's six thousand miles away in a hospital, and you're moving in on him."

"George—" Vinnie began, and paused abruptly. It was as though he had decided his approach was unsatisfactory, and wanted to start all over again. "Look, it's time we got realistic about everything. I mean, that's the point, isn't it? The man is flat on his back, out of it. It's like the captain of the ship all of a sudden not there anymore. Well, somebody has to take the wheel, right?"

"He's been away for months," George said. "Everything's gone smoothly, everything's working. So why rock the boat?" He could not help smiling with the nautical image. "Everything's shipshape."

Vinnie said almost gently, "The Jews are out, George. That's all there is to it."

Gerson opened his mouth to speak, but Vinnie waved him silent. "Now don't start giving me all the bullshit about how ungrateful all us Italians are, and how you Jews made all the *gelt* for us poor dumb wops. Well, Georgie boy, we both know you couldn't have done it without us. No way! We got married, and we lived together happy and prosperous. But now it's time for the divorce. And please don't tell me how we're taking advantage of a situation—"

There was a soft knock at the door. Betty Gerson entered. "Excuse me, I wondered if perhaps I couldn't get you something? A drink, Mr. Tomasino?"

"Not for me, thank you, Mrs. Gerson. I'm fine."

"It's all right, Betty," Gerson said. "Everything's all right." He smiled reassuringly, but Betty remained in the doorway. "Go ahead, dear, we'll be through soon." Betty stepped uncertainly away, and Gerson called after her. "Tell Joseph to hang around. I might need him."

Betty stood another uncertain moment, then left. Vinnie said, "Joseph? Your nigger driver?"

"I usually send him home after he drops me off at night," Gerson said.

"So why do you think you'll need him?"

"I might have to go back into town," Gerson said. He felt foolish, as though caught in a lie.

"Oh," Vinnie said, as though believing it. He glanced at the closed door, then sat down again. "Now, George, as far as Leo goes, he's an old man. An *alter kocker*." He grinned; he enjoyed using Yiddish expressions with the Jews; it made them uncomfortable. "He's got all the money he'll ever need, believe me, more than all of us together. He don't have a beef, you know it. He's still a partner, and he'll still keep getting dividends." Once more, Vinnie paused to think, and then carefully added, "Except we'll have to do something about that sooner or later. I mean, we'll buy him out. All legal and fair, I give you my word."

Gerson's attorney's mind selected and discarded arguments, but it was like trying a case whose verdict was already in. He said, "Just how do you plan to deal with the Gaming Commission? They won't let you simply walk in with a new management."

"IDIC will sell the casinos to a new corporation," Vinnie said. "You know how everything in Vegas is getting to be all corporations. Ours is as pure as GM."

"You're kidding yourself," Gerson said. "They'll go through the papers and sooner or later find the real owners. Then you'll have ninety days to dissolve. We'll all end up on the street."

"George, it would take a dozen Wall Street lawyers two dozen years to plow through all the companies and holding companies and partnerships. Don't worry about it."

"IDIC can sell only if Leo, who's the majority stockholder, approves," Gerson said. "I'm not so sure he will."

"The man had a heart attack," Vinnie said. "He's too sick to do his job. Not only that, he's out of the country and he can't come back. I got a feeling that under those conditions he can be voted out of a management position. He'll still have his stock, but no control. Don't forget, there are laws in this country that protect the other stockholders," he added quite seriously.

"It'll take time for all the legal machinery to move," Gerson said. "The applications, the board meetings, all of it. It's not as simple as your people moving in, and ours moving out.

"George, IDIC is not a public corporation. They can hire anybody they want, as long as the names get approved by the Gaming Commission," Vinnie said, and smiled. "And they will."

"What you're asking is that we make it easy for you," Gerson said. "The trouble is, I can't speak for Leo."

"We're in no hurry, George. I just want my guys out there on the spot to . . . observe. And then when they get the word, they can move right in. Like Paul said this morning, it should be a smooth transition."

Gerson said, "I'll have to repeat myself, Vinnie. I can't speak for Leo."

Vinnie shook his head. "I don't expect you to, George. All I want from you is to see your people cooperate. That's all. No problems, please." He smiled again and held out his hands. "Okay?"

No problems, Gerson thought. The very words renewed his strength and courage. Vinnie feared "problems," which meant he realized Leo's organization was still strong enough to fight. But how to fight? Shoot them all down with machine guns? All that went out ten years ago, twenty. Or did it?

Gerson said, "I'll tell our people in Vegas."

He hated himself for saying it, but had no choice. At least not until he could consult with Leo. If, indeed, Leo could ever again be consulted. It was at that moment, perhaps for the very first time in all the years,

George Gerson realized how helpless he was—how helpless they all were—without Leo.

The ship's captain.

2.

From his window in the west wing of the hospital Leo could see all Tel Aviv spread out below. During the day the city sparkled in the sun. At night it glowed. Even from here, he felt its vitality. It, like him, was alive, and whenever he thought of this he placed his hand on his heart to feel the beat.

Not that he was surprised to be alive; he never once had doubted his ability to survive the heart attack. He knew he would. Not that it could not happen to him; it could, and would, but not this time.

He had been in the hospital two weeks, and thought about this each day, and was thinking about it again now, standing at the window gazing out at the lights of the distant city. It was past midnight, so although he immediately recognized the voice, the presence of another person in the room startled him.

"You've already had your exercise today. Why aren't you in bed?" It was Avi, in the doorway, leaning against the doorframe. His green surgical gown was splotched with blood. The mask hung from his neck like a sweat-stained ascot.

"Who'd you slice up this time?" Leo asked.

"Some poor bastard with a ruptured spleen," Avi said. "A crazy taxi driver. Drove his cab into a light standard in Allenby Square. Drunk. Got me up out of a sound sleep."

"Nobody forced you to go to medical school," Leo said.

"Get back in bed, for Christ's sake," Avi said, walking over and smoothing down the bed sheets. "The nurse comes in and finds you running around she'll call me and get me out of another sound sleep!"

Leo got back into bed and drew the covers up around him. "How about a cigarette?" he asked.

"I'll have a few cartons sent in," Avi said. He sank wearily into a chair beside the bed. "You look good."

"Thanks," Leo said. "When do I get out?"

"Two weeks," Avi said. "Maybe less. We'll see."

"I want out now," Leo said. "I feel fine."

"What's your hurry?"

"Life," Leo said. "Living."

"That's interesting," said Avi. "I've yet to see a man recovering from an MI"—he raised a cautionary finger—"*if* he recovers, who doesn't regard life and living with a new, far more perceptive clarity. They have a fresh respect and appreciation for life and its fragility. They no longer take it for granted."

"We had that conversation, Doctor," Leo said. "The first day I was out of intensive care."

"I know," said Avi. "I always give the speech at least three times during a patient's hospitalization. As they feel stronger, they tend to forget."

"I have to get out of here," Leo said.

"You will," Avi said. He pushed himself up out of the chair. "Two more weeks."

"At least get me a telephone. I have urgent business."

"Your only urgent business right now is to stay quiet," Avi said, leaving. "Don't get out of bed anymore tonight. Not even for the can. Use the bedpan."

Leo stayed awake long after Avi left. He had refused the nightly sedative, so knew he would not immediately sleep, but he was not tired anyway. He wanted a telephone. He wanted to talk to Gerson, and to Vincent Tomasino and Paul Calvelli. He knew something was happening in Vegas. It was only common sense. His illness had provided the Alliance the chance for the move they had waited years to make. He decided to demand Avi discharge him.

Renata and Carla were there the following afternoon when Avi came in. Leo, sitting in an easy chair in robe and slippers, rose to confront him.

"I feel fine. I want to go home."

"That's all he's talked about since we've been here," Renata said. "Will you please explain the facts of life to him? I mean life with a capital 'L.' "

"I did," Avi said. "Last night."

Carla said, "Daddy, please stop being so stubborn. You're acting like a child."

"Thank you," Leo said, and to Avi, "Do you discharge me, or do I just walk out?"

Avi glanced unhappily at Renata. He sighed. "All right. I'll discharge you."

"Avi!" Carla said, shocked.

But Avi knew what he was doing. He watched interestedly as Leo brushed past Renata and Carla to the closet. Leo removed his shirt, jacket, and slacks from the hangers and carried them into the bathroom. He closed the door behind him.

"Why are you letting him do it?" Renata asked Avi.

Avi placed a finger to his lips for silence and nodded at the bathroom door. All watched the door, waiting. It opened now, slowly. Leo appeared, pale and shaken. His shirt, buttoned crookedly, was on over his pajama bottoms. He clutched the towel rack on the rear of the door for support. He gasped for breath.

Both women, alarmed, started out of their chairs toward Leo.

"It's all right," Avi said calmly, gesturing them not to assist Leo 'Slightly tired, are you, Leo?"

"I'm fine," Leo said. "I just need to rest a second.'

"Yes," Avi said. "Why don't you get back into bed? You'll feel much better."

"Don't worry about it," Leo said. He stepped away from the door. He stood a moment, then started across the room. All at once he swerved and reached behind him to grasp the bathroom door handle.

"Avi!" Renata cried angrily.

"Maybe he's right," Leo said. His voice was weak, almost distant. "I'll get back in bed for a minute."

Renata helped him remove his shirt while Carla retrieved the pajama top from the bathroom floor. The women helped Leo into the top, buttoned it, and then got him back into bed.

"Why did you let him do it?" Carla asked Avi. "He could have had another attack!"

"The only attack he'll have is one of intelligence," Avi said. He looked at Leo. "He's intelligent enough, I'm sure, to recognize his own limitations. Am I correct, Mr. Gorodetsky?"

Leo was still weak, but spoke with conviction. "If there's one thing I can't stand, it's a smartass Jewish doctor!"

Whether or not he recognized his own limitations then, or indeed ever, he did recognize for the first time the seriousness of this particular heart attack, and for the first time it frightened him.

Because he knew he had pressed the luck. The sucker play. He had won, but was not clever enough to quit. He felt frail and vulnerable, amateurish, playing into his enemies' hands. He could not beat them as an old, sick man. And certainly not as a dead one.

No, live to fight another day.

He stayed in bed another two weeks. He did speak with George Gerson, whom Avi had explicitly instructed not to discuss business. Gerson stubbornly evaded Leo's questions, although with Avi's permission informed Leo of Esther's deterioration. She weighed less than ninety pounds and recognized no one. The real tragedy was that she might linger this way for years.

Leo recuperated steadily. But not for three months, until the spring of 1962, did Avi pronounced him fully recovered, although with some residual problems. Mild angina, hypertension, and the start of a duodenal ulcer. But for all of this, he felt better than he had in years. And with good reason. He had after all beaten another count, the biggest one of all.

In April, George Gerson and his wife came to Israel. With dozens of papers and tax forms, stock proxies, and other business matters to be reviewed. Including certain power-of-attorney transfers for Esther's affairs. She had the best of care, and now they could only wait for her to die.

Gerson completed these matters before presenting Leo the really bad news: he had been ousted from the Council. Voted out, with the casinos for all practical purposes under full Alliance management.

The day was overcast, but warm. Renata had taken Betty Gerson into Tel Aviv to visit Carla and the baby, and George had accompanied Leo on his daily three-mile walk on the beach. Afterward they drove into Herzliya for lunch. Leo, defying Avi's orders to avoid eggs, ordered a mushroom omelet. What the hell, Gerson's visit was an occasion.

"Yes, I suppose it is," Gerson said, and took a deep, careful breath. And told him about the Alliance.

For all Leo's reaction, Gerson might have been discussing John F. Kennedy's threat to enforce public-school integration with federal troops in Mississippi and Alabama. Or even repeating Joe Valachi's fanciful tales of the Cosa Nostra, which Leo had read about in the American newspapers and found so amusing.

When Gerson finished, Leo said, "It doesn't surprise me."

"It doesn't seem to bother you, either," Gerson said.

Leo poked at the omelet. "Too well done. I hate overcooked eggs." He pushed the plate away. "You're wrong, it does bother me. But what can I do about it? I can't set foot back in the States. By the way, what about the janitor, Collins? Have you reached him yet?"

"We're working on it."

"You put Jack Maynard on it?"

"Oh, yes. He's on it."

"Then I'm not worried," Leo said. "But I'll tell you something. Whether or not Jack is successful, if he reaches Collins or not, I think I'm beginning to accept the reality of my own situation. Now what do you think of that?"

"I think it's terrific," Gerson said. He wanted to believe Leo, but knew him too well. Although hearing Leo's next words, Gerson began thinking that perhaps Leo might be accepting the realities after all.

". . . so I'm not top dog anymore," he was saying. "So what? Listen, I got off the tiger and it didn't eat me up. I have money, and now I have my health. And a wife I love, who loves me."

No, Gerson thought suspiciously. It is just too much, too easy. I do not believe him. But even as Gerson thought this, Leo continued, "And, George, you know what? I really like it here. I've already applied for citizenship. I have friends in high places, don't forget. Golda Meir had us to dinner last week. She said she didn't anticipate any problems. As a Jew, I'm entitled to dual citizenship. I've been thinking maybe I'd like to settle here for good. Watch my grandchildren grow up. Even my *shiksa* wife likes the country, even though she claims you can't find a decent bagel here."

"Then maybe she should have you put up a bagel plant," Gerson said dryly. "To go along with some of the other investments she asked me to make for her. Were they her idea, or yours? The chocolate factory, and a quarter of a million in that Fiat dealership?"

"I only advised her; the final decisions were hers," Leo said. "And remind me to talk to you later about one I want to make. A big one. A pharmaceutical plant. They're doing incredible things. I want to invest in the future of this country, George."

"Leo, you've got enough money to probably buy it," Gerson said. "I mean, the whole country."

"Maybe that's not such a bad idea, George." Leo said, joking. "I'll open a casino or two, eh?"

"You can't."

"Why not?"

"It's against the law," Gerson said. He grinned at Leo, appreciating his own joke.

But Leo did not grin back. "You know why I'm thinking of settling here, George?" He patted his pockets for cigarettes. A reflex. "Another law," he muttered. "No more cigarettes. Yes, let me tell you why I might live here someday. Because I think that this is a place where a Jew can enjoy the freedom of America, and at the same time be a Jew with no religious connotation. If you discount the handful of zealots and the Hassidic maniacs waiting for the Messiah, nobody gives a damn whether you believe in God or the New York Yankees or the Haifa Maccabees. You're a Jew, so you belong. It's for me, George, and I can live without the casinos."

The King is dead, Gerson thought. Long live the King. He knew he should have been pleased, and relieved, for it meant that he, too, could retire to a safe and secure old age. But seeing Leo so readily surrender saddened Gerson. It was like watching a champion involuntarily retire at his peak, not from honest defeat but from some insidious circumstance beyond his control.

Gerson should have known better.

Several months later, shortly after President Kennedy forced the Russians to remove their Cuban missiles, Gerson informed Leo that the Alliance was about to make a very generous offer for the purchase of all Leo's holdings. A buy-out. Leo was not at all disturbed, and agreed to discuss it. He asked Gerson to have Vincent Tomasino phone him.

Vinnie phoned that same day. A polite, pleasant conversation. In fact, Vinnie suggested—Leo's health permitting, of course—they meet in person. A neutral location. They could talk it all out face to face, Leo, Vinnie, and Paul Calvelli.

A date was set for the following month, in Nassau. Leo then instructed Gerson to bring $2 million in cash immediately to Nassau. A campaign contribution to the black nationalist leader, Gregory Peters. An extravagant sum, but it might almost guarantee Peters's Freedom Party a victory in the January elections.

"This is how you retire, Leo?" Gerson asked.

"Please don't argue, George," Leo said. "These calls are expensive. Oh, and round up the *Renata's* crew for me."

"You're bringing the boat to Israel?"

"No, George. She's staying right there in Nassau. I'll be entertaining on her."

3.

Paul Calvelli said, "As God is my judge, Leo, I never saw you looking better!"

"He's right," Vincent Tomasino said. "Hey, if a heart attack makes a guy look that healthy, maybe we should all have one."

"Not even in a joke," Leo said, raising his glass in a toast. They clicked glasses and drank the champagne, Leo thinking that if he could wish heart attacks on anybody it would be these two. He knew they were very uncomfortable in their street clothes, which was why he had not invited them to remove their jackets. But Vinnie did anyway, draping the jacket over the back of his chair, grimacing as his fingers brushed the jacket's armpits; they were stained with a blue-black ring of perspiration.

George Gerson came on deck, striding past the two husky young men attired in business suits standing stolidly at the fantail rail. They had accompanied Vincent Tomasino and Paul Calvelli, and at no time—not even in the bathroom—was either man out of their sight.

"Sorry to keep everybody waiting," George said. "But I had to take that call. From New York," he said to Leo. "They accepted our price on the building."

"The Central Park West apartment I lived in," Leo explained to the others. "I owned the building. We just sold it."

"*Mazel tov*," Vinnie said. "I hope you made a bundle."

"He did," Gerson said. "Now, where were we?"

"In the middle of the goddam ocean!" Vinnie said, pleased with his humor, and drinking down his champagne. Leo immediately refilled the glass. It was a mediocre vintage, but Vinnie did not know the difference. Leo simply believed the occasion demanded something more elegant than dago red.

They were not exactly in the middle of the ocean but anchored a half mile out in Nassau bay, on the *Renata*. It was a comfortably warm afternoon, with a calm but steady breeze slowly swinging the big schooner around in water so clear you could follow the anchor chain all the way down to the bottom.

Across the water, gazing past the little cat's-paws on the surface rippling gently in the wind, New Providence Island resembled an artist's painting. Small boats clustered at the pier, and the white-tiled roof of the pink Customs and Immigration Building towering over the low, flat-roofed structures lining the pier. Beyond were the larger commercial buildings in Nassau town, and beyond them, along the beach, the high-rise hotels.

Leo had been here nearly a week, without Renata. She had remained in Tel Aviv to stay with Carla who was pregnant again. Six months, and experiencing some slight staining. Avi insisted she go to bed and stay there. She felt good otherwise, and Avi was sure it would be an uncomplicated delivery. Renata's presence gave them both an additional sense of security.

Avi was not at all worried about Leo. A sixty-two-year-old man, after an MI that less than twelve months ago almost killed him, looking and acting now ten years younger. Trim, not a sign of flab, the sole concession to his age being a few more facial lines and wrinkles and slightly more gray in a nearly full head of hair.

It was this very revitalization Vincent Tomasino found so disconcerting. He had expected to see a sick, tired old man, and was therefore unprepared for Leo's initial resistance. Not at the money offered for the stock—$30 million in cash, which Leo admitted fair and generous —but Leo's attitude.

". . . so you expect me to take the money, and just walk off into the sunset?" Leo said, after the mechanics of the transfer had been explained.

Vincent Tomasino and Paul Calvelli exchanged grim glances. Paul said, "Leo, we've always respected each other. And you know that personally I couldn't be fonder of my own brother. But, Leo, we're businessmen. This is purely business."

"That's why you removed me from the Council?" Leo asked. "Because we're businessmen?"

"We removed you from the Council, Leo, for two good reasons," Vinnie said. "Your health, and your troubles with the Justice Department. Now why are you making us go all through this again?"

"I wanted to hear it from your own lips," Leo said. He enjoyed making them squirm, but cautioned himself not to be too overconfident. These were not stupid men. "I wanted to hear it firsthand."

"All right, you heard it," Vinnie said.

Leo glanced at Gerson, who looked nervously away, down at the papers piled on the table in front of his open attaché case. Gerson knew what Leo planned to say next, and disapproved.

"I still have an organization," Leo said carefully. He addressed Vinnie, and then Paul. "They're working with you right now only because I haven't told them not to. I also have my judges and policemen. Politicians, and newspapermen." He faced Vinnie again. "If I give the word, you'll have some problems."

Vinnie's face darkened. "We made you a decent offer, Leo."

"Yes, you could make problems, Leo," Paul Calvelli said. He sounded almost conciliatory. "But in the end we'll win. You have to know that."

"And a lot of your people won't ever see the light of day again," Vinnie said.

"So it's not an offer you're making me," Leo said. "It's an ultimatum."

Paul said, "For God's sake, Leo, does it have to come down to that?"

"—call it whatever you want," Vinnie said, his voice hard and flat. He glanced past Leo to the two perspiring young men as though to illustrate his point. "But unless you want those bright guys of yours splattered all over the street, you'll officially tell them you're retired. Then everybody gets to live happily ever after."

"Including you," Leo said easily.

"Yeah, Leo, including me," said Vincent Tomasino. He reached for the champagne bottle and poured himself half a glass. He drank it down in a single swallow, slammed the empty glass on the marble-topped table, and continued talking without pausing for breath. "The trouble with you, with all of you," he said, pointing at Gerson, "is you got it into your heads that nobody plays rough anymore! We're too big and too rich and too important for it now. Only the small-timers do it, the ones the FBI chases around, the drug pushers and the sharks, and the enforcers. Let me clue you in. We're still the experts. The stakes are just too big here to fuck around with, Leo!"

It was a long, loud speech, and he paused, almost as though surprised at his own vehemence. "For Christ's sake, Leo," he continued now, quieter, almost friendly. "Sit back and enjoy your old age."

For a moment no one spoke. It was so quiet the only sound was the creaking, like the squeak of tight shoes, of the masts swaying in the breeze, and the motor launch tied to the schooner's gangway stairs banging woodenly against the hull.

George Gerson said, "Let us think about it—"

"—there's nothing to think about," Vinnie said, his voice hard again.

"Vinnie's right," Paul Calvelli said. "We want an answer now. Be reasonable, Leo."

Suddenly, with no warning, Leo slammed his fist on the table. "Stop treating me like one of your soldiers! You're always telling me how we respect each other, so let's act like it! Now George asked for time to think about it. You don't want to grant us that small courtesy, then go back to New York and sit and wonder what I'll do!"

Leo's outburst startled the two young men at the rail. Paul Calvelli relaxed them with a wave of his hand as Vinnie said, "Hey, Leo, slow up. You don't want another heart attack."

"Don't worry about my heart," Leo said. "Now give me until tomorrow. You want to stay down here, you can stay on the boat, or I'll fix you up at the hotel. I'll even get you laid."

Vincent Tomasino and Paul Calvelli looked at each other. Vinnie's tiny eyes glittered coldly behind the glasses. "We'll go back to New York." He glanced at his watch. "Tomorrow, no later than three o'clock, you let me know."

"George will call you," Leo said.

Vinnie studied Leo, then nodded. It was like a signal to relax. They chatted a few moments, and then the men moved to leave. Vinnie stepped to the gangway gate. He peered down the stairs at the launch. The coxswain, Leo's schooner captain, was already at the wheel. The two young men also waited in the launch.

Vinnie said to Leo, "You don't mind, I'd like you to ride with us." He smiled narrowly. "I think you can understand."

Leo returned the smile. "Vinnie, under the circumstances, I wouldn't trust you, either. It'll be my pleasure." He said to Gerson, "You want to come along? We can have dinner ashore. Or maybe you'd rather eat on the boat?"

Gerson realized the question was rhetorical. Leo was telling him not to go ashore. He said, "I'll stay aboard. I like Franco's cooking."

"Ask him to make some game hens," Leo said. "Broiled." And he went down the stairs into the launch. Vincent Tomasino and Paul Calvelli followed.

Gerson, wondering why Leo wanted him to remain on board, watched the launch pull away. After a moment he ran into the pilot house for binoculars. He returned to the rail and trained the glasses on the launch.

The two young men in the rear were huddled over against the continual spray. Leo and the others were seated just behind the coxswain. Vincent Tomasino and Paul Calvelli looked stiff and uncomfortable in their business suits. Leo appeared quite at ease, his white knit shirt billowing in the wind, his hair flying rakishly about.

Just as the launch approached the point where it would be unseen from the boat, Gerson felt a sudden twinge of fear. He had suddenly remembered, preparing for the meeting, Leo saying that of the two, Vincent Tomasino and Paul Calvelli, Paul was the weak link. Paul, said Leo, had no stomach for trouble. If Paul was the only one to deal with, a deal could be made.

The launch rounded the point and headed straight for the pier which was busy with lobster and snapper boats in from the day's fishing. The coxswain steered the launch past the fishing vessels to the visitor's slip, sliding in behind a small Chris Craft.

As the coxswain cut the launch's engine and tossed a line up onto the pier, a small cream-colored Bahamian Constabulary car drove up and parked on the roadway immediately off the pier. Three uniformed black policemen got out. Their white pith helmets and white tunics were spotless. The brass buttons of their tunics flashed like mirrors in the sun, and their black trousers were pressed to a knife-edge crease. Their black shoes gleamed.

The policemen walked toward the arriving launch. Leo stepped onto the pier, turning to give Vinnie a hand. Seeing the policemen, Vinnie tensed; a reflex, of course. The two young men vaulted nimbly from the launch to flank Vinnie and Paul.

One policeman raised a hand. "Which one of you gentlemen is Mr. Tomasino?"

"I'm Tomasino," said Vinnie, annoyed. Under his breath he said to Leo, "What the fuck do these jigaboos want?"

"I don't know, but for God's sake, don't start anything," Leo said, and glanced at the two young men with a warning frown.

The policeman said to Vinnie, "Sir, would you mind stepping over here, please?" He indicated an area on the pier near the Chris Craft.

"What seems to be the problem, Corporal?" Leo asked the policeman. "This man is my guest."

"A few questions, that's all," the policeman said. "Routine."

Leo said quietly to Vinnie, "Whatever it is, I'll take care of it."

Vinnie hesitated an instant, then sighed with exasperation and started across the pier. He gestured the two young men to accompany him. The other two policemen joined the young men and now all followed the first policeman toward the Chris Craft. Paul Calvelli moved as though to join Vinnie, but Leo grasped his arm. A gesture of concern, a suggestion not to interfere. A quite normal gesture.

Even as Leo touched Paul Calvelli's sleeve, on the pier the first policeman whirled around to face Vincent Tomasino. In the policeman's hand now was a large, ugly Webley service revolver. In the same instant, both young men reached into their jackets but before their fingers even curled around the handles of the weapons in their shoulder holsters, the other two policemen had fired three slugs into each young man's chest and stomach. Simultaneously, the first policeman fired the Webley into Vincent Tomasino's face. Two shots, discharged so rapidly they sounded as one. The first struck Vinnie's upper lip. The trajectory carried it upward through the soft gum tissue, straight into his brain. The second shot, slightly higher, into the ridge of the nose, traversed Vinnie's skull. The entry points of both bullets resembled small, red-rimmed puncture holes, but the second bullet emerged at the back of Vinnie's head, bursting it open like a split melon in a shower of red shredded flesh, white bone fragments, and gray brain matter.

One of the two young men had immediately toppled backward into the water. The impact of the bullets slammed the other young man backward into the hawser post on the pier, which broke his fall and hurtled him forward again. He fell facedown on the pier. His hand, crumpled under his body, still gripped the handle of the revolver he had been unable to draw. An ever widening puddle of viscous, crimson-black liquid formed on the back of his jacket, oozing from the two large, ragged holes in the jacket fabric.

Literally before Vincent Tomasino's dead body struck the planked pier floor, and before either young man was down, and while the wisps of gunpowder smoke still swirled whitely in the air directly above the bodies, the three policemen had turned and walked briskly back to their car. They were gone and out of sight almost before the first female witness screamed.

From all directions, people rushed in, shouting, crying, clustering in confusion and morbid curiosity around the bodies. Paul Calvelli, stunned, unable to move or even speak, allowed Leo to guide him away, back to the waiting launch.

The coxswain had jumped up onto the dock at the first gunshots but was too far away for a clear view. All he saw was Leo and Paul Calvelli hurrying toward him through the crowd, Leo making a winding motion of hands, a signal to start the launch motor. The coxswain scrambled back into the launch and started the engine.

"What the hell happened . . . ?" he asked as Leo and Paul boarded.

"I'll tell you about it later," Leo said. "Move! Fast!" He pushed Paul into the rear of the launch where the roar of the engine and rush of wind would prevent the coxswain from overhearing. He shouted into Paul's ear. "We talked about gratitude before, Paul. I want you to remember the word! It's what you feel about someone who saves your life! Will you remember that word, Paul? Gratitude?"

Paul Calvelli said nothing. He looked back at the pier receding rapidly in the distance. He could still see the crowd, and several police cars just then arriving.

Leo said, "You can be top man in the Alliance now, Paul. But only if you gather and consolidate your power. You need me for that. I'll pledge my whole organization. A hundred percent cooperation! But I keep my casino points, and I'm reinstated with the Council. That's the price! Think it over!" He patted Paul's shoulder and smiled. "I'll give you a whole day."

Paul Calvelli heard and understood it all quite clearly. Far across the water, on the pier, he could still make out the flashing red lights atop the roofs of the police cars. The launch was too far out at sea for him to hear the sirens.

With Leo's support Paul Calvelli absorbed Vincent Tomasino's family into his own and became the most powerful man in the Alliance. In return, Leo was reinstated to the Council, and the Alliance people withdrawn from Las Vegas.

To be sure, it was not all that easy, nor did Leo expect it to be. While he knew he could direct IDIC operations from overseas—expanding them as well, particularly in London where casino gambling would soon be legalized—his position within the Alliance could be maintained only if he returned to the United States. And he had to return before Paul Calvelli felt secure enough to once again move on IDIC. It was only a matter of time.

How much time was the question, and that could only be determined by the man whose very existence precluded Leo's return.

Albert Collins.

28

FOR more than two years, since the summer of 1963, each evening promptly at 6:45, Staff Sergeant Leonard Houghton had brought Albert Collins his supper. Houghton, balancing the food tray and his little vinyl medical kit, climbed the three flights of stairs to the executive suite in the BOQ. The air policeman seated at a card table-desk at the top of the stairway would inspect the tray and the kit contents, then gesture Houghton to continue. A plainclothes federal marshal rose from his chair outside the suite to open the door.

An unchanging ritual.

But all in a day's work. This was good duty here at Hamilton Air Force Base. A five-minute ride to Sausalito, and less than eleven miles from San Francisco, where he shared an apartment with a woman who danced topless in a North Beach bar.

A medic, Houghton's main function was to monitor Albert Collins's condition, which had progressed into emphysema, and to give a daily prednisone injection. Since the medication was administered before the evening meal, it therefore fell to Houghton to deliver the food tray.

Houghton knocked gently on the door and entered the three-room suite. A bedroom with a modern, tiled bathroom, a kitchenette, a small but well-furnished dining room, and a comfortable living room with a picture window overlooking San Pablo Bay. Across the water was the Bay Bridge and the lights of San Francisco. Albert, as often at this time of day, stood at the window

"You can put the chow in the dining room," Albert said. He turned to face Houghton. "So, Sarge, how you doing?"

"Not bad, Albert, not bad." Houghton could never bring himself to address Albert Collins as "mister." Bad enough having to "sir" these spade officers. But a civilian, never.

"Hey, Albert, you see on the TV that blackout back east?" Houghton asked. "The whole fucking city of New York! No elevators, no subways, not even traffic lights. The electricity just started coming back on after four hours. Some fun, huh?"

"Some of it's still blacked out," Albert said. "They don't expect it back on till probably morning."

"Bet you're glad you're here, not there, huh?" Houghton stepped into the dining room and placed the tray on the table that the CQ had already set. "Roll up the sleeve, fella."

Albert rolled up his sleeve as Houghton, unzipping the vinyl kit, returned to the living room. He took out the syringe, prepared it, and plunged the needle into Albert Collins's waiting arm. He withdrew the syringe and removed the needle from the barrel. He dropped the needle, intact, back into the kit and zipped it closed.

"You sure do that good," Albert said. "I never feel even a twinge."

"That's because I'm an expert, Albert," Houghton said, thinking this was precisely what his girl, Lynette, always said whenever he gave her a shot of morphine. "You're an expert, Lenny darling." Although lately she hadn't been saying it too often; their supply was low. Impossible, for three weeks now, to steal any from the dispensary. The new nurse, a short-haired, flat-chested major who Houghton was sure was a bull-dyke, ran a daily inventory.

Already, Lynette had to buy some off the street, horse instead of morphine, which although providing her a better high, neither she nor Houghton could afford. He would have to think of something soon. He certainly did not want her fooling around with anybody else just to get the stuff. He knew she would.

Staff Sergeant Houghton's dislike of Albert Collins was mutual. Albert did not know Houghton thought of him as a spade, but he sensed Houghton's contempt. Albert assumed Houghton considered him a stool pigeon, a not unreasonable assumption under the circumstances. A man living under the protection of the U.S. government. It seemed hard to believe that four years had passed since the lawyer from Washington, Martin Raab, had knocked on Albert's Harlem apartment door with an offer of immunity from prosecution if Albert would testify that Jules Jefferson paid him $25,000 to fix the jury in the Leo Gorodetsky case.

It was like finding gold in the street. Albert reasoned that if they paid him $25,000 to do it, his silence should be worth twice as much. He went straight to Jules Jefferson. Jules agreed with Albert's reasoning, said he foresaw no problem, and had only to clear it with The People.

That same afternoon, on 125th Street, a delivery truck narrowly missed running Albert down. No accident, because at the grocery store on his way home after work he met his landlady. She said two of his friends were waiting for him in his room, and two others in a car parked a few doors away from the house.

Albert did not return home that night, or ever again. He spent a year in Detroit under a different name, but was careless, and one day it started all over. Strangers asking questions about him. So he went to the FBI. And now lived like a king, alimony and child-support payments all taken care of. He read and watched TV and listened to the radio. And watched the big air-force jets take off and land.

Raab promised that after the trial the government would continue the payments to the wives and children, and also arrange a good, well-paying job in a strange city. And continued medical treatment. A whole new life. It was called the Federal Witness Protection Program.

2.

Lynette Trask had been in San Francisco three years. She was twenty-eight, five four, 130 pounds, with a twenty-four-inch waist and breasts somebody once said could make a grown man weep with joy. For eight hours of gyrating on the runway-bar at Dukes, on Washington Street, she averaged with tips slightly more than $200 weekly. Five years ago a man in Gardena, California, turned her on to drugs. First pot, then acid, and only in the past two years the hard stuff.

Eleven months ago when she met Leonard Houghton she was in a methadone program. His easy access to morphine started her off again. She had been mainlining ever since. He was a nice enough guy, maybe a little too short and fat for her taste, but easy to live with, and un-demanding, never suspecting that all her sexual groaning and moaning was a performance, an Academy Award one at that. Besides, she knew he was madly in love with her, which certainly helped what a county social worker called "self-image." He also paid the rent.

Additionally, he never objected to her occasionally dating a customer. He knew it was strictly business. She never charged less than thirty dollars, and was very particular who she went with. No creeps, freaks, or Greeks.

She was thinking about this very endeavor during her first break of the evening, at almost the same moment Leonard Houghton and Albert Collins were discussing the great Manhattan blackout. Wearing the loose kimono required offstage, she sat in a rear booth with a customer. A young, big, good-looking sun-bleached blond guy with the deepest, bluest eyes Lynette ever saw on a man. He had been here five consecutive nights. Just to watch her dance, he said. Frankly, he said, he loved her tits.

". . . hey, come on," Lynette said. "Just 'cause I work in a place like this, doesn't mean I shouldn't be respected."

The blond man, who had introduced himself as Dan Meecham, laughed in her face. "Do us both a favor? Cut the crap." He plucked a single crumpled bill from his shirt pocket and flattened it on the table, palm over the corners to momentarily obscure the denomination. Then he made a Y of his fingers so she could see the number.

100.

"What time do you get off?" he asked.

"I think I better call the manager," she said.

He placed his fingers to her lips. "I said, no crap. Don't worry, I'm not vice."

"I get off at two," she said promptly. "You have a place, or you want a hotel?"

"Your place," he said. "I mean, where you live."

"No way," she said. "I live with my boyfriend."

"So let him watch."

"Oh, Christ!" he said, dismayed. "One of those."

He folded the bill in half and slid it across the table to her. "In advance," he said. "Yes, or no?"

She stared at the money, the numerals 100 on the edge. She seldom saw that kind of money. It bought at least five sticks.

"Tell you what," said the blond man. He brought another bill from his pocket, another hundred. "Let the boy friend go in first. *I* watch. Then I go in."

"Oh, Jesus!" said Lynette.

The blond man slid the second bill to her. "I was in the navy," he said. He winked. "I like wet decks."

"Oh, Jesus!" Lynette said again. But the idea all at once excited her. So did two hundred dollars. She had never in her life made that much for a trick. And one she might enjoy, yet.

"I don't know if he'll go for it," she said, but knew he would. Leonard Houghton would do anything she wanted. Suddenly, her whole body felt cold and clammy, and tense. The warm, unfamiliar sexual excitement of the previous moment was gone. Her nerves screamed for relief. She needed something, and now. She knew she had exactly twelve dollars in her purse; she already owed Cully, the doorman who supplied her, fifty. She cupped both bills in her palm and closed her fist. "Okay," she said.

The blond man who called himself Dan Meecham, but whose real name was Jack Maynard, was a partner in a San Diego-based organization called Osgood & Associates. It was a collection agency. Founded and funded twelve years before by Leo Gorodetsky, Osgood's efforts were devoted exclusively to the collection of overdue or ignored gambling markers. But only those of high rollers, and then only for amounts exceeding $10,000. Adhering to a firm policy set down by Leo, not once in twelve years had any form of violence or extortion been employed, or any threatened.

For all that, Osgood's rate of failure was under four percent. It had developed highly sophisticated collection procedures, actually psychological in nature, based on the proven premise that a gambling debt was a debt of honor. Also the gamblers knew that welshing on a Barclay or Oasis marker spelled instant barring from all Nevada casinos.

On occasion, however, Osgood & Associates were assigned projects of a less psychological kind. A cheating 21 dealer, for example, or a nimble-fingered card mechanic, or a greedy security man with a penchant for beating up hookers and rolling their clients. Or even the handful of naïve men and women who now and then foolishly implemented what they believed ingenious methods of robbing a casino or its executives. In such cases the approach was not at all sophisticated and hardly psychological.

Osgood & Associates, then, was assigned to find and deal with Albert Collins. As managing partner, Jack Maynard personally directed the operation. A thirty-eight-year-old former U.S. Marine, a decorated Korean War veteran, Maynard had started as a night desk clerk at the Barclay. Within a year he was a casino host, and a year later assistant credit manager. In that capacity he had on his own initiative discounted by fifty percent the $100,000 marker of a Mexico City high roller. Leo, in Las Vegas at the time, demanded an explanation.

"I'm curious to know why you chose to give away fifty thousand dollars of the casino's money," Leo had said.

"I didn't give the money away, Mr. Gorodetsky," Jack Maynard had coolly replied. "I invested it. If you'll look over at the baccarat pit, you'll see the individual in question playing at the number-six spot. Playing with him are two friends who never played here before. Between them, they're in to us for over a hundred thirty-five thousand."

Before Leo could acidly ask how much Maynard planned to settle *those* markers for, Maynard had continued, "They put up two hundred thousand front money. In cash. That was the deal I made with him. Cash up front."

The moral was of course obvious. As were the figures. Leo decided Jack Maynard the ideal man for Osgood & Associates.

Finding Albert Collins was simply a matter of legwork and determination. Finding Lynette Trask was an incredible stroke of luck.

Routinely researching the people surrounding Albert led Maynard to Staff Sergeant Leonard Houghton, and then to Lynette. The moment Maynard saw her and recognized her as a drug addict, he knew exactly how, and with whom, to proceed.

That night, Jack Maynard arrived at Houghton's Powell Street apartment two hours before Lynette finished work. Houghton was awake and waiting. Lynette had phoned him earlier. The sergeant was himself not a little intrigued at the kinky prospect. And if it made Lynette happy, it made him happy.

It was easier than Jack Maynard anticipated. He had to rough Leonard Houghton up slightly. A few expertly placed kidney blows. Nothing that would show, but would remind Houghton of the wisdom of silence, and the minimum ten-year-hard-labor sentence for the theft of government narcotics. It also persuaded the sergeant to participate in the delicate operation planned by Jack Maynard for the next few days.

Lynette was genuinely disappointed when she came home and was told the john had called to cancel the date. But he said that for her time and trouble she could keep the money. She never noticed Houghton's turmoil. She was too high from the shot she took just before leaving the club.

The following evening, in compliance with Jack Maynard's instructions, Houghton gave Albert Collins his regular prednisone injection. But only five milligrams, not the usual twenty. The same small dosage the next day, and the next. By the morning of the fourth day the reduced medication had caused Albert to develop a potentially serious lung infection. The base medical officer ordered a consultation with a San Francisco pulmonary specialist.

Accompanied by two air policemen and two plainclothes marshals, Albert was taken to Dr. Myron Flanders at the University of California Medical Center. Dr. Flanders and three other physicians saw private patients in a suite on the ground floor of a doctor's building opposite the Medical Center on Parnassus Street.

While the APs waited in the corridor, one marshal escorted Albert into the small, utilitarian waiting room. The other marshal checked the corridor, the stairwell, and the lavatories.

Five people were in the waiting room. An elderly man with a black nurse, a teenage boy, and a couple in their early thirties. The couple was well-dressed, the man in an expensive brown tweed suit; the woman, a strikingly attractive redhead, in a tailored blue blazer and gray flannel skirt. Her purse, a large alligator shoulder bag, was on the floor under her chair. She was reading a *National Geographic*. The man sat gazing glumly at a glass-framed Wyeth reproduction on the wall.

The receptionist, a pleasant, middle-aged woman wearing oversize rimless glasses, said Dr. Flanders would see Albert immediately. She buzzed open the door to the inner offices. The marshal and Albert entered and were shown to an examining room.

In the corridor outside the suite, in the alcove fronting the men's room, the second marshal deposited a dime into the public telephone. He was calling his office in the Federal Building to report his present location. There was no dial tone. He dropped in a quarter now, but still no tone. The phone was out of order. He retrieved the coins and started back to the doctors' suite.

In Dr. Flanders's examining room a nurse asked Albert to strip to the waist. The marshal helped Albert remove his shirt. The nurse prepared the doctor's examining instruments.

In the waiting room another nurse appeared at the door. A stout, motherly woman, but professionally aloof. "Mr. Shallert?" she said to the well-dressed man. "Dr. Mindlin will see you now, sir."

"I'd like my wife to come with me," the man said.

"Certainly," said the nurse, unsmiling. She gestured the couple to step past her into the inner area. "How are you?" she asked the man.

"That's what I want to find out," he said wryly.

"Yes, well I'm sure you're in the best of health," the nurse said, and closed the door.

The instant the door clicked shut, the redheaded woman drew a snub-nosed revolver from the alligator purse. She held it to the nurse's head and spoke in a quiet, flat voice. "Just shut up and you won't be hurt!"

The man, reaching into the redhead's open purse and removing a silencer, and another revolver, a longer-barreled .32, said in an equally calm voice as he screwed the silencer onto the revolver barrel, "Take us to the room where the black man is."

The nurse moved shakily down the long narrow hallway. The man and woman followed. The redhead said, "Just show us what room, and then step aside."

At the same time, in the waiting room, the second marshal returned. He strode to the receptionist's counter. "The public phone's out of order," he said. "Could I use yours? Won't take me but a second."

"I think that might be arranged," the receptionist said. She fluffed the back of her hair; the marshal was a big, leathery-skinned man with the look of a bachelor. She decided not to buzz him in, but to open the door herself. She thought it might be interesting to stand close to him. "Just come around in back here." She got up and opened the door. The marshal stepped into the inner office.

At this exact instant, at the far end of the hallway, the motherly nurse pointed to the door of Albert Collins's examination room. The well-dressed man reached for the doorknob, while the redhead pushed the nurse slightly aside but continued holding the gun to her head. The well-dressed man's back, and the redhead's, were to the marshal who had just entered the inner office for the telephone. The marshal's brain received and transmitted this image to his eyes, and simultaneously flashed other signals to other muscles. His hand reached for his gun, his knees flexed in preparation for an attack crouch, and his larynx formed a word.

"Freeze!"

The well-dressed man whirled, gun hand sweeping around toward the marshal. The redhead also whirled, but awkwardly, stumbling against the motherly nurse who stood between her and the marshal. The marshal, service revolver gripped with both hands, fired straight down the hallway. Both bullets smashed into the center of the well-dressed man's chest, spinning him halfway around and catapulting him sideways into the examining-room door, the weight of his body bursting open the door, tearing it completely off its hinges so it crashed forward onto the examining room floor.

Through the open doorframe the redhead saw, too late, the marshal in the examining room leveling his gun at her. She had no chance to shoulder the nurse around in front of her as a shield. The marshal fired a single shot into the side of the redheaded woman's head.

The entire incident began and ended in less than three seconds. The man and the redhead were killed instantly. The nurse and Albert Collins were uninjured.

A getaway car was discovered parked in the underground garage next to a doorway directly off the office suite. They could have killed Albert Collins in the same three seconds, and been safely away in the next three. But for an out-of-order public telephone, the operation should and would have succeeded; it was that audacious and well planned.

Fingerprints identified the man as Stanley Peter Chalmers, age thirty-five, a British national, long suspected of IRA connections. The woman, Emily Adele Simpson, twenty-seven, was an American citizen with no known police record. No other information on them existed. As a San Francisco police captain remarked, the two could almost have come from another planet.

And the details were made no clearer in a note from Staff Sergeant Leonard Houghton. In this note he confessed his role, but claimed he did not know the blond blue-eyed man who blackmailed him into the conspiracy, and had seen him only that one time. He very gallantly did not involve Lynette Trask.

The note was found on Houghton's body in the front seat of a commissary panel truck parked on the base behind the enlisted men's mess hall. One end of a garden hose was attached to the vehicle's exhaust pipe. The other end extended into the car through a small aperture in the left front window stuffed with towels to make it airtight. The truck's engine was still running.

No one ever quite determined if these events were related to an incident just two days later in Detroit. Thomas Stohlmeyer never kept a luncheon appointment with his attorney and two UATW officials at the Steak Out, a popular Woodward Avenue restaurant. Stohlmeyer did not return home that evening, or the next day. Or ever. He had vanished without a trace.

In truth, Stohlmeyer's disappearance and the attempt on Albert Collins's life were totally unrelated. But it suited Martin Raab's purposes to believe otherwise. To him, it was merely one more example of Leo Gorodetsky's arrogance and contempt, and further reason why this fugitive from justice must absolutely be brought to trial.

Raab petitioned the State Department to demand Leo's extradition from Israel.

---- *29* ----

H E was only half listening; he knew most of what Gerson had to say, anyway. He was gazing absently across the full length of the bar's parquet floor to the polished-brass batwing doors where two very chic women had just entered from the hotel lobby. The women chatted an instant with the tuxedoed maître d', who escorted them to a nearby table. They were fine-looking women, with a certain poise and self-assurance he believed unique to Paris women.

". . . so the bottom line is politics," Gerson was saying. "Leo, do you understand what I'm saying?"

"The bottom line is politics," Leo said, studying the women. Your vision, old boy, he told himself; wear your glasses! Closer, they were not as interesting. Middle forties, he guessed, younger than Renata and not nearly as attractive. He glanced at his watch: 7:05. Renata should be returning soon from her afternoon of shopping with Carla. He sat back now in the soft-leathered armchair and smiled at Gerson. "Bottom line? What a phrase. I wonder what social and economic pressures create this new language?"

Gerson drew in an exasperated breath. "Leo, I'm talking about an attempt, a very serious attempt, on the part of the government of the United States to extradite you! What the hell does that have to do with a new language?"

"I'm sorry, George. Please go on."

"But talk about language, I saw a copy of the State Department note," Gerson said. "It certainly wasn't couched in any diplomatic language. 'Any undue delay in honoring this request will be viewed with extreme disfavor by the United States government.' "

"George, I saw that note. The *original*, in fact. In fact, I've seen them all, from the very first one, after the Albert Collins business. I saw that first note in the foreign minister's office in Tel Aviv. She showed it to me herself. She invited me to lunch to talk about it."

"And told you not to worry about it, I know," said Gerson. "But that was a year and a half ago; things have changed. Golda's not foreign minister anymore. Abba Eban is. He has a whole different political philosophy, and he's nowhere near as tough and pragmatic. He's liable to buckle under the pressure."

"I've been assured not to worry about it, so I'm not worrying. Besides, with the Egyptians mobilizing and Nasser screaming about Pan Arabic unity, the Israelis have enough to think about."

"Leo, the heat comes from the very top. The White House. Raab has Brickhill's support. Brickhill is on the Senate Armed Services Committee. Johnson needs Brickhill's support to convince Congress to send more troops to Vietnam. Goddamit, Leo, they can squeeze the Israelis on this if they want to. And I'm afraid they want to!"

"Stop working yourself up, George. Your blood pressure."

"Stop taking it so lightly, then."

"Look, I don't have to tell you how much we've invested in the State of Israel. I'm under no illusions they're allowing me to stay there out of love, or even because as a Jew I'm entitled to refuge under the Law of Return. It's a question of business. They're businessmen."

"You're too sanguine about it, Leo," Gerson said. "No, worse. Naïve. I think you're being naïve."

"The United States made a classic error trying to push the Israelis," Leo said. "May I quote Mrs. Meir? 'If you want to see how stubborn an Israeli can be, merely demand something of him.' "

"Another Gorodetsky Law?" Gerson asked dryly.

"In this part of the world they're called commandments," Leo said, looking past Gerson to the chic women. They had just been served *Cinzano sur glace*, which Leo was also drinking, and which he heard was the latest rage in Paris. That amused him; he had enjoyed Cinzano over ice for years. He held up his nearly empty glass and rattled the ice. The waiter immediately nodded in acknowledgment.

"Want another, George?" Leo asked.

Gerson glanced at his half-finished martini. "Not yet, thanks. I learned a long time ago with you not to have the second drink until we're finished with our business."

They were in the bar of the Hotel Lancaster, a hotel not unfamiliar to Leo. It was where he first met Robert MacGowan. He stayed here whenever he came to Paris, not out of sentiment, but for the sedate luxury and superb service. He always welcomed an excuse to visit the city. The excuse this time was to meet Gerson.

The usual papers to sign, forms to fill. And, more important, Gerson's operational reports. Business was booming, and Paul Calvelli and the Alliance seemed content enough. Of course, as long as the profits continued—and Leo remained overseas—they might remain content.

Might.

For it was really all balanced on the head of a pin, all the apparent cooperation and goodwill between Leo and the Alliance. Dependent upon a dozen different personalities, probabilities, and possibilities. Younger, more aggressive Alliance people might at any time push Paul Calvelli into moving to absorb IDIC. It would almost certainly happen should Leo return to the United States.

And yet unless he did eventually return, they would move on him. Rock and hard place. Not to mention the warrant awaiting him the moment he set foot in the United States.

Double rock, double hard place.

But if Leo was concerned about power, or who held it, it certainly was not evident. He appeared to be enjoying himself. He ran the European operations. He had just opened a huge, plush casino in London, and purchased a half share of one in Lebanon. Negotiations were under way for a hotel in Yugoslavia.

Gerson said now, "One of the Vegas papers played up the extradition note. So Ben ran an editorial accusing Brickhill of electioneering; they loath each other, you know. Ben's thinking of running for the Senate himself, he tells me."

"Not a bad idea," Leo said. "He'd make a good senator."

"A Jewish senator from the state of Nevada? That'll be the day." Gerson paused as the waiter brought Leo's drink. Then, "That Vegas story on your extradition made Paul Calvelli very nervous. Bad publicity, he said. I told him there was no chance of your being extradited. He doesn't know about the White House pressure, and I wasn't about to tell him."

"Paul Calvelli is a horse's ass," Leo said. "My five-year-old grand-daughter has more brains."

Gerson bristled with frustration. "I'm just not getting through to you, am I?"

"I hear you," Leo said. "We have a different perspective on things, that's all."

"Leo, you can't sit back and rely on the assurances of your Israeli friends," Gerson said. "The Law of Return is one thing. The awesome influence of the United States of America is quite another."

"Awesome influence," Leo repeated. "You're getting poetic in your old age, George."

Gerson waved his hands helplessly. "I think maybe it's time for the second drink."

Leo gestured for the waiter, saying, "When have you ever known me to sit back when it was contrary to my interests?"

Gerson said nothing. He regarded Leo unhappily.

"So stop fretting," Leo said. "I know what I'm doing."

"All right, Leo, if you say so," Gerson said. He smiled. "So how are the children? What's the little one's name? Rima?"

"They're great," Leo said. "Great kids. The little one's name is Rivka, after my oldest sister. She was some terrific girl, Rivka." He had considered asking Avi and Carla to name the baby after Esther who had died shortly before the child's birth, but his first glimpse of the infant told him she was Rivka. "Her birthday's next week."

"I'll remind Betty," Gerson said. "We'll send something."

"I'm sorry now I didn't keep the *Renata*," Leo said, half seriously. "That could have been my present." At Renata's urging, the yacht was sold recently to an American movie director. Renata said it was too lovely a vessel simply to languish in a Nassau boatyard. Let someone else enjoy it.

". . . I thought you were supposed to be off those?" Gerson was saying.

Leo lit the cigarette, vaguely aware of Gerson's admonishment, thinking, I am sixty-seven years old, so why worry about cigarettes killing me? I have survived numerous other, far more immediate attempts to kill me. Not only that, but I have buried most of those making the attempts. Those who violated Gorodetsky's Law.

"George, nothing is forever," he said. But he mashed out the cigarette. It was after all a no-percentage play, and he really had all but quit smoking.

"I'd feel better if I thought you meant it," Gerson said.

"What?" Leo asked. "Quit smoking?"

"Yes, Leo, that's right," Gerson said. "Smoking."

When Renata and Carla arrived, laden with bundles—mostly clothes for the children, some shirts for Avi—they had an aperitif, and then went upstairs to dress for dinner. Gerson was staying across the street at the Hotel California. He would meet them later at Père Jacques, a restaurant on Avenue Marignon Leo liked.

From the living room of their third-floor suite, Leo gazed out at the Champs Élysées. He never tired of the view, or the noise. The stream of automobile headlights moving endlessly up and down the boulevard, the sidewalks bustling with life and vitality. He could not quite see Fouquet's from here, but could envision it. The crowded terrace, waiters gliding smoothly in and around the tables.

April in Paris, he thought. Except it was not April, but late May. Well, early summer in Paris. What difference? Any season in Paris was good, although October was not so good because it, and Fouquet's, always reminded him of that night with Charlotte Daniels. He had heard she married a doctor, a prominent San Franciscan. Then he heard they were in a serious automobile accident in Canada. He hadn't had the slightest curiosity whether she was dead or alive.

Who cares? he remembered saying at the time. "Who cares?" he repeated now, aloud, and went into the bedroom to see how much longer Renata would be.

She sat at the dressing-table mirror applying makeup. She glanced at Leo in the mirror and said, "What did he want? George?"

"What do you mean, 'What did he want?'" Leo observed himself in the mirror and twisted sideways to knot his tie. He smoothed back his hair; it was almost totally gray. But still thick. He smiled to himself, remembering Harry's concern over increasing hair loss. Poor Harry. Poor, dumb Harry.

"I mean, what did he want?" She turned to face him. "I know something's going on, Leo, and it isn't routine business."

"I'm sorry, but it is," Leo said. He bent to kiss her cheek, inhaling deeply her perfume. "Shalimar?"

"Isn't that what you said—what is the term nowadays—turns you on?"

"Ah, yes, the new language," he said. "You're a beautiful woman, you know that? Yes, Shalimar turns me on." He smiled ruefully. "I only wish I could carry out more of those turn-ons for you."

"Am I complaining?" she asked. She turned again, and smiled back at him in the mirror. "Isn't six times a week enough for any woman?"

"You wish," he said, and thought *once* a week, if you're lucky. If *I'm* lucky, he corrected himself. "How long before you're ready?"

Renata fitted her eye-shadow brush carefully into the molded compartment of the plastic mascara case on the dressing table. She faced him directly. "Leo, I've never interfered, or imposed my own feelings. But I know you, and I know George Gerson. He's worried about something."

"George is always worried about something," Leo said. "His latest, big worry is that the Arabs are about to start a war."

"When will you stop shutting me out? I'm part of you, part of your life. I'm tired of being closed off. What happens to you, happens to me."

He did not know what to say. She had never, not in all the years, even implied being shut out of his life. On the contrary, she had always seemed to accept the little charade that his business life and their personal lives were totally separate entities.

She said, "I don't want to go back to America, and I don't want you to."

"I wasn't planning to," he said. "Not for a while."

"You can't go back, Leo. Ever!"

Again, he did not know what to say. He wanted to be angry with her, but felt no anger. He wanted to resent the demanding tone of her voice, but felt no resentment. He wanted to say she was wrong about him shutting her out of his life. He wanted to say he had shared everything with her. His life, his love, his innermost thoughts. Everything. He did not say this because he knew it was not true.

"They'll kill you," she said. She spoke so matter-of-factly it frightened him. "They're only waiting for you to come back so they can kill you."

They looked at each other. It was suddenly so quiet that from an adjacent room he could hear the metallic click of a door closing, and through the open window the soft, steady rush of boulevard traffic.

No pretense now, no charade. Now it was out in the open. And he was glad. He wondered why he had allowed it to continue as long as it had, knowing all the time that it was a charade. A silly game they played. No, a game he alone played. A delusion he held. She had always recognized him for who and what he was. She had always known that reality. He idly wondered why she chose this time and place to finally, officially as it were, end the charade. But then, what better time and place than Paris on a lovely early summer evening.

And it was not an end, but a beginning. Of a new and more honest relationship. He loved her for it. He wanted to reach out and take her into his arms. But first, now that it was all out in the open, he knew he must confide to her the truth. More accurately, confirm a truth he knew she was already aware of. The reason he could not return yet.

He said, "If they wanted to kill me, Renata, they wouldn't have to wait for me to come back. That's not the problem. There's a man named Albert Collins who's been tucked safely away—"

"—yes, so safely now even *you* can't find him!"

"—so I don't plan to go back so soon," he finished.

She shook her head impatiently. Under the light trained on the dressing table, he noticed for the first time strands of white in her blond hair. He touched her hair gently.

"I have no immediate plans to go back," he said.

"It may be out of your hands," she said. "George told me about this latest extradition note."

"I happen to know that just two days ago, the day we left Tel Aviv, Washington was officially informed that as a Jew, I am entitled to refuge under the Law of Return," he said. "I've also, officially, applied for Israeli citizenship."

"Why didn't you tell me?"

"I wanted it to be a surprise." Leo's words were several sentences behind his brain, which was repeating to him George Gerson's warning of the awesome influence of the United States government, of which he was well aware and secretly feared. He also knew he should be confiding this fear to Renata, sharing it with her, but knew he would not. He wondered why. Pride? Shame? What was shameful about fear? Would he be seen through different eyes? Would he be considered less a man, less a *shtarker*? Even as a child he never allowed people to know he was afraid.

"The pride of children," he said aloud. The sound of his own voice surprised him, and the words embarrassed him. "Get dressed," he added quickly. "I'm hungry."

They arrived at the restaurant a half hour late. Carla had been trying to telephone Avi but the lines were out. When finally she did get through they were cut off after only a minute. But Avi said the children were fine and everything was all right, although Carla detected a certain strange note in his voice, as though he wanted to tell her something but could not.

Carla related all this at dinner. Leo sat back and listened; he loved the sound of Carla's voice. A low, intense voice that commanded your attention while never demanding it. She had grown into a beautiful woman, he thought. Tall and slim, at thirty-eight she looked ten years younger. Her shoulder-length chestnut hair shone with a healthy gloss, and her skin with a soft smoothness. She had never compromised the eyebrows, the famous heavy brown Gorodetsky eyebrows; they blended perfectly with the deep, long-lashed, wide-set eyes and flawless nose.

". . . I think Avi was trying to tell me he's been called up," she was saying. "He couldn't say it in so many words because of the censorship."

George Gerson said, "I did hear on the BBC a rumor that Nasser asked the UN to withdraw their observation units from the Sinai."

"We heard the same rumor in Tel Aviv," Leo said. "That's all it is, a rumor."

"Another Nasser bluff," Renata said. "The Israelis are used to all that rhetoric."

"I'm not so sure this time it is rhetoric," Carla said. "Daddy, didn't you say the Arabs are more united now than ever before? For the first time they're not bickering with each other?"

Leo laughed. "That was before Nasser accused King Hussein of being a traitor and CIA agent."

"But in the meantime Nasser's mobilized his army," Gerson said. "I hope it's only for maneuvers."

"He's trying to impress the Russians," Leo said. "Believe me, if a crisis were brewing, I'd know about it. It's nothing. Avi hasn't been called up, no one has."

"Even if he was called up, that doesn't mean the war is starting," Renata said. "This so-called 'crisis' has been going on for more than two weeks."

"Doctors are the last to be called up," Carla said. She pushed her demitasse cup away. "Tomorrow, I'm going back." She looked at Renata for support. "We shouldn't have left Israel at a time like this."

Leo said, "When we get back to the hotel, try phoning again. You'll see I'm right. Nothing's happened."

Carla did call, and succeeded in getting through. Avi assured her he had not been called up, although he did believe something was in the wind. He did not believe it would happen immediately, so he wanted Carla to continue as planned. Two weeks with Leo and Renata in Paris, London, and Dubrovnik. She needed the change. The children were with his parents, who adored them and spoiled them outrageously.

"You see, I told you. Everything's all right," Leo said. "Listen to your old man."

He rose early next morning and walked to the *Herald Tribune* office a few doors away. He bought a paper, folded it without looking at the front page, and went into a nearby bistro for coffee and a croissant. He sat on a terrace table and unfolded the newspaper. The glaring headlines sprang up at him.

ISRAEL IN FULL MOBILIZATION
AS EGYPTIANS BLOCKADE TIRAN STRAIT!

2.

That morning, Leo drove Sari to school. The school bus simply did not show up; only later was it learned bus and driver were requisitioned to transport a battalion of reserve tankers to their Negev depot. So Leo took the child to school. Rivka, the five-year-old, went along for the ride. During Avi's tour of army duty, Carla and both girls were staying with Leo and Renata in Herzlia.

Two weeks before, when Israel went to full mobilization, Leo and Renata had immediately returned with Carla to Tel Aviv. A week later, the last week in May, Avi was called up. His mobile surgical unit was attached to the Golani Brigade on the Syrian border. He had phoned only the previous afternoon saying he had to go into Tel Aviv for supplies and might drop in on them for dinner Monday evening. He also said war was imminent. The only question was which side would strike first, and where.

"Some war," Leo had said. "You come home from the front whenever you feel like it."

"The whole damn country is the front line!" Avi had replied.

This Monday morning, after dropping Sari at school Leo and Rivka listened to the car radio, a Tchaikovsky ballet on *Kol Yisrael*. Rivka said the music bored her. Leo said it was too bad she inherited only her mother's good looks and stubbornness, not her musical talent. Rivka said she wanted to be a doctor like her father. All at once the radio went dead. A few minutes later it came back on with a female announcer broadcasting in terse Hebrew. Leo asked Rivka to translate.

" 'The oranges are ready.' 'The child is named Zipora. . . .' 'The fishing is good. . . .' " Rivka giggled. "Isn't that funny, Poppy?" Both children called him Poppy, addressing him in English, although more often they used *Saba*, Hebrew for "Grandfather."

Leo recognized the radio messages as coded deployment instructions for civilian defense units. It meant the war had begun.

He raced the Chevrolet sedan through the wide, tree-lined Herzliya streets to the house. He and Rivka were almost at the front door when, in the distance, he heard the first jets. He stood a moment, frozen, peering up at the sky. The banshee wail was louder, and for a sickening instant he thought it might be an enemy attack. And then, their shrill jet whine now ear-shattering, he saw them. Three Mystères flashing past along the beach. On their desert-camouflaged fuselages was the Star of David roundel.

Leo ran into the house. Carla stood at the kitchen window gazing after the airplanes. The portable radio on the breakfast counter was tuned to *Kol Yisrael*, the same female voice reading the cryptic Hebrew messages.

"It's started," Carla said.

"I think so," Leo said. In the distance, the sound of more jets. That was when he rushed to the roof to watch. The sight of those airplanes with the Star of David filled him with a sense of awe. And pride. A different pride than he felt in 1948. Then he was an American Jew, helping other Jews create a nation. Here, now, nineteen years later, it was different. Now, although still certainly—now and forever—an American, he was also part of this new land. His grandchildren were a part of it. They belonged. He belonged.

All morning the Mystères and Mirages screamed low over the beach. They flew in Vs of three and sometimes six, and once twelve. They headed north, maintaining near wave-top altitude so that the Judean hills behind them shielded them from Syrian and Jordanian radar. They continued north only a few more minutes, then swung left, due west out over the Mediterranean but still far enough north to evade Egyptian radar. Then, well abeam Alexandria, they turned south in a great sweeping arc that brought them, finally, over land. Over Egypt, and the airfields where the fighters and bombers of the Egyptian Air Force were invitingly lined wing to wing on the tarmacs, or parked nakedly in their revetments.

In three hours it was over.

The entire Egyptian Air Force, some four hundred first-line aircraft, was destroyed, ninety percent of it on the ground. Four hours later, many of the same Israeli jets attacked Syrian and Jordanian airfields. Their air forces, too, were knocked out the first day.

Oddly enough, Avi did appear for dinner that first evening. After collecting his supplies he had to wait several hours for an ambulance to be repaired. He would drive the ambulance back to his unit on the Syrian border. In the meantime he borrowed a hospital orderly's car for this brief visit to his family.

Avi Schiff was a tall, deceptively slender, dark-complexioned man with curly black hair, a square, strong face, and bright, lively, very warm eyes.

At forty-one, he was chief of surgery at the Hakirya Hospital, and a reserve major in the IDF.

Leo had never quite decided if he liked Avi for himself, or because Avi had been so good for Carla. Or simply because they enjoyed more of a peer relationship than one of father and son-in-law. They argued incessantly, sometimes heatedly, mostly about politics, religion, and Israel.

Avi felt the Arabs, like the Jews, deserved their own homeland. Leo said the Arabs had their chance, but walked away in '48; now let them eat *pita*!

Avi believed in God, although in a broad, agnostic sense, and this evening over the hurried dinner challenged Leo. "When we take Jerusalem, you go and visit the Wailing Wall," he said. "I'm willing to bet twenty Israeli pounds you'll change your mind about the existence of God."

Renata said, "The Arab Legion will have something to say about that. The Jordanians still hold the Old City."

"Not for long," Avi said. "They were foolhardy enough to join in the war after we begged them not to. We'll take Jerusalem, believe me; it's one of our prime objectives. Do you know how many years since a Jew was allowed to pray at the Wailing Wall?"

The question was answered by seven-year-old Sari. "One thousand eight hundred and ninety-seven years, Poppy!"

"One thousand eight hundred and ninety-seven years," Leo said to Avi.

Avi pinched Sari's cheek affectionately and said, "You make sure you see it, Leo. The Wall makes everybody think differently."

"Poppy doesn't believe in religion!" Sari said, delighted to reveal an adult's secret.

"Ah, but it's not a question of religion," Avi said. "It's about being a Jew."

"I'm a Jew," Leo said. "Seeing the Wall won't make me a better one."

Avi smiled knowingly, and changed the subject. He left shortly afterward, promising to phone the moment he could. Carla packed sandwiches and fruit for him, and a thermos of coffee. The drive to Tiberias would take him most of the night.

The roads were clogged with military traffic. Tank carriers, APCs, trucks, buses. Anything that could move had been pressed into service. Avi wished he had remembered to bring a transistor radio, but it really was unnecessary. At every road junction or traffic delay someone reported the latest news.

General Ariel Sharon, rolling into the Sinai, already had engaged a large enemy armored force. In the north, they were pushing into the West Bank and into Jerusalem. Nothing could stop them, it seemed.

Casualties surprisingly light.

The preemptive aerial attack had crushed the Arabs, although you would not think so from Cairo or Damascus radio. One flinty-eyed old MP at a crossroads shared a few minutes of his radio with Avi. A propaganda broadcast in Hebrew from Damascus.

". . . Jews running for their lives before our valiant soldiers!" the Arab announcer was exclaiming. "The sands of our motherland are littered with the wreckage of your cowardly planes that attacked us so treacherously! And we have retaliated with our full might. Tel Aviv is in flames! The entire Jewish army has been routed!"

The MP laughed and spat on the ground. "Have you ever heard such atrocious Hebrew?" he asked.

Avi gave the MP a package of cigarettes and half a chicken sandwich and drove on. He wanted to make Tiberias by dawn; quiet front or not, he was sure there would be casualties. Sporadic artillery, snipers, random mortar fire. There were always casualties.

He kept thinking of Leo. He loved the man like his own father. More, sometimes. Yes, of course, he knew what was said about him in America. Gangster, killer. He remembered one conversation in the hospital shortly before Leo was discharged. Avi had seen a light in Leo's room and stopped in.

Leo was reading. Avi remembered the book, a novel, *Marjorie Morningstar*. A marvelous piece of writing, Leo said. About a Jewish girl in America. A girl not unlike Carla. And then Leo put down the book and said, "I want to tell you, I'm grateful for what you've done for her."

"Grateful?" Avi had said. "There's nothing to be grateful for. I love her."

"You've made her a person all unto herself," Leo said.

"She was always a person," Avi said.

"She was Leo Gorodetsky's daughter," Leo said. "That's not an easy thing to live down."

"Leo, she's proud of being your daughter."

"The daughter of a gangster?" Leo removed his reading glasses and placed them atop the book. "A killer?"

"No one believes those stories. Certainly not Carla."

"Do you?"

Avi was sitting on the bed edge facing Leo. "Does it make any difference?" he asked.

"The stories happen to be true," Leo said. "Some of them."

Avi said nothing.

"I had a friend once," Leo said. "Whenever he was accused of it, of being a gangster and killer, he always said, 'But we only kill each other.' "

"Look, Leo, this is not necessary—"

"—I don't say this to justify or rationalize what I've done, or am supposed to have done," Leo went on. "But it's an important truth that's too often overlooked. Ignored, I suppose, for the convenience and comfort of the hypocrites and moralists so they can excuse their own weaknesses, their own corruption. We're a corrupt species, Avi, living in a corrupt world."

"Only because we allow ourselves to be corrupted," Avi said.

Leo had smiled. Avi had made the point for him.

Now, driving the ambulance, Avi wondered why all that had come into his mind. He thought it was related to his urging Leo to see the Wall. Avi remembered he had felt almost as though compelled to tell Leo about the Wall. A strange, driving compulsion. Only hours later, with the sun rimming the eastern sky when he reached the schoolhouse temporarily housing his unit, did he realize why he wanted Leo to visit the Wall. Not for any religious purpose, but as his, Avi's, surrogate.

Because Avi feared he would never again see the Wall himself. He feared he would not survive to see it.

For an instant his fingers seemed frozen to the ambulance steering wheel. He felt his pulse racing, pounding through his fingertips. He knew he was behaving like some ignorant, superstitious recruit, but these sensations were not unfamiliar. He recalled them from '56, at Suez. And before that, as a young rifleman, in '48. Each time, certain he would be killed.

Certain, again, now.

But a day later, and for the next four days, the premonition was swept away in the increasing ferocity of the war. The Golani Brigade went into action, their objective to seize the Syrian heights overlooking farms and kibbutz settlements on Israel's northern frontier. The surgical-unit helicopters landed only yards behind the lines. More often than not, Avi operated in the midst of an artillery or mortar attack. Once two medics standing three feet away were hit with a shell that miraculously left Avi unscratched. The blast did not even knock him down. In between operations he dozed, or hastily enjoyed a C-ration—he liked the Hershey chocolate square, and the Kraft cheese snack with the little crackers— or simply rested. He forgot about the Wall.

Leo did not forget it. On Wednesday, three days after the war started, with 100,000 Egyptians cut off in the Sinai and the Jordanian army neutralized, the Israelis took the Old City of Jerusalem.

And the Wall.

On Thursday, the fourth day, Ben Sylbert, personally covering the war for his own *Las Vegas Record*, arrived in Israel. He was on his way to Jerusalem. Leo asked to accompany him.

Renata, aghast, said, "Leo, are you crazy?"

"Probably," Leo said. "I want to see the city."

"But they're still fighting!" Carla said. "You'll see it next week when they've cleared everything away."

Leo said, "Please! Stop treating me like a feeble old man. I'm in the best of health. Nothing will happen to me." He turned to Ben. "Fix it for me."

"What is it with you?" Ben asked. "You getting religious in your old age?"

"Fix it, Ben," Leo said.

Ben obtained war correspondent's credentials for Leo, and that same afternoon they drove to the city in a jeep festooned with "Press" flags. Both wore civilian clothes, but with "C" brassards.

"So we won't get shot as Arabs," Ben explained.

"You kidding?" the jeep driver said. He was an American, Milton Rubin, a photographer Ben had hired in London. "All we have to do to prove we're Jews is unzipper our flies!"

They entered the Old City from the east through St. Stephen's Gate. Israeli tanks were parked on both sides of the entrance, and the narrow road leading to the gate was littered with burned-out Jordanian half-tracks and trucks. To the north a great pall of greasy black smoke rose from an ammunition dump attacked only a few hours before by Israeli jets. Groups of bewildered, vacant-eyed Arab Legionnaires, hands clasped behind their necks, marched past under the guns of Israeli paratroopers. In the midst of all this, small Arab shops were already reopening, their proprietors standing smiling in the doorways, waving to Israelis moving in both directions. Black-veiled Arab women, balancing on their heads stone jugs of water, walked obliviously on the cobblestones in the middle of the street.

Rubin drove the jeep down the Via Dolorosa, around the ancient stone wall surrounding the Dome of the Rock, then swung left, past more smoldering Jordanian vehicles, into another street of Arab shops opening for business.

And then they reached the Wall.

The instant he saw it Leo understood what Avi meant.

It was a small, crumbling section of the larger rectangular wall protecting the Dome of the Rock. It rose some thirty feet high in huge, roughhewn stone blocks mottled with outgrowths of green vines and vegetation and seemed somehow different from the larger wall, almost as though under a separate light. The stones themselves shone brightly in the afternoon sun, some rust-colored, others nearly stark white.

Behind the Wall the sky was outlined with minaret towers, and the gilded, rounded roofs of mosques. But the Wall in the foreground seemed to stand alone, like a three-dimensional object in a flat tableau, a magnet pulling you toward it.

Hundreds of soldiers clustered three and four deep at the Wall. Some wore *tallisim*, some had wound phylacteries around their foreheads and arms. The tasseled fringe of one soldier's *tallis* was entangled in the muzzle of a bazooka slung over his shoulder. Others, clutching their rifles for support, knelt with their faces pressed to the stones. Some stood swaying in prayer. Many sang, many wept, while a few only quietly gazed at it.

"Take a good look," Ben Sylbert said. "The last time this happened was two thousand years ago. There's a legend that when the Romans tried to knock the Wall down, the tears of six angels hardened into a cement that fell into the cracks of the stones so nobody could ever break them apart."

Leo said nothing. He felt himself gripped by a power he could not see and did not understand. It reminded him of the day of Steve's death, when something—that same, or similar, power—drew him into a synagogue. But that day he had cursed God. Not now; now, this had nothing to do with God. It transcended God.

Avi was right, he thought. It was about being a Jew. He stepped closer. He wanted to go near the Wall, touch it, but thought he should not. He had not earned the right. He, unlike those soldiers, had not risked his life to get here. He had the strange feeling something might happen to him if he actually touched the stones.

You are talking like a fool, he told himself. A goddam—yes, say it, *god*dam!—religious fool. Or an old man, he told himself. An old man near the end, and beginning to wonder if he should not hedge the bet.

He stepped back and asked Ben, "What are those slips of paper they keep tucking into the Wall?" Almost every soldier had jotted something on a piece of paper, folded the paper, then inserted it into the crevices of the stones.

"Wishes, prayers, names of loved ones," Ben said. "You write down what you hope will happen, or the name of somebody you want God to remember."

Black magic, Leo thought, but did not say it, aware now he was walking forward, brushing past soldiers, wondering why he did this, wondering where he found the strength to propel his legs. Wondering whose fingers were feeling the cool roughness of the stones blinding his eyes, whose ears were hearing the chorus of voices around him chanting in Hebrew.

He did not know how long he remained there, but knew it was a long while. And he had decided to insert one of those slips of paper into the Wall himself. He borrowed a sheet of notepaper from a bearded soldier with an Australian bush-style hat, and the soldier's pencil.

On the paper he wrote *Steven Gordon*.

Three days later Leo returned to Jerusalem. To the Wall. To write another name on another slip of paper and fit it into a crevice near the right side of the Wall where the corners formed an L that shadowed that part of the Wall from the sun.

The name this time was *Avi Schiff*.

3.

On the sixth day, the last—with the Syrians in full retreat from the Golan—an eighteen-year-old paratrooper was brought into Avi's field hospital. Lodged in the boy's chest, just under the rib cage, was a live

20-mm explosive shell. A helicopter waited to carry him back to Tel Aviv but Avi feared any undue movement or even vibration might detonate the bullet. With all fighting in this sector virtually ended, conditions for the surgery were favorable.

After anesthetizing the soldier, Avi ordered everyone from the tent. X rays had located the exact site of the bullet; it would not be a difficult procedure. He probed briefly, and found it. The instant he pulled it free it exploded.

Killing them both.

Once again, Leo Gorodetsky would say Kaddish for a son.

The bright morning sun warmed Carla's face. Far below, beyond the hilltop overlooking the city of Haifa where the cemetery was located, and beyond the whitewashed buildings on the waterfront and ships packed in the harbor like toy boats, the water glittered blue and green. She heard the rabbi's deep, sonorous voice, but could not seem to translate the Hebrew words into English. She glanced away now, at the grave site. The plain pine box, covered with the white and blue Star of David flag, rested precariously on two wooden planks straddling the freshly dug hole. Mounds of gray, rocky dirt were piled on either side. The dirt smelled old and musty.

She stood alone. She wanted to be alone. Avi's white-haired parents were a few feet away, shocked and disbelieving, the seventy-five-year-old father staring glassily at the casket; the mother's head bowed, her face contorted in grief. Opposite Carla, on the other side of the grave, Sari and Rivka stood with Leo and Renata, each child clutching a grandparent's hand. On Leo's left was Ben Sylbert. Behind them were several officers and some nurses. It reminded Carla vaguely of her brother's military funeral. More accurately, the memorial service: Steven's body was never recovered. Only Carla, Leo, and Ellie—and a U.S. Army honor guard—attended.

She looked at Leo and smiled wanly. She knew that he, too, was thinking of that other service. His eyes were red, and although she had not seen him cry she idly wondered if he would break down. She thought not, at least not in public. Renata had not cried; she said she refused to allow herself to because it would upset the children. But they cried anyway. Most of last night. Carla tried to comfort them. The words sounded empty and hollow.

I should cry, she thought. It will make me feel better. Feel better? she thought. That was almost funny, almost a joke. Well, I will probably cry, she thought. Later. I have my whole life to cry.

She gazed past Leo, at the row upon row of other fresh graves. Propped into each mound was a little metal stick resembling a miniature signpost. It contained a white card on which was written in Hebrew the soldier's name, dates of birth and death. This would later be replaced by a simple stone plaque with the same information carved into the stone below the sword and leaf emblem of the Israel Defense Forces. A grateful nation's tribute, she thought, remembering one of the officers telling her that the offensive in the north, of which Avi was in the forefront, had succeeded beyond the most optimistic expectations. She had politely replied that she was sure Avi would have been pleased. The officer said that that was what Avi died for. Now she thought she was not sure what he died for. She was not sure what any of them died for.

The rabbi's liturgy stopped. The rabbi, a portly, bearded man in an army captain's uniform, motioned to Avi's father and handed him a prayer book. The old man began reciting the Kaddish. When he finished, the rabbi started to resume his portion of the service. Suddenly Leo spoke quietly to the rabbi. The rabbi gave Leo the prayer book. Leo declined it, embarrassed, and removed a small plastic card from his pocket. A phonetic English pronunciation of the Hebrew words.

Now, hoarse and pausing frequently for breath, Leo read the Kaddish. Carla closed her eyes and listened. She imagined herself a little girl again, cradled in his arms. Shortly, another voice, the rabbi's, replaced Leo's, and Carla opened her eyes. Leo had stepped back, once more draping his arm around Rivka who huddled against him.

Then, abruptly, it was over. For a moment it was so quiet you could hear the rasp of people's breath, and the soft whine of the wind coming in from the sea, and the distant rumbling of city traffic.

Carla thought she might be sleepwalking. The wood planks supporting the box had been removed, and the box lowered into the grave. An army lieutenant folded the flag and placed it into her hands. She found herself moving forward, awkwardly gripping the flag while reaching down for a handful of earth. She did not fling the coarse dirt, but allowed it to sift gently through her fingers to the box.

That same evening Carla and Leo walked along the beach. A fine, clear evening with the ocean breeze warm and gentle. The tide was coming in, but still out far enough for the sand to remain firmly packed. They talked of the marvelous Israeli victory, and its impact on the future, and Israel's sudden new global prestige. Ben Sylbert said that in the United States, Israel—and Jews—were all at once figures of admiration and respect.

They talked of everything but what they knew they must eventually talk about. They had walked nearly all the way to the construction site of a new luxury hotel on the beach, which Leo had measured on his daily walk as exactly one and one half miles from the house.

"We better turn back," he said.

Carla stopped and looked at him in the dark. "Daddy, I can't tell you how much it meant when you said Kaddish."

He said nothing. He faced the water so the wind flowed directly into his face. He filled his lungs with the strong, clean air.

"You didn't have to, you know."

"I wanted to."

"Even though you don't believe in it?"

"He believed in it," Leo said. "I did it for him."

"No, Daddy, you did it for yourself."

Leo said nothing.

"Because you loved him," she said. "And because he loved you."

He nodded, but his mind was lost in another time, and he said, "Once, when you were a little girl, three or four, I guess, you had a nightmare and you rushed into our room. I held you in my arms and we talked, and you made me promise that I'd never let anything bad like that ever happen to you again."

"I think I remember that," she said.

"I didn't keep the promise, kid. I'm sorry."

It was then she wept. At first almost as a soft moan, and then with the tears, louder and louder, until finally she screamed. A low, harsh, wailing scream that echoed back at him as a mocking reminder of his own helplessness. He held her, weeping himself now, and they sank to the sand, clutching each other, swaying back and forth, back and forth.

Slowly, painfully, they adjusted their lives, as did hundreds of other Israeli wives and parents that year. The tiny nation suddenly was a giant, feared by its enemies, respected by its friends. The population swelled with eager Jewish immigrants. Industry and commerce boomed. Golda Meir was elected prime minister. The future looked bright.

That fall, Leo and Renata took Carla and the children to Switzerland for a month. The girls learned to ski, and began speaking French. Then all five went to Dubrovnik for the opening of the new hotel, the Adriatic Palace. A smash opening, the hotel fully booked. The casino's profits the first night exceeded $100,000.

Cash, American.

Leo could not recall a more pleasant or gratifying time. His health, and Renata's, was good. Carla's grief and sense of loss were steadily eased, replaced with the reality of life. The girls were marvelous.

Returning to Israel in November, in the Lod terminal Leo glanced absently at a *Jerusalem Post* headline: DE GAULLE HALTS ISRAEL ARMS DE-LIVERY. He had noticed the same story in the *Rome American* that morning and paid little attention. Just more high-level political maneuvering. It did not affect him.

He should have known better.

4.

Martin Raab was annoyed when Senator Charles Brickhill asked him to stop by at the senator's Georgetown house on his way home. It was Raab's fifty-fourth birthday, and he knew his wife planned a small family party. But Brickhill promised not to keep him long. He wanted Raab to meet someone. It might just have to do with the rumor that LBJ, displeased at Ramsey Clark's handling of the Martin Luther King assassination, would replace his attorney general. Charles Brickhill had often expressed a desire to see Martin Raab head the Justice Department.

The meeting involved Brickhill's desire, all right, and Raab's ambition, but in an entirely different area. The man Raab met in the senator's living room that April evening in 1968 was a short, dark, very compact, forty-year-old Israeli named Uri Malitt. He was a colonel in the Israeli Air Force, and an assistant military attaché with the Israeli Embassy.

No time was wasted on amenities. After an exchange of introductions, Brickhill said, "Marty, the Israelis have made a formal request to us for arms. In fact, they've presented us with a whole shopping list."

Uri Malitt, speaking with only a slight Israeli accent, said, "Airplanes are the top priority. We had bought and paid for sixty French Mirages, you know. The aircraft were ready for delivery; in fact, six had already left the Dassault factory and were at a military airfield in Lyons waiting for Israeli pilots. De Gaulle canceled the shipment."

"Replacements are urgently needed," Brickhill said to Raab. "The war depleted almost the total reserve strength of the Israeli Air Force. France was their main source of supply. Now, apparently, it's off."

"And we believe it's to stay off," Malitt said. "With his domestic problems, reliance on Arab oil, and pressure from Algeria"—he grimaced —"not to mention that latent, almost genetic antisemitism of the French, De Gaulle finds it expedient to back away from us."

"Far away," said Brickhill.

Malitt poured the remainder of a bottle of club soda into his glass. "But it may be a blessing in disguise," he went on. "We believe our Mirages to be obsolete anyway. The Russians are resupplying the Egyptians and Syrians with advanced MiGs and much more sophisticated antiaircraft. We desperately need American Phantoms."

Raab wondered how Israel's need for American arms concerned him. He finished his martini and declined Brickhill's gesture for a refill. "All I need is for some eager District cop to stop me for driving under the influence."

Brickhill smiled. His once red hair had thinned to almost gossamer strands of white crisscrossing his freckled scalp. The skin of his face glowed with a smooth translucence. He said, "I have suggested to Colonel Malitt that the United States might be more receptive to his government's request if his government were to see its way clear to honoring a request of ours."

Raab's heart began beating faster. "Gorodetsky," he said. "Leo Gorodetsky."

"Yes," said Brickhill. "As part of the package."

Raab said, "I find it hard to believe that the United States government has finally recognized the importance of bringing Leo Gorodetsky to justice."

"Believe it," Brickhill said. "It's true."

There was a catch to it; there had to be. Raab said, "But under the Law of Return he's entitled to Israeli citizenship. They've been quite definite about that."

Uri Malitt said, "The Law of Return does not apply to those whose past criminal activities might pose a danger to public safety."

Raab was unimpressed. "We're aware of that provision, and we've reminded the Israelis of it a number of times in the past."

Malitt cleared his throat. "It may be that Mr. Gorodetsky's background was never thoroughly investigated."

Raab wanted to say, It also may be that Israel did not need American Phantoms until now. He did not say this, not for fear of offending or embarrassing the Israeli colonel, but because a strange and disconcerting thought had just occurred to him.

He felt sorry for Leo.

He strained to analyze this, as Brickhill was saying, "Colonel Malitt assures me he'll discuss the matter directly with Mrs. Meir. I'll personally inform the ambassador."

Raab nodded inattentively. He was remembering the day, so many years ago, when he told Leo how ashamed he was that Leo was a Jew. But now, aware of all Leo had done for Israel and the Jews, these same Jews now so unblinkingly prepared to sell him out, Raab was himself slightly ashamed.

Raab's discomfort was gone almost before it started. Leo Gorodetsky deserved whatever he got. Senator Brickhill read Raab's mind.

Brickhill grinned. "Nice birthday present, eh?"

— 30 —

LEO was in the driveway when the car with diplomatic plates pulled up at the house. Zahav bounded from the yard, barking. Leo quieted the dog and stepped out to the sidewalk to meet the young man who seemed uncomfortable, almost nervous as he presented a calling card.

"Mr. Gorodetsky, I'm Will Braswell, sir."

Engraved in the center of the card was the crest of the U.S. State Department, and in the lower left corner, small blue letters: EMBASSY OF THE UNITED STATES OF AMERICA. And the embassy's address: 71, Hayarkon Street, Tel Aviv, Israel. In the lower right corner, **Willard L. Braswell, Vice Consul**.

Williard Braswell fidgeted as Leo slipped the card into his shirt pocket and studied him. He was very young, a boy really, wearing a rumpled seersucker suit, button-down blue oxford cloth shirt, and regimental tie. And white-buck shoes.

Leo said, "All right, so what can I do for you?"

Braswell appeared at a loss. He patted down the crown of his thick black hair, which immediately sprang up again. Zahav growled. Braswell stepped worriedly back.

"He won't hurt you," Leo said, and to the dog, "Down!"

Zahav tensed, but Leo slapped the dog's rump gently. Zahav immediately knelt at Leo's feet. Willard Braswell said, "Nice animal. What's his name?"

"Zahav," Leo said.

"That's Hebrew for 'red,' isn't it, sir?"

" 'Gold,' " Leo said. "It means 'gold.' Do you want to come inside?"

"Sir, my business will take only a moment," Braswell said. He cleared his throat. "I'm going to have to ask for your passport."

At that instant, Renata emerged from the house. Willard Braswell nodded politely and said, "Ma'am."

Leo said, "He's from the embassy. He wants my passport."

"Your passport?" Renata said. She looked at Braswell. "What on earth for?"

Braswell removed a folded piece of paper from his pocket. The bottom was serrated where it had been torn from the telex machine. He handed it to Leo.

Leo read it and silently gave it to Renata who read it aloud. " 'U.S. Embassy, Tel Aviv. United States passport number 103835, issued Leo Gorodetsky, is hereby amended under Section 215b, United States Immigration and Naturalization Act, restricting travel to any country other than the United States. Document to be surrendered for appropriate endorsements ASAP. Signed, Woodruff, Passport Division.' "

Renata, bemused, returned the paper to Braswell. He folded it and put it back into his pocket. He said to Leo, "May I have the passport, please, sir?"

At Leo's feet Zahav, sensing the tension, growled and moved to rise. Leo knelt to pat him.

"Sir, the passport?" Braswell said, almost as a plea.

"Don't you dare give it to him!" Renata said, and to Braswell, "You need a reason to ask for a passport. What is the reason?"

"Ma'am, I'm sorry, I'm only following orders—"

"—get out!" Renata said.

Leo laughed quietly. Renata's anger touched him; she was being protective. "Relax," he said. "Everybody relax. Why don't I go over to the embassy and talk to the ambassador? He's a friend of mine, you know."

"Sir, the ambassador is in Geneva and won't be back for several days. I tried to reach him all morning about this."

"Well," Leo said easily, "I'm not giving you the passport until I speak with someone in authority."

"Sir," Braswell said, and paused. He was very nervous. "The deputy chief of mission instructed me to comply with the telex."

"Well, you can jolly well trot on back to the deputy chief of mission and tell him to come here himself and get it!" Renata said.

Again, Renata's anger made Leo laugh. It seemed to disconcert Willard Braswell entirely. "I'll relay your message," he said, and without another word turned, hurried to the car, and drove away. Zahav scrambled up to chase the car a short distance, then trotted back.

Renata shook her head grimly. "They'll never give up."

"They know the Israelis won't extradite me," Leo said. "But if they did," he continued, thinking aloud, "I'd have no passport to travel. I'd be able to go only to one place. The States."

"I think, Leo, you'd better see the prime minister," Renata said. "As soon as possible."

"ASAP," he said quietly, aloud to himself.

"I beg your pardon?"

"ASAP," he said. "In the dispatch from Washington, it said they wanted my passport surrendered ASAP. A-S-A-P: as-soon-as-possible."

The prime minister, who had already been informed of the passport revocation, did see him ASAP. But not, as before, in her friendly kitchen, although they did meet in an eating place. In Jaffa, a small Arab café fronting the beach. She arrived in a convoy of three late-model Plymouth sedans. Golda, in the center car, waited while four burly security men, two from each end car, jumped out and strode into the café. The security men, all young, wore open collared sport shirts under their jackets, and two carried unconcealed Uzi machine pistols.

The café consisted of two sections. One, the larger, main room had six tables and wire-backed chairs, and three booths. The other section was a small, trellis-ceilinged dining area in the courtyard. It could be entered only from the main room.

As arranged, Leo waited in the courtyard, alone, seated at a large picnic-bench-style table. A moment after two security men assumed positions near the stone archway separating the two rooms, Golda Meir entered.

"You see what's happened to me?" she said. She waved a hand at the guards. "It's a wonder I'm allowed to go to the bathroom alone!" She reached into her purse for a cigarette and lighter, lit the cigarette, inhaled, and said to Leo, "You're not smoking?"

"I'm cutting down," he said. "Doctor's orders."

"I should, too," she said. "But to hell with it. I'm surprised you took so long to see me."

"I didn't think it would get this serious," he said. "It is, isn't it?"

"Yes." Flat, no equivocation. Yes. Before Leo could speak, she continued, "I wanted this opportunity to explain personally to you what's happened."

"I know what's happened," Leo said. He strained to keep the anger and hurt from his voice. He had promised himself to remain calm. Cool, calm, logical. "You're knuckling under."

"Yes." Again, flat, unequivocal. "I have no choice."

Leo said nothing. He craved a cigarette but refused to indulge himself.

"*We* have no choice," Golda corrected herself. "Israel. Israel has no choice."

"Are you trying to tell me, Mrs. Meir, that you honestly believe the

United States government considers me—my extradition—so important that it would make it the price of a billion-dollar arms deal?"

"You're suggesting they might be bluffing?"

"Of course!"

Golda, puffing on her cigarette, studied him a long moment. Then, "You're a gambler." It was a statement, prefacing a point to be made. "Is it a good gamble for me to risk the procurement of desperately needed military supplies on the possibility—no, the probability, I'll concede that much—that it is all bluff and bluster? What are we talking about, Leo? I realize it might sound melodramatic, but isn't that what it comes down to: your freedom versus the security of this country? Now please tell me: is it a good gamble?"

The logic astonished Leo. The word *sophistry* flashed into his mind, but did not enable him to refute the logic, nor the prime minister's next words.

"I know what you've done for this country, and even your personal sacrifices. And, for what it's worth, we're eternally grateful." She waved a freshly lit cigarette at him. "Yes, this is a hell of a way to show it. But, Leo, it's a matter of plain, simple, hard business. Now that, I'm certain, is something you understand."

Business.

"And I'll tell you something else," she said. "No matter how deep our gratitude and appreciation, sentimentality for old times and old friends cannot be allowed to interfere in matters of state."

Business.

She reached across the table and clasped his hand. "I'm sorry," she said. "Truly, truly sorry."

He said nothing, but was thinking, Yes, it is obvious how sorry you are, how truly, truly sorry. So sorry that you feel it would be indiscreet to have a three-minute conversation with me at any place other than this place where we are unlikely to be seen together.

She glanced impatiently past him to a security man talking into a hand-held transceiver. She looked at her watch. "I'm late for an appointment, Leo." She rose.

He did not rise with her, but looked at her and said, "I'm sorry, too."

She nodded, then turned and started away. At the archway she stopped. She came back to the table. "You know," she said carefully, "we are after all a country of laws. You have the right to petition the Supreme Court to review your claim for refuge under the Law of Return." The parchment-like skin of her face crinkled in a wry smile. "It might be quite a while before the case is heard."

After she left he sat staring at the little white and red flowers entwined in the vines of the overhead trellis. From the other room he heard occasional laughter and the steellike clicking of dinnerware. He also heard the hard, flat, midwestern ring of her voice.

Business. A matter of plain, simple business.

No wonder Ben Gurion once called Golda Meir the best man in his cabinet. Surprisingly, Leo felt no bitterness. He wanted to feel bitter, but could not. Instead, he felt old and tired. Too tired to fight. A strange, new, frightening feeling.

"Tiger," he said aloud, but almost in a whisper. "The ride is getting rough. Rougher," he corrected himself. "I'm falling off."

And feeling sorry for yourself.

Yes, it seems so, doesn't it?

Then you have to keep fighting.

Who? he asked. Who do I fight? How, and with what?

But he remembered what she said about the Supreme Court, and remembered he had many friends in high places in Israel. If Golda Meir could be pressured by a few do-gooding hypocrites in the United States, then she could also be pressured by her own countrymen. More so.

And she had practically spelled it out for him, hadn't she? She said it might take a long time for the Supreme Court.

It took more than a year.

But in the end—and he realized it long before the end—it was inevitable. As Golda Meir said, it was business. Plain and simple business. Despite the fact that he had received a full pardon for the only crime of which he was ever convicted, a youthful indiscretion, the Supreme Court of Israel ruled that his background and associations with known criminal elements posed a danger to the public safety. His claim for refuge under the Law of Return was rejected.

The Israeli government honored the terms of their extradition treaty with the United States. Leo Gorodetsky was given thirty days to settle his affairs and leave the country.

2.

Below, the coast fell away sharply as the airplane climbed out over the water. Although mid-December, the day was sunny and the beaches crowded. Renata, at the window, said softly, "It's too far north."

"What's too far north?" Leo asked.

"I was wondering if we could see Herzliya from here. I wanted one last look at the house."

He gazed past her out the window. After a moment he sat back. "You're right," he said. "Too far north."

She rested her hand on his. They sat in the front section of the El Al 707, alone but for the pretty stewardess preparing coffee in the forward galley. They were the only passengers in the huge, empty cabin. Leo had chartered the airplane—for a cool $60,000. Not because he particularly desired an airliner all to himself, but because of a slight change in destination. As the two FBI agents who were following him had learned to their chagrin.

Thinking of the agents, he laughed. It was worth $60,000 just to see their expressions of utter astonishment and dismay when they had confronted him and Renata in the Lod terminal. One, a stolid, crewcutted man in his early thirties, flashing his identification plaque, had said, "We'll be on the plane with you, sir."

"What plane is that?" Leo had asked innocently.

"The one you're flying back to New York on," said the second agent. He was slightly younger, but dressed similarly. They were almost conspicuous in their plain, neat, natural-shouldered suit jackets and narrow-brimmed felt hats.

"TWA Eight-oh-five," the first FBI agent said.

"I canceled that booking," Leo said. "As a matter of fact, I'm not going to the States."

"Excuse me, sir," said the first man. "You're under an extradition order. You are not permitted to travel anywhere other than to the continental United States."

Leo removed a large folded document from his pocket, opened it, and presented it to the first man. "Read it and weep, boys."

The document was a gift from Golda Meir. An Israeli Interior Ministry travel permit entitling Leo to visit any country granting him entry. A final gesture of friendship and appreciation.

Not to mention, perhaps, guilt.

Now, watching the Seat Belt and No Smoking signs going off, he unbuckled his seat belt and brought the special travel permit from his pocket again. He unfolded it and spread it on his lap.

"You keep looking at that as though you're afraid the words might change," Renata said.

"As though it might be written in invisible ink?" he said. "No, I was wondering how Mr. Hoover will explain this to Marty Raab. How the fugitive escaped so easily. Not that Mr. Hoover is obliged to explain anything, or even would, to an assistant attorney general. But somebody will sure as hell want to know how this was done"—he tapped the paper gently—"without the United States knowing about it."

"Someone slipped up," she said. "Thank God!"

No, not God, he thought, Golda Meir.

Just then Ray Newman emerged from the flight deck. Part of the charter deal was that the pilot would be Ray Newman. Although Leo frequently flew El Al, somehow it was never with Ray Newman. Nor had he ever seen him in uniform, the charcoal gray jacket with the embroidered silver wings just above the left breast pocket, the wings with the Star of David in the center. And the gray cap with the silver scrambled eggs on the leather visor.

"A real *shtarker*," Leo said, fingering the four black captain's stripes on Ray's jacket sleeve. "A little different from the old PBY days, I think."

"A little," Ray said, and to Renata, "How you doing, Mrs. Gorodetsky?"

"I'm sad to be leaving, but glad for where we're going."

Ray removed his cap and perched on the armrest of the chair on the opposite aisle. "It should be a smooth flight. We'll be in Lisbon just after noontime. Shouldn't be on the ground more than an hour for refueling, and then we'll be on our way."

"What time do you estimate Nassau?" Leo asked.

"Weather permitting, approximately two P.M., Nassau time."

After Ray returned to the cockpit and the stewardess served coffee and croissants, Leo decided to nap. He moved across the aisle, removing the center armrest so he could stretch out on the two wide first-class seats.

He slept almost all the way to Lisbon, and then again during the over-water flight. Renata awakened him an hour out of Nassau. He washed, shaved with his electric razor, changed shirts, and even put on a tie. A blue and white polka dot blending nicely with his blue blazer and gray flannel slacks.

"Very handsome," Renata remarked. "You'll make a fine impression on Mr. Peters."

"Only one thing impresses Mr. Peters," Leo said. "Money."

"I don't believe that's unique to him," she said.

"Not hardly," Leo said. "By the way, they're arranging a villa for us just outside of town. On the north side, overlooking the whole harbor."

"I can't wait."

I can, Leo thought, but did not say it, and instead looked out the window, down at the ocean. They were so high, 31,000 feet, the water resembled a vast, almost smooth, blue-and-green-dappled sheet of glass curving gently with the horizon.

Leo was certainly not displeased that money impressed Mr. Peters. Gregory Peters, the one-time Grand Bahamian Hotel busboy now a power in the Bahamian government. It was he, after a brief negotiation with George Gerson, who pulled the strings admitting Leo to the Bahamas.

Price of admission, $5 million. Cash.

Renata was unaware of this, and Leo wanted her to remain unaware. The fact that he had to bribe his way into a country embarrassed him. More accurately, shamed him. The big man, the King, the Czar.

The Pariah.

Far in the distance where the blue sky merged with the dark horizon, a series of small, thin black lines appeared. The lines gradually expanded as though rising up from the ocean until they extended the entire length of the horizon. And became New Providence Island, and the Nassau skyline.

The instant the airplane touched down and began rolling, three police cars, lights flashing, wheeled onto the runway and raced after her. Leo unfastened his seat belt and hurried up the aisle to the flight deck. In the left seat, Ray Newman listened intently to tower instructions as he steered the airplane off the runway and onto a taxiway. On each side of the airplane was a police car, and a third police car directly ahead. They were escorting the airplane. But not to the terminal.

"What the hell's going on?" Leo asked.

Ray flicked a switch on the overhead instrument panel. The calypso-accented voice of the tower operator crackled loud and clear over the cockpit loudspeakers.

". . . I say again, El Al Four-zero-three is to follow the vehicles to a designated parking area. Please comply."

Ray spoke into his microphone. "Understood, tower, but we request disembarkation of our passengers at the terminal."

"Negative, Four-zero-three. An immigration officer will board your aircraft."

"Roger," Ray said. He slammed the microphone into its receptacle and tore off his earphones. "Shit!"

The police car in front of the airplane had stopped, and a white-helmeted policeman stood signaling them to halt. Ray braked to a stop and pulled back the thrust levers. The copilot began shutting down the engines and generators. The jet-whine of the turbines decreased in pitch like the voice on a record slowing on a turntable, quieter and hoarser until, finally, silent.

A small ramp-stairway truck raced down the taxiway to the airplane's rear passenger door. "Okay, let's see what it's all about," Ray said. He removed his shoulder harness and slid back his seat.

Leo felt his throat tighten and his body stiffen with the familiar chill of anger. He followed Ray into the cabin. They walked down the aisle past Renata. "What's wrong?" she asked.

"I don't know," Leo called after her, but he did know. He simply did not want to believe it.

The stewardess had already opened the door for the stairway truck, which was backed snugly up to the fuselage. In a moment the policeman entered. Just behind him was a young black man in rumpled civilian clothes. He addressed Ray.

"I have orders not to permit your passengers to leave the aircraft, or for the aircraft to remain here "

"What the hell are you talking about?" Leo said. 'I have permission!"

The plainclothesman again addressed Ray. "These are my orders. You must refuel the aircraft and depart immediately."

"Whose orders?" Leo asked. "I've been invited to this country by Gregory Peters personally!"

"Sir, these orders were issued by Mr. Peters."

Leo drew in his breath to speak, but then glanced at Renata who had joined them at the door. Her face was wrinkled in bewilderment. "They won't let us get off?" she asked quietly.

Leo's legs felt suddenly weak. He reached blindly behind him for the armrest of a chair. Ray grasped Leo's arm, but Leo pushed him away. "I want to talk to Mr. Peters," he said to the plainclothesman. "Now."

"I'm sorry, sir." The black man was cool, and very professional. "Mr. Peters is unavailable. He did, however, leave specific instructions regarding this matter." He turned to Ray. "Now, Captain, a refueling truck will arrive here shortly. You may file your flight plan via radio to the control tower."

"Flight plan to where?" Ray asked. "This airplane is scheduled to return to Israel."

"Then I suppose that is where you will file for. Good day, sir," the plainclothesman said, and moved to leave.

"Just a minute," Leo said. He had pulled his wallet from his jacket pocket and was counting out hundred-dollar bills. Three, which he held out to the plainclothesman. "I want to make some phone calls."

The uniformed policeman, standing silently in the doorway, stared at the money. He looked at the plainclothesman, who was also staring at the money. For a crazy instant Leo imagined one of them snatching the money and fleeing down the stairs.

The plainclothesman raised one hand, palm up. "Please, sir, I can't allow you to leave the plane." He turned and hurried down the ramp stairway.

Leo crumpled the bills in his fist. The entire cabin spun before his eyes. He sank into the chair. Renata and Ray Newman stood at the open door watching the ramp truck drive away. Then Renata noticed Leo. She sat beside him and placed her hand on his cheek.

"You're burning up!"

"The son of a bitch!" he said. He opened his fist and gazed at the money, now rolled into a soggy green ball. "The double-crossing son of a bitch!"

But even as the words spilled from his lips, he knew Gregory Peters had double-crossed him only technically. He knew what had happened. Five million was not enough, or fifty million. The awesome influence of the United States of America.

". . . needs a doctor," Renata was saying.

"I'll radio the tower," Ray said, and started up the aisle.

Leo caught Ray's sleeve. "I'm all right!" He rose, gripping the back of the chair, and struggled to separate the thousand thoughts flowing through his mind. Especially the five million dollars. Gerson had delivered it to Peters in cash. All right, they'd get it back somehow. Another part of his mind pondered the big problem. Where to go.

"The Wandering Jew," he said, with a quiet, harsh laugh. "No, The Dutchman! The Flying Dutchman. You remember that story. The Dutch sea captain who's consigned through all eternity to sail the seven seas. That's me. I'm the goddam Flying Dutchman!" He laughed again, and said to Ray, "The Flying Jew, I mean."

Ray said nothing.

"Where do we go?" Leo asked.

Ray shook his head helplessly.

Ray Newman filed for Tel Aviv, via Lisbon, but revised his flight plan in midair. Panama now. They landed, and actually entered the terminal where Leo telephoned a high government official he knew. This time he offered $10 million. The official felt confident he could prevail upon President Torrijos. Less than half an hour later a man from the Panamanian Interior Ministry arrived. Accompanied by an American vice-consul.

The Panamanian regretfully informed Leo that because he lacked an entry visa, none could presently be issued. Of course, should he desire to submit his application at a later date—with evidence that he possessed a valid passport of the country of his residence—it would most certainly receive full consideration. The American vice-consul was present to see that Leo's rights as an American citizen were protected.

After arranging with El Al to continue the charter—at a cost of $2,000 per hour for aircraft and crew—they went to Costa Rica, where George Gerson had preceded Leo's arrival to negotiate with the appropriate authorities. The Costa Ricans apologetically refused Gerson's client entrance into their country.

Guatemala. No amount of money acceptable.

Venezuela. Ben Sylbert's contacts were utilized, and Ben himself flew to Caracas. There, for sure, money talked. Leo's party checked into two suites at the Tamanac Intercontinental Hotel.

For the first time in nearly a week everyone enjoyed a full night's sleep. Leo woke early and, alone, had coffee and strolled the broad, tree-lined boulevard. He wanted to be alone, to think. The whole week had been a nightmare, a gallery of horrors.

All week the angina pains had worsened. Nitroglycerin eased the pain, but not completely. He had no intention of seeing a doctor, at least not until he was settled.

Ben said the story of Leo's saga had been picked up by the newspapers, and the FBI had men at the hotel. They skulked about, waiting like hovering vultures.

What surprised Leo—speaking of vultures, he thought—was the silence from New York, from Paul Calvelli. Not a single word, not even a message of admonition for all the embarrassing publicity. Well, Leo Gorodetsky still controlled IDIC, which controlled the Vegas hotels, so he could handle Paul Calvelli.

After walking what he estimated a mile, he retraced his steps back to the Tamanac. The walk and fresh air helped to clarify his thinking. The first order of business was to find a good place to live here in Caracas.

Then he would relax. Sleep a whole week. And deal with the problems

one at a time. By the time he reached the hotel he believed he had all
the future moves fairly well planned. The Venezuelans would grant him
the necessary *laissez-passer* to travel freely, enabling him to continue
strengthening his European operations while maintaining his position
within the Alliance. At the same time, an all-out public-relations campaign in Israel would eventually pressure Golda Meir to grant him citizenship. Yes, it would all work out.

The first person he saw in the hotel lobby was Ben Sylbert. One look
at Ben's grim face, and Leo knew all the well-planned future moves were
useless. His temples pounded, anginal pain squeezed his left shoulder
and arm like an electric shock.

"Leo . . ." Ben's voice fell to a weary sigh. "It's off."

Leo stood staring at him. The pain was gone almost as fast it came,
but seemed to have sapped all his strength. He leaned against one of
the mosaic-tiled lobby pillars.

"I don't know what happened," Ben said. "It was set, fixed, in the bag.
Straight from the very top."

It was an effort to talk. "Come on, Ben, you know what happened.
We both know. Good old Uncle Sam."

"They want you out of this country in twenty-four hours," Ben said.
"It's that bastard Charlie Brickhill, and his Justice Department stooges.
I can't believe they'd be this vindictive. I fucking well cannot believe it!"

"The Flying Jew," Leo said quietly. He marveled at his own calmness.
"Well," he said, forcing a smile. "What's the next stop?"

The question was answered a few minutes later by Ray Newman. "Leo,
I've been ordered to take the airplane back to Israel. 'Without further
delay,' " he quoted.

"I guess El Al doesn't need my business," Leo said. The initial $60,000
charter price had so far escalated into nearly $400,000, every cent of it
paid daily into the airline's New York office.

"Tell me what you want me to do," Ray said. "You want to go someplace
else, I'll fly you there. You say so, Leo, I'll hold on to the airplane until
they drag it away from us."

"Where would we go, Ray?" Leo said. It was rhetorical, and Leo did
not expect a reply, nor did Ray offer one. "I think, kid, the game's over.
Last of the ninth, two out, and they just called strike three on me."

Ray said nothing.

"And you know what?" Leo said. "I'm tired. I am very, very tired."

The Flying Jew.

A rowdy group of newsmen crowded the Pan American Airways terminal at Los Angeles International airport. At Leo's insistence Renata
had gone on ahead the previous day. He did not want her subjected to
the humiliation of his being arrested. She had agreed to await his release
on bail at the house Ben Sylbert rented for them in Beverly Hills.

Leo and two FBI agents were the last passengers through the jetway. Leo looked haggard, clothes wrinkled, shirt collar unbuttoned. The two agents, both big men, dwarfed Leo. Deliberately chosen for that very purpose, he believed. The cameras began grinding, flashbulbs popped, reporters surged forward.

Uniformed policemen and federal marshals formed a protective ring around him during the arrest formalities. Over the voices screaming questions and requests for statements he strained to concentrate on the charges being read. The sounds all blended into a single, waterfall-like roaring in his ears. He hardly realized he was handcuffed, hustled through the terminal to a car outside, and driven to the Federal Building in West Los Angeles for booking and fingerprinting.

And placed in a holding cell for several hours, his release on bail delayed on some technicality or other. But finally George Gerson and a local attorney appeared. He was freed on a $750,000 cash bond.

When he arrived at the house, a handsome Georgian Colonial on a pleasant street overlooking the Beverly Hills Hotel, Renata insisted that he go to bed immediately. He slept twelve hours and woke amazingly refreshed and, for the first time in days, with an appetite. The good feeling remained, and he began looking forward to preparing his defense with the attorneys Robert Lewis Peyton had sent out for preliminary consultations.

And then, three days later, his luck cycle swung back to win. George Gerson, who had returned to New York, phoned. "Leo, you'll never believe it. I just got a call from Ben Sylbert, who just spoke to a friend of his in Washington." Gerson took a deep breath. "Leo, Albert Collins is dead."

Leo said nothing. He did not know what to say, or think.

"He's dead, Leo," Gerson said. "Last night. Natural causes. The government's trying to keep it quiet, and they'll still go ahead and try to prosecute. But their case is gone. You've won!"

They celebrated that evening at Chasen's, where Leo drank and ate too much, but did not experience even mild anginal pain. He felt marvelous. And with good reason: he had won. He watched the 11 o'clock television news, and part of an old movie, and fell into a deep, dreamless sleep. The pain awakened him. And he was warm, and then cold, then warm again. His whole body was wet with perspiration.

He lay staring at the luminous dial of the radio clock on the bed table: 3:35. The numerals glowed in the dark. The 5 flicked to 6: 3:36.

The anginal pain, which a moment ago had been severe, now was only a dull, constant ache that he knew would soon turn bad again. He tried to sit up, but could not. He wanted to reach for the bottle of nitro pills next to the radio. He never remembered feeling so tired, so weak. He continued staring at the clock, but could not focus his eyes.

"Leo . . . ?" Renata sat up in bed beside him. "Leo, what is it?"

He tried to turn to her, but could not. He could not breathe. He thought he was suffocating. He forced himself to turn, and to sit up. He could not see her, only a wall of red, revolving faster and faster with a sound so like jet engines he thought he might be back on the airplane. The sound increased in pitch until it blocked all other sound, and the whirring redness brightened until it was a blur of blinding, flashing, crimson light that stabbed into his eyes and plunged into his chest.

He said, "It hurts like hell! God, but it hurts!"

He heard her voice as a distant echo, and he thought she was saying, "But we won. How could this happen if we won?" Just before the red wall became black, he realized it was not Renata speaking the words, but himself thinking them.

How could this happen if we won?

He never heard her scream.

3.

Ralph Calvelli said, "Pop, all I know is what I read. I'm not there, so I'm not acquainted with the clinical details. I can only speak in generalities."

"So speak in generalities," Paul Calvelli said. He shifted the telephone to his other hand. "What is this 'bypass' operation? And what are his chances?"

"I think they said it was a quadruple?"

"That's right. Quadruple."

"Well, that means none of the arteries carrying blood to the heart are doing their job. In Mr. Gorodetsky's case they're probably close to a hundred percent blocked. What the operation does is replace those clogged arteries with new ones that they take, usually, from the veins of the legs. In other words, they bypass the old, bad ones. It's a relatively new procedure, but there's been considerable success. We've had good results with it out here."

Out here was Cleveland, Ohio, where thirty-five-year-old Ralph Calvelli, M.D., practiced medicine. He was an internist, and a good one. Although specializing in pulmonary diseases, he knew enough about the new bypass procedure to explain it in lay terms to his father. Leo Gorodetsky was a business associate of Paul's, so Paul's concern was understandable. Leo had suffered a massive coronary two days before, and was operated on the same evening.

". . . but what are his chances?" Paul was saying.

"Frankly, not good," Ralph said, and added cautiously, "From what I understand, that is. I mean, his age, and prior history. This is the second one, isn't it?"

"Second one, yes," Paul said. "The last one nearly killed him, too."

"He's hard to kill, I guess," Ralph said innocently. Paul breathed heavily into the phone; it sounded more like a sigh of resignation to Ralph.

"Look, Pop, I know how you feel, but please don't you get upset."

"I'm okay, Ralph, don't worry about me."

"Well, just so you understand the facts," Ralph said. "I mean, prepare yourself for the worst and hope for the best."

"Good advice, boy," Paul said. "How's Kim?"

"Terrific," Ralph said. "I'll give her your love."

"And the little guy?"

"Almost as tall as his mother. Nine years old, can you believe it?"

"Okay, Ralph, thanks a lot."

"Give Mom a kiss," Ralph said.

"I will," Paul said. "Oh, Ralph, you'll love this one: what's the only difference between Cleveland and the *Titanic*?"

"I'll bite," Ralph said. "What's the difference?"

"The *Titanic* had decent restaurants! Talk to you soon." Paul hung up and leaned back in his chair. The call to his physician son was only one of many he made that day to various cities around the country. He had been here in his office in the Hamilton Building since early afternoon, engaged in those other, far more important phone calls. And one long lunch meeting with fellow Alliance Council members.

They had reached some hard decisions.

The slender gray-haired nurse insisted Renata come to the cafeteria for coffee. "You've sat here three solid hours, Mrs. Gorodetsky," she said. "He's heavily sedated, and won't wake for hours yet. So at least get a breath of fresh air."

"My . . . daughter is due here any time," Renata said. She could not bring herself to say stepdaughter. She forced a smile. "She's flying all the way from Israel with her two children. She won't know where to find me."

"We'll leave word at the desk," said the nurse, whose name was Doreen Buckner. She supervised the Cardiac Intensive Care Unit at the Mt. Sinai facility of Cedars-Sinai Medical Center.

Doreen Buckner had great empathy for the nice-looking English lady whose husband was not expected to survive. Ten years ago a heart attack killed Doreen Buckner's own husband. Bypass surgery, unknown in those days, might have saved him. It certainly had helped Leo Gorodetsky; whether or not it saved him, only the next four or five days would tell. All that really kept him alive now, the surgeon said, was the man's incredible will to live.

A refusal to die.

Renata allowed the nurse to cajole her from Leo's bedside. In truth, she welcomed a brief respite. All the tubes protruding from his body, and his face under the transparent plastic oyxgen tent so deathly pale, and the ominous metronomic beep and glaring red numerals of the machines monitoring him. Numbers continually changing with the indifference of a stock-market quotation display. And the sharp, almost acrid odors enveloping the entire room, the four other beds, each bed within its own small curtained alcove.

Renata and Doreen Buckner went into the corridor and waited for the elevator. The nurse chattered away about the fine December Los Angeles weather, and Christmas plans. Renata only half listened; she had just realized, shocked, that exactly ten days ago their odyssey from Tel Aviv had begun. The odyssey of horror and frustration.

One week and three days.

She wondered how many miles they had traveled. She must ask Ray Newman when next they met. The elevator door opened. Renata blindly stepped forward—and nearly collided with Carla. For a confused instant neither recognized the other, and then a small voice called out, "*Savta* Renata!"

It was Sari, clutching Rivka's hand, which was clutched in Carla's. A moment of pandemonium as the women embraced and the girls danced happily around Renata. Doreen Buckner went to the cafeteria alone.

Carla, although exhausted from the long flight, changing planes at three different airports, and shepherding the girls, had nevertheless come directly from LAX to the hospital. Now, while Renata sat with the children in the waiting room, Carla went into the intensive care unit.

She remained with Leo only a few discouraging minutes. When she returned to the waiting room, Rivka was asleep on Renata's lap. Sari sat staring hypnotically at the clock on the opposite wall. One other person was in the room. A man, early thirties, close-cropped hair, dark-gray suit and tie. He sat uncomfortably, eyes fixed on a *Life* magazine in his lap.

"Justice Department," Renata said, deliberately loud, to Carla. The man pretended not to hear. "They're afraid the criminal might leave the intensive care unit and jump his bail." Then, for the man's benefit, Renata added, "That is the term, I believe: 'jump bail'?"

The man's discomfort was so obvious Carla almost felt sorry for him. She sat beside Renata and held her hand. "He's dying, isn't he?"

Sari's head whirled. She said to her mother, "*Sava* is dying? You said he was sick, that's all!"

"I said he was very sick," Carla said. "When people are very sick sometimes they die."

Renata said to Carla, "They say if he gets through the next few days, he'll have a chance. The surgery was very successful."

"But the patient died," Carla said.

Renata started replying, then stopped; she was weary of platitudes and homilies. She honestly did not believe Leo would die, but to say so was itself a platitude. Sari spared her the effort by changing the subject.

Sari said to Renata, "We had to leave Zahav at *Savta* Ziporah's house."

"I'm sure they'll take good care of him," Renata said. Ziporah was Sari's paternal grandmother, Avi's mother.

"I hope they feed him at the right time," Sari said. She looked at the clock again. "Eight-thirty. What time is that at home?"

Renata tried to compute the time difference in her mind. She was so exhausted the figures swam before her eyes. "Ten hours ahead, aren't they?" she asked Carla.

"I think so," Carla said.

"That makes it six-thirty in the morning," Renata said to Sari.

"Six-thirty in the morning there," Sari said, frowning. "Eight-thirty at night here. When will they know if Poppy dies?"

"He's not going to die, darling," Renata said. "Not so easily."

"That's good," Sari said, and turned to gaze at the clock again.

It was also 8:30 in San Diego where, in the floodlighted driveway of the Torrey Pines Racquet Club, Jack Maynard watched his one-week-old red Corvette race to a brake-screeching halt before him. The shiny-faced college-kid parking attendant, leaving the lights on and motor running, leaped from the car and grinningly confronted Jack Maynard.

"Your chariot awaits, sir!"

Maynard tossed his canvas tote bag into the Corvette through the open window. "Let me ask you something," he said to the kid. "If that was your car, would you cowboy it around this driveway like that?"

"Mr. Maynard, if those wheels were mine, I'd cowboy it everywhere!"

Maynard sighed. He had slept only three hours the previous night, and been in meetings all day; if Leo Gorodetsky died, Jack Maynard had much to do, fast. Mainly, securing his own status in the corporation, which certainly had not been enhanced by the botched Albert Collins job. But Leo not only held Jack blameless for that, he had slated him for the eventual presidency of IDIC.

Jack Maynard had thought about this, his future, most of that day, remaining in his office until well after six, when he drove to the club. Three grueling sets of racquetball had not relaxed him, only left him sore and drained of energy. And the single beer afterward made him drowsy.

And now a wise-mouthed parking lot attendant. He wanted to tell the kid if he ever caught him abusing the car like this again he'd break both his arms. But it suddenly seemed too much trouble. Even too much trouble not to tip him. He flipped the boy a quarter, got into the car, and drove away.

He loved the car. Far more than the Jaguar he traded for it, and the Porsche before that. It could do 120 mph in the flat. The only object more desirable than a beautiful, fast, well-constructed automobile was a beautiful, fast, well-constructed woman. Like Charlene, his first wife, a former Radio City Music Hall Rockette, now married to the owner of three Florida television stations.

The narrow two-lane road wound through the hills like a roller coaster, with heavy spring steel barricades emplaced where the road curved sharply and fell off in a sheer, almost vertical two-hundred-foot drop to the rocky beach below. Now, on an upgrade, the Corvette's headlights shining emptily into the sky, Maynard shifted into second and floored the accelerator. He concentrated on the yellow center line, and thought about Charlene, and also the possibility of entering a road-rally race; he did not want to think about business or Leo Gorodetsky. Atop the hill he shifted back into third, then fourth for the brief straightaway.

He did not see the jeep that appeared from a brush-obscured side road and slid in behind him; its lights were out. Just as he downshifted to descend he felt the jarring thud of the jeep's broad, push-plate bumper striking the Corvette's rear bumper. He whirled to glance through the back window. He caught only a glimpse of the Corvette's red taillights reflected in the jeep's windshield. Now, turning front again, in the rear-view mirror he saw the same blurred red reflection. He did not know two men were in the jeep, one training a rifle on the Corvette.

But he knew he had to get away, fast. He jammed the gearshift lever back into fourth. The Corvette sped smoothly down the steep grade. At that instant the man in the jeep fired the rifle. The bullet shattered the Corvette's right side mirror. Jack Maynard flung an arm reflexively across his face. The Corvette, racing down the slope, reached another sharp curve. Maynard hit the brakes, but could not swing the wheel around soon enough. The Corvette hurtled through the spring-steel barrier and flew off the road.

Airborne, it seemed to hover horizontally an instant. Then it tipped forward and plummeted down toward the beach. To Jack Maynard it was an eternity, time enough for a million thoughts. He tried desperately to sort them out, but through the jumble of thoughts one in particular kept looming bright and clear. The way they had gotten him was so simple it was almost brilliant. He admired its cleanliness.

The beautiful red Corvette struck the rocks on the beach, caromed into the air, skidded across a shore-break ditch, doors disintegrating, tires shredding, hood flying off, and smashed to a halt right side up against another rock outcropping. For a moment the only sound was the steady soft hiss of air from ruptured hoses. And then the fuel tank exploded.

High above the beach the two men in the jeep watched the Corvette burn. After a moment they drove off. The jeep's headlights were on now, although really not needed. The road was brightly illuminated in the glare of the flames of the car burning on the beach.

Shortly before this, at precisely 8:37, in Las Vegas, Art Lewis received the phone call. He noted the time because he was lying in bed listening to KLVR, Ben Sylbert's FM station, featuring a program of oldies but goodies, including several Bea Wain vocals. When Bea Wain sang "My Reverie," or "Deep Purple," it sent Art's mind back to more pleasant times.

Not more lucrative times, to be sure, but in many ways more pleasant.

Then, before the war, Art—whose class of 1935 Roxbury, Massachusetts, High School classmates knew him as Avram Levitan—sometimes actually enjoyed being a bookie's runner. No pressure, no worries, just do your job and collect your weekly $17. Thirty-five years later, as the Barclay's general manager, he took down $100,000 annually, plus stock options, but sometimes certainly did not enjoy it. The last few days were a prime example.

Leo Gorodetsky supposedly dying. And everybody nervous about their jobs, although for most of them Leo's death should mean no great change. Even with him out of the country since 1962, eight years, his companies functioned like the well-oiled machines they were. Business went on.

But Leo dead meant a change for Art Lewis. More responsibility. Art would have to step in and take over full control of the Vegas operations, both the Barclay and the Oasis. Art knew Leo considered him a key man, strong enough to deal with the New York people, yet remain independent of them.

He closed his eyes, the better to appreciate Bea Wain. "Que Será, Será," "What Will Be, Will Be." Which, he thought, as the phone rang, was exactly the situation. What will be, will be. He was not worried.

The phone rang again, the private line.

Chuck Emery, Barclay shift boss. Two men from New York were in the hotel. They wanted to see Art immediately. Art told Chuck to put one of them on the phone.

It was Mike Severino, Paul Calvelli's number-one underboss. Polite, but insistent, Mike said he had a message from Paul that should be delivered in person. If it was more convenient he could drive out to Art's house.

"No, stay there. I'll be right over," Art said. "Put Chuck back on." To Chuck Emery, Art said, "Get the chief of security and have him wait with you in the office. Have him call the sheriff and get a few deputies into the hotel. Just in case."

"Yes, sir," Chuck Emery said.

"Just stay cool," Art said, and hung up. He switched off the radio, splashed water on his face, and combed his hair. He was dressed, so needed only to slip into his shoes and pull on a sweater.

He went out to the carport. He stood an instant, shivering in the bitter desert cold, debating whether to return to the house for a jacket or even an overcoat. He decided the car heater would warm him fast enough.

He got into the Seville and turned the starter key. In the millisecond between the explosion and his death the only thought in his mind was relief that his wife was at her weekly Las Vegas Country Club pan game. Otherwise her car, a 1969 robin's-egg blue Mercedes 280 convertible, would have been parked beside the Seville and blown to pieces.

Five minutes before this, in Chicago, at 10:42 P.M. Central Time, another man had received another phone call. Phillip Stolzberg, forty-seven, was president of Trans-American News Bureau, an IDIC division that since 1932 had operated the race wire. Phil Stolzberg had attracted Leo's attention more than twenty years before when, as Trans-American New Orleans branch manager, he refused to hire a young third cousin of Harry Wise's. Harry, furious, demanded that Leo order Phil to hire the boy.

Clearly unintimidated, Phil explained to Leo that this particular boy was wholly unqualified for the job. Furthermore, Phil disliked him. If Phil could not hire and fire his own personnel, perhaps Leo should find another New Orleans manager.

Leo had no intention of losing a man with guts enough to defy Harry Wise. And Leo's instinct proved correct. Phil Stolzberg proved an invaluable executive, continually upgrading the race-wire service and broadening its operation with constant, clever innovation. He had recently signed five eastern tracks for direct telecasts exclusively into the horse rooms of the Barclay and the Oasis.

This evening, in the living room of the same Skokie, Illinois, home they had occupied for eighteen years, Phil Stolzberg and his wife watched a rerun of a Bing Crosby Christmas movie on WGN-TV. Phil endured the movie only because he was waiting for the eleven o'clock news. He had an idea the newscast might mention Leo.

In point of fact, Leo's illness was not mentioned; it was not considered newsworthy enough for national television. But Phil Stolzberg did not watch the eleven o'clock news, anyway. Sixteen minutes before the news came on he received the telephone call.

"Is this the Phillip Stolzberg residence?" A man, brusque, authoritative. "Sir, I'm Sergeant Kowalski, Skokie Police. We're holding your son—"

"—hold it," Phil said calmly into the phone. "My son is at a basketball game in Evanston." Cary Stolzberg, seventeen, was a senior at Skokie High, a high honors student and star basketball guard. He had been offered athletic scholarships to three colleges.

"No, Mr. Stolzberg," the policeman said. "He's here, and I'm sorry to say on a drug charge. Now before he's booked—"

"—I know my son," Phil interrupted. "He's never so much as even looked at drugs. Not even marijuana! You've got the wrong kid."

The policeman was patient. "Mr. Stolzberg, I realize your boy has never been in trouble before. That's why I want to give him and you this opportunity. You come down and talk it over. Maybe it can all be straightened out."

Ah, yes, now Phil understood. A shakedown. He felt both anger and relief. He glanced at his worried wife and said into the phone, "All right, I'll come over."

He hung up and explained the situation to his wife. These bastards, knowing who you were and that publicity was the last thing you wanted, made an art of extortion. There was no need for concern. He would pay them off and get Cary out.

It occurred to him when he stepped outside that he should have insisted on speaking with Cary. It was the last thought of his life. The gunman stepped from the shadows of the tall hedges separating his driveway from the neighbor's, and at point-blank range pumped two shotgun shells into Phillip Stolzberg's face and upper body. The gunman jumped into a car that had suddenly appeared in the street. Barbara Stolzberg, who rushed outside at the sound of the gunshots, was unable to describe the getaway vehicle.

The headlights of George Gerson's car illuminated the washing machine at the far end of the garage. The machine had been there for months now. The Goodwill people, summoned to pick it up, simply never showed up. He reminded himself to phone them once more. If they did not come in three days he would have it hauled away for junk.

He got out of the car, an El Dorado Caddy, careful the door did not bump the door of Betty's Mercedes. He locked the car and walked across the concrete floor. He reached the garage entrance and flicked the switch to close the overhead door at the exact instant the Caddy's headlights automatically went off. The clever little device never failed to please him, as did the car itself. It had replaced the Imperial a year ago when his longtime chauffeur, Joseph, retired. Gerson had decided to do his own driving again. It made him feel younger, less dependent.

And he had a hunch he'd better start feeling less dependent from now on about everything. During the day he spoke three times with Renata. Each time the news was worse. He had flown back to New York the day of Leo's heart attack and simply could not muster the strength to return to Los Angeles. Not for a few days at least. Or until Leo died.

He glanced at his wristwatch under the front porch light: 11:50. He had been at the office since ten that morning. He would have one drink, phone Renata again—it was only 8:50 in California—and then go to bed. Hopefully to sleep, hopefully not too overtired for sleep.

He opened the door with his key, entered the foyer, snapped the latch shut, and started into the library. From the open door of the master bedroom at the end of the long hall he saw the familiar, flickering light of the television.

"Betty?" he called.

No reply.

He stepped tentatively into the library, groping for the light switch on the wall. But just as his fingers found the grooved circular rheostat button, he decided to forgo the drink. He would phone Renata from the bedroom. He walked down the hall, again calling, "Betty?"

Again, no reply. Approaching the bedroom he heard the sound of television voices. A movie. The bedroom door was halfway open, the room dark but for the light from the television screen. Betty lay huddled on her side, in her dressing gown, atop the tufted white satin bedspread.

"Betty," he called, louder. "Get up and get under the blankets, dear—" the last word froze on his lips. A bright scene on the television screen had illuminated the entire room for a split instant, just long enough for Gerson to see his wife's wide open eyes staring unseeingly, and the white bedspread under her ear stained blotchy red.

What George Gerson never saw was the bulky figure of the man behind him placing the muzzle of a long-barreled .22 revolver with a five-inch silencer against the nape of his neck. Only one shot was fired. It made a sound like the splatting hiss of an air gun.

Doreen Buckner knew it was long distance from the hollow, echoed rumble of the connection. And the man who called, a New Yorker. She recognized the accent; what they called a Bronx, or Brooklyn, accent. His polite, almost deferential tone somehow did not match the quiet hoarseness of his voice.

Replying to his question, she said, "I'm sorry, but if you're not immediate family, I'm not allowed to give any details." As she talked, she noted the time of day in the log: 9:10 P.M.

"No, no, I understand," said the man on the phone. "All I wanted was to give him a message."

"Well, all right," Doreen said. "I suppose I can do that."

"Good," said the man. "Just tell him Paul called. Tell him there's nothing to worry about, and he'll be okay."

Doreen wrote the message on a scratch pad. "I'll give him the message," she said.

"It's important," the man, who was of course Paul Calvelli, said. "It's very important that he know this. He will be okay."

"Is there anything else?"

"No, thank you very much," Paul said, and then quickly added, "Oh, yes, tell him it was only business. Did you get that? Only business."

"Only business, I'll tell him."

"Thank you," Paul said, and hung up.

Doreen sat a moment staring at the words she had written. Then she glanced at the monitor board. Leo Gorodetsky's pulse was still slow, but increasing steadily. The other readings were equally encouraging. She had a sudden good feeling about his recovery. Over the years she had developed an almost unerring instinct. You somehow knew when a corner was turned, one way or the other. She would have liked to confide this to his wife and daughter in the waiting room. It would be good for them. Perhaps tomorrow, or the day after, when she knew for sure.

She tore the sheet off the scratch pad, folded it neatly, and paper-clipped it to Leo's status file. She thought it was a nice message, and probably meant his friends had prayed for him. She did not understand the last of it, the part about "only business." She assumed Mr. Gorodetsky would understand it.

Paul Calvelli knew Leo would understand it. After hanging up from Doreen Buckner, he walked to the window overlooking the street and gazed out. The street was deserted but for his car parked in front of the building, and the driver at the wheel.

One after the other the calls had come in that evening. From San Diego, Vegas, Chicago, Riverdale. And three other cities, including London. The one he felt bad about was Gerson. The wife, that is. The craziest luck. She had gone outside to empty a trashcan at the exact instant the hit man arrived. They nearly bumped into each other. He said she got a clear look at his face. No choice but to take her inside and wait for George. That was the only unplanned part of the whole operation.

It was over, all of it, finally. Leo was finished. Paul smiled grimly to himself, remembering how he argued with the Council about hitting Leo. They wanted to do Leo, too, just to wrap it all up.

"What for?" Paul had asked. "Once his people are gone, who'll ever dare support him again?"

"Why take a chance?" someone had asked.

"What chance?" Paul said. "He's liable to die, anyway."

"He might not."

"It doesn't matter," Paul said. "Even if he lives, he's finished. He's like Cassius Clay with his hands cut off. Ted Williams without a bat. Hey, Casanova with no balls!"

In the end Paul prevailed. He was glad. After all, he did owe Leo. For Nassau, when Leo chose to hit Vinnie Tomasino instead of Paul. It would have been just as easy for Leo to do them both. True, Leo saved Paul's life strictly for business reasons, but that did not change the fact.

So now they were even.

And there was not the slightest doubt in Paul Calvelli's mind that Leo, alive, posed no danger. Not anymore, not with his whole organization cut out from under him. And since the government's case against him had collapsed, no danger of him getting on a witness stand and trying to save himself by telling tales out of school.

No, Paul thought, the king was dead. It was all over. Besides, he had nothing personal against Leo. In truth, he had always liked him. What was done needed to be done.

Business, strictly business.

PART SEVEN

GORODETSKY'S LAW

WHAT impressed Susan Edelman was the old man's alertness, his grasp of the present. They were just concluding a long, quite emotional discussion of the Israeli invasion of Lebanon.

". . . and please remember one thing, young lady," he said. "Think of the past two thousand years, particularly the Holocaust, and compare the pitiful image of the Jew then to the warrior image of the Jew now. A figure of power, feared and respected. Which image is preferable? Now you think about that. Think carefully, please, and objectively." He smiled. He had a nice smile that warmed his eyes, which were surprisingly bright and clear.

"All right, Mr. Gorodetsky," she said. "I'll try."

"Good," he said, and reached down to pat the dog at his feet. "You hear, Zahav, she'll try."

The dog, an ancient golden retriever, nuzzled against the old man's legs. The pair, the old man and the old dog, were here on the beach in Venice almost every day. On the same bench just opposite the Israel Levin Senior Adult Center. At the same time, between three and four in the afternoon, depending upon the season. Now, in October, with the sun setting earlier, he came at the earlier hour.

Susan Edelman, a social worker devoting eight hours a week of volunteer time to the center, knew the old man only as Mr. Gorodetsky. An extremely wealthy man who lived with his wife in an expensive condo on the bluffs in Santa Monica. She also knew he contributed generously to the center—a social club for elderly Jews—and to the synagogue on the Venice promenade, although attending neither facility. He also never, to her knowledge anyway, associated with any of the people. If they tried to engage him in conversation he politely but firmly discouraged them. Once when she asked him why, he had replied, "It's not necessary, thank you." With a finality that warned her not to pursue the subject.

Now, glancing at his watch, Leo said, "It's five to four." He pointed to the senior adult center. "You'd better see to your charges."

"Will you be here tomorrow?" she asked. She rose and smiled down at him. "I'll have my rebuttal prepared by then."

"No rebuttal," he said. "Facts cannot be rebutted. When I say that thanks to Israel's military prowess, the Jew is no longer a pitiful stereotype, that is a fact. I don't condemn the Lebanon adventure, nor do I approve it. I reserve judgment until I have more information."

"We'll continue it tomorrow," she said. They shook hands and she left. She crossed the boardwalk to the adult center, still feeling the pressure of his handshake. An extraordinarily firm grip for a man his age. Eighty-three, he said. For months she had promised herself to learn more about him, but really did not know where to start. Although little by little, bit by bit, he told her things about himself.

He had told her about his daughter and grown granddaughters living in Israel. And the dog, Zahav, although bearing a Hebrew name, was American born and bred, namesake of a similar dog, now of course long dead, that had lived in Israel. Years ago, when his granddaughters visited him on his seventy-third birthday, they had given him another golden-retriever pup. Because of the startling resemblance to the Israeli dog, the new one was given the same name. Ten now, an advanced age for large breeds, Zahav suffered from severe arthritis, an ailment unfortunately shared with his master.

The old man had also told Susan Edelman that his son and son-in-law were killed in different wars; his wife was English, and Gentile, although probably a far better Jew than most.

Leo, gazing after her, watching her enter the center, knew how curious she was about him. He enjoyed providing just a small bit of information here, a hint of something else there. He liked her and knew she liked him, and knew sooner or later she would find out who he was. More accurately, *had been*. Her reaction would be interesting. Character-revealing.

All she had to do was go to the library or the newspaper morgue.

Morgue, a very appropriate word.

Yes, you knew you were old when you opened the newspaper each morning first to the obituary page to see whom you had outlived today. Which included many, he thought, pushing himself up now and wrapping Zahav's leash around his wrist.

"Come on, you old wreck," he said to Zahav. "Time to go." Zahav struggled to his feet, stretched his forelegs, nuzzled Leo's leg again, and was ready to move.

They started along the boardwalk. It was warm, the setting sun still fairly bright and the beach crowded with sunbathers and surfers, the boardwalk with roller skaters, bicyclists, and joggers. He had promised Renata to be home before 4:30, so there was plenty of time.

He walked slowly but easily, nodding to joggers whose faces had become familiar over the years. A lot of years, thirteen. He quite literally had watched some of those faces grow old, as they in turn watched his.

"Tell you what," he said to the dog as they reached the Santa Monica portion of the boardwalk. "We'll rest a few minutes here and sit and look out at the water."

He sat on the nearest bench and gestured Zahav down. The dog immediately lay on the concrete platform at Leo's feet. It always reminded Leo of the original Zahav, who loved lying in the sand, which would have earned this Zahav a thirty-five-dollar fine. Santa Monica dogs were not allowed on the beach proper. Leo wondered if they were still allowed on the Herzliya beach. He often thought of Herzliya and Israel these days. Another sign, of course, of the approaching End. Because, in the End, he would finally settle in Israel.

Buried beside his mother in the Tel Aviv cemetery.

Provisions of his will. In return for bequeathing the State of Israel the bulk of his estate, the State of Israel would allow him to be buried there.

A kind of posthumous Law of Return.

He wondered what pretty little Susan Edelman would say when she read that in his obituary.

Obituary? he asked himself. What makes you so sure you'll even have one?

Come on, he answered himself, it'll be big news.

You think.

Wasn't I big news for years? What about when old Albert Collins died? They mentioned my name more than his. He smiled, remembering hearing how Martin Raab, realizing the government's case against Leo was also dead, flew into an absolute rage that day.

Raab's rage might have been even worse seven years later had he read his own obituary. Leo's name was mentioned prominently in that, too. Poor son of a bitch went out with cancer, the same lung cancer that killed old Sal Bracci. Poetic justice of some kind.

Justice was not quite served, however, in the other son of a bitch's case, Charlie Brickhill. He, older than Leo, was still alive. Retired from the Senate after making a run for the presidency. Never made it past the primaries. Leo regretted not being a New York resident at the time. He would have enjoyed voting against him.

He moved to rise. Zahav also reluctantly got up. "We're both getting

there, old guy," Leo said. They started walking along the boardwalk
again.

A blue and white Santa Monica police cruiser drove through the adjacent parking lot. The young black policeman carefully scrutinized the
people on the boardwalk and in the cars. Looking for drugs, Leo thought,
and shook his head sadly.

The young black cop nodded at Leo, and Leo waved in reply. He saw
this same cop frequently here at the beach. He wondered if the cop
knew him. He thought not. Not many recognized him nowadays. For a
while, after he and Renata first moved to Santa Monica, the police regularly visited. L.A. police, usually, and sometimes FBI.

These visits always followed some newsworthy crime or other. Leo
was unfailingly courteous, responding to any and all questions.

". . . gentlemen," he would say. "How would I know anything about
it? How could I know? I've never engaged in anything other than gambling. Other than, of course, some bootlegging. But everyone did it, you
know. Where do you think Joe Kennedy made his money? Or the Bronf-
mans? How do you think Moe Annenberg got so rich? Not from oil
wells, believe me."

Or some Las Vegas skimming scandal. "Organized crime?" he would
say. "What the hell would I know about that? I don't even remember
the last time I was in Vegas! I sold all my points years ago. They tell me
it's all corporations now. They run it with computers. Listen, they even
have electronic slot machines."

True, all too true, including his not having been there in years. It was
a big city now. Half a million population, Ben Sylbert said when last
they talked. Half a million! How Harry would have crowed about that.
Leo could almost hear him. "See, Kleyner, just like I said!"

The police car drove through the parking lot and out the Ocean Park
Boulevard exit. It would return in exactly one hour, Leo knew. Smart,
patrolling regularly. What did they call it? High profile.

High profile.

That was Vegas, all right. He thought that one of these days, maybe
just for the fun of it, he and Renata should take a trip there to see what
it looked like now. She would enjoy it. They would stay at the Barclay,
now owned and operated by a giant international conglomerate. The
Alliance had been out for years. He wondered if the new Barclay management would comp him. Probably not. Probably they wouldn't even
know who he was.

Low profile.

Which was what he became after Paul Calvelli's masterful coup. Paul
was another he had outlived, by two years already, a peaceful death in
his own bed. Strangely, Leo never really resented what happened. In
truth, he admired it. Wiping him out in one fast series of simultaneous
hits. Given the chance, Leo would have done the same.

When he finally had accepted it, Leo welcomed retirement. If for nothing else, Renata's sake. It was not the worst kind of life. He knew time was passing him by, anyway. It was the way of things.

"Hey, mister, for Christ's sake, watch it!" A skater, a droopy-mustached young man with long hair tied messily into a bun, nearly collided with him. And just missed Zahav, who scampered indignantly away.

"You should be on the bike path!" Leo said.

"Fuck off, you old fart!" the skater, who was now far past, shouted.

Leo stared angrily after him. Then he patted the dog, gripped the leash, and resumed walking. Old fart, he thought, and laughed. The anger was gone, replaced by mild chagrin.

Sticks and stones, he thought, and told himself, You'll never learn.

Not now, he answered himself. I'm too old to learn.

The thought comforted him, although he knew it was only a lazy man's excuse. A lazy old man, he corrected himself, quickening his pace as he realized the sun was suddenly much lower. He had dawdled too long. Renata would worry if he was late. Only the other day she commented that he seemed to lose track of time. He did not disagree, suggesting that this was not uncommon to the elderly. Something about the metabolism slowing down. Time speeding up.

Which reminded him of tomorrow morning's doctor's appointment. The regular monthly checkup, which he considered a nuisance and waste of time. For eighty-three his health was excellent. Not a single problem since the operation thirteen years ago. Not even a twinge. Except of course for the arthritis, really not all that bad. But no heart problems, and the blood pressure good. So what do I have to complain about?

Who's complaining?

Renata will, he thought, when I come barreling in so late. He began walking even faster, deciding to take a shortcut through the tunnel under the pier. It would get him over to Ocean Avenue ten minutes faster.

He turned off the promenade and onto the bike path. On the ocean the sun was a huge dull orange ball hovering above the horizon. He stopped to gaze at it. He loved this time of day, when for one brief moment all time seemed to stop.

The sun fell lower. Now it was only a yellow disk glittering on the water. Leo yanked Zahav's leash and started toward the tunnel again. He entered, peering down the length of the narrow walkway at the light at the opposite end.

The light at the end of the tunnel, he thought, and tugged the leash. Zahav, growling nervously, had abruptly halted.

"What's the matter?" Leo asked, and rubbed the dog's haunch. "Arthritis, I'll bet. Tomorrow, instead of me going to the doctor, I think we'll take you." He pulled the leash again. Zahav obediently moved forward.

Almost in the very center of the tunnel Zahav growled again. Two

figures loomed up directly ahead. Two boys. Closer now, in the dim
tunnel light, Leo saw they were blacks. Kids, no more than twelve
or thirteen, one quite tall, both very thin and wiry. They loped rather
than walked.

Both were on the far left, apparently giving Leo and the dog plenty
of room. Suddenly one, the taller, swung into the very middle of the
walkway.

"Hey, man, I need a quarter."

Leo stopped and looked at him. The other boy also stepped over. "I
need a quarter, too, man," he said.

Zahav growled quietly, his body tense. Leo patted him, and fished in
his pocket for change. A quarter, he thought. When I was that age,
I asked for a penny. He said, "Sure, I have a quarter. One for each
of you."

Leo brought the coins from his pocket, but pulled some dollar bills
out with them. The bills fluttered to the concrete. Dropping the coins
into the taller boy's outstretched palm, Leo bent to retrieve the bills. The
shorter boy had already scooped them up.

Leo held out his hand. "I'll take those, please."

The boy teasingly moved the bills clutched in his fist out of Leo's
reach. Zahav interpreted the gesture as hostile. Growling, he charged
toward the boy. The dog's momentum jerked the leash loose from Leo's
fingers. It happened so fast the boy could not step aside.

"No, Zahav!" Leo shouted. "Down!"

But too late. The dog nipped the boy's ankle. Even in the poor tunnel
light Leo saw it all as clearly as though under a spotlight. The boy's
sneakered foot went back and then forward. The toe struck the dog just
under his chest. Zahav was a big dog, but the boy kicked him hard enough
to send him skidding along the walkway into the tiled tunnel wall. The
dog shrieked with pain.

Leo went cold with anger. He slapped the boy's face. The boy staggered
backward, and Leo started across the tunnel toward the dog. At that
instant the other boy, the taller, brought a knife from his pocket. A small
switchblade, which he snapped open with a flick of his wrist. As Leo
moved past him, the boy leaned forward and plunged the blade into his
stomach.

Leo felt only a dull pain, like a pinch. He continued toward the dog,
then all at once stopped. He stood, facing the boys. They were staring
at his stomach. He looked down. The shiny mother-of-pearl knife handle
protruded from his shirt just above his trouser band. He saw no blood.
Curious, he lowered his head to see more clearly. His own body shadowed
the light; he could make out only the vague form of the knife handle.

The sense of total clarity that always accompanied the cold anger had
not come this time. Something was happening that he did not understand. He still felt chilled, but a different kind of cold now. It extended

down into his legs, which felt paralyzed. He wanted to pull the knife handle out of his stomach, and imagined himself doing it, and told himself to do it, but his arms refused to obey the order.

He peered, bemused, at his stomach. He did not look up when the boys ran off but knew they had gone. The slapping sound of their sneakers on the concrete walkway echoed hollowly through the tunnel.

He raised his head to gaze after them, straining to see better, seeing only the oval of the tunnel entrance, which seemed blurred. He was vaguely aware of Zahav standing beside him. Leo did not believe the dog seriously injured, but decided he would take him to the vet tomorrow for sure.

Again, he looked at his stomach. He saw only a blur of red, but too bright for blood. The red wall in front of his eyes. Dull red now. It is all wrong, he thought. Everything is wrong. It is a terrible, foolish mistake.

He toppled forward onto the concrete. He lay face down in the center of the tunnel. Zahav, confused, whimpered and began licking Leo's face. Leo did not move. After a moment Zahav lay down beside Leo, but alert, prepared to thwart any further offense.

The light from both tunnel entrances faded as the sun sank completely below the horizon. A few minutes later, with the sun down, the whole tunnel was dark.

All Futura Books are available at your bookshop or
newsagent, or can be ordered from the following address:
Futura Books, Cash Sales Department,
P.O. Box 11, Falmouth, Cornwall TR10 9EN.

Please send cheque or postal order (no currency), and
allow 60p for postage and packing for the first book
plus 25p for the second book and 15p for each additional
book ordered up to a maximum charge of £1.90 in U.K.

B.F.P.O. customers please allow 60p for
the first book, 25p for the second book plus 15p per
copy for the next 7 books, thereafter 9p per book

Overseas customers, including Eire, please allow £1.25
for postage and packing for the first book, 75p for the
second book and 28p for each subsequent title ordered.